LION OF EVERMORE

Book 3

DARK RAVEN CHRONICLES

by

Steven Hutton

BODDINGTON & ROYALL

Lion of Evermore

First published in Great Britain
by Books Illustrated Ltd

This paperback edition published 2018
1 3 5 7 9 10 8 6 4 2
Text and illustrations copyright © Steve Hutton

ISBN: 978-1-9164203-2-8

Printed and bound by CPI Group (UK) Ltd, Croydon, CR0 4YY

BODDINGTON & ROYALL

www.**DarkRavenChronicles**.com

"Countless times I have walked Evermore.
Yet no matter which door I choose, beyond it I die again,
and a mere lifetime later I find myself where I started
— with a door before me and a choice to be made.'

Clovis Augmentrum
Coven-father, Temple-of-Unity, Vega

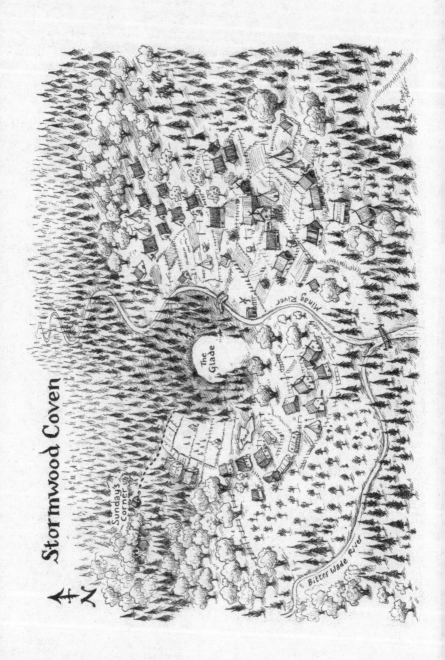

Stormwood Coven

PROLOGUE

The rotten heart of witchdom

Witches hold that when the last universe was old, the star-dragon was left unchecked to rampage and destroy. It was a terrible beast that ate all matter and time, a creature so vast that its wings were light-years across and it could swallow galaxies whole. It consumed everything that ever was, and then it even began to eat itself, compacting all creation into a tiny speck until it was so dense that it exploded with incredible violence. The star-dragon was torn apart, and once again a new universe was born from the ashes of the old. Although matter could not survive the cataclysm, other expressions of energy could: *ideas*. Two Ideas survived unscathed and they set about rebuilding the universe: the Idea-of-Life, and the Idea-of-Death. Life brought impetus, while Death brought change.

The first world they made was Vega the Blessed, where they left priceless seeds. Inside each rested serpent-twins, and it was their dreams that would infuse barren worlds with life. To spread these miraculous gifts through the stars, Life and Death created the first witches, and because they were more animal than human they became known as Therions. The young universe unfolded and all seemed well.

Unbeknown to all however, another Idea had survived, and it watched creation with envy. The Idea-of-Self sought to manipulate this new universe as it had the old one. It tainted all it touched and whispered dreams of superiority, and tragically some of Vega's first witches succumbed. In time these witches ultimately saw themselves as greater than their fellows. They formed a secret society named the Unitari and infiltrated the noble covens of Vega. Loyal witches continued to believe Vega was blessed but secretly it had become the rotten heart of witchdom.

Aeons passed before the Unitari finally made their move – to capture a stupendous relic. This incredible prize was a sacred vessel containing a god who could open any doorway. But he was guarded by Vega's greatest coven, thus first they had to kill its loyal witches and crucially its coven-father. . . a formidable witch named Clovis.

CHAPTER ONE

The lion, the god, and the flower

'See with your heart, not your eyes, they cannot be trusted.'
Traditional witch saying

It must be a terrible thing to forget who you are, but on rare occasions, remembering is surely more terrible yet. Janus looked out through the glass not realising he had forgotten who he was, and therefore content in his ignorance. He watched the comings and goings of Stormwood-coven with acute interest, oblivious to his true purpose. As always Clovis was the centre of his attention, but even when Clovis was out of sight he sensed what he was doing, which frequently revolved around Kolfinnia. Janus still couldn't decide if he liked her or not. She was young but wise, level but lively, and clearly the warrior's affection for her ran deep, which only kindled his resentment further. *Love him with all your heart, silly Kolfinnia*, he plotted, t*he final parting will simply be more painful*.

Janus certainly hadn't changed for the better. He had waited patiently for the perfect moment to make Clovis return him to Vega as promised. Yes, he could have done it any time he chose, but the perfect moment for the trickster god was when Clovis had become so dear to them, that losing him would be devastating. So he let them establish Stormwood, their new coven. He watched them put down roots, build homes, plant crops, and mend the wounds left from Kittiwake. He watched them say prayers for their lost friends and prayers for the sleeping dragon-twins. He watched them all grow to love Clovis, especially Kolfinnia.

Janus became a mere spectator to the life of Stormwood-coven but he didn't care. He kept his peace, content to be an onlooker while they found new joy in rebuilding what the Illuminata had taken from them. Janus was ready to ruin all of that and break their hearts, when suddenly everything changed.

It was Midsummer's Day 1887. Janus wasn't a witch, so he cared little for long days, short days, or even no days at all, but that Midsummer's Day was different. Kolfinnia and Clovis had been consumed with preparations to sabotage the Illuminata's tournament at Salisbury. There was little time and a mountain of work. Janus watched their efforts with amusement. He knew the chances of victory were slim and he saw how Kolfinnia's fears followed her like her own shadow, along with the guilt. She was sending witches into danger, while she was compelled to remain at Stormwood. Clovis meanwhile was so absorbed with training his witches that he had all but forgotten Janus. *I see there's a new love in your life Clovis. Shall we ask her to come to Vega with us? I doubt she will, the trip is one way, but I long to see your face when she speaks a resounding 'no'. Do coven-fathers weep? I think they might, Clovis, I think they might.*

While Janus plotted, the witches of Stormwood sent their loved ones into the fight, and while Kolfinnia and Clovis agonised over events at Salisbury, something else even more significant, yet utterly unexpected, happened. A very special flower opened. The Flowering-of-Fate.

A lone witch and her dear champion had defied the Patternmaker. Freewill's victory sent a shockwave through the esoteric universe, unlocking ancient doors, one of which lay dormant inside the mind of the trickster god. And the real Janus, the one who had been buried for aeons, at last slipped free. The moment it happened he was dreaming, and today on the longest day, while witches died at Wellesley Hall, the god of doorways was dreaming of a real life memory. It was the day that the heart of witchdom was struck by treachery. The day Clovis became a fugitive. . .

"Clovis, behind you!" Tiber roared.

Clovis swung his sword without thinking and beheaded his assailant in one swipe. The corpse stood a moment, still clutching its sword and not yet comprehending its death. No blood flowed but a last puff of air rushed from the severed windpipe, the soul's final journey perhaps, then the corpse toppled and Clovis recognised the rolling head even before it had come to a stop. It was Arriu, one of the temple masters. Just this morning he shared prayers with him for the serpent-twins. "This is insane!" he panted.

"No, this is treachery." Tiber was his chief Ward and closest companion. He towered over him by six inches and his fur was iron black. He sidestepped Arriu's corpse, careful not to look the severed head in the eyes, which twitched and fluttered in their sockets. "It's vital we keep moving."

"He mentored me from my earliest years." Clovis stared down at his former teacher in disbelief. "I killed him."

"He *deceived* you from your earliest years. He and many like him were *not* the witches we long believed. We *have* to keep moving."

"But I killed him."

"Coven-father – *Clovis!*" he hissed when he failed to move.

Clovis shook his head clear. The scale of the treachery left him numb, and he wasn't sure what to believe any longer. He sheathed his sword. "You're right, keep moving."

Both set off at a pace through the Exillon hall, which was now disconcertingly quiet. An hour ago it had been pandemonium, as witches loyal to Vega were caught unawares and cut down by their brethren while engaged in prayers. Their bodies still littered the marble floor. Many of them hadn't even had time to draw their swords, and Clovis saw many friends amongst them. Strangely though he felt nothing. The fury would come later, but right now he was running on instincts, and they told him to get Janus away from the Temple-of-Unity as fast as possible.

They rounded the arched gateway to the Exillon hall and down the mile-long corridor ahead they saw distant flames billowing from the Pallacus Sanctum, the coven library. "They're destroying all our records!" Aghast, he started towards the desecration.

"Just words on paper." Tiber grabbed him.

"But it's our history, our purpose!"

"No!" He whirled him around. "Our coven was a lie Clovis, all these centuries, all they ever wanted was to poison Janus! Our history is *their* history, the Unitari!"

Clovis looked into his dark face, loath to accept the unthinkable. His beloved coven, The Temple-of-Unity, had been infiltrated by Self from the start. "The Temple was a cover."

"I'm sorry." Tiber could smell his confusion and pain. "But maybe a few loyal witches can still win the day."

That ignited him. "Get Janus," he growled.

"Aye, Janus!" He bared his teeth and clenched a clawed fist. They could still avenge their brothers if they put Janus out of Acola's reach. They set off at a run, with the sound of their armour ringing down the empty halls. "The way to the Spiral-gate will be heavily guarded," he panted as they ran.

"Janus is not at the Spiral-gate," Clovis revealed.

He skidded to a halt. "Not there?"

"No, he's. . ." Trust was a fragile thing this day.

"Where?"

Clovis was breathing too fast and sweat stung his eyes. "I moved him."

"Clovis?" he squinted at him. "I have to know, where did you move Janus to?"

Don't tell him! an inner voice insisted and Clovis didn't know if it was paranoia or sixth sense, by the sleeping twins it might even be the voice of Self for all he knew.

"Clovis, tell me." His eyes widened to glittering moons.

Lots of good things had died this day, but he was determined his friendship with Tiber wouldn't be one of them. Clovis chose to ignore his paranoia. "I moved Janus in secret two days ago, to the Crossway-cortex."

Tiber's muzzle twitched and his ears pricked forwards.

Now we'll see: sixth sense, or paranoia? Clovis couldn't differentiate, and in readiness he touched the hilt of his sword.

Tiber relaxed and dipped his head respectfully. "A shrewd move."

"Paranoia be damned," Clovis swallowed his tensions and Tiber frowned. "Never mind, nobody knows he's there, we can beat them to it."

They broke into a run and then a sprint, and finally both drew their lightning-staffs. They flew down the magnificent halls that had once been their coven, but now where smoke from ransacked rooms blackened the air and bodies littered the floors.

The Viloress was a covered bridge that joined the Exillon hall to the Novex, the fortress that constituted the coven's official headquarters. The bridge comprised one hundred and fifty-six stone arches offering spectacular views across the gardens far below, where acres of cherry trees formed a sea of blossom. Clovis had loved this place from childhood. It was here, that as a stubborn young witch, he'd leapt into thin air with his lightning-staff in his first attempt at flight. The danger he faced then was exhilarating, now it was insidious and suffocating. *Vega is rotten,*he repeated, still not quite grasping it. With that came another even more desolate notion. *Who am I? If the coven I've served all my life was a lie, then who – and what – am I without it?*

Thankfully the answer would have to wait. They had reached the cascade of water concealing the entrance to the Novex beyond. This glittering curtain was named Evermore's Tears. To pass through it, signified the visitor was cleansed and worthy, but today Clovis saw it anew. "Evermore weeps indeed," he accused.

"I'll go first." Tiber charged through without pause. Water poured down his armour and splashed against the flags darkening them, and Clovis imagined blood spraying against marble. "Clovis!" he beckoned from behind the waterfall.

Clovis followed, alert for danger. For a moment the sound of rushing water surrounded him, a throwback to life in the womb, and then he was through. He shook the water from his mane, feeling not in the least bit cleansed. The first thing he saw were the huge doors to the Spiral-gate hanging open. "Acola's up there, looking for Janus," he realised and suddenly he wanted to race up there and plunge his sword into the traitor's heart.

"Then let him search, he won't find." Tiber padded softly across the hall and stood at the foot of the Spiral-gate. From the chamber high above, they heard the clash of weapons and roars of pain and fury.

"My witches are up there, defending an empty room!" His urge was to charge into the fight.

"Then don't waste their blood." Tiber set off in the opposite direction, towards the Crossway-cortex.

Clovis listened to Acola's traitors killing the last of his loyal witches. "I want to kill him." His heart pounded and his hand went to his sword.

"No!" Ever the more cool-headed, Tiber hurried back to his side. "The snake has struck, now we have to stop the poison spreading, not waste time running after it!"

Clovis didn't seem to hear. He bared his teeth and tasted the air. Yes, Acola was up there. Acola the snow-white lion whose heart it now transpired was blacker than soulless sin. Now the shock was ebbing, and the fury welling up in its place was almost uncontrollable. "The dark lion masquerades in white. I want to kill him!" Hatred distorted his words.

Tiber tugged at his arm, but it was like hauling a huge stone. "Even if you do, the Unitari still win if they seize Janus. Don't give in to rage!"

"No!" Clovis bared his gleaming fangs. Foam erupted in a spray and splattered across his muzzle. He flattened his ears, threw back his head and roared, "KILL HIM!"

"CLOVIS!" Tiber hauled him around until they were face to face. His eyes were dangerous slits and his tongue lolled red and steaming. "How did you know?" he demanded.

The unexpected question fazed him. Clovis blinked, his pupils dilated and his muzzle sagged slowly, covering those fearsome teeth. "Know?"

"How did you know to move Janus?"

"Move Janus," he mumbled and wiped the froth from his furred chin, ashamed now. "I had a dream," he confided. "I dreamed of taking Janus through Evermore to a special door. I didn't know it was a premonition, but as a precaution, I moved Janus."

"Then to the Crossway-cortex, and let's fulfil this dream of yours!" He tugged on his arm, keen to lead him away.

Clovis gave a decisive nod and sprinted ahead. Tiber followed and they left behind them the sounds of fighting above where good witches, good friends, were dying to defend an empty room.

Half way down the gallery leading to the Crossway-cortex, they arrived at the circular glass hall known as the Orchard. Many delicate orchids were grown here for their medicinal nectar and the blue dye from their petals. Normally Clovis found it the most peaceful place in the whole coven, but today it rang with terrified screams. "Tiber!" He pulled his staff to a halt. The smell of crushed orchids was overpowering, and when his feet hit the ground he heard the crunch of broken glass. Tiber dropped to his side and together they rushed within, drawn by the horrible cries.

Clovis evaluated everything in an instant. He saw novice Elsu lying in a sea of broken glass, smashed pots and trampled flowers. The young witch was wounded and struggling to reach his sword, while his assailant stomped through the debris towards him, feeling not a shred of fear or pain, but then again how could it, the thing was not really alive. It was a monster conjured by their enemies, a monster known as an amalga. "Elsu!" Clovis charged.

"VEGA!" Tiber bellowed, overjoyed to finally have an enemy to fight – and what an enemy.

Amalga were compositions of anything the conjurer found at hand, and driven by a spell-bottle buried deep in their innards. The one stalking Elsu was made of shattered glass. It towered almost eight feet high, lumbering on unfeeling legs, like a mountain of killing blades on the move. All it had to do was fall on him and he would be sliced to bloody rags.

"Elsu, stay down!" Clovis hurtled forwards.

Complying instantly, Elsu buried his head as the amalga now looked in Clovis's direction and swung an arm towards him. Clovis charged and threw himself to the ground, sliding through a carpet of debris and driving his sword at the creature's leg. The blade sailed through its ankle. Glass screamed against steel and the creature swayed dangerously. The amalga thundered its arm down to counter the fall, but now Tiber was ready to strike. His sword whirled and its wrist shattered.

"Back!" Clovis rolled away from the collapsing giant. Glass sliced his palms and knees and now fresh blood added to the pungent odour of crushed orchids.

Tiber grabbed Elsu by the scruff, as a cat takes its kitten, and hauled him aside. "Stay back!"

The amalga hit the ground but didn't break. It thrashed and jerked as it tried to right itself, gouging scars in the marble, and the sound of screeching glass echoed around the hall.

"Clovis, down!" Tiber suddenly shoved him aside.

Claws, tipped with wicked shards, whistled past inches from Clovis's face, and for a surreal moment he saw his fractured reflection snarling back at him.

As the creature swung at Clovis, Tiber detected a tell-tale flicker of green deep inside it and seized the opportunity. He thrust his staff and pierced it dead centre. More glass broke, this time the crucial spell-bottle, and the amalga's life ended in a violent explosion and a wave of debris. Clovis barely had time to look away before a sheet of shards and powdered glass swept over him, and only his thick fur saved him from injury. The creature's death song echoed around the Orchard and trailed away to the bright tinkle of falling glass, before silence settled at last.

Tiber looked about in horror. "Dark magic, here, in our own coven."

"Their coven you mean," Clovis panted, shaking slivers from his fur. "Elsu!" He helped him to his feet.

Elsu struggled upright, looking bewildered but still stubbornly clutching his sword. "My thanks Coven-father," he mumbled, ashamed.

Clovis inspected his wounds, which wasn't easy. Elsu's coat was desert-red, making blood hard to see. However, as a novice his mane was cropped short, and here Clovis saw several angry gashes. No wonder Elsu reeked of blood, he thought. "You're hurt," he said, going to tend his wounds.

"I'm fine Coven-father," he recoiled, feeling he'd failed them both.

"Where were you this morning?" Tiber interrupted.

"I was on the Ashfalda, making sunrise observations. When I came back I found this. . . this madness!" he swept an arm across the devastation.

"The Unitari have struck," Clovis explained. "Acola was their agent all along."

His pupils narrowed. "Ward Acola? A traitor?"

Clovis closed his eyes and nodded once. "Traitor." Each time he said it, it became more real.

"Can you move?" Tiber checked.

"Yes." Elsu sheathed his sword while trying to conceal his tremors.

"Then escape," Clovis ordered. "This place is no longer ours. Tiber and I are out to put Janus beyond Acola's reach."

"Then let me help you!"

"You can. Leave at once and head to Wester-Sol. My sister is coven-mother there, and if I know Neeri she'll have given the traitors a run for their money."

"You mean this reaches beyond our own coven?" The scale of the treachery was only just dawning on him.

"Almost certainly. All of them," Tiber predicted, "to make sure survivors don't band together."

"And fight back!" Inspired, Elsu went for his sword again.

Clovis stopped him. "We'll fight back alright, but not with steel, not yet. This is my last command – find Neeri. Tell her that her brother has taken Janus." He clasped Elsu's arm and found his coat sticky with more blood.

"Last command," Elsu accepted sadly.

"And I wouldn't trust it to anyone else." He managed a smile.

"We have to move," Tiber reminded him softly.

"Find my sister, she'll rally the survivors. This isn't over yet," Clovis promised.

Elsu flushed with pride. "It's an honour to serve you Coven-father."

"Not me, the twins." He tapped the twin dragons on his bloodied robe, the coven's emblem. "Serve the sleeping twins, give *them* reason to be proud of Vega again."

"Blessings on you novice," Tiber added in farewell, then without another word he and Clovis turned and ran.

Elsu watched them go. "Dragons be with you both," he wished them, and then he was left alone in the ruins of a temple that was never really his.

The Novex was built on an extinct volcanic plug, the sides of which were incredibly sheer, and the Crossway-cortex was a citadel of towers on its western side. The towers were the coven's highest point and from their narrow windows one might enjoy the view over the Ashfalda plains, but only if the viewer had a head for heights. It was a terrifying three thousand feet to the river Osara below.

"This one." Clovis shoved the heavy oak door aside and started up the spiral. Tiber followed, careful to close the door and disguise their passing.

"Why here?" he heard himself ask. It was cave-black, but their eyes missed nothing.

"Intuition." Clovis steadied his scabbard to stop it rattling. Three small doors stood at the first gallery, each housing unremarkable storerooms. The brooms here were strictly for cleaning and sweeping. There were a total of five galleries in the tower, but Clovis had moved Janus to the least important room in the first gallery. "In here." He pressed his ear to the door listening for sounds from inside. "Maybe they knew and they're already waiting." He half hoped they were.

"Hmm, no sign of entry," Tiber noted the even dust on the floor.

"Trust nothing." He felt for the binding words he'd secreted into the wooden door.

"What was the manner of your dream?" Tiber asked quietly as he worked.

Clovis thought back. "I saw the first portent in the dark mirror while contemplating. I saw many doors, millions of them. They all opened a fraction, then slammed shut before I could glimpse what lay beyond. Then the vision faded to reveal a beautiful flower – the petals were alternately black and gold and the centre was brilliant blue."

"Profound indeed," Tiber agreed. "But its meaning?"

"It was too symbolic, but my dream was more explicit. I saw myself running upwards through Evermore with Janus and I was carrying Tempest also." At this he touched the lightning-staff strung over his shoulder. His thunder-sprite was worryingly quiet. *Shock?* he thought.

"But where to?"

"That I can't answer." He listened as the hidden words of magic called back to him. "But there was only one door on Evermore I was bound for."

"Yes?" Tiber waited.

"It was wooden and small, insignificant even. But the word on it will stand 'til the end of creation."

"Word?" Tiber was fascinated. "A real word, or just part of the dream?"

"I'm convinced it's real. . . it exists there, on Evermore."

Tiber flinched. "But it would take a living soul to leave any kind of message in the netherworld of Evermore." The implications were astonishing.

"Oh I know," Clovis grinned. "It cost me a few night's sleep, yet if correct, some wanderer *did* travel there and forewarn us."

"Then what was the word?" It was ridiculous, but he imagined the stones around them leaning closer to listen.

Clovis took a breath. "Rowan."

"Rowan?" Tiber frowned. It meant nothing to him. "Like the tree you mean?"

"Perhaps, or a person or place. I don't know." At this the lock clicked softly. "Be ready," he warned, then gripped the handle and gave a gentle push.

Clovis believed signs were not to be ignored. He moved Janus out of respect for that rule, not because he genuinely believed something bad was going to happen. But now look at them – their coven in ruins, and pursued by lifelong 'friends' who wanted to slit their throats. The door swung open and he stepped inside to find it unchanged.

"Where is he?" Tiber scanned the crates and ceremonial armour hanging on the racks. "Where's Janus?"

Clovis could almost hear the trickster god chuckling to himself. He knew today's massacre would delight the heartless little imp. Janus might be a mighty relic of cosmic significance, but in truth he hated him. He went to a shelf lined with jars of powdered sage, and pried the middle one free. He reached into the gap and slid a wholly different jar into view. It was a sealed octagonal vessel, fashioned of glass that was pitted and ancient looking, and with no apparent lid. Inside, some greenish liquid seemed to circulate under its own will, and suspended in that fluid was a small figure carved from what appeared to be stone. It was dark and squat with diminutive arms and legs, more like vestigial limbs than the real thing. The body was portly and its chubby face bore only rudimentary features. The eyes were just crescent slits, as if the figure was laughing at some secret only he knew.

"Janus." Tiber managed a small bow despite his distaste.

Clovis set the vessel upon a bronze chest and the green liquid played across the ceiling like sunlight on water. "Janus, do you see now why I moved you?"

Janus spun merrily and his smug face whirled past like a leering carousel horse. "But I have missed all the excitement," he whined. "Tell me, was the fighting brutal? Oh I do hope so!"

Why? Clovis thought to himself. *Why do we guard this spoiled bastard with our lives and lavish upon him respect grossly out of measure to his worth? Why have my friends been murdered today just to preserve his miserable life?* He grew angry thinking such things. It did no good, and of course he already knew the answer. "Janus, the Unitari have finally showed their hand."

"They were amongst you all along I see. Hiding in plain sight eh?" he tittered.

Tiber flinched as if slapped, while Clovis just scrutinised the mocking face behind the glass, as it wheeled by. "If they find you they will take you."

"I have only your word for that Clovis."

"Shall we put it to the test? Shall we wait for Acola's traitors to search here? They will eventually."

"Only the damned dare open this vessel," he boasted.

"Even that might not be enough to protect you oh mighty Janus." He bowed his head to hide his anger and when he looked up again Janus had stopped and was studying him.

"It would take more than a mere witch to kill a god," he accused acidly.

"It has been 'mere witches' who have kept you safe this long, and we two 'mere witches' are all you have to spirit you away before Acola finds you."

"Two? From a coven of seventy-eight I believe?" Janus sounded unimpressed. "Were they *all* traitors, or were they all just killed like rats?"

Clovis was about to retaliate when he heard the distant clang of armour. They didn't have long. "Tiber, watch the door."

Glad to be away, Tiber went and peered out onto the landing, where he detected movement. "I hear them," he whispered.

Clovis looked to the tower's single window. Outside, through leaded glass as intricate as a dragonfly wing, he saw that it was a beautiful day, but it didn't inspire him at all. "Tiber and I are leaving, we're taking you from this place."

"Simple flying staffs will not put you beyond the reach of your foes," Janus sympathised.

Clovis hated to agree, but he was right. They needed a more decisive departure, and he had one in mind. "That is why you Janus must help us. Open a door to Evermore." Tiber never made a sound, but Clovis could hear his thudding heart pick up in pace. Both of them were equally scared by the idea of walking in that place.

"You ask a great deal," he stated.

"They will kill you," he said flatly. Or *worse*, he added silently.

"And if I choose not to travel through Evermore?"

"You will."

"Oh will I?" he scoffed. "A witch commands a god this day? And what makes you so certain?"

"It is one of the few great doors you have never opened. Have you never wondered?" He was going to add '*what lies beyond*', when Janus interrupted.

"You imply I have not the power to achieve such a feat!"

Clovis was weary of games. "I'm certain you have, are you not a god after all?"

Now Janus wondered if he was being toyed with. It was a new sensation, and one he didn't enjoy. "There is no door I cannot unlock Clovis," he stated with certainty.

Clovis tapped the glass. "Oh but there is. . . this very vessel. It cannot be opened except by a witch and only then with the right intent."

"Clovis they're coming!" Tiber hissed.

He was on his feet in a second, sword drawn. "There's little time to consider, and I'd advise you not to wait until Tiber and I are lifeless corpses before you decide," he smiled coldly and went to his companion.

"Well, will he?" Tiber asked.

Clovis's silence was answer enough. He peered out through the crack. The gallery was empty, but it wouldn't be for long. The sound of marching feet rolled down to them from the spiral stair. Their enemies had been lurking on the floor above. "Acola must have drafted in mercenaries to bolster his ranks."

"I never liked him you know," Tiber confided, "his mane was always too neat."

Clovis gave a sardonic laugh, "You're a good judge of character. Perhaps you should have been coven-father instead."

Tiber was silent for a moment and when he spoke it was of their demise, "We could open the vessel, deprive them of the god?"

Clovis smiled sadly. "A noble plan but you know the vessel brims with poison, it would kill us both."

"I'm ready," he promised truthfully.

"I don't doubt it, but remember without the proper ritual Janus might well die also, and even if he didn't it would send a very incomplete being into the heavens, and who knows what a child with untold power could do." He looked back at the vessel. "He's not evolved enough to ascend, and perhaps we were fools to ever believe he would be."

Tiber sensed movement outside, and he shut the door softly and secured the lock. "They'll have to get through it first."

Both stood back, swords ready. Outside they could hear footsteps and guessed their enemies numbered a dozen. Predictably, they heard the first of the three storeroom doors thud open, followed by muffled voices as they inspected inside. "One," Clovis counted. Seconds later came another hefty thud as someone kicked open the next door.

"Two." Tiber took a step back.

Now the voices congregated right outside. Tiber flattened his ears and Clovis felt his hackles rise. The door rocked as someone kicked it, but it didn't give.

"Three," Janus chortled.

Clovis suppressed the urge to send the jar crashing to the floor. *They don't know,* he thought. If the Unitari suspected they were hiding they would have searched with more caution. The door rocked again, harder this time and both witches retreated and stood before the bronze chest, swords raised. "You were right Tiber. If the worst happens, smash the vessel," Clovis whispered. "No matter the consequences."

Tiber grunted an acknowledgement.

All was quiet for a moment, when suddenly the door was hit a third time, but not by any boot. A sword cleaved through the solid oak like butter, whistling through the wood as it went and leaving a surgically neat slit a yard long. "They'll split it with the next stroke," Clovis warned.

"All this fuss over little old me!" Janus trilled softly.

Clovis bit his tongue and waited. The door was hit again, and he saw the blade sail down it like a shark's fin, slicing it in two. A heavy boot came next. The two halves crashed to the floor, and loyal and treacherous came face to face at last.

There was a brief moment of total clarity so balanced that it seemed almost theatrical. Outside, a dozen traitors and mercenaries led by novice-ward Hexim stood staring in at a bland storeroom, only to be confronted with none other than Coven-father Clovis and Chief-ward Tiber. His eyes flicked from one to the other, as he wondered who the more deadly opponent was. That instant, everyone knew this was going to be a fight to the death. "Clovis. . . Tiber. . ." he uttered.

Clovis saw a dozen hostile faces, including former friends, regard him uncertainly. He smelled their fear and felt his fury rise in response. Behind Hexim's band, he saw further amalga creatures lumber into the gallery. He regarded them with disgust, before turning his full stare against Hexim. "Resorting to black magic now I see novice? And who taught you such wickedness, Acola perhaps?"

"Where is Janus?" he asked warily.

"Janus is here. Come claim him if you dare. Traitor."

He shuffled backwards and his sword wavered. "Hand him over and we'll spare you both."

"Claim him!" Clovis ordered.

Hexim flattened his ears and growled in response, but still he refused to move. His companions were no better. They looked to him for orders, before eyeing one another nervously.

"Treacherous *and* cowardly? How little we have in common brother." Clovis crouched, ready.

Hexim's company clutched their swords and the amalga twitched in anticipation. They were building their nerve to charge. Hexim looked beyond his former coven-father to the vessel resting on the chest, and upon seeing the prize of all prizes greed boosted his courage. "Hand over Janus, I shan't ask again."

"CLAIM HIM!" Clovis's roar echoed up the tower, mocking them all.

Torn by fear and hate of that fear, Hexim sprang forwards and his followers surged after him. "Unitari!" he roared in defiance.

"Finally!" Clovis ran to meet them, when out of nowhere something black barged him aside.

"Take Janus and go!" Tiber crashed into the wall of enemies, swinging his sword with brutal force. Hexim screamed as he was split from shoulder to waist, but his death-call was drowned out by Tiber's roar.

"Take Janus and go!" He ploughed into the thick of them, slashing repeatedly. Limbs, heads, hands and swords began to litter the floor, while screams and roars resounded off the walls. Blood rolled in waves and steel flashed as Tiber cut down the very witches he helped train. He swung his blade and an opponent's chest disgorged organs and blood. That blade swung again, and another lost his head from the eyes up, leaving a standing corpse with a slack mouthed expression. It teetered then slumped down into a spreading sea of gore that sloshed over the floor. Frantic, the survivors pressed in, knowing death would follow if they didn't act. Tiber vanished from sight as they surged over him. "GO!" his muffled cry came again.

The coven's primary command was to protect Janus, and against all his wishes Clovis obeyed it. He whirled around to see Janus spinning delightedly, drunk with self-importance. "All this fuss over me!" he laughed.

Clovis bellowed in fury and charged. He snatched the vessel from the chest, leaving deep scratches in the bronze, and bounded towards the window. Behind him, he heard a solitary roar from Tiber, followed by a different and utterly unexpected roar.

"VEGA!" the roar came, and despite everything he recognised that voice, which to his frantic brain sounded impossibly familiar.

It can't be! he thought, both frightened and astounded by the paradox. The voice had sounded like. . .

"The Janus vessel, he has it!" a sudden scream came, as the traitors at last forced a way into the room.

Somewhere, Tiber was still bellowing defiantly and that impossible voice came again. "FOR VEGA!"

Clovis was compelled to see, but rather than waste a second, he hurled himself full force at the window. He smashed through the glass and sailed through thin air until momentum yielded to gravity and he began to fall three thousand feet to the river Osara below. Roars of outrage followed, but quickly diminished as he dropped faster and faster. He rolled in space and the Ashfalda's broad pastures flipped places with the sky. He saw the Crossway-cortex rushing away from him at terrific speed, framed by blue sky and innocent clouds. *Tiber's up there,* he thought sadly.

A tiny figure leaned out of the window. Clovis caught the tail end of a cry, but it was stolen by the wind roaring in his ears and whipping through his mane. This was his last gambit. The fall would kill him and ready or not Janus would be released.

Realising his suicidal plan, Janus finally ceased laughing. "Fly Clovis, take your staff and fly!" he shrieked. It was a long way down and there was time enough for the little god to contemplate existence outside his lifelong cocoon. "Fly Clovis! I order you to fly!"

"You failed Acola." Clovis closed his eyes to the cliff walls racing by and clenched his jaw against the bile-inducing inertia. *Both Janus and I will die.*

His last thought was quieter than a whisper in a hurricane, but Janus heard it clearly and he had no intention of being cast out of his protective shell. "Curse you witch!" There was only one way out of this he knew, and he began to spin faster and faster until the vessel was just a matrix of bubbles and it throbbed like a nest of soldier-bees.

Clovis gripped it for dear life as he tumbled downwards, understanding that Janus god of doorways was opening that unknown door he had tempted him with: the gateway to Evermore. His life was no longer his to control, and he surrendered to fate knowing he would either die or find himself transported to Evermore's steps. But Acola had lost regardless, and Clovis managed a smile as the killing earth rushed closer.

Janus dreamed on, approaching the moment when they had materialised on Evermore's steps followed by amalga, which had jumped in pursuit and were inadvertently carried through.

Outside, Stormwood was gripped by tension as everyone agonised over the battle at Salisbury. Both Kolfinnia and Clovis strained to see through the miles using magical means, but there were strange forces at work at Salisbury and the picture was heavily veiled. None of them sensed the incredible event rushing towards them. Amid the cannons, krakens, and valkyries, another hard fought battle was taking place between an even greater god and his former servant.

The Timekeeper had defied the Patternmaker in order to save a single witch, and in doing so he won a bitter concession. The battle over Sunday's life had set the precedent. The Patternmaker had grudgingly yielded and although it represented only a fraction of his all-consuming control it was enough. A new law had been written: *If the will is sufficiently strong, one's own fate might be written.* It was this shockwave that now rolled across the esoteric realm like the first rain in an eternal desert, or more aptly like the opening of a magnificent flower, a flower bearing black garb, golden hair and brilliant blue eyes.

At Salisbury, that very flower was fighting for her life and the Book-of-Nine were watching their creations rampage out of control, while at Stormwood, Kolfinnia was lost in tormented prayers. Little wonder they didn't sense the event. But Janus did. The Flowering-of-Fate expanded into the cosmos, and those with an ear to listen heard it as a whisper promising redemption.

Janus was alone in Clovis's quarters when it happened. The room was a simple wooden hut nestling in the branches of a tree. Sunlight pooled through the single window, where a shutter rocked gently in the breeze, which had carried in a few dandelion seeds. To look at the place one might think its owner was a hermit, not a great coven-father. Clovis owned little, yet his most valuable possession sat on his bunk bathed in sunlight. The sacred vessel glinted in the sun, casting green reflections across the walls. Janus was turning lazily, savouring the moment he had heroically opened the gate to Evermore and saved Clovis's life, when someone or something whispered to him.

"Look back."

The voice came not from outside the glass, but from within. Janus knew that was impossible, the vessel was sealed to the outside universe. "Who is there?" He awoke from his daydream with a start. "Clovis?" But the hut was empty except for a single bee that had sailed in from the heat outside. The strange words brushed against him again, as harmless as drifting clouds, but he suddenly felt afraid, like a child left alone.

"Look back."

He flinched and bumped against the glass making a small 'tink' sound. "Clovis, is this your idea of a joke?"

"Look back!" the voice urged again, and most worryingly the view of the room began to fade as if the sun was being eclipsed.

"Clovis, enough of this trickery! Where are you?" He spun left and right, but the unnatural darkness was eating up the walls, the window and the trees outside.

The whispers continued their loving message. *"Look,"* they said, *"look back master of doorways and see what you left behind. See the one door you were born to open."*

Now the outer world was as dark as night and Janus realised something awful, but vital, was coming. He saw stars shining in the blackness and understood this was a view of remotest space and time. The whispers were fading now as they travelled onwards taking their message with them, but the door they had unlocked was swinging wide and like it or not he was going to see what lay behind it. *"Look back master of doorways and see the one door you were born to open."*

"No!" he protested. "I don't want to see! CLOVIS!"

It must be a terrible thing to forget who you are but on rare occasions remembering is surely more terrible yet. Janus saw his missing past in one devastating revelation. He saw that even gods weren't eternal. They were born and died like all creatures and sometimes they died a terrible death. He spun violently and crashed against the glass making the fluid churn.

There was blackness all around, but the void wasn't inert. He saw an omnipotent being striding through the cosmos sowing a miraculous gift through creation. Whoever he was, his intent was nothing short of holy. He crossed galaxies in a single stride and where he passed divisions were obliterated and harmony reigned. The will to serve the Self was replaced with the will to listen to conscience. World after world received the wanderer's gift, which Janus saw as a very special door indeed, joining the one with the all. *See the one door you were born to open.* He watched the god-like wanderer until it finally dawned on him what he was seeing. This being was him. But if so, then how had he been reduced to this imprisoned relic? "No!" he pleaded, knowing what would happen next. "I don't want to know!"

The memory replayed in grotesque detail, projected across the canvas of space like a lantern show, and it felt to kill him afresh. It was the day he had been murdered.

Self, his killer, believed him dead and no longer a threat, but it was wrong. A fragment survived, a shard of bone from his skull was left adrift in the universe and inside it was preserved an echo of the true Janus.

He might have drifted forever, half-living, half-dead, but the witches of Vega had come to his aid. They rescued this shard and shaped it into his infant likeness, then sealed him safely away with the intention of raising him back to completeness, but the shock of his murder obliterated his memory. He was left a cold and selfish trickster, tainted by Self. The witches of Vega lamented that a great force for good had been extinguished, but they did not give up hope. They believed that one day he would remember his purpose, and until then they swore to protect the wounded god. To this end they built their greatest coven around him and populated it with their strongest witches.

Self meanwhile lurked in the outer blackness. It had slept long because a god takes much digesting, but when it awoke it began to sense disturbing tremors. A tiny crumb of Janus had survived, and so Self devised an even more repellent plan. It would poison him to suit its own ends, and thus it began a long slow process of infiltration. It corrupted the more susceptible witches of Vega, those with a taste for pride, and in time the Temple-of-Unity became the unwitting host to its servants. As generations passed they grew stronger and took the coven's illustrious name and inverted it. They called themselves Unitari and secretly worked so Janus never remembered his former greatness. . . until today.

"No, I refuse!" Janus wailed. Under Self's influence the universe had gone astray. Consciousness became divided and unending conflict became the norm. The brain now sat within the skull in two separate halves, the connection with the cosmos was diminished and the third eye was condemned to eternal slumber. The 'one door' was no physical barrier, but the third eye itself. He alone could revive it and so open the doorway between the left and right sides of the mind. Consciousness would be healed, and Self's influence would crumble, but the task mocked him. He wanted to be the other Janus again, fickle and selfish, but now the Flowering had revealed the truth, it couldn't be taken back. In the blink of an eye he went from deceiver to saviour and the revelation was agony. "The door has opened, I see it!" He began his maniac spinning again, before finally he struck the glass so hard that the whole vessel rocked and he lost consciousness.

The jar on Clovis's bunk stilled and the fluid inside settled again. Janus drifted gently to the bottom and the swirling bubbles dissipated. He lay there, knowing and seeing nothing. The only witness was a solitary bee. She circled the room indifferent to his plight, until the lure of the open window pulled her through towards the summer skies beyond and Janus was left alone in the black.

CHAPTER TWO

A feast of knowledge

*'When the last Therions withdrew to the faded-realm, man's link
with his animal kin was broken. Ever since, he has been at war
with the creatures he shares this world with.'*
Orro Bas, Burning Heart of the united iron-fairy nations

Another storm had just passed, leaving the earth smelling renewed and
the grass bent double with rain. But while the green hills and sparkling
seas of Britain's southwest appear the picture of tranquillity, only nine
months ago something terrible happened here.

From the highest cliffs, where a ring of stones stands in defiance of time,
the views are magnificent, and in the hidden valley below sits a ruined tin
mine. This was the site of Kittiwake-coven, founded by Kolfinnia and Clovis
and defended to the end with witches' blood. Those same witches are gone
and the buildings are just tumbled wrecks, but not due to the storms that
batter this coast. This destruction was caused by gunpowder and cannons.
The few walls that remain are scarred with bullet holes, and flooded craters
pockmark the ground, but already frogs and pond-skaters have claimed
them. Greenery has returned to renew what the Illuminata first scorched
then Ruination withered. But frogs and birds aren't the only life here.

Someone has erected a cluster of large wooden huts in the crook of the
bay and defended them with a robust barricade. A small flag flies over the
largest of the buildings and tellingly it bears the crest of a unicorn and a

dragon chained to a thunderbolt. In the end it might be true to say that the Illuminata *did* conquer Kittiwake-coven, but only the blighted corpse of it, and since October last year they have relentlessly dissected that corpse, struggling to find answers but so far uncovering only ghosts.

Captain Kelly surveyed the sea with his telescope, taking in the whole bay. As always his attention was drawn to the sea stack at the bay's western edge. Why he couldn't say, but it appeared to be watching somehow. "Not so much as a row boat," he sighed. Security was his duty, but in reality he was hoping for the supply ship. They hadn't had word from London since the Salisbury tournament two weeks ago. The garrison had pay and rations until the end of July, and Kelly knew that would hold them until then, despite London's ominous silence. *But what of August, what then?* He asked himself this question a lot.

"Anything sir?"

Kelly looked to his sergeant, named Patrick Shipley; a stocky man with large ears and earnest eyes. "Nothing. Not a thing." He slid the telescope closed.

"What do we do sir?"

"Do?" he pretended.

"When August 1st comes around. I mean it's one thing to follow your duty, but another entirely when you don't even know what your duty's meant to be! If you take my meaning sir."

"Orders will come Sergeant." He tried to sound certain.

But will pay and rations? Shipley thought sourly.

"I'll advise Barda to send another courier to Goldhawk." Kelly cast a wary glance towards the camp huts. He didn't like the idea of tangling with Barda.

"Last 'un went off ten days ago, should've been back long since," Shipley rubbed at his doughy chin. "You don't think he –,"

"No," Kelly interrupted. "He didn't."

Shipley nodded half-heartedly. Nobody said it, but everyone thought it: desertion. But who could blame them? Two weeks ago the Illuminata had waged a tournament, an era-defining event, but they'd had not a squeak from Goldhawk. Maybe London was no longer the heart of the

Illuminata Empire? If that was so Kelly could watch until doomsday, but a boat loaded with pay and grub would never appear on that horizon. The garrison had been abandoned.

"They haven't forgotten us, mark my words," Kelly feigned a smile.

Shipley looked about the lonely coast. The sky seemed broody, and huge clouds prowled across it like giants spoiling for a fight. "No people and no tavern for fifteen miles. Not the best posting I ever had."

"There are plenty of worse places to be posted." Kelly squinted at the horizon, still willing the ship to appear. He disliked this place as much as the rest.

"But none so haunted I'll warrant," Shipley looked to the distant standing stones on the hill, and the derelict mine below, and thought of those who died here. Tales were rife, and for good reason, Kittiwake was a haunted coven where a mighty army had been turned to ash by God-only-knows what.

Kelly felt it too. "Just tales Sergeant, that's all." But he wondered. Odd things happened here. Five times this last month he'd found a pebble in his boot when dressing in the morning. It hadn't been there the night before, it was always in the left boot and by God he would swear it was the same stone. Always perfectly round, always the same pale blue, and always part of him desired to hold it and keep it, but always he threw it back into the dunes and always somehow it came back to him. He told nobody of it, although he suspected the rest experienced similar things. "Tales," he finished and wriggled the toes on his left foot, half expecting to feel a stone hidden there. "How's Private Yorke?"

Shipley shook his head. "Hasn't risen from his bed in two days."

"He say any more about this 'singing' he heard?"

"None."

"Anyone else heard it since?"

"No sir, just Yorke that time."

The pair looked out to sea again, contemplating the obvious.

"If I send his report back to Goldhawk, you know they'll have him committed," Kelly said truthfully. Yorke's account had disturbed them. While patrolling the cliffs near the standing stones he claimed a voice sang to him, and that he saw a black cat that turned into a lion of all things, a *black* lion. He ran back to camp blubbering like an imbecile and since then the only thing he'd said was, *'Thunder hails the headless king,'* over and over. Nobody had a clue what it meant. "I think that report should vanish on its way to London."

"I'll see to it sir." Shipley tugged at his collar. The evening wasn't far off, but the day was still muggy. "And *when* might we expect to send a courier back to Goldhawk?" he tactfully brought them back to their original question.

"I'll speak to Barda about the situation." While Kelly's tone was firm, his expression was less so. Everyone knew Barda wasn't a man to take advice.

Shipley rolled his eyes towards the largest hut, without moving his head. He didn't want Barda to think they'd been discussing him. "Soldier ought to have taken command of this operation sir, and Barda isn't no soldier."

"Watch your lip Sergeant."

He immediately straightened. "Sorry sir."

Kelly heaved a sigh. "You're right though." He tapped the telescope against his leg. "Barda's something else altogether."

Both men thought the same word at precisely the same instant, and if aware of it they might have smiled, but the word was too dark to warrant any humour. *'Magician'* is what captain and sergeant thought.

Magician to some, occult-scientist to others, either way Colm Barda was a rare sort. Most of Goldhawk's senior devisers had been killed the day Hobbs Ash had gone up in smoke. Now men like Barda were much sought after, for while knights could crush covens with guns and armour, devisers combated witchcraft with magic of their own. It had been men like Barda who had devised first-dawn, imbued the Fortitude with anti-magical properties, conceptualised machines driven by biological life essence, and of course turned prominent politicians to stone. Since last October Barda had been given all of Kittiwake-coven to study. He had an amply provisioned research post and a score of troops at his command. His orders were to determine what destroyed Krast's taskforce last year.

For the last eight months he had dutifully sent his findings back to Goldhawk where it was rumoured they had hired a rogue occultist to examine the krakens salvaged from here. Barda kept his reservations private, but he sneered at the idea of employing a mercenary occultist and his crude black magic. In truth he cared little if the French, Portuguese, or whoever, usurped the Illuminata. He could find rich employment with any of them and that, in the end, was what mattered most.

Right now the epic struggle between knights and witches was the furthest thing from his mind. Barda's interest was fixed on a humble snail. "Helicidae," he said, thinking how the Latin name neatly matched its whorled shell.

He took a pair of tongs and plucked the snail up from the Petri dish. The creature immediately withdrew to its shell, which was now numbered. He carefully catalogued each specimen recovered from the standing stones. The blight centred on them, and he was convinced answers would be unearthed there. "How artful nature is," he admired it, "yet how insensible."

He dropped the snail into a jar of hydrochloric acid, ruminating on how evolution had equipped it with a superb defence, but not enough intelligence to perceive abstract threats. "And that is why man will always conquer." Barda sat back to watch. This was less the scientist in him than the cruel little boy, the one who had listened to his sister's pitiful sobs rising up from the well rather than go fetch help.

A clatter in the corner diverted his attention.

He kept animals for his experiments, usually wild animals caught near the stones. At present he had a black cat in a crate by the door. The animal had toppled its water bowl. Barda saw the crate's wooden floor awash and heard a single soft 'meow' from its occupant. For over a month he had been feeding it food laced with ground rock taken from the stones. He suspected the rock had been affected by the blight and he wanted to see the effect of it on living tissue. Soon he would kill the cat and vivisect it.

The cat meowed again, but Barda didn't hear or care. He turned back to the dying snail. Already tiny bubbles were streaming up from the dissolving shell. Later he would study the gas released from the dissolved animal, as well as the effects of tide and moon on the residue, but right now the pretty curtain of rising bubbles in the jar captivated him.

"Colm! Get help please! Find papa, please! My leg, it's broken, I can't climb out!"

Pattie's cries rose up from his memory just like the glistening bubbles in the jar. *"Colm, pleeease!"*

"You should have promised Pattie," he said quietly.

Barda was daydreaming when there came a soft knock at the door followed by a voice. "Deviser Barda sir, it's Captain Kelly. I must speak with you."

"Come," he droned. Kelly entered, still holding the telescope. "Be quick Captain, I have important work." Barda stared at the undulating bubbles.

Kelly looked about him. Although really just a huge shed, the lab was packed with sophisticated equipment, not to mention unsavoury objects he couldn't identify. "Sir, I think it prudent we send another courier to Goldhawk, the situation is beginning to tell on the garrison's nerves."

Barda sighed impatiently, shoved back his chair and stood up. He was an imposing man, well over six feet tall, and his long grey hair streamed down his back while his bald scalp made him look brutish. A silver vial hung around his neck. Kelly knew for a fact it contained the ashes of a burned witch, but whether for symbolic of scientific reasons he didn't know. He wore heavy leather gauntlets and an apron. A thick belt loaded with cruel-looking examination tools was lashed around his ample waist. *Magician,* Kelly thought again.

"Situation?" Barda enquired icily.

"No word from London sir. Men need orders."

"While here under my command, my word is order enough."

"Right enough sir, but such won't feed and pay the men. If I could send a courier we might find out the situation at Goldhawk."

"Are their constitutions so frail that fear of low provisions sets them a shiver?" he sneered.

"It's wages to feed their families they're fearful for sir." Kelly was rattled, and now his anger exceeded his reservations.

"Are you questioning my command Captain?" He slid the gauntlets free and slapped them down against the bench.

"No sir." He tried a different tack. "But Goldhawk will expect your report. We could dispatch it with another request for re-supply."

Barda stroked his stubbly shin as he considered. Shaving soap was something else they were running low on. "Request denied," he said at last.

Kelly had anticipated resistance, but not outright refusal. He certainly hadn't anticipated the way his hand slid down to his revolver and the weight of the words that suddenly left his mouth, "Men's loyalty only goes so far sir." He found he was shaking. He also found to his surprise that he was relieved.

Barda glanced at the hand hovering over the holster, and sneered. "Have a care Captain, I've bested creatures that mere bullets would not scathe."

He looked totally calm Kelly thought. Was he bluffing? *Magician or man?* he thought again.

Barda slid a knife from the table and his mouth tightened into a thin slit. "There is pay and food until the end of the month you say?"

Kelly's fingers brushed at the revolver's handle. "Yes. As you well know. . . sir."

He examined the knife tip and pouted. "Then there's no cause to send a courier until August 1st."

"And by the time he should get back we'll have been without for at least a fortnight." Kelly gripped the revolver and the tension thickened like fog, broken only by the rumble of yet more thunder from outside.

"I doubt the garrison will resort to cannibalism. That'll be all Captain." Barda rammed the knife into the workbench, left it wavering there and turned back to the doomed snail.

"Colm, help me! I promise I won't tell papa!"

"But sir, for all we know London was beaten at Salisbury and the coffers are empty. Men need to know who's in charge or if they're going to be paid!" Without him realising it the revolver left its holster and was pointed in Barda's direction. Kelly wondered if his hands and mouth had taken on a life of their own because they were certainly doing things he'd never dreamed possible this morning. He thumbed back the hammer. The last warning gesture before he launched into treason and perhaps murder. As he did, a fresh bout of thunder shook the world outside. *Magician or man?* Now he'd have his answer. But Barda wasn't even listening.

The senior deviser was staring at the specimen jars on the table. There must have been two-dozen there, and all of them were moving. "Resonance!" He touched the vial around his neck.

Kelly saw it too. The contents of each jar were gently spiralling under their own power, all at the same rate, and all in a counter-clockwise direction. He saw dead butterflies, minerals, seedpods and shrapnel fragments, all circling silently inside their glass coffins. Suddenly a dreadful wailing sliced through the shed. Both men turned. The cat was yowling and staggering in circles, as if disorientated. Kelly could see it through the mesh. "What's wrong with it?" he asked in alarm.

"Resonance," Barda repeated. "Witchcraft you simpleton!"

"Witches?" He waved the gun around the room, expecting to see a witch right there.

Barda reached for his own revolver, amused by Kelly's bewilderment. "Never met a witch who was immune to bullets." He waved the gun in Kelly's direction. "Or a mutineer," he added threateningly. "Assemble the men. You want your pay, well today you're all going to earn it."

"Sir?"

"We're under attack you fool!" He ripped his tool belt and apron free. "Now move!" He gripped his collar and shoved him towards the door, and all the while the cat's mournful wails filled the room.

Kelly stumbled forwards feeling Barda's gun at his back, somehow understanding that whatever dark business had begun at haunted Kittiwake-coven, it was about to be concluded.

That dark business unknowingly began when a young man made a dangerous journey into the earth, guided by an untrustworthy god. Farona saved the serpent-twins and emerged to find his friends locked in battle, but they escaped thanks to that same god. Janus earned much gratitude from Clovis that day but he unwittingly earned something else as well. Far away, across unfathomable miles an insidious consciousness heard the earth open, followed by witches' footsteps on the spiral of Evermore and it recognised them as Janus's doing.

Self had at last found the missing god. It would return him to the Temple-of-Unity to complete his conditioning, but first he had to be recaptured. This very moment the chosen agent appointed this task was approaching the end of a long journey, intending to begin his search where Clovis had vanished. Kittiwake-coven was about to receive an unexpected visitor.

Along the coast all seemed normal. A flock of dunlins patrolled the undulating tide, and shafts of afternoon light raced across the waves like searchlights. A black-backed gull drifted overhead, scanning the shore for carrion. Spotting a drowned redshank, he swept down just in time to see off an opportunist raven who croaked indignantly, but the gull had his way and he settled down to eat.

A distant peal of thunder boomed eastwards, where dark clouds were advancing inland. Undaunted, the gull began tearing off chunks and shaking the sand loose before gulping them down. Occasionally he stopped to inspect the shore, troubled by his instincts. They were usually clear, but right now they were confused. They were telling him he might not be the undisputed king of the coast after all. *Danger! There is danger approaching!* they said. But nowhere did he see any.

Thunder rolled again, but closer now and it sounded 'crooked' as if this was the wrong kind of thunder. Without warning the dunlins burst into flight. Startled, the gull looked around. *Something is wrong here.* His instincts seemed supercharged now.

The landscape grew darker. He looked up, expecting to see thunderclouds but instead he saw a ragged hole in the sky where night replaced day and through it he saw alien stars twinkle. This was an image of night from somewhere else, somewhere far away. Thunder growled again, this time accompanied by an agonised scream, like a mother dying in childbirth. Instantly he abandoned the carrion, and was racing over the shore cackling in alarm. The sky-hole gaped wider, and the screaming grew louder. Something was about to happen that had never happened before.

The gull was lucky enough to miss what came next. The hole cast a dark funnel like a spotlight and everything within became as cold as deep space. The sand froze hard as iron and worms were desiccated in their burrows. Suddenly, this black-light revealed a living core, like a beating heart, and a wriggling shape began to materialise above the frozen sand. It was disturbingly humanoid, like a figure wrapped in a shroud, but before long other strange constructs began to appear, shielding it from view. First came the shadowy orb of a womb, framed by the curved bars of a rib cage, then the crenellated line of a backbone followed by the globular shapes of organs; a pair of kidneys, a stringy mop of intestines, a wedge-shaped slab that was the liver, and a thundering fist that was the heart. They steadily precipitated around the figure, until at last it vanished from sight.

The creature continued to materialise. A backbone stretched into a neck crowned with an unmistakably reptilian head, elongate and dragon-like. Eye sockets appeared cradling wild, staring eyes, followed by huge jaws, which sprang open to unleash a forked tongue and another agonised wail. Whatever this creature was it was in great pain. Muscles, veins and arteries branched and threaded themselves through the skeleton, stretching flesh over naked organs beneath. Wings appeared on its back and clawed feet on its four legs. Its heavy tail whipped back and forth, tearing up a shower of frozen sand, and now all across its flanks scales bubbled up and glittered as brightly as the stars above. This dragon was Acola's chariot and she had finally landed after a journey across the stars carrying the one charged with finding Janus.

She was elegant and magnificent. Every inch of her was pure white, everything: her claws, wings, scales and spines. Her eyes ought to have been ruby-red, but they were muddy brown with exhaustion. She emitted another roar and crashed down against the sand. The black-light faded and sunshine fell upon the dragon for the first, and last, time in her life. She had never felt the light of a sun, having been engineered solely to traverse the darkness of space.

For a while she lay there gasping and gripped by pain. A few gulls circled above, but they kept a distance. The breeze whistled through her spines and rippled her membranous wings. She forced an eye open and saw a living world after so long navigating the void. It was miracle enough to briefly banish the pain. She wanted to sample this new world and enjoy the sun against her scales, but without warning fresh pain ripped through her and she bellowed again. It was time to give birth.

This was no natural birth, but then again she was no natural animal and the thing inside her was not her offspring. He was an intruder who had stolen a ride across the stars hidden in her belly, safe from the harshness of space but now he wanted out.

She raised her head, gaped wide and heaved. Spittle flew, followed by droplets of blood. Her throat bulged as something slithered up from her innards, blocking her airway. Unable to breathe, she thrashed her head side-to-side, frantic to dislodge it. She strained until her eyes felt ready to rupture, and finally a bloody shower exploded from her mouth and the cocoon was ejected like a cork. It catapulted through the air and crashed down some twenty yards away, then she collapsed, too exhausted to realise that the pain had vanished.

The commotion seemed to be over. The gull returned and hovered a safe distance away, drawn by the smell of offal. He saw the strange cocoon lying on the sand. It smelled of fresh blood and lay still, apparently lifeless, and the gull was about to advance when it twitched. He hopped back with a strangled cry, blinked and cocked his head. He waited. The cocoon jerked again, harder this time and there came a growling sound from within. That sealed it. The gull had seen enough for one day and he heaved himself aloft and disappeared, shrieking as he went.

Something sharp punctured the cocoon and sliced an opening. Fluid jetted up and in a second the blade had split the membrane down the middle. It flopped open like a gruesome flower, and after a few seconds a head rose slowly into view and green eyes surveyed the landscape.

The outsider slithered from the cocoon, alert for danger and assessing everything around him. He lay belly down on the sand and raised his head. He was covered in black fur and his features were distinctly leonine. This traveller wasn't human, that much was obvious. In fact he was like no other being on Earth, except perhaps for one. . . a witch who had briefly lived here at Kittiwake-coven.

"Sergeant! Run up the red flag!" Kelly pulled the whistle from his pocket and delivered three sharp blasts.

Sergeant Shipley came running from the mess hut, rifle clutched to his chest. "Sir?"

"Barda says we're under attack, run the flag!" Kelly watched as Barda hurried around the camp taking readings with something akin to a compass. *If he is a magician, now's the time to prove it,* he thought.

"Red flag!" Shipley bellowed, and immediately three privates duly ran to hoist it. "Captain, there's half the company out on patrol." He looked about, expecting to see witches flooding over the barricade. "Can't do much with ten lads."

"We'll have to manage, and hope they see the flag." Kelly blasted his whistle three more times. "Company!" he shouted. Within seconds ten troopers stood to attention outside Barda's laboratory. The red flag flapped above, warning the whole camp of imminent attack. *To think all I had to worry about five minutes ago was wages and provisions,* he thought, watching the flag ripple, and briefly wondered why danger signs must always be the colour of blood.

"Form up," Shipley ordered and ten pairs of boots all stamped to attention. "Captain?" Shipley looked to his superior, who in turn looked to Barda.

"Deviser Barda, your orders?" Kelly listened to the echo of spent thunder and distant gulls, and dared hope it was a mistake.

Barda stood with his back to them, studying his instrument. Eventually he lifted an arm towards the sea. "It's coming from the shore."

Kelly swallowed a lump. "Company, it's likely there are witches advancing from the seaward side. Sergeant, take half the men and follow me. When we reach the dunes veer east, I'll turn west." He set off without waiting for an answer, dimly aware that Barda wasn't following. *Just a man after all,* he thought angrily. It seemed he had his answer.

The creature slowly stood upright. He was naked and plastered with secretions from the cocoon, and he swayed unsteadily. He was heavily built and covered from head to toe in short panther-black fur, which had an underlying red sheen like angry coals. Black whiskers dotted his cheeks and his eyes were living pools of emerald. Slit pupils looked out from them, appraising and calculating everything. His mane was shorn to the skin revealing a muscular neck, a wide forehead and short pointed ears. He flexed his muzzle in a grimace, and fearsome teeth flashed for an instant. The journey had been an ordeal and he needed time to recover, but time was short and there were rituals to finish before he was seen. He parted his jaws and tasted the air, sampling a host of sensations. Satisfied, he snapped his mouth shut and licked his lips, revealing a tongue that was thick and ruddy.

His name was Sef and unlike Clovis he had arrived prepared. Already shaking off the drowsiness of hibernation, he knelt and retrieved a pack from the ruptured cocoon. Inside were his sword, his staff, and a bundle of garments and other possessions. He worked quickly, twitching his huge head this way and that as he did, scanning for life. The sound of voices drifted over the dunes. Perhaps he'd been discovered already he thought, but it troubled him little. Evasion and killing were both arts he excelled in.

He drew his sword, which was slender, subtly curved and just as deadly as Clovis's, and crept over to the exhausted dragon. She concealed one last item and he must retrieve if he stood any chance of getting home again. He stood astride her head, gauging where to make his blow.

She forced an eye open and looked up, but Sef was just a blur against the sky. She tried to rise and confront him, recognising danger, but there was no strength in her and her claws just raked impotently against the sand. A last gasp escaped her lungs and her wings rippled with the passing wind. Sef selected his mark and with one swipe severed her head from her neck.

She saw the blue ocean one last time followed by the flash of steel, then nothing more. Such was her reward for a harsh lifetime of servitude. Sef might have been pleased to know that things weren't so different here on Earth either.

He worked fast. The voices were drawing closer and his instincts were coming back to life. He was already growing faster and more confident.

Her body continued to twitch as he slit open the abdomen. A jumble of organs spilled out and washed across his feet. Checking the shore one last time, he knelt and slid an arm into the cavity. He searched by touch, feeling bones and tissues press against his hand until at last, deep in her womb, he found what he wanted. It was small enough to fit inside his fist and could have easily been overlooked, but he had trained for this and knew just where to find it. He withdrew his clenched fist with a triumphant growl, shook the blood free, snatched up his possessions and ran.

"There!"

Shipley skidded to a halt. "Where?"

"There," Anderson repeated, pointing. "Something black ran into the dunes."

All five men dropped low, partly from training, partly from fear.

"Where?" Shipley whispered, wishing Kelly was with them, and hadn't split their forces.

Anderson pointed to a hillock two hundred yards along the shore.

"Dunno what it was. It was like a man but black all over."

"So not a man?" Shipley was already feeling out of his depth. Something 'black' and 'inhuman' were two words guaranteed to give him the creeps. He thought of the huge spiders that used to live in his grandfather's hay barn.

"A witch?" one of the others asked. It was Graves, who was little more than a youth.

"Dunno," Anderson replied unhelpfully. "But it vanished into the dunes right over there." Again there came that pointing finger and Shipley quietly cursed it, thinking it could well be leading them to their doom.

"Right lads, we keep to the dunes. Follow me." He half crawled, half ran, seeking cover in the grass, heading in the direction Anderson had indicated.

They heard it before anything else: gulls, lots of gulls. The sky was full of them, hundreds at least, but what was on the beach for them to squabble over was a mystery from here. Shipley tumbled into the marram grass chasing his breath.

"Stinks like Hell," Jones wrinkled his nose. Sure enough there was the rank and intimate odour of decay.

"Smells of something long dead," Clarke, the oldest, not to mention dourest, said grimly.

"There must be hundreds of birds. Whatever's dead it's big for sure." Jones made to climb the dune.

"Come back you oaf!" Shipley grabbed his foot and dragged him down. "Could be a trap. It's known witches can make animals do what they want." He looked up at a sky full of gulls. It looked like a crazy jigsaw of bird-shaped pieces.

"Gulls are drawn by blood," Clarke said gloomily. "Mark my words, blood. And that smell, it's death, mark my words."

"You're not bloody helping!" Shipley scowled. "I'm going up for a look, Anderson watch my back."

"Aye Sarge."

Shipley crawled up the shifting sands, dragging his rifle along. Tough dune grass pricked at his face as he went, and as he climbed higher more of the beach came into view, and that stink grew even stronger.

Already she was decomposing. It wasn't such a difficult thing to programme into her being. The Unitari's devisers were careful to always cover their tracks and within an hour the white dragon would be just a pool of slurry. There was enough of her left to give Sergeant Shipley a start however. "All the saint's bones!" he uttered and crossed himself.

"Sarge?" Jones hissed, "what you see?"

Shipley wasn't even sure himself. Just hundreds of gulls fighting over formidably large bones dripping with liquefied flesh. He waved them up and a moment later five men peered down at the gruesome spectacle.

"Dead whale?" Jones guessed.

"Na, wasn't here an hour ago. Already rotting. Looks like it's been here days," Shipley figured.

"A curse killed it," Clarke warned.

"Do you have to be so bloody cheerful?"

"He's got a point," Jones chipped in.

"No sign of that thing." Anderson was more interested in the dunes than the corpse on the beach. "Swear it ran this way."

"He's probably responsible for this too," Shipley nodded to the carnage below.

"It wasn't a 'he' Sarge, it was an 'it'."

"A witch's familiar," Clarke warned again. "Summoned by dark arts, able to kill with a curse and drag a soul screaming down to Lucifer."

Shipley rolled his eyes. *Gordon Clarke,* he thought wearily, *C Squad's very own angel of death.*

"Sarge?" Anderson pressed.

"Curse or no," he said stoically, "it's our job. We're going down there." He wriggled over the crest. The rest followed, and all five slithered down through wet grass and gritty sand, assailed by that stench and the scream of the gulls.

They huddled at the foot of the slope. Down here the stink was even worse. The air felt oily with rot and already swarmed with flies. A constant drizzle of guano rained down, and Shipley could hardly hear himself think for the noise.

"It's getting colder," Jones observed nervously.

At first Shipley thought the air was dark with flies, then it dawned on him that some kind of dark fog was growing there above the carcass, slowly draining the sun's warmth. Clarke said something, but it was lost in the din of the gulls. "What?" he snapped.

"Said it's getting darker and colder, there's a mist moving in."

He was right, Shipley saw. That strange mist was permeating the whole beach. It had a faint brown tinge to it, and reminded him of the diseased bedding he'd so often seen in battlefield infirmaries. Worse still, it was clearly thickening. *We'll get lost in that and nobody'll hear a thing with all those blasted gulls,* he thought, knowing they had to work fast.

"What is it?" Anderson whispered.

Shipley shook his head. "Fan out and search lads, before it gets too thick. Keep the next man in sight at all times, whistles at the ready." He set off before his courage failed him, heading towards the wreckage of flesh and bones, which even now was growing fainter in the menacing mist.

When Kelly saw reinforcements moving through the dunes towards him he breathed a sigh of relief. He raised a hand but didn't call out. Corporal Beckley did likewise and moved quietly towards them. "Good man," Kelly noted and signalled for his own unit to take cover in the grass.

Within a minute Beckley's squad joined them. "Saw the red flag sir, came back as quick as we could."

Kelly looked about, where now he had fourteen men. "See anything on your patrol?"

"Nothing sir, what's the situation?"

"Barda says we're under attack."

"Attack?" Beckley looked sceptical.

"So he says. I'm starting to think this is all a mistake. Nevertheless, we make a thorough search of the dunes and regroup with Sergeant Shipley."

"Where's Deviser Barda now sir?"

"Back at camp." Kelly heard a few cynical mutters, but let them pass. They were justified after all. "Right, fan out, make a search line, twenty yards between each man." He was on his feet and moving purposefully through the dunes. The remainder formed up on either side of him stretched out into a long line, looking for an enemy they were certain now didn't exist.

The mist burned his throat and he wanted to cough. It was like breathing carbolic vapour, but Sergeant Shipley pressed on. He could just see Clarke's silhouette to his right, while Jones hovered to his left. He just hoped both of them could see the next man beyond, namely Graves and Anderson. An unexpected shower of gull shit plastered his neck and shoulder. "Blast it!" he growled and tried to shrug the foul stuff off. He gripped his rifle harder. The air was clammy and faintly sticky, while underfoot was a revolting soup of decay.

Shipley's foot snagged against a bone as long as a scythe and he grimaced in disgust. Everywhere he looked he fancied he saw that black 'thing'; a shadow here, a fleeting shape there. He strained to hear anything through the gull's racket, wondering how even these scavengers could even think of eating this mess. He trod on something soft and rubbery, but didn't look down for fear of losing his lunch. So far he saw no sign of witches. In all his years he'd never even heard of witches employing tactics like this. Even at Solvgarad.

The mire underfoot grew thicker, and the smell more offensive. "There's nothing in here," he realised. "Whatever came this way is long gone." He reached for his whistle to call the search off when suddenly he heard a scream. He whirled to his right and just caught the vague shape of Clarke dropping to the ground and a shadow flitting away into the mist. "Clarke!" Now he blasted his whistle in a battle call and splashed through the quagmire towards him. He got halfway there when he heard a second scream, this time to his rear and knew without looking that it was Jones. He spun back in his direction and again there was that moving shape: black and so very fast. *Nothing can move that fast!* his mind insisted. *Nothing!* On impulse he raised his rifle and fired. "JONES!" he bellowed.

"Sarge!" A stricken voice answered, but it was Anderson who ran at him from the mist. His eyes were like saucers and he teeth were bared. "Sarge I saw it!"

"Where's Jones?"

"Killed him. It must have!"

There's that 'it' word again, Shipley thought with rising panic. The two stood back to back and Shipley's next whistle-blast stopped short, when Graves, the last of his squad, staggered over, dripping with filth.

"Sarge, it got Clarke, I fell," he blubbered, "it got him." The youngest of them was close to hysteria.

Shipley grabbed his collar. "Down, both of you." He all but threw them to the ground, where they knelt in a crude triangle facing outwards with their rifles raised. Shipley scanned the mist. The overpowering smell was making him dizzy and all he could hear were gulls. "What happened to Clarke?" he asked.

Graves wiped the mess from his face. "Dunno," he panted. "I saw him go down. Ran over but he was already dead. Heard your whistle and ran, but fell."

"You sure he was dead?"

"Head was gone," he stammered. "Gone."

Shipley saw how his rifle trembled. *Lad's got the frights. If we don't get out of here now we'll all get it,* he calculated. "Captain Kelly will have heard us lad. He's on his way Graves, you hear me?"

Graves said nothing.

"Graves!" he barked.

"Aye Sarge," he sobbed.

"We move together, back the way we came. Keep it tight. Understood?"

"Yes Sarge," they echoed together.

"Right, up." They stood slowly, and Shipley walked backwards covering their retreat, while either side of him Graves and Anderson faced into the mist, rifles ready for the terrible black 'thing' that hunted them.

Kelly and his men stopped in their tracks. They'd heard a single gunshot. "Shipley." He knew his sergeant was in trouble and this was no false alarm. "We're coming Sergeant." On his signal the search line drew close, formed two ranks and headed out at a run.

So far so good, Shipley thought. Something darted over the sand to his left. A quick glance told him it was just a gull, but Graves saw it too, and fear got the better of him.

"Sarge!" he screamed and fired. The discharge left Shipley's ears ringing and the bullet sent up a cloud of sand, while the gull flew off in a panic.

"What was it, what was it!" Anderson flapped.

"Just a bloody gull!" Shipley elbowed the rifle away. "Keep that thing down if you can't use it properly!"

"Sorry Sarge, I thought it was –,"

"Never mind. Keep moving." He listened hard, hearing only their squelching footfalls and the constant gulls.

"Are we far off?" Graves pleaded.

"Not far now lad."

"Really?"

"I promise." As soon as he made that promise he heard the rasp of sand on his left and suspected movement. "Anderson what was that?" The private didn't answer, and something about his footsteps sounded wrong. "Anderson, answer me!" As Shipley turned to see, something sailed past him and at first he thought it was just another gull but, when it hit the sand and rolled, he clearly saw that it was a human head. "Dear Christ!"

Anderson's headless body staggered a few more paces then slumped to the sand. Graves saw it from the corner of his eye, let out a terrified scream and fired again.

"Down!" Shipley roared and knocked the private to the ground and raised his rifle. There it was, coming right at him. *Something black and not human.*

Shipley got his first and only look at it just as steel flashed. The blade swept upwards in a scything arc, slicing his arms off at the elbows and taking most of his rifle with them. At the same instant his trigger finger squeezed as it obeyed a command from a brain it was no longer connected to, and what was left of the rifle roared a final time. The gun, now ruined, exploded and whirled away. His attacker was so fast that Shipley didn't have time to register his ruined arms or scream. *It's a panther,* he thought incredulously, *a bloody black panther.*

Steel flashed again and Shipley's head joined Anderson's face down in the sand.

Kelly kept running but he wasn't sure what he was running towards. It looked like fog, but it was unnaturally localised and an unhealthy brown colour, while a swarm of gulls circled above it. Muzzle flash danced in the murk, men screamed and gunshots rang out. "Sergeant!" He broke into a sprint, with his company close on his heels.

"Cover the Captain!" Corporal Beckley dropped to one knee, with his rifle trained on the wall of mist, but seeing nothing to fire at.

A figure approached from the mist, weaving drunkenly. "Stop and be known!" Kelly skidded to a stop. "I said stop!"

The figure continued towards him at a run, and then without warning another shot rang out, this time from the stranger.

Kelly felt a hammer blow to the chest and was thrown backwards. He hit the sand hard and had time to realise he'd been shot. *Witches don't carry guns?* he thought dimly. The front of his uniform grew dark and sticky with blood. Around him he could hear men screaming and shouting in confusion.

Kelly's attacker ran out of the mist, still clutching his rifle. It was Graves, now senseless with terror. "It killed the Sarge!" he screamed over and over. "Killed him dead!"

Kelly lay with his cheek pressed against the sand, feeling numb and dazed. Somewhere he could hear Corporal Beckley shouting his name and Graves screaming hysterically, but it all seemed so much fuss over nothing. Panic-stricken men crowded in, arguing about what to do for their Captain. Someone restrained the sobbing Graves and snatched his rifle away, and now the corporal was at his side, shaking him, trying to get a response, but it was such a huge effort to answer. Instead, he regarded the world from this curious angle where men towered over him like giants and sand grains glistened like stars. Just inches from his face sat a pebble and it came as no surprise to him to see that it was smooth, perfectly rounded, and a delicate blue colour. The neatness of it all elicited a faint parting smile. He dragged his hand up and clasped the little stone knowing this time he would keep it forever. "Haunted," he whispered, and then the world dimmed and he went off to join that shadowy realm.

The camp was eerily quiet and for a while the only thing Barda could hear were distant cries from the infirmary hut where Private Yorke languished in a witless state. *'Thunder hails the headless king.'* He had said nothing else for two days now.

After a very long ten minutes there came a rash of gunfire and the suggestion of screams. Barda couldn't be certain because there were an abnormal number of gulls circling close by. He waited patiently in his laboratory, hiding behind shelves laden with books and jars. Hiding was no use against the enemy heading this way, he knew that, but he also knew a trick or two from his long years battling witches. He had opened the silver vial around his neck and drawn a circle on the floor with the ash. There wasn't much and the circle was only just big enough for him to stand in. But he couldn't leave it. His life depended on it.

Barda stood perfectly still, feet together, revolver poised, eyes fixed on the door. *Never met a witch who was immune to bullets,* he thought with satisfaction, and whoever or whatever came through that door would be no different he told himself. *And never met a witch who'd see harm come to an animal.* Witches were known for their reverence of animals. Barda had tethered the cat to the bench leg. The disorientated animal continued to stagger in pointless circles. Occasionally it emitted a guttural wail, but for the most part the only sound was the click of its claws. It would be the first thing any witch would see when they came through that door, a momentary distraction, just long enough for him to aim and fire.

Without warning, the device in his hand rattled as the needle spun frantically, and the cat let out its most wrenching cry yet. The enemy was close. Barda smiled, and levelled the revolver at the door.

None of them had been suitable. Sef was searching for someone special, someone who had touched the hidden realm: a worker of magic. None of the men he killed on the beach were of that breed, and until he found one he would remain a stranger in this world.

He quickly readied himself, and now he wore simple black robes, boots and a belt. Around his neck he wore a small iron locket. It was a vital artefact, just like the thing taken from the dragon's womb, which was now safely concealed in his robes. He crouched in the dunes holding his lightning-staff, listening and sensing. Ahead, he spied a cluster of huts defended by a barricade, but the gates stood open. *A trap?* he wondered. Behind, back the way he'd come, Sef could hear men scream and shout. The confusion would occupy them for a while longer. He should leave, he knew, but right now he'd caught the scent of a magic-worker and he couldn't waste the opportunity.

He broke cover and darted forwards. As he drew closer to the largest hut, where the scent was strongest, he heard a pitiful wailing from inside and his hackles rose in response. He bounded onto the steps and pressed a clawed hand to the door, tasting what lay beyond. The scent was overpowering, but Sef was momentarily confused. His senses were telling him contradictory things. The creature inside wailed again and Sef hissed in reply, powerless to acknowledge its kindred call. Lying low on the step, he pushed the door open quietly and flowed inside like a living shadow.

Barda heard a soft thud outside and caught his breath. The cat wailed again, giving him chance to cock the revolver. Daylight first glinted around the door then pooled across the floor, as the door swung further open. Barda caught the sounds of distant shouting and even a stray rumble of thunder, then the sunlight was blotted out again as something entered.

Sef saw much in his first glance, but never a creature like the one before him. It was so alike but so different to him that for a fraction his concentration lapsed. The cat saw the intruder and hissed in fear. It leapt away, the twine snapped and the cat darted towards the daylight. But Sef was equally fast. His hand shot out with lightning speed and he snatched the cat from the floor, gripping it by the neck. He brought it closer to his face, overcome with curiosity. The cat hung suspended from his fist and the two supreme killers came eye-to-eye.

Barda watched in disbelief. The creature couldn't be what his eyes were telling him. They were extinct. The last confirmed one died at Solvgarad over twenty years ago. With peculiar regret he aimed the revolver. Perhaps he could kill it with minimal damage and have it stuffed he thought. Such a trophy would earn him great renown. In his excitement Barda didn't notice how the revolver's tip edged over the protective circle. It was less than a hair's width, but it made the tiniest hole in his protective barrier.

Sef suddenly detected another creature in the room: the magic-worker, and with speed that defied natural law he dropped the cat and whirled around.

Barda saw his error and fired. The gun exploded into life. The creature roared. And Barda screamed. The bullet went low, struck the iron locket around Sef's neck and ricocheted off, shattering it in the process. Heedless of the loss, Sef threw himself at Barda, and before the deviser had chance to fire again he was knocked to the floor where the creature pinned him with its deadly claws. Barda looked up into those bottomless green eyes, feeling like a doomed mouse. "No, you're extinct!" he accused.

Sef didn't understand a word, although this was the man he had scented, the one he needed. But he didn't need all of him.

"Your kind are dead!" Barda roared and struggled in his grip.

Without relinquishing his hold Sef reached for his sword.

"The Therions are dead!" Barda screamed.

The thing hissed in response and he saw the red cave of its mouth open up, surrounded by an arsenal of fearsome teeth.

"Dead! You hear me? Dead!" Never let it be said that Senior Deviser Colm Barda didn't go out screaming and shouting. Although the hand holding the revolver was pinned to the floor, he fired again and managed to hit the chair leg, which in other circumstances would have been an impressive shot.

The black creature didn't even flinch, instead the blade sliced through the air.

"Dead, you bastard, DEAD!" Barda screamed, and his last word was perfectly apt. His head rolled away as his body fired a third and final shot, this time hitting the empty cat cage.

The hut fell silent and the gun smoke cleared.

"D-e-a-d?" Sef repeated the word, liking the sound of it. He grabbed Barda's long grey hair and held his head aloft, examining his trophy. Now he had everything he wanted, although he bitterly regretted losing the locket. He just hoped what he'd come here for would be worth the trouble.

He paused on the step and surveyed the empty camp with Barda's head dangling from his fist. His keen eyes just caught sight of a black tail vanishing behind the infirmary hut. The cat had made good its escape, unlike Deviser Barda. Sef carefully dropped the head into a black sack that had a metallic lustre, and hauled it over his shoulder and made ready to leave. It was only then that he realised he was being watched. The effects of long sleep still plagued him, and he cursed himself for being so slow.

A gaunt looking man dressed in pyjamas was standing outside the infirmary. Sef watched him for a moment. He smelled of confusion and turmoil and he knew he wasn't a threat.

Private Yorke pointed towards the sack, and thunder rolled again as he did. "Thunder hails the headless king," he repeated groggily.

Sef dipped him a farewell bow as if understanding, and vanished behind the laboratory and out of sight.

By nightfall Sef had travelled a good distance, flying on his staff and mostly over empty countryside. Instincts took him roughly east, and as the sky was turning violet and the first stars showed, he took refuge on the wilderness coast around the Goonhilly Downs. The place was devoid of life but for sheep and birds, which suited him fine. He couldn't afford another confrontation, not now especially. He needed privacy and time for what would come next.

He sat in the dunes close to a ruined little abbey and opened the sack. He had brought only essential equipment from Vega. Of course he had his lightning-staff containing his mysterious thunder-sprite, his devastating sword, the prized locket known as a 'pact-of-grace', but now tragically broken, also the sacred object cut from the dragon's belly, and lastly this sinister device; the gelding-sack.

Currently it contained Barda's head, but Sef had brought it intending to catch a far more significant trophy. Once he had reclaimed Janus he would cut Clovis's head from his shoulders and he would take it back to Vega as proof of his victory and for Acola to interrogate, just as he now intended to interrogate Barda.

Sef tenderly withdrew the head and held it between his huge hands. It resembled a turnip dangling ropes of bloodied hair. Barda's glassy eyes stared up at him, but he wasn't entirely dead, such was the power of the gelding-sack. He still lived, barely, but even so he was living enough to interrogate.

It had been a long journey and Sef was hungry. The interrogation would serve two purposes, firstly to educate him about this world, and secondly to silence his growling belly, because unlike Clovis and other loyal witches Sef had never sworn the oath against eating flesh. He licked his lips and opened his jaws wide.

Senior Deviser Colm Barda was still vaguely conscious when the creature took its first bite. Agony rolled over him as fangs punctured flesh and bone, but he had no lungs with which to scream.

As it gulped down a chunk of cerebellum, Barda briefly experienced the bizarre sensation of being in two places at once, of still being inside his own skull yet also sliding down Sef's throat. With each bite Barda became less and Sef became more. His knowledge was digested, until finally all his memories streamed upwards into nothing, like bubbles from a dying snail or pleadings from a forgotten well.

Sef ate every last scrap. Barda's tongue told him the language of this world, his eyes told him everything they'd seen and read, his ears held the subtlety of both music and lies, his mind spilled its secrets for Sef to lap up, and when the feast of knowledge was done Sef curled up and fell into a deep sleep. When he next awoke he would know this world intimately and then the hunt for Clovis would begin with a vengeance.

Chapter Three

Safe in the storm

'Here is a miracle – take a handful of soil and watch living things spring from it.
And there is no soil so hard, nor wound so deep, that green things cannot
eventually heal it.'
'Almanac of Ever-Spring', a witch's text on garden matters

A lone crow glided high above England's borderlands, where gentle
pasture met the Black Mountains of Wales. The summer sky was flawless
and his viewpoint was unrivalled. He could see the world's private life
ticking away below and no drama was too small for his keen eyes, which
is precisely why crows were so valuable to witches. In exchange for shelter
and food, birds like him patrolled for miles around the hidden refuge
known as Stormwood-coven.

His own chief was named Harl, although that was merely the witches'
name for him. Crows had no need of names, human or otherwise, but
Harl had been absent from Stormwood for some weeks helping witches
coordinate their strike against the Illuminata. Crow-kind might not
comprehend precisely what the Illuminata were or stood for, but wherever
they went the world suffered and that was good enough reason for crows
to help witches.

As he continued his patrol, a raven called from greater heights above.
Stormwood's scout dipped his wings in respect. Ravens, not raptors, were
royalty amongst birds for they kept the Earth's memories safe and passed

them down the generations. The crow drifted on, flapping with lazy grace, while marking the landscape below.

He passed a succession of river-valleys and crumpled mountains, until finally the distinctive oval of Stormwood-coven rolled into view, looking like an island in an ocean of dark forest. Two small rivers ran through Stormwood; Minag from the north and Bitterwade from the east, and joined at the coven's southern edge creating a 'Y' shaped confluence.

Witches had started a new home here four months ago, secret to all outsiders. It was up to Harl's crows to lead witches through the hostile counties beyond to the safe harbour of Stormwood. Only trusted crows knew the way and this is how Kolfinnia kept its location secret.

At the coven's heart lay an ancient Iron Age fort. From ground level it was just a rough embankment, but from above it revealed itself as a great horseshoe-shaped construct. The south-eastern wall had long since collapsed and been reclaimed by nature, leaving a beautiful amphitheatre at the fort's centre that everyone had come to call the Glade. Ceremonies, debates and gatherings were held here, and during fair weather the Wildwood founding-banner was flown here. Made by Valonia, it acted as Kolfinnia's standard at the battle for Kittiwake and its presence was held to be very lucky. Beside the banner sat a huge flat stone, shaped like an anvil and appropriately dubbed likewise, and important announcements were made from here.

In its heyday the fort would have repelled all intruders but time had done what enemy warriors couldn't and trees had invaded the embankment around the Glade, clothing it with leafy buttresses and spires, like a green cathedral. While the fort was almost unrecognisable, its innards were surprisingly complete even after thousands of years. It was crisscrossed with tunnels and chambers and after some excavation the witches were beginning to find them eminently useful, not to mention magical. They had unearthed a good many prehistoric lions' claws, which many, including Kolfinnia, thought perfect for their lion-like coven-father.

Kolfinnia's witches had turned the forgotten land surrounding the fort into gardens, and what a sight it was. From his vantage point the crow saw a patchwork of vegetable plots, orchards, herb gardens, irrigation ditches, grain crops, medicinal plants beds, thatched huts of all shapes and sizes, treetop shelters, a smithy, grain store and even a vineyard and small brewery. Four months ago none of this had been here, then the witches had come and made it with hard toil and disciplined magic. They had built a new coven, and at the same time honoured an old one. Valonia's seasons; Snow-Thaw, Flower-Forth, Seed-Fall and Moon-Frost found an echo here. Everyone wore one of the season colours, even if it was just a strip of cloth tied around an arm or a hat, and so Wildwood's memory lived on. Although the ruined fort sat central to Stormwood, the Glade and the gardens were its beating heart and the witches that tended them were its lifeblood, and as always the gardens were busy.

The crow dropped lower, already feeling the security that comes with familiarity. He could even spot the ragged scarecrow that doubled as his nesting site and lookout post. If it had occurred to him he would have thought it darkly ironic that witches provided scarecrows for birds to make their homes in, while in the outer world he regularly saw his dead kin dangling from them as grim warnings. The smell of blooms, berries and a hundred other crops wafted up towards him. He swooped low, disturbing a flock of jackdaws, and cawed in welcome, simply glad to be home. A young girl kneeling in the blackcurrant bushes looked up as he sailed overhead. He would find Kolfinnia, report the day's findings and then be off to grab kitchen scraps before the best of the pickings were taken. The sun was shining, he had a safe home and plenty to eat. Yes, it was fair to say, that for this crow at least, life was good.

Emily Meadows heard a crow call. She looked up from picking blackcurrants, but he was already gone. "I wish I was a crow," she sulked, "I could spend all day flying, pinching shiny things and doing what I wanted, not picking berries." Her fingers were sticky and stained, and she was hot and tired.

She glanced over to where a strange but striking witch surveyed the gardens. Although she first laid eyes on him last autumn she still hadn't actually spoken with him, which only added to the mystery of Coven-father Clovis. She kept a distance because she was wary of him. To a seven-year old, Clovis not only looked like a lion but he was likely as dangerous as one, and it wasn't too far-fetched to imagine him snacking on disobedient young witches who didn't work sufficiently hard. Her fingers worked faster at this thought and she stole another glance in his direction. The gentle breeze tugged at his mane of steel-grey fur, and the sun glinted off the sword around his waist. He looked stern, almost terrible even, yet all of Stormwood owed him their lives. Nine months ago they had fought a savage battle and Clovis had found them an escape. He had taken them through Evermore, the stairway of the dead. Thereafter, they had wandered for a while before settling at what was to become Stormwood.

Next to Clovis stood a young woman with long dark hair and an elegant but serious face. Emily remembered when Kolfinnia had been filled with youthful dreams, but that was before Wildwood fell, before the battle for Kittiwake. Now she was Stormwood's coven-mother and duty, not dreams, filled her head. A crow landed nimbly on her shoulder, cackling and chattering. She welcomed him and listened to what he had to say before he flapped away again, lifting strands of her hair in a sweep of feathers.

Emily watched the pair of them. Coven-mother and coven-father seemed deep in conversation. Kolfinnia said something to Clovis and Emily heard him rumble something in reply. She noted from the way he smiled at her that he had a tender side, but still those glinting teeth set her wondering. . . did he really eat wayward little witches who would rather daydream than work?

She dropped more fruits into her collecting bowl. Her mind wasn't wholly on her work as usual. She sneaked another look around the gardens, this time alert for chief gardener Flora Greyswan. Flora was always reminding her how something called 'selfsuffishuncy' was vital. Emily understood, but on a beautiful July day the last thing she wanted was to gather blackcurrants, especially now. Last month had been a turbulent time, with witches leaving to attack a tournament on Kolfinnia's orders. Emily didn't fully grasp what was involved, but she knew it wasn't good. The witches had returned triumphant, most of them anyhow, and there was only one tale on everyone's lips – Blackwand.

Many survivors were still journeying to Stormwood, and it was common knowledge that *she* was on her way too. All of Stormwood waited for Blackwand to arrive; Blackwand, champion of witches, loved by fairy-kind, protected by giant bears, and even blessed by the strange denizens of Ruination, who, according to the wildest tales, had appeared when all seemed lost and helped turn the tide, or something like that. Emily couldn't be sure because the adults didn't like to talk of fighting when children were about. She gathered that some of the tales were dark, but it seemed there was nothing Blackwand couldn't do. From the sound of it she had practically defeated the Illuminata by herself, but best of all it was said that Blackwand was a solstice queen, the very same duty Emily enjoyed. She cheerfully imagined them being queens together and that common bond would be enough for Blackwand's magic to rub off on her. But waiting for the hero of the hour to finally arrive was deeply frustrating.

"Blackwand," Emily sighed, thinking blackcurrants were hardly as exciting. Noting the basket was full she stood and clapped the dirt from her hands. Through the rows of tomatoes she could see Flora. "Miss Flora?" she called politely.

A tall young woman rose from weeding the plants. She wore a headscarf against the sun, a satchel bursting with garden tools, and most conspicuously a patch over her left eye. Her fair hair was tied in a ponytail that reached below her waist and her smock was dusty with earth. "Yes Emily?"

"May I go to the stream for a drink?"

"There's plenty of water here Emmy."

"But the stream's a lot nicer and cooler."

Flora smiled shrewdly. "Emmy, when she gets here I think you'll know about it."

"When who gets here?" she pretended.

"Never mind, just don't fall in the stream and be back in ten minutes. And *only* ten minutes you hear, the currants need gathering while the moon's still waxing."

"Aye miss." Emily was already away, racing along the path between the cherry saplings.

"Ten minutes!" Flora shouted after her, already worrying. Just like her closest friend Kolfinnia, it seemed she was more cautious these days.

"That's Emily's fifth patrol today." Kolfinnia watched with amusement. "We hardly need crows watching over us with her running around."

"Blackwand has energized the whole coven," Clovis agreed.

She studied him for a moment, oblivious to the other witches going about their duties. "You seem serious today, or should I say 'these days'." A bond deeper than duty had grown between them, and although outwardly he remained the lone figure of authority, she knew better.

"I'm always serious," he insisted, and proved it with a deliberate frown.

"You used to be less serious, put it that way. In fact you weren't this brooding even before the battle at Kittiwake." She reconsidered, "What am I saying – you *enjoyed* the battle at Kittiwake."

He played along and roused a half-smile. "Perhaps."

"Clovis," she became serious, "what's troubling you?"

He just stared silently at the trees.

"Clovis, don't lock me out."

He shook his head. "It's Janus," he said eventually.

She took a sharp breath, "You're leaving then, to return him home as promised?"

"Not quite." He wrinkled his top lip and his whiskers bristled.

"So you're not leaving. . . yet?" she asked with fragile relief.

"Not yet." He looked at the well-beaten path at his feet. Since founding Stormwood the place had become their home, not just a camp readying for battle like Kittiwake. Despite its ominous name, both of them had found some well earned peace here. He wasn't sure how to articulate his worries and he was still trying when she spoke up.

"Clovis. We govern Stormwood together, we face problems the same way – together." She made to touch him.

"Kolfinnia," he stepped back from her. "When we left Kittiwake, it was to the racket of battle. I fully expected Janus to demand I return him home that very hour, but he didn't."

"And I thank Oak for that," she muttered, folding her arms.

"Even as we walked Evermore's steps he changed his bargain again. I'm sure you remember."

"Very well."

"Each day I've stayed has been a gift, but I knew he would eventually make me honour my promise, but what's unsettling is that so far he hasn't." He kicked a pebble by his toe. Close by, children were laughing as they pretended to fly lightning-staffs through the gardens, running with broom handles held between their legs.

"That's good though isn't it?" But she knew the longer he stayed the harder the parting would be.

"I'm used to him playing tricks, but now something's wrong. He's spoken not a word since the solstice, and neither does he move. I've never seen him like this before."

"Why didn't you say something sooner?"

"I didn't want to worry you."

"Do you think he's sick? Can a god even fall ill?" she added as an afterthought.

He shook his head. "Something tells me not."

"But if he was, then might he die?" The idea was horrible, but buried deep inside was a germ of relief. If Janus died Clovis would have to stay. *Don't be so petty!* she told herself.

"I simply don't know. I try to commune with him daily, and each time I'm greeted with silence."

"Huh! Sounds like he's sulking!"

He smiled faintly. "I know that side of him all too well, but this is something different. He drifts motionless, as if he doesn't perceive the outer world."

"So tell me, what are you most afraid of?"

"I wonder if he's considering something else."

"You think he wants to change the bargain he made with you, *again*?"

"It's quite possible, he has little regard for promises except for when he's the beneficiary."

Kolfinnia paused to greet several witches carrying water buckets and firewood. More survivors from the battle at Wellesley Hall had arrived and as always the coven celebrated their safe return. "So you think slippery Janus might ask even more from you than just taking him home?" she asked once they were gone.

"Slippery?" Occasionally he still struggled with the language, but by now his English was very good.

"It means hard to get a straight answer from."

"Ah, well put. But be careful what you say, he sleeps with one eye open." He tapped his nose meaningfully.

She looked back towards his quarters, a simple treetop shelter opposite her own which she had named Crow-top, and imagined Janus listening to all of Stormwood. *Trickster god,* she thought. "What more could he ask?"

He looked sad for a moment. He knew there was no more exacting price for taking Janus home. He was just glad she didn't know. "Of me, nothing more," he forewarned, "but I'm afraid he might devise a new price that involves others."

She gave a huff. "Like sending young Farona under the earth to save the serpent-twins all by himself! Yes, we all remember that nasty trick!"

"Something like that." In truth he feared Janus would target Kolfinnia herself, and this was why he concealed his affection for her, to protect her from the god's cruel sense of humour. "This strange stupor that's seized him, well it has me wondering the worst."

She patted his shoulder amiably before pulling her hair into a ponytail and collected her lightning-staff from next to a wheelbarrow. Immediately Skald emerged and sat at its tip blinking against the sunlight. "Don't let your worries run away with you," she advised, "whatever bridges Janus set before us we'll cross them together."

Together, he thought moodily. *That's what worries me because there's something you don't know Kolfinnia. The price for releasing Janus is a life, possibly yours if he demands you be involved.*

"Clovis?" She wondered what was going through his head. Skald turned to watch. Something about their coven-father seemed amiss today.

"Nothing." He gave her one of his best smiles, the kind that scared little witches who didn't know him better, and she relaxed. "Now, much to be done, there's still a welcome feast to prepare." He dipped her a little bow, turned on his heels and marched away through the gardens, aware of her concerned gaze against his back.

"What's he up to Skald?" she pondered. Clovis rounded the corner and vanished into a crowd of witches. "Skald, didn't you hear me?" She looked up and saw him peering intently across the gardens. "Skald what's wrong?"

"It can't be?" he scoffed.

"Can't be what?" She craned to see what had unsettled him. "And don't you dare say it's trouble!"

"We have visitors," he declared, still staring eastwards and spread his wings, not in warning, but anticipation. "Wildwood!" He stood erect, straining for a better view. "Kolfinnia, it's Wildwood!" In the next moment he was airborne and flying towards the trees.

Wildwood? The thought eclipsed everything else. Clovis, Janus, Blackwand, everything was forgotten. "Wildwood!" She broke into a run, ignoring the alarmed looks. "Flora!" she called at the top of her lungs. "Flora, it's Wildwood!" She charged after Skald in the direction of the trees even though there wasn't a soul to be seen there.

"Wildwood?" Flora looked up from her work, and in the next instant she was running, still clutching her trowel and with a basket of carrots hooked over one arm. She dropped them both without a care and sprinted after her. They had waited almost a year, but perhaps the lost survivors from Wildwood had come at last.

Emily really *was* thirsty, but why drink from the barrel when there was a refreshing stream close by? And if she happened to see Blackwand on her little jaunt, well so be it.

She made a meandering circuit through the Glade, remembering to touch the founding-banner for luck as she passed, and then skipped through the woods west of Stormwood. This was the very wood that gave the coven its name, although so far most of the saplings weren't much bigger than her. The seeds were taken from the trees that had given their lives to provide lightning-staffs for Kittiwake's defence. This was the wood Kolfinnia had planted in fulfilment of her promise, the wood Flora's special skills had nurtured, the wood marking Skald's stupendous storm. It was 'the wood of the storm'.

By the time she reached the stream Emily was ready to drink the whole thing dry. She knelt where the water was shallow and the nettles sparse. She briefly glimpsed her reflection in the stream, before she scooped at her own shimmering likeness and lifted a handful of water to her lips. The sensation was divine and she hurriedly reached for more. She drank without caution. Droplets darkened her dress, water-skaters piloted the stream and a woodpecker drummed from nearby as she drank. She wiped her mouth then went for a third helping, but instead of her own reflection she saw something unexpected staring back up at her.

A black stick was lying on the stream bed, undulating gently with the water's movement. It hadn't been there a moment ago.

She frowned. It was just a stick she thought, but intuition told her this was like no stick for a thousand miles about. "A wand?" The word bubbled up by itself.

The stick rocked in the current like a dog wagging its tail. *Yes, a wand, now claim me*, it seemed to say, *I've come so far to get home, take me. I am home.*

"A wand!" she grinned in realisation, and plunged her arm to the elbow and grasped it.

At last after so far, hrafn-dimmu once again felt the touch of a Wildwood witch. *I am home.*

She drew the wand from the water and as she did it seemed to grow in size and become heavier. Right away she knew this was no ordinary wand and in her small hand it looked like a sword. It was an incredible wand, eighteen inches of black ash. A tear glistened at her eye and her throat was suddenly tight. "Hrafn-dimmu," she whispered in disbelief.

The last time she had seen this wand it was buckled about the waist of Coven-mother Valonia Gulfoss. It had been Kolfinnia's beacon calling survivors to Kittiwake, but it had been subsequently lost and nobody knew to what fate, but there had been rumours, oh yes, plenty of rumours. Emily had secretly hoped to catch a glimpse of Blackwand but instead she found *the* black wand. It had been set to sail by a solstice queen facing grave danger and it seemed only right that another solstice queen should find it. "Kolfinnia! Kolfinnia!" She scrambled up from the stream and ran, holding the wand above her head, knowing this was a very special day indeed.

Although Emily had no way of knowing, the day was going to turn out to be far more special than anyone could have guessed. While she ran to show Kolfinnia her amazing discovery, Kolfinnia herself was already out of the gardens and charging into the forest, with Flora close behind.

"Kol, slow down!" Flora snatched the scarf from her head and dropped it without thought. "I can hardly keep up!"

"Skald says they're just ahead!" She crashed through bracken, sick with anticipation.

Flora saw a flash of blue, as Skald flitted from branch to branch. "But who, who's come? You think it's Frey?" She barged through twigs and brambles, scratching her face, but grinning madly.

"I don't know," Kolfinnia panted, "Wildwood is all he said!" She'd never asked, but once or twice Rowan had alluded to the fact that Wildwood's lost survivors were alive out there. Her friend, Freya Albright, and her crew of nine escaped Wildwood in a boat named Speedwell, but hadn't been heard from since. *But how will they have changed, what trials have they been through?* Her mind ran so fast it almost tripped over itself.

Suddenly a crow's call rang through the wood like a proclamation and Kolfinnia stopped dead. In a moment Flora was at her side, chasing her breath. "Kol?"

"It's one of Harl's crows," she gasped, peering into the trees ahead. Although the July sun rode high, down here shadows ruled, except for where sunlight sent down glowing shafts, but there was no sign of the elusive crow.

"There's Skald," Flora pointed to an oak. From here they could only see the back of him. He had spread his wings, something he usually did only in warning. Now Flora whispered, "What if it's not Wildwood witches, what if it's not witches at all?"

"We'll soon see." She gripped her staff ready.

They stood rigid, while above them Skald scanned the forest. All three waited in silence and Flora was about to speak when the crow called again, this time from much closer, and both witches forgot to breath when they saw a shadowy figure walking through the woods directly towards them.

"Kolfinnia!" Emily raced through the gardens looking for her coven-mother. "Kolfinnia I've found your wand!" Men, women, boys and girls all stopped their work and watched as she ran past waving something above her head. "Coven-mother!" she tried again, but it wasn't Stormwood's coven-mother she found, rather its coven-father, the one with the sharp teeth and the scary voice.

She rounded a willow fence and charged blindly into Clovis, sending him stumbling. He recovered in a second and whirled around with a fighter's grace. "What's the meaning of this!" he boomed.

The words died in her throat and she backed away with the wand clutched to her chest.

"Well?" he demanded, although softer this time.

She stared into his eyes. The pupils were black slits against the sun and she felt like a rabbit facing a stoat. Witches were gathering around them, but Emily couldn't take her eyes off him. And now she saw Tempest, his thunder-sprite, appear from the lightning-staff over his shoulder and sit watching curiously.

"Don't scare the girl to death," Tempest advised quietly.

Clovis glanced around. He was aware of young and old closing in, and he could tell from their scent that all of them feared the worst, namely that it was time to run again. The young girl looked no less afraid. He was about to roar at everyone to be about their business, when he remembered Tempest's advice. He cleared his throat and knelt before her. "It is Emily, is it not?" he rumbled softly.

She swallowed and looked from Tempest's hawkish face, back to Clovis's leonine one, not knowing who looked most frightening.

"Emily Meadows?" he elaborated, feeling a little self-conscious. Children weren't his strong point.

She stole a glance around. There was no sign of Kolfinnia, but a crowd was gathering. "Yes, Emily Meadows," she confirmed with a tiny nod.

"Solstice queen," someone in the crowd offered.

She looked to the voice, and saw Sally Crook's friendly face. Sally winked at her and she felt a touch of relief.

Clovis looked around at anxious witches, many clutching garden tools and looking ready to fight or run. "Ah, yes." He turned back to the girl. "Solstice queen." He smiled, hoping it would soothe her, but Emily just saw big teeth and thought of all the blackcurrants she should have picked. "And what does our little queen have there?" He gestured to the wand.

She looked down at hrafn-dimmu, having forgotten she was holding it. "I found this in the stream." She held it out and saw his eyes widen and sensed amazement sweep through the crowd.

"Kolfinnia's lost wand!" Sally uttered.

Clovis took it gently. "Kolfinnia's lost wand indeed," he marvelled, remembering the day she placed it at the sea stack's summit.

Emily watched him hold it up to the sun, inspecting it with wonder. "How did it get here?" she ventured, and heard a hundred whispered opinions.

He turned those bright eyes her way, and again she was the sole object of his attention. "Some wands are alive, they have a will of their own. Now take this back," he pressed the wand back into her hands, "because as the finder, *you* Emily should be the one to return it to Kolfinnia."

The sound of her name rumbling in his throat thrilled her. "Thank you," she murmured.

"You're learning," Tempest congratulated quietly.

Clovis concealed a smile and offered her his hand. "Let's go and find this wand's rightful companion shall we?"

She regarded that furred hand, more like a paw than a palm, and slowly eased her cautious fingers into it. He gently closed his hand around hers and she felt the touch of hard claws through that soft fur.

Sally caught his eye and offered him an approving smile. *The gentle lion,* she thought, and Clovis set off at a stately pace, hand in hand with Emily, leading a phalanx of amazed witches.

The figure stopped in shadows under the great pines, and spoke. "Kolfinnia?"

Kolfinnia recognised the voice. It was the past come alive, a relic from the world before the darkness, but it couldn't be, she told herself. The universe *couldn't* be so forgiving. Above, she heard Skald hiss in surprise, while Flora emitted a gasp.

"Kolfinnia Algra," the figure declared proudly. "Now coven-mother of Stormwood, and with her is Flora Greyswan, and Skald, thunder-sprite to the beloved Valonia Gulfoss."

It was Flora who found her tongue first. "Ward Saxon?" She advanced a step. "Hilda? Is that really you?"

Kolfinnia watched in disbelief as the figure emerged from the shadows and slid the pointed hat from her head. Her face hadn't changed, and those sparkling eyes and that fall of dark hair were just as she remembered. Immediately Kolfinnia's eyes swam with tears. It was Swanhilda Bridget Saxon.

"Kolfinnia and Flora. How my two finest witches have grown," Hilda looked from one witch to the other and back again smiling benignly, then her dignified expression slipped and the tears came. She opened her arms and they ran to her.

A discreet distance away a man stood with his jacket over his arm and a kitbag over his shoulder, watching their reunion. It had been a long journey from Wellesley Hall and the July weather wasn't kind to a middle-aged man with a steel kneecap, although he had slimmed a little thanks to his new-found lifestyle. Bertrand Hathwell lingered in the shade, listening to the branches swishing above. He knew all along that Hilda was going back to her own, and he wondered a lot about what that meant for him. He was a squire turned traitor, a witch-sympathiser, but would *they* sympathise with him? That question had cost him a lot of sleep.

He heard women laughing and occasionally crying. He looked out and saw the three still joined in a tight huddle. Already he felt like an outsider. "Shouldn't have bloody come here." He was as nervous as he could ever remember. Right then he almost turned and ran, bad knee or no bad knee. *Bugger it all*, he thought. He'd run off, change his name, settle down and find a job to suit his engineering skills, perhaps the railways or canals. But thoughts of steam engines sent his mind back to Hobbs Ash and Knight Superior Krast, his knight and ultimately the man he turned against and killed. "I don't belong here," he admitted. "What the hell was I thinking?" He took a step back towards his old life before realising he didn't have an old life. It was either this one or a new one. A rustle in the branches made him look up. He saw a strange creature peering down at him and knew it was a thunder-sprite, although he'd never seen one so close. Right away he gathered this creature didn't like him. "Good day," he said awkwardly.

Skald snorted and vanished into the leaves.

"Friendly bunch," he sighed, and wondered again if he was doing the right thing, but it was something Hilda had said yesterday that stopped him leaving.

"I look forward to introducing you to my family, Bertrand."

She never called him Bertrand, not once in the nine months since rescuing her from Kittiwake and escaping to France. He dared to hope her feelings about him were changing at last. He had come through war and fire. He wasn't going to quit now. He waited for Hilda's signal, then the hard work would *really* begin.

They shared a long, breathless hug, all of them lost for words, before Hilda finally withdrew and cupped a hand to Kolfinnia's cheek, the other to Flora's, regarding them both intently. All three of them had been crying. "Val would be proud of you both."

"I never dared dream to see you again," Kolfinnia sniffed. That's when Hilda noticed something odd: a small scar on her left cheek, shaped like an hourglass.

"One should never be afraid to dream," Hilda said absently and smoothed a thumb over the scar, now moist with tears. "You hurt your face?"

"Silly accident chopping wood, never mind it. We've plenty to tell you!" Kolfinnia beamed, oblivious to her curious gaze, and she grabbed her in yet another crushing embrace, prompting Flora to join in.

"Plenty to talk about," Hilda laughed, Kolfinnia's strange scar forgotten, and gently eased herself free.

"Come on," Kolfinnia tugged her hand. "There are *so* many people I want you to meet, and lots of old faces too! And Clovis, just wait 'til you meet Clovis!"

"You must have been travelling for ages." Flora was already taking her possessions, which comprised a satchel, a rolled blanket and two small cooking pans. "I'll make you the best meal you ever ate and the deepest bath you've ever seen."

"Wait, there's someone I want you to meet first." Now she had come to the hard part just like Hathwell. She turned and coughed loudly. "Mr Hathwell!" she called.

Immediately both witches stiffened.

Hathwell? Kolfinnia thought. *Rowan spoke of him.*

"Hathwell?" Flora repeated.

When the realisation finally hit, Kolfinnia reeled. "Hathwell? The Knight Superior's squire! Hilda? You don't mean to say you brought a –,"

"Wait," she interrupted. "It's not as it looks."

All three watched the trees expectantly, and after a moment Hathwell stepped out like a reluctant performer onto a very big stage.

Kolfinnia's eyes narrowed and she swallowed loudly. Flora stepped to her side and they closed ranks. This was the man, according to Rowan, who'd tried to help them while imprisoned at Hobbs Ash. "Hathwell," she uttered, facing him at last. Despite his help he was once allied with the monsters who'd interrogated Rowan, destroyed Wildwood and murdered her friends. She growled something unpleasant.

Hilda leaned closer. "Please, I understand, but without him Kittiwake-coven and perhaps even the serpent-twins would have been captured."

"But, still, you brought him *here*?" She spoke in a low voice, surveying the man only twenty yards away. To her he was everything she wasn't.

"Mr Hathwell," Hilda announced pleasantly, ignoring her. "These are two of my finest friends." She shot Kolfinnia a loaded look.

No mention of 'Bertrand' now, he thought glumly. He smiled and started forwards, discreetly drying his sweaty palms against his trousers ready to shake hands, or whatever witches did. Suddenly he realised he knew almost nothing about their customs.

"He was our man on the inside, keeping the airships from discovering our position at Wellesley Hall," Hilda boasted loudly. "And he was the last one to speak to Valonia," she added quietly. The two young witches exchanged glances. " . . .And he put an end to the Knight Superior," she finished in a whisper.

Kolfinnia didn't have time to acknowledge this incredible news because he was almost with them. She saw the way he limped and the deep worry-lines on his brow. He looked ashamed, and with good reason she thought. Meanwhile Flora unconsciously touched her eye-patch as painful memories stirred.

"Miss Flora, Miss Kolfinnia." He felt he already knew them. "Hilda has spoken of you both a great deal."

Hilda watched closely. Kolfinnia's face remained wooden, while Flora looked wary.

There was a long silence that Kolfinnia knew she had to fill somehow. She took a step forward and reached out to her former enemy. "Welcome to Stormwood Mr Hathwell."

He looked to Hilda for support but her expression told him this was something he had to do alone. "Good day, Coven-mother." He grasped her hand firmly, but the rehearsed line sounded rickety.

She delivered a short and reluctant handshake. "Just Kolfinnia will suffice." She withdrew her hand, resisting the urge to wipe it on her dress.

He was about to invite her to call him 'Bertrand' but from the look on her face he reconsidered. "Honoured Miss Kolfinnia," he yielded, and held on to his smile even as his innards churned.

"And this is Flora," Hilda declared. "It's by her skills that the coven remains self-sufficient and so hidden."

Flora advanced a step, more curious than afraid. "Mr Hathwell," she offered him the merest nod.

"Miss Flora." He made a decent job of ignoring her wounded eye.

She looked him up and down. "You were a squire were you not?"

"A squire?" He couldn't decide if she intended to sound so blunt. "Aye miss."

"Well, you'll be swapping rifles for rakes here at Stormwood."

He rubbed at his neck and managed his first genuine smile. "I helped my father grow cabbage and kale when I was a lad, but the rabbits got the better part of it."

"Good with greenery *and* animals? Perhaps we'll make a witch of you yet," Hilda observed.

Flora took a small trowel from her work apron. "Here, a welcome gift. You'll have cause to use it a lot I promise." She tossed it over.

His reflexes were keen and he caught it neatly. "An olive branch," he heard himself say.

"Just a trowel sadly, it's hard growing olives in Wales." Flora's joke released the tension a little.

"Cabbage and kale it is then," he waved the trowel and looked around the group where Flora's faint smile glimmered like the sun behind the fog of Kolfinnia's suspicion.

There was a rustle of leaves and Skald glided down onto a nearby branch. "Valonia always said greenery heals the heart." At the mention of her name they became silent.

"She taught me a great deal," Hathwell confessed.

"She must have for you to come all this way." Skald locked eyes with him. "She also said: sow the seeds of forgiveness and nurture them." At this he looked Kolfinnia's way.

She smiled diplomatically, first at Skald and Hathwell, before offering Hilda the real thing. "This is truly a miraculous day. Thank the twins you came back to us." She took the older woman's hand, while Flora, gazing at her adoringly again, took the other.

"Welcome home Ward Saxon," Skald said gruffly, but with great heart.

"Welcome home," Flora sighed happily.

"Welcome home," Kolfinnia affirmed. She took Hilda's elbow and led her away.

Hathwell watched them set off without him, feeling somewhat dejected but thinking it could have been a lot worse. He slipped the trowel into his pocket and ran a hand through his hair. "For better or worse," he promised himself and started after them, towards his new home.

Hathwell thought he knew about witches, but his first look at Stormwood told him otherwise. He might have marched into dozens of vanquished covens as Krast's squire, but he'd never seen a *living* coven, where witches honoured the serpent-twins, grew their food with love and lived richer lives than the vast majority in the outside world. Hilda and her young friends continued ahead, lost in conversation, but he simply stood and admired the sight. "So," he nodded in appreciation, "this is how a coven *should* look."

A few passers-by eyed him suspiciously, perhaps with good cause, he thought. Firstly there was his ever-present sense of guilt, and secondly he wasn't dressed like them. He wore a black waistcoat over his white shirt, with the sleeves rolled to his elbows. He looked more like a railway foreman, while everyone else seemed to be wearing pioneer clothes, wand-sheathes, carrying lightning-staffs, or wore charms or symbolic tattoos. Clearly he was a stranger, but still he earned a few polite smiles. "Afternoon." He greeted a young lad shoving a wheelbarrow.

"Blessed be," the boy muttered and passed quickly. A scruffy dog trailed after him, and even that regarded Hathwell warily.

Afternoon? he thought, *is that how witches greet one another?* It dawned on him that if he didn't even know how these people said 'good-day' then he really did have a mountain to climb. He held back as Hilda and the others continued through the gardens, which heaved with fruits and flowers, medicinal and culinary herbs, vegetables and legume crops. "Gardeners," he marvelled. All these years the Illuminata had persecuted witches, and what did they really do in their hidden covens: they grew food, simple as that.

Looking along the path, glowing with sunlight and criss-crossed by bees and hoverflies, he saw another group of witches heading towards Hilda and the others. It was the leader of this group that caught his eye. He frowned, then blinked, shielded his eyes from the sun and stared hard, wondering if memory and illusion were merging, but no, he was right. Leading this new group was a witch who wasn't human. He was distinctly lion-like. The last time he saw such a creature was in a very dark place, and they were supposed to be extinct. "My God, a Therion," he exhaled. The lion warrior must have been over a hundred yards away, but as the words left his lips he looked in his direction. The distance was too far to be sure but Hathwell had the distinct sense that he had quickly been assessed. The crowds shifted again, the lion warrior looked elsewhere and Hathwell breathed a sigh of relief. He watched as the Therion greeted Kolfinnia and a crowd gathered around, chattering and jostling and eventually Hilda and the others were lost from sight.

He stood in the now empty gardens trying to make sense of what he'd just seen. *The last one died at Solvgarad,* he told himself, but clearly he was wrong. *How could an extinct race more myth than fact, show up here in the wooded hills of Wales?* he struggled.

How indeed, his worries voiced.

"Kolfinnia!" Clovis looked elated. "Emily has a surprise for you!" He shooed the girl forwards.

"Me first!" Kolfinnia didn't see Emily or her incredible gift. "Hilly's come back!" She took her elbow and ushered her forwards. "I can't believe it, Hilda's come back! My lost friend!" She thought she was going to cry all over again, while Hilda stood gazing around, looking overwhelmed. "Hilda. . . this is Clovis!" Kolfinnia boasted.

"Our coven-father," Flora added.

Clovis cleared his throat and framed his words. "It is an honour to finally meet the woman who trained such a witch as Kolfinnia."

Hilda admired him while concealing her amazement. "I've already heard tales about your bravery Clovis." It briefly occurred to her to introduce Hathwell, but after a quick inspection she didn't see him and soon forgot the idea, and before she had chance to say more she was bombarded by the inevitable barrage of questions.

'Where have you been?' 'Were you at Salisbury?' 'Did you see Blackwand?' 'Are there any other witches with you?' 'My cousin's still missing, please say you've seen him.' 'Someone get Hilda's lightning-staff, tell her thunder-sprite she's come home at last!'

"Please everyone, give Hilda a moment, you'll drown her in questions," Kolfinnia took charge.

Eventually they settled and regarded Hilda expectantly. "It's good to be home," was all she managed, before bowing her head and wiping her eyes.

Flora embraced her as the crowd began to cheer and clap, and Clovis took his chance. "Kolfinnia," he drew her aside. "Emily has a gift for you." He looked down and saw the girl's somewhat dejected face.

Kolfinnia tore her eyes from the spectacle. Now Sally Crook was hugging Hilda like a bear, by the end of the day the poor woman would be bruised all over, she thought. "Forgive me Emmy," she apologised, and knelt to hear her better. "You've something for me?"

"I found this," Emily held out the wand, feeling now it wasn't nearly as important as Hilda coming home. "It was in the stream."

"Found?" She looked from the girl's sombre face to the object in her hands and saw a part of herself that she had left behind, and in a heartbeat she was complete again. "Oh Emmy!" she reached out and took it, and now she was trembling. "Hrafn-dimmu – Raven's wand," she uttered the sacred name and pressed the wand to her cheek, bowed to hide her tears and thought of Valonia, everything else forgotten.

"Your black wand," Emily added.

But Kolfinnia didn't hear. She knelt in the middle of the joyous throng and remembered Kittiwake, the screams and the gunfire, but mostly she remembered Valonia.

Emily looked up at Clovis, afraid she'd done something wrong. "Hilda and the black wand have come home on the same day." She wondered if that was significant.

Clovis returned her smile. "Well done Emily. Something tells me there's a reason the wand was found by our solstice queen."

She didn't know what that reason might be, but her smile widened. A very important black wand had come home, and one might smile in wonder at fate's subtle but irresistible weave, for none of them knew that at that very moment, another Blackwand was heading towards Stormwood and she was only a day's journey away.

"Mr Hathwell?" a gentle voice came, and an equally gentle hand slipped easily into his. The small fingers were warm and trusting.

He was shaken from his dark thoughts and knew straight away who it was even before he looked down. Although it had only been nine months she had grown a lot to his eye. First his heart leapt in gladness, then clenched in shame. "Rowan."

She wore an almost identical russet dress to the one he remembered, which made the memories all too raw, and of course her feet were still bare. She stood hand in hand with him, watching the happy gathering but saying nothing, and both thought of Valonia. *"You don't need a wand to be a witch,"* she told him as she lay dying. They seemed the only ones not joining the crowd.

"Do you like my hair?" she enquired at last. Her shoulder length chestnut hair was restored.

He regarded her as if this was the most important question in the world, and in many ways it was. "It makes you look older," he flattered.

She gave him the kind of sunny smile that made him regret not becoming a parent. "I'm never going to have it cut again," she promised and pushed her long fringe back to demonstrate. "It'll grow to my feet."

He was glad her hair had re-grown, not only because she looked like herself again, but it also hid the scar left from her interrogation. "It's lovely to see you again Rowan. Hilda's come, did you know?"

"I know," she smiled and squeezed his hand. "Everyone's dying to see her, so I'll go see her a bit later." It seemed she didn't have to hug Ward Saxon to celebrate her presence. Hathwell thought that so mature that suddenly he felt he was the child clasping *her* adult hand. "I know you helped us at Kittiwake. And I know you were the last one to see to Valonia," she said from nowhere, swinging their joined hands idly as she spoke

"That's true," he confessed.

"And I knew you were coming."

He swallowed. "Are you glad I came?"

"I knew Hilda was coming too," she evaded.

"Hilda belongs here." He wanted to add that 'he didn't' but thought it snivelling.

"Do you like cor-jets?" She took his hand fully in hers and held it fast.

His smile returned. "Cor-jets?"

"Baby marrows, well-to-do folk call them 'cor-jets'," she quoted Ada Crabbe's garden wisdom from a lifetime ago. "I'm growing some, would you like to see?"

He cast a parting look at the crowd. Somewhere in there was the woman he loved, but who'd forgotten all about him. He shook his reservations away. "Aye, it's been a long walk from Salisbury. Do cor-jets taste nice?"

"Come and see!" She pulled on his arm. "I've got my own garden, and my own wheelbarrow too."

He drew Flora's trowel from his coat. "And I've got my own trowel."

Rowan laughed and skipped away. He followed, and together they wandered through the gardens leaving the crowds behind, and Hathwell was relieved to have found at least one friend at Stormwood.

CHAPTER FOUR

The raven's secret

'When I realised that my enemy was just like me I had little reason to want him dead."
Testimony of infantryman John Colly
Executed for refusing orders during Balkan campaign, 1861

She ate well and talked a great deal. The Welcome feast was held in the heart of the old fort, in that beautiful amphitheatre known as the Glade. First came prayers for those who died at Salisbury then came the celebrations for their victory and to welcome the living home, and what celebrations they were.

Now Kolfinnia was tired but contented in a way she hadn't known for a long time. July 6th would go down as a very special day indeed. Hilda had enjoyed the evening, while Mr Hathwell had looked strained she thought. Talk had turned to battle, to Salisbury and to loved-ones lost, and of course Blackwand. Tales about her shot back and forth across the bonfire, growing in stature with each telling. Hilda had actually met the great woman and was hounded for every detail.

'What's her real name Hilda?' 'Is she really as beautiful as the sun?' 'They say she can down a kraken with just one look, can she? I bet she can!' 'Is Ben really travelling with her?' 'Happen they're in love! Tell us Hilda, are they in love?'

The questions came thick and fast, but she just smiled patiently and told them they would find out in good time. It was a given fact that Blackwand was on her way, accompanied by Stormwood's very own Benedict Collins.

In light of all the action at Salisbury, Stormwood's numbers had swelled to one hundred and forty-nine, including a few from the continent. Many of them would leave for their home covens once the excitement had passed, but even so she felt a twinge of sadness to know that by autumn Stormwood would shrink to a contingent of about forty. Still, she told herself, forty was a good number and she couldn't wish for a better family around her.

More wood was thrown on the fire, more food was served and more ale was poured. Many had taken what they could from the ruins of Wellesley Hall, and Oliver Blunt caused a stir when he revealed a curious yellow fruit called a banana. It was mostly brown rather than yellow now, but nobody had ever seen one and he couldn't have made a bigger impression if he'd turned up with the crown jewels themselves. He elected to eat it right there and began munching on it before someone pointed out that it needed peeling. Kolfinnia had laughed so hard that she showered Clovis with ale.

'All those treasures lying around that place and you pick up a banana!' Sally joked.

'Seen one golden thingy you've seen 'em all, but I haven't never seen a banana,' Oliver shrugged as he passed chucks of the rare fruit around.

Kolfinnia left the Glade and ambled back through the gardens barefoot, carrying her tattered old boots, wearing a dreamy smile and smelling faintly of the bonfire. Tonight she didn't need a lantern to find her way because the moon was over half full. Moths and bats pursued and evaded one another against a backdrop of stars, while around her the gardens were full of night scents and the occasional bark of a distant fox. She patted her wand-sheath where hrafn-dimmu was snugly fixed, just to make sure it was safe. She had drunk four mugs of ale this evening and her memory was pleasantly foggy. Something black and white shambled across her path, sniffing as it went. "Goodnight Mr Brock," she chuckled.

"Walking home alone?" someone asked, and for a bizarre moment she thought it was the badger. She turned and saw Farona loping after her, his face lit by the lantern he carried. From the look of it she guessed he had drunk more than her.

"You've come to chaperon me?"

"Much as I'd love to, I've more pressing duties."

"More pressing than my honour?" she tried not to slur.

"Aye, I'm off to fetch a few bottles of wine, the ale's run out." He jerked his head back towards the fort where she could see the bonfire twinkling through the trees and hear the sound of laughter and music.

"Not Bridget's carrot wine I hope?"

He nodded guiltily.

She groaned, "There'll be plenty of pounding heads in the morning."

"Not least of which is Clovis. He was dancing with Sally Crook when I left."

She sniggered and looked back at the distant fire, tempted to see him dance a jig, but Rowan was waiting. "Keep an eye on him. Tell me how badly he embarrasses himself."

He looked serious and made a mock salute. "Consider it done." He surprised her then by leaning forwards and planting a kiss on her cheek, then wandered off in search of wine, swaying dangerously as he did.

She continued on her way, thinking how much he had changed since his fateful encounter with the serpent-twins, and wondering when he might finally get around to resolving his feelings for Flora. There wasn't much that escaped her attention, even after a few ales.

Back at Crow-top, she found Albert Parry sitting in a branch, guarding her tree house just where she left him. "Any trouble Albert?" She stifled a yawn. The day's excitement was catching up with her.

"No, Miss Kolfinnia." He hooked a foot in the rope ladder and came down, descending nimbly for a man of seventy-one. Mally, his faithful Jack Russell uncurled from where she was sleeping in the grass and went and sat by his ankle.

"And Rowan?"

"Fast asleep these last three hours," he stroked his beard, sounding satisfied.

"You're a treasure." She gave him a lingering hug, then kissed his hairy cheek, already knowing she would wince at the memory when sober. "The feast's far from over, why don't you go and take some leave?"

"Nay thanks coven-mother, I had my share of grub earlier, and besides I've tasted Bridget's wine." He slung his satchel over his shoulder and picked up his hat. Mally got to her feet and whined impatiently.

"Then I'll bid you both goodnight and the twin's blessings on you," she tried to be a little more formal, but he gave her a cheeky wink that made her blush.

"Blessing on you too miss," he tipped his hat and set off into the darkness singing a Welsh folk song, with Mally at his heels.

She waited to make sure he had gone. "You've humiliated yourself enough tonight," she muttered. The last thing Stormwood needed to see was their coven-mother lying in a drunken heap at the bottom of her own rope ladder with her dress over her head. She anchored a foot on the first rung, lifted herself up and started to climb, knowing Rowan was sleeping above and trying to be as quiet as possible.

"Is it snowing?" Rowan murmured, half asleep.

Kolfinnia slumped down on her bunk and lit a candle. It took her three matches before she succeeded. "No, it's just a dream. Go back to sleep, I'm sorry to wake you." She set the candleholder on a stool next to her bed, and the tiny shelter glowed in its welcome light.

"I dreamed of a snowstorm, and there was broken glass all in my knee." Rowan wriggled around under her blankets to face her. She even cupped her knee to make sure. Her eyes were vulnerable and her face pale. "Was the feast good?"

"Broken glass in your knee?" Granted her wits were dull tonight, but she still thought that an odd, even prophetic, dream.

"Was the feast good?" Rowan badgered.

"Yes, lots of news to catch up on."

"And lots of ale to drink?"

"I wouldn't know," she pretended.

Rowan rubbed at her eyes. "When I'm older will you let me stay up late, and drink ale and throw wood on the fire?"

She smiled as she dropped the hatch across the hole in the floor, and then she pulled her ponytail free letting her dark hair tumble down her back. "You'll be eight in November, maybe we'll let you stay up then."

"And the ale?"

"Ohh! You'll have to be nine at least for that," she yawned, feeling too tired to change into her nightdress, and considering sleeping in her clothes.

"I'm glad Hilda's back," Rowan added, but she looked serious.

"Didn't you enjoy your afternoon with her?" she asked delicately, imagining survivors of Hobbs Ash might share painful memories. "You showed her around Stormwood didn't you?"

"Mmm. She loved the Glade and the little water mill. We talked for ages as well. It's lovely to have someone to talk to again," she alluded to their capture.

Kolfinnia respected her privacy, but on impulse, she unbuckled her wand-sheath. "I've a surprise for you. Someone else came home today."

Rowan frowned and sat upright, now fully awake. "Who?"

"You don't know?" she teased.

"You told me not to look!" Her face brightened. "Tell me!"

She slipped the sheath from around her waist, and flopped down onto her own bunk. "Hrafn-dimmu came home today." She held it out.

Rowan took it and her smile faded. "Valonia's wand."

"Valonia's," she agreed wistfully. "But I didn't tell you to make you sad. Emily found it in the stream. It was just lying there."

Rowan shuffled out of the blankets and dangled her legs over the bunk. She was wearing mismatched bed socks. She gazed down at the sheath knowing great mysteries were hidden inside, mysteries she could unlock if she wanted.

Kolfinnia leaned back on her elbows and tickled Rowan's feet with her toes. "It's a special night, would you like to break a rule and use that gift of yours?"

She smiled guardedly, "You really have drunk lots of ale."

She laughed, "Tell me where it's been since October last year."

"Everything?"

Serious now, she shook her head. "No, you know the golden rule, if it becomes bad we look away."

Rowan said nothing.

"Rowan promise me, or I'll put Raven's wand right to bed," she warned, not that that would stop the girl from knowing if she wanted to.

"Alright, I promise."

Satisfied, she went and knelt before Rowan's bed where she cupped her hands on the girl's knees. They were rough and scabby from garden work.

"Amaze me then."

The two shared excited smiles before Rowan unfastened the wooden toggle and drew out a wand of black ash a foot and a half long and held it tight in her hands.

'Dear champion. . .'

Like it or not, Rowan saw everything from the day hrafn-dimmu vanished to the moment it had arrived at Stormwood that morning. She tried to remember their golden rule but it all exploded in an instant, everything, dark and light all mixed together and the light was like the naked sun while the dark went on forever. Rowan saw how one event led to another like a line of dominoes, starting with the reason why Sunday had taken the wand and descended into that chamber to confront the Timekeeper. It was all because of her treacherous note. "It's come so far," she whispered. "From here to the black sands of the north." She seemed unaware that she was speaking and Kolfinnia watched with growing unease. "From life to death and back again."

"Rowan you're not making sense, better let go sweetheart." Worried now, she tried to take the wand back but the girl gripped it fast.

"The sand is so black."

"Rowan let go," she tried again, but Rowan stared ahead at nothing, powerless to tell hrafn-dimmu's tale.

"It began with her note, the one that told the soldiers how to find Kittiwake." Her voice was flat and distant.

Horrified, and suddenly very sober, Kolfinnia wrenched the wand from her grip and put it out of the way. "Rowan?" she grabbed her shoulders and gave her a shake. "Row – I don't want you to look any more." But it was too late. She'd already seen everything.

Rowan looked her way, with fat tears rolling down her cheeks, but she seemed unaware of these too. "She died to put things right, but she didn't die, she was brought back and woke up in a cold, faraway place." She began to sob and Kolfinnia scooped her up, laid her down on the bunk and wrapped her arms around her.

They lay like that for some time, with Rowan crying softly and Kolfinnia rocking her gently, shattered by her revelation. She wanted to know the rest, but at what cost? *What horrors did she see?* she wondered, and cursed whoever had given her this 'gift'. *So Kittiwake was betrayed after all.* The thought mocked her for not guessing sooner. She peered back at Raven's wand, not knowing whether to hate it, revere it, or pity it. "Curse the black wand," she vented.

"No. Blackwand saved us." Rowan looked out from behind her hands. Her face was red and her eyes puffy.

"Rowan, it doesn't matter. Tell me in the morning, but not now."

"She died to put it right. Died to save us." She wriggled free and sat on the crumpled blankets with her knees pulled to her chest. It appeared that Rowan couldn't wait until morning.

"Who did?"

"The solstice queen just wanted what was best for Hethra and Halla, but she forgot that witches matter too." Rowan was reluctant to name her. Having tasted the depths of her sacrifice, this felt like telling tales.

"Sunday?" Kolfinnia guessed.

Rowan nodded faintly. "She went to see the great spider at the end, when everyone at Kittiwake was trying to escape. . . when you'd been shot."

Kolfinnia's hand went to her chest. There was still a small scar there from where a bullet had ripped through her. Why had she never given any thought as to how she had so miraculously recovered? "Yes I was shot." She had almost forgotten, but how could one forget such a thing?

"You were dying," Rowan clarified, "and if you died, I died too."

"Dying," she echoed woodenly. Had she forgotten or had something forgotten for her, she wondered?

"But she went and swapped her thread for yours. The moment you were saved, she died. And because you didn't die, then I didn't either," Rowan revealed. Kolfinnia fought back the tears, but Rowan was compelled to go on and in the end Kolfinnia's tears won. "We lived and she died. But the great spider changed after meeting her. He saw something he'd never seen before and he began to think things he didn't *know* he could think, and so he made up his mind."

"What did he do?" Kolfinnia wiped her eyes.

Rowan looked around, afraid of being overheard. "He said 'no' to the Patternmaker."

"He refused fate?"

"Yes. He made her thread whole again and she woke up, not dead anymore! And she was holding the black wand, it took her back to its home, Valonia's home in the north. That's where she woke up and that's where it all began!"

"There's more?"

She nodded firmly. "The Patternmaker was *so* angry. He sent a horrible thing to kill the great spider and kill the solstice queen all over again, but for good this time."

"Sunday?"

"Blackwand," Rowan corrected. "Blackwand she called herself and she found three monsters that were really men and she freed them, but they followed her because of their love for her."

"And came to Salisbury." Now it all began to make sense. She'd heard the accounts of Blackwand's incredible allies.

Rowan nodded again. "Without them, the Book-of-Nine would have won and Victor Thorpe would own the Illuminata. But worst is that the world would be full of valkyries and death." She recited the words without grasping them.

"Book-of-Nine? Valkyries?" she shook her head, "Rowan, what are they?"

She concentrated on the word and something beyond that door of knowing bayed to be let in. She knew it was a valkyrie and if she saw it she would scream. She denied that door and looked away as taught. "I can't tell you."

"I understand."

"But if Thorpe won, then other Illuminata families would be making Ruin armies of their own to beat him, and everything would get out of control."

"I understand Row, really, there's no need to look more."

"But I want you to know just how much we owe her." She looked at her small hands, now glistening with tears. "Blackwand saved you and me, she saved the man-bears, and then she came home and saved us all from Vorus and her valkyries."

Kolfinnia had no idea what Vorus was, but had the feeling that she didn't want to know. She reached up and stroked the girl's face. "I'm sorry I asked you to look, so *so* sorry."

"It's her we should be sorry for. She wonders if she'll ever be happy again. She wants to love Ben but her secret is getting in the way."

"Ben?" she realised. Benedict Collins, one of the trusted witches she'd sent to spy on London. *Tell us Hilda – are Ben and Blackwand in love?* The campfire gossip appeared to be correct.

"He's coming here, with Blackwand. He's told her it can be her new home."

Kolfinnia looked worried. *I've already embraced one traitor today, can I find room in my heart for two?* She thought of Hathwell. He was so out of place that she pitied him.

"She's not a traitor," Rowan insisted.

"That's not polite," she scolded, guessing the girl had just known her thoughts. "And you don't know she isn't."

Rowan looked thoughtful for a moment, then she confessed something that had been on her mind a very long time. "Esta Salt died because of me."

"Row, don't –,"

"I made a mistake," she insisted, "just like Blackwand did."

"That's not the same!" She was angry now. "That's not the same at all, Row, you're just a. . ." *'Child'* is what she wanted to say but Rowan had never been just a child. "It's not the same!" she finished hotly.

"But it is. If I hadn't run off from Valonia she wouldn't have been caught, and neither would the others, but then Ada wouldn't have broken that evil machine that hurt Hethra and Halla." She looked down at her hands again. "Sometimes I think it takes a wrong thing to stop even worse things happening."

Kolfinnia struggled for a retort but couldn't find one and was left wondering which of them really should be coven-mother. "Where is she now?" she asked at last.

"She'll be here tomorrow," she sniffed.

Kolfinnia took her hands, which were now clammy with tears. "This is our secret, understand, never to leave this room. A secret between us, and we're like sisters aren't we Row. Sisters trust each other."

Rowan nodded meekly. "And you're *her* sister now."

She suddenly felt cold. "Me?"

Rowan reached up and stroked the little scar on Kolfinnia's cheek. It was shaped like an hourglass and now she understood why. "That's why you have this."

Kolfinnia touched it, frightened of its significance and now wishing she could rub it away. "No. That was just an accident chopping wood."

"No it isn't. You're fated sisters: she died for you, you lived for her. The Timekeeper made it, to remind you both how much you mean to each other."

Scared and confused, Kolfinnia grabbed the blankets and went to wrap her up again. "It's late and we can talk more in the morning. I want you to sleep now."

Rowan let out a weighty sigh and flopped back onto her bunk and amazingly she curled up and readied for sleep. As Kolfinnia squeezed in next to her, Rowan's eyes grew heavy. "Don't be angry with her," she murmured.

"Just sleep. It's late." She kissed her goodnight, knowing she wouldn't get a wink of sleep herself.

Rowan's breathing eased and her eyes finally closed. The night drew on, and outside light rain pattered against the thatch, while inside Crow-top the candle died and Kolfinnia turned the momentous news over and over, trying to make it fit her world.

Some time in the early hours Rowan stirred in her sleep. "Janus heard the Flowering," she sighed without waking.

Kolfinnia's heart jumped. *The Flowering.* It sounded beautiful, but from nowhere she thought of Clovis and felt a crippling pang of loss. She curled closer to Rowan, who remained blissfully asleep and tried to picture herself governing Stormwood alone – a woman not yet even nineteen – but that wasn't what frightened her so much. No man she had yet met could match him, and she simply didn't want to lose him. *Am I in love?* she dared ask herself, and then closed her heart and ears to any possible answer, because she knew it wouldn't be good.

Clovis returned to Stormwood somewhere between midnight and dawn. He had indeed danced with Sally Crook, and many others, and enjoyed the feast, but afterwards came penance. Laughter and ale were all well and good, but when the festivities ended he decided to wander the woods and recover his mindfulness, and also nurse his sore head. He went with Tempest and although they walked in the blackest woods Clovis saw all. He carried his staff over his shoulder, where Tempest sat staring up at the moon through the trees. "One day the trail will lead them here," Tempest reminded him. Alone together, they spoke their native language again.

"I know," he sighed ruefully, "we've stayed too long as it is." They continued in silence. Kolfinnia didn't know it, but he regularly walked these woods at night looking for answers. "We should go before the end of summer," he decided.

"When will you tell her?"

"Perhaps today. I've been less than truthful, but now it's time to tell all. The omens are good: Salisbury is won and her friend Hilda is back. We shall take Janus far away. With him gone they shan't be able to track him here, and Stormwood will be safe."

"And if Janus awakens in the meantime and demands you return him to Vega?"

He halted. They were close to home now and he didn't want his words overheard, native or not. "One way or another that day will come, and if the Temple is held by our enemies we won't stand a chance, you understand that don't you?"

"We only have to live long enough to open the vessel," Tempest said defiantly.

"You know the price for that as well as I do."

"The opener of the vessel shall pay with their life," he recited the legend.

Clovis stared off towards Crow-top through the pre-dawn shadows. "She can't be involved."

"Agreed. And even if he awakens from this strange sleep, is Janus ready to be released upon the universe?"

"No. But it would still be better than letting the Unitari seize him. Imagine if they completed their plans and perverted him to their purpose? He might eventually be loosened only to sing Self's foul song. There wouldn't be a compassionate soul left in creation." Both of them considered this bleak prospect. "But we can't go anywhere until he awakens," he sighed, "and who's to say how long that will be?"

"And if you can't reach him, if he remains sleeping? Would you take to a life stranded on this world?"

Clovis considered this. "Stormwood would make a good home."

"But as you said Janus can't remain here. Asleep or not, the Unitari will one day track him down."

He groaned. Already his words were coming back to haunt him. If he could find a well deep enough he would happily hurl Janus down it and be rid of him. "Then we either wander this world with a sleeping god until the day we die, or rouse him and go back to Vega where we'll face untold dangers, but as you say," he took a deep breath, "he can't stay here." He had a sobering image of himself as an old witch wandering the Earth without an ally or even another of his kind. "And neither can we," he added under his breath.

Tempest suppressed a shudder. "Let's talk of better things. . . everyone was surprised to see what a fine dancer you are."

Clovis caught the tale-end of the memory and winced. "How many saw?"

"Plenty!" he chirped. "Never seen so many slack mouths and goggle eyes."

"Did Kolfinnia see?"

"No, but I noticed that artist lad, Connor, making a few sketches."

"Perfect!" he rumbled, "Blackmail material!"

"He made a good likeness of you. . ."

"Don't gloat!" He rubbed his tired eyes. "Were they really so shocked?"

"It cheered them up," Tempest consoled, "sometimes a shock to the system is a good thing."

'Shock,' Clovis reflected and suddenly stopped. That was the missing, even magical, word. "Shock!"

"It wasn't *that* scandalous," Tempest downplayed.

"Can it be so simple?"

"What be so simple?"

"Janus. His silence and inertia – is it shock?" The implications set his heart racing.

"What could shock him so badly as to leave him senseless?" Tempest ventured uneasily.

"By Hethra's tail, did he?" He spun around to face his tree house.

Tempest fluttered to the ground. "Did he what?"

"Did he awaken?" he stared down at him.

Tempest scrambled backwards. "The real Janus. . . *woke up?*"

"Woke up and saw his past." Clovis saw how all the pieces made sense. "And the shock has robbed his mind. Janus could already be whole again!"

Now both of them looked towards Clovis's shelter, just as dawn was warming the eastern sky. Was it possible that after aeons of waiting, Janus had remembered his purpose, here, far from home, and in a humble shack? Clovis *knew* he had, and he burst into flight, now crashing through the undergrowth without a care.

"Clovis!" Tempest watched in disbelief before scampering after him, back to where a restored god drifted alone in a dark and silent world.

If he expected a chorus of trumpets and a heavenly light Clovis was to be disappointed. He was a practical witch who had little time for ceremony, but still he climbed the rope ladder with trepidation. *How many witches lived and died on Vega waiting for this very moment?* he thought giddily. The hatch loomed closer. It was just a plain opening, but what universe did it now lead into? If he was right, then the Janus waiting up there wasn't as any witch of Vega had known in millions of years. He slowed at the last rung, finding it a massive effort to cross the threshold.

"What's wrong?" Tempest hissed from his shoulder.

"This moment," he whispered, "is like the hub of a wheel with many fates radiating from it." He peered into the darkness above. "What fate awaits us?"

Inspired and frightened, Tempest replied, "We'll never find out if we stay here. . ."

Clovis licked his lips then pulled himself higher. The rope creaked and the ladder swayed. The opening embraced them and they vanished into the darkness.

The sacred vessel was just where he left it, and in dawn's frail light it looked dark and empty and for a wild moment he imagined Janus had slipped free. "But which Janus is it?" he heard himself ask. "The unifier or the trickster?" He sat with his legs hanging through the hatch and his eyes fixed on the vessel.

Tempest hopped forwards and halted just short of the bunk. "Whoever's in there, they're still lost."

"Then today we find out." Clovis climbed up and padded softly over, where he knelt respectfully. "We find out just which Janus we have here." He studied the figure behind the glass, suspended in dark and motionless liquid. There wasn't even the faintest aura of life.

"But how? We've tried all we know."

Clovis bared his teeth. "Almost all. There is still the Lady."

He growled uneasily, "Not good!"

"If this is the Janus we've long awaited, he'll know her name and respond to it." He ran a finger down the vessel and his claw whistled against the glass.

Tempest looked around. "But others might be listening too!"

"Forgive me Janus, but we must," he apologised, just in case the vessel's occupant was not the selfish monster he'd long detested. He grabbed his blanket and bundled the vessel inside. "We find somewhere quiet and discover the truth. Today." He made back for the ladder, while Tempest cast another nervous glance around before flapping after him.

Back on solid ground Clovis set off with the vessel clamped under his arm. Dawn's light was rousing the coven and he walked fast, aiming to be away before he was spotted. Even the singing birds sounded like an alarm call.

"Where are we headed?" Tempest hopped through the grass, itching to enter the staff and fly.

"Anywhere where we can't bring trouble to Stormwood." He stole a look around, and his heart sank when he saw someone approaching. "By all the dragon's scales! They drink all night and rise at dawn. Don't these witches ever sleep!" he cursed quietly.

"It's Farona," Tempest informed him.

Sure enough, the flame-haired youth was striding towards them. They didn't know, but he was on a special quest of his own this morning after making an important decision last night. It was a fearsome task he'd set himself and he needed all the courage he could get. He waved when he saw them. "Coven-father." Farona found it hard work sounding bright when his head pounded and his throat ached. It had been a good night, but all good things had a price. "Blessings on you both."

"An early start I see," Clovis curbed his impatience. He couldn't just breeze past him. It was improper, and besides, he felt a special kinship with him. "Farona, would you tell Kolfinnia I shall be away for the day."

He eyed the bundle under his arm, knowing exactly what doors it could open. "You will come back won't you?"

He couldn't help but smile. "I have no plans to leave you today." It was as close to the truth as he could come.

"I'll tell her," he promised.

Clovis could smell fear emanating from him, and had a shrewd idea why. "Farona," he began tactfully, "you travelled with Janus at Kittiwake, you even saw Hethra and Halla with your own eyes."

"It was my privilege," he said proudly.

"There are very few who have travelled with Janus alone." He indicated the three of them, "And all such individuals are standing right here."

He stood a few inches higher. "So few? I didn't realise."

"You faced great danger when you went below. Do you remember what Janus said to you then?"

"He said many things." *Most of which were cruel,* he added silently.

"Something you told me comes to mind. He said: if you pass every doorway without being bold enough to open it, your life will be very dull. Remember that?"

"Yes," he smiled, touched that he remembered.

"So with that in mind just find her and tell her." He gave the young man's shoulder a friendly pat.

"Find who?"

"It's early and my head hurts," he smiled cannily, "just tell her, and open that door."

He looked first baffled then guilty. "How did you know?"

"It's not important. Just tell her. The outcome is immaterial, only the deed counts."

Farona steeled himself. "I will. Thank you coven-father."

Clovis hoisted the bundle under his arm. "Blessings on you Farona. Tell Kolfinnia I shall be back." The group broke up and went their separate ways, all of them equally frightened. Coven-father was off to awaken a god using the name of a sacred woman, while Farona had some other sacred name on his mind. He was going to find Flora and tell her something important.

She was surprised to find that she had slept. Kolfinnia had fallen asleep curled around Rowan and now her shoulders throbbed with cramp. Wincing, she slid her arms free as the girl slept on, then pinched the bridge of her nose and rubbed her eyes and lay looking up at the thatched branches. Here and there sunlight glimmered and she made a mental note to ensure the roof was weatherproof before winter, then she reluctantly turned her mind to her other problem: Sunday, what was she going to do about Sunday? She stroked the little scar on her cheek as she thought. Back in April she cut her cheek while chopping wood. It had bled a lot but an hour later it was forgotten. But now she wondered. *What else happened on that April day? Where was Sunday and what was she doing right then that bound us together?*

'Fated sisters,' Rowan had said and she had no reason to doubt her. Well, if they *were* sisters she would deal with this in a family manner, quietly and sensitively. With that decision made, she gently disengaged from Rowan and began readying for a difficult day. As soon as she stood, her head boomed. She winced again, this time at the memory of kissing Albert Parry and pressed a hand to her aching head and sighed. It wasn't just the situation with Sunday that was delicate. Kolfinnia silently cursed whoever had invented ale, and then set about freshening up.

Skald watched her buckle hrafn-dimmu around her waist and she sensed his interest. "We're whole again," she whispered, careful not to wake Rowan.

He stretched and nodded wisely. "What will you do about Sunday?" he asked from nowhere.

She was ready for this. "The last person Valonia saw was a former enemy. But she treated him as an equal."

Skald stirred and sat upright. "And?"

"And I'm going to do the same."

He closed his eyes and sighed deeply, "Then Valonia is still with us. Her wisdom lives in you."

Skald wasn't known for compliments, and she almost blushed. "I really have to get going. Will you watch over Rowan?"

"I think I can manage it," he said dryly.

She smirked, both in affection and irritation, before collecting the last of her things and clambering down Crow-top's ladder – tripping on the last rung. "This autumn I'm going to have bloody stairs made!" she complained, hoping nobody had seen her. Satisfied, she surveyed the gardens.

On the garden's edge she saw Leonard Sanding inspecting his crop. He came at seven every morning on the dot, as did May Smallword and Eileen Bishop, these latter two were just hunched shapes between the rows of corn. "Seven o'clock," Kolfinnia observed. Already the morning was late, and today was significant. "Today Blackwand arrives," she reminded herself, but first she had to find Clovis. Her head was full of worries stirred up by something called 'the Flowering'. "What does that even mean?" She couldn't ask Rowan, the girl was upset enough. "Clovis will know," she convinced herself, and set off to find him.

By seven-thirty she had circled the gardens and called at Clovis's quarters only to find a bunk not slept in and no sign of Janus either. By nine o'clock the gardens were busy and the children were beginning their spell-lessons, and she was consumed with worry. In her mind he had gone, simple as that. She asked everyone to the point where she began to feel like the abandoned wife who's last to know her husband has run away. If coven-mother didn't know where her counterpart was then what sort of coven-mother was she, she reasoned? Her age didn't help either. Being Britain's youngest coven-head was a constant weight, like having a heap of criticisms hanging over her ready to fall, but to her troubled mind this matter came a distant second, because whatever 'the Flowering' was, it had taken Clovis.

Aside from hunting Clovis, she was confronted with Stormwood's routine business. She was asked again who should get the coveted garden-plot closest to the pond where the frogs kept the slugs under control. One by one she dealt with sensitive issues and disputes, always aware of her age and determined not to fall. Many enquiries seemed trivial, but it was important that everyone's voice counted. After mediating over slug control, rationing firewood, investigating rumoured fairy sightings, looking for lost wands and scheduling laundry duty, Clovis was still very much on her mind. At last she found someone she hadn't asked and wouldn't feel silly in front of.

"Farona, have you seen Clovis? Sometimes I swear he just vanishes like any other cat!" she rolled her eyes in mock dismay, trying to hide the real thing.

He looked preoccupied. "Aye, I saw him first thing this morning."

"Oh?"

"And he said to tell you he'll be away for the day." He cast a furtive glance around the gardens.

"Did he say where?"

"Sorry no, just that he'll be back later. I'd have told you sooner," he hurried to apologise, "but I've been looking for, erm. . . Flora."

"Flo, why?"

He regretted mentioning her now. "Erm, nothing really, I was going to help gather nettles for steeping, that's all."

"Well, I'll tell her you're looking for her, yes?"

"No need! I'm sure I'll run into her. Good day coven-mother." He offered her a fleeting smile and swept past.

"Farona, is all well?" she called after him.

He turned back, "All's well. All's fine!"

She watched him march away, thinking he was as much a mystery as Clovis. "Men," she despaired, as she pulled a headscarf from her pocket and tied it in place. She took in the trees around Stormwood and its ancient fort. Somewhere out there Clovis was conspiring with Janus. He had slipped away without telling her and that's what worried her most. "Don't you dare go walking Evermore without telling me." She rolled up her sleeves ready for work and ready to forget her worries, or at least try.

After such a lively night it might be reasonable for all of Stormwood to be slow to rise, but not all its witches had indulged so heartily and many knew effective remedies for sore heads. By the time Kolfinnia was wandering Stormwood looking for Clovis there were already a score of witches in the gardens inspecting the crops and letting mother nature work her magic or helping things along with a little magic of their own.

Hathwell, unlike many others, wasn't worse for wear. He spent the evening nursing a mug of ale and trying hard to make small talk with wary strangers. At midnight he slipped away and bedded down in one of the temporary camps at the Glade's edge. He slept under canvas, surrounded by snoring men and boys, who wouldn't have much to say to him even if they were awake. He doubted if Hilda had even noticed he'd gone. At dawn he came down to the gardens where he now officially had a plot of his own. Granted it was just a scrap of soil in the corner of Rowan's garden, but her gesture had reassured him about his new home. At Rowan's prompting he had planted a plum stone. She said she knew enough magic to give it a boost, but couldn't do it while he was watching. He enquired if it was a secret, but when she blushed he realised she was simply too shy to do it in front of him, and so he left her to it. That was yesterday evening. Now there was a sturdy little sapling where he had planted his stone. It stood about a foot high and had all of four leaves, but it was miracle enough to him.

"Good Lord," he smiled. "Good Lord she did it." He reached out and stroked one of the leaves. It was quite most incredible thing he'd ever seen – well almost. There was the small matter of the Therion. He thought Clovis was even more impossible than the plum tree. Where as Kolfinnia had endured a night worrying about the future, his mind had turned to the past, to Eastern Europe and to Solvgarad.

The coven they fought there had almost defeated them. Eventually Krast won the day, but the battle was savage and in retribution they showed the captives no mercy. The witches of Solvgarad had likewise fought hard, and perhaps the reason they displayed such incredible courage was that they were led by a warrior just like the one Hathwell had met yesterday: a Therion.

Therions were the 'beast people' who owned the world before man, or as some had it they were God's rejects before he perfected the human form. Either way, in the end the battle's outcome was inevitable. The coven was destroyed and the Therion's corpse was carted back to London as a prized curiosity. The last of his kind would spend eternity sealed behind glass at Goldhawk Row.

Therions had gradually been seen less and less in the world. Now and again one was sighted, but by the Middle Ages the Therions were just the stuff of fantasy, that is until one showed up in Solvgarad. According to Illuminata doctrine that was the day the Therions had become officially extinct but here at Stormwood the past had come alive to accuse him, and the past had emerald eyes.

"What is it?" Hathwell looked down at the witch in fascination, thinking it looked like a cross between a lion and a man. He, or rather it, was riddled with bullet holes.

"Dead, that's what it is," Field Commander Hood declared and prodded the creature with his foot. "And just as well too."

Hathwell didn't have a fraction of Hood's field service, even though he was Knight-Superior's squire. He knelt for a closer look. "Yes but what is it?"

"I told you — dead." The older man turned and surveyed the battlefield. Less than an hour ago it looked like the knights were doomed. Hood counted at least ten fallen krakens still pumping black smoke into the air, while riderless horses trotted through the wreckage and wounded men called out for medics. It had been a hard fight he thought, the hardest of his long years. He looked back at the Knight Superior's young squire still examining the corpse. "Therion," he said, a touch superstitiously.

"A what?" Hathwell wiped sweat from his face.

"Therionthrope," Hood elaborated. "Man-beasts. There was a time when the world was overrun with the filthy things. Folk tales have it that it was them what taught witches all they know of magic. Probably rutted with 'em too."

"I've never heard of them, let alone seen one." Hathwell resisted the urge to stroke the creature's mane. The fur was a magnificent dappled red-ochre, but gritty and blood soaked now. Its emerald eyes stared skywards, and even though they'd taken on the milky cast of the recent dead they looked resolute. 'Where are you from?' he wondered, but the Therion's secrets were lost.

"This might well be the very last one," Hood added, somewhat proudly. "And good for us. See how the coven rallied around the thing and made their final push?" He glanced to where the dead witches were being piled for burning, and the wretched survivors were being herded into a group. "We'd have come out of this without a scratch if not for the Therion. Take my word for it."

"I suppose," he agreed faintly. Images of women and children hurling themselves into the fight still burned in his mind, and would do so for the rest of his days. With or without the Therion the witches of Solvgarad had been fearless.

"Eyes front!" Hood suddenly stood erect.

Hathwell got to his feet slowly and saw Knight Superior Krast heading their way. He looked unmoved by the carnage around him. His uniform was stippled with mud and there was a slight tear in the sleeve. Hathwell had never seen him walk away *from a battle with so much as sweat on his brow. Today though he looked positively bedraggled, and it was that, not the dead, the dying and the roaring fires, that finally brought it home to him just how close they'd come to defeat.* "Knight Superior," *he saluted.*

"Sir!" *Hood stood parade ground stiff as if his life depended on it.*

Krast ignored their salutes. "Hathwell. Purity's left furnace stack is damaged. Can it be field-repaired?" *He flicked his eyes left, where two hundred yards away stood the looming shape of his own kraken. It was the only machine on the battlefield painted white, but now it was mostly black from mud and gun smoke.*

"I'll need to make a closer inspection sir, but it's doubtful."

He sighed in irritation and swept a bony hand across his crown. His dark hair was thinning even though he was barely in his forties, and the more it receded the more of those strange golden scars showed. "Then have her dismantled and ready for transport by sunset."

"Aye sir."

He was about to turn away when he stopped. "And what do we have here?" *He finally noticed the corpse at his feet, hardly surprising considering the number of dead littering the ground.* "Good God, a Therion!" *He sounded like a man who had just received a gift.* "A supremely rare beast, no wonder the witches of Solvgarad fought like animals — they were led by one."

"I've never seen one sir." *Hathwell found the creature's emerald gaze unsettling.*

"And you'll likely never see another," *Krast stared down in fascination.* "It's believed they were long since extinct."

'They probably are now,' Hathwell thought.

"Hood," *Krast ordered.*

"Sir." *He almost jumped out of his skin in an attempt to stand taller.*

"Have this thing boxed up and sent back to London before it rots." *He regarded the lion-like face for a moment and acknowledged the passing of a race.* "It'll make an impressive trophy wouldn't you say."

"And the prisoners sir?" *Hood asked dutifully.* "Are they to be taken back too?"

His eyes became slits. He didn't want word of their near defeat reaching London. He couldn't risk it. "No captives today Hood."

Hathwell suppressed a hiss of shock. He knew what was coming.

"Sir?" *Hood was less quick on the uptake.*

"No survivors." *Krast casually teased a stray thread from his ripped uniform.*

"They gave us a run for our money, I concede that, but we can't let this spread. The covens will only become bolder. Have them executed as an example."

"Right away sir." Hood snapped another salute.

After a last look at the Therion, Krast made to leave, but stopped after just a few paces. "And Hood — make it clean and quick. I'm not a cruel man." He said this last with unblemished conviction.

Hathwell watched him wander away through the smoke, probably back to the field kitchen to find an early breakfast, then turned his attention to where tattered men, women and children were being rounded up for processing, but they would never reach those cells. 'No survivors of Solvgarad,' he thought, and right then he didn't envy Hood one bit. "I best attend Knight Superior's kraken." Hathwell slipped gratefully away from him and his terrible duty lest it taint him further, and set off across the battlefield all the while imagining the Therion's emerald eyes following him.

'One day you will pay Bertrand Hathwell,' it seemed to call after him, and Hathwell knew it was right; one day he would.

The memory passed and he found himself staring at the little plum sapling again. Somewhere he could hear a child laughing, a butterfly flitted past and the sun was already warm on his neck. It was going to be another beautiful day. "I paid in full," he heard himself say, and the image of Krast lying trapped in his wrecked kraken came back to him, followed by the sound of a single gunshot. "And you paid too." It should have made him feel better but he just felt weary.

"Lost somewhere nice?" someone asked.

He turned and smiled helplessly. It was Hilda.

"You looked a hundred miles away."

"Just thinking." He saw she was wearing a work smock and her fabulously long dark hair was restrained under a headscarf. She carried a basket of onion bulbs and a garden rake. "You look to have a day's work ahead of you," he indicated her tools.

"What were you thinking about?" She leaned on her rake, wearing a curious smile.

"It was a pleasant night last night, your friends are very hospitable," he rambled.

"Hathwell." A frown replaced her smile and he saw he wasn't going to get off so lightly.

"If you must know I was thinking of Kittiwake."

She nodded vaguely, "And what part of that day were you thinking about?"

He wasn't sure if she was testing his loyalty, stabbing his conscience or confiding in him like a friend. In short, Hilda was a wonderful mystery to him. "Truthfully?"

"Is there any other way?"

He met her gaze fully. "I was thinking of the moment I shot Knight Superior Krast."

She swayed a little at his bluntness then recovered her poise. "You never speak of that."

"It's nothing I'm proud of."

"Then what are you proud of Bertrand?"

There it was again, that magical word that had him in knots: his own name from her lips. "I'm proud that I met Valonia one last time."

Her smile resurfaced at the name. "She was an extraordinary woman, and a good friend." Hilda stood looking down at the basket in her hands and sad memories floated around them like lost wishes.

"Need a hand with those?" he said eventually, pointing to the onions.

She disregarded the question and looked past him to the little sapling. "I see you've made a start."

"Rowan helped me," he admitted with meaning.

"Plums and onions don't make the best bedfellows." She slung her rake over her shoulder and hoisted the basket up her arm.

"Aye." That old feeling of dejection washed over him again. *You're the sweet plum I bet, and I'm the bloody rank onion,* he thought moodily, and the less said about the implications of 'bedfellows' the better.

"But rhubarb and plums are another matter entirely," she continued, "Kolfinnia's already given me a good area to plant in. Rhubarb's easy to grow." She cocked her head towards her own plot and set off.

He grasped her meaning and suddenly felt foolish for being sullen. He turned back to his plum tree. "I'll be back to water you later," he promised it.

"Careful what you say to plants, they understand you," she called over her shoulder.

"Really?" He hurried after her.

"Oh yes, it was said that Valonia's tree knew *all* her secrets!"

He didn't know if she was teasing him and he didn't care. It was a beautiful day and he was here with Hilda. Everything seemed so perfect that he was even able to forget the Therion's accusing gaze for a while and that was fine for Hathwell.

He dreamed, but these were not his dreams. In his dream he was called 'Colm' and his older sister had fallen down a well on her tenth birthday.

In his dream Colm kept quiet about Pattie's whereabouts, because on that August day as a boy he'd been the one who'd pushed her. He remembered her screaming, followed the sound of breaking wood, but it wasn't breaking wood it was bone. Pattie broke her leg and begged for Colm to fetch papa, but Colm just crouched by the well, torn by indecision.

He was scared Pattie would tell papa he'd pushed her, but satisfied because she had teased him all morning with her new birthday present: a fabulous hobbyhorse. She called it Starglade and although Colm thought the name was silly, its bright eyes, painted face and bushy mane were irresistible to a five year-old. At that moment in his life it was his dearest desire. Pattie galloped through cornfields and poppy meadows and never once let him ride it. She deserved to stay down that stinking well, Colm thought, and when she'd been down there long enough and swore never to tell papa, then he would go and bring help. She deserved it, he reminded himself. But she refused to promise, and such a simple promise too. All she did was snivel and beg, but she never promised. In the end when darkness was creeping over the marshes and fireflies darted around the weeping willows Colm ran back home, devising a tale as he went.

'Pattie ran into the woods papa, riding Starglade. I told her to slow down, I couldn't keep up, but she left me behind. I was so scared being left by myself! And Pattie rode away and left me and I couldn't find her!'

That very night and all the next day the villagers searched every corner of Easingford Cross but Patricia Barda had simply vanished.

Colm waited. Even at five he could calculate and devise, skills that would serve him well in later life. He would return to Pattie at early evening and tell her the village had given up looking for her, and if he didn't tell papa where she was then nobody would ever find her. Then she had to promise.

Dread quickly invaded the Barda household. Colm watched his mother anxiously pace the halls of Cross Manor, while her husband Earnest coordinated the desperate search for their missing daughter. The search went on even as thunder rolled. It continued unabated even as the rain began to fall, but when the summer storm turned into an unprecedented flash flood, even resolute Earnest Barda was forced back home.

Colm watched rain batter the windows and lightning torture the sky, enjoying the drama and quite forgetting his sister. The world outside had become a maelstrom of untamed water, while Cross Manor became a gloomy dungeon lit by candles. Gravel and leaves were hurled against the glass. The roof sprung a dozen leaks. Thunder rocked the earth and streams and rivers found a fury they hadn't known in over a century. They delighted in tumbling walls, bridges and riverbanks, flooding cellars and invading fields of wheat and barley. Cart tracks turned to rivers of sludge, sheep and cows were swept away, hillsides slipped and crumbled, and even age-old wells that had stood disused for years began to fill once more.

Colm couldn't go and make Pattie promise that evening as planned, but he earned an extra goodnight kiss from his distraught mother, who clung to him now as never before, and he slept well that night. Colm believed he could grow accustomed to life as an only child.

The next morning the sun had returned and the world was scarred by heavy rains. Colm found it easy to slip away while the grown-ups began their searching again, but when he arrived at the forgotten well in the woods he found to his puzzlement that now it brimmed with dark water. He dipped his hand in, but it was so muddy he couldn't even see his own fingers. He knew then that Pattie would never come out of the well.

"Serves her right," he absolved himself. "She should've promised." Regretfully he buried her hobbyhorse in the woods, knowing in some vague way it could get him into trouble if found, and set off for home, already looking forward to his breakfast.

Sef awoke, still savouring the stolen dream. Desires and treachery fascinated him.

"You slept a long time," a voice rebuked.

He ignored the remark, sat up and flexed his powerful arms. It was overcast and the shore was empty. Barda's murderous memory wasn't the only interesting thing he had digested. There was the small matter of the Martian artefact too.

"Dawn was an hour ago," the voice continued.

Sef turned to Iso, his thunder-sprite, almost replied, then changed his mind.

"The creature's mind, did it tell you anything of Clovis?" Iso pestered.

Sef stood and looked around. *Goonhilly Downs,* he thought, now knowing the name and language of these isles.

"Sef. Answer me."

"Nothing," he replied in English.

His thunder-sprite scowled. "Very amusing, but speak words we can both understand." He couldn't comprehend. It was Sef who had devoured Barda's mind, not him.

He switched back to their native language. "The place where we arrived, it was a coven. There was a battle. Eyewitness survivors say a creature was with these witches. It could only be Clovis."

"He has found allies here?" Iso was perturbed.

"Yes. And they escaped using Janus."

"When?"

"By the calendar of this place nine months ago."

"So long! Then there's no time to waste. We must locate his trail."

"No, first we must go to London."

"London?" Iso shook his head.

"A city of great importance."

"Is Clovis there?"

Sef stared at the horizon. Already he knew London well because Barda had known London well. "No," he said at last.

Iso looked unimpressed. "Then why go there?"

"We have lost this," he tapped the chain around his neck where the locket known as the pact-of-grace had once been. "There is something in London that might work instead." He thought of the Martian relic he'd inadvertently seen in Barda's memories. *How fortunate,* he mused.

"The pact is the least of our worries."

"For now. But should the unthinkable happen and Clovis decides to open the vessel, then we will need it."

"He won't."

"You don't know that for sure," Sef dismissed him.

Iso spread his wings and stretched, looking unconcerned. "Clovis will not open the vessel here. He will return to Vega."

"Where our kinsmen await in great numbers. But if he does open the vessel here," he lifted a finger, "I am the only one to stop him."

"London might be a costly delay."

"No. A vital detour." He picked up his staff, the signal to be off.

"And what is this thing in London that can replace the pact-of-grace?"

"A rare artefact, holding an even rarer soul." He kept the details vague.

"The creature's mind told you that?" Iso looked to the now empty gelding-sack. "He was so learned?"

"Learned?" Sef barked a derisory laugh.

"Then who was he?"

"Barda. His name was Barda. As a boy he murdered his sister." He looked wistful for a moment. "A resourceful man. A pity I had to kill him."

"Man?"

"The beings that hold this world to be their own," Sef elaborated.

"Their minds, are they strong?" Iso wanted to know more about them.

"I have but tasted one."

"And?"

He thought of the hobbyhorse and how desire for it had led to murder. They were a weak species, but still he marvelled at how such a young boy could be so ruthless and cunning. Yes, under other circumstances he and Barda could have been allies. "Like all beings Iso, desire will always defeat them," he concluded.

Iso laughed sardonically, "The same the worlds over."

"Praised be Lord Self."

"Praised be Lord Self," Iso added respectfully.

Sef nodded in satisfaction. Yes, it was true to say he understood this world and the men that swarmed across it. He held the staff at arm's length. "Now fly," he ordered.

In one interrogation Sef had learned a great deal. He understood that men dominated and races like himself were dubbed 'Therions'. Now they were considered extinct and for the most part only knights and witches believed they had ever existed at all. In short, Sef was going to have trouble blending in, but there were ways around that.

He flew high and fast, seemingly immune to the cold wind. His sprite was undaunted also, for Iso was no natural sprite. No loyal thunder-sprite would serve the Unitari, hence to maintain their cover they secretly bred their own sprites. Iso, like all of his kind, had been born of artificial lightning generated by advanced technology. During their countless centuries of plotting, the Unitari's generated sprites had watched over them, but not for protection. It was rare but not unknown for Unitari to show sympathies for the Temple's true purpose. These rogues were eliminated, and invariably it was their thunder-sprites who betrayed them. Sef knew that Iso would report all he'd done here on Earth. He was as much a spy as a sprite, and Sef often resented him as much as he needed him.

"How long is our journey?" So far Sef hadn't said, which displeased Iso.

"Two hundred miles." Sef watched the land roll by far below.

"It would be prudent for me to know the customs of this land. It would hamper our purpose if I were to be left ignorant."

Sef growled in irritation.

"Acola will ask questions upon our return. I wish only to speak the best of you Sef."

"You're right," he agreed grudgingly. "But speed is now our goal. I shall share what I learned from Barda when we take shelter tonight. Not before."

"Of course you will." His tone was annoyingly smug.

Sef guarded his anger and instead scanned the landscape below, knowing somewhere in this land there was a lion and a god, and he intended to subdue both. How fortunate then that he should stumble upon a forgotten time bomb just waiting for him in London. Lord Self was guiding his path indeed.

Chapter Five

Blackwand of Stormwood

'It took a great fall to elevate me to great heights'
Sunday Evelyn Flowers, Solstice queen - Regal-Fox coven, Surrey

Clovis set off westwards to where mountains edged the horizon. First, he went on foot, but after passing the way-bewares and leaving Stormwood behind he took to the air. Luckily the hills beyond were veiled in dawn mist and the valleys obscured. He could fly without fear, but as a precaution he travelled higher than normal, where the air was cold and the winds were wild. He made good speed and after a short time the land became more mountainous, and he judged himself far enough from Stormwood, or anyone else for that matter, to begin. He selected a foreboding ridge of exposed rock and touched down. "This is far enough." He shook dew from his mane. The mist had thickened into a fog. It was damp and gloomy but at least it concealed them.

The lightning-staff flashed once and Tempest dropped to the ground, surveyed the scene and stretched. "Charming place."

"Mountains have a will of their own," he ruled, looking around. Peaks soared into the fog around him, and everywhere was shattered rock. Close by he could hear running water and he caught the smell of something rank, probably one of the grazing animals had died, he thought. Sure enough tufts of rotten wool clung to the rocks like mould. "Poor wretch," he muttered, and thought of dying up here exiled from greenery and warmth.

He scented the air for traces of people but found none. "We are alone," he said, satisfied.

"Let's begin." Tempest wanted this over with.

Clovis sat down on a rock and pulled his cloak around himself. He rummaged in his pack and set the vessel down before him. Janus hadn't changed. He still drifted askew and silent and Clovis sighed heavily. He half hoped the journey might shake him awake and they wouldn't have to go through with this.

"No salt circle?" Tempest asked.

Clovis shook his head. "Nothing can protect us if HE is listening. We take our chances and leave as fast as we can."

Tempest looked around at the thickening fog. "How could he not listen," he warned.

Clovis pressed a finger to his lips. "Try not to think of it, it might only draw attention. . ."

"Agreed." He closed his beak, and instead kept watch on the swirling mists.

Clovis hunched over and cupped the vessel between his hands. "Now it's you and I Janus." He shut his eyes, took a cleansing breath and cleared his mind. His heart slowed as he concentrated, feeling for Janus through the glass. Clovis had a very important but very brief message to deliver to the god. It was just one word. It was the name of a woman. She too had been murdered and her killer had also been a powerful and wrathful entity. She had been killed long ago but nothing of her survived, and unlike Janus, she remained dead, to the detriment of all.

Clovis poured his will through the glass until it surrounded Janus. He hoped the name would be enough, but as potent as it was Janus was virtually lifeless and Clovis wondered if there was anything left to wake up. *Please great Lady,* he thought without naming her, *please bring Janus back to me*. He leaned closer and spoke that one most dangerous word: the name of the Lady.

The Temple-of-Unity was founded to revive the murdered Janus. Later it had been infiltrated by disciples of Self and corrupted, but there was one other secret the Temple protected, and neither Self nor Acola, or any other treacherous soul managed to defile it.

Within the Temple coven there was *another* coven, smaller, secret and elite. Clovis had been a witch of this coven also, although not its coven-father. That honour went to his closest friend Tiber, and on the occasions the coven had met in secret, it was Clovis who called *him* coven-father. This coven had no name, for it was dedicated to a Lady whose name, though beautiful, meant death for anyone who dare speak it. The Lady was the original voice of the cosmos and the female counterpart to Janus. The two were husband and wife, but because her boundless compassion made her so fair, another god desired her. This jealous and possessive god forged a pact with Self and it was agreed that Self would kill Janus and this other would then take the Lady for his pleasure. Darkest legends say it was none other than the Patternmaker who lusted after her.

On the day Janus was murdered the balance of good in the universe shifted fatally towards darkness. The Lady refused to marry her husband's killer and as punishment he chained her to the eleven moons of Tythan, and as they circled the gas giant she was slowly and agonizingly torn to pieces. Ever after, whenever her murderer heard her name spoken anywhere in the cosmos he unleashed his fury, killing anyone who might still revere her. In this way he erased her from conscious memory and her once beautiful name became synonymous with death.

No great goodness is ever forgotten however, and despite the danger her name was passed down the generations in secret codes entrusted to secret covens. Even those who worshipped her would likely go their whole lives without saying her name, just as Clovis expected to, until today. He leaned closer, misting the glass with his breath and spoke the most dangerous word in creation, the name of the Lady.

'Ȧrȯı̇ả'

The world outside rolled by as it ever had. It was still a symphony of countless sensations, but Janus didn't detect a single one. His tiny world consisted of a numbing void and his only companion was a staggering sense of grief. The landscape was a monotonous plain as grey as the empty sky. He stared towards the horizon, too dismayed to believe anything might lay beyond it and the only thought that circled his head was the word 'Self'. Around and around it went with crushing tedium and each time it passed it erased a little more of him until his own name was just a hollow word with no form.

'Janus - Self - Janus - Self - Janus - Self - Janus.' Over and over it came. One name he hated while the other was becoming a mystery to him. This might have gone on forever but for something new: a third name came into his world like a thunderbolt. It was a name he had longed to speak for aeons, but even he couldn't risk saying it aloud. Αριδιά.

Suddenly the world rocked and the sky split open with a terrible roar. The grey peeled back to show swirling mist and ragged mountain peaks. A hundred different sensations poured in. The light hurt his eyes. Janus was overwhelmed by the smell of wet rock and damp moss and he felt a chill but welcome wind. Then a figure loomed up, a figure he recognised.

Clovis hissed, "I saw him move, I swear!"

"Are you sure?" Tempest fluttered down to see and just then both of them heard a familiar voice.

"Clo–vis?" It was Janus.

Clovis couldn't help but smile. "Ja –," he started, but didn't finish because suddenly he felt the mountain tremble. "He heard us," he barked, "MOVE!" Clovis snatched up the jar, while Tempest dived into the staff. He mounted, and as his feet left the ground he felt the very mountain heave like a wave. Just as they launched, Clovis gaped at the sight of the whole mountainside sliding like wet sand. In the next instant they were tearing down the mountain's flank, blinded by fog and racing for their lives as rocks began to shift and tumble with disastrous force. He *had* been listening and a landslide was a very efficient way to silence The Lady's worshippers. Clovis pulled the staff up, while the atrocious noise reached up like giant fists, pounding the very air around them. He risked a look down and saw massive boulders, spindly trees and even unfortunate sheep being swept away in a great churning wave. *Bastard!* he thought wrathfully. To keep his secret, the Lady's killer cast a far reaching net of death and devastation.

As they rocketed forwards, the mist and dust thinned and the sound of Armageddon faded. Clovis saw numerous small valleys nestling between adjacent peaks, and he judged them far enough away and set a course towards them, all the while wondering which Janus he carried with him: the trickster or the saviour?

Less than ten minutes later he found out. They landed in a wooded glen next to a peaceful stream, but Clovis remained hyper-cautious. From across the valley he could hear the distant thunder of falling rocks, but now it was fading just like the mist. "He listens always," he accused and set the vessel down in the wet grass.

Tempest appeared, looking breathless. "I never want to try that again." He looked around, alert for danger and didn't speak above a whisper. "But it worked at least."

"Speak no more of it, it might only draw his attention again." Clovis sat and caught his breath, and after a while he sensed he was being watched.

"Clovis." It was Janus.

Relieved and afraid, he knelt, and Tempest crouched beside him. "Janus, I am glad to see you recovered."

"Recovered?" he repeated. The word had far deeper meaning than Clovis realised. Janus knew that he had drifted unconscious for over two weeks, he knew how Clovis had worried, how a girl had discovered a black wand and how Blackwand herself was coming, but most crucial of all he knew *himself* again. He was not a relic or a treasure, he was Janus god of doorways, born to unify the splintered mind, but he had been murdered along with his beloved yet nameless wife. "Recovered, in a manner, yes," he reflected.

Clovis quickly realised that this wasn't Janus at all. Instead it seemed that this was the promised Janus the Temple's founders had long awaited. If so, then it was no exaggeration to say that this moment had been anticipated for endless generations. Right away witch and sprite bowed their heads. "Janus, master of doorways?" It was both a greeting and an open question. They stayed that way until Janus finally spoke.

"Why did you never tell me?"

It is him! Clovis looked up. "My Lord?" he struggled.

"I am nobody's Lord."

He was unaccustomed to such humility. "Janus, what could I tell you of that unforgivable atrocity?"

"The truth."

He took a moment to prepare. "The truth is you were slain and your great purpose forgotten."

"And your coven rescued me?" He drifted closer to the glass until he was almost touching it. "Did you?"

"We did."

"Hoping I would one day remember?"

"One day, yes."

"And this is all that remains of me?" he regarded himself. "A trinket of bone, the last scrap of my own corpse?" The question was heartbreaking.

Witch and sprite exchanged mortified looks. "Your physical body was ravaged beyond resurrection." Clovis felt tears moisten his eyes. "The resulting shock banished your mind, and in its place. . ."

"In its place a monster held sway," he concluded.

Clovis bowed again, but this time to hide his face. There was no denying it, or the shame it must now cause the restored god.

"Answer me Clovis, please."

He readied himself. "Yes Janus." He didn't look up.

"Why?" he asked softly. "Why did I *not* remember?"

"We did not realise," Clovis was loath to admit. "We thought you were safe, but the Temple was infiltrated. Down the centuries the Unitari secretly suppressed your rightful self." He let this awful news sink in. "I am sorry Janus, we failed you," he added quietly, staring at the grass.

Janus considered this. "Then praise Blackwand," he said gratefully.

Clovis flattened his ears. "Blackwand?"

"Your forefathers rescued my broken body Clovis, but she rescued my mind."

"She did?"

"She challenged the Patternmaker, and she won."

He had never heard the like. "Fate yielded to freewill?"

"Yes, and in doing so a magnificent flower opened. And I heard it."

"And awoke," Clovis understood now.

"Almost. The awakening will only be fully realised when this vessel is opened," he dictated gravely. "Until then I remain incomplete. The poisoned portion of my mind still resides in here."

He swirled in the fluid and Clovis imagined all the lies he'd ever told floating in there with him, ready to corrupt him again. Yes, the vessel was tainted. Janus must leave it and the sooner the better. He stared sadly at the liquid in the jar. "The vessel is protected Janus, the fluid that gives you life is death to anyone who touches it."

"I am sorry," he said gently. "But this vessel must be opened. I shall ascend and leave my tainted self behind."

"I know," he affirmed. "Then now is the hour to take you home and break the seal."

"No. The Temple-of-Unity will be crawling with your enemies."

"Let me worry about that," he growled.

"Courage still abounds in you I see, but alas you wouldn't live long enough to break the seal."

"There will be many loyal witches in hiding, if we could rally them we could reclaim the Temple."

"No," Janus interrupted, "your plan is too precarious and there's no time."

"No time?" he frowned.

"Already there is an agent of Self here. I have tasted his poison at work in the world."

"A Unitari, here?" he hissed, and at his side Tempest growled.

"Clovis, this is what I ask of you."

Both witch and sprite noted how he said 'ask' not 'want'. He had indeed changed. "Yes Janus?"

"The Flowering had done more than just break my silence, it has pierced the Patternmaker's armour. With enough fortitude a soul might choose its own fate."

Clovis blinked, "Truly?"

"I hope so, because in light of it I have made a choice of my own."

He took a deep breath. "You are ready to ascend?"

"I am."

"Then we *must* return to Vega."

"And as I said, no." Janus sank slowly to the bottom, and stared out at him.

Clovis wasn't sure if this was the damaged side of Janus speaking now or not. "But Janus, Vega has been prepared for this day since the beginning –,"

"The ascension will take place here," he interrupted.

Now he wasn't sure if he'd heard right. "Here, Earth?"

"He can't!" Tempest whispered.

"I have chosen," Janus repeated.

Clovis grappled for excuses, "But this world is a mystery to me, I have no idea of where the fairy-nations lie or what magical laws apply, but on Vega all such concerns are in hand."

"You'll find a way Clovis, you always do. But be quick, the Unitari will find you in time."

Clovis touched his sword. "I'd like to see him try."

"Don't underestimate them."

"We shall deal with him," Clovis promised.

"You are the only witch who knows the proper ritual Clovis. It must be here and it must be you," he added regretfully. "I am sorry."

Clovis sighed. *And the day I break the vessel I walk Evermore again, but this time amongst the host of the deceased,* he thought and his gaze drifted back to that green fluid again and he wondered distantly what it might smell and taste like, and whether it would kill him quickly. He hoped it would. "I will find a way," he promised, and at his side Tempest hung his head in sorrow, because Clovis always kept his promises.

The last of Stormwood's crows came home that evening, and the last witches from Salisbury came with him. Harl had guided Benedict Collins and Sunday Flowers safely for many miles, and with their arrival the campaign against the Illuminata's tournament would officially be over. For the most part it was a victorious ending but Kolfinnia was as nervous as she could remember. She had asked Rowan to keep Blackwand's impending arrival secret. Firstly because she wasn't sure how to confront her, and secondly because after coming through so much would she want a grand welcome? The old Sunday certainly would, but from what Rowan had said this was a very different woman altogether and Kolfinnia discovered something that surprised her: she was excited about her arrival.

"Still no sign of Clovis?" Kolfinnia asked. It was now early evening and Stormwood enjoyed the afterglow of a glorious summer's day.

Flora stabbed her spade into the ground and stretched. "No," she grunted, "and a strong back like his would be handy in the garden."

"He's been gone all day." She scanned the woods for the hundredth time. Flora's wasn't convinced, "What's really wrong?"

"I told you, it's Clovis." It was only a half-lie she told herself.

"He often vanishes. I wouldn't worry about it, cats like wandering off."

She managed a smile. "Don't let him hear you say that."

"What did he say anyway?"

"He left a message with Farona early this morning and then vanished. Did he find you by the way?"

"Who?"

"Farona was looking for you earlier."

She shook her head. "I've had my head down in the gardens, maybe I missed him."

"Maybe," she sighed and glanced towards the distant hills again, knowing Ben and Sunday were very close now. *Just when I need him most, Clovis goes off by himself.*

"You keep looking east, you're expecting someone?"

"No." This time it was a full-lie, and she pretended to go back to her work.

"Kol, are you alright?"

"Fine." The biggest lie of all. Her stomach churned and she felt sick. Sunday was coming, and Clovis was likely negotiating with Janus about leaving, what could be worse, she wondered? "Really I'm fine."

"Hmm."

"You're worrying over nothing," Kolfinnia promised and just when she was beginning to believe it, a flurry of activity on the garden's edge made her jump. This was it. She looked over to where a crowd was gathering and when she heard a crow call that sealed it. "That's Harl." That could only mean Ben and Sunday had arrived. *Blackwand,* she told herself, *nobody's supposed to know Sunday is Blackwand yet.*

She was about to suggest they go take a look, when Sally Crook came rushing over with news. "Kolfinnia! You'll never guess!"

Flora hastily wiped her hands on her apron in a bid to look presentable. "Is it Blackwand? Please tell me it's not, I look a mess!"

"It's Ben!" Sally gasped. "And yes, she's with him! She's just up the glen, be here in a few minutes." She flapped an arm towards the hills.

Blackwand, Kolfinnia practised, *her name is Blackwand.* She couldn't spoil the surprise. All of Stormwood had waited weeks for this. "Where's Ben?"

"Come on!" Sally heaved on her arm. "Come on, Ben's here right now!"

Kolfinnia could see the crowd swelling rapidly. "Come on then!" She dropped her hoe, turned and ran after her. Flora came close behind, laughing, while Kolfinnia was mute with anticipation.

A discreet distance away Farona watched them go. He had tried no less than five times to approach her but on each occasion someone had bumbled along and ruined everything. Each time it happened he cursed, veered off and circled the coven, steadily building his courage for another try. He watched Flora and Kolfinnia vanish into the crowds and sighed, "Another time Flora, I promise you that." He plucked a few rocket leaves from the vegetable beds and chewed on them thoughtfully as he wandered down there to see what all the fuss was about.

"Ben!" Kolfinnia shoved through the crowds. "Ben!"

"Let coven-mother through!" someone called, "Let her through!"

The crush of bodies eased, but the noise was deafening. "Ben!" She squeezed through the last well-wishers and abruptly found herself face to face with Benedict Collins. His face was tanned and he had a week's stubble on his chin. He looked happy and refreshed, like a man home from holiday, not battle, and she knew why. *Don't you dare break his heart Sunday,* she thought protectively.

"Coven-mother!" He grabbed her in a fierce hug. His laughter rang in her ear and his beard scratched her cheek. She found she liked it and thought how lucky Sunday was. "Kolfinnia, I can't tell you how happy I am to be home!"

"Welcome home," she cried over the crowd, "I promise I'll never send you in to such danger again." She held him tight. "Never, I promise!"

"Don't fret!" He leaned back and beamed at her. "It was the best piece of luck I've ever had and I owe it all to you!"

Before she had chance to reply Flora barged forwards and threw herself at him. "Ben!"

"Flo!" He caught her neatly and swung her around just as the crowd pressed in again. Kolfinnia heard Flora's laughter followed by the meaty thud of countless backslapping welcomes. All around her people were cheering and breaking into song, and inevitably ale was called for. It was going to be another long and lively night.

Kolfinnia stood a little way back wearing a dazed smile, chasing her breath and taking stock as Ben revelled in his homecoming. Despite the joyous mood her mind kept drifting back to Clovis. "He can't leave us," she said to nobody, and by 'us' she meant 'me'. She was tempted to go and look for him again, but then something stopped her. Everything had gone quiet. The crowd's voice faded, and an expectant hush settled over Stormwood like the first winter snow. It could only mean one thing. "Blackwand." She took a deep breath and prepared to meet her fated sister.

Ahead of her, everyone fell quiet and the last mutterings died away. The crowd parted and as if on cue everyone, including Ben, turned to where a new figure now approached through the gardens. She carried a battered lightning-staff and walked with her sprite perched on her shoulder. She was dressed in black and her eyes burned glacier-blue. A silver hammer glinted at her neck, while her hair shone like ripe barley and was pinned with combs fashioned like foxes. She looked like a Viking queen, Kolfinnia thought. A soft gasp escaped the crowds. The rumours were true, Blackwand really was as beautiful as she was brave.

Kolfinnia started towards her through an avenue of reverential onlookers. As she drew closer she saw both the familiar and the new in her. She looked as she remembered, but there the similarity stopped and a new Sunday held sway, one lit by an inner light. No wonder Ben loved her, she thought. Sunday saw her at last and visibly stiffened, yet of all the gathered spectators only Kolfinnia noticed. It seemed that every face in the crowd was under some adoring spell of Blackwand's making, and only Sunday and Kolfinnia were truly awake.

Strike flapped away from Sunday's shoulder and up into the surrounding trees, which now thronged with dozens of sprites, while Blackwand continued her fateful last journey. Closer and closer they came, former opponents now bound by threads of fate. Kolfinnia even imagined the Timekeeper somewhere alone in the dark, weaving this last word in Sunday's journey, ensuring the end was as it should be. She felt a wall of energy, first touching her then enveloping her and she knew without doubt that Sunday Flowers really *had* died in the Timekeeper's cavern and whoever had awoken on those lonely black sands was another woman entirely, one she would be proud to call sister.

The two came together. Sunday looked searchingly into her face. She was about to speak when she saw the tiny scar on her cheek. She blinked in shock and swayed minutely. "Coven-mother?"

"Blackwand." Now she was closer she could likewise see the faint smudge where her own special scar had once been.

Sunday saw Kolfinnia scrutinising her, and understood that somehow she *knew*. She knew her terrible past. "Kolfinnia –," she began.

Kolfinnia silenced her with an embrace. "Welcome home," she whispered, "sister." It was a greeting solely for her, while everyone else looked on blissfully unaware.

"Kolfinnia," she stumbled again, but tears got the better of her. "Kolfinnia, I. . ."

"It's alright," she hugged tighter, "it's alright because we're sisters."

Somehow the crowd realised this was the only introduction they were going to get and an approving roar went up led by Ben. "Blackwand of Stormwood!" they chanted.

Sunday and Kolfinnia stood as one and both felt the touch of a weaving spider one last time followed by a whisper, *'Dear champion.'* At last they parted and regarded one another's teary face. The crowd thundered on, cheering, whistling and applauding. Blackwand, saviour of witchdom, had finally come. The two women saw nothing but the other and even the deafening crowds were forgotten.

'I'm sorry,' Sunday mouthed.

Kolfinnia wiped her eyes and smiled warmly, "You're home now."

As their smiles turned to grins the crowds went wild. It seemed everything was as it ought to be and Kolfinnia felt a huge weight slide from her shoulders, glad that she had a new sister.

Harry Cotter guessed he had an hour of daylight left. Just time to check the last traps, but it had rained most of the day, he felt wretched and wanted to go home. *Check them traps Cotter lad,* he told himself.

He set down his shotgun, crouched by the riverside and pushed aside beds of pungent wild garlic hoping the trap had bagged something sweet. Nothing, and no tracks either. "Huh," he sniffed. Billy Tote had bragged that Benton's estate boasted wild otters, and fashionable London ladies adored otter fur. "That lying Tote, bet he spun the yarn so as he can tell the regulars in the Bull how dim Harold Cotter went out a' catching otters and earned himself naught but a cold." He had checked the trap three nights running now. Four would be pushing his luck. He retrieved the trap, disarmed it, dropped it into a sack and decided to set off home.

Darkness was chasing daylight and he avoided the footpaths and tracks, keeping instead to the woods. Cotter knew these woods intimately. He had poached here his whole life and had no fear of the dark, just unfriendly gamekeepers with shotguns. But tonight was different.

Without knowing why, he stopped and looked over his shoulder. He saw only trees, but still he gave an involuntary shudder. "Devil's luck to turn back," he chided himself. He swept his cap from his head, mopped his brow, then hooked it back in place. He felt chill. Maybe he was getting a fever after all. "Bloody Tote," he swallowed and made to set off again when he heard a branch snap. He stopped dead. It had sounded like a big branch. "Someone there?" he called out. *Pipe down!* his mind insisted, *You're not here by invite!*

The trees had darkened into a mat of tangled branches, reminding him of branching veins painted across a cow's stomach. He willed his feet to move, and after some hesitation they shambled forwards once more and he tore his eyes from the woods behind and turned around. . . right into the face of a demon.

Iso watched him finish the interrogation. They had covered a good distance and found somewhere to spend the night. That is until a man had stumbled upon their hiding place. Sef was angry at being discovered and wasted no time in killing the intruder.

Sef gulped down the last of Harry Cotter's tongue, then let out a contented growl and sat back. It was fully night now, but Sef missed nothing. A night creature armed with prickles snuffled through the undergrowth to his left, but he ignored it. His belly was full and his mind was still digesting all he'd learned.

"Was the man of any use?" Iso enquired.

Sef yawned and began mopping at the mess around his muzzle. "He was nothing like Barda. Just a peasant of no value."

"Then it was a waste of time killing him. Others might come looking for him," he sniped.

Sef shrugged, "Nobody will come. He was not important."

"Surely you must have discovered something useful? The meal took you long enough!" Iso sat on a branch and regarded the dark sky. He didn't recognise any of the stars. "Where is this place for instance?"

"Lord-Ben-tons-Es-tate."

"Ben-tons?" he snorted. "Until you share what you've learned, the language of this land is meaningless."

"All in good time Iso," he purred.

"And how far to London?"

He considered. "Three, perhaps fours days."

"I hope it's worth it."

"It is. Without the pact-of-grace we cannot enter the fairy-nations, and as you well know, that is where Clovis must open the vessel."

"If we catch Clovis first, we won't have to."

"And if he gets wind of us and decides to open the vessel?"

"He won't," Iso interrupted, tired of repeating himself.

"Yet if he does, then we will have no way to catch him."

"How could he possibly do that without a pact of his own!"

"Remember, Clovis has joined a coven. He already has the advantage over us. It's likely the witches he's allied with will know ways to help him." Sef let out a rumbling growl, "If only I could interrogate a *real* witch."

Iso grumbled something in reply, but he was right. A quest to London might be essential after all. "And what can replace the pact-of-grace?"

He looked away from Cotter's headless corpse and toyed with the broken chain about his neck. The pact was a contract of passage to the fairy-nations, or 'faded-realm' as some had it, but now it was broken and useless. "We seek a stone."

"That's all?"

"It is no mere rock. It came from one of the spheres and it holds the last member of a war-like race."

"I see now. And this creature can bargain a passage to the faded-realm for us?"

Sef laughed, "Bargain? You speak like a politician! No, this creature will help us invade."

Iso looked mildly impressed. "And the Barda man, his mind was so knowledgeable that it told you this?"

"No!" Sef looked affronted. "Barda simply saw the stone once in a museum. It was but a novelty to his eyes, but I see his memories deeper than he ever knew. Without my instincts the stone's value would go unknown."

"Yes, yes," he placated, "what else did he see? Tell me!"

Sef licked the blood from his rough palms and sharp claws. Cotter was worthless but his blood was deliciously salty. "You are right. It is time to educate you to the ways of this world." He rose and stretched. He wouldn't let Iso have everything of course. Both Barda and Cotter had many memories celebrating envy and greed, and Sef wanted to keep those savouries for himself. No, Iso would taste only what was necessary for their mission: language and history and such like. He bent and hung his head. After a few moments he began to heave and pant, while Iso watched with hungry eyes. Sef coughed and spluttered and finally regurgitated a slab of semi-digested flesh. It splattered to the ground and glistened amongst the leaves and twigs. "Eat well," he wiped his muzzle and went back and sat alone in the dark.

Iso swooped down, chattering like an excited magpie, and began to tear at it. He enjoyed interrogations as much as Sef did.

As Iso ate and learned, Sef retrieved a small object from his robes. The night was fully black now but he saw perfectly. He turned the small object over in his hands, smoothing its contours, and when he held it to his ear he could hear a fluttering heart within. This tiny heart would eventually take him home, for the stone was an egg and inside slept a dragon just like the one he'd taken it from. When Janus was recaptured and the gelding-sack bulged with Clovis's head, Sef would set the egg to mature. It would hatch and grow to adulthood in mere days, and then it would carry him across the stars to Vega. Acola had forbidden him from using Janus to return home, that privilege was saved for Lords only, so Sef would have to endure months of hibernation again.

He hadn't thought to be resentful of this until he'd tasted Barda's desire. The boy wanted the hobbyhorse and he'd killed to get it. Sef admired that. *How simple would it be to return home with Janus in the wink of an eye, kill Acola and take his place?* He put the unsettling thought aside for now, but couldn't help but wonder if the thought garnered the approval of his god, Lord Self, watching from across the blackness of space.

A night creature barked somewhere in the woods. Barda's stolen thoughts told him it was a fox, probably drawn to Cotter's corpse, and Sef smiled at the omen. He clenched the egg in his fist and leaned closer to it, making sure his fickle sprite couldn't hear him. "Let me serve the Self within, my Lord. Let me have the coven-father's head. And let *me* have the honour of interrogating him," he whispered.

If Clovis could be toppled, Acola could too. Lord Self always rewarded selfish desires, it was its nature, and Sef knew his god wouldn't fail him.

She had another sore head. Clovis had returned late last night when Blackwand's welcome feast was already in full swing. Perhaps Kolfinnia wouldn't have celebrated so much if she hadn't been so relieved. Clovis had seemed distant, but with all the excitement she barely had time to speak to him. She was just glad to have him back. "Did Valonia celebrate so much?" she asked Hilda. "I don't think I can stand much more happiness."

Hilda looked up from her laundry. They were sitting in the Glade, arms to the elbows in soapy water. "Oh yes, but she knew a trick or two to sort a woolly head."

"I wish you'd share it." Last night's bonfire still smouldered, the riotous songs still throbbed in her head, and everything had the faint smell of ale, smoke and wine, hence the laundry.

"Think yourself lucky, if the Illuminata had won then there'd be nothing to celebrate."

She sat back, rubbed at her shoulder and looked around. "Have you seen Sunday this morning?"

"Blackwand is recovering," Hilda smirked. "She only retired a couple of hours ago."

"I thought they'd never let her leave," Kolfinnia smiled, "she must have danced with every witch at Stormwood, including Farona – he almost keeled over when he finally learned who Blackwand was."

"Everyone's wanted to meet her for so long. And although just a newcomer here myself, I have to say that all of Stormwood feels different."

"You noticed that too?"

"Everyone has I suspect. Stormwood feels," she paused, with her arms still submerged in soapy water, "it feels balanced."

Kolfinnia flashed her a puzzled smile.

"Not only do we have the hero of Salisbury, we also have the hero of Kittiwake." She reached out and patted her knee, leaving a wet print on her dress.

"Thank you," she accepted graciously.

"Balance," Hilda said again. "A coven with two such heroes – well it feels invulnerable."

"Please!" she blushed, brushing droplets from her knee.

"It's almost as if you two are sisters," she remarked lightly, not seeing Kolfinnia's smile fade a fraction. "And she's a knack for telling tales," she grunted as she wrung a sleeve dry.

"I almost felt I was there." Everyone had been amazed, entranced and horrified by Sunday's account.

"So did I, and remember I *was* there." Hilda hauled her smock out of the barrel and a cascade of soapy water rolled off it.

"Some of her tales were dark."

Hilda gave the smock a shake, and rainbow droplets briefly danced around them. "I suspect the very darkest tales will never be told."

Kolfinnia thought of the Timekeeper and the truth behind Kittiwake. "I'd put money on that." She leaned closer and smiled secretly, "Did you see her and Ben?"

"Of course!" Hilda rolled her eyes. "I suppose you think I'm too old to spot such things?"

Kolfinnia laughed and found herself thinking of Mr Hathwell. *And I'm not too young to spot such things either Hilly,* she smiled privately. "We might be having our first marriage at Stormwood?" she ventured.

"For pity's sake give the girl time to settle in," she clucked, but for some reason she pictured Hathwell's honest face and wondered what he was up to. "That's the last of it." She collected her laundry and slopped it into a basket. "By the way, did Clovis say where he'd been yesterday?"

She frowned, "No, he didn't."

"Try charm it out of him."

"I haven't Sunday's flair!"

Hilda's smile faded and she looked thoughtful. "Kolfinnia, I hope you don't mind, but after all you've told me, do you think he's getting ready to leave?"

She swallowed back her dread, "Maybe. I need to speak to him."

"Do that," she urged. "And if you need an ear to confide in. . ." She arched an eyebrow. It wasn't just Sunday and Ben she'd noticed.

"Thank you." The two witches stood, clutching their washing baskets, regarding one another. "Why's life never simple?"

"Oh it is," she said with total faith, "it's just people that aren't."

Kolfinnia smiled. "It's *so* good to have you home."

"It's a good home to come back to."

Kolfinnia kissed her farewell and left to find Clovis, wanting some answers, while Hilda went to see how an old squire was getting along.

She found Clovis on the old fortress wall. He was deep in conversation with a young witch named Connor Williams, and not over cheeky sketches of dancing coven-fathers either. "Clovis?" She made sure to sound cheery, but her heart galloped.

He turned her way but didn't smile. "That will be all Connor," he dismissed the young man.

"Coven-mother," Connor greeted her as he passed.

She waited for him to depart before beginning. "Still planning where to dig?"

"There are tunnels under here that would make good store houses." He thudded his foot against the ground. *Or defensive positions,* he thought darkly.

She looked out over the Glade. From up here, surrounded by trees, she felt somewhat detached from the rest of the coven. The bonfire still puffed wisps of smoke like a volcanic fissure, and she could see lanterns still hanging from trees and posts. Last night had been joyous, but today was different. "You're leaving aren't you?"

He heaved a sigh.

"Clovis?" she persisted.

"Yes, I'm leaving."

"Oh." She concealed her shock. "When?" she added quietly.

"As soon as I can."

She looked down at Hilda's wet hand print on her dress. It had dried to a heart-shaped blotch. "And when were you planning on telling me?"

He watched swallows dart and swoop through the trees, but didn't answer.

She dug deep for her courage. "Whatever you might need, just ask."

He smiled now. It took a brave soul to face loss with grace. "My plans have changed."

"Changed?"

The hopeful look on her face wounded him. "Janus is not going back to Vega."

"Not going back?" Now she looked confused as well as hurt. "Clovis – be plain with me."

He rubbed at his chin and flicked an ear. "Where to begin?" he sighed.

She gave him a moment, listening to the wind in the trees. Laughter floated across the Glade and she hoped one day she'd have cause to laugh again. "Clo –,"

"Please," he lifted a hand. "Janus has heard something he called 'The Flowering'."

"Flowering!" she stifled her shock.

"You know of it?"

"Rowan mentioned it, the other night."

He nodded. "Hmm, he says it is intimately connected with Blackwand."

"Sunday hasn't said anything of it. Then again, last night was so hectic."

"I'm sure she will. She's not the woman I remember," he managed a small smile.

"I'll ask her about it." She looked at him expectantly. "Go on."

"Janus heard this Flowering, and he has. . . changed."

"And now he doesn't wish to return to Vega?" Her insides felt icy. "Has he devised something even more terrible as way of payment?" she accused.

"This is nothing to do with payment. That Janus, the one you knew, is all but vanquished. As I say, he has changed."

She rested a hand on his arm. "What's he asked of you?"

"To be released."

She took a step back. "Then why wait, simply open the vessel right here! He'll be free and you –," She almost said it – *Can stay with me*.

"If it were that simple I would. Believe me. But the vessel can only be opened in accordance with strict laws. It must happen at a certain place. And I, and I alone, must open it." He said nothing of the cost, but he briefly wondered again, *Will death come quickly?*

She saw his dilemma. "And on Vega you knew where this place was?"

He grunted something and nodded.

"But not here, not this world?" she pressed.

He nodded again and cast her a sideways look. "And so I need your help."

A bee hurried past and she thought of Lilain and of barghests. "Anything," she promised.

He regarded her tenderly, wishing things could be different, and began to tell her what he needed.

Life might be simple according to Hilda Saxon, but it was seldom fair. At least that was Emily Meadow's view of life right now. Last night she caught a brief look at Blackwand and then all the pip-staffs were hurried off to bed and the grown-ups celebrated long into the night. No, it wasn't fair at all she thought as she picked yet more blackcurrants. Blackwand had finally come and she had missed all the excitement. She sighed and carried on picking, thinking of blackcurrant tart, when another kind of 'black' altogether addressed her from nowhere.

"You're a queen aren't you?"

Emily jumped and looked around, right into the face of Blackwand. "Erm, miss?" she stammered.

"Emily Meadows I'm told, Stormwood's solstice queen?" Sunday smiled and crouched down next to her.

Emily thought of giant bears and terrible war machines. This was Blackwand she told herself, and she was speaking to *her*. But she couldn't think of a single thing to say.

"I'm sorry," Sunday looked embarrassed, "I didn't mean to intrude." She stood, intending to leave her in peace.

"Yes, I'm a queen!" Emily blurted. "A queen of the solstice, just like you, erm, Miss Blackwand."

"Just 'Sunday' will do." She lowered herself back down again. Many curious heads turned their way. It seemed Sunday would always be a magnet for attention. "And you found the wand I'm told?"

"Your black wand," Emily said respectfully.

"Not mine." Sunday picked a few blackcurrants as she spoke. "I only borrowed it. It's back with Kolfinnia now. And I'm glad *you* found it."

"Me?" she blushed.

"Hrafn-dimmu saved a certain solstice queen many times. So I'm glad another solstice queen found it, and helped it come home."

Instantly Emily felt like they were a team. "I knew it was special when I saw it. I told Miss Flora I was going for a drink by the stream, but really..."

"Yes?"

"Really I was looking for you!" she confided.

Sunday laughed, "And you found Raven's wand instead."

"Why did you send it away?" she asked carefully.

Sunday considered. "Because I was going somewhere dangerous and I feared it would be captured."

The girl stared at her stained fingers, looking worried. "So if you're Sunday now, will Blackwand ever come back?"

Sunday clasped her hand. "Blackwand is right beside you and every other witch of Stormwood, sometimes she is Sunday but *always* she is Blackwand." The two queens shared a moment of union, surrounded by the hum of insects and the aroma of blackcurrants. "Now tell me," Sunday brightened, "my solstice was thoroughly unpleasant. Tell me how *you* honoured the sun's day?"

Emily grinned and started to tell Blackwand how all of Stormwood had cheered as she'd lit the solstice bonfire, and how she'd carried the fire torch all by herself. Sunday picked blackcurrants, listened and smiled, and remembered what it really meant to be a witch.

Clovis had told her a great deal but omitted a great deal more, saying only that he would return home after releasing Janus. Thankfully

Kolfinnia never asked how, and he certainly didn't have the heart to lie to her. "So, you see my path is a crooked one," he finished.

"Not one I envy." She worked hard to keep a level demeanour. "So Janus can only be released at a given location within the boundaries of the fairy-nations?" she clarified.

"Yes. For ages past that place was meant to be the fairy-nations of Vega, but he has chosen Earth." He folded his arms and sighed. "But I do not know where Earth's fairy-nations are, or how to get there."

"The faded-realm we call it." She teased a hand through her hair, thinking hard. "I'm not very knowledgeable in fairy lore. I'll have to ask some of the others. Do I have your permission?"

"I shall let you select, but be discreet."

"Let me speak with a few people, and we'll reconvene to discuss it as a council."

"Agreed. But I must be away soon, before the end of the month at the latest." He thought of the foe that was tracking him even now.

"I'll speak with Hilly." She pulled an apple from her satchel and polished it against her dress. Her cool manner helped cover her hurt.

"Kolfinnia. . . I am sorry."

"Sorry?" she pretended.

"This is very hard for me also."

"We all knew this day would come." She took a bite of apple, striving to appear casual. "Leave it with me, we'll put our heads together and find out what you need to know." She turned to leave.

"Kolfinnia!"

She glanced back.

"Thank you, keeper of Raven's wand," he dipped his head.

She forced down a mouthful of apple, and an equally reluctant smile. "You're welcome, Lion of Evermore." She caught his surprised smile, but turned to hide her face and went to organize his leaving.

She didn't return to Stormwood right away. Instead she wandered the overgrown fort, taking refuge in the trees. She couldn't face anyone right now. As she passed each towering trunk, she caressed the bark and read their memories. Perhaps she was looking for something to lift her, or maybe hoping to find a time when someone somewhere felt sadder than she did now.

At last she halted. Her feet didn't know which way to take her, and her mind ached. She leaned against a tree and the uneaten apple dropped to the ground quickly followed by a lone tear. For a while she fought against the grief, but when a small hand found its way into hers she couldn't stop herself. She slumped to the ground, weighed down. Rowan slid her arms around her and Kolfinnia repaid the gesture, and the two clung to one another beneath the shady pines. "Clovis is leaving," she spoke the awful news.

"I know," Rowan said simply, "I know."

CHAPTER SIX

'What is your dearest desire?'

'Wanting is more potent that having.'
'Higher Forms of Magic - a witch's meditations on daily life'
Author unknown

It was dark and he wasn't sure if he was dreaming or awake. Everything was muddled. There were big gaps, punctuated by bizarre memories that couldn't possibly be real. The memory of locking the rectory door seemed vivid enough, but then everything went topsy-turvy. There was some black demon. He saw it briefly, catching the glimmer of fangs and emerald eyes, and then something like lightning flashed and the earth and sky swapped places. Of course that was absurd. It must have been a dream he told himself. After that everything was dark, a shroud seemed to cover his face and he couldn't move.

He was still pondering these things when daylight suddenly blazed from nowhere. He wanted to cry out, but he couldn't make a sound. Rough hands, like paws, grabbed his head and pulled. The sunlight hurt his eyes. The demon loomed into view again and now he knew he wasn't dreaming. He screamed, but nothing escaped his lips. He felt a hot tongue rasp his cheek, and then sharp teeth crack his skull like a boiled egg. He screamed the Lord's name again and again, but without a sound. It seemed the Lord wasn't listening today. Teeth crunched and bone splintered and Sef began another interrogation.

This one he savoured, considering each mouthful, learning all it had to divulge before swallowing and tearing away another chunk.

"It is risky to slay a shaman," Iso warned when he'd finished.

Sef sat in meditation, listening to new insights circle his consciousness. The vicar of Looe had been his fourth interrogation, and with each one he knew this world better.

"Didn't you hear me? It is bad luck to kill a shaman." Iso crawled up onto a rotten stump and surveyed the darkening woods.

"I heard you." Sef opened his eyes when suddenly a pang clenched in his gut. The mind had some seriously bitter flavours. He leaned over with his head between his legs, groaning and feeling nauseous.

"Sef, what's wrong?"

He grunted something and began to heave. A moment later he ejected a mound of steaming flesh and wiped his face in disgust. "Rancid!"

Agitated, Iso hopped closer. "What! What's wrong?"

Sef retched again and gasped. He swept saliva from his muzzle and sat up. "The shaman, his god is a god of love and selflessness," he grimaced and his long tongue snaked out. He could still taste the rotten flavour.

This was bad, Iso knew. "Selflessness? If the men of this world worship such a god. . ." He looked around the empty woods, suddenly afraid.

"Calm yourself," he sneered. "Their god teaches these things but hardly a soul practises them."

"Won't their god be angry?"

Sef flopped back against the tree. "That Iso is the great mystery of men. Their god says one thing, they do another. Nobody sees this as wrong."

Iso relaxed. "Then we have nothing to fear."

"The witches will be different," he warned. "And Clovis has joined a coven of them. But there are more ways to fight than magic and steel. Desire can be the most potent weapon of all." He said no more, but instead sat alone with his thoughts, thinking how Barda had concealed his sister's death. *Lord Self is everywhere,* he thought joyously. *Even a child can murder in his name. There isn't a soul who cannot be tempted by desire to serve the Self within. No woman, or man, or witch. Not even Clovis.*

Four days later, that same dark figure stood atop the highest pinnacles of Westminster, surveying the city. Smoke hung over the city like a bad dream. The sun was just a ruddy disc sinking against the sea of smoke. Soon it would be dark and he would wait out the night and strike at dawn. The air up here was cleaner, but still the fumes stung his nostrils. They had reached their first goal in the pursuit of Clovis, and the gelding-sack had been filled and emptied no less than ten times. Sef's understanding of this world now went beyond a mere lifetime's worth.

"The city smells of fear," Iso noted.

"It was recently besieged by the Blackwand witch," Sef reminded him.

"What if she's still here?"

"Barda believed she was caught and hanged. I have no reason to dispute that."

"But what if she wasn't?"

Sef frowned at his worries. "Then we'll kill her and interrogate her." He found himself relishing the prospect. He curled up against the roof slates, undaunted by the dizzying heights, and drew the tiny dragon egg from his robes.

"Do not drop it," Iso fussed.

He shot him a withering look before turning his attention back to the egg. He turned it between his fingers, so tenderly, that it seemed impossible those same hands could have ended so many lives, and then without warning he tossed it in the air and caught it neatly in his palm.

"Don't be such a fool!" Iso spat.

"Why? You think this is our only way home?"

"It is disrespectful."

"You have such little faith in me. Once we have Janus we could travel to Vega in an instant."

"That's forbidden!"

Sef just shrugged, and returned the egg to the safety of his robes. "Then pray no harm comes to our carriage."

"We'll go tonight and take the stone?" Iso changed the subject.

"No. Just before dawn. Then be away. I want to awaken the stone's sleeper in daylight."

"If it still lives."

"Ever the pessimist," Sef bared his fangs in a silent laugh. "Can't you hear its song?"

He cocked his head and listened. "No," he replied gloomily.

"It's very close now."

"The museum."

"Mmm," Sef looked westwards, towards the Museum of Natural History. Barda had been there just six years previous when it had opened. "A striking building," he complimented, despite never having set foot in it.

"Barda's opinion or yours?"

"Mine!" he stated indignantly. "Barda had no eye for beauty or form."

"Then I leave you to enjoy the 'beauty and form' of London until we set out. I'm going to rest." Iso went and curled up against the balustrade leaving Sef alone.

Westminster's landmark clock boomed the hour of four announcing dawn. Sef felt the stonework vibrate in harmony with the chimes. To his keen senses it felt like the footsteps of an approaching giant. He had watched all night and enjoyed the hundreds of different sounds and aromas that wafted up from the city below. He detected running feet and shrill whistles as lawmen pursued their quarry, rats sniffing and squeaking over drowned gulls along the Thames, laughter – both genuine and pretend, the tinkle of a pub piano and the stink of back-alley sex and watered down gin. A flock of pigeons flew past in a rustle of wings and his eyes narrowed as he followed their course. He licked his lips, feeling hungry again. "Iso!" he commanded.

Immediately the sprite woke up. "The hour has come?"

"We go."

"Good," he yawned, "then you can tell me what is so special about the sleeper within."

"With Self's blessing I can *show* you."

Sef mounted his lightning-staff and silently launched from the spire. A second later he was just a black shape streaking high across the city, bound for London's grandest museum, intent on stealing its most dangerous artefact.

A train chugged its way out of South Kensington and headed north towards Bayswater. Sef sat on the museum's wide roof ledge and watched it draw a line of steam as it went. He liked the sound it made, it sounded single-minded.

He watched it vanish into the early dawn, and then he quietly dropped down onto the window ledge below, pulled his hood up over his head, broke the glass, twisted the catch and slipped inside.

He had entered through the window nearest his goal. Once inside, the gallery was just yards away. He pushed the doors open and entered, making no attempt to conceal his presence. This gallery was crammed with geological specimens. He passed rows of cabinets packed with crystals and rocks, some of them very rare, but it wasn't pretty gems he was looking for. The item was calling and he knew exactly where it was even in the half-light streaming in through the decorative windows. The humming grew louder and he followed in quickening strides until he found himself standing before a cabinet filled with dull-looking rocks. One of them however wasn't dull. In fact it literally pulsed with life. Sef stood looking down at a lump of reddish-brown rock about the size of an apple. It was sitting in a bed of cotton wool, cradled in a wooden tray. He was hardly able to credit that it had come so far, or concealed such a terrible creature. The specimen label was written in a neat script. "Ironstone, Natal, Africa. 1803," he read aloud. "They named you wrong." He shook his head disapprovingly. This wasn't mere ironstone. It wasn't even of Earth origin. It had fallen from the red planet centuries before and there was something inside vital to his cause. "Thank you Deviser Barda," he gloated.

He jabbed his fist through the glass. The noise was brief but harsh. Shards tumbled down but Sef hardly heard them over the meteorite's exotic song and now the barrier was broken it sounded louder than ever. He reached inside and as soon as he touched it he felt the creature hibernating within and he smiled in satisfaction. *Yes, still alive. You and I, two travellers who journeyed through space.* He was about to take it, when a voice stopped him.

"You've no permission to be here!"

Sef turned, and saw a night-guard standing between the towering cases. He was holding a lantern, but clearly he thought the night was over without incident, because it wasn't lit. How wrong he was. "The museum isn't open until nine o'clock. Who let you in here? Speak up now, or I'll be calling the bobbies." He stepped out into the open. Sef saw he was tall and well built, but middle-aged and probably slow and clumsy.

"Kill him." The lightning-staff buzzed with Iso's anticipation.

Sef stood silently, considering.

"Didn't you hear me? Kill him and leave."

"No. Not yet. I wish to test a theory," he thought in return.

"Theory? This is not some coven spell-class, kill him, take the meteorite and go."

"No. It is Lord Self's will." Sef reached up and slowly lowered his hood.

"This is jeopardising our mission!" Iso protested vainly.

The guard stepped closer, saw the broken glass and immediately drew a short club from his belt. "Thief!" he shouted, but from the way his voice echoed around the huge hall it seemed unlikely anybody would hear. "Thief!" Now he reached for his whistle and blew, but when Sef's hood at last fell, revealing his face, the whistle blast drew off into a strangled rattle. "Dear God Jesus!" The whistle clattered to the floor and the man stumbled back a step.

"There is no need for alarm." Sef slowly drew his wand from his belt. Now he would see.

"What are you doing!" Iso hissed.

He pointed the wand and it emitted a harsh buzzing sound. "No need for alarm at all, is there. . ." he listened to what the wand was telling him. "James?" he finished. His voice had taken on a soothing candour, and his eyes dilated and contracted in time with the man's breathing.

Iso watched helplessly. Sef was using magic when he should have used brawn. *Reckless!* he thought, but fascinating nevertheless.

Jim Worthing backed away. It was a man, it spoke, it even knew his name, but it looked just like a panther. He thought of the stuffed beast sat snarling in the museum's mammal hall. The black thing with the gaping red throat and dazzling fangs gave him the shivers, and now his eyes were telling him the thing had slipped its case and changed into a man, a man whose eyes burned jungle green. "I'm dreaming?" he asked, and bumped a specimen case as he backed away. Had he drunk one too many stouts the night before he wondered? *That green, it goes on forever, like a jungle.* He thought the creature's eyes looked like the gateway to Eden itself. "Who are you?" he heard his mouth ask, but he wasn't the least bit concerned as to the answer. He found he wanted to go closer and walk into Eden, the everlasting jungle. His feet even shuffled forward an inch.

"Good," Sef smiled, making sure not to show his teeth. "No cause for alarm, what matters is desire. Picture your dearest desire James Worthing." Now his words seemed to float through the air and encircle his victim, like the coils of a snake.

"Desire?" Worthing repeated.

"Every man has a dearest desire." The wand continued its work, and now Sef began to perceive his desires, and how to exploit them.

"Desire." Worthing saw his own dearest desire reflected back to him. It was hiding deep in that luminous jungle behind the stranger's eyes. It had been there forever, obscured by distractions and vain pursuits, but now he saw it plainly. "Desire."

"Ah! Now I see," Sef smiled again, and this time his fangs glinted. "You dream of sailing through the open blue do you not?" He gazed purposefully at the grand windows. Outside the dawn sky was pristine.

"Yes." Worthing looked to the windows wearing a peaceful expression. "Fly."

He's done it, Iso thought, *praise be Lord Self.*

The floodgates opened and Sef's wand told him everything. "Your father's farm in Tonbridge, remember how as a boy you watched the rooks and wished you could fly like them? Or the summer you visited the Highlands, recall that exhilaration of standing at the highest summit. You were but eleven years old." Sef understood that his dreams of flight stemmed from a single incident far more earthbound – Molly. "Haven't you always dreamed of flying? Is that not your dearest desire?"

A smile flickered across his lips. "Yes, flying like a bird."

"I envy you!" Sef confided.

"Envy?"

"Because you *can* fly."

"Can?"

"Oh yes, you *have* your heart's desire. Show me," he instigated. "Show me how easily you can fly James Worthing." He gestured towards the windows.

Worthing dropped the lantern with a clatter, and the club came next, then he turned and shuffled towards the window, kicking both out of the way. The club rolled away like a black sausage and vanished under one of the cabinets, while the now broken lantern left a trail of oil where his marching feet knocked it aside.

"Yes, have no fear," Sef encouraged, anxious to witness the madness he had unleashed.

Jim Worthing thought of that glorious summer in Scotland. He had met a girl. Molly she was called. She was a year older than him but they played in the hay meadows near Perth, and eventually their play had become more serious and they had kissed. It was his first kiss and he felt he was flying. He had been unknowingly searching for that lost feeling all of his life, and now at last he could really fly, because the panther-man had told him. He had seen it hiding in the jungle of Eden.

He climbed up onto the stone windowsill with a grunt and stood facing the stained-glass panel, looking out at the beckoning cityscape beyond. He fumbled with the heavy latch, determined to have his reward, to feel that very first kiss again, to feel the air rush across his wings. But the catch was jammed and a frustrated snarl rose up in his throat.

"Never mind the catch." Sef was losing patience. "The glass is no barrier to you, simply break it, break it and fly free!"

Worthing slapped a hand against the glass then another, and then he began to batter it with his fists, landing heavy blows like a man in a pub brawl. The lead buckled and the coloured glass cracked and ran red from his broken knuckles, but he didn't feel a thing: all he knew was that after a lifetime of dreaming he could at last fly. Again and again he punched and kicked the glass, ripping chunks of it loose as he clawed his way through to Eden beyond.

Sef watched in morbid fascination. "Yes Molly is there for you, now fly!"

James Henry Worthing, fifty-one years old, father of three and a patient and devoted husband, crawled through the broken glass. He didn't feel shards slice his clothes and flesh, or snag in his hair and drag tufts of it loose. All he felt was the cooling breeze against his face and all he saw was a dawn so promising that his eyes brimmed with tears. He planted one foot on the stone sill outside then pulled his other leg through the jagged hole, tearing his trousers as he did, and stood facing his desire with nothing to hold him back.

"Fly," Sef whispered.

"Fly," Iso added.

He cried out in vindication, and flew.

Sef watched the figure leap into space and drop from sight. Worthing had his dearest desire. He might have only had it for a few seconds, but better a few seconds of bliss than a lifetime of drudgery Sef believed. Feeling a sense of wholesome satisfaction, he took the meteorite, dropped it into the gelding-sack and left.

Clovis had wisely put Hathwell's engineering skills to use. He and three others were excavating a collapsed opening in the fort. Work was going well and although the conversation was minimal the others were taking orders from a squire without complaint. Thankfully, the trees shaded them against the sun, but the clay here was heavy and red, and Hathwell's hands and boots were ruddy with the stuff. It vaguely reminded him of blood.

"It's the iron," Albert Parry explained, noting his interest. "Plenty of iron artefacts buried here and that's why the earth's red. If I had the knack for seeing 'em, I reckon there'll be a throng of iron-fairies right under our noses." He reached down and scratched Mally's head. The little dog was also matted with clay.

"Iron-fairies?" Hathwell was fascinated.

"Patrons of iron, hidden a breath away in the faded-realm," Albert said as if stating the obvious. "Surely you knows that?"

"I only know about engineering," he apologised. "But I know we'll need timber to shore up the roof before we go further." He wiped his brow and took stock. "Good progress this morning."

"Aye, not bad," May Stone and Amelia Felling agreed in unison.

Hathwell hadn't worked with women before and although they seldom spoke they were polite at least. He couldn't take his eyes off Amelia's thunder-sprite, who sat on a mossy stone, nibbling pinecones.

Again, Albert saw his curiosity. "Lightning eats wood. Feed a sprite a piney a day and he'll be spitting fire 'til bedtime."

"Oh, I see," he smiled faintly. He couldn't imagine the delicate-looking creature bringing down a kraken, but experience told him otherwise.

"We'll need a bar to pry out the big stones," Albert indicated the tunnel as he lit his pipe.

"And more workers to heave them out," someone else stated, and even before he turned Hathwell knew it was Clovis. The others all touched their temples and Hathwell found himself doing the same, although he didn't grasp the significance.

Clovis returned the gesture before turning to him. "Would the fort make a good defensive position Mr Hathwell?" It sounded like 'Hack-Well' in his rough tongue. They all turned his way, curious to know how their enemies might attack.

He cleared his throat, "Erm, in all honesty no."

"No?"

"They would block up the entrances, seal you in and pound it with artillery."

"As I thought," his eyes narrowed. "Your verdict?"

"Well, erm, as a storehouse and shelter, the fort is superb, but as a refuge it's a trap."

"And as a decoy?" Clovis asked.

Hathwell understood, and smiled at his cunning. "Make sure the enemy sees you retreating to the fort?"

"And while they waste time besieging it, we leave through the back door," Clovis surmised.

Hathwell nodded. "So when do we start digging an escape tunnel?"

"A new tunnel?" Albert asked.

"We've just started on this one!" May protested.

"The new one will start at the fort's centre and head out into the woods," Hathwell explained. "Am I right?'

Clovis grunted an agreement. "Three hundred yards at least, longer if possible."

"Sorry 'father, but you want a new tunnel three hundred yards long? That'll take months!" Albert's pipe hung from his bottom lip and even Mally whined.

"We have the time. There's no risk of imminent attack . . . is there?" He put Hathwell on the spot.

"Likely the knights are fighting amongst themselves. Witches'll be the least of their worries for now."

"Then we'll survey the surrounding woods and decide where best to set the tunnel." Coven-father and squire shared a moment's respect for one another's skills. "Blessed be," he finished formally.

"Blessed be," they all echoed, including Hathwell.

No sooner had he left, than they received another visitor. Hilda arrived carrying water, fruit and fresh bread. "Refreshments!" she announced and set the bucket down. Albert took the ladle and helped himself to a drink and shared his bread with Mally. May and Amelia quickly joined him and the three flopped down for a well-earned break, leaving Hathwell watching Clovis marching back across the Glade.

"He's a determined soul," Hilda noted.

"I'd expect no less from a Therion," he said with respect.

"Therion? I didn't know the Knighthood briefed their staff on mythical beings?"

"They don't," he admitted. "I saw one once years ago. It was said it was the last of its kind."

"And mayhap it was. Clovis came from elsewhere I'm told."

"Not the faded-realm? Isn't that where the Therions went to escape persecution?"

She raised an eyebrow. "My! You've done much reading, I'm impressed."

He almost blushed, but made sure not to say what he'd been reading or why, thinking of last summer locked away at Goldhawk researching the serpent-twins for Krast.

"Hathwell," she asked after a long pause, "where did you see a Therion?"

He made sure the rest weren't listening. "Solvgarad." He saw she wasn't familiar with the name. "You won't have heard of it, the Illuminata covered it up."

"Things didn't go well for them I assume?"

"Hence they covered it up."

She looked off into the distance, considering this, and as she did he admired her. Today her dark hair was fastened in a plait that reached to her calves, and she wore an open neck smock and a long grey skirt. They were just work clothes, but he thought she could outshine any Illuminata Countess any day. He was enjoying his daydream when Albert got up and stretched.

"Right back to it, best get Clovis's tunnel dug before the Knights come calling and have us fleeing like rabbits down holes!" He chuckled at his joke, but Hathwell detected accusing glances from the others. He didn't dare look at Hilda, lest she wore a similar expression, and so he clung to his daydream, grabbed his shovel and went back to work.

The Forbes Dyke iron bridge had collapsed only two years after being built, largely because it was built by two different rail companies who couldn't agree on anything, and also because it used low-grade steel. After suffering heavy losses to rival firms, the Lower-Midlands, and the South-England-Counties railway corporations had decided not to repair the bridge. The line fell into disuse and the two operators were swallowed up by larger interests. Now all that remained of the once impressive structure was a tangled mess of bent girders lying at the foot of the Brooklee Gorge, half submerged in the River Tyst.

They were some thirty-five miles north of London now and at last the landscape looked suited to his task. Sef dropped from altitude into the shady gorge. The twisted girders rising from the Tyst looked like petrified serpents, pitted with corrosion and matted with debris from past floods. Considering what was about to transpire, he couldn't have chosen a better place. "This is good." He selected a girder bent like an upturned fish hook, and sat at the top. After a quick look around, he was satisfied they were alone.

Iso joined him, relieved to be free of the staff's confines. "A dour place," he remarked, looking up at the gorge's sheer walls.

"A place of iron," Sef sounded pleased.

"Why did you not just kill the guard?"

Sef drew the meteorite from the gelding-sack and admired it. "I told you, I was testing a theory."

"It was risky."

"But successful."

"But why?"

He growled impatiently, "Because Clovis has found himself allies, perhaps too many for steel alone to kill, but desire. . . you saw how easily it led the Worthing man to his death."

"And the stone?" Iso raised his hooked beak to it and sniffed. It smelled inert. "Explain its true nature."

"It is a unique species of fairy as I said."

Iso looked around, unimpressed. "There are fairies around us in countless numbers unseen, what makes this one noteworthy?"

"Again, as I said, it is the last of its kind. It fell from the red world."

"A fairy from another biosphere," he realised.

"Indeed. But it is doubly unique. This creature was the by-product of a war-like civilization." He turned the stone over in his hands.

Iso searched his stolen knowledge. "There is much fanciful speculation on the part of the men as to life on the spheres."

"And all of it wrong. I told you they are backwards."

"So there is no life on Mars, the red world?"

"Maybe not now. But there was, and their destructive nature finally consumed them."

"And they made the fairy?" Iso thought of the Gokstahl generator his kind were created in.

"No."

"I tire of asking questions!" he said curtly.

Sef purred in amusement. "I theorize the creature *evolved* as a consequence of centuries of warfare. Natural iron-fairies, as you know, gather the souls of iron, but after prolonged conditions of war a new iron-fairy evolved, one dedicated to the iron alloys manufactured for weapons." He looked around ruefully. "Conditions here are similar, mayhap an identical creature will also soon evolve here as it did on the red world."

"It is naturally hostile then?" Iso gazed at the rock.

"I'm counting on it." Sef imagined it wasn't just hostile but utterly voracious and infectious. "With it we can meet Clovis's army with a force of our own."

"And what will become of this world once the war-fairy is set loose and we leave?"

Sef shrugged, "It will suffer the same fate as the red world? Who knows? Either way it is of no matter to us."

"But a fairy of iron? How might creatures attracted to iron defeat men?"

Sef sighed, "Have you learned so little from me?"

Iso just glowered back at him.

"Because," he continued, holding the rock up for him to see, "this creature has a taste for *living-iron*."

"Blood!" Iso finally realised.

Sef nodded. "And those iron-fairies of the faded-realm that it infects will succumb to the same thirst. And in light of losing the pact-of-grace, this creature will allow us to force our way in."

"Now I begin to see."

"We are gathering allies just as Clovis has, and when it comes to it, we shall pit our allies against his. His witches will either be devoured, or choke on their own desires." He tapped his wand with meaning.

"How did you know these things?" Iso asked suspiciously.

Sef's lips peeled back in savage smile. "Lord Self controls my fate. I see now that he broke the pact-of-grace and sent me the Barda man so I might find this far greater treasure instead."

Iso was naturally sceptical, but he now began to wonder if this wasn't so. "You have done well Sef," he conceded grudgingly.

"Speak no more. I have important work," he dismissed him.

Iso clambered further up the girder and began preening himself, seemingly unconcerned, but paying close attention. Sef took a small knife from his robes, splayed his left hand and sliced the fleshy pads. The knife quickly vanished back into his robes, and now he grasped the meteorite with his bleeding hand and squeezed hard. Iso saw blood well up between his fingers, glisten in the black fur, and then run down the rock in dark droplets. . . and the war-fairy of the red planet, that hadn't tasted life in untold years, began to awaken.

Feri had collected iron souls since – well, since forever. He didn't remember being young or a time when things were different. He was Feri, an iron-fairy, and when the tiniest specks of iron corroded to nothing then their souls were released and he would gather them and escort them to the mystical spiral of Evermore where they would be reused in the grand purpose of All and Everything. Yes, Feri was an iron-fairy and he knew his business well.

Some time ago there had been a sudden abundance of dying iron in this part of the world, and he and thousands like him had been busily shepherding it from this forest of mangled girders. There was plenty of iron for everyone so things seldom got rough. Fairies could be vicious and territorial when souls were in short supply, but not so here. In fact, the iron was so abundant that other fairies had migrated in from outside areas, something that would normally result in open conflict, but everyone had enough to keep the peace. The more Feri thought about it the more it seemed that where humans went their iron went with them.

He whirred his wings, which resembled rusted kitchen knives, and turned his chisel-shaped head to where a Therion was sat amongst the iron. Feri saw both worlds at once, the faded-realm that was his natural home, and Earth, where men lived. He had seen Therions before in the faded-realm many times, but he hadn't seen one walk the Earth in many years, which was precisely where this mysterious black Therion was right now.

Feri looked around. Herds of fairies grazed the iron, collecting souls, and a few moss-fairies wearing caps of verdant green were picking at the tiny plant colonies. It was a familiar sight, but something wasn't right. Suddenly he felt hungry, and for something he'd never tasted or desired, and the hunger seemed to be radiating from the Therion sitting quietly in their midst.

He tried to ignore the feeling and continue gathering, but when another pang gripped him he growled in discomfort. His mind told him the food he needed was hot and red, living-iron, but that was impossible: that was the food of the old universe, a dark age of barbarism. Feri stopped again and watched uneasily as the hungry cloud continued to bleed from the Therion like a slit artery.

"Feri?"

He turned. It was Alsa, a primrose-fairy.

"Is something amiss?" She dropped gently down beside him and folded her delicate yellow wings. Her skin was pale gold and a crown of petal-like fins grew from her head and down her back. She crawled closer on all fours, swishing her stem-like tail in agitation. While Feri had skin like chain mail and an angular body, Alsa was elegant and pretty.

"Alsa?" He looked into her concerned face. Her kind was less numerous here, but he knew her well. "The Therion, you see him?"

"I see him."

"Does he look strange to your eyes?"

She considered a moment. "I cannot say so, although it is unheard of for one of them to be seen on Earth," she noted, but not unduly bothered. It was him she was worried about. "But never mind that Feri, you look ill. Again I ask: is something amiss?"

He was touched by her concern and rightly suspected that she liked him, but species difference forbade them from being one. He watched the

Therion, mesmerized by the shadow creeping out from the stone. "Can't you see the hunger growing around him?" he asked, unable to take his eyes off it.

"Hunger?" she looked about. "I see a Therion sitting amid the iron and no more. Feri I'm worried. You speak in riddles and you look drained."

Drained, he thought, *drained and hungry Alsa.* The shadow continued to blossom and he bared his teeth and hissed softly. The world was turning red.

Sef placed the bloody meteorite gently on the ironwork and it rocked a fraction as something inside shifted. Suddenly, the whole thing began to unfurl like a dormant crab, scraping angrily against the metal as it did. The meteorite hadn't simply carried the sleeper to Earth. It was the sleeper.

"It awakens!" Iso gasped.

Sef hadn't expected anything less, and watched his child begin to grow.

A pair of wings erupted like blades, followed by stocky limbs, all of them the texture and colour of beaten iron. It awoke with the sound of grinding metal and looked nothing like the fanciful fairies of bedtime stories, but instead resembled a living suit of armour. It uncurled fully and its head creaked into view and turned his way. The creature's face was all but featureless, except for a slit mouth and two tiny eyes that burned like molten metal.

Now the desire for living-iron was so strong that Feri was trembling. The Therion was still sitting hunched over a rock, but when Feri saw it move and uncurl the pangs in his gut became unbearable. "Alsa!" he groaned and doubled over.

"Feri!" She went to haul him back and in her panic she didn't notice how every other iron-fairy there was similarly debilitated. "Feri, tell me what's wrong!"

He screwed up his eyes against the pain, breathing fast and shallow. His mouth suddenly felt as dry and as dead as this rusted iron, and the idea of gathering souls and eating of their goodwill suddenly seemed revolting to him. His throat felt swollen and lined with broken glass, and there was only one thing that could ease the burning. There came a squeak of pain from right beside him and he opened his eyes to see his fellows also suffering. Iron-fairies all around were falling, bent by pain. They dropped into the grass, and rattled against stones or plopped into puddles in a shower of tiny armoured bodies.

"Feri!" Alsa pleaded. She tried to help him up, but he was far too heavy for a delicate primrose-fairy.

The rock! The Therion's rock is a plague! Feri's intuition screamed through a fog of crippling hunger. "Leave Alsa!" he gurgled.

"Feri, I'm going to find help, I'm going for the witches."

"Leave!" he pleaded, but now he sounded like a snarling animal and Alsa hardly recognised him.

Sef raised his wounded hand. The war-fairy struggled forwards on all fours, sounding like clanking chains and spreading its razor-tipped wings. It crawled within touching distance and smelled his bloodied fingers. He could hear tiny snorting sounds as it sniffed at him. Without warning, he suddenly seized the creature and clenched his fist around it. It was like taking hold of a handful of nails, but he squeezed harder until the blood flowed and the fairy shrieked. "I am Sef of the Unitari," he said through clenched teeth. "You live again by my blood. You are mine understand? Mine!" The fairy hissed and struggled in his fist. "Understand?" He squeezed so hard that his vision crackled and the fairy screamed. "Your name!" Sef demanded.

It gurgled something in reply.

"AGAIN!"

"Chentek," it rasped, clearer this time.

"Chentek, good." Sef opened his hand feeling metal blades dragged from his flesh, and dropped the fairy like a stone.

It landed in his pooled blood, and squatted there, staring at him with naked hatred. It looked even more menacing now that it glistened red. After a moment it sat up gargoyle-like on its haunches, regarded him with those burning eyes, and hissed, "Sef. Unitari."

Sef saw its throat glowing with fire, and jaws lined with tiny pointed teeth like bullets. "Perfect," he smiled.

Alsa struggled to lift him but she just wasn't strong enough. Around her, other fays were likewise confused and scared. Ink-cap-fairies, water-fairies and willow-fairies, to name but a few, were struggling to assist the iron-fairies, despite their own bewilderment.

"Heili!" Alsa screamed, seeing one of her own. "Heili, come help me, Feri is hurt!"

The primrose-fairy fluttered over and joined her. They heaved in unison, but they were made to lift nothing heavier than the souls of petals and pollen, and neither of them could even roll Feri onto his back.

"The world is red!" he snarled and opened his mouth wide and Alsa was horrified to see the glow of a fire burning deep in his throat.

Heili jumped back, scared out of her wits now. "Why's he saying that, what's happening to them?"

"I don't know, but help us, go find witches," she pleaded.

"Witches?" Heili's yellow eyes rolled with fear. "But there are no witches here."

"Just find some! One even, just one!"

Just then Feri convulsed. "THE WORLD TURNS RED!" he rasped. Even more chilling was listening to thousands of others take up the chant. *"THE WORLD TURNS RED! THE WORLD TURNS RED!"*

"Go!" Alsa screamed.

Heili turned and fled. Alsa didn't know if she was running away in terror or rushing off in search of witches, but she had the awful feeling that it didn't matter now.

As Heili vanished, Alsa heard a scream followed by a chorus of savage howls and turned to see a dandelion-fairy sink below a scrum of iron-fairies. She watched, numb with shock, as the pack tore the unfortunate creature apart, slashing and hacking until they glistened with blood. "No, they can't!" She wanted to close her eyes, but they were frozen wide and she saw horrible things she didn't want to see. All around her the iron-fairies were rising up in ferocious packs and attacking those who'd come to help them. She saw two buttercup-fairies dragged under, and heard their petrified squeals followed by snarls and the sound of tearing and ripping. "No, they can't!" she pleaded. One of the moss-fairies scrambled away, bleating in panic, but he was snagged by iron hands and dragged back.

The pack attacked him instantly, frenziedly biting his flesh and then setting on one another, crazed by blood. "They can't!" She was mad with terror. These were iron-fairies, many of them she knew. They gathered souls. No fairy had eaten flesh since the early times. It was bestial. It was forbidden. "They can't!" she screamed again. But it appeared they could.

Sef saw Chentek's story in crimson-soaked detail, and he was right. The war-fairy evolved from iron-fairies as a result of prolonged war. When the beings of Mars were not engaged in outright war they enforced societies based on suppression and brutality. It was that constant flow of blood and despair that nurtured hybrids like Chentek, and in the end their planet was overrun with war-fairies. The beings of Mars were the architects of their own downfall, and even in the end, when swarms of ravenous fays swept from city to city, they still failed to understand how this calamity had come to be. Survivors fled to Earth, but now stripped of their great technology they forgot the past and tragically began to build societies just like those that had destroyed them.

Sef found the irony so sublime it was comic and he smiled gratefully and opened his eyes. "A war-fairy of the red planet," he regarded his new servant. The war-fairy licked Sef's blood from his clawed hands, then stopped and cocked his head, hearing something for his ears only.

"I smell blood," Iso added quietly.

"Mine," Sef said flatly.

"No, different." He scanned the shady gorge. All seemed peaceful and quiet, but he suspected the façade was only skin deep. "There is blood here," he warned.

Sef turned to Chentek. "Your doing?"

The war-fairy just peered at him.

"There is blood all around us." Smelling it so strongly yet unable to see it made Iso nervous. "Can't you detect it?"

Sef looked at his injured palm. If not his blood then whose, he wondered? Then it dawned on him and he frowned. "The faded-realm. Perhaps the infection's already spreading?" Sef turned to Chentek. "Is this your doing?" He went to grasp the fairy and it backed away, growling.

"Living-iron," the war-fairy rasped, and each word sounded like a metal file.

"Perhaps he means—," Iso began.

"Shh!" Sef listened. His hearing was sensitive, but this task demanded he listen with senses far beyond the six he was born with. He listened with magic and eavesdropped on that place a heartbeat away: the faded-realm. It took a second to adjust, but there it was, the sound of screaming and the rank odour of blood. The infection had begun.

A hand suddenly clamped around her wrist. Alsa screamed and looked down into Feri's face. Her gentle friend was gone and some monster had replaced him. "Feri, no! It's me, Alsa!" she howled.

"LIVING-IRON!" He lunged and locked his jaws around her throat, cutting off her scream. Her blood gushed across his face and down his throat.

She tried to push him away but her fingers slipped over his glistening hide. "Feri – please," she choked.

Excited, he found new strength and threw her down and pounced on her, ripping and slashing, turning her beautiful wings to tatters and crushing her stem-like limbs. Alsa saw the world turn grey, just as Feri saw it turn red. Evermore was calling and she would journey there not as guide for delicate flower-souls but amongst the host of the dead. "Fe-ri, ple-as-e," she gasped a final time, before her former friend, and secret sweetheart, joined with her in a manner more terrible and intimate than she ever knew possible.

The iron-fairies of the Brooklee Gorge slaughtered every fairy within their territory that wasn't like them, and when they were done they were stained with carnage, and the hunger still burned.

Sef jumped to his feet. "Iso!" He pulled his staff from his shoulders and the thunder-sprite instantly vanished ready to fight. As he attuned further to the faded-realm, the sound of fighting grew louder and the stink of slaughter became suffocating. He stood ready, watching the Earth slowly peel back and reveal the atrocities unfolding only a whisker away. And it was a massacre.

Iso gasped at the spectacle. Even Sef was momentarily stunned.

The whole of Brooklee Gorge was coated with blood, it dripped from grass and trees and even the air was hazy with it. The screaming had dwindled to groans and whimpers from the few who lay dying. The rest had been eaten. And everywhere, on every inch of iron, every twisted bough, clinging to grassy stems and squatting on every rock and stone, there were iron-fairies, hundreds of thousands of them. All of them sat watching. All of them splattered red.

"Sef!" Iso cried.

Sef smiled and his eyes twinkled. "Afraid Iso?" he taunted.

The thunder-sprite said nothing, feeling angry and ashamed.

Chentek shuffled forwards, and Sef understood it was time to claim them all. "Chentek brings you the thirst for living-iron," he addressed the horde, "but *I* am the one who brings you Chentek. He has no will but for my word."

Chentek hissed spitefully, but the Therion was right. Sef's blood had resurrected him, and now Sef's word was his god. He was no better than a slave.

Now Sef had his army, one that could invade the faded-realm or butcher its way across this miserable land, turning witches to scraps as it went. "Heed this Iso and be sure to tell Acola all you see here, Janus is already mine."

Iso saw infected fairies without number and knew he was right, while Chentek sat by his master's heel, radiating sickness and hatred.

She was getting good at climbing Crow-top's ladder, although she still intended to have steps built this autumn. Kolfinnia pulled herself up through the hatchway and sat on the edge, and that's when she saw she wasn't alone.

"I'm sorry." Sunday had been waiting on her bunk and now she stood up. "There was nobody around and I just needed a moment's peace."

Kolfinnia climbed to her feet and coughed nervously. "It's good to see you, I haven't had chance to speak with you in private."

"I've been busy," she explained shyly.

"And no wonder. All of witchdom is talking about you."

The two stood facing one another across the hole in the floor, trying not to think too deeply or saying anything too sensitive. Sunday had a hundred questions while Kolfinnia felt she had a thousand. "You have a lovely home," Sunday ventured.

She looked about. Crow-top comprised two tiny rooms joined by a corridor short enough to cross in one stride. The smallest room was packed with books and clothes, baskets and jars, while the larger room contained her and Rowan's bunks. "I'm pleased you like it. It's small but cosy."

Sunday smiled nervously as she gathered herself. "Firstly, thank you. The welcome I've received is. . . well it's magical," she finished.

Kolfinnia fidgeted. "Magic should be regal as somebody once said." She eyed the faint scar on her cheek. The hourglass was long gone but the Timekeeper's mark was still very much on her.

Sunday's expression was caught somewhere between happy and terrified. "You *know* what happened last October?" she was compelled to ask, terrible or not.

Kolfinnia guessed this was her real reason for coming, and she considered before answering. "I know that neither I nor Rowan would be here today if not for you."

Sunday looked at the floor and nodded mutely.

"Black suits you," Kolfinnia complimented lightly.

She relaxed a little. "It's all the rage in London, maybe because it's good for concealing the dirt." Now she dared look into her face, and her eyes rested on her scarred cheek. She raised her hand, thought better of it and lowered it again. "Forgive me, but how did that happen?"

Kolfinnia stepped past her, sat on her bunk and patted the blankets inviting her to do the same. Sunday lowered herself down wearing a fragile smile. They sat side by side and Sunday listened to the gently creaking branches, and the clack of staffs outside and Clovis barking orders. "I was chopping wood," Kolfinnia said at last. "Would you believe it, a big spider crawled out just at the wrong moment. I swung wide so I wouldn't kill it, and so hit the log at a bad angle. A shard flew up and cut my face." She traced a finger across her embroidered dress as she spoke. "I didn't think anything of it at the time, it was only recently I knew what it meant."

Sunday sighed, "Yes, I would believe it. Coincidences."

"Coincidence, the language of the universe," Kolfinnia smiled, thinking of Valonia.

"But are you sure it wasn't because you're just scared of spiders?" she teased.

"No! I like spiders, one of them in particular."

"Dear champion," Sunday said longingly and stroked her chin as she thought. "Kolfinnia," she said finally, "I have a message for you and it's from him."

"The Timekeeper?"

Sunday nodded.

'Luck be with you in battle tomorrow Kolfinnia.' Those were his last words to her. He bent the rules to give her a coded warning, and then he broke them completely to resurrect Sunday. "What does he say?" She imagined him weaving right now.

She reached into her black waistcoat and drew out a square of folded paper. "This is the Flowering-of-Fate. Kolfinnia?" She saw astonishment and despair written on her face. The note wasn't meant to elicit anything like that. "Kolfinnia, what's wrong?"

"The Flowering," she cupped her mouth suddenly remembering.

"You already know of it?"

"No, but Rowan said Janus heard something called 'the Flowering'."

"The god of doorways, Clovis's relic you mean?"

"Yes. It changed him, for the better I believe. May I see it?"

"Then I hope it will change you too, and all of witchdom and beyond." She handed over the promise of a god written on a scrap of paper. "I give you the Flowering-of-Fate."

Kolfinnia opened it, all the while trembling, and read it several times, and there it was for all to see: Sunday's handwriting dictating the will of fate.

Sunday Evelyn Flowers and Lightning-Strikes-Lonesome-Ash. I have watched over you both, and for a time I believed your threads would be broken once more. In the end however, pity prevailed, and the Patternmaker yielded. But the legacy your courage has forged shall be this; The Patternmaker concedes individuals shall be free to determine their own fates, providing they believe ardently enough. Earth has needed such a Flowering of Fate for a very long time, and only your sacrifice and love made it possible. I would watch you further Sunday, but it appears fate has brought you a new protector. May your days with Ben be long and happy, until at last your thread is woven no more.

"It's beautiful," she recovered. "He did this for you?"

"Yes," she said simply.

"Dear champion." She understood now, and for a second she was envious. *What it must be like to have a protector like that?* She wiped her eyes. "When word of this spreads, Stormwood will be besieged. Witches'll come from far and wide to see this."

"I think he gave it to me as a mission. To spread the word," she explained. "To show people, not just witches, that fate doesn't control all, freewill can change the universe. He watched over me, right through the darkest moments, and even when –," she faltered, then abruptly ceased.

"Sunday?" Without thinking they joined hands and Kolfinnia saw that she'd been wrong. Sunday hadn't just saved them from valkyries, bullets or cannons: she'd shaken the very gods.

"He watched over me," she said finally.

"And this note is proof of it. You can begin here, show all of Stormwood what you've helped create."

Sunday looked up to the branches. "Soon," she sighed, "there are unfinished matters, loose threads you might say, and they need to be concluded first. May I?"

Kolfinnia gladly handed the note back, and Sunday carefully hid it again. *Unfinished business.* Kolfinnia thought of Ben. "Whatever happens I meant what I said – welcome home."

"And whatever happens I meant what I said – thank you."

They chatted pleasantly for a while and swapped stories, gossip, news, and by the end they were no different to any other sisters catching up. Eventually, Sunday stood and stretched away the last of her tension. "I had better get on, if Emily doesn't see me every few hours she thinks the sky will fall."

Kolfinnia got to her feet. "Next time you call, I'll have a kettle on the boil," she promised, before a shy smile touched her lips.

"What?" Sunday guessed.

"Sunday, this is difficult, but I really have to ask. . ."

"Yes?" She looked defensive.

"Did you *really* rob the Bank of England?"

She offered her an impish grin, "I never knew money was so heavy, Strike and I were glad to be rid of it!" Kolfinnia burst out laughing and before long

Sunday joined her. "I'll leave you to your duties coven-mother," she said at last and went and sat by the hatch, ready to descend.

"Watch your footing," Kolfinnia advised.

Sunday gave her a knowing look. "Oh, I've fallen from far greater heights than this." She winked and then dropped out of sight leaving Kolfinnia wearing a satisfied smile and feeling contented for the first time in many weeks.

Chapter Seven

Unfinished business

'I risked all I had and lost it. Yet I still won.'
Witch proverb

A large troupe of children had gathered under the founding-banner in
the Glade, and Benedict Collins was amongst them. They giggled at the
grown-up in their midst, but he took it all with good humour. Nothing
could upset him these days. In fact things were as good as they ever had
been for the young man and he had one person to thank for that: Sunday.

Today she was taking a class in the open air; an advanced class in 'fairy
lore', which is why Kolfinnia watched from the Glade's edge with acute
interest. Clovis needed to understand the fairy-nations, and here was their
own conduit to that realm. She had been thinking for days about who
would be best suited for the job and she could have kicked herself for not
thinking of Sunday before, although getting a private moment with her
was often impossible. Adoring children (not to mention dogs, thunder-
sprites and adults) seemed to follow her wherever she went.

There was a flurry of chatter, and Kolfinnia saw their teacher enter the
Glade and make her way towards her pupils. Sunday came barefoot, wearing
short black trousers and a long black shirt, with her knife and newly carved
wand fastened to her belt. Her silver hammer and fox never left her neck,
but today her hair was tied in a sensible ponytail. As she approached,
many children rushed to her, leaving Ben all the more conspicuous. She

shepherded them back with kindly patience and Kolfinnia sighed. Things might be bad but at least Sunday was here, Stormwood's living talisman. Hilda had been right; the coven didn't just feel balanced, it felt energized.

"Taking an interest in fairies?" Flora passed, shoving a wheelbarrow loaded with broken pots, followed by a gloomy looking boy called Jole.

Kolfinnia looked his way. "Cheer up Jole, there'll be another class tomorrow."

"Yes coven-mother," he nodded politely, but the look on his face told her he didn't rate garden work as highly as fairy spotting.

Flora rolled her eyes. "Sunday gets the spotters, I get all the potters." She ruffled his hair. "Come on Jole, plants can be just as exciting as fairies. Kolfinnia?"

"I'll stay and watch if it's all the same to you."

"Let me know if you see one." She grasped the barrow and set off, with Jole plodding along behind.

"Oh, you'll hear me scream, be sure of that." In all her years Kolfinnia had never seen a fairy fully, but her enthusiasm was false. The rest might shriek joyfully if one appeared, but right now she felt hardly able to muster a smile.

"And so," Sunday continued, "fairy kind live right beside us in the faded-realm, and they only appear to us earthbound people when it suits them. But!" she raised a finger and all the children, including Ben, waited. "A witch can learn to see the faded-realm and all the wonderful beings that dwell there. So always be polite about fairies because you never know when one might be watching." A young hand went up. "Yes Peter?"

"Miss Sunday Blackwand, how long does it take to learn?" Peter Sparks sat cross-legged and rocked excitedly as he spoke.

"It can take a day or a lifetime Peter, it depends on how determined or skilled the witch is." Another hand went up. "Yes, erm?" Sunday looked for the hand's owner. "Emily," she smiled when she saw Stormwood's diminutive solstice queen.

"What fairies have you seen Miss Sunday?" Her question boosted the air of excitement.

She took a deep breath. "Let me see now, it depends on the place. Water-fairies wouldn't be so numerous in the desert, or you wouldn't find many corn-fairies at the top of a mountain. But the fairies I've seen most are," she paused theatrically, "frost-fairies."

Plenty of 'oohs' and 'ahhs' followed.

"Will they be here now, watching us?" Emily looked around, imagining them.

"Remember, time and place. In cold snowy lands you'll find them by the bucket load, but here, they hibernate until winter comes." She thought of Neet and smiled. "But I think someone else just as special is watching us," she added secretly. The children hushed and looked around. Were there fairies with them already, they wondered? "I see coven-mother Algra watching our lesson." Her eyes darted to a figure standing in the trees, and everyone turned. Some sat straighter, many giggled, but all of them waved, including Ben. "Now, are you ready to see this place?" Sunday announced when they'd settled. They cheered in answer and she smiled when she heard Ben join them. It appeared children and grown-ups alike were ready for their lesson.

Kolfinnia was watching when everyone suddenly turned her way and waved. "Sunday," she smiled to herself, and waved back. The children finally settled and began with a blessing for Hethra and Halla, and then all of them started the long slow job of sensing the faded-realm. *This could take all day,* she thought knowing she ought to be off but determined to speak with Sunday.

As the children and Ben learned to see fairies, Kolfinnia stood lost in thought and most of her thoughts weren't pleasant. Clovis was leaving and so far only Rowan knew. "Thank Halla's scales for Blackwand," she muttered. Losing Clovis was devastating, but she took solace in knowing that Blackwand was staying. "And she's here for good," she told herself.

She was brooding on these things when she heard a scream. She was running with her wand drawn even before she knew it. Ahead of her, the children were rushing around in excitement and she slowed from a sprint to a jog, while her poor heart continued to thud in confusion. "Berries-be-red!" she gasped upon hearing the laughter. She'd heard too many screams this last year.

"I saw one right there!" Emily Meadows was jumping up and down. "There, right there!" She pointed to an empty patch of grass. All eyes strained to see any sign of movement, but it remained just plain old grass. Whatever Emily had seen, she'd seen alone.

"What was it like?" Sunday dropped to her side. "Don't leave anything out!" The rest clustered in until she was surrounded. Ben's cheerful face peered over her shoulder and in no time Kolfinnia was there too.

Emily took her time. "Erm, well, it walked on all fours, it was green and there were yellowy spines down its back, oh, and it had a long tail and its face was like a flower but yellowy too."

"Buttercup!" Ben guessed. "Must have been a buttercup-fairy." Sure enough there were plenty of buttercups in the glade.

"Hmm," Kolfinnia added doubtfully. "Sounds more like primrose to me."

"Primrose, yes!" a few supporters chanted.

"Did it look more like a primrose or a buttercup?" Ben asked.

Emily tried to think. It had happened so fast. "I really can't say," she admitted reluctantly.

"The type isn't important," Sunday took her hand. "What matters is you saw one, and you saw one because you tried so hard it *wanted* you to see it." She heard disappointed moans from the rest. "Roll up those long faces!" she lectured gently. "There'll be plenty more lessons ahead." Emily grinned and Sunday gave her a congratulatory hug. "Well done little queen," she winked.

After much debate and chatter Sunday declared the lesson ended.

"You're not going to try again?" Kolfinnia watched children run through the Glade, all the while alert for fairies.

"I'll never settle that lot again this afternoon," she looked after them nostalgically.

Ben wanted to hug her, but he controlled himself. "A born teacher," he complimented, and discreetly brushed his fingertips against hers. "You know there were moments back then when I almost felt there was a fairy right next to me."

"Really? I'm so pleased. They'll come to you when it's right."

Suddenly Kolfinnia felt intrusive. "Erm, Sunday, may I have a moment?"

"Of course." She brushed a tiny kiss against his face. "It's your turn to cook tonight," she reminded him.

"I only know baked potatoes," he apologised.

"Which always taste sweeter when made by someone else." The way she looked at him made Kolfinnia look away out of respect for their privacy.

"Blessings on you Ben," she bid him.

"Hethra light your path coven-mother," he wished her, and left them alone.

"I need your advice," Kolfinnia asked when he'd gone.

Sunday regarded her 'younger sister' and smiled. "Just ask."

They walked the Glade's perimeter and Stormwood's witches saw its two young heroes in debate and believed all was well, but Kolfinnia knew better.

"I can't believe Clovis is leaving." Sunday grasped her pain and the coven's loss.

"I need advice and I thought of you. Clovis is going to the faded-realm with Janus, and there are so many empty gaps."

"Who else have you asked?"

"So far only you, but I thought of Hilda too."

"Mmm, wise choice."

"If I organize a council; me, Hilly and Clovis, sprites included, would you come?"

Sunday didn't hesitate. "It'd be an honour."

Kolfinnia relaxed. "Thank Hethra that Stormwood still has Blackwand."

"For now at least," she revealed.

Ice slithered down her back. "For now?"

She folded her arms. "The welcome I've been given has been overwhelming, but there's one last thing I must do before I can call Stormwood my home." She chewed at her lip. "Kolfinnia, I've decided – I have to tell Ben."

No! her instincts screamed. *He'll reject her, then she'll leave all of us! She can't leave! Order her not to tell Ben. Order her: a coven command!* She reeled at the dreadful news and the urge to interfere danced on the tip of her tongue, but what she said next would have had Valonia aglow with pride, "You're right. You should tell him."

She nodded rapidly, but now she looked terrified. "I know, but what if he turns his back on me?"

Kolfinnia listened to the founding-banner flutter in the breeze. It seemed immune to fleeting human problems. If only she could be more like it, or the woman who'd stitched it. "If he's the man you believe him to be then he won't. If he rejects you for a mistake you've amply paid for, then he's someone else and not meant for you." Now she was stony and commanding, just like the Valonia of old. The pair stood in silence considering all they had to lose and at last Kolfinnia noticed her visitor loitering on the Glade's edge. "Rowan's waiting, I'd better go."

Sunday looked in the girl's direction. "Rowan knows," she observed.

Kolfinnia had used the expression so many times that it had become a phrase. She didn't know if Sunday meant their current plight or whether the girl had some inkling as to the outcome. Either way she couldn't have spoken truer words. She looked her in the eye. "I think we've both endured far worse than this."

A spark of defiance joined them, and Sunday touched the hammer around her neck. "You wouldn't believe the things I've seen," she confessed.

"Tell me one day, if it's just you and I, no Ben, no Clovis, we'll drink a toast to the twins and forget our woes."

"Thank you," Sunday accepted humbly.

"Good luck," Kolfinnia wished her, and then they embraced, both of them wondering where fate would take them next.

There were three of them kneeling in a row, weeding the young pea shoots, and although Farona was normally the friendliest of witches, right then he sincerely wished Kathy Tooley would just bugger off.

Without any hint of planning or contrivance, here he was with Flora, right by her side, close enough to smell her scented soap. Corn grew tall and leafy on either side of them. The sun was shining, Flora was in a playful mood, it was private and it was perfect, all he had to do was open his mouth and tell her, except for bloody Kathy Tooley.

Middle-aged Kathy was a likeable sort but Farona had 'liked' her for the last two hours and was exhausted by the effort. She chattered constantly and was fond of jokes, bad ones, and he didn't think he could force another laugh. Worse still, she had the annoying habit of somehow manoeuvring herself between him and Flora, and every time he devised a clever way to get back by her side Kathy would manage to squeeze between them again.

Flora worked happily, oblivious to his frustration and seemingly delighted by Kathy's painful banter. Occasionally, Flora would bump against him when she reached over to deposit weeds in the bucket and when she did her hair brushed his cheek and he thought he would faint.

Kathy jabbed him in the ribs. "Need some ducks in here," she declared loudly.

"Why's that Kathy?" His smile was for Flora's benefit only. Right now he just wanted to ram the weed bucket on Kathy's head and stop her infernal twittering.

"Ducks keep the slugs down you know." She jabbed his ribs again, which were now quite sore. "Ain't that right Flora? Ducks," she shouted even though Flora was right beside her, "they keep the slugs down."

"That they do, but I prefer to use spells to keep them away. I don't like the idea of anything getting eaten."

"So do I!" Farona agreed earnestly. Flora looked up and smiled at him.

"Eurgh! Imagine eating a slug!" Kathy stuck her tongue out and her elbow did its prodding thing again. Farona groaned inwardly. "Hey, I say imagine that, Rona lad." She always fuddled his name and it came out sounding like 'Rona' – a distinctly girlish name. "You know why ducks eat slugs?"

"Go on, tell me Kathy," he sighed.

"Cos' they're quackers!" She honked with laughter. "Get it? Quackers!"

Lord Hethra just kill me now! he pleaded silently. If there was anything worse than a bad joke it was having one explained. He was depressed to hear Flora's genuine laughter.

"Oh, Kathy, I swear your jokes are more numerous than the weeds!" she chuckled.

"A witch should sow laughter wherever she goes." Kathy had many homespun expressions, which Farona found as trying as her jokes.

He stretched, aiming for an out-of-reach dandelion. The pose was somewhat undignified.

"Oh! Hey, Flora look!" Kathy pointed a thumb at him. "Bottoms up!"

Horrified, he straightened so fast that his head came up straight through the pea plants.

"Bottoms up!" Kathy was shaking with laughter and Farona eyed the weed bucket again.

It'll fit, by God-Oak it'll fit and if it doesn't I'll bray it down with a spade until it does. He imagined Kathy with the bucket on her head, and a stream of chatter still blaring from it. He mopped sweat from his face and ran a hand through his hair, and turned to see Flora studying him. "Bottoms up!" he laughed feebly.

"I promise I didn't look," she assured him.

He was ready to excuse himself and put an end to the torment when salvation fell into his lap.

"Well, begging your pardon Miss Flora, but I'll be off," Kathy stood and rubbed at the small of her back.

She's going? She's really going? His heart jumped. He would be alone with Flora.

"There's some willow hurdles need a little fixing, and it's murder on my back all this kneeling down," Kathy explained.

"You've been a sweetheart Kathy," Flora looked up. "Couldn't have done it without you."

"Yes. We've got a lot done today." Now Farona's smile was genuine.

"Bottoms up Rona!" Kathy laughed and because he was out of elbow range she gave his bottom a friendly prod with her toe. She collected her hat and waddled away through the corn still laughing, leaving him alone with a curious feeling of dread and elation.

Flora sat up and stretched and Farona made sure not to look at the nice things happening across the front of her dress. She drew a flask from her satchel and offered it over. "Nettle tea?"

"Why not." He jabbed the trowel into the earth and took the flask. "Lovely," he declared after a sip and passed it back, not wanting to guzzle it all.

"Thank you." She gave him a shy smile.

He struggled for something to say and now the silence sounded too loud. He was about to fill that silence with the boldest and scariest thing he would ever say when she started first.

"There's something I want to tell you," she said.

His heart didn't jump this time. It stopped dead. "There is?"

"Mmm." She took her handkerchief and moistened the corner. "There's a big smudge of dirt on your cheek."

"Oh, there is." The tension was killing him.

She shuffled closer on her knees, cupped his chin and began to scrub at his dirty face. Her face was only inches from his. If he wanted he could just lean forwards and kiss her. She finished, leaned back and appraised him. "There, you're handsome again."

Her hand slid from under his chin and he imagined his chance slipping away just as easily. He had to act he told himself, but he was struck helpless by her proximity. *I may never be this close to her again,* he thought, *especially if she says no, then I'll have to find lots of reasons not to work in the gardens.* But each moment's delay ate up more of his precious opportunity.

"Just tell her!" Clovis's advice boomed in his ears.

It's not that bloody easy! he fought himself.

She caught his intense gaze. "Something wrong?"

All things considered he recovered admirably. "Not at all, I was just making sure you didn't have a few smudges of your own."

She laughed and uncorked the flask again, took a drink and looked at the ground thoughtfully.

"Flora?" She looked pensive, he thought.

"I was just thinking." She stroked the earth tenderly. He saw how her elegant fingers were dirty with honest work and he wondered again what he would do if she said 'no'. "I was thinking that right under us there are two sleeping dragons."

"Hmm," he agreed faintly. *And other things too,* he thought of carnivorous larvae.

"And you're the only witch who's ever seen them." Now she admired him. "I shouldn't be, but I'm jealous."

He regarded the earth, thinking of all the horrors and miracles below, and only he and Wester had seen them.

"I've heard the tales of course, but what was it *really* like?" She sat back and wrapped her arms around her knees, waiting.

What can I say? he thought. *'Never mind the twins Flora, those hallowed dragons that give life. Never mind them because I so badly want to kiss you?'* He sat copying her with his arms around his knees. Her face was open and receptive, and her lips were parted in the faintest smile. He still wanted to kiss her and tell her something important, but here was a chance to tell her something far greater. He put his desires aside and began. "It was so magnificent that I could hardly look at them."

Her mouth spread into a beautiful smile and he began his tale.

The following hour was almost as dizzying and wonderful as seeing the twins themselves. Speaking of Hethra and Halla eased his nerves, and she gained a truer picture of him. Incredible memories poured out of him and he even found himself telling her things that he'd never revealed before, and best of all it was just the two of them. They shared the flask and the sunshine like the only two people on Earth. "Just before we left the crumbling cavern I turned, and watched them slip away into the deep fire." He wiped an eye. "It was the saddest but happiest moment of my life." For a while the gardens were gone, and he saw that cavern and its vast diamond one last time, then the image faded and there he was, sitting in the sun with Flora.

She was so rapt that she hadn't noticed a butterfly resting on her shoulder. She searched his face, seeing so many new and admirable qualities there. "I think you're wonderful," she said at last.

His heart didn't jump or flutter this time, it just beat steadily and the words he'd been groping for now seemed so clear and he opened his mouth to say them, "Flora, I –,"

"Farona!"

Both of them jumped and turned to see Clovis approaching, and a misplaced sense of guilt washed over them. Flora scrambled to her feet and the butterfly fluttered away, while Farona got up slowly.

"Farona, we're ready to start weapon practice. You asked me to let you know." Clovis looked from one to the other and his blunder dawned on him. "Erm, but of course finish what you're doing here first though," he added quickly.

"I was just packing up anyway," Flora pretended. She turned to the young man who until just today she had regarded as a mere youth. "Thank you, I felt I was there."

Oddly he felt happy. "It was a pleasure to take you there." Yes, she might turn him down, but there was only one who'd seen what he'd seen and nobody could take that away from him.

Flora excused herself and left.

"Erm, my apologies," Clovis patched-up when she was out of earshot.

Farona stared after her until she was out of sight. "I almost said it coven-father." He looked pleased rather than crushed.

"I promise next time I'll knock." He gave him a friendly pat. "Now, weapon practice beckons."

Farona collected his things and then stood looking thoughtful. "Why do ducks eat slugs?" he said from nowhere.

Clovis scratched his chin. "Hmm." He liked philosophical debate. "Because of the intrinsic nature of life and death, and the constant flow of cosmic energy."

Farona just laughed, "Try again!"

They left the gardens locked in deep debate, well one of them was at least, and as they left the butterfly returned, landed on a flower and drank deeply. If Clovis had chanced upon it he might remark that 'persistence always wins through in the end,' and on this occasion he would be right.

"Your hands are shaking," Wake said unhelpfully. Ben gave him a withering look and went back to his work. He was carving tiny oak leaves, or at least trying to when a certain annoying thunder-sprite would let him. "Peppermint's good for nerves, maybe you ought to try some?" he rambled.

"Wake!" He sat upright and tossed the chisel onto the bench.

"Sorry – continue, I shan't say another word."

He mumbled something, retrieved the chisel and started again, but Wake was right. "Anyway," he added without looking up, "I think I've a right to be nervous."

"They look very nice," he complimented, meaning the little charms. "She'll like them."

"I hope she does more than 'like them'."

Wake hummed in agreement and took a quick look through the window. His task was to make sure Sunday didn't catch him. She'd know right away what he was doing and this was supposed to be a secret. "So when will you, erm, well you know. . ."

"Don't know yet," he grunted, trying to keep the chisel level. "This week, this month, this year? I can't say." He swapped chisels and thumbed the tip, making sure it was keen. "I've been thinking and I reckon it's best to—"

"She's here!" Wake spluttered.

Ben frantically bundled everything up. "You're supposed to be on watch!"

"I know, I know!" He flapped up and hid amongst the rafters.

He heard her soft footfalls, and looked up to see the door swing open and Sunday look in. He snatched his hand away from the bundle just in time. "Sunday!"

"There you are." Her smile was precarious, he thought. "I've been looking everywhere."

He jumped to his feet and placed himself between her and the bench. "Looking for me? You should've just asked Rowan." He summoned his best innocent smile, and just as well her mind was elsewhere because it wasn't that convincing. He went to kiss her, but his embrace also helped him direct her away from the bench and to sit her down with her back to it. "You look troubled?"

She sat beside him and clasped his hands. Now the words she'd prepared abandoned her, leaving a sinking stone in her chest. *The Flowering,* the better part of her mind insisted, *use the Flowering to weave a fate of your choosing!* But just like beleaguered Farona, she found that it just wasn't that easy. How could she focus on magic *and* bare her soul at the same time? "Ben, I wanted to share something with you. It's been on my mind all day. I wanted to say, that. . ." She paused to catch her breath while blood drummed in her temples. "Well, Ben, it's just that. . ."

"Sunday. It's alright. I know."

"You do?" she gulped.

"And I'm not jealous. You must understand that."

"Jealous?" Now she was confused.

"Today's lesson in fairies of the faded-realm. I know you see them quicker and easier than me and I know why."

"Really?" She felt disconnected, convinced that any second he was going to reveal her dark secret and she was powerless to stop him.

"The trials of being Blackwand, they changed you." He stroked her hand tenderly. Should he ask her now he wondered?

"Ben. . ." How she wanted to be rid of her secret, but how it curled around her heart and gripped even tighter.

"I'm not jealous," he said again, "fays come to you because they know your heart's pure."

I can't stand this! She pulled away, covering her hasty withdrawal with a pretend smile. "And they'll come to you eventually." She patted his cheek. "I knew you wouldn't be jealous, but it's been worrying me a little," she lied. He reached for her again, but she stood and backed away. "So, shall we eat before or after sleeping-spells tonight?"

The sudden change of direction threw him. "Erm, how about after?"

"Splendid." She leaned over and planted a kiss against his cheek, desperate to leave before the tears showed. That's when she noticed the small bundle on the bench behind him. She saw a tiny carved oak leaf and the tip of a chisel jutting out of the bag, and she knew, *He's carving a Solemn-circle.*

Alerted, he shifted sideways to hide his secret, thinking that's why she looked so preoccupied. "After sleeping-spells then."

"Blessed be," she wished him.

"Blessed be," he called after her as she left. The door banged and she was gone.

"I think you escaped by a gnat's wing," Wake said from above.

He looked up and let out a huge sigh, "Yes, all things considered that went very well."

She closed the door and first jogged before breaking into a run, not towards the coven but into the woods. The dam had burst and she was crying, but she was Blackwand and Stormwood couldn't see her this way. At last, confident she was alone, she collapsed against a tree with her hands on her knees, bent over and feeling sick with guilt. "He's making me a Solemn-circle," she despaired. It could mean only one thing; at some point Ben was going to ask her to marry him, and until she unburdened herself she could never say yes.

Kolfinnia walked right in to it; a full-blown dispute, and it centred on Mr Hathwell of all people. She had gone to find Hilda and ask her to join her secret council, but instead she found Hathwell standing at the centre of a mob, with a red cheek from where he'd been soundly slapped. The shouting stopped as soon as she appeared, and the crowd parted to reveal a fiery woman named Scarlet Tanner. "Explain!" Already she wasn't in the best of moods today.

"Him!" Scarlet pointed right into Hathwell's face. "Why the Saxon woman brought him I'll never know."

He put an end to the Knight Superior. Hilda's news still left her with a chill. Kolfinnia quickly appraised the situation. The work party was supposed to be excavating the fort. She saw spades all around and knew for a fact that Scarlet hadn't been assigned to this work. She'd come up here looking for trouble. Albert Parry was standing next to Hathwell, with a reassuring hand on his shoulder. Clearly he had a few supporters of his own here. "Did Mr Hathwell assault you in some way Scarlet?" In truth she had little liking for the woman. She was sour and quick to accuse.

Scarlet stood facing her enemy. "He'd be lying dead if he had," she vowed coldly.

"Then why did you strike him?"

"He's one of them isn't he!" she spat. "A filthy squire!

"So you hit him for that?"

"Good enough reason, I lost a good son to the likes of him!" She clenched her fists and a few heads nodded and a few voices add their support.

Kolfinnia singled one of them out. "You, Sam Goodstock, you agree with Scarlet?"

He looked at his feet. "Aye, a bit coven-mother."

"Anyone else?" Feet shuffled and eyes were averted, but nobody spoke up. For a moment Kolfinnia didn't recognise any of them. "Sam, you were given excavation duty this morning. Mr Hathwell is an engineer, you're supposed to take instructions from him."

"I did!" he protested.

"Even though you think he's no right to be here?" Now she was almost as angry as Scarlet. "You mean to tell me that you'd take orders from a man you had no respect for?"

"Well, I didn't quite say that Kolf –,"

"Coven-mother!" she boomed, "I am your coven-mother and you'll address me as such!" Uneasy glances rippled through them. She had seldom been so angry. "Men who take bad orders are as guilty as the ones who give them!

You're supposed to be witches, you're supposed to set the example. And you Scarlet, you hit a man who caused you no harm. Just as the Illuminata killed the good witch who was your son, even though he'd done them no harm. I see no difference between you."

"Aye," Albert added softly.

"Why he came here I'll never know," Scarlet said again, glaring at him in disgust.

"He came because I brought him," someone said.

All heads turned to see Hilda watching closely.

Scarlet lowered her fists. "Shunt have brought him, Hilda! He's not a witch!" she blustered.

"Hilda? You may address me as 'the Saxon woman' if that's your preference." She stepped closer and folded her arms. "Men who take orders from those they do not respect, and women who have differing names for those they believe aren't listening." Her tone was sad. "This is a coven, not a camp, and you are witches not soldiers. Those who wish to indulge in such behaviour might find a more fitting position within the Illuminata's ranks." Now she came and stood by Hathwell's side. "Mr Hathwell didn't like those values either. Imagine then how sorry he must be to see such behaviour here of all places. Your coven-mother is right; you are witches, you set the example."

"Hear, hear," Albert muttered, and he wasn't alone.

"Coven-mother, your verdict?" Hilda prompted. It was time for her to settle this.

Kolfinnia thought hard and acted likewise. "Those that do not wish to take instruction from Mr Hathwell are welcome to decline, but by the same token I deem any such witch to be in doubt of my own instructions, and therefore they are welcome to leave the protection of Stormwood." Shocked gasps followed. She was talking about banishment. "Furthermore – Scarlet, you lost a son. Mr Hathwell, you lost your sense of security. And while the two do not balance out I concede both parties have lost something dear to them. Scarlet, tonight you will help Mr Hathwell know our ways better and show him how we say sleeping-spells for Hethra and Halla. Mr Hathwell, if you wish to remain at Stormwood then you'll take up the good work Scarlet's son began before he was unjustly killed, and therefore you will join us in saying sleeping-spells from now on. For the good of the coven and the twins, your coven-mother has spoken," she finished formally.

Scarlet forced herself to look at the man she had to sit beside tonight. It was proper for her to say 'I accept' and so end the dispute, although it would be a bitter pill to swallow. She was about to do the right thing when Hathwell surprised everyone and spoke first.

"I'm sorry for your loss, but I didn't kill your son Ms Tanner," he explained, "I killed the Knight Superior." Albert's hand slid from his shoulder, and Scarlet's mouth fell open. Hathwell took up his spade. "I'll see all of you at dusk, and while I can't promise I'll make a good job of saying 'sleeping-spells' I'll try my best, because that's what old soldiers do. Now if you'll excuse me I've a plum tree to tend." He marched past them all, ignoring everyone, even Hilda, and went in search of the one person who seemed to understand him: Rowan.

Kolfinnia was still shaking when Hilda found a quiet moment with her. "You did well. Your judgement was even and firm." She looked pleased.

"Did he really? Did he really kill Krast?"

Children passed carrying spell bottles. Hilda waited for the chatter and tinkle of glass to fade before she answered. "I told you. Point blank, right between the eyes."

She drew a sharp breath. "That's awful."

The older woman nodded in agreement. "It saddens me to see death of any kind, even Samuel Krast, but it would sadden me more to see a man like him still walk the Earth."

"A terrible day," she murmured to nobody.

"Take heart! You performed admirably."

"It's not Mr Hathwell's dispute I'm troubled by."

"Oh?"

"Clovis is leaving." She hung her head.

"My dear," she cupped her elbow, "I'm sorry, I know how much he means to you and Stormwood."

"That's not the worst of it. He's leaving to complete unfinished business. And very soon now."

"And there's no chance he'll return once this business is settled?" she posed gently.

"No." She had pretended, Hethra knew she had, but the answer was plain. Win or lose, live or die, Clovis was leaving.

"So how may I help?"

Kolfinnia managed a laugh. "You know me well."

"I always knew when you were building up to asking for something, like the time you and Flora wanted to make your own tree house and it took you days to ask if you could have that tatty old rug of mine to furnish it with."

She smiled at the memory, but it didn't last long. "Clovis has to take Janus away from here and release him."

"Ahh, the mysterious Janus. Yes, I've heard about him. And where must he take this imprisoned god?"

"He has to travel to the fairy-nations."

"The faded-realm?" Hilda considered a moment. "Of course, where else."

"You know?"

"Hmm. Clovis is a Therion, and although it's been many years since such magnificent beings walked amongst us, they are still to be found in the faded-realm." She looked about her where Therions and fairies might very well walk unseen right now. "A place of profound peace I believe."

Kolfinnia came alive, "See, I knew you'd know about the place! Will you come to a select gathering? Clovis needs to find out all he can before he. . ." She closed her mouth before the word could come out.

Hilda regarded her lovingly. *Poor Kolfinnia,* she thought, *not the first witch to fall for a Therion, and doubtful she'll be the last.* She nodded once. "I'll come."

"I've asked Sunday too."

"Again, your judgement's sound. She has a special link with fairies I'm told."

Just hope she stays long enough to attend the meeting! Kolfinnia made sure to keep that horrible thought to herself. "So myself, you, Sunday and Clovis, sprites too. Nobody else is to know for now."

"Then tell me when you're ready." She drew a pair of work gloves from her shoulder bag and put them on. "In the meantime I'm off to the gardens."

"You've done your share of garden work today though?"

"Yes, but I suspect there's a man there watering a plum sapling, and I think he'll need a few pointers in how we conduct our sleeping-spells," she offered her a crafty smile.

"Ah, yes," her mouth puckered. "I did sort of drop him in it didn't I?"

"Even but firm. That's the way to govern," she reminded her.

"That one," Hathwell pointed to Rowan's left hand this time, but she opened it to reveal an empty palm, again.

"Sorry!"

"That's ten times I've been wrong in a row, even that must count for something?"

Her laughter said it all.

The sapling had been thoroughly watered. He wanted her to do some magic, and see the tree shoot up, but she just laughed as if he'd asked something impossible. The guessing game wasn't going well either. If he found the plum stone she promised to 'do' her garden magic for him, but so far no luck.

"You're too trusting Mr Hathwell," Hilda sympathised.

"Hilda!" Rowan dropped from the log, and ran to her.

"Hilda." Hathwell stood and straightened his waistcoat.

"She might look the picture of sweetness, but little Rowan can be as slippery as a toad in a butter tub." She stroked the girl's hair from her eyes. "I think she got the better of you Mr Hathwell."

"She's a knack for winning, I'll say that."

Hilda snaked a hand down the back of Rowan's tunic making her laugh helplessly. "Rather she's got a knack for hiding things." And drew out the plum stone and tossed it over to him.

He caught it in one hand. "Well Rowan Barefoot, to think you took advantage of a helpless old man!"

Helpless? I think not, Hilda thought, and imagined a lone rifle shot.

"Mr Hathwell wanted me to show him some magic," Rowan explained.

"And you can." Hilda drew up a bucket, flipped it over and sat down regally, as if it was her throne. "Tonight Mr Hathwell's joining us for the sleeping-spells. And so we're going to show him how it's done."

"Mr Hathwell's going to learn magic!" Rowan looked delighted, while Hathwell just looked worried.

She made sure to look him in the eye. "Yes, Mr Hathwell is going to learn magic and be a proper witch."

He swallowed and sat down, ready for his first lesson.

While Hathwell was tutored in the gentle art of sleeping-spells, Clovis led a master class in the brutal art of weapon practice. "No! Again!" he bellowed, and marched into their midst, grabbed the staff in Farona's hands and shoved it below his waist. "Too high, always too high! Keep your lower half defended at all times!" he snarled before stalking away.

Farona blew an exhausted sigh. It was hot and today's lesson had been hard. It was almost as if Clovis expected invasion any second.

"He's a grumpy old moggy today," Morag Heron said from the corner of her mouth.

Farona grunted in agreement and held his staff in readiness once more.

"Again!" Clovis boomed and forty-seven witches all thrust their staffs at imaginary foes.

Kolfinnia watched from a little way off. Albert Parry was next to her, again with Mally at his feet. "You'd think we're going into battle, not just recovering from one," he said as he lit his pipe.

"He's just determined to make Stormwood as strong as possible," she defended him, but Albert was right. Clovis was making sure he left them prepared.

"Aye, suppose so coven-mother. Either way we're lucky to have him."

"Not for long," she said quietly. Thankfully Albert was a touch deaf.

"I remember my grandfather said there were Therions all over long ago, he even saw them sometimes as a boy, but I haven't seen one in years." He sucked noisily on the pipe. "Mermaid it was, over across on Skye. Just sitting on a skerry she was, combing her hair," he smiled dreamily. "Fairest lassie I ever saw. I hid in the rocks and watched her for hours."

"Would you have watched for as long if 'she' had been a 'he'?" she smirked.

"By Halla's prickly leaves no! That'd be disrespectful!"

Her smile won through. "Other than Clovis, I've never seen a Therion." She wondered what others of his race were like.

"To the shame of us all."

"Shame?"

"As men folk spread, Therions retreated to the faded world. Bit by bit they vanished to escape us." He chewed on the pipe stem. "Aye vanished they did." And Mally whined in agreement.

Kolfinnia wondered if she ought to ask him to their special meeting. She was mulling this over when Clovis called an end to the gruelling session. "Excuse me Albert, I need a word with our coven-father."

He just stared off into the distance, reminiscing about mermaids. She left him with his daydream and went to intercept Clovis before he slipped away, certain he'd been avoiding her these last few days.

"Clovis!" She hurried after him. All around, exhausted witches were slumped in the grass or heaving buckets of water over their heads. The lesson had been hot and hard, and she knew why.

He glanced back but didn't stop. "How go the excavations at the fort?"

She caught him up. "Slow down!"

His eyes were everywhere, assessing everything. "And the excavations?" he enquired again.

"Apart from some tension between our resident squire and one of the others, they go well."

"How did Hathwell take it?"

"With restraint. I was impressed."

"Then he'll make a witch yet." He pointed to the overgrown fort with his staff. "I've recommended to him about digging an escape tunnel."

"An escape tunnel?" He was growing obsessed she thought. She didn't like warrior-Clovis as much as witch-Clovis.

"Perhaps more than one."

"Stop it!" She tugged at his arm, and he stopped and stared at her. "Stop what?"

"You know what. We *will* learn to live without you." *I will learn to live without you,* she thought and deliberately stepped away from him.

"This coven must have all the strengths the former ones did not. You must learn from the past."

"And it will. But this coven is first and foremost a home, not a fortress."

"Ha!" he scoffed, and those formidable teeth came into view. "A home is useless unless it's secure. Look what happened to you last year."

"I know why you're afraid," she confided, leaning closer.

Her concern disarmed him, and she saw the hurt on his face. "I just have to know that you'll be safe."

"I've asked Sunday and Hilda to come to our meeting," she tried to sound positive.

"Then we'll begin."

"Tonight?" she asked apprehensively.

He didn't answer straight away. Instead he took in the gardens in the evening sun and listened to the sound of the little corn mill at work and the rhythmic tap of hammers in the smithy. He didn't want to leave. He didn't want to open the vessel. He didn't want to die. "Tomorrow," he decided.

She masked her relief and recovered her poise. "Then if you'll pardon me I have sleeping-spells to lead. Goodnight coven-father."

"Goodnight coven-mother."

Stormwood's two leaders went their separate ways, but thinking the same dark thoughts.

Sleeping-spells were said in the Glade if the weather was kind. Tonight was warm and the evening had a contented glow to it. All of Stormwood made their way to the Glade, with a nervous Bertrand Hathwell amongst them. Of course news travels fast and he noticed how formerly suspicious glances had been replaced by different ones, ranging from admiration to disbelief. *'Point blank, right between the eyes.'* He didn't like to think about it because part of him would always hate himself for betraying his knight.

Kolfinnia was standing on the Anvil stone by the founding-banner, ready to begin, but tonight she felt jittery. It had been a fraught day; Clovis's looming departure, Hathwell's confrontation, and now Sunday and Ben weighed heavily on her mind. "So much unfinished business," she said to nobody as the crowds began to gather.

"Weather certainly brings them out," Hilda noted, but Kolfinnia didn't reply. "Kolfinnia, are you feeling shipshape, you look troubled?"

"What?" She was scanning the crowds, looking for two faces in particular, and anxious because she couldn't see them. "Sorry, unfinished business, that's all."

Hilda looked around. By now witches were kneeling or sitting around the banner, ready to send their love to Hethra and Halla. "Clovis?"

She took in the Glade. Neither Ben nor Sunday was there. *'I've decided, I'm going to tell Ben.'* "She's telling him tonight," Kolfinnia realised, and looked westwards. Sunday and Ben shared a small dwelling just the other side of the trees. "Hilly, lead the sleeping-spells for me."

"But I was going to keep an eye on Hathwell, Kolfinnia what's –,"

"Please, there's no time to explain, sorry I've got to go." She jumped down and was running before she'd even finished. Intuition told her that if she didn't hurry, by nightfall Blackwand would be gone.

Hilda watched her run off into the deepening dusk. "Hilly?" the name dawned on her and she smiled. "She's getting more like Valonia every day."

Maybe it wasn't her business, unfinished or otherwise, but Kolfinnia couldn't let Sunday face this alone. "Rowan understood, but will Ben?" she asked nobody, hiding in the cover of the trees. She was watching Sunday's small hut, which lay just outside the main coven and had come to be known as 'Sunday's Corner'. She briefly wished Skald was there. "No, this is sisterly duty," she reminded herself and watched the lantern-light in the window, imagining the heartbreak unfolding inside.

"We should get going." Ben stood by the door, grasping the handle. Sunday was sitting on the edge of her bunk, and although they shared this little house, they had separate beds. But if things went as Sunday suspected, then they'd never even share another word, let alone a marriage-bed one day.

"Did you enjoy the fairy lesson today Ben?" She stared at her feet.

"Not as much as little Emmy, she nearly jumped out of her skin, but yes. And I meant what I said; I'm envious of your skills, not envious *for* them." He wasn't sure what she was driving at, but she looked so forlorn it pained him. "Sunday?" He knelt before her and rested his hands on her knees, and was shocked to see she was almost crying.

"But you didn't see a fairy?" She spoke so quietly he could hardly hear her.

"No, I didn't. Sunday what's wrong?" He clasped her hands, and was alarmed by how cold she felt. Had she got wind of his special surprise he wondered?

She looked into his face. "Fairies see the world differently, it's said they can see souls. And if you were a fairy you'd see *my* soul."

"And a feast for the eyes it would be too." His false cheer didn't work however. "Sunday what's wrong?"

"And if you did see my soul you'd see it had once been broken then made anew," she persisted. "You asked me where I went after the battle for Kittiwake, you said nobody knew and it was a miracle I turned up alive."

"Sunday, you're scaring me."

"One short summer or a lifetime of winter, you once said." She was powerless to stop now. "I'd never heard such beautiful words, even in the hell of London and Salisbury they gave me hope. But now the choice is yours: summer or winter? Do you know why I took my leave at Kittiwake?"

"Sunday, please."

"Summer may surely die if I tell you, but winter will always reign if I don't. Ben, I left Kittiwake to go and make amends for a terrible mistake." The dam burst, and out poured the most terrible words she would ever say.

A universe away, on a different plane of reality, Sunday's dear champion listened to her heartbreak. If he could he would tease the threads just right and weave a happy outcome, but sometimes tangled threads were necessary. He watched with his remaining seven eyes, and even he didn't know what would follow. He detected another thread close by, drawn by compassion. *And a good and loyal sister you are Kolfinnia,* he thought like a proud father. He watched as Sunday's confession was woven and Ben's heart broke.

The light in the window flickered. Someone was moving, but Kolfinnia didn't hear raised voices or an argument, and she found that much more worrying. She ducked behind the trees when she heard the door bang open, and saw a tall figure march out and into the darkness. "Ben," she knew. Sympathy for him and anger towards him briefly fought, then her thoughts turned to Sunday. "I'm losing Clovis, I'll not lose Blackwand too," she vowed, and hurried across the darkening gardens towards Sunday's Corner.

Each knew the other was there before mundane things like eyes and ears told them so.

"I've heard of Blackwand's many brave feats, but by far that was the bravest," Kolfinnia was humbled.

Sunday looked up from packing her things. "Kolfinnia."

"You can't leave." She filled the doorway, barring her departure.

Sunday smiled, but clearly she'd been crying. "I risked all I had and lost it. . ."

". . .Yet I still won," she finished.

Sunday just shook her head in despair.

"This isn't for me, Stormwood needs you. Everyone takes strength from just seeing you, you can't leave."

"I can't go through my life knowing I failed him." She looked to the floor where tiny carved oak leaves lay forgotten. Ben had thrown them across the room in anger. "I failed," she whispered.

"Failed?" Her anger soared. "If you hadn't been washed up on that beach, the world would be swarming with valkyries! We'd all be dead if your past hadn't led you there."

Sunday stood, now with her belongings over her shoulder. She was dressed in black once more and carried her black staff. Strike was hidden inside but Kolfinnia could have sworn the staff glistened with tears. "I'm touched by your loyalty. But my bravery only goes so far. I can't go the rest of my days looking upon him."

Although loath to admit it Kolfinnia understood a fraction of her pain, and she surrendered. "Let me escort you to the coven boundary at least, but I need to fetch my staff first. Skald will want to say goodbye."

Sunday looked around the homely shack. "Very well," she agreed under pressure, "but please hurry."

Kolfinnia darted away with no intentions of getting her staff or anything else. She ran as fast as she could though the gathering darkness, following Ben's trail.

"Am I doing this right?" Hathwell's manner was frosty. Just because Scarlet was showing him the ropes didn't mean he had to like her.

"Just relax and think about breathing steady." She didn't open her eyes.

Everywhere he looked Hathwell saw men, women and children sitting or kneeling in the Glade, and from their peaceful expressions they were doing something that he wasn't. Hilda sat in the centre. She'd begun the invocation, and she would end it shortly. The spell didn't last long. Between start and finish he was meant to do or feel something, but he was buggered if he knew what. He closed his eyes and did as he was told, and so he didn't see Scarlet peep at him.

Right between the eyes. She appraised him again, and again found him mysterious. She looked away quickly when he caught her watching. "Put your palms down on the grass," she said from the corner of her mouth.

"Why?" he whispered.

"You'll feel the twins. They'll come to you. Now, shhh!" She returned to her meditation.

He pulled a face and pressed harder against the soft grass. He thought of all the soldiers and witches who died fighting over Hethra and Halla. *Were they even real?* he asked himself again. Real or not, lives were lost, and surely that defined 'real' better than anything else he thought.

He was pondering these things when he was distracted. Something tickled his palm. Three times he lifted his hand and looked, but it was damp with dew and nothing more. He tried again and this time he didn't deny the sensation but listened to it. *Valkyries rampant at Salisbury, he thought, Kittiwake's witches spilling their blood. Surely all that death must have been for something? Surely right under my hands there really are dreaming dragons?* The tickling spread to both palms now and it wasn't random.

du-dum - du-dum - du-dum - du-dum - du-dum

It was the touch of a beating heart. Hathwell snatched his hands away, feeling both scared and elated.

Scarlet opened an eye. "That was them," she almost smiled.

He looked first at his palms and then the grass. It was almost dark now and the attendants were lighting the lanterns. Someone was singing softly as the spell drew to an end, it was Hilda, and witches were waking and stretching. *That was the sound of Krast's grand prize.* His head spun at the enormity of it. "The sound of life," he said aloud, forgetting he wasn't alone.

Scarlet eyed him again, wondering. "Same time tomorrow," she finished abruptly and took her leave.

He knelt in the dewy grass still staring at his palms, and eventually became aware of someone standing over him. He looked up. Hilda looked youthful in the lantern light. "Welcome to Stormwood." She held out a hand, and when he was on his feet she didn't let go, instead she led him away to the Glade's edge where tables were being laden with food. It was time for supper.

People often behave strangely when they're upset, and witches are no exception. Ben stomped along, heedless of the dark, or the snagging pine roots underfoot. More than once he stumbled, but he was too angry and hurt to notice. If he'd set out with a purpose in mind, then perhaps Kolfinnia wouldn't have found him and things might have turned out very differently, but his upset made him predictable.

"You'll fall and break a bone, the fort's a dangerous place after dark." Kolfinnia drew closer, holding her wand up for light.

He turned and she saw his face was almost unrecognisable, and his cheeks glistened. "You knew," he guessed, and wiped an arm across his eyes before turning away.

She went and stood at his back. "Ben I can't talk to a face I can't see."

He angled around just enough, and she could see he was shaking. "She was a hero to all of us."

"She still is."

"Still is? How could you have her here! How could you let me even be near her, knowing what you know?" The Solemn-circle seemed so mocking now.

Far off, Kolfinnia could hear laughter and chatter as the supper tables were being laid. Above her an owl hooted and she remembered some small detail from the past. "Remember how Arthur Conrad left you with a bloody nose on the eve of battle at Kittiwake?"

"So?" he argued,

"For a moment you doubted. Many did, including me. We all doubt sometimes, we all do things we later regret."

"You can't possibly equate that with *her* crime!" he retorted.

"What she did she did for the twins, no matter how twisted it was."

"You're defending her!"

"No, I'm explaining. People change."

"People change?" he sneered. "Nobody changes that much."

"No?" she regarded him steadily. "There's a man saying sleeping-spells with us tonight who served the Knight Superior for over twenty years. .. before finally shooting him between the eyes."

He twitched in shock. "Hathwell? I'd no idea."

"Yes – Hathwell."

Uncertainty gnawed at him. "He's a good man," he struggled, "and a brave one, his help at Salisbury was crucial."

"Even though he used to be Illuminata?"

Ben had no answer for this.

"Yes," she resumed. "Valonia trusted him, and with good reason. His actions saved her, and perhaps all of Kittiwake. She trusted him, Hilda trusted him with her life at Salisbury, along with hundreds of other witches including you, and I trust him. Just as I trust Sunday."

He collapsed against a tree and let the air rush from his chest. "I love her, Kolfinnia," he said at last.

"Which is precisely why you must forgive her. And be quick, she's readying to leave."

He clutched his head in turmoil. "I just don't know if I can!"

"You know of her miraculous note, the Flowering-of-Fate?" she asked, and his silence told her 'yes'. "We can choose our own fates Ben. Sunday earned us that right, so choose to be the witch she fell in love with, or choose to abandon her and for Stormwood to lose her." Now she stood arms folded, even looking like Valonia. "The rest is up to you. And don't fall in the dark and break a leg, we're short on medicines," she added before turning to leave.

He watched her wand-light until it was gone, and as it vanished so too his head cleared enough, and Benedict Collins made up his mind.

She waited as long as she dare, but she was in no mood for heartbreaking goodbyes, even with her fated sister. Sunday left Stormwood behind. She had imagined a happy lifetime here, but in reality her dream had lasted less than two weeks.

"Where do we go now?" Strike asked.

She clutched her staff for all its worth. He was her only friend now. "I don't know," she answered truthfully, but anywhere far from hurt was good to her.

They were almost at Stormwood's magical boundary. She could hear the way-beware's song on the breeze, and once she passed them she told herself there would be no going back.

"He was wrong, you know," Strike added, *"wrong to say what he said and storm off like that."*

"Thank you," she swallowed, but kept up her pace. The pain in her heart was worse than anything she'd felt even in the darkest moments at Salisbury. Mercifully, the way-beware's song grew stronger. Once past them she pretended her pain would stay behind.

At last she heard someone crashing through the undergrowth behind and her stomach flipped. "No Kolfinnia!" she moaned. "Just leave me be!" But the sounds grew closer, and finally a branch broke in the dark as someone tripped over. "Kolfinnia, you'll kill yourself, go back for Oak's sake and let me go!"

"Sunday!" Rough hands grabbed her and spun her around.

"Ben!" Agony and joy overwhelmed her.

He didn't speak, he couldn't, but instead he just grabbed her in a desperate embrace. She wanted to push him away, but found herself holding him just as tight. "I don't want winter forever," he whispered hoarsely. "I want summer, and I only want it with you."

Her lightning-staff fell to the ground unnoticed. Fortunately Strike didn't take offence easily. He appeared quietly, feeling wrung-out but satisfied, and left them to their silent forgiveness and went and sat a little way off. The first stars twinkled in the blackness above and of course Arinidia the spider was foremost amongst them. He listened to the way-bewares' haunting melody. It drifted through his head as delicate as silken threads and he thought of spiders and smiled to himself. Before long he was thinking of supper and looking forward to getting home.

CHAPTER EIGHT

Brimstone

'Oak endures!'
Traditional fairy war cry

The lion lifted his huge head and listened. Caesar was a bedraggled lion that had spent all his life in Pascal Masson's travelling circus. Towns and cities, countries and seasons, went by, but the bars never changed. If anyone were to ask his dearest desire it would surely be for freedom. He heard the sound again, like the chattering of a million roosting starlings, but then lost interest and dropped his head between his paws and found release in sleep as the rain continued to fall.

Madam Mystique wasn't her real name of course but it looked good on the poster. Madam Mystique, or rather Lizzie Trent, had worked this circus for almost a decade. The work was repetitive and the folk she worked alongside had worse manners than the caged animals, but her real purpose wasn't to spin fortunes for a penny a time or anything else the sign on her caravan said.

She wasn't a real fortune-teller of course, but then again Ringmaster Masson wasn't even French, he was from Southampton, but his accent was convincing enough. Despite the circus's lack of authenticity, she did rub shoulders with *real* magical folk on occasion and that's where all the travelling paid off. Witches knew Lizzie as a 'Smoke': someone in the wider world who acted as a go-between when they needed information or goods or such like. And as a Smoke and fortune-teller she travelled all of Europe and enjoyed secret contact with many covens, as well as trying to keep an eye on the animals' welfare as best she could. She had lived with threat of capture for years and the idea of waking up in an Illuminata cell was never far from her mind, but her loyalty was to witches.

Lizzie was plundering the shelves in her tiny caravan that acted as workplace and home. She needed a smoke before tonight's performance, but from the sound of the rain and the sound of the town's name she didn't expect a busy evening. The circus had never been to Gobsley before, and she already suspected they wouldn't go back. "For one night only," she muttered as she rifled the dresser. At last she found pipe and tobacco, and just as she sat down she heard footsteps on the ladder outside her door. "I'm busy love, come back at six, show doesn't start 'til then." She didn't have the heart to feign a French accent tonight. That would come after a couple of brandies, but first a smoke. She lit the match and suddenly heard what sounded like a flock of starlings outside, despite the pouring rain, and a loud banging at the door followed. She lit her pipe and extinguished the match with a brisk puff. "Come back at six!" she shouted.

"I am king of winter and my leaves never fall," a voice came.

She froze. That was code, and it could only be a witch. "A moment please stranger!" She leapt to her feet, turned down the lanterns and pulled her veil up over her face. She didn't want to see or be seen. It could be dangerous for both parties. She took her place behind the card table and slipped a hand underneath. The pistol was there as always. *Just in case,* she told herself. One day her secret caller might not be what they claimed to be. "Would you care for a Smoke stranger?" she called. This too was code, and she gripped the pistol and waited for the door to open.

Open it did and a cloaked figure slipped inside. He was concealed by shadows and Lizzie made sure to keep her own face hidden behind the veil. "I am in need of help madam, and I saw the oak and holly leaves painted upon this wagon." He alluded to the secret symbols alerting witches to her allegiance, but his voice was gruff and almost bestial, she thought.

"Then sit seeker and tell me how I may help." Under the table her finger stroked the trigger in readiness.

"I seek a coven madam, the closest to these whereabouts. I am in haste to find fellow witches to aid my cause." Still he didn't move.

Lizzie was uncertain. Outside she heard the lion roar even through the pounding rain and there was that whirring sound again, like millions of flying insects. "Witches sir? I know nothing of brooms and spells." This was intended to elicit a coded response. Her finger was as taut as it could be. An ounce more pressure and the pistol would fire.

He chuckled and it sounded like a hungry wolf, "Come now Ms Mystique. It isn't your desire to deceive me is it? I'll wager you have more tantalizing desires than that."

She saw movement. He was holding something and it was pointed her way. "Stay where you are sir," she warned. "I know nothing of witches and you're trespassing here. Masson!" she cried.

"Shh!" Something in his hand buzzed like a bone-saw, and instantly she felt sleepy. "Desire Madam, tell me your dearest desire."

Her fingers melted from the pistol and her arm flopped into her lap. "Desire," she mumbled, now feeling stony and forgetful.

"Oh yes," he agreed hungrily. "Freedom is your desire, but not for you." He was curious. The chattering sound outside intensified and Lizzie heard a scream but her brain didn't register it. "You desire to set the lion free." Such a selfless act was so alien that it intrigued him. "You know where Masson keeps the keys?" That buzzing sound came again and her stupor fell away leaving her with a desperate urge to fulfil her dearest desire.

"I do." She almost jumped to her feet, intending to fetch them.

"A moment first Madam," he held up a hand, and in her confused state she didn't see that it was furred and the fingers were tipped with claws. "Covens, you know of them I assume?"

"I know." Outside the rain hammered down, the screaming grew louder and the lion roared in pain and her anxiety peaked. She must get to him.

"Tell me then, where is the closest coven to this place? I promise I shan't tell a soul, your secret is safe with me." And of course he meant it.

"Brimstone-coven, twenty miles northwest, hidden in Tresslain woods. Torrance Rowley is coven-father." She wrung her hands helplessly. "Please sir, Caesar needs me."

"Yes," he sympathised, "now go, and let him at last taste freedom."

Lizzie hurried past him in such a rush that she didn't notice his emerald eyes or panther-black fur. She was consumed by desire for the wellbeing of another. Sef found this somewhat disturbing and he stood lost in thought for a moment. He hadn't counted on such acts of selflessness. It could be a problem later he told himself.

She ran clutching the master keys from Masson's' caravan. The rain fell in waves and pounded the ground into a sheet of mud and she slipped and stumbled across it oblivious to the screams all around her. She didn't even register the crimson slurry underfoot where blood mixed with mud, or how her fellow performers clawed at the air as voracious fairies assailed them. Her desire was such that she didn't even feel the first bites from Chentek's iron-fairies, or how they swarmed across her back in the driving rain and tangled in her hair. Caesar's wagon was just up ahead and the aged animal was rolling and thrashing in pain, as he too fell under the ravenous swarm.

"Caesar!" She fumbled for the right key as she ran, not seeing the myriad bites across her hands, or the bizarre creatures that crawled across her skin. She was numb to the pain and knew only her dearest desire. As more of them landed to feed, her legs buckled under the weight. She lost her footing and tumbled forwards into the bloody filth.

Lizzie hit the ground and the keys splashed down into a puddle. The bright steel glinted through the red waters. She reached out but her hands were little more than ragged claws now. The iron-fairies were stripping her away to nothing, but still desire defeated her pain. *Caesar! I'm coming to set you free at last!* she thought, unable to speak now as her face was drowned under a biting mask. She tried to right herself, but sinew-by-sinew her arms were unhooked and her body was ruthlessly demolished and she collapsed in the mud, yet still her desire blazed. *Caesar! Set – you – free!*

The horde devoured every drop of living-iron and by the end Lizzie Trent was just a desire without a body. The world turned black and the last thing she heard was the lion's agonised roars lost in the endless rain.

Sef sat inside the caravan deep in thought. The screams were dwindling now but the rain fell heavier than ever. There was a distant rumble of thunder and Iso pricked his ears. "You have what you need. We must find this Brimstone-coven she spoke of," Iso urged.

Sef didn't hear, or didn't want to. He sat on the edge of Lizzie's bunk idly turning something over in his hand. It was a tarot card. Her deck lay on the card table, its fortune telling days were over.

"Sef! We go and find this coven, and our first clue to Clovis's whereabouts. Aren't you listening?" He flapped up onto the table, scattering the cards. "Sef?"

"I hear you," he replied moodily. Something had unsettled him, something buried so deep he didn't even see it: the terrifying notion of a universe where selfless acts prevailed. "Desire," he mused.

"Desire defeated her, as you said it would." Iso didn't see any reason to be concerned.

"Selflessness," he whispered and gave an involuntary shiver. The card dropped from his hand as he stood. It landed face up on the table and Iso saw it depicted two swords and he thought of Clovis and Sef, and of the inevitable duel that must come.

Torrance Rowley sat outside his tent enjoying the morning sun, adjusted the mirror and tried again. He hated shaving.

"You missed a bit uncle," someone gibed.

He looked away from the wrinkled face in the mirror, and to Marcus's youthful face. "Someone without a whisker to their name advises *me* on shaving?"

"Sorry coven-father." Marcus thought he looked comical with soap plastered all over his scalp and he tried not to smile. Rowley's razor blade hadn't touched his face in over twenty years but he kept his skull as smooth as a crystal ball.

"You won't be young forever Marcus," he chuckled to himself and went back to shaving.

"And that forest sitting below your chin could do with a weed," he continued, unperturbed.

"Just like your mother, full of advice nobody wants to hear," he sighed. Marcus's mother, his sister, had been a great loss, leaving him as the ten year-old's only relative, but Brimstone was his extended family and each loved the other.

"I'm away to do the washing uncle." He held up an empty laundry basket as evidence. Rowley had badgered him about it all morning.

"Get that bed-shaped, no-good, Janice to lend a hand." He skilfully swiped the blade over his head as he spoke.

"She's already out gathering berries."

"Huh! And likely eatin' them all too." Marcus left with a smile, leaving his uncle to finish his morning ritual and after a few more strokes with the razor he was done. "Rowley lad, you've done it again." He admired his perfectly smooth scalp and patted it fondly, before packing his kit away, dousing a cloth and finishing with a wet rub down.

Brimstone-coven wasn't named for the devil as many would think, but for the butterflies here. Like Kolfinnia, his original home was gone. Brimstone was less than six months old, but it had the feel of a familiar sanctuary and was home to almost a dozen witches including himself and Marcus. It was good to be back. Last month he and some others went fighting again, this time at Salisbury, before returning home.

Now he was looking forward to a long period of peace. The Illuminata's claws had been blunted, the hysteria about witchcraft was ebbing and Brimstone was well hidden and protected by spells. In fact, Rowley was so confident of their safety, that he'd begun a long term plan of building stone and turf huts, thinking they'd be more snug when the winter set in, and all the winters after that.

A small group was making ready to set off on a short patrol. Rowley's chief ward, Bernard Wessex, was leading them out. The two had been friends since boyhood and the only thing that set them apart physically was that Rowley's beard was an inch longer and Bernard's arms were heavily tattooed with dragons: Oak and Holly of course. "See if you can find us some yarrow." Rowley finished rubbing his scalp and noted blood on the towel. "Can't be perfect every time," he shrugged.

"I'd sooner keep an eye out for intruders." Wessex, the more practical of the pair, scowled.

"You worry too much Bern."

"These are dangerous days," he reminded him.

"They *were* dangerous days and the worst is over. Didn't we survive the monsters of Salisbury and come home without a scratch?"

"Many good witches didn't," Wessex put a hand to his heart.

"Aye," Rowley did likewise. "Blessings on 'em, may they find a worthy door on Evermore. But in the meantime we've a coven to run and yarrow's good for wounds."

"I'll add it to my list," he huffed, and turned to where a small party of witches were making their way through the trees towards them. Three men and two women, all of them barely in their twenties. He ushered them over and began his briefing. "Now remember, keep to wooded cover, keep talk to a minimum and keep the next person in sight at all times."

"Ward Wessex is right," Rowley smiled at the young faces. "But it's a gathering party not a war party. So try and enjoy the day too, and some yarrow wouldn't go amiss."

"Can never be too careful." Wessex patted his wand and knife, and the troupe set off. Each bid their coven-father good morning as they passed and Rowley watched them go thinking the next generation of witches had little to fear, they were resolute, wily and strong. He took a deep breath, held it a moment, then released it with a happy sigh. Yes, he dared believe Britain's witches had turned a corner and their luck was on the up.

Marcus could have washed in the stream above the waterfall but he liked the pool below and the way the thundering water echoed around the rocks. He picked his way down the banks, which were slick with last year's sycamore leaves, carrying the heavy laundry basket over his shoulder. It would be twice as heavy when he was done and he knew he'd have to make two trips back. He tried a fully laden basket once and ended up slithering down the slope and into the pool. He'd had to wash his own clothes afterwards and he was wet through and exhausted when he got back, but pride stopped him telling anyone why the laundry had taken all day.

Once in the shady pool he kicked off his boots, rolled up his trousers, steeled himself and waded in. Although the weather was hot, the water seemed immune to puny things like physics and it felt wilfully cold. He hissed through clenched teeth as the waters climbed his bare legs. This was his real reason for coming here: to test himself. He still didn't have his own lightning-staff, and was considered too young to fight, and so he endured the cold just as the adults endured battle in the name of witchcraft, but there was another more tender reason also. His mother, Elwen, was born under the sign of the fish. Whenever he was near water he imagined she was close by watching over him.

He stood still, letting the roaring falls fill his head and the waters chill his blood, using both to find stillness. After a while he didn't feel the cold any longer and the rushing waters felt to carry away his troubles. *Even the most mundane tasks, if done with care, can honour the serpent-twins*, father Rowley often said. With this in mind, Marcus took up the soap and began scrubbing.

Rowley unpacked his chisels and set to work again. They had found a fallen tree a week ago and he had already started carving it, beginning with Halla's sublime face. He was sat astride the trunk lovingly adding her holly-shaped scales when someone addressed him.

"How's Marcus?" Beth Waring stood admiring his work.

Rowley looked around. "Washing laundry."

"Again?"

"It's a ritual for the lad." Marcus might think he didn't know, but he did.

Beth nodded sadly, "Blessings on Elwen."

"Blessings on her," he echoed, and then stretched and appraised his progress. "I'm thinking Beth, come winter solstice I might take Marcus on a trip to Stormwood for their winter feast. And I'm hoping he might get to meet Clovis."

"Oh yes, the fabled Therion. Is he all they say?"

"Like a storm in a bottle!" he whistled and shook his head, thinking of his brief visit to Stormwood earlier that year.

"It's a hazardous journey for a lad in midwinter though."

He threw his hands up. "I keep saying – the dust is settling and witches are the least of the Knighthood's worries."

"Ever the optimist!"

"I do my best." He gazed down at Halla's serene face. *Am I right my Lady? Is this most recent nightmare ended?* Halla stared up at him from the wood grain, but just like her living counterpart she maintained her inscrutable silence.

"Well, there's the moaning sod's yarrow." Wessex used phrases like 'moaning sod' with affection. He handed it over to Sam Danby, who put it in his satchel.

"Yarrow's meant to be a favourite of fairies, isn't it?" Like the rest, twenty year-old Sam adored Ward Wessex.

"Fairies love the stuff, and they make a fearsome brew with it." Wessex passed around a jar of damson preserve and everyone dipped their bread in it. They were taking a rest in a hollow surrounded by trees.

"Really?"

He looked at each of them in turn. If he hadn't been a witch he'd have been on the stage. He loved tales and drama, and best of all his tales were true. "Let me assure you Sam Dandy, Marion Elcott, Frederick Penbridge, Louisa Stour and Charles Keeping, that I can say with hand on heart that I have not only communed with fairies but I have supped with them too. And a thimble-full of yarrow ale as made by the flint-fairies of Penrith was strong enough to lay me on my back. I woke up three days later with a crow thinking I was a dead 'un, and robbing the pennies from my pocket. No word of a lie." They all knew it was true. Wessex was a witch who'd been places and done things.

"I've tried the spells, but I've never glimpsed the faded-realm," Marion admitted.

Wessex would never say, but youthful Marion was his favourite. She reminded him of his own daughter, but her strong likeness meant fresh grief. "Such spells aren't only about seeing fairies Marion lass, to see the faded-realm is to see a whole and secret world. No wonder many witches never master it." They all looked glum at this. "But rest assured, as long as Brimstone stands I'll endeavour to school you all in the knack. Just think twice before you accept a drink from them."

"Have you ever walked in the faded-realm?" Frederick knew this bordered on the impossible, but with a man like Wessex there was half a chance.

"Sadly nay," he confessed. "One would need a pact-of-grace, not just to get there but stay safe once within their borders. Fairies can be wicked folk on their own turf."

They suddenly had a hundred questions about this but Wessex put the lid back on the jar, and the conversation, and stood up. "Come on. We'll scout out to Temple Monkton and back, but from here on it's ears open and mouths closed." He set off without another word and his adoring witches filed after him like cubs behind a bear.

Marcus concentrated on scrubbing each garment, knowing in his heart that his mother was watching and wanting to make her proud. And because he took his duties to heart he didn't feel the water's icy touch, which in turn meant that Chentek didn't see him.

He was wringing dry a pair of trousers, and getting drenched in the process, when he heard a noise that caused his skin to bristle with goose bumps. It sounded like the chattering of a million birds, a hungry sound full of malign intent. He froze, clutching the wet garments, and rolled his eyes upwards. There wasn't a bird in the sky but the noise grew louder. *Stay still, stay cold.* The voice might have been intuition, but Marcus knew otherwise.

The ridge above was a dark crescent against the sky, and nowhere did he see a single bird even though his ears screamed with them, but as he watched, a lone figure skulked into view. Right away he knew it wasn't human. It was just a black shape moving swiftly from tree to tree, and two other creatures crawled along behind it. Both looked disconcertingly like giant spiders. *Stay still, stay cold.* The waters rolled over his lower body, cooling his core and masking him and he knew his mother was in those waters protecting him. The black figure slithered out of view, followed by the two crawling things. He dare not move to follow their progress, and so he remained frozen in the innocent act of washing, a deceptive snapshot of a peaceful life that was soon to be shattered.

They formed a rough line and patrolled the woods using spells just as Wessex had shown them. They strove to see the faded-realm behind the day-to-day world, and catch the signs and signals that only a witch can see. With patience and effort Marion could see glowing trails where a vixen in heat had passed hours before. Frederick heard an owl's steady heartbeat from the branches high above, as it snoozed away the sunlight hours. Charles tasted a poet's heartfelt words spoken to his beloved when they had frequented this place a night ago. Louisa could hear the delicate tinkle of bells announcing a fairy wedding somewhere tantalizingly close. Sam was privileged to see a raft of dandelion seeds carried by the breeze briefly form the face of Lord Hethra himself.

Miracles were all around them, yet the most incredible miracle was wholly dependent on chance. If he hadn't looked in that direction with just the right intent, Wessex would have missed it and Heili would have died alone. She had curled up amongst a cluster of primroses. A small soul, hidden from earthly eyes and too weak to call for help, concealed by the very flowers she was born to shepherd. It was a miracle indeed that he saw her.

"By Hethra's grace what's this?" He knelt and scooped something up. The others were roused from their magical patrol and quickly clustered around. To their eyes, attuned though they were, Wessex held nothing but thin air.

"Ward Wessex?" Sam didn't like the look on his face. "What is it?"

Wessex spoke to the fairy, already knowing she was dying, "Small soul, what in Oak's name became of you?" He seemingly spoke to nothing, which unnerved his companions even more.

Heili forced open an eye and looked his way. "The iron-fays," she uttered.

"What does he see?" Sam couldn't see a thing.

"Shhh!" Marion hissed, "It's a fay, it must be. He's found one."

"A real fairy?" Charles knew nobody, not even a witch, just 'found' a fairy. Something dreadful must have happened.

Five witches struggled to see what Wessex held so tenderly and Marion cried aloud when a tiny figure flickered in and out of view: a primrose-fairy stained with blood.

"The Therion has a rock. It breeds lust for living-iron," Heili gasped. She had flown far and been pursued ruthlessly. Her wings hung in gauzy shreds and her eyes were dull with pain. "The war-fairy's army, it's coming here. Beware. . ." Her last words drained out of her, along with her life, leaving a horrified Wessex holding her lifeless body.

"Ward Wessex?" Sam gripped his shoulder.

"Poor soul." He was a tough man but now his cheeks were wet with tears. "Poor thing, to come so far." He lowered her body back into the primroses.

"Ward Wessex!" Louisa tugged at his sleeve, shaking him out of his trance. "Bernard!"

"There was a fairy," he explained at last. "Didn't any of you see her?"

"Ward Wessex, *look!*" Marion gripped his arm. "Look!"

He tore his eyes off Heili's little body and looked. "Dear Oak save us," he whispered.

The whole wood was full of fairies.

He counted his breaths and only when he got to a hundred did he dare to look. The chattering sound had passed and the ridge was empty. The black creature and the crawling things were gone. He sprang into life and dropped the sodden clothes into the water, forgotten now. He charged through the pool, clambered onto the bank and ran, heedless of the slippery rocks and leaves, knowing he had to get back to his uncle before it was too late.

Wessex had never seen so many. Every species of the wood must have been there, and in vast numbers. He saw fairies of oak, beech, ash, elder, holly, limestone, granite, quartz, spider-silk, celandine, copper, peppermint, sorrel, sunlight, dandelion, toadstool and fungi, and a hundred others he'd never set eyes on before. Every fairy of the wood was sat watching them. The trees hung thick with them and the woodland floor was covered so completely that not a blade of grass showed. Without thinking he dropped to one knee and bowed, and a moment later his witches followed. All six knelt, knowing only something calamitous could prompt an entire nation to reveal itself so completely. Although bowed, Wessex detected a faint glow and he looked up to see an oak-fairy regarding him, but this was no ordinary oak-fairy. His four wings were as oak leaves, and twisting horns like branches sprouted from his noble brow. He burned with an inner fire as vivid as young acorns and carried a slender staff tipped with acorns cups. Wessex understood immediately this was none other than the wood's Burning Heart.

"You are Ward Wessex?" His voice was like the rustle of leaves.

He risked a fuller look. "Aye, I am Wessex, Ward of Brimstone-coven."

"I am Kercus, the Burning Heart of Tresslain Wood," he announced and floated closer.

Wessex was stunned. Names were power, so why would a fairy just reveal itself and offer its name on a plate, especially a Burning Heart? Something was very wrong indeed. "Lord Kercus, let me say how honoured –,"

"War is coming," he interrupted.

He looked again to where Heili lay amongst the primroses, angry now. "What vile thing did this?"

"All nations are at risk," Kercus warned. "A Therion brings an army of iron-fays, led by a war-fairy never seen before on this sphere. Already many millions of our kin it has slaughtered. They head to Brimstone as we speak."

"Rowley's practically all alone back there!" he spluttered.

Kercus's green eyes burned. "To stop the infection, the war-fairy must die. We cannot do this alone." Now he came to the hard part, "Will witches fight with us?"

For a man like Wessex there was only one possible answer to that, and a second later six witches raced through the woods heedless of secrecy, flying at reckless speed and leading a vast army of fairies. Wessex had been right to be cautious; last year's nightmare was far from over. In fact, it had only just begun.

"Curious?" Rowley set down his chisels and looked to the sky. It sounded like the heavens were full of angry starlings, but all he saw were harmless clouds. He slid from the trunk and stood in a carpet of wood shavings, listening. The noise was growing louder and a feeling of dread stirred in his belly. "Something's wrong," he said to nobody and reached for his wand, but a fraction too late.

"That won't be necessary Torrance Rowley." The voice was like iron wrapped in silk.

He spun around and confronted a Therion. *Clovis?* he thought, bewildered. "Clovis, yes, tell me of him," the stranger asked, alerted.

Rowley raised his wand, but couldn't quite remember the spell he wanted. "Who are you?" It took great effort to summon the words, and the woods seemed to be fading, leaving the Therion's emerald eyes looking even brighter. He didn't even register the two amalga creeping forwards to flank their master. One conjured from ropes, the other from chains. Both resembled huge spiders.

"Who I am isn't worth telling." Sef couldn't risk killing him. He needed his head. "What *is* of consequence is desire, Torrance Rowley. Tell me your desires."

"I am a witch and sworn to protect this coven," he challenged, but the funny thing was he couldn't remember the coven's name.

"You are tired Torrance, tired of grief." As he spoke Sef shook open the neck of the gelding-sack ready to fill it. "I know why your heart is heavy, and I know how to make it light again."

Elwen? he wondered. Hadn't he just glimpsed her there in the stranger's emerald gaze? *Elwen, is that you?*

"Yes," Sef promised, gliding ever closer and reaching for his sword. "Yes, you can have Elwen back, a mother for Marcus, and a sister for a coven-father."

"Elwen." His arm melted and his wand pointed impotently at his feet. *Is that possible, can this thing bring her back?*

"Oh yes," Sef promised. Rowley's desire was so plain he could taste it. "I promise that you and Elwen will be reunited very soon." The first inch of steel glided from its scabbard and Sef smiled. This was a lot easier than he'd anticipated.

Rowley watched the endless green jungle grow deeper and closer, ready to swallow him, and waiting there for him was Elwen. The stranger appeared to offer his dearest desire, but something in his words nettled Rowley, like a slippery contract or a cruel riddle. *But Elwen's dead,* he thought. *How can we possibly be reunited?* A tiny spark flickered through the haze. *We'll only be reunited when I too am. . . dead.* The spark became a flame. Dead. That's what the stranger promised: death. Rowley penetrated the deceit, the drowsiness melted and he swung his wand accompanied by a furious roar.

Sef was terrifyingly fast. He dipped backwards, whipping his sword free in the same instant, and slashing at Rowley's unprotected belly. Steel bit through flesh, but not mortally. It was imperative he wasn't killed.

Rowley didn't feel the strike. The steel was too sharp and his fury was too great, instead he lunged with his wand and commanded the air to disperse, creating a powerful vacuum. Sef's sensitive ears bulged with the pressure change. The world went utterly silent and he didn't even hear his own agonised scream. He staggered free, before the vacuum sucked his eyes from their sockets, and struck again, this time with a brutal fist, that slammed into Rowley's jaw.

Rowley saw stars and the world rocked. The next thing he knew he was laying amid the wood shavings and the black Therion was towering over him, but he looked disorientated. Rowley clawed at his belt, aiming for his knife, but his hand just groped over his bloody shirtfront. That's when he finally saw that he'd been wounded. Instead, he raised his wand just as the first of Chentek's slaves landed on his chest, and the amalga's first limbs began to snake towards him.

Sef shook away the pain and saw Chentek's host crawling on Rowley's front. He landed hard, knees either side of the old man and swept them aside. "No! Feed only on my command! This one is MINE!" He gripped Rowley's neck and shoved his head back, aiming for a clear strike at his throat. Iron-fairies buzzed around him, crazed by blood. Sef raised the blade, just as Rowley jabbed his wand into his ribs.

"DIE!" he spat, and his intent exploded through the wand.

This vacuum ripped the air from Sef's lungs. His chest froze and the sword stroke went wide and sent up a harmless shower of leaves. A dry gasp escaped his mouth and he collapsed across Rowley, but although he fought for breath, he still gripped him tight.

Rowley was weakening. Already he'd lost much blood and the Therion was dreadfully strong. He jabbed the wand again, but the magic was fading. Sef countered it with will alone, and disgorged the spell in a torrent of stale vapour. He could breathe again, but his chest burned with pain. This had quickly become personal. He wouldn't slice his head off, he'd tear it off with his bare hands. Sef bared his fangs and sank his claws deeper, intending to rip the head free, but a certain 'bed-shaped' witch had just returned from collecting berries, and she had other ideas.

Janice Strong never went anywhere without her lightning-staff and today was one of those days she thanked Hethra and Halla for never breaking that rule. "YOU'LL NOT LAY A FINGER ON HIM!" she shrieked. Sef looked around, but there was nothing he could do to stop the staff crashing into his ribs and the sprite inside from doing what sprites do best.

Janice screamed, the staff blazed and Sef roared. He was flung bodily across the clearing and hammered into the beech Rowley had been carving, while the sinister amalga were hurled backwards like toppled trees. For a surreal moment, witches, Therions and fairies saw nothing but the brilliant afterimage of lightning, while the wood rocked beneath a cracking peal of thunder.

"Father Rowley!" Janice dropped to his side. "Father!"

"Find Wessex, get everyone away from here," he coughed a spray of blood.

She tried to lift him. "Marcus, Jonathon, Katie!" she screamed for help.

"Leave me," he groaned. "Find Wessex, go!"

"No!" she sobbed, hauling him upright. A peek from the corner of her eye told her that the Therion wasn't dead. She could see it writhing on the ground. Worse still, bizarre things looking like living ropes or chains were flailing in the undergrowth. "Got to get you up and away!"

"GO!" Rowley slapped at her shoulder. He also saw the Therion slowly getting to his feet. *By Oak! The thing must be made of stone to survive such an attack!* It was a horrible thought.

Sef clambered up, trailing smoke from singed fur. Janice Strong had hurt him more than any witch he could remember. "Chentek!" he slobbered, "leave the man, but strip that bitch to the bone!"

Janice turned to see the Therion kneeling up, raving in some language she didn't understand, while around her the whirring noise became deafening. Suddenly the sky turned black, as quick as a snuffed candle. But that blackness wasn't inert: it comprised endless tiny bodies. Chentek's swarm dropped on her, driven mindless by the stink of living-iron.

In the next instant she was smothered in tearing jaws and pain exploded through her. She screamed and staggered around the clearing, clawing at them, but in mere seconds Janice was eaten to the bone and another soul began its journey to Evermore. A last flash of lightning was her thunder-sprite returning to his realm, proof, if any were needed that Janice Strong lived no longer.

Sef lumbered towards Rowley, still smoking, and burning with hatred. An old man and a hag had defied him, and that was intolerable. He saw iron-fairies swarming around him and the amalga were crawling back to his side. Once he had Rowley the fairies could ravage his corpse, perhaps he'd even make the old bastard watch them feast before he dropped his severed head into the gelding-sack. "Coven-father Torrance Rowley," he wiped blood from his face. "Let me reveal to you *my* dearest desire." He staggered to where Rowley was struggling to reach his wand. "*My* dearest desire is to make your pain last from now until this miserable world ends." He stood over Rowley with a foot on his chest and aimed his sword, but for the second time that day his desires were thwarted.

"KILL THEM ALL!" Wessex charged into the clearing, leading five witches and an army of fairies whose numbers were without end. The battle for Brimstone-coven had only just begun.

What followed became legend. Magic and steel had clashed on many occasions, but seldom had magic clashed against magic in battle.

"Kill them all!" Wessex drove towards the Therion, while Kercus's army scattered to engage the iron-fairies. Seeing the ghoulish thing stooping over his friend, and the spider-looking amalga hovering close by, fury consumed him. "OAK ENDURES!" he roared.

Sef readied himself. As Wessex powered his staff in a stinging blow, he countered expertly with his devastating sword, slicing the staff in half.

The lightning-staff exploded and both witch and Therion were sprayed with flying shards. Splinters embedded themselves in Sef's muzzle and Wessex's cheek. At the very same instant lightning blinded everyone and thunder roared so loud that Sef's ears bulged and pain filled his head. Wessex was thrown hard and skidded through a carpet of leaves, leaving a trail of fresh earth. A brilliant spark shot upwards and he watched in despair as Torn, his thunder-sprite of a lifetime's companionship, streaked upwards and homewards.

Sef blinked away the dazzling blindness, only to see Wessex bearing down on him: wand drawn and teeth bared. Without thinking he whirled his blade, but Wessex's wand hit home a millisecond sooner and the spell was unleashed. A divine wind blasted Sef off his feet threw him across the clearing and slammed him against the beech trunk. He was almost bent double, before the spell's momentum flipped him over and sent him spinning through the air.

Wessex wasted no time, not even to see if Rowley was alive. He vaulted the beech, grabbing a chisel as he went, and charged Sef again. The thing was pushing itself upright, but it looked dazed and Wessex took his chance.

He dropped clean onto its back and brought the chisel down hard at the base of his skull. The blow was vicious and flesh parted and bone glinted, but the chisel didn't part the vertebrae. Sef wailed in pure agony, and empowered by fury he jerked upright, sending Wessex tumbling back, and he whirled his sword. Wessex rolled sideways at the last moment, and 'luckily' for him the blade sliced through his arm and not through his chest. His forearm was cleaved right through between the elbow and the wrist and it dropped to the ground where it clenched once and then lay still.

Sef would have killed him right there, but a scream drew his attention. Marion charged into the fight, aiming her staff for the kill. He had less than a second to calculate the threat, but it was enough and Wessex saw the inevitable unfold in cruel detail.

"Mari no!" He tried to shove himself up, forgetting his severed right arm, and fell back. "Mari!" The scream left his mouth just as Sef's sword powered forwards.

"Ward Wessex!" Marion never even saw it. All she saw was her beloved Ward lying in his own blood, and perhaps compassion got the better of her. The last thing she saw was the glint of fangs as Sef's steel pierced her heart, and then mercifully she saw no more.

"MARI!" He saw her flop sideways and crash to the ground and the Therion turn its attention back to him, but he was ready. He knew how to harness his anger, and by Oak he had a mountain of it. He disregarded his severed arm, coven-father Rowley, and even Marion, and jabbed the wand towards the creature and this time called upon Hethra's grace to finish the murdering bastard. "OAKEN LORD DEFEND THIS REALM!" he bellowed.

Instantly, branches were ripped from the surrounding trees and sent spinning. Every tree there with rotten limbs or storm damaged boughs willingly lent them to the fight. Sef saw his peril and staggered backwards, sword drawn. He screamed and roared, as he fought desperately to swipe them aside, and ended up lashing blindly at all and everything.

Wessex lay in a growing pool of blood, listening to the Therion's furious screams. Twigs, leaves and branches whipped overhead like bullets and the Therion was lost in a vortex of wreckage. Wessex saw the world through a glaze of tears, but he steeled himself against the pain and gave his all to keep the spell flowing. *I'll see you soon Mari,* he promised her, but first he had a monster to kill.

Wessex's young witches saw their Ward hurtle towards the Therion, and much as they longed to fight by his side they had an evil of their own to combat; two hideous constructs lumbering from the undergrowth. Both resembled giant spiders, but made from chains or ropes, and they moved with relentless speed. Charles screamed and veered right, closely followed by Sam, and both of them set upon the thing that rattled like chains, while Frederick and Louisa went left to tackle the one writhing like a nest of snakes.

"What in Oak's name is it!" Sam yelled.

"Magic!" Charles jabbed his staff. Sparks flew and the creature jerked. Sam joined him, dodging flailing chains as he went.

"Sam!" Charles's warning didn't come soon enough.

A chain lashed against his skull, and he saw stars and stumbled backwards. "Charlie!" he groaned, and hit the ground clutching his head with blood streaming from between his fingers.

Enraged, Charles snatched his friend's staff and attacked again, now armed with a pair of thunder-sprites. "THIS IS OUR COVEN!" he screamed, and where the staffs connected, iron sparked. He pressed again, dancing through the creature's whirling arms, trying to strike the body. Something was in there turning dead iron into a living weapon. "This is our coven!" he howled and thrust at something that glittered green and cold. The staff never delivered its killing blow because suddenly his feet were pulled from under him. He fell face-down and instantly more chains slithered over him, squeezing the breath from his lungs. He tried to cry out but a worthless gasp was all he could manage. The chains constricted and he heard bones break and screamed so hard he felt sick, but no sound escaped his lips. In the next horrible instant both staffs were ripped from his hands and he assumed the creature had taken them. But it wasn't the amalga.

"LET HIM GO!" Despite being almost blinded by blood, Sam picked up where he'd left off, and plunged both staffs, right into the monster's heart.

The explosion was deadly. The spell-bottle shattered and the amalga ruptured. Sam was pelted with shrapnel travelling at incredible speed, and killed instantly. His body was thrown across the clearing where it landed in a crumpled pile.

Charles was scorched by the blast and the bonds loosened as the amalga died, but he was too badly injured to escape. "Sam!" he struggled again, but earned only agony, and so he lay there broken and helpless, as all around him witches battled for their lives.

Both Frederick and Louisa heard wrenching screams and the unmistakable sound of a lightning-staff being broken. For a second the world filled with light and shook with thunder. Neither of them knew if a witch had died or delivered a victorious blow. Their once peaceful coven was in chaos, as monsters tore the place apart and a hundred snaking ropes tried to throttle the life from them.

"Try get behind it!" Frederick commanded.

"It hasn't even got a face," she screamed back, "which *is* the behind?"

They'd hit the amalga at least six times, and although many of the ropes were ablaze still it lashed at them with savage strength. Fire might finish it, but not soon enough.

A rope whipped from nowhere and Louisa was brought to her knees, but her scream was instantly strangled as another rope slithered around her neck and constricted.

"LOU!" Frederik tried to run to her, only to have a curtain of ropes engulf him. His limbs were lashed tight, he tripped over his own legs, and before he knew it a rope was worming its way around his throat like a tentacle. "Lou!" Both struggled madly, but the amalga, now trailing smoke and flames, had them pinned and very soon those ropes would kill them as surely as a hangman's noose.

There was a great deal of bravery that day, but all of them would have died the instant they entered the clearing if not for Kercus.

His army of fairies seemed endless. Kercus could see the witches battling the Therion. Branches flew and lightning flashed, and circling everyone, like a vast cloud hungry for blood was Chentek's army. "Kill them!" Kercus roared, all the while scanning the fight below looking for that one prime infector: Chentek himself.

The fairies of Tresslain Wood plunged right into Chentek's horde. The two opposing forces clashed like continents, and the animals of the wood scattered in terror. The trees groaned under the sheer numbers fighting on their branches. Iron-fairies mauled and savaged their cousins until they dripped with blood, but the Burning Heart's forces continued to surge onwards.

Pine-fairies spat dagger needles, and fungus-fairies blew acrid spore-clouds like smoky veils, blotting out everything. Wasp-fairies and nettle-fairies sprayed their victims with scalding venom or gnashed with crushing mandibles. Oak-fairies like Kercus himself wrapped their foes tight in branch-like limbs and cracked open their iron shells as surely as roots break stone, while the stone-fairies themselves were only too keen to pit rock against iron. Fists, claws, talons and jaws punched and snapped. Stone blunted iron just as iron cracked stone, and although they were delicate and virtually helpless, innumerable species of flower-fairy waded into the fight swarming over their enemies and overwhelming them with sheer numbers. But the cost was high. Heads, wings and tiny limbs rained down along with a deluge of blood and the wood was filled with the screams, but the iron-fairies were too crazed and too numerous. The tide was turning in their favour. There was only one way to stop this madness and Kercus searched the heaving landscape of bodies looking for the source of the infection.

And there in the maelstrom of battle he saw Chentek, looking like a burning ember. The war-fairy was crouched on Rowley's body, like a dog guarding the best meat. Seizing his chance, Kercus drove downward like an arrow, weaving through desperate scenes of carnage, but never taking his eyes off that glowing target. He crashed through the iron-fairies surrounding their master, catching them unawares, and right into Chentek. The two rolled away locking in combat and landed in the leaf litter where they continued their struggle. Kercus coiled his rooted arms around the creature's neck and hauled with all his strength. Chentek screamed and there came the sound of creaking iron, but Kercus was woefully outnumbered and iron-fairies dropped on him like rain. "This is not your realm!" he snarled into the war-fairy's face.

"Very soon, it will be!" He reached up and gripped his arms with vice-like claws and squeezed.

Kercus roared as Chentek first broke his arms and then ripped them away. Undaunted, he raised his legs, planted his feet squarely on Chentek's chest and they spread like roots, prying under his armoured hide. "Oak endures!" Kercus screamed. Those tendrils came within a whisker of piercing his heart. Chentek bellowed in pain and the iron-fairies attacked with renewed frenzy, tearing Kercus free. "Oak endures!" he chanted to the end, hoping Hethra and Halla themselves would hear him, as Chentek clutched at his wounded gut and lurched away. "OAK ENDURES!" Kercus managed a final time as his enemies closed in. In seconds his body was just tattered fragments, leaving Chentek to crawl away, and Tresslain Wood bereft of its Burning Heart.

Very soon iron had its victory and the brave fairies of Tresslain Wood were first forced back, then routed and finally slaughtered. They fell in vast numbers, some fled, others crawled away to die but all of them understood the grave consequence of defeat. If Chentek's infection couldn't be stopped, then the entire world would be consumed.

As more fairies fell, more iron-fairies disengaged and descended to fight the witches. As the amalga choked the life out of the unfortunate Louisa and Frederick, Brimstone's last witches finally arrived, drawn from their duties by the dreadful sounds of fighting.

Katie Hemlock fell battling the last amalga. By now it was a burning torch, yet it still possessed enough strength to wrestle her to the ground, but not before she had dealt it a deathblow. The amalga collapsed in a bonfire of flaming rope, as the iron-fairies descended to finish the exhausted witches.

Beth Waring and Jonathon Priest, the last of Brimstone's fighters, charged Sef directly, and although he was battered and depleted he still managed to cut them down with ease.

Wessex collapsed against the ground, not from effort, but from the weight of iron-fairies attacking him, and the furious winds abated at last. By now he was soaked in blood and Sef watched, equally bloodied and breathless as the stubborn old witch was finally finished. Shattered and mangled branches lay all around him, and tattered leaves and blood continued to drift down. Sef turned and surveyed the battlefield. The fight had lasted less than eight minutes, but even he'd never seen anything like it. Begrudgingly, he lifted his sword in salute to Wessex, who by now was smothered in squabbling iron-fairies. "Die well." He spat a mouthful of blood and set off back to Rowley, stepping over dead and dying as he went to take what he came here for.

Rowley looked up at the dark figure standing against the sky. His lower body was soaked with blood and he felt numb with shock. He knew he wouldn't last much longer. "Oak damn you Therion," he rasped.

Sef regarded him coldly and then spoke to Chentek, lurking nearby. "I told you to feed when I gave the order."

He looked up from nursing his own wounds. "Chentek has no need of orders."

Sef swatted him away with the flat of his sword, and the war-fairy landed amid the fairy corpses from where he glowered at him. "Now coven-father," Sef resumed, "we have unfinished business."

Rowley saw the trees were thick with iron-fairies, but he saw something else also, and tried to divert his gaze before Sef noticed.

Sef looked around, however. There was a boy standing at the clearing's edge, holding a lightning-staff. "Boy?"

"Marcus!" Rowley tried to sit up. "Go lad!"

Sef shoved him down with a kick and turned the boy's way again. "Come closer boy and I promise I'll make it quick." Sef held out a hand, wondering briefly how the iron-fairies had missed this scrap of a child. "I said come boy!" he growled.

Marcus backed away.

Rowley saw the boy was holding his old lightning-staff. He must have taken it on his way to help him. If he could stay alive long enough the lad could gain a head start. "Fly Marcus!" he begged, "just go and find her!" He prayed Marcus knew who 'her' was. *Kolfinnia!* he thought pleadingly. *Fly to Kolfinnia!*

"COME!" Sef demanded.

"GO!" Rowley barked his last order.

Marcus backed away another step.

"Chentek: kill the child!" Sef ordered, but the war-fairy just stared up at him and none of the iron-fairies so much as twitched a wing in answer.

"Chentek, kill him!"

"GO!" Rowley agonised and tried again to sit up.

"Down!" Sef thumped him flat on his back, but when he turned again he saw the boy had gone. He snarled in frustration and turned his anger on Rowley. "I'll kill you and then the boy," he vowed.

Rowley erupted a gruff laugh, and took a last look at the carved face of Halla the holly dragon gazing down at him. "You don't know where he's gone."

"I'll find out soon enough." He raised his sword. A second later Rowley's head left his body and a few drops of blood splattered against Halla's beautiful yet impassive face, where they glistened amongst her scales like the first berries of autumn.

CHAPTER NINE

Lions in the Glade

- and a meeting of the minds

'Hurt of others is the greatest balm I know.'
Unitari saying

Today was the day. Kolfinnia had woken up with butterflies in her
stomach, and a headache from all her worrying. Today, they would hold
their important meeting and by dusk Clovis might be wandering away from
Stormwood forever. "That'll be fine Albert, thank you," she directed him.

"Don't want the wind getting under it and it sailing away coven-mother."
He gave the guy lines another tug to make sure, and then appraised the
little pavilion. "There, fit for a dragon."

"No dragons today, just witches." Her smile was nervous and fleeting. "I
think we ought to roll the sides up, that way we can enjoy the breeze," she
suggested, and set to it aided by Albert. A cool breeze would be welcome,
but she also didn't want the coven thinking their leaders were being
secretive. She wanted everything just right, and so they had the pavilion
to shade them, and an odd assortment of cushions placed around a cloth
lain with refreshments. There was already a wasp hovering near the jam,
making it an almost perfect picture of summer. She could see witches
coming and going around the Glade's edge, while the Glade itself was a
deserted sea of dandelions and buttercups. They had their privacy but no

doubt everyone would be curious. Kolfinnia stepped out from the pavilion and shaded her eyes against the sun. "Albert, do you have the time?"

"A quarter before noon," he said after a quick inspection of his pocket watch. "Will that be all Mother Algra?" He wanted to ask other things, like; 'what's this special meeting about?' and 'why do you look so grave?' In the end he settled for something less blunt. "Is everything alright miss? You don't seem yourself."

She looked away from the founding-banner, flapping merrily close by. "Don't I?"

"Just saying what my eyes see, and they see a young woman with a heavy heart."

She returned his smile. "Maybe those eyes might prefer other sights, like bathing mermaids perhaps?"

He grinned, "I'm too old, and the world's bereft of such wonders now."

Not in the faded-realm, she thought. *In the faded-realm there's whole nations of fairies and Therions, and that's where Clovis is heading.*

"Well I'll be off miss, and good luck," he excused himself, and Mally sprang up in readiness.

"Good luck?" she pretended.

"With your important picnic." He offered her a little bow and left her wondering.

The next ten minutes saw the butterflies in her stomach flutter so hard that she worried she might take off.

"Try to relax," Skald advised.

She turned. He was sitting atop his staff, driven into the grass beside the pavilion. "I'll try," she promised emptily.

"At least the matter with Sunday is resolved," he reminded her.

"Hmm," she smiled at last. "Blackwand's here to stay now." Surprisingly she did feel better. She looked down to the picnic and saw a thrush had taken an interest in the scones. It didn't matter she knew, besides, the tension had robbed her of her appetite.

"They're coming," he informed her.

She turned as calmly as she could, and saw Clovis, Hilda and Sunday making their way across the Glade, all of them carrying their staffs. "Do I look coven-motherly enough?" she asked discreetly.

"Try not to fidget."

There was no time to reply. Her guests had arrived. "Sunday, Hilly, Clovis!" she hugged each in turn and invited them to sit. Each planted their lightning-staff at one of the pavilion's corners, and within minutes they were surrounded by thunder-sprites. Kolfinnia saw how the wind lifted their feathers and rustled the founding-banner, and she couldn't picture a less casual picnic. At last, when everyone was seated she began, "Firstly, my thanks for coming, and for Hethra and Halla blessing us with such a beautiful day." She touched her temple and the others did likewise. "Clovis, would you like me to begin?" she invited.

"This problem is mine coven-mother, and I'm obliged to explain myself." His manner was formal today. He took something from his shoulder bag and placed it in the middle of the picnic cloth. It was a flat pebble with an eye painted on it. "This," he patted the stone, "is the cause of my problem."

Kolfinnia felt excluded by the word 'my' and not 'our'.

"Some of what follows you will know," he continued, "but much will be new to you. As you know, I came here almost a year ago, forced to flee my home by treachery. I would have likely died if not for this," he tapped the pebble again.

"It's Janus, isn't it?" Sunday guessed.

He nodded. "I brought this to represent him, and I chose an eye because his true task is, and always was, to open the third eye that has long slept. When that happens, souls will hear their conscience again and the entity we call Self will lose its stranglehold over creation."

"Blessed be," Kolfinnia uttered, as astounded looks flitted between them.

"Janus was *always* meant to ascend to the stars," Clovis outlined, "to open that last great door. But something went wrong and he suffered a dark and total amnesia. His true self has only just returned." He looked deliberately in Sunday's direction, "And all thanks to Blackwand."

"The Flowering-of-Fate?" she returned his stare. "Am I right?"

"Sunday," he prompted, "I think now is the time."

"I was going to wait for the right moment, but. . ." She stole a breath and drew the special note from her waistcoat. "This is the Flowering," she made known, and carefully passed it to Clovis.

He read it with wonder and woe. It had awoken Janus, but that meant death for him. "There exists nothing like this in all creation," he said softly.

Hilda read it next and for a while she was silent, and then she appraised Sunday anew. "Why did you not say?" Her voice conveyed admiration and sorrow.

Sunday watched a chaffinch steal a crumb and smiled faintly. "The Timekeeper sent me this message when I finally arrived at Stormwood. Even in the thick of it at Salisbury and London, I had no idea an even greater battle was being fought – between freewill and fate."

Kolfinnia read it last, and once again she felt the touch of the infinite and her eyes grew misty. "There's a time and place for everything," she swallowed back her emotions. "I think it only proper that Sunday be the one to make this known to witchdom at an hour of her choosing."

"It would be my honour." She retrieved the note, brushing Kolfinnia's fingers as she did.

The Flowering had left him wonderstruck and Clovis took a moment to collect his thoughts. "And so," he began, when he found his tongue again, "because of The Flowering, Janus has awoken and asks to be released, and this is where I need your help." He looked at each of them in turn, and then back to the painted pebble and its staring eye. "On Vega this day was long prepared for, but Janus, true to his old nature, has surprised us all again. He asks to be set free here, on Earth. But I cannot simply break the vessel. I must take Janus to the faded-realm." As they sat in weighty silence, he took a scone and gobbled it in one go. "Very good, Kolfinnia!" he mumbled through the crumbs.

She laughed and her gloom melted. "Eat, everyone, before Clovis takes the lion's share." The others joined in, and suddenly even Kolfinnia felt hungry. They ate, drank and chatted for a while. The thunder-sprites sailed down from their staffs and joined them, and before long the meeting almost felt like any other summer picnic.

"So, I'm told you can see fairies Sunday?" Clovis finished his fifth scone and drained a second beaker of tea.

"It depends how much wine I've had," she joked, "but more precisely, I think fairies see *me* and choose to show themselves, perhaps in light of what happened."

"Happened?" Hilda repeated. "You had business with fairies?"

Her smile shrank. "I found myself in a land of frost-fairies. I owed one of them my life, and repaid him with a favour that changed all their fortunes, and mine too." She nibbled a scone thoughtfully.

"I see," Hilda caught her reticence, and pressed no further.

"Clovis has need of fairy knowledge," Kolfinnia explained, bringing them back to business. "I'm hoping that if we put our heads together we'll find the answers."

Clovis brushed crumbs from his whiskery cheeks. "Janus can only be released within the boundaries of the fairy-nations, this 'faded-realm' you call it."

"Why so?" Sunday ventured.

He took a moment to think. "Long ago each world was tied to the universe in the way a newborn is tied by an umbilical cord. This 'umbilical' connected each world to the next, creating the matrix of the living universe. These special places still exist, even if they are but shadows and memories, and Earth will have such a place of its own, but hidden within the faded-realm."

"The navel of the world," Sunday pondered.

"Correct."

"And you want us to help you find it," Hilda gathered.

"Find it yes, but not to go there. That is my task alone."

"Must it be alone?" Sunday asked, mostly for her friend's sake.

"It must. There are dangers, most tellingly from one of my own kind." He considered long before speaking. "I didn't tell you before, and maybe I should, but someone has come to take Janus."

"You mean those that tried to steal him in the first place?" Kolfinnia guessed.

"Indeed."

"How did he get all the way across the stars?" Sunday asked.

"By forbidden science not suited to picnic conversation," he warned. "Sef will use whatever cursed magic he can. He'll stop at nothing to claim Janus, he'd leave Earth as a withered husk if it suited his plans."

"That's terrifying!" Kolfinnia was even more afraid for him now.

"You said 'Sef', so you already know his name?" Hilda interrupted.

"Sef is merely his title: one dedicated to Lord Self. Unless I recognise him, his real name shall always remain a mystery."

"Why so?"

"Because I shall not bother to ask it before I kill him." His answer was so casual it was chilling, and he moved on quickly. "But first I need to cross to the faded-realm. Once there I hope to negotiate a passage to the place of ascension, this cosmic connection I mentioned."

"Valonia always called the faded-realm 'a dream within a dream'," Hilda remembered. "Do you dream Kolfinnia?" she turned her way.

She smiled at the odd question. "Well, yes of course."

"And have you ever had one of those peculiar dreams when you *dreamed* of dreaming?" Now Sunday and Clovis listened too.

"A dream within a dream? Yes I think I've sometimes had those strange kind of dreams," she considered.

"Very powerful are such dreams, they create a world of their own." She made the sign of Oak. "A world of their own," she repeated, almost religiously.

Now Kolfinnia grasped it. "Hethra and Halla, they dream in that strange way sometimes don't they?"

"They do," she smiled, watching her unravel the puzzle.

"Their dream is *our* world, all that's around us, but their dream *within* a dream is the faded-realm." Her own explanation sounded amazing.

"And soon Clovis will go into that strange place, a dream inside a dream." She turned to him, but he looked away sadly.

"Yes, but how to get to such an abstract world?" Kolfinnia wondered. "Seeing fairies and Therions is one thing, but to venture bodily into their world? I've never heard it done."

"Valonia knew someone who'd once walked there," Hilda confirmed. "And it's much simpler than one might think, all the traveller needs is a pact-of-grace."

Sunday understood instantly. "Fairies can be very hostile. Is a 'pact-of-grace' some kind of permission to go there?"

"Spot on," Hilda confirmed. "Someone carrying one could travel the length and breadth of the faded-realm unmolested."

"A pact always takes the form of a locket, embossed with the seal of one of the fairy-nations," Clovis explained.

"What's inside the locket?" Sunday asked.

"You keep asking the darker questions Miss Blackwand," he half-smiled. Sunday blushed and shrugged.

"So our first task is to find you a pact?" Kolfinnia surmised.

"It seems so," he agreed.

"Therions gradually retreated to the faded-realm, until now they're not seen at all," Sunday recapped sadly. "But surely one of them would have had a pact, to let them come and go, yes?"

"Yes," Clovis agreed, "but, if as you say they're now all vanished, that does not help us." He sat thinking hard.

"You know, we could just ask Rowan?" she added tactfully.

Clovis growled warily, "The girl sees much, but I worry about what might see *her* in return."

"I couldn't agree more," Kolfinnia backed him. "Whatever infernal gift she's got it's more like a curse. I don't like her using it."

"Then we have to find out for ourselves," Hilda proposed.

Clovis racked his brains, while Sunday and Kolfinnia delved deep into memory, hoping for any scrap of information about the elusive 'pact-of-grace'. But Hilda beat them all too it. "I think I know just the person!" she clicked her fingers, "set another cushion Kolfinnia. I'll be back shortly with an extra guest." She rose to her feet wearing a confident smile.

"Hilly? Where are you going?"

"To find someone who might well know where we can get a pact-of-grace."

Clovis was his usual unflappable self, while Sunday, who'd seen far stranger things, also looked unconcerned, but Kolfinnia still couldn't quite believe the situation. Here they were holding their profoundly magical meeting and now their newest guest was none other than the Knight Superior's former squire. "I thank you for coming, Mr Hathwell," she heard herself say.

He was still muddy from excavation works. When Hilda had come and asked 'for a hand with something', he imagined heaving sacks around, or mending a broken spade. He certainly hadn't pictured this. "It's a pleasure to be of assistance," he said truthfully, sipping his nettle-tea, but baffled as to why they needed him.

"Mr Hathwell, what you'll hear is sensitive and must not be spoken of for now," Kolfinnia stressed.

"I understand."

"We're gathered to discuss a possible venture into a place called the faded-realm. Hilda indicates that you've at least heard of the place."

He looked at their expectant faces, feeling very much out of his depth. "Yes, I've read about such a place, it's the supposed realm of fairies, and where the Therion races retreated to." His eyes were drawn to Clovis's impassive face and he saw another Therion, this one lying on a battlefield in Solvgarad.

"Those are the rumours, yes," she agreed. "Hilda tells us you might even know of the whereabouts of a genuine Therion?"

Now he understood, and he looked down at his hands. "Yes," he said quietly.

"Go on," Clovis commanded.

"It was a long time ago."

"What species of Therion?"

"One like, erm. . ."

"Like me," he finished for him.

"Yes, like you. He led a coven against the knights at Solvgarad."

"What happened to him?"

Hathwell looked to Hilda. *Why are you making me do this?* he seemed to say.

"Tell them," she encouraged.

"Must I?"

"This is no trial, we're not here to debate the past."

He took a deep breath. "All of them were killed. The Therion was considered a rarity and Krast had him taken back to London."

"He's still there?" Clovis quizzed him.

"No. Eventually he was moved to Krast's family estate, a place called Helthorn Castle near Edinburgh." He saw Clovis's puzzled frown. "A city in Scotland, way north of here," he clarified.

He nodded in understanding. "And the dead Therion, is he still there, at this Helthorn?"

Hathwell steeled himself. "As far as I know yes. Krast kept him as a trophy."

"Was the Therion stripped of valuables?" Clovis pressed.

He set the teacup down with a rattle and a retort, "I'm no bloody grave robber!"

"Nobody claims you are," Hilda soothed. "Please just answer as best you can."

He took a breath, held it and let it out slowly. "As far as I know everything was preserved as found."

"Then he might still have it!" Clovis sensed the first goal was within his grasp. He turned to Hathwell. "You know where this place is?"

"Of course."

"I'd ask you to take me there."

The rest all gasped in unison. "Clovis, I don't believe anyone's explained to Mr Hathwell how dangerous this might be!" Hilda protested, thinking of the horrible creature only known as 'Sef', and now the others were adding their opinions. Sunday and Kolfinnia were both talking at once and Clovis was trying to talk over the top of them, and the sprites were chipping in with their own verdicts until the peaceful picnic became a heated debate.

None of this registered to Hathwell though. All he'd heard was the worry in Hilda's voice and his heart jumped like a spring-hare. "I'll go!" he shouted. All of them turned to him. "I'll go," he offered again, softer this time. "Besides, I'm the only one who knows where it is."

"Then it's settled." Clovis looked ready to leave right then.

"Almost," Hilda interjected, "if Mr Hathwell's guiding you, then I'm coming too."

Hathwell almost choked on his tea.

"For what purpose!" Clovis argued.

She cast Hathwell a peculiar look that he couldn't decipher. "Because the mission's dangerous and he'll need someone to accompany him back to Stormwood."

"No! It's out of the question." Clovis made a sweeping gesture with his arm, attempting to quash the matter.

"He'll need a guide to get back" she stressed.

Hathwell was flattered, but a little overwhelmed. "It's alright Hilda, I shall go as I promised and return alone."

"I don't think you know just what dangers you'll face."

Kolfinnia saw her chance. "Well if Hilly's going I'm coming too."

"What!" Clovis looked from one to the other, utterly confounded. "No! This is no summer outing, it is a dangerous quest."

"Which is why we're coming." Hilda took Kolfinnia's hand, ". . .Both of us."

"Can I come too?" Sunday added innocently.

Frustration got the better of him, and Clovis just spluttered a stream of half-words.

"No," Kolfinnia ruled. "While we're gone I want you to remain – as Stormwood's coven-mother." The choice was so natural that she said it without thinking. "Will you?"

Sunday was taken aback, but not from vexation. "I'd be honoured," she managed at last.

"No!" Clovis jumped to his feet. "No I refuse to take so many!"

Hilda took a scone, looking totally composed. "Clovis, there's one thing you must know about Earth's witches, the women in particular – they are stubborn creatures that always get their way."

Kolfinnia concealed a smile. "Always," she added, and then also took a scone.

Clovis looked to Tempest and then Skald. "Tell them," he fought back, "tell them they can't come!" Both sprites exchanged wary glances, but it was Strike who swayed the argument.

"Sunday paid a hard toll to win the Flowering-of-Fate." He spoke quietly, remembering all they'd been through. "Kolfinnia and Hilda have the right to decide their own fates, if not, then the Flowering is worth nothing and Janus might as well slip back into forgetfulness." He looked up at his witch, who regarded him tenderly.

"Well put," she complimented.

Strike's words convinced Clovis that he wasn't going to win this. "We four then," he agreed with deep reluctance, staring down at the pebble and its unavoidable eye.

"We four. Clovis's own pride of Lions." Kolfinnia stood and collected the empty kettle.

"Are we done?" Sunday was surprised.

"Hardly, there's one small matter we haven't discussed and I think a fresh pot is in order." She looked down at their bemused faces. "Has anyone given any thought as to how Mr Hathwell will get to Edinburgh without a lightning-staff?"

The realisation dawned on them. "Ah, I see your point," Sunday began. "Well I've travelled far and I know the benefit of a good disguise."

"And of money," Hilda said. "Horrible stuff that it is."

"So we need to organize both, and very soon," Clovis dictated. "Anything else?"

"Trains would be faster and less conspicuous," Hathwell suggested.

"For which we'll need money," Hilda reminded them.

"As I say, more to discuss. I'll fetch some tea." Kolfinnia left them to stretch their limbs, while she went to fill the kettle. Stormwood's coven-mother marched happily across the Glade wearing a huge grin. Yes, Clovis was leaving and dangers lay ahead, but at least she was going with him.

He desired comfort, thinking he'd earned it, and so he took refuge in a tiny cottage overlooking a cornfield. The animals in the adjoining barn bleated and lowed, but the cottage's former occupiers were silent. The man was blind and his wife was corrupted by disease. Both were old and Sef killed them with no feeling other than vengeful satisfaction for what Rowley had put him through, but satisfaction wasn't his only motive. By forbidden arts, he used their meagre life essence to help mend his wounds. He left their drained bodies lying where they fell, and now he could hear crows squabbling outside.

Iso sat by the open shutters, where a little window box was luxuriant with herbs, and watched the cornfields glow vermilion in the setting sun. Chentek and his swarm hid in the trees and thatch, where they scurried and scratched like a plague of mice. They were sated for now, and so they ought to be, they had dined on a coven of witches and a whole nation of fairies.

Sef sat next to the kitchen range, which was still hot, nursing his wounds and his ego. When he'd attacked Brimstone that morning, he hadn't expected to earn so much as a sweat, let alone a scratch. Now however, each breath felt like a knife in his chest and his lungs puffed like broken bellows. Janice's staff had scorched his abdomen, and he felt physically and mentally drained by Wessex's magic. No wonder he'd delayed this moment all day. Interrogating a commoner was one thing, but a witch was something else entirely. He cast a hateful glance at the gelding-sack, knowing he'd have to consume the contents and relishing it as much as a mouthful of glass. The witch was still very much alive and if Rowley's mind put up a similar fight to his body then this promised to be a hard meal.

"Time's wasting," Iso hurried him. "Interrogate the witch and we shall have a clear path to Clovis."

Sef coughed and spat. At least the blood was gone. He snagged the sack and dragged it closer. "The witch won't just hand over his knowledge."

"He is but a single witch. You killed a whole coven today, surely one mind will be easily quelled?" Iso dressed the accusation in a compliment.

He looked at the sack, thinking of the battle within.

"You're afraid?" Iso smirked.

Sef was about to retort when his ears alerted him to someone outside. He was on his feet in an instant, sword drawn, and Iso scurried across the pot sink and vanished into his lightning-staff. Sef backed into the corner where the shadows were deepest, watched the door and waited. The footsteps were light and playful, and he calculated it was a child. A shadow fell across the threshold, a diminutive shadow, and Sef relaxed. It was a child. He drew his wand now feeling spiteful and cruel. Rowley had hurt him. . . surely a little indulgence was justified, he thought?

"Granddad?" a scared voice came.

Sef pointed the wand at the doorway. "In here," he growled.

Drawn by the voice, the boy stepped into view and right into Sef's firing line. His wand made that buzzing sound again and scanned the boy's hidden desires. They streamed up through the wand and into Sef's brain where he sampled and sorted them and selected the most potent. And what a desire it was.

"Granddad?" The boy switched the basket he was holding to his other hand, with no idea his inner world had just been breached. But he heard a strange buzzing sound and imagined a bloated wasp hovering in the dark kitchen. "Granddad, you there?"

"Your grandfather is not here William," Sef's voice drifted out of the shadows.

"He's not?" Already the wand was subduing him. It never occurred to ask who the stranger was, or how he knew his name.

"Pain is like rain," Sef quoted mysteriously. "It runs downwards."

"Sir?" He strained to see who was there, but all he saw was the suggestion of two green eyes like lanterns.

"Come closer," Sef ordered, and he obeyed. "Your grandfather beat your father, who in turn beats you. Is that not so?" He drank in William Kind's short and tragic life, and already he felt calmer.

William knew no other life. It hadn't struck him that there might even be another life, until now. The stranger was right: pain runs downwards.

"I see your pain boy, and I see a way to make that rain run *upwards*, would you like that?" His voice was loaded with sympathy.

William nodded once.

"Is that your dearest desire?" For Sef, these words were like the signature on the contract. "Is it?"

"Yes." William's fist unfurled and the basket of apples fell, spilling rosy fruits across the uneven tiles.

Sef watched them roll in all directions. "Yes what?"

"Yes. My dearest desire," he mumbled emptily.

"You can make the rain run *upwards* William, send that pain back where it came from, and beating fists will beat no more, when the heart that drives them beats its last. Understand?"

"I understand." He shuffled forwards and kicked an apple away into the darkness. Outside, the sky was a slab of blood red.

Sef drew a knife from his robes and tossed it over. It clattered against the floor right by his feet. "Take it. Stop that beating heart, and the beating fists will also stop."

William stooped to collect it, but then stopped. He was only nine years-old, but somewhere not so deep down he knew the word 'murder', and he hesitated.

Sef frowned. "You will become him. You will have sons and daughters of your own, and the rain will run downwards. You will do to them what Cedric Kind has done to you."

"I will?"

"Oh yes. . . unless you heed me. Do it tonight, while he sleeps," Sef concealed a smile.

William bent and cautiously took the knife.

"Brave lad. Now go William. Defy God, and make the rain fall upwards." He shoved his will through the wand and drilled it into the boy's head, eclipsing all selflessness. He wanted to hurt Rowley through this helpless child.

William dropped the knife into his threadbare jacket and backed away, but just before reaching the door he turned. "I brought apples for Gran' to make a pie with."

"You're a good boy William. I'll see that Betty gets them," he lied.

He turned and walked away into the deepening dusk, following a very dark path. Sef listened to his footfalls grow fainter, until they were swallowed by the clamour of crows. After a quarter of a mile even his ears couldn't catch them, and William was left to face his fate alone.

"Again – reckless," Iso condemned when they were alone.

Sef limped to the table and flopped down, ignoring him.

Iso landed in front of him. "I said reckless. The boy might recover and tell others we are here."

He regarded him with contempt. "I thought you were a thunder-sprite, not an old mother hen."

"Acola will not be pleased when I –,"

"Damn Acola!" he hurled him off the table with a powerful swipe.

Iso shook away the indignation and flapped up onto the sink a safe distance away. "You take unnecessary risks Sef, and gamble when you've already won. You should have killed the brat. Have you forgotten why we came so far? Janus and Clovis still elude you."

"Don't lecture me little mother hen! I serve only Lord Self. And William has gone to do the Lord's work. That's a lesson even the mighty Acola would do well to remember."

Iso glowered at him, silently swearing he would convey every word back to Acola. "As you wish," he dismissed the matter.

"Now. As you fear our discovery so constantly, keep watch while I conduct the interrogation," Sef shooed him away, and pulled the gelding-sack closer. It was time for coven-father Rowley to divulge his secrets.

After they hammered out the details, the meeting in the Glade broke up. "May I tell Ben what we discussed?" Sunday asked, watching the others wander off.

Kolfinnia caught her meaning. "Things were a little shaky when I saw you last night, is all well?"

She smiled bashfully, "Very well."

"Then yes, tell him." She was happy for her, but Clovis was drifting away, and he'd been subdued since being overruled about them coming along. "But keep it to yourselves until tonight." She didn't wait for a reply but jogged after him, only to find Rowan waiting patiently by the founding-banner.

"Have you all made up your minds?" she asked worriedly.

"Yes. I'll tell you as we go. There's a lot to get ready." And to prove it she set off after Clovis at a brisk pace, trailing Rowan beside her. "Clovis!" She bounded up to him.

"Coven-mother." He paced along, carrying his staff.

"You're still mad at me aren't you."

"I am going to explain the situation to Janus," he replied curtly.

"Will he approve do you think?"

He gazed down at Rowan and knew better than to lie before her. "I think he will."

"I know you're worried about our safety," she began.

He cleared his throat. "Mr Hathwell's help is crucial, and while your company is a blessing I'm troubled."

"Troubled?"

"That both you and Hilda are coming for the wrong reasons."

"*Wrong* reasons?"

"The Sef will use desire to undo us. Perhaps I'll stop him first, but be warned. Know your desires else they'll undo you." He hoped her concerns were selfless. If they weren't, then Sef would have readymade weapons against them. "Now, if you'll excuse me." He stalked away without looking back, leaving Kolfinnia fuming and Rowan puzzled.

By early evening the coven was buzzing with gossip, all of it stirred up by a cryptic notice pinned to Crow-top's tree trunk. "What's it say Sal?" Albert hadn't brought his glasses.

Sally Crook took the note. "It's a coven-mother's request." This constituted a legal document in coven politics. Albert helped her onto a little stool and she stood and read aloud for all of them.

Witches of Stormwood, your coven-mother & father are engaged in planning a mission of the most urgent nature. Rest assured that Stormwood is in no danger, but to this end we ask for your assistance. Firstly we are in need of any surplus clothing of the kind that might have been taken from the ruins of Wellesley Hall. The garments must be in fine order and be clean. Secondly, we are in want of silver trinkets such as jewellery and cutlery.

By decree of Kolfinnia Catherine Algra and Clovis Augmentrum.

Blessings on Stormwood and its witches.

"Silver titbits and old clothes?" Albert scratched his head.

"Not just any. They've got to look like lords' and ladies' garments," Sally tapped the note again, as everyone gathered closer.

"Suits, bonnets and dresses and such like?" he pondered.

"I expect so," she shrugged.

"But who's got owt like that?" someone chipped in.

Sally looked around. "I know you have for one thing, Brian Siddle. Didn't you take a ladies' gown and corset from Wellesley Hall before we ran for it!" The crowd exploded with laughter.

Brian, a young man with a squint, flushed crimson. "Me mam needs 'em for a rag-rug!" he protested.

"Aye I'll believe you. It wasn't your colour anyhow," she countered.

"It wer for a rag-rug!" His complaints were swallowed up by more laughter, and Sally gestured for a little quiet.

"Now then, I know Wellesley was a hard fight, and whatever you took away from that place was nothing compared to what *it* took away from you." They calmed down at the memories. "But Kolfinnia's obviously got some serious business on the boil, and so if anyone's got anything they ransacked that might help her, I say hand it over." Cheers and claps greeted this. "You heard the note: good quality clothes and silver odds n' ends. Now off you go!" The crowd dispersed and Sally caught Brian's arm. "You still got that dress?"

"Might have," he shrugged, "I just grabbed whatever I could that day."

"And why not. No harm in takin' a few rags and trinkets. I think we paid in blood for all and more besides." She was serious now. "And I was only jestin', I think you'd look lovely in maroon."

He just gave her a wry smile. "Me mam said it wer no good for raggin' anyhow, the weave's too fine." He sauntered away to fetch what plunder might be useful, leaving Sally wondering about Kolfinnia's plans.

"You said I would find a way Janus, and I have." Clovis sat cross-legged before the vessel in the privacy of his shelter. The carved figure hovered motionless in the fluid, saving his strength. Clovis briefly wondered how it must feel to be surrounded by every lie and hurtful thing you ever said. "Don't worry Janus, soon we'll set you free. I promise." He bowed respectfully, and when he looked up he saw the figure slowly turn once. Janus had heard. He was about to leave when Janus spoke, and while it must have taken great effort, the price was worth it. Janus reminded him of something important, and as soon as he finished, he returned to silence again. "You truly are the master of doorways," Clovis thanked him, feeling better about Kolfinnia coming along now. Now all he had to do was swallow his pride and go and tell her.

The pavilion in the Glade became the coven's rallying point, and witches deposited useful plunder there. 'A mission of the most urgent nature' was the phrase on everyone's lips, and as might be expected there was a murmur of disquiet around Stormwood.

By nine that evening, sacks and bundles surrounded the pavilion. The activities briefly stopped for sleeping-spells, during which Hathwell again sat beside Scarlet Tanner, and again felt that magical pulsing in his palms. Once the lanterns were lit and the spells were said, Stormwood continued gathering, speculating and worrying. By ten o'clock, when it was too dark to carry on, Kolfinnia summoned everyone, young and old, to the Glade and explained their plans. In light of her spat with Clovis she had planned a rather dry speech, but as they gathered he took her aside for a quiet word. "Kolfinnia, a word in the pavilion please?"

Right away she readied for an argument. "Make it quick, everyone's waiting." She disappeared through the tent flaps and he followed. Inside, the plunder from Wellesley Hall looked like a pirate's hoard. Somewhere amongst it, she hoped were items that would help their madcap plan. "Go on?" she hurried him.

"I told Janus of our plans."

"And?"

"He approves."

"Good." She made to leave but he took her arm.

"He said something else."

She raised her eyebrows impatiently.

"He reminded me that I shouldn't mistake friendship for desire," he smiled bashfully. "I'm glad you're coming." He saw her smile faintly and considered his work done. "Now, time to tell all." He gave her shoulder a friendly pat and vanished back outside, leaving her somewhat bewildered.

You're a mystery Clovis, a total mystery, she thought.

Outside again, Clovis helped her up onto the Anvil. She returned his smile and then gazed out across the Glade, which was now a sea of twinkling candles and lanterns, and where over a hundred witches watched intently. She cleared her throat and began. "Firstly – my thanks to all of Stormwood for your efforts," she pointed to the bulging pavilion. "And now I'll repay your trust and tell you just why we need such things. Last October many of you fought at Kittiwake, and although there was much bravery that day, in the end it would have all been in vain if not for one witch. Without Clovis and his miraculous companion Janus, we would have made a final stand amid those stones – and we'd have been buried there." Muted supports and a few handclaps drifted up. "And now, at last, we have the chance to help Clovis just as he helped us. The time has come for our beloved coven-father to leave us, as we all knew one day he would." She promised herself she wouldn't cry, but already she could feel her throat swell. She swallowed and continued. "Clovis is journeying northwards, and taking Janus with him in order to set him free. But he will need a disguise and provisions to travel as secretly as he may. Hence the goods you've donated are for his benefit. But our brave Lion of Evermore is not going alone." She made sure not to look his way in case she faltered. "Myself and Ward Hilda Saxon will be going also, and Mr Hathwell is to be our guide."

Now came the biggest shock of all. Both coven-father *and* mother were leaving. This was bad news indeed, and very unlucky.

"She can't leave too!" A child spoke up.

Kolfinnia looked down. It was Emily Meadows, and Sunday was standing with her arms around her, and next to her was of course Ben. "Have no fears, any of you" she soothed them, "I'd be forced to stay if not for one exceptional witch who I trust like no other, and I'm happy to leave Stormwood in her hands. While I'm gone this coven will be governed and protected by none other than Blackwand herself," she said proudly.

The applause quickly swelled, and Sunday looked around, bemused but flattered.

Kolfinnia signalled for quiet and continued, "And so we leave you in safe hands, and tomorrow we prepare our expedition, and with Hethra and Halla's blessings we'll start out in two days' time." She hastily finished with a few stirring words, sparking more applause, before stepping down and finding herself at Clovis's side.

"Well said." He gave her one of his trademark hugs, the kind that leave the recipient with sore ribs.

"I hope you didn't mind?" she asked over the noise.

"Mind?"

"Lion of Evermore?"

He smiled, "It sounds heroic, perhaps I'll call myself that when I get back to Vega." His smiled widened but his heart sank. He had no doubt that he would be a Lion of Evermore, but a ghostly one that nobody would see again, and again he thought of the poisoned vessel, *Will death come quickly?*

"Clovis?" she asked, full of concern.

He said nothing, but did something he'd never done before. He leaned over and gently kissed her cheek. She was stunned, and still struggling for a reply, when a tide of questioning witches surrounded her, and he slipped away without an answer. She laughed and smiled as best she could, but her mind was like a stormy lake. Something about his gesture frightened her, and when it finally hit home her heart juddered: he had just given her a goodbye kiss.

The deed was done, and although what was left of Torrance Rowley now rested within the dark maze of Sef's gut, his mind refused to yield.

Torrance Rowley sat cross-legged in a leafy glade surrounded by towering oaks and a dense thicket of holly. He was contemplative and calm, but he knew that very soon the one who'd killed him would come seeking the knowledge he'd killed him for. His body was destroyed, but just as Sef suspected: his mind was still robust. It was certainly strong enough for him to construct this metaphysical fortress. But now the black Therion lurked at the glade's edge, searching for chinks in his armour.

Rowley knew in his heart that the Therion would eventually overwhelm him. When that happened, his mind would crack open and his spirit would fly to Evermore, leaving all his memories for the creature's taking, but he also knew something else. He knew the longer he withstood the enemy, the closer Marcus got to Stormwood. He sat and listened to confident feet creep through the bracken, and he could feel the Therion's eyes on him.

"Torrance Rowley?" Sef called softly.

He ignored him and focused on keeping the illusion alive. As long as he prevailed, the forest would persist.

"I know you hear me," he tried again, "Lizzie Trent sent me. She told me where to find you."

Division, Rowley thought. *He's using division to break down the forest.* The trees had become the metaphor for his sovereignty over his own mind.

"I killed you Rowley, and when I've conquered your mind I'll find Marcus and kill him too," Sef provoked.

"Marcus will live a long and happy life," he growled, unable to stop himself, and the forest trembled for a moment. Rowley curbed his anger, and directed his reserves back to his defences.

"Where did the boy go?" Sef ruminated. "You sent him somewhere safe. Now where might that be?"

Rowley diverted his mind to the forest.

Sef heard branches creak and leaves rustle, and the light dimmed as the canopy thickened. He spat in anger and stepped back as the trees increased their girth and the barbed holly grew even pricklier. "You cannot keep me out forever!"

"We'll see about that." He never looked around.

"Eventually, you *will* go to Evermore Torrance Rowley, and leave behind all the secrets I killed you for." Sef saw the old man flicker, before growing solid again, and he smiled. "Already you weaken," he pouted. "Be kind to yourself. Your defence of Brimstone was heroic, but now you must find peace. No one would begrudge you that."

Rowley swallowed his uncertainties.

Sef saw how the gentle blade was deadlier than the forceful thrust, and continued, "I salute you. I confess in all my years I've seldom met such a warrior." All souls had a spark of vanity somewhere he knew, and Rowley would be no exception. If he could just ignite that spark it might illuminate deeper levels, like a match thrown down a well. "I shall remember your bravery. Even this construct is a wonder. It must require such strength to maintain it." He patted a tree trunk with pretend affection. "But it must be so draining, and after so hard a fight."

Rowley's thoughts turned to Wessex, and the oaks briefly flushed with autumnal colours, before turning a vigorous green again.

Sef noted it and smiled. "This fight isn't yours coven-father. I came here only to find a criminal, a witch named Clovis. He took something of great importance from my coven. He is a thief, and when I am done here I shall return home. I mean no harm to Earth's witches."

No harm? He thought of the massacre at Brimstone and his anger shifted the oaks, as if by a strong wind, and the leaves briefly glowed red.

"I see you disagree." Sef's tone was reasonable. "I only took such drastic action because Clovis has so completely beguiled you, that no witch would betray him." He tried to push through the holly thicket, but the branches were like iron rods. "Clovis the thief and his outrageous lies have cost the lives of good witches." He shook his head sorrowfully. "Truly nobody is what they seem – are they Torrance?"

Rowley tried to block out the words crawling in his ears.

"And those we love most, in the end hurt us most." Sef licked his lips, and delivered his most poisoned message, "Even Ward Wessex was not all he seemed."

Rowley readied himself for the worst.

"Lizzie Trent told me much. You were a fine opponent Rowley, a pity Wessex never treated you as a fine friend. Your wife Clara, she never told you did she?"

Rowley frowned and the trees wavered for an instant.

"Clara and Wessex were secret lovers." He inched closer as he spoke, and now the thicket was springy and the leaves were tender.

Rowley couldn't disarm such potent lies *and* maintain the forest simultaneously. He bolstered his defences again, but not before the Therion had crept even closer. The thicket recovered its strength, leaving Sef snagged in the middle. "Soon I'll be with you Torrance Rowley!" he hissed.

Rowley sat in the glade, breathing fast and dripping with sweat, and knew the Therion was right. *Fly fast Marcus lad, fly fast and don't look back.* He must get to Kolfinnia before the Therion breached his defences, because when he did, there was nothing to stop the creature from finding Stormwood, and Rowley wondered if even Britain's strongest coven could withstand Sef and his ferocious swarm.

CHAPTER TEN

The witch within

'Skin-deep eyes see only lies.'
Traditional witch saying

One day, that's all they had. One day to prepare, and then they would set out, travelling with only borrowed garments and alter egos to shield them from a hostile world. Rowan seemed fascinated by all the secrecy however. "So you'll dress up as a rich lady?" Her cheeky smile suggested this would be something to see.

"You think I can't pass myself off as a woman of refinement?" Kolfinnia combed the girl's hair as she spoke. They had risen early and were sat on the bunk under Skald's watchful eye.

"And Clovis will be a baron?" She struggled to get this straight in her mind.

"Clovis doesn't look like any man alive, but he looks like a baron. Understand?"

"But I don't understand!"

"A baron is a rich man whose family didn't mix much," Skald elaborated. Both of them looked up to the sound of his voice, somewhere amongst the branches. "And because of that, he has a 'royal' disease, one that makes a man look very hairy, like a bear."

"Or a lion." Kolfinnia knew the plan was tenuous, but it was the best they had. Rowan just scowled, which didn't help.

"I like it." Skald dropped down onto the bunk, along with a few leaves.

"Sometimes the stranger something looks, the more people ignore it."

"Baron Clovis Krast from Hungary," Kolfinnia recited. "With a rare blood disorder. It isn't entirely unknown."

"He's a hungry Baron then?"

"Not that kind of hungry."

"And Mr Hathwell and Hilda are meant to be married!" Rowan covered her smile. This was delightfully scandalous for a child.

"Yes, husband and wife. He turned as red as cherry when Hilda suggested it."

"And now he's your father!" This time she laughed aloud.

Kolfinnia carried on combing and tried not to smile. This was meant to be serious, and having a child pick holes in your only plan didn't bode well. "Baron Clovis Krast is going to Helthorn Castle to claim his share of the family inheritance. Mr and Mrs Saxon are his entourage, and young Catherine Saxon is their daughter," she pointed to herself.

Rowan just giggled again, and Kolfinnia and Skald swapped telling looks. Skald went and perched on the bed head. "You only need your disguises long enough to get inside and find the Therion. If he doesn't have this pact-of-grace then you'll have left before anyone even knows there's no such person as 'Baron Clovis Krast'." He stressed the plan's simplicity.

"Have you chosen a dress?" Rowan asked suddenly.

"There isn't much choice, but I have my eye on one. It's a lovely maroon colour."

"You should just go as you are, you're pretty enough."

"Thank you, but we'd be spotted quicker than a hare can hop. And Mr Hathwell says Helthorn won't be empty. It'll be full of people and soldiers. We have to look right or we'll never get inside."

"Who lives there now?" She wondered if Krast had any children, and immediately felt sorry for them.

"People hoping to claim the place. When Krast died he left a huge mess behind. Now Mr Hathwell says there's an executive fighting over his property."

"Executive?"

"A group of people, all arguing and hoping to grab what he left," Kolfinnia explained.

"Oh! Like evil uncles and wicked stepmothers?"

She smiled at the fairytale trappings. "Something like that." She finished combing and pulled her hair into a ponytail. "Your hair grows by the day."

"I told you, I'm growing it to my feet."

"Like Hilda."

"You know why she's really going don't you," Rowan confided.

"I can guess. Now, let's look at you." She turned her about and noted again that it wasn't just her hair that was growing.

"You'll be alright won't you, all four of you?" Rowan played with a button on her tunic, looking worried. "I don't like the name. 'Helthorn' sounds bad."

"I know," she admitted, "but with the twins' blessing we'll be home within a week, two at most." She bent and kissed her, glad that the girl kept her word and didn't peep. If she had, she would know how afraid she was; afraid that they'd be caught, and also afraid they wouldn't and Clovis would leave. *Either way the devil wins,* she thought. "Now come on. There's a lot to get done today."

The pair climbed down the ladder, closing the hatch behind them, while Skald sailed down gracefully from the open window and Kolfinnia began her last day at Stormwood.

"Mr Hathwell?" someone called him.

Hathwell dropped the silver candlestick back into the sack of loot, and looked around to see Albert Parry. "Ah, good morning Albert. A fine haul," he indicated the assorted goods.

"It'd have burned to nothing if folks hadn't taken it." Albert didn't want him thinking witches were pirates by nature.

"I suppose."

"And a lot of useful stuff in there too." As a witch, Albert believed their true value was how recyclable they were.

"I hope so. But precious little in the way of coins." Hathwell fished in his pocket and brought out a few crowns and shillings he'd recovered.

"That's where I come in handy," Albert tapped his nose. "Miss Kolfinnia asked me to use the silver to make money for your journey."

Hathwell thought the idea of forging coins was quite exciting. "And you want me to lend a hand?"

"I hope so. I haven't had a penny to my name for over thirty years. Do people still use pennies?"

"Some don't even have that much."

Albert shook his head. "Anyhow, I work metal and we have a modest smithy. Would you help me sort the best bits of silver?"

"Forgery's punishable by hanging you know."

"Huh! Being poor's punishable by hanging in this land, lad!"

Hathwell retrieved the candlestick, pleased to see an Illuminata crest on it. "Perfect. We'll have this for starters."

Albert rubbed his hands. "I love a good rummage!"

"You're a magpie!" Hathwell complimented, and just like magpies, the pair set about selecting the best treasure.

"Hilda, I can't possibly do that!" Kolfinnia stood clutching the scissors feeling like someone ordered her to destroy a masterpiece.

"I thought you were going to help me get ready?" she complained.

"Ready yes, but not this." She waved the scissors disapprovingly.

"Oh just the bottom two feet, nothing drastic," she said breezily.

"Flora?"

Both of them turned to Flora to mediate, making her wish she hadn't agreed to help Hilda prepare her disguise. Hilda sat on a battered stool in the pavilion wearing only a long white smock. Her fabulous hair fell loose and trailed to the ground behind her. She had perhaps wisely decided to have it 'trimmed' as she put it, to help their cause. "It's not fair." Flora admired her hair.

"By which I conclude you think it a prudent, if regrettable, course of action?" Hilda noted.

Flora nodded reluctantly. Yes she thought, they already had Clovis to smuggle through the outer world, they didn't need further distractions. "I suppose so. . ."

"Chop away!" Hilda ordered pleasantly.

Kolfinnia shot her friend a horrified look, but received only a hopeless shrug in answer. "Very well then." She knelt and took a handful of Hilda's hair, and feeling like a fiend she began to cut. Flora knelt beside her and offered her the comb.

"Mr and Mrs Saxon have to look like ordinary rich people," Hilda chatted as she worked.

"You sound excited?" Flora smiled.

"In truth I am. I've never been to Edinburgh, or stayed in a hotel and never travelled on a train. I feel like a child again!"

"You're not worried, you know, about what might happen?"

She considered. "I think Hathwell's right, and if we're suspected it'll be as family rivals rather than witches. As far as I know, no witch has walked into the lion's den like this, which makes me believe it will work."

"Apt description," Kolfinnia murmured between snips.

"It's funny, but when he first came I wondered if a squire could ever fit in here, now though he's essential to Clovis's plan." Flora suddenly had a terrible thought, "Hey! You don't think it's a trap do you?"

Hilda laughed aloud, making Kolfinnia squeak in alarm. "Keep still!"

"No, he's not a schemer," Hilda chuckled.

"You're fond of him aren't you?" Flora gathered.

She brushed a stray hair from her lap and looked serious. "Those day at Hobbs Ash with Valonia and the others. I see now that they might have been even darker if not for his help."

Kolfinnia didn't like the mood. "Pass the comb please Flo." Flora dutifully handed it over. A few more cuts and it was done. "There!" Kolfinnia exhaled in relief.

Hilda stood and tossed her newly cut hair. "My word, it feels so light!"

"Turn around," Kolfinnia suggested nervously.

She obliged, showing off her new hair, which now reached just to her hips. "Well?"

"Very practical," Flora approved, "and you got a straight line too."

Hilda took a brush and started combing. "Thank you Kolfinnia, I know it wasn't easy."

"What shall I do with this, it's so beautiful." She looked sadly at the mound of hair.

"Leave it out for the crows, they always need nest material," she said happily. "Now then?"

Both women appraised her. "If anything you look younger," Flora noted.

Kolfinnia gladly put the scissors aside. "You look wonderful, just don't ask me to cut anything else."

"Now, I can't go to Edinburgh in my nightdress, so who'll help me pick out something from all this jumble?"

Feeling happier, they helped Ward Saxon begin the job of becoming Mrs Saxon.

It took them less than an hour, and Hilda knew unerringly which garments were tasteful and more importantly fashionable. *Clovis might look like a lion but I assure you nothing will rouse suspicion more than an unfashionable dress,* she warned. Kolfinnia thought the outer world was so odd that she was probably right. They helped her dress, slowly covering up the witch within with the trappings of a society that feared them.

"There." Both Kolfinnia and Flora stood back.

"Well, how do I look?" Hilda wore a long black skirt with a soft bustle and a matching black blouse with princess puff sleeves and slender cuffs and a white lacy collar showed at her neck. The whole ensemble was figure flattering and smart and with her hair pinned in a tidy bun she was almost unrecognisable. She finished the outfit with a pair of matching gloves and a wide brimmed hat adorned with a handy veil.

"I wouldn't recognise you," Flora said softly.

"Nor I." Kolfinnia suddenly remembered that this was no mere dressing-up party. "You look elegant, and just a little austere, mother," she added, getting into character.

"Ah, very good Catherine, but speak when spoken to child," Hilda practised.

"Is that how people really behave?" Flora scowled.

"Explains a great deal doesn't it," Hilda agreed sadly. "Now, shall we take my new attire for a constitutional?" She picked out a parasol and smirked at their confused expressions. "You'll have to learn to talk like a lady too Kolfinnia. . . a stroll around the coven, that's what I mean."

Kolfinnia obliged by opening the pavilion, and Flora stood opposite, both of them holding the canvas aside as Mrs Saxon emerged into the daylight.

There was sudden and unexpected applause and Kolfinnia was startled to see a huge crowd. All of them had been waiting patiently for their appearance. Hilda opened her parasol and rested it neatly on her shoulder, prompting a few whistles. Kolfinnia offered her an arm and she slipped her own through it and they began their tour of the Glade to the tune of laughter and cheers. Nobody was more surprised than Hathwell. He stood with his mouth agape, watching her. "Good morning dear husband," she winked as they passed.

"Father," Kolfinnia added respectfully.

He watched his new family parade by, and one or two onlookers even gave him an appreciative nod or a 'thumbs-up'.

"Bloody hell!" Albert Parry admired her. "She's a fine looking lass."

He couldn't stop himself grinning. "That's no way to talk about my wife!"

"Bloody hell," Albert said again, and now he had a new daydream to add to the one about mermaids.

Hathwell let out a long sigh, and just like Kolfinnia, when the brevity passed, he felt anxious. They were going into the heart of the Illuminata's world and no amount of planning could protect against bad luck. "Best get on," he told himself and went to fetch more silver, all the while thinking about the elegant lady with the parasol.

Hilda's admirers followed her around the Glade and afterwards she retired to change and alter her garments, making it easier to reach her wand for one thing.

Kolfinnia was joined by Sunday as she took stock of their efforts so far. "Here, a going away present." Sunday handed over a bundle of papers.

"What are they?"

"Albert's forgery skills are admirable, but these are the real thing."

"From your visit to the bank?" she smiled craftily.

"Just a few spares," Sunday shrugged. "Might be helpful on the journey."

She thumbed through the wad of five-pound notes. "There must be over two hundred pounds here!"

"You could buy your own train with that, couldn't you?" Flora guessed.

"Or bribe people," Sunday incited with relish, earning a respectful glance from Flora.

"So Albert's working on the coins," Kolfinnia summarised. "Sally's made contact with our Smoke, who'll meet us tomorrow, and Mr Hathwell's drawing each of us a map, should we be separated. That just leaves my own disguise." She counted off the tasks with her fingers.

"And that's where I come in!" Sunday had been itching for this moment. "Simply *having* money isn't enough. As an aristocrat you'll be expected to look like a high-class young woman."

"Well, I've chosen a nice dress."

"Won't be enough."

"It won't?"

"I can help you look like a well-bred lady," Sunday promised.

"You mean I don't already?" She felt vaguely deflated.

"You will I promise. Let me help you get ready, select your garments and prepare your complexion." She sounded energized, and beside her Flora concealed a smile.

"Why what's wrong with my complexion?" She imagined herself as a ruddy-faced peasant. "Flo?"

"Well, I suppose Sunday's got a point," she admitted. "It wouldn't hurt to cover up as much of Kolfinnia the witch as possible would it? I mean, only for a short time." In truth she worried a lot about this whole venture.

Sunday resumed, "Part of your disguise means looking like a lady who hasn't even *seen* dirt, let alone collected it under her fingernails."

"What!" Now she splayed her fingers and held them out, imagining navvy's hands. "I look fine, don't I?"

"Fine yes, but radiant? Hmm. . . not quite."

"Oh," Kolfinnia slumped.

"Don't worry about a thing! Now tell me truthfully, is there anybody you'd trust more to make you look regal?" Sunday looked around purposefully.

"Erm, well, Flo?"

"Don't look at me!" Flora sidestepped the issue.

"Indeed," Sunday eyed her dirty work clothes, although not unkindly.

"Oh, I see!" Flora retorted, enjoying the exchange. "That old chestnut – finery's more important than food eh?"

Sunday held up her hands. "Admit it Flo, on this occasion finery's vital to the plan's success. Garden magic comes a close second."

"How close?" she smirked, setting her hands on her hips.

Sunday made a tiny gap between her finger and thumb, "Very, *very* close, but still second – sorry."

"Right!" She turned and addressed anyone within earshot. "If Sunday can yield a score of turnips before noon, then she can prettify Kolfinnia to her heart's content!"

"Hang on!" Kolfinnia protested.

"A wager?" Sunday beamed.

"A wager!" Flora confirmed.

"Done!" she accepted.

"Erm, haven't you forgotten someone?" Kolfinnia tried again, but when she saw the pair shake hands she knew they had.

Sunday turned to her excitedly, "Fret not, I won't fail you. I'm adept in garden magic too!"

"They've got to be firm but sweet," Flora interjected.

"I hope you're talking about the turnips?" Sunday teased.

"Oh yes, I can't be wagered for any old turnips can I," Kolfinnia grumbled.

"I shall see you later Flora, with a score of the finest turnips you ever saw," Sunday vowed, and set off towards the gardens.

"They'd better be, my standards are very high!" Flora called after her.

"As are mine!" she returned over her shoulder.

While Sunday planted turnips under Flora's watchful gaze, and while Hilda began sewing, Clovis went and recruited Hathwell for a job. "Albert, I need Mr Hathwell's assistance. May I borrow him?"

Albert was heating a small crucible of silver, while Hathwell had been chopping old spoons into melt-sized chunks. "Aye, I reckon I've enough ingots for a while," he agreed. Clovis said no more, but left the little smithy and its heat and headed into the woods.

"You're not looking for garments in the pavilion?" Hathwell asked as he followed.

"I already have." He held up a sack.

Hathwell followed beyond the Glade and into the old fort with growing unease. At last, when they were a good distance into the woods, he stopped and emptied the sack onto the ground. "There's much I don't know about your world, Mr Hathwell, and much I don't know about you. I want to know what sort of man is going on a dangerous mission with me. Are you honest, brave, sly or cowardly? I know very little, which bothers me." He prodded the clothes with his foot. "Instruct me how to wear these garments and in the process maybe I'll learn a little more about you too."

Hathwell liked his directness. "Well, you don't want dirt on them for starters." He gathered them up, brushed off the pine needles and laid them over a branch.

They spoke little as Hathwell first helped him with trousers, then waistcoat, frock coat and even shoes. All of them were black, which suited the mood. Beneath it all though, he wore his mail shirt and breastplate, and just as well the clothes were on the large side. "Ready for anything I see," Hathwell noted.

Clovis rapped the metal under his shirt. "There's no coming back Mr Hathwell. I'm obliged to take all I'll need." This of course had many meanings.

They continued in silence and Hathwell was starting to wonder how this was helping Clovis get to know him.

"The Therion you once saw," Clovis asked at last.

Here it comes, he thought.

"Did Krast kill him?"

He shook his head. "Bullets fell like rain that day, it could have been anyone."

"Why did it take you so long?"

He frowned, "The battle?"

"You know what I mean," Clovis said impatiently.

He brushed grit from his coat and straightened a lapel before answering. "It was meeting Valonia that changed me."

"But the seeds were already there," he pondered, "so why did it take so long?"

Hathwell knew only truth would suffice. "I was a very different man then. I did my duty without question, and I killed strangers who'd never done me any harm." It wasn't a boast.

"But something inside always told you it was wrong?" Clovis never took his eyes off him as he fastened the waistcoat buttons.

"Yes," he said at length. "Was that conscience?"

"All souls have one, although some speak louder than others." He shrugged the coat into place, and if anything he looked even more impressive in the sombre outfit. "Do you know what makes a witch a witch, Mr Hathwell?"

"You're going to tell me I assume?" He handed over a pair of gloves.

"A witch always listens to conscience."

"And conscience is the language of the inner god," he finished.

"Very good." He pulled the gloves over his powerful hands concealing the claws and fur. "Valonia told you that?"

He considered a moment. "Maybe, I don't remember. It just seemed the right answer."

"The right answer always comes when you listen to conscience, even if that answer is terrible. My scarf please." He indicated the length of black material and Hathwell passed it over.

"Was it conscience that told me to kill Krast?"

"Conscience told you he'd have caused havoc if he carried on living. You did only what you thought was best." He wrapped the scarf around his lower face, leaving just his amber eyes and the crest of his mane showing. "Lastly, my hat."

"Why are you telling me all of this? Because I'm ignorant of your ways?" He couldn't conceal his resentment.

Clovis smiled behind the mask. "I'm telling you because by helping me you'll be playing your part in freeing Janus. And when he does what he was born to do, then souls everywhere will eventually listen to conscience again."

He swallowed his reservations. "A great undertaking then."

"None greater." He fixed the top hat in place. "Now, Baron Clovis Krast is a 'freak' by the standards of this world. He dislikes attention and so keeps covered up."

Hathwell had to agree. All that showed was a pair of gleaming eyes, framed by dense fur. "Won't you be too hot?"

"My real home is what you would call a desert."

Hathwell circled him. The simple disguise was far more effective than he dared hope, until you looked Baron Krast in the eyes that is. "It'll work," he said truthfully.

Clovis made a satisfied 'hmm' sound and then without warning he turned and left.

"Is that it, we're done?" Hathwell stumbled after him.

"We're done." He had learned what he wanted to know.

Hathwell watched the immaculately dressed man stride through the woods, knowing it wasn't a man at all, and the effect was unnerving. "Yes, this might actually work," he told himself.

It was a day for gifts, although sadly most of them marked their leaving, and Kolfinnia received another keepsake, this time from Ben. "Here, there wasn't much time, but I wanted to give you something." He handed over a small velvet bag tied at the neck.

"A going away gift?" She took it and began to open it.

"More a 'thank you' gift."

She peered at him inquisitively.

"For helping me see sense, for giving me the chance of summer rather than winter."

She didn't catch the oblique reference, but then she didn't have to. "I only helped you act on the decision you'd already chosen."

He smiled reluctantly, "You get more mystical by the day; being coven-mother's having an effect on you."

Smiling, she opened the bag and poured a stream of shiny pebbles into her palm. Each was painted with the symbol of Oak. "Ben they're beautiful," she sniffed. "Thank you."

"I hope they bring you luck."

She returned them to the bag, making sure not to lose any. "You know I didn't mean to say you'd done something wrong when I said how you wanted to leave Kittiwake before the battle." This had bothered her later.

"I never thought that," he said truthfully.

"You're one of the bravest witches I know, as well as the most humble."

"Humble?"

"You know what I mean. You never speak of it, but the others tell me of Salisbury, and how you were always in the thick of the fighting."

His smiled slipped.

"Aye, maybe, but I'd have lost my last 'battle' if you hadn't helped me."

"You make a good pair. Two heroes." She embraced him, and he wondered about her meaning of 'pair' and smiled happily to himself.

A lot of people had learned of Sunday's wager and so the gardens were busy and all attention was focused on a humble row of turnips.

Flora counted them. Sure enough there were twenty, and she'd seen Sunday plant them herself. They were adequate, if a little small. She took one and sliced it, while everyone waited anxiously, especially Sunday and Kolfinnia. She nibbled it critically. The texture was firm but the taste was just on the wrong side of sweet. She looked at the expectant faces. *What harm's a little fun,* she thought? "They're delicious," she pretended, "Sunday wins!"

"What!" Kolfinnia exploded, but she was drowned out by fresh applause.

Sunday smiled triumphantly. "This way your ladyship," and she took Kolfinnia's hand and led her away.

Kolfinnia looked around for help, but saw only sympathetic smirks. When Flora winked at her though, she knew. *Flora bloody Greyswan, I'll get you back for this,* she thought without meaning it, and was trailed along behind Sunday to the privacy of the pavilion, as nervous as she could remember.

The pavilion was closed up, but a curious crowd was gathering. "Don't let anyone in." Kolfinnia poked her head through the flaps to where Farona stood guard. She reasoned he was a gentleman and so the perfect sentry.

"Quite a crowd gathering. What if they get ugly and rush the tent?"

"Just keep them out. Use your lightning-staff if you have to!"

His smile never faltered. "Think of it as a compliment, after all, I don't see anyone outside Mr Hathwell's tent."

"That's because he's still at the smithy. Nobody but Sunday gets in or out, understood?"

"Nobody?"

"Nobody."

"What if I'm offered a bribe? Some plump turnips for instance?"

She pulled a face and vanished back inside.

"This is going to be a sight," Skald chuckled. As always he sat atop his staff, watching in amusement.

"Oh no, I can't do this if Skald's watching!" She was ready to call it off.

"My apologies Skald." Sunday picked up a towel. "These are hallowed rituals pertaining to the sacred feminine."

"Come again?" he snapped his beak.

"It means 'women only'." She threw the towel over him and heard him mutter something rude, before he vanished into the staff and the towel flopped down empty. "Right, try this on." She scooped up her chosen dress and pushed it into her arms.

Kolfinnia admired the satin. It was maroon and finely made, and she had to admit was looked very luxurious, but when she looked up it was to see Sunday leaving. "Now where are you off to?"

"To get the powders and paints," she replied mysteriously. "Oh, and before you put that on – those go on first." She pointed to a heap of frilly fabrics on the chest.

Kolfinnia looked horrified. "There's enough there for ship sails!"

"Every last petticoat. I shan't be long," she smiled and left.

"Skald, are you still mad at me?" Kolfinnia asked when she'd gone, but there was no reply from the staff. "I see you are – just don't look!" she warned, and got to work. She found the undergarments baffling and it took her ages to work out how to fasten the stockings to the corset, and when she finally did she felt spring-loaded. "I wouldn't get ten yards in this death-trap." She wriggled free and elected to wear short trousers and a vest underneath instead, and of course her wand and knife.

Just as she finished dressing, canvas rustled and Sunday returned carrying the rest of her finery. "Oh my!" she admired her.

"You approve?" She turned full circle.

"Absolutely!" Sunday held up a small mirror for her.

Kolfinnia regarded herself. The bodice and skirt were cut in one piece while the sleeves were plain and close fitting, and most importantly long enough to cover her Hethra and Halla tattoos. The outfit looked and felt exceptionally comfortable but elegant. "It's far nicer than I imagined it'd be. . . I'm almost glad you won the bet now."

"Hang on – what's this?" The neckline was just low enough to reveal a tell-tale strap. "Kolfinnia?" Sunday scowled.

"Oh, you might as well know the rest. . ." And she lifted the dress to reveal her shorts underneath.

"Oh Kol!" Sunday shook her head and gestured to the discarded underwear. "You know, according to Flora's wager I can *make* you wear those."

"Try it," she warned.

She just smiled. "Didn't you enjoy dressing up for feasts when you were a girl? I know I did." She began rummaging through the box.

Kolfinnia smiled at the memory. "Yes, but this is different. These things," she tugged at the dress, "they're not of *our* world. Everything about them is to do with what's on top and the person wearing them gets forgotten."

Sunday looked up. "But when *you* wear them you'll do so with a purpose no other woman ever aspired to."

"I will?"

"Of course," she swelled, "you're a witch!"

Inspired, Kolfinnia remembered her duty, but frowned at the devilish corset. "I'm still not wearing it."

"Quite right," she agreed, "but keep it, it might come in handy one day."

"Well having tried it on I can assure you it'd make a first rate catapult to repel invaders."

"What would you fire at them though?"

Kolfinnia smirked, "Turnips perhaps?"

Sunday's laughter was infectious and before long both of them were enjoying the joke. Farona stood guard outside listening to their mirth and wondering what women found so fascinating about clothes.

Her hair seemed to take forever, and once Sunday had finished she started on her face, beginning with whitener. "I'll look like a China doll if you go on," Kolfinnia protested.

"You've lived and worked outdoors your whole life."

"So?"

"So, ladies don't work and therefore seldom go outside."

"That sounds dreadful," she pulled a face.

"Hold still, and because they don't go outside they look pale."

"Pale and sickly!"

"Pale and fashionable."

"It's fashionable to look ill?"

"No, it's fashionable to look rich." Sunday continued applying the powder, this time concealing the small hourglass scar on her cheek, and she thought of how Victor Thorpe had destroyed her own.

"Sunday, you alright?" Kolfinnia asked, concerned.

"I. . . was just thinking."

"About the past?" She sensed where Sunday's thoughts were taking her. "You know, Rowan described us as fated sisters."

"I like that." She idly adjusted a lock of her hair. "Three fated sisters."

"Three? Yes, I suppose her fate's bound with ours, I never thought of it that way. Three of us." She found the idea comforting, but Sunday looked pensive and she knew why. "Ben trusts you. Rowan trusts you. And I trust you with the most crucial thing of all."

"Which is?"

"To make me look like a lady and not a scarecrow."

Sunday smiled and started adding rouge to her cheeks.

"First you paint me white then you colour me in again. It's nonsensical!"

"Keep still."

"Bossy sister," she muttered.

"I heard that. Now. . ." She leaned back to appraise her work.

Kolfinnia stared up at her. "I look like a doll don't I?" She imagined some gruesome fairground dummy.

Sunday picked up the mirror with a satisfied smile. "You trust me?"

"I trust you."

"Then see." She relinquished the mirror.

Kolfinnia took it but there was something wrong. The woman she saw reflected there couldn't be her. Her hair was arranged in an elaborate style of curls and loops and her face was that of someone who'd never known a moment's hardship or heartbreak. This *couldn't* be her. . .

"I told you I wouldn't fail you," Sunday promised.

Kolfinnia was transfixed. "And I knew I was right to trust you." And although nobody asked him, Skald listened from the staff and added his silent agreement.

A whole day now, Iso thought. A whole day and Sef hadn't moved an inch. He sat like one engaged in meaningful meditation, but Iso knew better. Inside him lurked a foreign mind, a witch within, and Sef was struggling to crack it open. It had never taken so long before and Iso was just beginning to realise what a stubborn old bastard Rowley must be.

He listened to the harsh chatter of iron-fairies outside. They had consumed a few pathetic sheep and now they were growing restless again, while Chentek sat on the kitchen table as inert as a lump of coal. If Sef didn't surface soon the iron-fairies would become a problem. "Hurry Sef," he hissed, not wanting Chentek to hear. He didn't trust the creature. *What would he do if Sef died?* he wondered. Would he simply return to a catatonic state, or would he be free to ravage the Earth? He shot the creature a sideways glance. It looked asleep, but he imagined a spiteful furnace boiling away inside, craving for blood and war. *What if it escaped Earth and spread through the stars? he thought. Iron is everywhere. Everything would turn red.*

Iso banished those disturbing thoughts, and looked back at Sef. As he did, he didn't see Chentek open an eye and study him, and by the time Iso looked his way again Chentek had returned to the pretence of sleep.

Thoughts of Hethra and Halla kept the monster at bay, but only just. Rowley concentrated on a modest lad he'd met at Stormwood, who'd seen the twins with his own eyes. Even in his current state he found that sublime. No wonder that creature wanted Janus so badly, he thought.

"Rowley," Sef called innocently. The creature had been doing this for hours. "Rowley, tell me how the boy slipped past me, and maybe I'll forget him."

Rowley guarded his thoughts. If he paid too much mind to why Marcus had evaded those awful fairies, then that would be just another thought for Sef to steal, and both of them knew this.

"I'll find him in good time," Sef promised. "I've interrogated so many others, and learned so much."

"Murdered them and stole their memories," he shot back.

"Ah, but what memories! And now I remember where I heard the name

'Rowley' before. You had a sister didn't you?"

Not this, please not this! Rowley clenched his fists. It was getting harder to maintain the forest.

"Elwen. Such a beautiful name." Sef tested the holly branches and they bent slightly. He was breaking him down. "A beautiful name, yet her end was anything but."

Lies! But the Therion knew her name. Was it possible, he wondered?

"I met a man named Barda: a deviser. I know that word means something to you." He began to shoulder his way through the disintegrating holly.

Marcus lad, I hope by Oak's sacred boughs you're far enough away by now! This was too much to bear.

"Devisers extract answers from witches with tight lips," he tormented, "Elwen was a witch, but by the end her lips weren't sealed. Before she died, she told them everything."

No! He bent double and the forest flickered like a cheap lantern show.

"I saw all within Barda's mind." Sef pressed forwards, one more step and he'd be in. Holly leaves raked him, but now they seemed listless. "And after they learned all they wanted, she was hanged. She looked to the empty sky, hoping to see you, but in the end she died alone." At last his foot crossed from the tangled hollies and into the glade.

Rowley felt his presence like hot breath on his neck, and responded with all he had. *A boy saw Hethra and Halla, a mere lad! Come on Rowley! What will Wessex say when you see him on Evermore's steps? If a lad can see the gods you can stop this bastard a while longer yet!* He balled his fists and held them high. "NOT YET!" he roared.

The holly whipped about Sef's wrists and ankles, and his foot stopped short of breaking into the glade completely. He snarled and struggled, but the holly burst into berries and the spines lengthened like blades. They stabbed and sliced him and he screamed in frustration, "Rowley! You're dying old man, you think you can keep this up much longer?"

"Not yet!" Rowley laughed softly to himself.

Sef calmed himself, and hung there, ensnared and covered in cuts but just feet from the old man. His breathing slowed and he returned to his slow, insidious poisoning. "Soon I'll be with you," he whispered.

Rowley fought for every second he could, while somewhere out there a terrified boy flew like an arrow towards Kolfinnia, carrying dire warning.

Kolfinnia heard canvas flap, and turned to see Flora enter. "Sorry to intrude, I just –," she stopped. "Kolty?"

"Miss Catherine Saxon if you please," Sunday introduced her.

Kolfinnia lowered the mirror and stood up carefully. "Well?" She turned on the spot accompanied by the ghostly rustle of satin.

Flora took in the dress, its soft bustle and lustrous sheen and gaped at the new Kolfinnia. Her hair was pinned high and arranged in a sophisticated style of curls and ringlets, and an assortment of tasteful jewellery added to the effect. But it was her face that stole the show. Flora saw a Kolfinnia who'd been born in another time and place. The witch within was gone. "It's incredible."

"Thank you," Sunday accepted modestly. "Although I had first rate materials to work with," she complimented her friend.

Kolfinnia took a few steps. "It's a little restrictive."

Sunday folded her arms. "Hmm, should you need speed you can just strip off and run."

Flora had a vivid image of her escaping in just her under-things and smirked. "A little extreme isn't it?"

"You've not seen what she considers underwear," Sunday rolled her eyes.

Looking pleased, Kolfinnia lifted the dress to reveal trousers, vest and her wand.

"Ah! Now there's the witch I know!" Flora pointed.

She let the fabric drop, before suddenly looking serious. "Hold on? I just thought, how did you get past my sentry?"

"Farona knows me," she replied, and a mysterious smile touched her lips. "Isn't it time you took a promenade around the coven?"

"An excellent idea!" Sunday agreed, eager to premier her efforts.

Flora stood back and grasped the flap. "Ready?"

"Here goes." Kolfinnia swallowed her nerves and made her grand debut. The first thing she saw was a man in black wearing a top hat. *Clovis?*

She opened her mouth to speak but the crowd stole her voice. The applause was wild and the children screamed in excitement, even the boys, and Kolfinnia blushed at the chorus of whistles.

Clovis removed his hat and sauntered over. "Kolfinnia?"

"Yes, it's me."

"Much excitement."

"Let them celebrate!" she shouted over the din.

"Celebrate a dangerous mission?"

She leaned closer. "They're saying their goodbyes," she explained, worrying that if she had to spell it out for him she might cry and spoil Sunday's hard work.

Now he understood and he offered her an arm. "Forgive me."

She joined him and they started out, but she could feel his tension. "Relax, let them say goodbye properly." She was glad the crowd couldn't hear the sadness in her voice.

It took courage to play along. Clovis wasn't an exhibitionist and perhaps he had more in common with 'Baron Clovis Krast' than he cared for. He put aside his reservations and waved to the crowd. Halfway around the Glade, Hathwell joined them, now looking distinguished in a suit of his own.

"Father," Kolfinnia greeted him with a demure bow.

He hobbled forwards. His false knee had been painful lately, but his stylish cane both suited the disguise and helped him walk. "Daughter," he openly admired her.

"Mr Saxon," Clovis tipped the brim of his hat. "I think it proper a daughter accompanies her father." He passed her to his waiting arm.

"My Lord." He gladly took the elegant young woman, knowing this was as much serious practise as it was play. The three continued, smiling and waving, pretending and lamenting. Enjoying their last day at Stormwood.

One witch however didn't join the procession. Rowan sat against a pine in the old fort watching the activity in the Glade below. She thought Kolfinnia looked beautiful, while Mr Hathwell looked so dignified, and Clovis so aristocratic. All of them looked perfectly dressed for a mysterious place named 'Helthorn Castle'. If she wanted, she could know what this 'Helthorn' was like. If she wanted, she could smell the carpets and touch the furniture, the paintings and statues. If she wanted she could see every pot and pan in the vast kitchens, and count the horses in the sprawling stable block. And if she wanted she could count the soldiers and their guns and gleaming bayonets. Her dearest friends were going to walk right into their midst, and if they made just one mistake then Helthorn would be their tomb. And so she didn't look, but instead enjoyed the celebration, all the while trying not to wonder how many of those four Lions would come back alive.

The evening meal was by contrast a sober affair, although it was officially a farewell feast. Clovis and the others returned to their familiar clothes, and the baggage gathered inside the pavilion was proof to all that they were leaving tomorrow. While everyone enjoyed their meal, he took time to ascend his treetop shelter and speak with Janus. The small god rarely awoke now, although this time his hibernation was deliberate. "You found a way Clovis," he said dreamily.

He leaned back against the branches and released a sigh, "I wish it were just you and I."

"I think it noble that you haven't told her," Janus commended.

"And I never will."

"A happy ending," Tempest added, thinking this was one lie they could live with.

"And as I say, noble," Janus repeated.

Tempest watched the coven darken to dusk as Clovis passed the time cleaning his sword and other equipment. He found a strip of blue cloth amongst his few things. He'd worn it at Kittiwake along with his Moon-Frost witches. "Those were dark days," he thought aloud, "but I'd take a hundred of them in trade for this."

"I am sorry," Janus said again. "Truly I am."

Clovis shot his thunder-sprite a knowing look. "We'd better show our faces at the meal, lest they suspect." Tempest flapped down to his side and Clovis brushed a tender finger across his brow. "Thank you for never doubting me."

"Thank you for never giving me cause," he replied.

Clovis turned, "We'll leave you to rest Janus." But when he looked he saw that Janus had slipped away again. He sighed, and covered the priceless artefact over with a blanket. "Come on Tem'. Let's go eat."

The pair dropped silently from their shelter and set off to join the feast, but neither had any appetite for food or company.

The Glade had seen many bonfires of late, but this one was different. Tonight's was to mark a departure, not a return. The celebration was tinged with sadness, but at the last minute Kolfinnia had decided how to enliven it. Tonight, Sunday was to present her with hrafn-dimmu in the wand's official hand over. The two shared a moment in the pavilion before the exchange. "I'll never forget this wand," Sunday cradled it in her hands.

"I've a feeling it'll outlive us all. Raven's wand is no ordinary wand."

"Oh I know that well." Sunday slipped it into her wand-sheath.

"You're ready?"

"Ready." She pulled the black scarf up over her face. She'd blacked her eyes with soot and her hair was again plaited with crow feathers, and everything she wore was black. Oddly enough, the idea had been Kolfinnia's.

"So this is the Blackwand the Illuminata saw?" Kolfinnia appraised her. "No wonder they feared you."

"I didn't think I'd ever wear these things again."

"And how does it feel?"

"Hmm," she considered, "a little last season."

Laughing, Kolfinnia straightened her hat for her. "You know the wand's as much yours now as it is mine. Tonight's really. . ."

"I know. . . just for show," she finished. "Take their minds off the other."

"Yes, the other," she sighed.

"Kolfinnia –," Sunday was about to tell her something private but joyous, when suddenly the flaps opened and Farona looked in.

"Not disturbing anything am I? It's just that everyone's waiting."

Sunday bit her lip. She'd promised not to tell anyone yet anyway. "We'll be along presently Farona, thank you." The young man vanished as quickly as he'd appeared.

"What were you going to say?" Kolfinnia asked.

"It's gone now, sorry," she pretended, "can't have been important."

"Oh. Well, let's not keep our crowd waiting."

"After you." Her news could keep. Anyway, it might be nicer to announce her and Ben's marriage plans when Kolfinnia got home, she thought.

Stormwood expected Sunday and Kolfinnia, what they got was Blackwand herself. As soon as she stepped out of the pavilion the crowd exploded with cheers and both witches had been wrong: this wasn't just for show. The coven was losing Clovis, and uncertainty was rife. The woman in black now marching into the torch-lit Glade was as their new hope.

Both went and stood under the founding-banner and when the cheers died away Kolfinnia knelt before Sunday who drew hrafn-dimmu from its sheath and then she too knelt. She offered her the wand and when Kolfinnia grasped it the two were briefly joined. Finally Sunday relinquished the wand and Kolfinnia stood and held it up for everyone to see, and with that it was done.

The crowd started cheering and Sunday got to her feet. Hrafn-dimmu had officially come home and tomorrow it would embark on its latest journey, this time to Helthorn Castle. "A salute to Clovis!" Kolfinnia raised the wand.

"Clovis!" A roar went up.

Clovis stood bathed in the bonfire's glow and returned their salute. He drained his mug in one go, acknowledging his last ale at Stormwood. The crowd's appreciation was deafening and before it had died down fiddle music started up and a fresh cask was opened. Tonight's merriment helped conceal the pain and Clovis was happy to play along.

"Clovis?" Kolfinnia thought he looked old in the torchlight.

"Nice touch." He waved his empty mug to where Sunday was being accosted by excited children. "Your idea?"

"I wanted them to know they're in good hands."

"They always were."

She smiled gratefully. "I have a gift for you." She took something like a miniature silver snuffbox from her dress. "We want you to take a piece of each of us home, back to the stars."

"And what is this?" Gently, he took the little box.

"Don't open it!" she cautioned. "It might blow away. It's very delicate."

"It's beautiful." He admired the entwined dragons of oak and holly on the lid.

"Inside is a piece of each of us. Everyone's taken a sliver of their staff or their wand. The fragments were burned, and the ash is inside. Part of hrafn-dimmu is in there too, part of me." She closed his hands around the silver box. "When you get home, open it, release the contents to the wind and think of us. Think of me." In this way she hoped they might still be together, no matter how remote.

"I've never heard the like." But he wouldn't open the box on Vega because he wasn't going back there. "Kolfinnia. . ." He almost told her, just as Sunday almost divulged her wedding news, but unlike her, he had nothing of comfort to offer. "I will think of you all when I open the box on Vega." He lied because he had to, but the smile he won from her was genuine.

"When I look up at the stars and see Vega, I'll know part of me is there." Now she was glad of the noisy crowds. "Don't forget."

"I won't forget." This wasn't a lie at least.

Suddenly, she was lost for anything further to say and she feared if she tried she might say something regrettable. "I must go see if Row's alright," she pardoned herself and left.

He stood by the roaring bonfire, holding the little box. "Fate," he said softly. If the Flowering was at all true then why was it that he must open another vessel and not the one Kolfinnia had given him? *Because freewill is not free at all – it costs.*

With that thought, he slipped the gift into his clothes and joined the crowds, pretending to be enjoying himself.

Chapter Eleven

Disparate journeys

*'The world may come tumbling down around a person's ears,
while for others all seems well. Therefore, who says that
two worlds cannot exist side by side?'*
Arla Sojun - World-Fall coven, Powys

Iso didn't know what to do. That made him angry, which in turn
aggravated his indecision. He'd lost count of the hours Sef had been
slumped against the wall. Occasionally he moaned or twitched but for
the most part he lay motionless, and all the while Chentek's fairies grew
more boisterous. "Reckless," he grumbled and glanced Chentek's way
again. The war-fairy appeared as lifeless as Sef. "Reckless to restore such
a thing to life. Clovis probably isn't anywhere near the faded-realm and
we won't even need it after all this." He made sure to keep his voice low.
Suddenly Sef twitched, making him jump.

"Rowlll. . ." he groaned.

"Finish it soon," Iso willed him. Sef heard nothing, but lay on the floor
where his epic fight was at last drawing to a conclusion.

A man can only fight for so long and Rowley knew the fight was over
when the sound of rustling branches ceased. He opened his eyes to see
his forest fortress dissolving all around him. He'd done his best he told
himself, but that didn't dampen the sense of failure. *Sorry Marcus, sorry
Bern*, he apologised. Whatever happened back on Earth wasn't his to

influence any longer. *So sorry Marcus, I'll give Elwen your love, and do so until the day you come to give it her in person, long may that day be coming.* His peaceful thoughts were disturbed by the sound of panting and slobbering, and he turned to see the Therion clawing his way into the glade.

"I won! You're dead witch, dead!" Sef howled, but Rowley's ascension had begun and all the Therion's bluster seemed unimportant now, although he had one last trick up his sleeve.

You want my memories? Try these. He made sure the first memories the creature would taste were very unpleasant indeed. *A parting gift you might say.*

In an instant, Rowley's soul found itself on Evermore's steps amid the majesty of eternity, while Sef pounced greedily on his abandoned memories.

In the little cottage where the range was now stony cold, Sef jerked and gasped and sat up clutching his head, groaning in pain.

"At last!" Iso dropped to his side. "Sef! Are you done? It's time we were away!" He jabbed him with questions, but Sef heard not a single one.

A stream of stolen memories pulsed through his mind, and Rowley had made sure the most recent came first. Sef saw yesterday's battle from Rowley's viewpoint, and of course saw himself battered and beaten. Worse still, he felt the old man's satisfaction at his humiliation, but now the filthy witch was gone and there was nothing he could do about it. "Bastard!" he seethed, still clutching his head, "you sly bastard!" Sef sat waiting for it to pass like a migraine, and wishing Rowley were still alive so he could kill him all over again. After a while he relaxed, but cautiously as though he expected a fresh attack any moment.

"Sef?" Iso was likewise cautious. He didn't want to be knocked sideways again. "Sef, do you hear me?" He grunted something in reply. "What?"

Sef looked up. "Stormwood," he exhaled, "Clovis is at Stormwood."

"Stormwood?"

Sef saw it all now. "A coven, hidden in the black mountains of a country called Wales."

"Not too far I hope?"

"Close enough, a few days' travel." As he climbed to his feet a hundred different wounds yelled at him. "Stormwood is large, ten times bigger than Rowley's, and well defended too." Suddenly a name came to him,

"Kol-fin-nia?" Along with it, came the image of a young woman with dark hair and earnest eyes. He stopped and blinked and then grinned despite the pain: this wasn't just any woman. "Oh this is perfect!" he laughed.

"What? What's perfect?" Iso demanded.

He flexed his huge arms and rolled his head and neck. Bones cracked and wounds complained, but the pain refreshed him. "I can see him. I can see Clovis just as Rowley saw him. And I see the way he looks at *her*."

"Her?" Iso bounded onto the table.

"He has found love." He shuddered with laughter.

"Another Therion?"

"Better, Kolfinnia is a young woman, the coven's head. And he loves her dearly."

"They are two?" Iso said with revulsion.

"No, not flesh-love, they are much more. I see the way he looks at her – theirs is soul-love." He looked to the cottage's crumbling ceiling and saw beyond. "Thank you Lord Self." What a gift he thought, all he had to do was capture Kolfinnia and Clovis would be his. Desire had undone the great coven-father.

"Then we leave right now!"

"No not yet, attacking Stormwood will involve total battle. Chentek!" Immediately the war-fairy uncurled and scuttled around to face him. "Call your dogs, we're leaving."

"To Stormwood?" Iso repeated hopefully.

"No little hen, to Basingford Iron Works, where we swell our ranks."

"But what if Clovis leaves this 'Stormwood' in the meantime?"

"No matter. We shall gather iron-fays as we travel westwards. And when we get to Stormwood the skies will be black with them. Even if Clovis is gone there will be many witches to interrogate. One of them will lead us to him."

"And the rest will be devoured!" Iso trilled.

"All but one," Sef brooded. "All but one." *Kol-fin-nia*. He would ravage her, flay her, then eat her alive. Then only after Clovis had witnessed her agonising death would he interrogate him. When his knowledge was consumed he would take Janus and return to Vega, where he would kill Acola in the name of Lord Self. "Greatness calls." He bared his fangs in a macabre smile and Iso wondered at his thoughts and began to worry.

Kolfinnia had a distinct feeling of déjà-vu. Over a year ago she had met with Hilda early one morning at Wildwood when the dew was fresh, and together five of them had set out to find the Hand-of-Fate. Now here she was – under dawn's glow again and facing a perilous mission, only this time the whole coven had risen to say farewell.

She didn't speak as she led Rowan to the Glade, and Skald sat on her shoulder likewise silent. Yesterday's sense of jocularity had vanished. Ahead, Kolfinnia could see the Glade filled with subdued onlookers, while her companions and honour guard awaited her in the middle. "Row, I want you to behave for Sunday while I'm gone, understood?" She tried to sound breezy.

"Sunday's made a nice bed for me." Rowan didn't want to leave Crow-top and move in with Ben and Sunday, but neither could she stay there alone. Just like Kolfinnia, she tried to sound positive. "When you get back we'll go home again won't we?"

"Of course we will. And if you ask Sunday nicely I'll wager she has some special tales that she hasn't told anyone else."

Rowan almost smiled. "I want to hear about taking the bears to the bank."

She patted the banknotes in her satchel and smiled. "Oh yes, that's a good one." They were almost there. Another fifty yards and their departure would become real. "And help her around the coven, just as I showed you."

"I will."

"And no looking," Skald added fatherly.

"Skald's right, no looking, no matter how tempting it might be." Kolfinnia didn't want her glimpsing their fates if they didn't return. "Promise?"

"Alright I promise!" Rowan groaned.

Ahead, she saw Clovis step forward. He was wearing wayfarer grey and his armour was concealed under his cloak. Hilda was dressed similarly, and only Mr Hathwell looked himself, in a white shirt and black waistcoat. Beside them they had gathered their baggage. After half a day's march they would reach Longtown and meet their guide, a Smoke named simply 'John'. He would take them to Hereford, where they would don their disguises and board the first of numerous trains.

"Coven-mother," Clovis greeted her with a fierce hug, while Hathwell's embrace was uncertain and Hilda's was tender.

"So, we're ready?"

"Ready," he confirmed.

"They're waiting," she indicated the crowd.

Clovis stepped up onto the Anvil and turned to the crowd, where he saw many teary faces. *This is really goodbye,* he thought. "My friends, my family. I don't need to remind you that Janus helped all of us escape last year, and now you have helped me fulfil my promise to him. I came here by tragedy, but found triumph in your company and it has been my honour to serve you all." He heard a few sniffles, and he struggled, determined not to join them. "Although I leave you, I want you all to know that the cause is great. Janus will eventually change creation for the better. And should your magic be strong enough one day, then I would ask you to come to Vega where I assure you I shall repay your hospitality a thousand fold." He smiled sadly knowing he wouldn't be there to greet them even if they did. "All I ask is that you don't bring any of Bridget's carrot wine." They laughed softly at this and ended with gentle applause. Many of them were crying freely now. "Kolfinnia?" he invited.

Now it was her turn, and she joined him on the Anvil. "Magic strong enough to reach the stars? That sounds like a spell well worth learning." Incredibly, the mad idea gave her hope. She drew hrafn-dimmu and thought of all the people it had touched, and now it was beginning another journey. "I take this black wand on my journey, safe in the knowledge that another Blackwand watches over you. I know coven-mother Flowers will prove to be Stormwood's greatest asset and a witch's best friend."

"Blessed be," Sunday murmured. Next to her Ben held her hand tight.

"Now, the day's young but our journey's long. Look for us, and with the twin's grace we'll be with you again soon," Kolfinnia finished and the pair stepped down again.

Their honour guard stepped forwards now; Sunday, Flora, Sally, Albert, Farona and of course Rowan. They would escort them to Stormwood's boundary and help carry their things. After that they would be on their own.

She couldn't face another sad word, and so without any further goodbyes Kolfinnia collected her baggage and led them out, closely followed by the rest. Each of them touched the sacred founding-banner as they departed, and Kolfinnia listened to her feet whisper through the grass and felt weighed down by sorrow, not for what they might face, but for the prospect of returning without Clovis. After a while she detected singing.

"Kolfinnia?" Rowan heard it too.

"Keep walking," Skald advised kindly.

"Yes, keep walking." Kolfinnia swallowed her regrets and held Rowan's hand tighter, and she walked away from Stormwood as the whole coven began to sing quietly. The 'Ballad of Oak and Holly' drifted after her and its haunting melody accompanied them even after they had left the Glade and filed through the gardens. It continued still, until at last they entered the surrounding forest, and then the hymn was nothing but a sweet memory.

This was a day for many journeys. Some were sad, others were bloody, but young Marcus Rowley's journey was simply frantic.

He took his uncle's lightning-staff and fled. Rowley's sprite, Hammer, knew the way to Stormwood and flew hard, but Rowley was so badly wounded and painfully interrogated that Hammer suffered too. He couldn't find his speed and needed frequent rests. When darkness came he couldn't fly at all and so Marcus bedded down under a haystack and waited for morning. For boy and sprite, that was the longest night of their lives and although he was barely ten years-old, Marcus understood well enough that Hammer only lingered in this realm because his uncle was still alive, but alive how? He tried not to imagine the torments he must be going through. *'Torrance fights the Therion's magic, but he can't fight for long,'* Hammer told him. He could have told him much more, but the boy didn't need nightmares.

As soon as the sun rose, they were off again but things had gone badly wrong almost at once. After less than a mile the lightning-staff dropped and suddenly Marcus found himself tumbling to the earth. *This is it,* he thought. *My uncle is dead.*

He crash-landed in a cornfield, scattering a flock of jackdaws, but thankfully the tough plants broke the worst of his fall. He struggled to his feet, dazed and shaken. "Hammer!" He stumbled through the dense plants and found his staff. It hadn't broken but he knew it was as useless as if it had. "Hammer?" A groan drew his attention and he headed towards it. "Hammer, I'm coming!" He shouldered the thick stems aside and found the thunder-sprite sprawled amongst corn heads, trembling and moaning. Right away he scooped him up into his arms. "Hammer, speak to me."

"I can't stay. Go westward," he panted, "Stormwood is westward, in those mountains."

In a panic, he looked all around but saw only a wall of corn stalks. "Hammer, I don't know where to go, please don't go yet, please! Where do I go?"

"West. Find Kolfinnia," he managed a last time.

Marcus pressed on with no sense of direction, still cradling the thunder-sprite, and in the next instant he was blinded as Waves-Hammer-Rocky-Shore returned to the thunder-heights. When the brilliance passed he found himself alone, cradling nothing at all, as fine hail swirled around him "No! Hammer, uncle, Ward Wessex!" He implored countless names, but none of them could help. He was alone.

A hare sprinted from cover and bounded away, startled by a muddy boy crashing through the corn. When Marcus at last emerged he saw an endless vista of fields and hedges and what he first took to be a cloudbank hugging the horizon. After a closer look he realised the clouds were in fact a line of low hills. *Mountains?* he hoped. They certainly lay in the right direction, but they appeared to be miles away.

He was alerted by a flash of brown and white, and glimpsed the hare racing along a hedgerow, heading west. He took it as a sign. A moment later his tired legs carried him after the fleet-footed hare, and he staggered on under a dawn sky, hoping Stormwood was hidden somewhere in those distant hills.

The banter was pleasant but punctuated by weighty silences. Everyone felt time running away, and a tangible sense of sorrow following like a cloud. Soon the Lions and their escort would reach the way-beware circle, where they would part company and continue alone. As she walked along holding Rowan's hand Kolfinnia drank in the woods for perhaps the last time. The way-bewares were close, in fact now she could hear their song.

"Do you remember?" Rowan asked softly.

Kolfinnia smiled. "That's the day we met: putting out way-bewares. Of course I remember."

"I liked that day."

"Me too."

Silence returned and thoughts returned to departures and loss.

"This Smoke we're meeting, what's he like?" Hilda asked, mostly to make conversation.

Kolfinnia adjusted her baggage into a more comfortable position. "Oh, John and his whole family have been friends to witches for generations. I've actually never met him, but Albert knows him and rates him highly, he'll take us to Hereford where our journey really starts."

"Albert, this John, is he a fine fellow?" Hilda asked over her shoulder.

"No fear. He's a staunch Welsh man like myself and he's been a Smoke around this district since boyhood. There's none more loyal Miss Hilda," he vouched, and Mally yapped in agreement.

"How come he never joined a coven?" Sunday ventured.

"Says he's more service to us out there, keeping an ear and an eye open."

"Sunday," Clovis asked suddenly from up front.

"Yes?"

"If I were you, I'd think of doubling the number of way-bewares." He was wary and his eyes were everywhere.

"Isn't that a little heavy handed?" Kolfinnia countered.

"There's a Sef out there somewhere," he reminded them.

"You haven't said much about this Sef. What's he like?" It was Farona who asked what everyone wanted to know. Uniquely he seemed able to ask blunt questions of Clovis and not irritate him, and all ears turned to listen.

Clovis chose his words carefully, remembering Rowan. "I don't know who he is, and perhaps I won't recognise him either, but Sef are cunning and adept in magical arts that true witches disown."

"Such as?" It was Farona again.

He sighed. "They serve the entity known as Self, and any action, no matter how vile, is considered a blessing to their god if it indulges the practitioner's desires."

Intrigued, Farona hurried and drew level with him. "So a Sef thinks their god approves when they do whatever they like?"

"Indeed."

"That's typical god behaviour for yer!" Sally spoke up.

"Not surprisingly there are many fanatical adherents to the cult of Self." Clovis felt ashamed that he and the Sef were of the same race. *But there will be one less before this is over,* he promised himself.

"Plenty of men who behave like that here," Kolfinnia lamented.

"And women," Hathwell added without thinking.

"Really?" Hilda enquired smartly.

"Erm, well, I assume, that's all."

"So enlighten me, what selfish temptresses have you had dealings with?"

He wasn't sure if she was teasing. "Well, I only meant. . . well, you know."

"Oh look out Hilly," Sally grinned, "that husband of yours knows some rum women."

"I hope not," she objected.

Hathwell caught her expression, which looked a little too real for comfort. *Is that jealousy?* he wondered.

"Self is in all souls," Clovis cautioned, dispelling the mirth. "All souls."

"Even witches?" Kolfinnia asked.

"I said all." He stepped over a fallen log without looking back.

"Then how can one fight it?" Flora didn't like the idea at all.

He stopped and turned. It was important that they understand. "Face it and know Yourself, not Self."

They considered this for a moment, and Hathwell grasped it first. "Listen to conscience." Now he understood their conversation in the woods yesterday.

Clovis smiled, "And you said you weren't a witch Mr Hathwell."

"You know you can call me Bertrand, all of you." Again he looked Hilda's way, but now she appeared more interested in their surroundings.

"I already struggle to think of you as Mr Saxon, a third name will only add to my labours." Clovis was so dry it was impossible to say if he was enjoying a joke.

"We're almost there," Kolfinnia cut in. "I can hear them for certain now."

They all stood quietly and listened and there it was; an ethereal chorus. "The way-bewares." Sunday knew it better than most and she shivered.

"Then this is where we say goodbye." Clovis turned to them and now it was real, now he was leaving. His companions gathered by his side, while the escorts shuffled closer for comfort, creating two distinct parties, each with very different paths to take.

"I can't believe I'll never see you again." The reality of the parting suddenly hit Sunday.

"Never," Flora echoed.

Clovis regarded them warmly. "Never? The mind might have its limits, but magic does not. Who's to say a soul cannot travel the stars in the blink of an eye?"

"Blessings on you Clovis." Sunday stepped forwards and embraced him and when she withdrew his mane sparkled with her tears.

"No. Blessings on *you* Blackwand. Without the Flowering, Janus would be trapped forever."

Sally came next. "I don't know what would have happened at Kittiwake if you hadn't been there."

"You would have found a way, witches always do." He held her close, thinking of his own plight. "Blessings on you Sally Crook."

"Goodbye Clovis." She stepped back, wiping her eyes and Albert came forwards.

"I'll have that tunnel dug by autumn, mark my words," he promised.

Clovis embraced him, but gently, he was an old man after all. "Save the hardest digging for when Mr Hathwell gets back."

"I like the sound of that," Albert grinned. "Say hello to those mermaids for me."

"I'll give them your love," he winked.

Flora's goodbye came next and clearly she was nervous. "I've grown a special rose, and I'm going to name it after you," she revealed.

His smile broadened. "Then I trust it has thorns an inch long and grows anywhere."

"No," she laughed, "its petals are amber, like your eyes."

"My thanks, garden mistress." Thankfully, his fur concealed his red face and he kissed her softly. Now he turned to Farona. "If he were not deep in slumber I know Janus would wish to say goodbye to you himself."

"It was a privilege to know both of you." He offered his hand and his voice wavered.

Clovis ignored it and wrapped his arms around him and delivered a crushing hug. "Remember what I told you," he whispered confidentially, "tell her, and open that door."

"I will, and wherever it leads I'll think of you."

"Only if it's a happy ending," he slapped his shoulder. "Now, our guide will be waiting. Kolfinnia?"

There was one last goodbye and she knelt level with Rowan. "I'll see you again soon, Row. Please don't worry about us."

She touched a finger to her special scar. "I won't. He's always watching over you."

"Then all will be well, and this time at least I get to say goodbye."

"Just so you can say hello again one day soon." Rowan looked downcast but composed.

"Some day soon." She kissed her and they shared a lingering hug. At last she withdrew, stood and brushed the girl's hair away from her eyes. "It grows by the day," she marvelled. "Take care of her Blackwand." She gently directed her over to Sunday's side.

"Ben and I won't let her out of our sight." Sunday slid an arm around her shoulder. "And make sure you wear that dress like I showed you, and don't forget how to prepare your complexion," she fussed.

"I know – regally."

"And no looking," Clovis wagged a finger at Rowan.

She gave him a warm and wise smile, "I'm glad you picked the door that brought you here."

He thought of that mysterious door. 'ROWAN'. Even now he still didn't understand it. "There was only one door I ever wanted to pick – yours," he smiled down at her, still wondering.

"Flo, I want to see the gardens laden with produce when I get back." Kolfinnia heaved her baggage onto her shoulder.

"Leave it to me, and there'll be Clovis-roses everywhere."

"And I'll water your plum tree Mr Hathwell," Rowan promised.

"We'll share the first plums when I get home." He hadn't called it 'home' before, and now he was just beginning to see what he would be missing.

"And all of you remember. . ." Kolfinnia looked each of them in the eye. "Stormwood is yours, enjoy its blessings and look for us soon." Now she felt the urge to go. It took great courage but she turned her back on them. "Clovis, shall we?"

"The journey begins," he agreed, and the rest took up their baggage. He offered Sunday's party a slight bow, thinking more words would only delay them, and then he left them. Stormwood's Lions set off heavyhearted and heavy loaded. It was nine miles to where they would meet John and many more miles after that.

"Don't look back," Clovis said quietly.

"Until I come this way again." Kolfinnia clung to her staff.

"You'll be home before you know it," Skald tried to lift her.

"But without Clovis," she thought back and this time he had no answer.

The four left bound for dangers unknown, and this time their departure wasn't to a chorus of singing witches but the emotive and otherworldly song of the way-bewares. Pace by pace Stormwood dwindled and soon the trees swallowed them up and the song was just another bittersweet reminder of home.

Their escort watched until they were out of sight.

"I worry when she goes off without me. I lost her once, will I find her a second time?" Flora said to herself.

"She has Clovis, he'll keep her safe," Farona promised.

"Yes," she sighed. "Just as he kept us safe at Kittiwake. I'll miss him so much."

"I never saw that, the fighting and all. I was below with Janus."

She stared at the trees ahead, wondering and worrying already. "I'd love to hear that story again, of you and the twins."

He also stared at the vacant tree line, imagining the four who had disappeared beyond it. "It would be my pleasure."

"A summer evening by the river can be a beautiful place for tales," she suggested.

"Then I'll see you there one evening soon."

"Just you and I?"

"Just you and I," he promised.

The two joined hands and Farona realised he'd just opened that door Clovis had told him of, and the wonder of it was he'd stepped through without even trying.

Mally whined and Albert reached down and scratched her ear. "Cheer up my lovely," he sniffed.

"Albert, you crying?" Sally noticed.

"No," he lied. "Just a touch of pine-fever. Anyhow, day's wasting and there's a tunnel to dig."

"Don't forget to leave some work for Mr Hathwell."

"He's nothing but a slip of a lad, work like that would break his back!"

Sally took in his bony arms and wrinkled face, but knew without doubt he was right. She looked to the trees, still smiling, half expecting to see something, but they kept their secret. "Valonia was right," she told herself. "A fine choice for coven-mother."

"Come on girl," Albert tapped his leg and Mally trotted after him. He couldn't bear to look at those empty trees any longer, and if he did his 'pine-fever' would only get worse.

Rowan also watched the trees longingly, but for her out of sight did not mean out of range. If she wanted she could know every step of their journey. And because that door was available to her she didn't need to open it, just knowing it was there was enough.

"Are they alright?" Sunday asked.

Rowan reached up and offered her a comforting hand. "Sad, but determined."

Sunday knew to ask no more.

"Did you really rob a bank?" Rowan asked lightly.

She gave a small laugh, "I did it for noble reasons."

"You threw it all away didn't you?"

"It was more use where I left it than where I found it."

"All those poor city people."

"Sounds like you know the tale already?" she pretended.

"But I want to hear it from you," Rowan squeezed her hand.

"Come on then. We'll put a kettle on and coven-mother will tell you a tale of bears that could tear down fortresses." She looked in the direction they had gone one last time, struck by the parallel of the Lions heading north, just as she and the berserks had travelled south. *Keep her safe dear champion,* she wished silently.

Hand in hand, girl and woman led the honour guard away from the trees and the hostile world beyond, and started back towards Kolfinnia's empty tree house, missing her already.

Now he finally had Clovis's scent Sef was relentless. He flew towards another bloody confrontation, but this time with mere men. Basingford Ironworks employed almost four hundred workers, but before nightfall not even a brick would be left standing.

Since Brimstone, a powerful idea had dogged him, one so deeply heretical yet irresistible that he shielded it from Iso at all costs. *What if I kept Janus for myself?* He was convinced Lord Self was guiding him with blessedly suspicious thoughts. He banked the lightning-staff westwards, keeping to high altitude. Speed was his goal now, but Stormwood was a fortress, and if by chance Clovis wasn't there any longer he might have to interrogate every last witch to learn his whereabouts. He needed reinforcements.

"How much further?" Iso complained.

"You'll know when we get there."

"Witches and sprites should share what they know!"

"I am no witch!" he shouted over the wind.

Chentek sat on his shoulder shielded from the wind and cackled. "Sprite complains again?"

Iso ignored him. *"The thing is too ambitious, you should kill it when we're done,"* he warned silently.

"Your constant fears tire me." Sef likewise kept his answer quiet.

"If it escapes your control, none of us will ever get back to Vega."

"We need his forces." Although invisible, a vast plague of iron-fays followed alongside in the faded-realm. He looked down and detected a township through the gauzy clouds. "We're close." He began his descent towards rows of terraced houses and plumes of factory smog.

"So this is Basingford?"

"Mark it well. The town is about to die."

"A whole town?" Iso questioned uneasily.

"Chentek's children must be nourished."

"Nourished!" Chentek cackled hungrily.

The cloud was thicker now and his view obscured, but the noise and smells from below told a hundred stories. On his shoulder the war-fairy chattered excitedly and in response the air filled with rustling wings and clacking teeth.

Their journey took them directly over two high ridges and down the accompanying valleys. After what seemed like much work and little headway, they finally dropped through a rocky outcrop known as the Black Darren and saw a settlement resting on the hilly plain below.

"That's Longtown?" Hathwell asked as they unpacked their provisions.

"Yes, John will be expecting us on the eastern road, under an old elm by a bridge." Kolfinnia took a swig from the bottle before passing it to Clovis.

"Is it far?" He tried not to sound sullen. Already his bad knee was telling him it had done enough hiking for one day.

"It's all downhill from here," Hilda said between mouthfuls.

"This isn't the way we came is it?" He alluded to their journey from Salisbury just weeks before.

"No, but take heart, you're officially back in England." She passed him a hunk of bread.

He didn't take heart. He was a wanted traitor in England, probably Wales and Scotland too. The Illuminata was everywhere.

"We should be gone." Clovis stood and eyed the distant township. "It would be very bad to miss our escort."

Hathwell checked his pocket watch. "But there's plenty of time?"

"It's best we're gone." He appeared uncharacteristically edgy. The others swapped worried glances, reluctantly finished their break and hauled their bags into place.

"Rain's coming," Skald informed Kolfinnia silently.

She looked to the clear sky, knowing he was right, slung her staff and picked her way through the rocks. The rest followed and the Lions slowly descended the Black Darren and down into England.

Just like poor Madam Mystique, 'John' wasn't his real name, but Smokes were cautious and judging from the pentacle brand on his forearm he'd once been punished for helping suspected witches. John was somewhere in his late thirties, with pale eyes and a lean face half hidden by a beard. He had a reserved manner and Kolfinnia had been uncertain of him when they'd met. He spoke Welsh, not English, but Albert had been right about his loyalties because he spoke Pegalia fluently. After a short while in his company, Kolfinnia happily admitted she'd been wrong. "There was a coven up at the fort centuries back," he informed her.

She sat beside him on his cart, which swayed as it trundled along. The horse was a huge shire named Langdon, whose immaculate condition further reassured her of his character. "A coven, really? I'd not heard that tale."

"You should've. After all, it was Albert who told me."

"I'll ask him about it when I get back."

"I'll tell you," he offered.

"You've always lived in the Black Mountains?" she ventured, noting the pentacle scar again.

"Always," he said simply.

She looked behind, to the others in the covered cart, and Hilda waved her hand in a 'go on' gesture, wanting to hear the story. "So when did witches first come to the fort?"

"It's been empty centuries, but it's held that Merlin had a coven there. He named it Lion's Glade on account of the claws buried in the fort. He lived a long time there, and there are still ancient lion claws inside the fort."

"Mmm, yes I've seen a few of them." She was intrigued.

"Well the claws came from a Lion that visited the coven each midwinter night, year after year. He was as large as a horse, but well-disposed and very wise. He taught Merlin magic from beyond the stars and the Lion's annual visit became a celebration for the coven." John rocked in time with the cart and Kolfinnia found herself hooked on his every word. "The Lion never revealed his name to anyone, and so their mysterious visitor became known simply as 'the Lion'."

One year though he didn't come and Merlin was distraught and the mood around the coven became gloomy. The witches got on as best they could, and they had a lot to do because in those days people revered them as healers and wise ones. Pregnant women welcomed the skills of a witch-wife, and ailing crops could be revived if a kindly witch was around to lend a hand. Despite all of this to keep him busy though, Merlin still worried about the Lion. At last, after twelve months, when midwinter came again he waited expectantly, wondering if his friend would come.

As the first snows began to fall the Lion walked into the clearing. Merlin was overjoyed, but right away he saw something was wrong. The Lion's head and mane were streaked with blood. As Merlin tended to his wounds the Lion explained that some of his distant tribe had forsaken the path of true magic and a terrible war had broken out amongst the stars.

Merlin mended the Lion's wounds and in doing so he removed claws left behind from the Lion's battles. Merlin wanted him to stay and recover, but the Lion refused, saying that a war of magic raged across the heavens, and he was sorely needed. The Lion left that very same night, but Merlin saw how he hobbled slightly and he no longer held his head high.

Year after year the Lion returned on midwinter's night, always bloody from battle, and Merlin removed yet more of those savage claws, lodged in his wounds. He buried them in the old fort, but as the years went by the Lion grew older and the heap of claws grew bigger and bigger and Merlin wondered how much longer his old friend could endure.

The next year, after twelve months of waiting, the Lion dragged himself into the clearing, bleeding from countless wounds, and this time Merlin took a hundred claws from his neck and muzzle; because the Lion always confronted his enemies head on. As he cleaned away the blood, the Lion told him the enemy had almost been beaten, but they had fled across the universe to spread their corruption in secret. The Lion struggled to his feet, saying his duty was to hunt them down and he staggered out of the clearing. As he left he finally told Merlin his name, and swore he would return, no more a lion but whatever shape he should wear upon his next incarnation. Merlin never disclosed the Lion's true name, but it's said that somewhere in the old fort he carved it upon a stone in his honour, for he never came again after that night. And the 'Lion's Stone' remains hidden to this day.

"His name?" Kolfinnia wiped a tear away.

"Aye, but don't ask me miss, the stone's never been uncovered."

She turned about and saw Hilda and Clovis's stunned faces. She dried her eyes before asking, "How many people know we're there?"

He shook his head. "Rest assured, just me and the boy."

She didn't ask who 'the boy' was. "And what happened to them, the witches I mean?"

"They fell out in the end. The Lion's loss was a terrible blow. Merlin wasn't the same man and when he died nobody could decide who should be in charge, and so they argued and finally one by one they left."

"That's a sad end for a coven."

"Self," Clovis interjected from behind. "It can ruin even the strongest heart." Maybe it was chance, but just then the first raindrops arrived and the shower quickly turned heavy.

"Sit in the back miss," John advised, already getting wet. "I can manage."

"Very well, thank you." She crawled through the canvas and sat beside Clovis.

"That's an unusual language." Hathwell hadn't grasped a word of what had just been said.

Hilda looked proud. "Pegalia is spoken only by witches and magical creatures. Even the Illuminata don't know it."

"And what was he saying?"

Hilda felt sad again. "A tale about Stormwood's past."

"Can you teach me the language?" he asked.

She appraised him. "I'll consider it," she smiled.

"That song they sang as we left. Could you teach me that?"

"The Ballad of Oak and Holly? It's as close as witches have to a formal hymn. It's very old, very beautiful."

"But can you teach me the words?"

Before she could answer, John barked something, and Kolfinnia's mouth tightened. "John says there's another cart approaching, keep quiet." She dropped the canvas sheet both front and back and they listened to approaching hooves and rain patter on the tarpaulin. Likely it was just another trader, but now Stormwood was behind them every sound had her on edge. Drumming hooves passed without incident but they all noticed how John didn't greet the stranger by name.

"We must be out of John's district now," Hilda murmured.

"I wonder where we are?" Kolfinnia pondered.

Hathwell took out his pocket watch. "It's mid-afternoon. Maybe an hour or two more to Hereford?"

"Do you know the place?" Clovis asked.

"No, but it won't be hard finding lodgings for the night. I'll make the arrangements. You might speak Pegalia but I speak plainly," he smiled. "And tomorrow we board our train."

"We'll have to change clothes before we approach lodging houses." Clovis gestured to their witches' attire and his muddy cloak.

Hathwell looked about. "There's space enough in here, we don't need full costume, just something respectable." Clovis looked satisfied, but the others certainly weren't.

"What? You expect me to undress in here, in front of you both?" Kolfinnia laughed, unsure if they were playing a prank.

Hathwell and Clovis exchanged bemused looks. "Yes," they said in unison.

Hilda looked mortified. "Are you quite serious?" she became frosty.

"Well, I suppose we could step out when we get close to Hereford, let you change in private?" Hathwell suggested tactfully.

"Erm, yes," Clovis coughed. "I'm certain the rain will have stopped by then."

Both women smiled triumphantly. "You're true gents," Kolfinnia thanked them.

Hathwell managed a smile, all the while listening to the rain grow heavier.

Doctor Joshua Barnes had seen service in the Crimean War, but he'd never seen the likes of today's disaster. Living close by in neighbouring Crompton Stone, he'd been one of the first on the scene, having only been informed by the constable that Basingford Ironworks had suffered some kind of explosion. He knew the town well, and so was all the more horrified when he arrived with the constable to find it unrecognisable.

"Where's the town gone? My God, where's the town!" He stood on the bridge leading into Basingford and dropped his bag without noticing. All of Basingford seemed to be ablaze; houses, trees and factories, and the fiercest fires were raging where the ironworks once stood. "What happened?" he gaped. "And where are all the fire dousers and, and. . ." He suddenly realised there was nobody around. No survivors, no wounded and most disturbingly not even any bodies. "Where is everyone? Tell me, where are they?" He felt irrationally angry with Constable Shaw.

Shaw had to shout over the racket of sundering wood, "Dunno sir, lad in the marshes raised the alarm, and I came to find you."

A nearby house collapsed in flames and Barnes jumped back. "What happened?" he stuttered again.

Shaw said nothing because he didn't know what to say, and started out across the bridge towards the inferno. There was even burning wreckage floating in the canal, and fine ash was falling like black snow. Barnes collected his bag, which looked ridiculously inadequate, and trudged after him.

The road led to the town square and every building that faced onto it was a raging inferno. The inn, the butcher's, the magistrate's court, the town hall and even the police station were being devoured. The heat was tremendous and the air was filled with terrifying bangs and groans as more buildings succumbed. "We'll never get to the works!" Barnes waved a hand off where the sky was blackest and the fires were almost white with heat.

"Look!" Shaw grabbed his arm.

Barnes saw it too: someone lying by the water trough in the square. "Come on!" Relieved that he might have some purpose at last, he set off.

Doctor and constable ran across the square, dodging wreckage, and ducking when a roof collapsed or a window exploded. Barnes saw liquid fire jet up like geysers from ruptured gas mains, and heard hefty booms from the direction of the tanning works. As they stumbled across the cobbles he dimly registered that they were glossy with something wet, but what he didn't know.

"Is he alive?" Shaw shouted as they approached.

Barnes shielded his face from the worst of the heat, dropped to the patient's side and rolled him over. "Good God," he whispered.

"Is he alive?" Shaw repeated, and then saw for himself. "Jesus!" he exclaimed and then mumbled an apology. "What happened to him?"

Barnes seemed oblivious to his blasphemy, and even the heat. His hand hovered over his bag, but he had no need to open it. This poor wretch was beyond help. "This man hasn't been burned?" He wasn't even sure if it was a man or not, the body looked like a pile of butcher's scraps swaddled in rags. The face was cratered with so many tiny wounds that there were no features left. Barnes imagined iron fragments travelling at tremendous speed, but the victim lay too far from the supposed explosion.

"Poor sod's been ravaged!" Shaw tugged at his chinstrap, feeling queasy. "Explosion did that?"

"I fear not," Barnes shook his head. The heat was stifling and he cupped a handful of water from the trough to soothe his brow, but when he looked it was so tainted with blood that it almost looked like wine. "Lord!" he flung the stuff aside in disgust. He looked around, squinting in the heat. *What in God's name happened here?* he wondered fearfully. He forced himself to examine the body again and lifted a flap of clothing aside. It was heavy with blood and made a slurping sound as he peeled it away. And just then something flew out and sprang on his front and hooked itself there, making chattering sounds.

Both men screamed and Barnes rolled onto his back, flapping wildly at it. "Get it off! Get it off!"

Shaw didn't have time to think. He simply grabbed the tiny creature, thinking it was a rat, and flung it to the cobbles and brought a boot down on it. There was a short squeak followed by a peculiarly metallic crunch. "Got the little bleeder!"

Barnes clambered up. "Good God, what was that?" He swept at his clothes, making sure there were no more and then looked at his hands and saw they were red with blood. In fact he was bloodied all over. "The cobbles?" he realised. The slick coating on the road was blood. It was everywhere.

Shaw reached down and scraped the dead thing off the ground. "Is it a rat?" Now he wasn't so sure, and he held it out for him to see.

Barnes saw a creature no bigger than a sparrow. It had wings like knife blades, and its whole body had the heavy sheen of iron. He first thought it was a bird, but it couldn't be. "It has limbs?" he peered closer, fascinated and repulsed. "God knows what the unnatural thing is?"

"I thought it was a rat." Shaw looked closer and saw a pointed shark-like face and crumpled arms and legs. It reminded him of a tiny winged dog.

Barnes looked from the tiny corpse, to the bloody one by the trough. "It ate him?" he wondered aloud.

"Ate?" Shaw suddenly flung the thing aside and rubbed his hands on his uniform. They too, were now ruddy with blood. "Pardon my boldness sir, but might we be thinking of getting back, waiting for the rescue crews from Crompton Stone?" he swallowed.

"Yes," Barnes agreed hazily. The heat and the fear were suffocating. "Nothing we can do here, get back, yes." Shaw drew his whistle and gave a few short blasts. Barnes wasn't sure if he was signalling to survivors or just trying to appear useful. Either way it wasn't going to make a jot of difference to Basingford. The town had been destroyed as surely as if old Hob himself had arisen and done it in person. Doctor and constable skidded and lurched over the slippery cobbles, wondering where the town's folk had gone, all the while plagued by the dreadful notion that the answer lay under their feet.

John halted along a quiet track, but the cost for the women's privacy was for both Hathwell and Clovis to stand in the rain. They themselves later changed in the back of the cart as it trundled the last few miles into Hereford. Like the others, they wore the minimum needed to complete their disguises. John shouted something through the canvas. "He says we're close now. Less than a mile," Hilda translated.

Hathwell suddenly felt nervous. His clothes felt too hot and too tight, and he kept eyeing Clovis, no longer sure if his disguise was credible.

"You have your doubts?" he asked through his scarf.

Hathwell looked to the women. Even without the finishing touches of hair and complexion they looked radiant, but how would the world take a man like Clovis? "Let me do the talking, and stay close to Hilda, she's meant to be your escort after all. And don't speak if you can help it."

"I know," he grumbled.

If there was a 'nervous bug' going around Kolfinnia felt she'd caught a dose of it. "John's going to take the cart right into the stables. We can get out while Mr Hathwell secures a room and be inside again before anyone sees us."

"Until we get to Helthorn itself I recommend you don't use the name 'Krast'," Hilda advised.

"Agreed." Clovis pulled the top hat into place followed by the gloves.

"John will help us in with our things, we're not supposed to handle our own baggage. It would look wrong," Kolfinnia reminded them.

Hathwell prodded the bundle of lightning-staffs. "The Baron enjoys shooting: a good plan." The canvas bundle could easily be mistaken for shotguns.

"It was the best I could think of," Kolfinnia apologised. When she'd first explained the concept of shooting wildlife for entertainment, Clovis had believed it was a twisted joke and she only wished it was.

Before long Kolfinnia heard a distant whistle and knew it must be the railway. Voices suddenly sounded beyond the canvas, but faded quickly as Langdon trotted on. "Nothing to worry about," Hilda murmured, catching her apprehension.

"Thank you mother," she rehearsed. Now she could hear the cathedral bells and the rattle of iron on cobbles as the track yielded to road. New aromas assailed her, chiefly the smell of hay, cattle and dung. Clovis meanwhile smelled bread, roasting meat and chimney smoke as the city gradually drew them into its embrace, but his keen senses also detected things beyond the reach of the others; a barking dog, a blacksmith's hammer, the sullied river, a crying infant, subdued birdsong and of course the tang of apples.

Hathwell felt a subtle shift in his worth. Now the others looked to him to navigate them through the etiquette of Victorian society. *I won't let Hilda down,* he promised himself.

The cart lurched as they turned a corner, and even the light seemed different and Kolfinnia guessed that buildings now loomed over them. She heard John shout some encouragement to Langdon and stray words drifting by from countless voices, all of them dressed in unfamiliar accents. *How many people out there would take a few shillings for betraying a witch?*

Her palms felt clammy.

"All's well," Hilda eased her.

She returned the smile as best she could, as Clovis made small adjustments to his attire. She might not speak Welsh, but when the cart swayed again she understood John's command perfectly, "Whoa!"

"We're here." She checked her dress and pulled her shawl higher. Hilda fixed her hat and veil, as Clovis pulled his scarf up and his hat brim down.

"Remember, leave the baggage to John and the talk to me. I'll be back as quick as I can." Hathwell buttoned his coat and collected his cane, and vanished through the flaps, giving the others a tantalising glimpse of a courtyard, before the view was obscured again. The cart rocked as he stepped down. They heard his shoes click across the cobbles and the regular tap of his cane, they sounded confident, as if he'd stepped from a carriage, not a cart, and then he was lost in the whirl of outside sounds.

"Sit tight," Clovis ordered.

Kolfinnia slipped her gloves on, covering Ben's bag of charms around her wrist, and sat back to wait, while Hilda sat with her hands in her lap, eyes closed, taking in all the new sensations. "Do you think Mr Hathwell will be –,"

"Shh!" Clovis touched his lips.

She bit her tongue as their guide went about the simple yet perilous business of securing a room for the night.

He fell asleep under a little bridge next to a lively river, but Marcus only slept because he was too broken to go on. Three times he'd spotted a hare racing over the landscape and followed it, desperate to believe that some force somewhere must have taken pity on him. Rain clouds obscured the mountains he'd seen earlier, leaving him with no idea where he was heading, but he followed the hare and dared to hope.

Far away another traveller halted for the night. He had detoured from his route in order to attack the choicest locations, and now several counties lay between him and his goal, but he would make up the lost ground and already he commanded a force sufficient to destroy Stormwood many times over. Sef sat in deep meditation reflecting on all that had transpired. He savoured the day's events, remembering the screams and the raging fires at Basingford and later in Handford and Lowes Water. Insignificant iron towns that had been wiped off the map and their occupants rendered and fed to his army. That night while Marcus endured nightmares, Sef's dreams were righteous and revivifying.

Kolfinnia lay in her bed. Beside her, Hilda slept peacefully. For seven shillings each they had a comfortable room, hot water and even a bath. All she'd seen of the Prince of Wales hotel was the threadbare carpet and dowdy wallpaper as Hathwell had whisked her up the stairs. She'd been too frightened to look up, and only minutes after leaving the shelter of John's cart she'd locked the door to their room on the first floor and offloaded with a huge sigh of relief.

That night, as the rain drummed on the windows and filled the gutters, she had lain down with her lightning-staff and held a silent communion with Skald. Every sound in the corridor outside was alien and every shadow that played across the ceiling portended danger. *This is how it must have been for Sunday in London, alone and lost,* she told herself.

"You're not alone," a voice comforted, *"Sunday had her berserks, you have your Lions."*

"Thank you Skald." She caressed her staff, feeling the runes Valonia had carved there, and listened to Hilda's soft breathing and the rain outside. She imagined Evermore and whether Valonia was watching, and hoping that if she were she'd still be proud of her 'little wolf mother'.

Skald heard her too, and knew for a fact that she would.

CHAPTER TWELVE

The age of iron

*"The iron of Britain's mills will run like a molten river
to encompass the whole world."*
Clarence Hoxley - Minister for Industry, 1854-61

Stormwood awoke to its first day without them, and tried to get on as normal.

"I'm making a wicker star, with coltsfoot flowers for when Kolfinnia gets back," Emily revealed as they patrolled the forest.

"Which I'm sure will be sooner than you think." Sally had taken Emily Meadows along to collect wild garlic and ground rosebay. Albert Parry ambled along a short way behind.

"It's a pity we can't go out all the way to the coven's edge," Emily sighed.

"Coven-mother Flowers wants us to stay close for now, until she's had more way-bewares made." Sally thought of the Sef everyone had been warned about. She stooped to collect some tender borage leaves and shared one with Emily. "Once everything's back to normal we'll see about going a little further."

"We've got nothing to worry about with Blackwand protecting us!" Emily nibbled the borage.

"That's 'coven-mother Flowers', please try to remember Emmy," she reminded her yet again.

"Coven-mother Blackwand's a solstice queen like me!"

"Yes I know," Sally replied patiently. "Albert! Don't get too far behind."

Mally caught up first, and shoved her nose into Sally's waiting palm and wagged her tail, Albert sauntered along soon after. "We're ten minutes from Stormwood, what could go amiss?"

She didn't like baited questions. "Nothing as long as we keep our wits."

"Mally knows when things aren't right an' look at her!" The little dog was now rolling among the buttercups. "She's happy."

For some reason Sally felt nervy. *Just the new routine,* she told herself. "Grab a handful of that bittercress will you Emmy?" The girl obliged and the trio plus their dog wandered on.

They traced the westward course of the Bitterwade River and as they went the pines grew wild and unruly. Old trunks lay in tangled heaps and the river sliced its way through a rocky gorge. Plentiful rosebay grew amongst the branches and ferns. "I think that's far enough." Sally unpacked her kit. "We'll gather what we need here."

"There's better forage further up. Leaves as big as your hand," Albert tempted.

"No. Here's fine." She looked around, and without thinking she drew Emily close, while Mally scurried through the trees sniffing and digging.

"Sal?" Albert leaned on his lightning-staff, peering at her.

"It's nothing," she pretended. *The trees. . . today they look untrustworthy,* she thought secretly.

Albert followed her gaze. "Something wrong?"

"No, it's nothing." This time she added a smile, more for Emily's sake. "Come on, mother-Blackwand won't be happy if we get back late and empty handed."

"You called her 'mother-Blackwand'," Emily sniggered.

"Our secret," she winked and passed them each a sack and they began foraging.

The Prince of Wales hotel served very little that would appeal to a disciple of magic. "What's black pudding?" Kolfinnia whispered to Hathwell, thinking it sounded nice.

"You'd be better not knowing," he dissuaded her.

There were three of them for breakfast. Clovis remained in his room where they planned to take some food up for him. Kolfinnia surveyed the dining hall. It was lavishly decorated, but it was her fellow guests she kept an eye on. *Who are they and what are their professions? Did they earn a reward for betraying witches last autumn?* Her thoughts were caustic and suspicious.

"Don't keep looking, you'll draw attention." Hilda casually sipped her water. Kolfinnia straightened and fidgeted with her napkin, until Hilda's disapproving gaze made her stop. The waiter drifted over. He was about Kolfinnia's age, with striking blue eyes and neatly combed fair hair, and he made a poor job of pretending he wasn't interested in her.

"Would madam, miss and sir care to order?" he invited.

Hathwell took charge. "Our party are of a religious persuasion that forbids the eating of flesh, have you something suitable?" Hilda watched him, impressed by his confidence.

The young man looked undecided. "I shall have to speak with the cook sir, pardon me."

"Be quick," he grunted, and shooed the lad away.

"You're enjoying this aren't you?" Hilda smiled behind her napkin.

"Just practising for later. Helthorn will test us all."

"I didn't like him!" Kolfinnia hissed. "He kept looking at me. Do you think he knows?"

Hilda was touched by her innocence. "Catherine dearest, I think perhaps he found you more bewitching than witch."

She frowned as she pondered this, and she was still pondering it when the waiter returned with a selection of muffins, fruit, toast and preserves. The young man also offered her a shy smile and she finally guessed Hilda's meaning. Breakfast was plain but sufficient, and Kolfinnia wrapped some in her napkin for Clovis, and hid it in the folds of her dress.

The journey from the hotel to the train station was less than quarter of a mile and so they opted to walk, but every step of it brought new sights and sounds, and to her surprise Kolfinnia found their deception vaguely exciting. "Nobody's sparing us a second glance," she whispered to Hilda. Both walked in front with Clovis and Hathwell behind. She could hear the metallic tap of Hathwell's cane over the rustle of her dress.

"I told you." Hilda's parasol was propped over her shoulder, mostly to help shield Clovis. "When people look, they don't just use their eyes, but their hearts and minds too. Set your mind to be invisible and people will simply see past you."

She groaned, "I seem to have forgotten my basic teachings."

"Well now's the time to reacquaint yourself."

She did so, and saw without being seen. She was just a young woman in the street, she pretended, hardly worth a second glance.

"Left here," Hathwell grunted.

The party swung left, passing a platoon of soldiers marching in the other direction, and Kolfinnia took a sharp breath.

"Just parade drill," Hilda noted their bright red uniforms, and Kolfinnia pretended not to see them as they stomped past.

One building caught her eye. There was a carved coat of arms above the sandstone portico, and she shuddered when she recognised the unicorn and a dragon chained to a thunderbolt. *The Illuminata!*

"You seem surprised?" Hathwell said discreetly. "They own almost everything and influence the little they don't own."

"What *is* that building?" she asked.

"Courthouse."

"But don't expect justice," Hilda quipped.

Kolfinnia strolled on, reassured by the feel of hrafn-dimmu under her dress. She could see the train station at the end of a narrow street, and plumes of steam rising up from behind the buildings. *Almost there*, she told herself. A man in a brown suit and carrying a hatbox shot Clovis a curious look as they passed, and then he was gone. The station crept closer and now she could see a huge crowd outside. "Trouble?" she worried.

"That's normal," Hathwell calmed her. "Getting tickets can be a lengthy ordeal. Most of these people will be looking for second and third class tickets."

"We'll find a general room and await you there." Hilda twirled her parasol and adjusted her veil.

The street grew more congested, and their progress slowed until Kolfinnia found herself walking right alongside strangers. "Lucky heather?"

someone asked. She turned to see an old woman wearing a ragged shawl and lace bonnet. She was clutching a sprig of heather, with her other hand held out expectantly. "Lucky heather my dear, penny well spent will bring luck and blessings, bring you the man of your dreams."

Kolfinnia fished in her dress, found a shilling and pressed it into the woman's hand and took the heather. "Keep it. Are you a devotee of the twins?" she ventured.

The woman first smiled at the shilling then frowned at the question. "The twins?"

She knew to say no more. "My mistake, thank you."

The shilling vanished into her apron and the old woman waved a gnarled hand in her direction and barked a husky laugh. "Lucky heather. It'll bring you your heart's desire my dear!"

Heart's desire? Kolfinnia smiled, while from behind she could almost feel Clovis's angry glare.

The three waited in the general room while Hathwell bought tickets. He adopted the Illuminata approach, and barged to the front of the queue, ignoring the shouts of protest and bribed the ticket master, and it worked a treat. When the whistle blew for boarding, a station porter arrived to carry their baggage. Albert's silver had clearly passed its first test.

Their accommodation was a six-seat compartment in the first class carriage, and Hathwell had wisely bought six tickets so they could have complete privacy. Kolfinnia had felt nervous when the guard had locked the doors and sealed them in. *"To prevent anyone accidentally falling out,"* Hathwell had explained.

She saw many people trooping past the sumptuous carriages, heading for the lesser accommodation to the rear. Most of them looked despondent and transitory, perhaps travelling to find work. She briefly caught sight of a man walking between two constables and noted the glint of handcuffs about his wrists, which only added to her paranoia. After a woman wearing a bonnet had banged on the window trying to sell them sherry and walnuts from a wooden tray, the whistle had blown and at last the train had rolled out of Hereford bound for Birmingham. Kolfinnia had felt vaguely guilty watching the woman shrink from view, and the look of resignation on her face stayed with her the rest of the day. This is how the poor scraped a living she realised. After Birmingham would come Manchester, then Leeds and York. Once there they would find another hotel and catch a train to Edinburgh tomorrow morning.

Kolfinnia leaned back into her velvet seat once more. They were deep and separated by hefty arm and headrests, and when she reclined she couldn't see the others, and she felt trapped. Sitting on her bustle also made things uncomfortable. Clovis sat next to her, although she couldn't see him, and Hilda and Hathwell sat opposite.

She leaned closer to the window and gazed out through the glass, which was now studded with raindrops. "So this is Britain?" She had never travelled so far and so fast. *The train goes as fast as a sprite can fly,* she thought with mixed feelings, and checked a glance at their lightning-staffs secured in the rack above. It appeared that no corner of the country was untouched by man, and what others might call pastoral was to her an agricultural wasteland stripped of its native forest. *The days of the wildwood are ending, this really is the age of iron.* The thought brought a lump to her throat.

Mile after mile, she bore witness to the subjugated landscape. Fences and fields swept by in profusion. Some of those fields extended to the horizon and were nothing but grassy deserts grazed by sheep. She saw windmills rolling their huge blades and drovers shepherding their animals along narrow lanes. Canals snaked across the land, piloted by barges drawing thin lines of smoke as they went. Muddy tracks, scarred by cartwheels, led to quarries and mines, each looking like shotgun wounds on the landscape. Signal boxes and station houses, with their deep eaves and narrow chimneys, flashed past, as did smart-looking platforms lined with milk churns, crates and hand-barrows. The train hurtled under bridges thick with ivy and through deep embankments bristling with brambles. Thirsty steam trains thundered past, rushing from one water tower to the next, as they distributed materials across the heart of the empire. Goods yards whisked by, and Kolfinnia saw mountains of coal with men scurrying around them, like ants working to serve their queen empress. She saw cemeteries where the dead speak their last through carved epitaphs, sheltered by majestic yews, and ominous mills with darkened windows and cobbled streets textured like lizard skin.

Kolfinnia saw much, all of it accompanied by the endless silvery rails on their throne of ballast. *The age of iron.* She closed her eyes and wished she could awaken at Wildwood, but iron's empire was relentless and Wildwood was long dead.

"Penny for them?"

She was roused from her daydream to see Hilda watching her over the cover of her book; Emily Brontë's 'Wuthering Heights'. "How's the book?" she enquired.

Hilda regarded it thoughtfully. "It astounds me how desire can make sensible folks insensible."

"Isn't it a love story?"

"It's more accurately a story of people who mistake desire for love, but what desire!"

"And in consequence they do foolish things?" Clovis guessed. He lay in his seat with his coat over his head trying to sleep.

Kolfinnia scowled, "You make it sound like people never fall in love on Vega."

He pulled the coat down just enough to see her. "They don't. We have evolved beyond that."

Hilda smiled wryly, while Kolfinnia was left baffled. "How are our funds Mr Hathwell?" she changed the subject.

"Sorry?" He looked up from a copy of The Times he'd found at the station.

"Money. We have enough yes?"

"Yes. I trust you didn't mind me buying six seats?"

She rested her book in her lap. "No, it's a fine idea, but can we afford it all the way to Edinburgh and back?"

He regarded her again in her Victorian finery, and thought about what Clovis had said of love. He did love her, and despite what Clovis might say he knew he would wish her happiness even if she found another. How much more 'unconditional' could he be, he wondered?

"Husband?" She dragged him from his thoughts.

"Yes, sorry." He folded the newspaper. "I'm confident we've enough."

"Good. I don't want to have to walk back from Manchester."

"If we're frugal," he added, "and don't use the most expensive hotels."

Her face fell. "Pity, I was rather getting used to baths, beds and trains."

"Desire comes in many forms, not always flesh and blood," Clovis warned again.

"Oh Clovis! You're like a dour soothsayer!" Kolfinnia leaned forward to meet his gaze. The others muttered similar things, even Hathwell.

He saw that he was outnumbered. "Forgive me. I'm anxious that's all." But that wasn't all. Thoughts of opening the vessel haunted him, and talk of love unsettled him also. There were many things he loved and didn't want to leave behind. At this he cast a glance at Kolfinnia. "Maybe love isn't so foolish after all," he conceded.

"Desire or love, they both make for a rattling read," Hilda patted the book.

"Really?" Kolfinnia thought it suddenly looked very interesting.

"You've never read this?" she raised an eyebrow.

"No."

"Even Valonia enjoyed a little fiction once in a while. This was one of her favourites."

Fascinated, Kolfinnia leaned closer. "Even Valonia read about wild, reckless things like love?" She gave Clovis a 'told-you-so' glance.

"Dickens was her favourite mostly, and of course the Sagas from her homeland, which are also crammed with people doing mad things for love." She regarded the book, remembering her friend. She was the last of Wildwood's Wards, and sometimes that hung heavy on her. As if in answer the carriage suddenly darkened as they raced under a bridge. The whistle blew and the darkness fled and light poured in again.

"Read us some," Kolfinnia suggested. "It'll pass the time."

Hilda straightened from her seat. "A splendid idea!" She opened the book again and cleared her throat. Kolfinnia waited in anticipation and Hathwell set aside the newspaper, relaxed and sank back into his seat, and even Clovis emerged from under his coat.

Hilda began, performing rather than just reading, and page-by-page, mile-by-mile, they were slowly drawn into a tale of destructive yet undeniable desire and each of them thought of the dark places they were going and what Clovis had said: *Self is in all souls.*

"And we tie the twigs on like this, so our little sentry has arms," Flora held up the finished way-beware for Sunday to see. Both of them were sat working in the gardens enjoying the weather and trying not to think too much.

"May I?" Sunday asked.

"Please do," she handed it over.

Sunday held it gently. "He reminds me of one I once had." It was made from a pine root and wore a headdress of jay feathers. Flora had carved two little eyes and a small but expressive mouth, and now she had just finished attaching the twigs for outstretched arms. "He already looks alive."

"Hmm, he's not alive yet. The spell's complex and needs a new moon."

Sunday traced a finger over the way-beware's inscrutable face. It didn't sing yet, but it would, and she knew the song would hurt her heart. "He's beautiful." She passed the doll back. "How many more to make?"

"Another thirty maybe."

"That's a lot of jay feathers."

"Yes, and jays don't give them lightly."

"Sunday!" someone called. Both witches looked around to see Ben dashing towards them, clearly worried. "Sunday!"

"Ben, what's wrong?"

He collapsed by her side, chasing his breath. "There's a lad come through the outer hills and crossed the coven boundary. He's looking for Kolfinnia. Says its urgent," he panted.

Right away she drew her wand. "Flora, send word that the coven is to be ready for possible attack."

"Attack?" She looked about the idyllic gardens.

"Call it instinct. And if it's not I'll look a fool and no more. Ben take me to him right away."

He was perhaps ten years old, muddy, exhausted and from the look on his face Sunday understood he was recently orphaned. "Kolfinnia!" he guessed when he saw her approaching.

She knelt and took him gently by the shoulders. "No. Kolfinnia is away. I command for now. Who are you?"

"Kolfinnia, I need Kolfinnia!" he remembered his uncle's last command.

"My name's Sunday," she tried to calm him. "Tell me yours."

He stopped and tried to remember. "Marcus," he stammered.

"Lad's wild with fright," Ben said softly.

"I know." She turned back to the boy. "Marcus, what do you need to tell Kolfinnia?" She was aware of a growing crowd and knew that whatever message he had wasn't going to be good and wasn't going to be private.

He took a deep breath and his long pent up warning gushed out of him, "There's a beast coming!" he sobbed, "a beast with a million fairies, and he's coming to Stormwood!" There was a stunned silence before he finally imparted the most painful news of all. "He killed my uncle!" Words now blurred into sobs and tears rolled down his muddy face and he collapsed against her.

Sunday grabbed him and she looked up to see dozens of stricken faces. "Marcus," she pulled back to face him, "Kolfinnia's not here, but *I* am and my other name is Blackwand, and no intruder crosses our boundary while I live and breathe." Now she felt the old anger rise up, and was shocked to realise that she liked it. "Ben, take charge of the coven defences!"

"What about you?"

"Sally's out gathering. I'm going after them." She turned to one of the others. "Scarlet, take Marcus, clean him and keep him safe."

"Aye coven-mother," she obliged, and Marcus found protective arms around him once more.

"Good luck." Sunday planted a kiss on Ben's cheek and then raced past them all, already directing her thoughts to Strike, *"Are you ready?"*

"Just like old times."

"Let's make Eirik proud!" she vowed, and touched the silver hammer at her neck.

"Sunday, be careful!" Ben shouted and then turned to the rest. "You heard her, let's move! Staffs, arrows, wands and fire!"

Marcus watched her too. He was dazed and exhausted, but something inside him flickered. *Blackwand,* he thought, *that's really her.* He'd heard the tales and from the sound of them he dared believe that she might be equal to the horror that was even now heading their way. *Kill the bastard, Blackwand. Do it for Uncle Torrance,* he thought, and felt both instantly ashamed and hopeful.

As she foraged she kept one eye on Emily and the other on the woods. Something wasn't right, but what she didn't know. *An enemy couldn't just walk into Stormwood unnoticed, not past the way-bewares and crows without so much as a murmur from any of them, could they?* She recalled what Clovis had said about Sef being adept in arcane arts. For a moment she paused and directed both eyes to the forest, but it wasn't her eyes that worried her. She could almost swear there was the distant chatter of angry starlings. *Could they?* she wondered again.

"Ward Crook?" Emily asked.

"Come on, we'll just fill that last sack and then be off." She looked over to where Albert was bent over in the grass. "Going well Albert?" He raised a hand in answer but didn't stop working. She was trying to frame herself, when Emily's next question made her freeze.

"I keep hearing birds, but I don't see any." She plucked a few more leaves, already seeming to disregard the idea.

Sally knew then. "Emmy," she said quietly, still monitoring the trees. "I want you to get your things. We're heading back. Never mind the gathering."

"Back? I could get loads more if you want."

"Never mind that," she repeated. "We're heading back." Her manner remained calm, but inside her nerves felt aflame. "Do it slowly and make sure not to rush."

Now she whispered. "Are we in danger?"

"No," she pretended, and heard the mournful sound of trees creaking in the breeze. But there was no breeze. "I'm going to tell Albert, and I want you to —"

Suddenly, they both heard those strange bird sounds again, but this time they weren't distant. It sounded to be right on top of them and Albert heard it too.

"Starlings seem mad at something?" He looked to the sky where there wasn't a bird to be seen.

"Albert!" Sally called casually. "We're breaking for lunch, come join us," she pretended.

"Be a minute. Man's business to attend." He stretched and wandered away into the trees.

"Oak damn it!" she cursed softly.

"Ward Crook." Emily shuffled closer. "What's wrong?"

"Just do what I told you Emmy." Sally saw movement in the grass. Her heart pounced, and then settled when she saw it was Mally. "Mally girl, come here, come on girl!" The dog came running over, and Sally grabbed her scruff.

"Mally doesn't seem scared?" Emily stroked the dog, more to comfort herself. "So everything's alright isn't it?"

"I don't know." She watched the trees, willing Albert to reappear. "Come on Albert, you haven't drunk that much tea," she hissed.

Woman and girl waited, and Mally whined gently when more pines creaked and that strange bird sound came again.

Sally was right; Albert hadn't drunk *that* much tea, but his seventy year-old bladder didn't work as well as it used to. He finished his business and retrieved his gathering sack, and his mind was just turning to lunch when he heard a voice, a perfectly reasonable and friendly voice.

"Tell me of Clovis."

He spun around. "Who's there?" There was a rustle of branches and not far away a figure stepped out.

"I seek Clovis and Kolfinnia. I am an old friend," the stranger claimed.

Albert squinted, but something was clouding his mind. "A friend?"

"Oh yes, an old friend," he chuckled. Darkness seemed to roll off the figure in waves, and in that darkness emerald eyes slid open like lanterns showing the way. The stranger took a step closer. "Clovis and Kolfinnia, where are they?"

Without knowing, Albert clutched his knife. His mind might be under siege, but his body still knew what to do. He shook his head, and the fuzziness cleared a little.

"Clovis and Kolfinnia," the stranger demanded again.

"Clovis and Kolfinnia aren't here, but come hither stranger and I'll divulge their destination to you." *Like hell I will,* he thought, and slid his knife behind him. Above him, he could hear what sounded like millions of birds whooshing through the air, and branches groaning.

"Oh yes. You'll tell me all you know." Sef smelled the old man's feint as strong as rank fish, and he *would* divulge Clovis's whereabouts, bite by bite. "You will tell me." He'd seen the girl in the clearing too, and wondered how tender she would be. His mouth watered at the prospect.

Sef closed the gap wearing a smile and now drawing his sword, and just as he reached striking range Albert made his move, only it wasn't the move Sef expected. He swung the sack stuffed with leaves into his field of vision, before slashing with his knife.

Surprised, Sef jerked back, and in the same instant he whipped his sword free and swung.

"SALLY, RUN!" Albert had time to roar, and he was still shouting a warning when his head was cut from his shoulders.

Sally heard a shout echo through the wood followed by a loud crack. She spun around to see Albert's lightning-staff, still propped by a tree, leap clean into the air and blaze with light. She screamed and covered her eyes as his thunder-sprite rocketed into the heavens, and in that instant she knew he was dead. Mally snarled and yapped, wriggled free, and darted off into the undergrowth towards her master. "Mally!" Emily cried. "Mally come back!"

An instant later Sally heard the terrible sound of Mally's growls turn to squeals, and then nothing. Now there were two of them. "EMILY, GET DOWN!" She shoved the girl to the ground, and whirled her staff just as some dark creature hurtled out of the woods towards her, while all around them the storm of screaming birds became deafening.

Flora could have sworn she'd seen lightning. It came from the west, the direction Sunday had gone and for a moment she had an awful premonition. Thunder rolled faintly and she knew a witch had died. "Lord Oak!"

"Then this is no false alarm," her sprite, Torrent, foretold.

"Did you see that?" Ben pointed a trembling finger.

"Sunday's fine, I know it."

"But that flash, and thunder as well, that can only mean a –,"

"Ben, snap out of it!" She couldn't let him say it. "She's fine, now help get the pip-staffs to shelter."

"I know, I know!" He wiped his mouth and looked eastwards again. *But what if?* It was too horrible to think about.

"Scarlet!" Flora caught sight of her running hand in hand with a boy she didn't recognise. "Gather all the children, hide in the woods around the Glade!"

"I'm already on with it!" she called back.

Although they'd never expected attack so soon, the plan was to form a defensive circle and keep the children secure in the Glade. That meant someone had to fight in dense woodland in the north however, and that someone was Ben. Flora had been allocated the west, John Spelt was given the south, but she didn't know who was manning the east. Fire was also part of their defence and she saw bonfires being lit around the perimeter.

"Bridget!" Flora hailed a witch pulling a chain of frightened children along after her. "Bridget, make sure nobody goes into the fort, the escape tunnels aren't finished!"

Bridget shouted some affirmative and carried on.

"Flora, I'm away," Ben shouted.

She threw her arms around him first. "Good luck."

"I'll see you soon." He pressed a kiss against her cheek, turned and ran, gathering his fighters as he went.

Flora faced west again, like it was some malevolent magnet drawing her attention. Everywhere, she saw witches running to mount their stations. Wand-arrows were prepared and lightning-staffs were shouldered. Firebrands were lit, charms and prayers were said, and bonfires now blazed at the coven's edge.

"Flora, all the pip-staffs are gathered in the woods. The rest are on the perimeter standing ready." It was Mary Fife, and beside her stood Morag Heron and a score of other veteran Wildwooders. "Coven-mother back yet?"

Flora almost told them about the lightning. "Not yet. Who's holding the east?"

"Sam Morris twisted his ankle – bloody oaf! Farona's taken over."

Farona? She pictured his face and suddenly understood what Ben had to lose. "Halla be with him."

"Halla be with all of us," Mary added.

"And not a moment too soon, look!" Morag pointed skywards, where a dark cloud, shaped like an anvil, was swelling to gigantic size.

"A storm cloud?" Flora wondered.

"Believe me, that's no storm," Torrent corrected.

"No. It's moving, look," Mary grasped, and all of them fell mute and watched. In fact a hush had fallen across the whole of Stormwood. Flora could hear children crying and the crackle of the bonfires. There was a sudden flurry of feathers, making everyone jump, and a crow landed amongst them, and immediately Mary went to him and listened to his news.

Flora looked west, where Sunday may be lying dead, and then east where Farona might soon follow. "I wish you were here Clovis," she whispered.

Mary stood up, looking pale. "Albert's been killed." There was a second of silence, then a barrage of exclamations. "Listen! The attacker's coming from the west."

"Then hadn't we best mass all our forces here?" Flora insisted.

"No. Attack may come from all sides eventually. We'll have to hold 'em here as best we can."

"But Sunday's gone west!"

"No!" Mary commanded. "We stay and hold here. Sunday can manage."

"Poor Albert!" someone sniffed.

"Will Sally be alright?" Flora asked.

"Of course!" Mary pretended. "Didn't we both topple krakens at Wildwood and then again at Kittiwake? The woman's bloody bullet-proof!"

Flora felt a chill and the landscape seemed to darken. A second later she knew why.

"The cloud!" Morag warned, "It's speeding up."

To their horror they saw she was right. It swirled and shifted like a vast flock of starlings, and it was so dense it seemed night had come early. "There must be millions!" Flora knew the number was woefully small to describe the spectacle.

"Listen," Mary uttered.

Now all of them heard it, the high-pitched chattering of churning metal, like countless blades being sharpened, and Flora realised something terrible. "It's hungry."

"Twins protect us," Mary made the sign of the Oak, and then the living storm above began to descend and that screeching sound grew closer.

It was a Therion, that much was clear, but not one like Clovis. "STAY DOWN!" Sally bellowed. At her feet, Emily cowered in the grass.

Sef hurdled a fallen tree and landed in the clearing, while Chentek's plague whirled in a vortex above and the noise was unbearable. "Clovis, I seek Clovis!" he shouted over the racket.

Sally said nothing, but brandished her staff.

"Don't tell it!" Emily whimpered.

"Give me Clovis and I shall spare you," Sef promised, "I shall spare all of Stormwood."

"Clovis warned us of you!" she retorted. "And how to defeat you!"

Sef gathered more from her words than she knew. Clovis clearly knew he was coming, and he must have left already. "Clovis lied. There is no force able to compete with Self. Why die to protect a liar?" He lowered his sword and edged forward a step.

"Don't trust him!" Emily hissed.

Sally had no such intention. "Help's on its way. Leave, or I'll cut you down right now." She tried not to let the girl see how badly she was shaking.

Sef's lips shrank back into a smile, and a tiny moan escaped her when she saw those terrible teeth. "There is room in the gelding-sack for two, old witch." He looked deliberately in Emily's direction and his tongue flopped out and slurped across his muzzle.

"Sally!" Emily moaned.

"LEAVE OR DIE!" Sally challenged with a roar.

"Not without the thing I came for – give me Clovis and Kolfinnia. Give me both of them and you'll live to see the sunset." He heard the iron-fays squeal in agitation, but he couldn't let them feed yet. "Clovis and the witch!" he demanded. "I shall not ask again!" He advanced, sword raised.

"Emily, run!" Sally hissed.

"I won't!"

"RUN!" She kicked the girl into action, but Emily just cowered in the grass. "For Oak's sake, just go girl!" Sally was close to breaking. The creature's green eyes seemed to burn, and the screaming vortex above drilled into her head. "GO!"

Sef had had enough. This witch was only slowing him down. "Self be mine!" he howled and charged.

"Sally!" Emily screamed.

Sally ran to meet his attack. She had scant seconds to think. *His lightning-staff's slung over his shoulder. He's only got his sword. If he cuts my staff in two we're done for. One good blast, that's all I need. Put him down then finish him.* In the next instant they met in battle.

Sef did just as she knew he would. He drove his sword towards her staff, intending to break it, and she even held it out as bait. At the last moment she veered right, drawing her staff out of harm's way and spinning full circle in the process, just as Clovis had taught them. Sef's momentum pulled him forwards, and now she was on his blind side and ready to strike his unprotected back.

Sef recovered, turned and finished the job. His sword sliced through her throat. Blood jetted up and the iron-fays screamed in frenzy.

Sally staggered backwards, clutching her neck, and saw Emily rush forwards, brandishing her wand. "Emmy, no!" she gurgled, and more blood flowed. She crashed down just as a sobbing Emily stabbed her wand into Sef's midsection. But her blow was weak and her magic was young in years. He swatted her aside contemptuously and she hit the ground hard.

Sally crawled forwards, still clutching her staff, but its magic was fast failing as her sprite weakened. *Emmy,* she thought, *can't let the thing take Emmy!*

Sef saw the dying witch crawling towards him and spat in her direction. "I shall attend to you later," he promised and then reached down and grabbed the terrified girl by the throat. Emily felt fingers strong enough to snap her bones clamp around her neck. She flailed for her wand again, but it lay broken in the grass. He hauled her off her feet and she dangled before him like a snared rabbit, and he pushed his face right into hers. "You will tell me all I want to know girl," he promised, and for good measure he rolled out his wet tongue and licked the terror-soaked sweat from her face.

"Fairies!" someone screamed.

Flora looked up again. Now she could see they weren't birds, they were some species of fairy, but she'd never believed there were so many in the world.

"Fire!" Mary ordered, "fight them off with fire!"

Flora was running to snatch a firebrand out of the brazier, when something landed on her shoulder and instantly began to bite. She swiped it aside, but her hand came away bloody. *Iron-fairies?* she thought, just as shouts and screams erupted all around as Chentek's feast began.

"Em. .m. . ." Sally grated, desperately trying to reach her.

Sef didn't even spare her a second look. He stared into Emily's terrified eyes, raised his sword and pressed it to her neck.

She sobbed and struggled, and looked into those emerald pits. All her desires seemed to wait for her in there, but there was only one thing she longed for right then and by chance, providence, or perhaps by Hethra and Halla themselves, she arrived.

Sef had heard the screams of the defiant, the dying, the brave and the mad down the years, but he'd never heard a scream like this one. He turned to his new attacker, still clutching the girl, and what he saw left him numb. He didn't even notice as his hand wilted and Emily dropped to the grass. *No!* His mind saw something both impossible and offensive. *No!*

"GET AWAY FROM HER!" Sunday blazed into the clearing, and dropped from her staff raving like a berserk.

He saw that she was fierce and beautiful, but that was not the force that so frightened him. It was the thing *around* her, the thing she couldn't even see herself. He saw the shape of a huge spider encircling her and knew who it must be. More incredible still, this witch was criss-crossed with unbreakable threads. Her soul had once been broken, but then mended with the ultimate selfless sacrifice. Lord Self had no power over her, and she had been mended so strong that her soul would never break again. *She cannot die?* He grappled with the impossibility and suddenly a voice boomed across his inner world and rocked his soul to the core.

"DEAR CHAMPION"

Sef clutched his head and screamed. "She cannot die!" he screamed again, this time at the gross breach of universal law and at his impending defeat, for he knew nothing could beat a woman with such a protector.

Even louder now, and the voice terrified him. Nothing could resist it. He staggered away from the impossible witch, snarling in fury before he turned and fled. Around him the horde sensed his defeat and began to disperse in a panic. Chentek tore after him, and their assault quickly became a rout.

Sunday saw the thing hiss and curse, before finally it turned and ran. She was given to chase, but Strike stopped her. *"The girl! Get her away from here!"*

She skidded to a halt and watched Sef shoot away through the trees on his staff. The giant cloud first dissolved into countless tiny bodies, and then followed its master before fading into nothing. "Emmy!" Sunday ran to where she was slumped in the grass, crying her heart out, and Sunday saw why. Sally Crook lay next to her in a pool of blood staring up at the sky. "NO!" Sunday dropped to her side and tried to lift her head and ignore the gaping wound across her throat. Sunday clasped her hand and felt the older woman clasp back. "Sally, Emmy's safe," she sobbed. "You saved her."

Sally twitched a smile, revealing bloody teeth, and she uttered something and Sunday leaned closer. "Alb-er-t," she grated.

"I won't leave him here." Sunday's tears fell and mingled with her blood. Beside her, Emily clutched her hand, crying uncontrollably.

Sally gave Sunday's hand a last squeeze and saw something miraculous around her; a vision as fine as smoke in sunlight, the shape of a weaving spider. She smiled fully this time, for she had much to smile about. Stormwood was saved, and Clovis had once shown her what lay beyond death. With this in mind, Sally Crook died fearless and contented.

She looked so peaceful it was hard for Sunday to believe she was dead, but when her lightning-staff quivered and a gentle light arose from it, she knew. Hail emerged and looked upon his friend a last time. "Hail, I'm sorry."

He never looked her way, having only eyes for Sally, and he spent his last seconds well, gazing upon that which he loved most yet which now lay bloodied and dead before him. In a brilliant flash he ascended. Thunder rumbled and Hail returned to his ancestral home.

Emily shuffled closer. "She's gone to Evermore?"

"She's gone." She drew the girl close and the two queens clung to one another and began to cry out their sorrows.

Strike crawled from his staff and went and said his own farewell to a fine witch and a fellow sprite. He touched the inert staff and Sally's lifeless face, and his thoughts mirrored those of young Marcus. *It's coming for you now Clovis, and I hope you kill it stone dead, and its death is hard and long.*

Sunday looked in the direction Sef had gone, and her thoughts were so in tune with Strike's that she knew what he was thinking and vehemently agreed. She kissed Emily's head and rocked her gently. "Kill it hard Clovis, and kill it forever," she whispered, and thankfully Emily was crying too hard to hear her dark wish.

Inexplicably, the swarm simply vanished. One moment Flora was surrounded by that terrifying sound, and the next, sunlight and silence poured in and Stormwood reappeared. She fell into the grass clutching her staff, still expecting attack but now feeling bewildered. "They're gone?" she blinked against the sudden light.

"Gone!" Torrent confirmed.

Quickly, she scrambled up, half expecting a trick. "Mary?" She looked around and saw equally confused witches looking to the skies. There was nothing up there but fluffy clouds. "What happened?"

Mary stood close by, breathing heavily and bleeding from numerous bites. Nobody it seemed had been too badly mauled. "I don't know." She wiped blood from her cheek. "But go check the pip-staffs are safe, and report back."

Flora ignored the bites on her hands, and set off at a run. Incredibly, the sun was shining and birds were singing again. It seemed surreal that only moments ago they were fighting for survival. As she ran through the coven, she dreaded the sight of wounded or dying, but everywhere was the same picture of incredulous witches who'd survived by the skin of their teeth.

"Flo!" someone called, "what the hell just happened?" It was Ben. "You're unhurt?"

He nodded vaguely, looking confused. "Is Sunday back?"

"Not yet, but she will be."

"She will?" he ached. "You've seen her?"

"Just trust me!" She sidestepped two puzzled-looking witches, both holding firebrands but with nothing to fight any longer.

"What happened?" one of them asked.

"We lived, that's what happened!" she panted.

"But how?" came the reply.

She was almost out of earshot now, running as fast as she could. "Ask Sunday when she gets here!" Now she was certain. Whatever had happened, Blackwand had won through, for who else could have turned the tide?

"Flora, did you see that, did you see those bloody fairies?" Sam Goodstock limped alongside her. There were bites on his cheeks and ears but otherwise he was unscathed.

"Saw them come, and saw them go," she grinned with relief. "I've got to go Sam, got to check the pip-staffs. See to the others." She veered off.

The first thing she saw was the founding-banner billowing in the Glade, proof if any were needed that Stormwood had endured. Children were already being shepherded out of the woods towards it. Scarlet was rounding them up, and shouting over the excited chatter. "Marion, hold your partner's hand and don't wander off! Jonathon, where's your brother? You're the older one, you're supposed to be looking after him!" Flora saw she was holding a child's hand. It was the muddy boy who'd come with the warning.

"Are the pip-staffs alright?" Flora gasped.

"They bloody would be if they stayed still long enough for me to count 'em!" she complained.

"And our guest?" She sank on her haunches level with the boy, whose slight build made him look much younger than ten.

"This is Marcus."

Flora smiled at him, but he didn't smile back. "Hello Marcus," she tried.

"Blackwand," he murmured. "Blackwand killed it?"

Flora and Scarlet swapped glances. "We'll find out soon enough. But for now stay here, yes?" He became silent again, and Flora took a moment with Scarlet. "Poor thing's in shock. Where's he from?"

"Not sure yet. Won't say."

Flora bent closer again. "Marcus, I've a friend, and she's been through things like you. Would you like me to find her?"

He just looked at the ground, stunned rather than sullen.

She turned back to Scarlet. "Keep him close. We'll get him shelter sorted."

"And this 'friend' of yours, can she help him?"

"I'm sure." Blackwand might have saved the coven, but Rowan might be just what was needed to save this boy. "I'll find her as soon as I can."

"Where you off now?"

"East." Flora broke into run, and what's more even she found her smile again. Their brush with danger had highlighted what was precious. She was off to find Farona and tell him something important.

He didn't know who they were and he didn't care, he simply killed them both to salve his wounded ego. Sef flew north at incredible speed, consumed by rage. At sunset he landed in remote farmland with no idea where he was. There was a cottage and maybe the young women had come from there, maybe not, he didn't care. He'd heard someone coming along the track as dusk was gathering. He heard their laughter and smelled sour milk and manure on them, and tormented by shame he struck them both. The first he cut down in an instant. The second had no time to scream before he pounced on her. She was strong and well made, and as he choked the life from her he imagined the blonde witch in black garb. He imagined it was *her* face turning red, *her* eyes bulging in terror and *her* bones snapping in his grip. When her struggles ended he dumped both bodies in a ditch and marched deeper into the woods looking for privacy and darkness equal to that in his soul. He sat in silent contemplation seeking Lord Self, but the girls' deaths left him feeling strangely inadequate. He could kill a hundred more and still today's shame would linger. How he *hated* that black witch. How he *feared* her.

Iso had never seen him so furious and he knew to keep quiet. Even Chentek withdrew into a state of semi-hibernation. The trees were heavy with iron-fairies but there wasn't a sound from any of them. Every living thing around Sef was cowed into silence. Birds and rats scurried into their holes. Even the insects in the leaf litter sensed his boiling hatred and stilled for fear of death.

Eventually, when his anger had simmered enough, he stood staring up at Vega, and shut out all other senses. The brilliant pinpoint became the centre of his awareness and he fell into a deep trance-like state. His breathing all but stopped and his body was as stone, but his mind raced out to the furthest black seeking answers from Lord Self. *Why had a lone witch defeated him? How is it that her guardian was the very weaver of fate? Where had Clovis gone and why?*

Sef stood inanimate, staring at the glimmering beacon of Vega. The darkness hours passed and he shifted not an inch, while inside his head plans and countermeasures, schemes and plots wove together to provide him the perfect solution. Just before dawn, his muzzle twitched and he blinked. Awareness tingled in his limbs once more and he smiled, revealing those ivory fangs. Lord Self had *indeed* told him what he must do.

Sef was going to the faded-realm. . . by force.

CHAPTER THIRTEEN

Lions alone

'A witch is a witch, be they in a coven of hundreds or alone in the world.'
Author unknown

Fortunately the hotel in York, suitably named The Royal Oak, adjoined
the train station, so they had little trouble navigating the crowds and
slipping inside. Kolfinnia felt less nervous when she ascended the stairs
this time. She was getting a feel for this way of life, although certainly
not a liking. "What time do we leave tomorrow?" All four were sitting in
Clovis's room, which was so big that it boasted its own drawing room.

"There's a train at ten, and the journey's about six hours." Hathwell had
done his homework.

Clovis was busy studying one of his diagrams of Helthorn Castle. "When
were you last there?" he checked again.

"It must be fifteen years or more."

"These are good diagrams," he complimented.

Kolfinnia pulled her shawl higher. Although it was July the room was
draughty. "How far from Edinburgh is this castle?"

"Hmm," he tapped his bottom lip. "Some twenty-five miles westwards,
near Falkirk."

"And when we get to Helthorn, how will we be presented?" Clovis continued.

"We'll be asked to sign declarations of intent, and then appointed
quarters until our claim is validated."

"Come again?" Kolfinnia asked.

He was about to elaborate when he noticed her shawl. "Would you like me to have a fire lit?"

She was touched by his concern. "No. I don't really want staff coming up here. Let's just keep it us for now."

"Of course. Well, a declaration is just a signed document to prove who we are."

"But we're not who we are. . ." She looked to the others, feeling worried.

"It's a formality, the declarations are checked by clerks in London. The process takes weeks. It's really to make sure of our identity for when the estate is broken up, and that could be years away."

"Oh, I see," she relaxed again. "And while all this paperwork's being sorted we're expected to stay at the castle, yes?"

"Yes, hence our quarters. There'll be numerous families there. Some will be willing to wait for a few years if needed."

"A few years!"

"Oh yes. One Austrian duchess lived at a palace in Belgrade for nineteen years before the will was finally sorted."

"I wouldn't waste my life sitting around a musty old castle." Hilda was reclining on a chaise longue, eating dates like a woman on holiday.

"That's not the worst of it. In the end her claim was rejected and she had to pay nineteen years worth of rent."

Clovis shook his head, "Your race continues to astound me."

"Not *our* race dear," Hilda corrected.

"Signing claims and taking quarters is just part of the act. I doubt we'll even sleep in the rooms they give us, let alone pay for them," Hathwell assured everyone.

"Well, that's the 'getting in' part taken care of," Kolfinnia said. "Question is what do we *do* when we get in there?"

"Hathwell and I locate this 'trophy Therion' while you prepare the distraction we spoke of," Clovis outlined. "Get the pact-of-grace, and get out fast."

"And then you'll leave." She instantly regretted saying it.

He ran a hand through his mane and looked at the floor. "I'll take the pact somewhere quiet, a place where I can cross to the faded-realm in secret."

He looked up and caught her eye, "But first I'll make sure you three are safely on your way."

Her smile was grateful but sad.

Hathwell pondered. "We'll come back via Glasgow. Less chance of being seen twice."

Hilda finished another date. "I've never been to Glasgow, this really is turning into a grand tour isn't it."

"By then we might be travelling third class," he warned. "Can you cope?"

"I've been holed up in worse places."

"I'm sure." He recalled Hobbs Ash and his brow became moist.

"I think our plans are concluded," Clovis stretched and stifled a yawn. "Sleep would be welcome."

"A wise option," Hilda agreed, now wiping her hands on a napkin. "Kolfinnia?"

"Yes, it's been a long day." She got to her feet. "Goodnight father, goodnight my Lord," she curtseyed to Clovis.

"Yes," he agreed. "We're getting closer, time to be different people. Goodnight Miss Saxon." He turned to Hilda, "And to you Mrs Saxon."

"My Lord," she offered him a similar curtsey.

"Mr Saxon, be so good as to show my guests out." Clovis found the pretence too sobering to muster a smile.

"This way my dear," Hathwell escorted them to the door and opened it for them. "Goodnight to you both."

"Goodnight dear husband," Hilda returned, and if she was feigning affection she made a very good job of it.

"Goodnight father," Kolfinnia bid him.

He gave an anxious shiver and watched his wife and young daughter glide past and return to their own room accompanied by the whisper of satin.

Stormwood's first reaction was disbelief, quickly followed by relief, but neither of these things lasted when news of Albert and Sally's deaths spread.

Sunday brought Emily home, and then returned with a heavily armed party to recover Sally, Albert and Mally. All three were taken home with honour, but also a profound sense of grief. Evil had come to their coven and two witches and an innocent animal had paid with their lives. Sally Crook and Albert Parry were the first witches to be buried at Stormwood. Mally was buried alongside her friend and all three were afforded a place along the perimeter of the Glade, and already their graves were adorned with candles and offerings. It wasn't a decision Sunday took lightly, knowing it would set the precedent for future burials, hopefully elderly witches who died a natural death.

"Here at least they're still with us. The Glade is the centre of the coven, and we should keep our dead central to our hearts." Sunday was giving an epitaph on the evening of the tragedy. She stood atop the Anvil, while the coven watched from the Glade. "We turned the evil aside today, blessed be the twins, and while Sally and Albert thwarted its wicked purpose we can safely assume the creature was in pursuit of Clovis. Many of you have asked me if the beast will return and relish the prospect, for there's much anger, but I implore you, don't succumb. Our vengeance will be for Clovis to be victorious, and for Kolfinnia's party to return to a peaceful and resilient Stormwood. Those that wish to see the beast defeated should send their love to Clovis, for it is he who will deliver the blow of justice that we all so long for. Peace be with Clovis and Stormwood, and blessings eternal on the twins," she concluded.

The applause was ardent but solemn. She stepped down and now Sally and Albert's friends waited to share their anecdotes. Traditionally, this was the moment when the mourners were encouraged to remember their fellows with humour. Sunday hoped this part would lift their spirits, and Oak knew they needed it.

Mary Fife climbed up onto the Anvil and began speaking fondly of Sally. Now she had the dubious distinction of being the only witch present who'd fought in Valonia's legendary defence of Wildwood.

"Do you think he'll come back, this Sef?" Ben asked quietly from her side.

Sunday took his hand. "No, in all honesty I don't. It's Clovis we must think of now."

He was quiet for a moment and she knew what he was thinking about. "Do you think it fled because of what you told me, you know – of becoming Blackwand?"

It was a good question, she thought. *Once again, perhaps my past mistake has yielded something good.* She certainly wanted to believe so. "Perhaps," she replied, and beside her Ben clasped her hand tighter and said no more.

Flora listened as Mary praised a woman she'd known her whole life, and memories of growing up with Sally Crook as her mentor made her cry.

Farona eased an arm around her shoulder and held her close. "Remember when Clovis showed you all the promise of Evermore. Sally's there now, and we'll go there too one day."

"I know," she sniffed. "And thank you." She leaned forwards and kissed him. It was brief and shy, but to Farona it was the start of a new life. He just wished he could tell Clovis where that door had led to and thank him with all his heart. The pair listened to Sally and Albert's greatest moments, understanding that whatever Sef was, amongst other things he deserved their pity, because he knew nothing as grand as friendship or love.

Gentle laughter spread through the crowd as Mary shared something witty and Sunday breathed a sigh of relief at last. *Stormwood endures, witches endure, Oak Endures,* she reflected. Another hand took hers and she looked down to see Rowan.

"I liked what you said before, about the dead being with us." She pressed against her, and unusually she was sucking her thumb.

Sunday held her close. "How's Marcus?"

"He's still sleeping."

"Has he told you anything?"

Her thumb slipped from her mouth, "He told me he followed a hare to find us. Lady Halla sent it for him. And he escaped the Sef by staying in the cold water."

"He told you that?" But Rowan just shrugged as if to say 'maybe', and as always the girl's talents mystified her. "Well, I know he'll be fine now he's got you to talk to."

"I'm glad to have something to take my mind off Kolfinnia." She considered a moment and then stunned them both when from nowhere she said quite evenly, "I like him. I think we'll get married one day."

She couldn't help it but Sunday started to laugh, and Ben followed. "I like a witch who knows their own mind," he grinned.

Rowan gave Sunday a curious look. Typically it was a 'knowing' kind of look, and Sunday half smiled. *She knows,* she thought, *she knows.*

On the Anvil, Mary was recounting how Sally had toppled krakens at Wildwood, and Sunday imagined the dangers awaiting Clovis and his Lions. She sighed again and held her little sister close. Both thought of their fated sister, and where she might be, and Sunday quietly asked the weaver of fate to watch over them, because one way or another Stormwood and its witches couldn't help them any longer.

****

Kolfinnia had set out into the wider world expecting exposure any moment, and on the morning they left York it finally came.

Their train hadn't even left the sidings thanks to a broken engine blocking the line. As the platforms grew more and more crowded, Kolfinnia grew ever more tense. It was hot, her clothes were suffocating and Clovis seemed too conspicuous. "How much longer?" she groaned, wafting her fan for all its worth.

"Hathwell's gone off to see what's happening, he won't be long," Hilda looked out from under her parasol.

"He went thirty minutes ago," she complained, watching the hands on the station clock creep forwards inch by inch, while frustratingly on other platforms engines rumbled past puffing clouds of steam. "I'm going to see if he's in trouble."

Hilda looked about. "Alright, but I can't leave Clovis alone." She practically stood in front of him to conceal him.

"I'll go alone, I won't be long."

"Crown me if trouble calls," she said from the corner of her mouth.

"It'll be loud enough to stand your hair on end," Kolfinnia pledged.

"Be careful," Clovis mumbled from behind his mask.

She wasted no time, heading straight for the Station Master's office, which was by now besieged by irate travellers. Hathwell was most likely caught in the middle of it, she reasoned. On the way she didn't notice the stocky man with the narrow nose, blotchy face and curly dark hair, but he noticed her. He tugged his cap down to hide his face, slipped his hands into his waistcoat pockets and fell in behind her, meandering through the crowd with predatory intent. When Kolfinnia moved around an obstruction he did the same. He saw nothing but the young woman in the maroon dress, and more specifically the dainty bag about her wrist. Victorian ladies always carried their most precious valuables in such bags. Donald Small was his name and he'd killed for less than a lady's purse in the past.

Last month he'd followed two women out of Kings Cross and trailed them through the narrow streets backing the station, knowing he had little time before they got to the busy Caledonian Road. At the last moment he'd made a grab at one's purse, but she'd screamed. Old Donny was ready though, oh yes. Quick as a flash he'd jabbed his knife into her ribs and dropped the slut to the cobbles. No more screaming, no more fuss, but her companion was off like a scalded cat. He took her bag and scarpered.

Ten streets later, out of puff and out of trouble, he'd slit open the little bag and found nought but bloody lavender inside. Nothing, not even a bloody shilling, just stinking dried lavender. He'd tossed the bag into the Thames and headed north, thinking he'd lay low for a while. He finally found himself in York and made sure to avoid trouble, that is until he'd seen the slut in the maroon dress waving her valuables around for all to see, and the temptation was too much.

As he stalked her he flexed his fingers in readiness. A few more steps and he would be right behind her. A quick snatch and he'd be off before she could even yell. Although he wanted to, he couldn't do more. *Pity, if I could get her down one of the side streets, I'd stick her with more than just my blade,* he fantasised.

"Hathwell?" Kolfinnia's impatience was growing. "Where are you?" She stopped and craned this way and that.

Small dipped behind a cart piled with suitcases, drew out a grubby hanky and pretended to wipe his nose, all the while keeping her locked in his sights. The velvet bag around her wrist dangled like a lure. "Christ, she's just askin' for it," he sneered. Her worried frown and meandering path told him that she didn't know the station, which made her vulnerable. She set off again, and he stuffed the handkerchief away and crept after her.

Kolfinnia glanced across the crowds towards the clock. Hilda and Clovis were off in that direction, but now it looked far away. If she didn't find Hathwell in the next minute she decided she'd head back. She sighed, pressed fingers to her hip and touched hrafn-dimmu under the satin. "We're both a long way from home," she mourned. There were whistles, thundering engines and voices all around her. Hathwell could be anywhere. "Oh this is hopeless."

Small read her like a book and took his chance.

She turned back, only to be shunted roughly as a man barged into her. At first she thought it was just rudeness, but suddenly her wrist was gripped and her arm yanked hard enough to throw her sideways. "Hey!"

Small seized the little bag, but it caught on her cuff buttons and tore open. Something tumbled out and he knew expertly that it wasn't valuables.

"Hey, stop, HELP!" She jerked back. The bag tore completely and the rest of her charm-pebbles spilled out and rattled over the flags. Now faces were turning her way.

Damn the slut! He let go, shoved her violently and ran.

She stumbled backwards, crashing into people, but hands grasped her, breaking her fall and a second later she was looking at York's station roof from a very undignified position.

"Good heavens! Miss, are you alright?" Enquires bombarded her, but her mind was on her charms. To her they screamed 'witch!' and now they were scattered across the station blaring her secret to the world.

"Allow me to assist you miss," another voice came.

She gathered her wits. "Yes, I'm fine, quite alright now." She struggled to fend off the questions and scoop up the little pebbles as she babbled her apology.

"Nasty fall, who was that brute? I ought to apprehend the blighter." A man in a top hat waved a cane in the direction her attacker had vanished, but he looked too old to offer chase. "I'll call a constable miss."

"No, no please sir there's no need." As she climbed to her feet she tried to drape the stones with her dress or kick them away out of sight. She was dimly aware of someone's hand on her elbow, supporting her.

"But the bounder tried to rob you!"

"No need I assure you," she stressed, "please don't call for the police."

"No need. I'm already here." This new voice was solid and calm and she turned to see a fair-haired man with a moustache and wearing a brown checked suit and a bowler hat. Straight away she saw that he was relatively young, and rather attractive, and then she realised that it was his hand on her elbow. "Allow me miss; Detective Sergeant Robertson, off duty I might add. Are you hurt?"

Police. The thought hit her like a spear. "My thanks Detective Sergeant," she smiled prettily, meanwhile easing a foot over the nearest pebble. *If he sees them I'm caught.*

Robertson gently eased his hand from her elbow, down her arm and to her wrist where he inspected the ruined bag. "Lost your valuables I see. It's best I call for a constable miss." He fumbled in his waistcoat for his whistle.

If he moved her cuff just a fraction more, she knew her Hethra tattoo would show. Despite her rising alarm, she slipped into her Catherine persona. "Really, Mr Robertson, your assistance is most kind but I fear the man is already long gone. I am unhurt and nothing of value was taken. Now forgive me, but I must return, for fear my train will depart without me." She withdrew and turned to go, knocking a pebble with her foot as she did, and winced at her blunder.

Without letting go of her hand, he stooped and picked it up. "This yours miss?" He examined the small stone and the mysterious symbol painted on it. "Curious artefact to have about one's person?" Something in his stare told her he knew a lie when he heard one.

'The Flowering!' The voice came from nowhere, or perhaps from a faraway cavern.

She understood at once, dispelled her doubts and reached for the prize. "Just trinkets sir. My uncle returned from Africa a year ago bringing them with him and bid me wear them for protection. A silly superstition I know, but Uncle Horace is so dear to me I simply had to indulge him." Deceit didn't empower her words, but will. She willed herself to *know* what Robertson would say next, understanding that if her will was sufficient then fate would be woven to match it. *'That's quite alright miss.'* She made herself know he would say it. *'That's quite alright miss.'* She had to *know* it.

Far away she imagined nimble legs weaving silken threads. *'That's quite alright miss.'*

Robertson frowned, examined the pebble again and let go of her hand. "That's quite alright miss," he relaxed and handed the stone over. "And maybe they worked, you're lucky not to have been hurt."

She gave him a shy smile, "My uncle will be over the moon to know his 'magic' protected me."

His smile broadened. For a moment he looked on the verge of saying something further, then he tapped his hat. "A good day to you miss." Then he was gone.

Kolfinnia watched his domed hat weave through the crowds and finally out of sight. "Dear champion?" she wondered, before setting off back to the others on rubbery legs, and with her heart still galloping.

A further thirty minutes later and they were at last ready to leave York. The carriage was once again plush but baking hot. Kolfinnia was settling down, glad to be out of public sight, when just then the guard opened their compartment and for a horrible moment she thought Robertson had sent constables to arrest them all. Instead, two late passengers boarded and suddenly the compartment felt very small and she wished Hathwell had bought those extra tickets after all. Both men ignored them as they hoisted their baggage onto the overhead racks, and after some theatrical fuss and mutterings about 'others taking up the baggage room', the pair took their seats facing one another: one next to Hilda and the other next to Hathwell. Kolfinnia stole a sideways glance, then checked the others. Hathwell was staring blankly at an old newspaper, pretending to read it, while Clovis, sat furthest away from the newcomers, was wrapped up as always and pretending to sleep.

As the pair settled down and retrieved their own newspapers, Kolfinnia examined them a little closer. Both looked the same age, around forty, and both wore country tweeds. Despite their neat clothes, both had dirty fingernails and muddy boots, which set her wondering.

The whistle blew and the train set off with a jolt. Sunlight swept in as they rolled out from under the station, and one of them finally noticed the odd-looking gentleman by the window. He didn't get much of a look because almost right away they entered a tunnel. Even in the dark and drowned out by the clatter of pistons, Kolfinnia could sense his curiosity. They exited the tunnel with another whistle blast and it came as no surprise to her to see both men now peering at Clovis over their newspapers. They swapped bemused looks and went back to reading.

The carriage was hot and she must have nodded off because the next thing she knew she heard voices. Kolfinnia sat motionless and listened before opening her eyes.

"I tell you, this infernal business has her trademarks all over it. Didn't she blight a northern steel town last month too?" The first voice was high pitched.

"Newspapers say the harlot was hanged and good riddance. Even the crows wouldn't peck at that she-devil's flesh. No, it was some foreign agents, anti-colonialists perhaps." The second voice had a moist sound about it and Kolfinnia imagined wet lips. She heard the rustle of newspapers. Were they debating some recent news article she wondered?

"Well think what you may," the first voice came again. "I for one see the truth of it – the Blackwand agitator had a hand in it. And even if she's dead, who's to say her raving devotees aren't behind it?"

Blackwand? Her heart felt to punch her ribs and she couldn't stop her eyes fluttering open. The first thing she saw was the stony mask of Hilda's face, who must have endured the whole conversation.

"I trust you're refreshed my dear?" she asked.

"Thank you mother, yes." She kept her voice low and tried to sink out of sight behind Hathwell's open newspaper. The man sitting beside Hilda glanced her way. What the other was doing she couldn't see. He held her gaze a fraction of a second longer than was comfortable, then redirected his attention to his paper. Kolfinnia laid her hands in her lap and touched hrafn-dimmu through her dress. She was burning to ask what had happened, what was Blackwand being accused of now?

"The authorities ought to have exterminated the heathen brutes," one sniffed.

"Evidently they didn't do a sufficient job and the canker grew back," the reply came.

Kolfinnia bristled. Hilda fixed her with a penetrating stare. *Don't say a word!*

she mouthed silently. Kolfinnia looked at the floor, dreading what they might say next.

"Might be agitators anywhere," one declared loudly. She didn't see, but she detected a kind of silent communication pass between them, followed by a pretend sigh. "It's stuffy in here. Happen I'll open a window." He was on his feet and aiming to shuffle past and open the window above Clovis's head.

"Please, allow me." Hilda quickly reached over and opened it for him, denying him the chance to inspect the mysterious Baron. "There, the fresh air will revive us all." She sat down and offered him a tight little smile.

"Obliged madam." He concealed his chagrin and returned to his seat. "A warm day to be so wrapped up is it not?" he addressed Hilda, but looked at Clovis. Kolfinnia felt a tingle of apprehension and heard Hathwell growl something.

"You refer to my travel companion sir? Alas, Mr Pegalia speaks no English," Hilda apologised. "And at present he is suffering from a malaise of the airways, and hence he must keep warm as per doctor's orders."

"Mr Peg-alia? Not an English name." His smile didn't soften the glint in his eyes.

"Hence why he speaks no English," she explained with aplomb.

"Funny looking chap." He noted the hairy skin around the eyes and wondered what abomination lurked under the mask. "Is he some kind of medical freak?"

Outraged by his rudeness, she nevertheless kept cool. "Mr Pegalia suffers a rare skin condition, exacerbated by man's innate tendency to persecute those different and unlike."

If he grasped her chastisement he didn't let on. Instead he cast a sly glance at his companion and before long they were talking about investments, racehorses and the poor state of the railways. Kolfinnia glanced Clovis's way. A pair of eyes flickered open in the dark cave under his hat, and as always his steady gaze was like looking into a calm pool and it soothed her.

The tortuous journey continued. All the way, Kolfinnia sensed their conversation was an act intended to inflame. Firm, and often crass, opinions were bandied about and newspapers were ruffled loudly. When they weren't insulting the poor or the unfortunate, they pretended to read.

Kolfinnia frequently caught them glancing Clovis's way, and each time she pressed her hand against her wand. Maybe she could turn their lying tongues to lead, she wondered darkly.

Finally, when they were approaching Durham the two men made to alight. One of them was caught by a coughing fit and Hilda stepped in smoothly. "Pardon me sir, but it sounds as if you have a bronchial indisposition. Here," she took a small tin from her dress and opened it. "These lozenges are medicinal. Please take one."

He dabbed his mouth with his handkerchief and recoiled from the offered tin and the tiny dark tablets inside. "What are they madam?"

"A potent curative called Valonia. Please be my guest."

Reluctantly, he took one.

"My compliments." She held his gaze and he was obliged to swallow the tiny pill down. To his surprise it was tasteless and vanished easily.

Hilda saw Durham Castle and Cathedral slide into view, followed mercifully by the platform. "Good day gentlemen."

They finally came to a halt and the door was thrown open by a station guard. Both spared a last glance at Clovis and then the door slammed and they were gone, whereupon Kolfinnia deflated like a punctured balloon. "At last! They were awful!"

Hathwell dropped his newspaper, revealing an admiring smile. "I thought *I* was supposed to be your guide? That was artful!"

Clovis slid his mask down an inch. "A curative called Valonia?" he smiled.

Hilda closed the tin. "Night-sorrel. Brought them by mistake. They're actually Albert's. He gives them to Mally."

"What for?"

"Why, chronic constipation my dear, what else," she smiled wickedly. "Let's hope he has enough pennies for the public amenities."

Hilda settled back and admired the view while the others started to laugh.

The day took a turn for the worse after they reached Berwick-upon-Tweed. Some obstruction further up the line meant they arrived in Edinburgh two hours late, and by now it was early evening. Seeing no other solution, Clovis reluctantly agreed to spend a third night in a hotel, this time in Edinburgh itself. But it took Hathwell over an hour to find vacant rooms, and all the while they had to wait at the station surrounded by crowds and fending off polite but probing attempts at conversation. In the end they took two rooms at the Falcon hotel in the heart of the city. The staff were unfriendly and the rooms expensive, but by now all they wanted was privacy and rest. Kolfinnia and Hilda shared their room with an adjoining single room taken by Hathwell, while Clovis had to take a single room further down the hall with instructions to only open the door upon a secret knock. He unpacked his lightning-staff and Kolfinnia did likewise, feeling she hadn't seen Skald in a month.

"A grand city," Skald watched the gaslights flicker into life on the streets below, while the castle's hulking outline dominated the skyline.

"Right now I'd settle for homely." Kolfinnia stood staring out of the window. She felt adrift and so wore her plain old Flower-Forth dress, now badly crumpled from its travels. "I'd give anything to be back at Stormwood." She let the lacy curtain fall back into place and Edinburgh was blotted out.

"Me too." Hilda sat sewing in a rocking chair under the gaslight.

Kolfinnia could hear the slurp of water in the next room, where Hathwell was taking a bath. Confident he wouldn't disturb them, she asked Hilda something that had been on her mind for some time, "Hilly, what will Clovis face in the faded-realm?"

The rocking chair ceased and her needle paused. "I've heard of witches walking the faded-realm, but never have I spoken to any. I believe it is a mirror of sorts."

"Mirror?"

"What happens here has consequences there. It might look similar to our world, but it'll be different, sometimes glaringly different, sometimes subtly so."

"I know little of the faded-realm," Kolfinnia revealed. Again, her young age felt to weigh her down.

Hilda adjusted her cushion. "It's reputed to be a land of countless wonders, fanciful I know, but the stories are hard to resist. Therion races of endless species, many like Clovis himself, but countless others – the Caprians are the goat-headed beings, the Bjoren are the bear-folk, then there are the bull-headed Mynos, the wolfen that many ignorant souls call 'werewolves'. There are mermaids and mermen we know collectively as Merlins. And don't forget the unicorns, the dragons, centaurs and the vampires."

"Vampires!" Kolfinnia cut in.

"The bat-headed priests dedicated to Hethra and Halla, and feed upon the 'blood of life', the energy of the cosmos. The vampire myth was always a way to smear them and their teachings."

"And what else?" Kolfinnia was fascinated.

Hilda set her chin in her hand and stared dreamily into space. "There are witches there too I'm told. Therion-witches, dedicated to the sleeping twins. Each village has its own witch, they don't have to live in secret, and Therions go to them for advice, spells or a hundred other things. It's a privileged place Clovis is going to."

Kolfinnia stroked Skald's brow absently. He arched his back and stretched. It had been a long journey for such an energetic soul. "But will he be safe Hilly?" she asked at last.

"You heard the Flowering. 'If the will is sufficiently strong'. And he has such a will."

She thought of her victory at York Station and felt a little better. "And tomorrow he goes there."

"Take heart. Whatever mysterious force brought him here watches over him yet I'm sure."

She sighed heavily, "Thank you."

"Now, would you like to check on Clovis or shall I?"

She regarded her Flower-Forth dress. "Perhaps you'd better."

Hilda got to her feet, making the chair rock lazily. "In that case, tell your dear father not to use all the hot water and I'll be back presently."

Kolfinnia saw her out and then made sure to bolt the door again. She couldn't help but smile when she heard Hathwell singing the Ballad of Oak and Holly from the bathroom. Hilda had kept her promise, and she was patiently teaching him Pegalia.

The following morning, nobody had an appetite for breakfast and instead kept to their rooms as Hathwell went about finding a driver to take them to the Helthorn Estate. It wasn't hard, but it cost. He found a driver named

William Spencer, but had to pay for the fellow's lodging and two days' wages because the return journey was too far for the horses in one day. Hathwell returned to the hotel and told the rest to get ready. They had a good two hours before Spencer called to collect them, but there was much to be done.

Kolfinnia's hour had come and she prepared her hair and complexion just as Sunday had shown her. Hilda likewise ensured her appearance left nothing to chance, and she lit the fire especially to have an iron to press her garments. While the women helped one another get ready, Clovis and Hathwell did the same. Shoes and buttons were polished to a high shine. Muddy marks were dabbed away from suits and shirts, gloves and hats. Those that had them, ensured wands were easily accessible and Hathwell packed their lightning-staffs and Clovis's sword securely, but with minimum bindings in case they needed them quickly.

Kolfinnia checked the clock on the mantle. It was half-past eleven. In fifteen minutes they would make their way downstairs and meet Spencer at the rear of the hotel. "How do I look?" she asked.

"Immaculate," Hilda admired the striking young woman who was Catherine Saxon. "Truly immaculate."

"Thank you," Kolfinnia blushed, and played with her fan nervously. "Shall I check on the others?"

"They'll come when they're ready." Hilda slid another pin into her hair. She took a deep breath. "If only Stormwood could see me now."

"They'd be very proud of you."

"They needn't be, I'm as nervous as I can remember." She lifted her dress and paced over to the door, listening for footsteps.

"Kolfinnia, take a moment," she patted the couch.

Reluctantly, she came and sat beside her, but kept one eye on the door, the other on the clock.

"This is a very testing day for all of us, but especially you and Clovis."

"Us both?" She toyed with the pendant around her neck, feeling like a pip-staff, not a coven-mother.

"He wishes to leave you no more than you wish it yourself." She took her hand. "And to face a dangerous mission and lose a loved one on the same day, well I defy anyone not to worry."

"Even coven-mothers?"

"Especially coven-mothers. Now, they'll be here any minute, and we don't want you to spoil that lovely face of yours." She reached for a handkerchief and passed it over.

"You can thank Sunday for that," Kolfinnia managed a laugh as she dabbed her eyes dry.

"And we can thank Hathwell for getting us this far."

She considered asking outright about him, when there was a discreet knock at the door.

"That's them." Hilda stood and smoothed the front of her outfit.

Kolfinnia hurried to the door, opened it a crack and saw Hathwell's serious face. "It's time," he declared, and with that the journey to Helthorn had really begun.

Helthorn hadn't changed, but upon seeing it again Hathwell felt the years pile against him like falling leaves.

"Hathwell," Clovis growled.

"Sorry?" He blinked away the memories.

"No time for daydreams."

"I know," he replied irritably, and slipped on the spectacles and top hat. Around him the others were busying nervous hands with last minute preparations.

"Everyone know their role?" Clovis checked.

"To the letter." Hilda lowered her veil another inch and checked her wand under her dress.

Kolfinnia listened to hooves and wheels crunch across gravel as the carriage turned past the gatehouse and along the drive. "It's so hot!" She wafted her fan, and now it wasn't just for show. "This 'distraction' we've planned, Hilda what if I can't do it?"

The older woman shook her head at the impossibility. "You're coven-mother – you will."

"But the heat? I'm starting to think it'll make the spell impossible!"

"You *will* triumph and the heat will only make our distraction all the more complete." She squeezed her hand. "You will triumph."

"I will triumph," she repeated, and peered out just in time to catch her first sight of Helthorn itself; a stark castle surrounded by heather-capped hills.

The rambling castle was built in the Scottish style and sat at the end of an avenue of towering fir trees. The walls were white and the roof was a mass of crenellated battlements, turrets, spires and chimney stacks. The castle was surrounded by numerous outbuildings, gravelled pathways and neatly cut lawns. "It looks formidable." She hadn't realised that she'd spoken.

"Then good for us we're infiltrating, not invading," Clovis remarked.

The carriage trundled past a white peacock grazing on the lawn, and then another, and then suddenly a fountain topped with a clock tower rolled into view and she realised that they had arrived.

"Let me talk. Speak only if necessary," Hathwell dictated again.

The carriage halted with a bump and the sudden silence felt ominous. Spencer dropped from his driving seat and they heard his crunching footsteps, then the door opened briskly. "We're here sirs, ma'am." He stood holding the door wide and lowered the step, inviting them to exit. "Shall I inform the estate Captain of your arrival sir?"

"No need." Hathwell climbed out of the carriage and proffered a hand to Hilda. "My dear?"

She slipped her gloved hand into his, lifted her dress and gracefully climbed down. She never made eye contact with Spencer but instead quickly appraised their surroundings. Kolfinnia came next and again Hathwell's hand was there to aid her. She looked every inch the noble young woman. "Thank you father," she mumbled. After a brief look around she mentally evaluated what she'd seen. *A platoon of soldiers to the west by the stables. Open lawns all round. It would be hard to find cover if we had to run for it.*

Clovis came last and Spencer worked hard not to stare. He dropped to the gravel and immediately went into his play-act. Kolfinnia had seen him practise, but it still astonished her. He slouched, and the power visibly drained from him and he seemed to shrink in stature. His stout arms fell limp by his side and to add to the effect he began to cough behind the mask. It sounded dry and feverish, and more importantly: contagious.

"I'll fetch your baggage sir," Spencer volunteered, taking a step back.

Hathwell nodded and the driver vanished behind his carriage and began to unfasten buckles and straps. All four stood looking around, but casually, as if this was just another castle similar to the many they'd seen before. All of them noted the soldiers executing some parade drill over by the stable block. The castle loomed over them, and Kolfinnia wondered what alien world waited inside. Here they were in the heart of Krast's empire, although that empire was now fragmented and decaying. *The man who tortured Rowan came from here.* Again she regarded the blank walls and imagined the corruption behind them. She caressed hrafn-dimmu again, and wished she could take it and crack these walls to rubble.

Just then Spencer appeared with their baggage. "Shall I call for one of the serving staff to have them taken to your rooms?" he asked.

"No, that won't be necessary. Leave them here, we'll find someone presently. For your trouble sir." Hathwell stuffed a banknote into his surprised hand and tapped his cane to his hat, hoping he would take the hint and leave without any further questions.

"God bless you sir!" Spencer was astounded at the hefty five-pound tip. "I'll take the horses for water and hay, then be on my way."

"Safe journey Mr Spencer," Hathwell wished him without looking around. Instead he drank in the castle and tasted a hundred different memories. *Noble knight, faithful squire*, he thought.

Kolfinnia's heart accelerated when she heard their carriage trundle off towards the stables. Their lifeline was leaving them behind, alone in the Illuminata's world. She couldn't take her eyes off the towering castle. Its white walls were almost blinding in the baking sun, and again she fanned herself to cool her nerves. *It looks so white, so pure. But its guts are black.*

"Hopefully we shan't linger," Hilda whispered from her side.

She was just about to answer when a voice called to them. "This estate is private sir, I have no record of visitors due this day?"

All of them turned to see a short man in tweeds and puffing on a pipe, marching towards them with a pair of gun dogs trailing after him. "Visitors aren't expected. Am I to believe there's been an error in the estate's register?" He had a soft Perth accent and chose his words diplomatically, but his tone made it sound like Helthorn never made mistakes and these strangers were certainly not welcome.

Hathwell slipped easily into character. "By the look of it there must be. Were you not expecting Baron Clovis Krast's party?" He leaned on his cane and looked the man directly in the eye. Hilda meanwhile shot the man her most indignant look, while Kolfinnia tried to look aloof. Clovis skulked at the back out of sight.

"Baron?"

"Baron Clovis Krast has travelled far from Hungary these last eleven days just to get here. Did you not get my telegram?"

"Telegram?"

"Damn it man don't repeat everything I say! I telegrammed six weeks ago detailing our visit, and I was sent a telegram from the Captain's office in reply, our arrival is expected. And might I add I find it most underhanded that the Baron was not informed sooner of the demise of the estate's former owner. Was it someone's intention to deny him his due of the will?"

"There's been no deception sir, I assure you!" he blustered.

"That remains to be seen. Whom am I addressing anyway?"

The man swiped the pipe from his mouth and stood straight. "Mclean sir, junior estate manager."

Junior, yes. Now he looked, Hathwell saw that he couldn't have been more than thirty. "Well Mclean, the Baron is drained from his long journey. His constitution is frail and he requires quarters at once."

At this Clovis coughed again, and Mclean spared him a wary look. There was the suggestion of furred skin and amber eyes above the man's mask. *He's not just ill, he's bloody deformed,* he thought.

One of Mclean's dogs was sniffing intently at Clovis's foot, that is until he growled softly and it scurried away with its tail tucked between its legs.

Hathwell made the introductions, "I am his chief retainer, Mr Bernard Saxon, and this is Hilda my lady wife, and Catherine my daughter." He indicated each of them in turn.

Mclean appraised them politely. "Miss, ma'am," he greeted them, before turning his attention to the Baron. "My Lord," he offered him a slight bow.

"The Baron thanks you but he speaks no English. My wife alone communes with him," Hathwell explained. "Now, the journey's been devilishly draining. I'd be glad if you would escort us to our quarters and we shall overlook the matter of this rude reception."

He looked anxious at this. Even one of his dogs whimpered. "I shall have to speak with the estate Captain sir, your details must be logged if your claim is to be verified," he paused, "I assume that is the nature of your visit?"

Hathwell managed a smile. "Claiming the Baron's portion can wait Mr Mclean, all I'm anxious to claim right now is a good bed, a bath and perhaps good whisky. I dare say the Baron feels the same way."

Mclean relaxed. "I'll have the staff make up some rooms and fetch your luggage. In the meantime, would you be so good as to accompany me to the estate office so I can take some particulars. You'll need to speak to the estate Captain later, although at present he's out shooting."

"Of course," Hathwell bluffed.

By now a couple of servants were marching over and just like Mclean they looked a little embarrassed to find guests when none were expected. Mclean tried again to assess what lay behind the Baron's mask, but when he looked directly into the man's eyes, he saw they were filled with a fire that had nothing to do with fever. *Baron Clovis Krast?* he thought uncertainly. "This way please," he invited.

Hathwell and Hilda exchanged furtive looks and then took their place either side of the Baron, with Kolfinnia behind as was proper. Then the party moved off after Mclean, trailed by servants carrying their baggage, all of them heading towards the dark entrance of Helthorn Castle.

An elderly man watched the party from one of the castle's narrow windows. Something caught his eye and it wasn't just the attractive women or their unannounced arrival. The man in the top hat, the one conversing with Mclean, seemed to rouse old memories. The strangers were being escorted to the entrance and the old man leaned closer to the window, removed his thick spectacles and polished them. He hadn't gained a clear view of his face but something about his stature, and that slight limp, kindled a memory. "Hathwell," he whispered absently. "Yes, he had a similar limp. Krast's squire, Hathwell, yes that was his name." But that was impossible because Hathwell had died at Kittiwake.

Still pondering this, he replaced his glasses. His name was Tobias Skulle and at one time he'd been a copyist at Goldhawk Row, but he now copied legal documents relating to this estate. He tapped his thin lips as he thought. Last summer, before the chaos, he had copied numerous papers for Hathwell as part of Krast's research. "It can't be him." The courtyard was empty now but he still gazed out through the glass. "It can't be?" A worried frown creased his already wrinkled brow. The Knight Superior had died at Kittiwake, shot in the head. It had been assumed a savage had found a rifle and murdered him in cold blood. The alternative idea was very worrying indeed.

That morning, across the veil in the faded-realm, where fairies are more numerous than raindrops, two young Therions were navigating the Severn in a small hollowed out canoe.

Mana and Geris were brothers. Both were Lutra, or river-Therions, much like otters. Like all Therion races, they understood that the faded-realm was their last refuge, because Hethra and Halla's world was overrun with men. They also knew that although men were constantly hungry for resources, they could never come here, for to do so would require great magic. It was a safeguard that had protected the realm since the beginning. Exceptionally skilled witches had come and gone down the years, teaching Therions and learning from them also. They were always few, and they were always welcome. But things were changing. A strange sense of pessimism was spreading. Therion-witches seemed forgetful of their duties, their skills enfeebled, and the belief in magic was waning. The whole realm had a feeling of being compressed somehow. Worse still, mysterious creatures had begun stalking the faded-realm. There was a new terror in the world: the Magnon. Perhaps it was this state of decay that had allowed the Magnon to flourish, or perhaps the Magnon had brought it with them. Either way, Therions were growing more resentful of their human cousins across the veil, and perhaps even witches too.

"Hold the boat steady." Mana surveyed the banks with a battered telescope.

"I am. It's you, you wriggle around too much," Geris complained.

The pair drifted onwards in their small canoe, with Mana watching and Geris silently paddling. The morning was still and there was a mist across the waters. Geris remembered how they had played here as children, racing their canoes for the sheer fun of it, but now their journey was born of duty. The village depended on such vigilance, for the Magnon were spreading.

"Any sign?" Geris asked softly.

Mana lowered the telescope and shook his broad head. He wrinkled his muzzle, tasted the air and sat back in the canoe. "Not a thing."

"Maybe Astar was wrong, maybe it wasn't a Magnon he saw?"

"But if it was then it might have already gone to seed, you know how fast they're said to spread."

Geris swept the paddle silently through the waters, surveying the banks with his yellow eyes. "Shall we make shore and hunt it on foot?"

Mana was about to agree when he twitched his black nose and growled.

"Magnon?" Geris hissed.

"Shh!" Both of them froze; Mana with a webbed finger held aloft to silence his brother, and Geris holding the dripping paddle over the water. The canoe glided on, and they heard a heron call from somewhere on the misty banks. "Don't you hear that?"

"The heron?"

"No you clot, listen!"

Now Geris heard it too. "That sounds like starlings?" The illusion was so strong that he looked up, expecting to see them, but the sky was rosy-gold and this was no time for any bird to roost. "Do Magnon make such a noise?"

"I don't know." Mana swivelled about, looking for the source of the sound. "But I don't like it, and it's getting louder."

Geris directed the canoe towards a reed bed and they took cover there. Both were armed with short swords, and although the blades were dull and unused, they gripped them now in earnest. The canoe bumped against the reeds and stopped. "What do we do?"

"Shh! I'm thinking." He was still thinking when a host of water-fairies crawled up out of the river and perched on the reeds. They were all staring intently at the woods on the opposite bank and making an ominous growling noise. Suddenly a school of dragonfly-fairies skimmed overhead in tight formation, heading for that same spot. The water-fairies launched themselves in pursuit, so aggressively that the reeds swayed and the water rippled. Before he had time to speak, Mana was stunned to see a swarm of willow-fairies dart overhead, again heading in the same direction. They must have been a hundred strong at least, and flying with purpose.

"I don't like this brother, don't like this at all." Geris drew his old sword, wishing he had a better one.

More water-fairies emerged and clambered up the reeds. Immediately they took off without giving the brothers a glance. "Hey!" Mana hissed, "Hey water-fay, what's going on?"

One of them turned his way. "An incursion!" he gargled, before chasing after his kin.

Mana looked about in horror. All along the estuary, vast flocks of fairies were now racing to battle. "Something has breached the faded-realm!" he gasped.

"Magnon?"

"Not this time."

"Men, you mean men are coming here?" Geris flapped.

"Something else." Mana watched the woods across the river grow dark with fairies, and then the inevitable sound of fighting ensued. Screams and howls echoed along the estuary, as more and more fairies joined the fight. The brothers crouched in the canoe, which now rocked with the churning waters whipped up by so many passing wings, and listened to the terrifying sounds of fighting opposite.

"In Halla's name! What's happening?" Geris cried. A moment later they saw their answer.

There was a figure striding through the woods. It was impossible to say who or what it was, but the fairies of the Estuary Nation couldn't get close enough to deliver a single blow. The intruder did not carry a pact-of-grace. By rights he should be dead, but he walked with impunity, protected by a vicious cloud that grew larger by the second. As the cloud swelled, the sound became louder: the clashing of a million blades, and the maddening chatter of crazed starlings. Geris smelled blood and now there was a red mist rising up and staining the trees.

When the first severed limbs and wings began to rain down on them, Geris finally lost his nerve. He snatched the paddle and began beating at the water with all his might, and even Mana, the braver of the pair, dropped his sword, took his paddle and joined him.

Behind them, they heard the sound of battle become the sound of slaughter. War cries became death cries, and the woods filled with agonised squeals and howls, and the brothers knew the Estuary Nation had been routed. Geris risked a look back and instantly wished he hadn't. The woods seethed with fighting bodies, and the last he saw was a black figure marching down to the water's edge. He roared at his brother to paddle faster, as they raced home with the most dreadful news: an intruder had breached the faded-realm, and all the fairies of the Estuary Nation were powerless to stop it.

Chapter Fourteen

Helthorn

'Strength, Justice, Honour and Mercy.'
Inscription above the entrance to Helthorn Castle

It was dark inside the wardrobe, but Claudia found that if she left the door ajar there was just enough light to soften the sense of confinement. She was playing hide and seek with Constantine and Oberon, and although she was the eldest, her two cousins bullied her into playing on this floor of the castle. She much preferred to play downstairs where she could explore the Grand Hall, the Games Room and the Music Room, or better still the gardens. Up here it was just one dull bedroom after another, but she often yielded to her cousins, and others, because it was the easiest way to avoid torment and teasing, for Claudia was cruelly blighted and cruelly named. The last two fingers on her right hand were fused into a single digit tipped with a hooked fingernail. Her playmates were quick to call her 'Claudia the claw'. In games of Catch they squealed with horrified delight, and ran like rabbits to avoid her touch. Claudia grew up surrounded by the wealthy and the elite, but she was resigned to a life of compliance, and now at the tender age of ten there was little childhood left in her.

She had chosen an empty room and hidden in this musty wardrobe, crammed with forgotten clothes. She pressed her face against the furs and waited, watching through the crack in the door and listening to her own soft breathing. Gradually, she became aware of voices and knew at once that it wasn't her spiteful cousins.

She peeped out, and her heart jumped when she saw the bedroom door open and a servant girl escort two guests into the room. Her brief glimpse told her that both guests were female. If they caught her here she would be severely punished. She fought the urge to run for it, and instead burrowed deeper into the clothes, pulled the door as closed as she dare and peered out through the minuscule crack.

"Right this way madam, miss," the servant obliged.

"Thank you," someone out of sight replied.

Claudia saw the servant deposit some luggage by the dressing table, curtsey and then leave. The door clicked closed and her heart fluttered in fear. She was trapped in here with the strangers. Powerless as always, she caught her breath and listened hard.

"I hope Clovis is alright." It was a young woman's voice.

"His room's directly opposite. It's Hathwell I'm concerned about." This second voice was also female, but somewhat authoritarian.

"At least he's been here before."

"You're right I know, but still, being around these people sickens me." The other voice sounded vehement and Claudia shivered. She leaned closer to the crack, but the room's new occupants remained just out of view, and despite her fear, the conversation intrigued her.

"What awful deals have been hammered out in this very room?" Hilda whispered as she surveyed the lavish chamber. The four-poster bed dominated. It was draped with heavy fabric the colour of unripe plums, and next to it sat a writing desk, complete with letter rack and a crystal clock. The walls were encrusted with paintings, and needlework depictions of angelic looking children. Opposite the bed stood a fireplace topped by an ornate mirror, and a voluminous wardrobe sat in each alcove either side of it. "What evils have transpired here?"

Kolfinnia chose not to think about it and instead lay their baggage on the bed and began opening it. She sighed wistfully upon seeing her staff again. Even before she'd taken it Skald appeared and shook himself all over. "Damned unpleasant way to travel," he groused. Five, Hilda's sprite, joined him, as did Tempest and within minutes of entering, the witches had filled the room with magic. The three sprites sat on the bed watching them get ready.

Kolfinnia admired the final treasure in their luggage: Clovis's sword, and she thought of what he'd said of the Sef and she shivered faintly. *'I shan't bother to ask his name before I kill him.'*

"Kolfinnia?" Hilda threw her hat and gloves onto the bed. "No time to waste, best begin."

She gave a mute nod, removed her shawl and then went and sat on the carpet below the window, where she could see the sky. If they were to succeed she had to paint that cheery blue canvas with snow clouds. It was possible of course, but there were so many distractions, and even her clothes felt wrong.

Hilda watched, resisting the urge to help. Kolfinnia was coven-mother now, while her role was to guide not interfere. She padded softly to the door and locked it. The room was quiet, as was the corridor outside. Hathwell was presenting their papers to Mclean, but soon he and Clovis would begin searching the castle, while Kolfinnia summoned their 'distraction'. A freak summer snowstorm was to be their cover for a fast escape. Hilda drew her wand as a precaution and stood watch over Kolfinnia, with no idea that a pair of young eyes observed her from the depths of the wardrobe.

Someone went and stood by the door and Claudia caught her first glimpse of the stern-sounding woman. She was her grandmother's age and she wore black and her dark hair was neatly arranged in a tidy bun. Her features were elegant and for a moment the girl was inexplicably drawn to her without knowing why. She craned forwards, straining to see that gruff male voice. Someone had complained about a 'rough journey', or something like that. *But I didn't see any men come in?* Just then there was a knock at the door, and as the woman turned to open it Claudia saw what she was holding and let out a tiny whimper. That stick in the woman's grasp looked awfully like a wand.

Hilda heard Hathwell's coded knock and swiftly let him in. Kolfinnia looked up, flashed him a worried smile, and then turned her attention back to the spell. "They believed you?" Hilda asked nervously.

"Our credentials are sound for now. Later they'll check with London and find out the truth."

"Pray to the twins we're long gone by then." She resisted the urge to embrace him. "You're ready?"

"Clovis is in his room. We'll come back once we've located the Therion." He twitched his eyes to where Kolfinnia sat by the window with her back to him. "And our escape plan?" he asked quietly.

"Coven-mother won't fail us," she promised, and he returned her smile and made for the door, but she took his arm. "Good luck," she added.

His impulse was to kiss her, but he knew it would be misunderstood. "And you too," he returned simply. Hilda let him out and locked the door again. Still clutching her wand, she went and sat down at the dressing table with a sigh, aware of Kolfinnia falling deeper and deeper into the spell, and watched the blue sky outside, anxious to see the first dark clouds.

Coven-mother? Claudia had heard a great deal, but that one word squeezed her heart. 'Coven'. And who lived in covens? *Witches!* The thought tightened her scalp and curdled her skin. *Ma'ma!* she whined silently. *I want to go home!* She'd never wanted to come to this remote castle and play with her cruel cousins. She didn't like the way her parents spent the days wrangling over the will of some long-lost relative she'd never heard of, and now she was trapped alone with evil women who were likely witches and might cut her guts out for sport. This wouldn't happen to Rebecca or Elizabeth or Sienna, or any of her other playmates, but she was 'Claudia the claw.' She slid silently to her haunches, her face wrinkled in despair and she began to cry.

Hathwell quietly slipped into Clovis's bedroom. The 'Baron' was standing in the shadows in the far corner, alert and watchful. "We are believed?" he echoed Hilda's question.

"For now."

"Then we begin." He prowled towards him, already slipping the mask up over his face and lowering his hat.

"We'll have to start below and work our way through the whole castle." But the idea of touring the entire building with Clovis in-tow worried him.

"Calm yourself, I'll be discreet," he grunted. He was anxious and wanted this over with, and he shouldered Hathwell aside and dipped out into the hallway. "It's clear. Come, we start." In the next instant he was gone.

Hathwell grimaced, closed the door and hurried after him. "At least keep by my side!" he grumbled. "I'm supposed to be showing you around, remember."

"What's downstairs?" Clovis observed the stag heads adorning the walls and sighed sadly.

"Function rooms. If Krast wanted to show off his trophy he would have installed it down there I'm sure."

"Trophy!" he growled.

"I hope Kolfinnia's making headway," he changed the subject.

"She is."

"How do you know?"

"It's getting colder," he said simply.

Hilda was trying not to count the minutes, when the door handle turned a fraction, making her jump. The sprites turned to see, but not Kolfinnia: she was by now too immersed in her spell. "Don't answer it!" Skald hissed.

Hilda watched the handle turn again, bolder this time. Someone obviously thought the room was empty. "What if it's a servant and they use a master key? They'll see everything!"

"Don't open it!" Skald repeated. Five and Tempest both rocked their heads in agreement.

"I can't risk it!" Without thinking she sprang up, unlocked the door and opened it a crack. "Who dares enter our chambers?" she demanded. Oddly the hallway appeared empty, but a stifled cry made her look down. There were two boys looking up at her as if she was an ogress.

"Please madam," one stuttered, "we're only playing."

"We thought the room was empty," the other squeaked.

"Then find a more appropriate playground, child." She made sure to block the doorway so they didn't see inside.

"But we can't find our cousin. She's hiding," one said faintly.

"Well she's not in here I assure you. Now, kindly go play elsewhere."

The pair, who had silvery-blonde hair and couldn't have been more than eight backed away in unison. Hilda closed the door softly without taking her eyes off them, and slid the bolt for good measure.

"Who was it?" Skald crept forwards to the edge of the bed.

"Nobody," she replied distractedly, troubled by a disturbing notion. *'She's hiding,'* one of them had said, and when the servant girl had shown them up here wasn't the door already unlocked? Now Skald caught her apprehension and he too scrutinised the room. When witch and sprite finally noted the wardrobe door ajar, their eyes locked and they reached the same conclusion. *Someone's in here with us.*

Hathwell took them down a small staircase lined with portraits, known as the Picture Staircase. As he passed the narrow windows he saw that outside was noticeably dimmer. "The sun's going in."

"The forecast is for snow," Clovis said with satisfaction.

"She's very skilled for one so young."

"She is."

Hathwell sensed his great affection, and sympathised.

They reached the bottom of the stairs and heard muffled voices from the adjacent Guard Room. "We'll start in the Earl's Room and cover this floor." Hathwell negotiated them through red-carpeted corridors, which bristled with yet more trophies.

"Is there any wildlife left outside?" Clovis noted scathingly.

"Krast never went shooting," he pointed out, "but his visitors were encouraged to fill these walls." Speaking of him awakened memories he'd forgotten, and all of them ended with the sound of that single gunshot. They crept stealthily past the Guard Room, but before they could enter the Earl's Room, two men emerged from the room beyond and ambled down the corridor towards them, lost in conversation. Hathwell stepped forward to conceal Clovis as best he could and greeted the men pleasantly. "Good afternoon sirs."

The pair looked up and saw them at last. The first was short and dark-haired, while the second was wiry and wore spectacles. The first one looked past him to Clovis and smiled thinly. "More vultures arrive at the carcass I see."

"Congenital vultures by the looks of it," the other stared at the masked stranger.

Hathwell bristled. "Fortunately the Baron speaks no English, else he'd give you a lesson in manners sir."

"Not even an English vulture!" the second snorted, and both of them shook with laughter and continued past.

"Congenital indeed!" Hathwell simmered as they pushed onwards. "Half of these men wed their cousins."

"Never mind," Clovis rumbled. "Just remember why we're here."

Kolfinnia lost herself to the spell, remembering everything Flora had taught her about hastening the elements. Her first task was the simplest yet the hardest. She had to create a speck of cold air high above the castle. This tiny anomaly would set a chain reaction and thus the storm would be born, but first she had to find an atmospheric pocket suited to her will. She scanned the skies listening for the voice of air and wind. At last she found a suitable candidate and offered her name as a gesture of goodwill. She could not force the air to change – she must *convince* it to do so. Her eyes were closed but she knew it was working because suggestions of cloud and snow came to her through hrafn-dimmu, which rested in her open palms and felt as cold as the grave. *Helthorn is Hel, and it will snow in Hel this day. August snows, snows in Hel,* she recited.

Hrafn-dimmu, a soul of the frozen north, broadcast her will into the world, enveloping Helthorn with her intent and a huge bubble of chill air began to condense around the castle.

Neither witch saw the sky begin to dim or the first snowflake fall. It fell silently against the turret of the Treasury Tower and lingered for a moment before the tiles, baked by an August sun, drank it away. Already staff and guests were commenting on the sudden cold, wondering how the sun had faded on such a glorious day. Many were drawn to the windows, disturbed to see a gauzy veil now reaching from horizon to horizon and the sun shielded behind it, creating a perfect disc of fire.

Hilda turned from Skald's worried face and surveyed the room, but all the while aware of that not-quite-closed wardrobe door. "The weather grows chill," she chatted pleasantly, maintaining her pretence. Skald and the others slunk to the edge of the bed and crouched out of sight.

She swept past the wardrobe without a glance and went and stood beside it, out of view. "Happen I'll call the staff and have a fire lit. July is only just out." As she spoke she slipped an arm silently towards the door handle, while in her other hand she readied her wand. After a final look at Skald she grasped the handle, hurled the door wide-open and leapt forwards.

The first thing Mclean did upon getting back to his office was to slip his coat jacket on. He'd just come from the stables and it was oddly chill outside. There was a weather front moving in, but none of the usual signs had preceded it. One moment it was blazing August sun and the next he could see his breath and the hairs on his arms stood on end. That wasn't the only unexpected frosty reception.

"Mclean." Skulle had raced to the estate office as fast as possible. If the new guest really was Bertrand Hathwell he didn't want him seeing him. "Mclean I need a word with you."

He sighed. He was only just relighting his pipe and now he got up from his desk. "Yes Mr Skulle, what is it?"

"Those new claimants – who were they?"

"Semi-noble from Hungary. He gave his name as Baron Clovis." He pulled his jacket tighter and looked to the windows. Sure enough the clouds were thickening.

Skulle frowned. "Never heard of a valid Krastian bloodline from Hungary before?" he tapped his chin.

"That's for Goldhawk to ascertain." He lit a match and touched it to his pipe.

"Did they seem odd to you?"

He extinguished the match with a shake and tossed it into the empty grate. "Only caught a glimpse of the Baron. Clearly an ill man, as well as a cursed one," he said between puffs.

"Cursed?"

"Some deformity. His face was very hairy from what I could see."

Skulle pursed his lips as he thought. "The man who vouched for them, did he give a name?"

"Just Mr Bernard Saxon."

"And his papers?"

"They seemed in order."

"Did he strike you as familiar?"

He sighed. Since arriving five months ago Skulle had nurtured the belief that he ran the whole estate. "No, why, do you believe him an impostor?"

He hung his head as he thought. "I saw him only fleetingly. I thought he was someone else."

"Oh? Who?"

He hesitated. If Hathwell had come here working for rival bloodlines, he alone wanted recognition for catching him.

"Out with it." He clenched his pipe between his teeth and put his hands on his hips.

"The former first secretary," Skulle said quickly.

Mclean almost spat the pipe from his mouth, "Hathwell? But he died with the Knight Superior last autumn!"

Skulle smiled coldly. "It was assumed so. Had you ever met him?"

"Well, no," he admitted.

"Then it *could* be him, and if it is then I can identify him." Skulle indicated the register, "Which rooms are they in?"

"Bidewell Room, second floor. The Baron is right across the hall." Mclean drew thoughtfully on his pipe, and then added, "Now listen Skulle, I won't have you going up there and accusing guests. If you're wrong you'll be for the chop, and me too if I let you hurl accusations around."

"Then we must be discreet," he plotted. "We take a couple of men and go up there quietly and create some pretence to see this Mr Saxon. I'll know him face to face."

"I don't want you disturbing the Baron."

"I'm not concerned with the Baron. Hathwell is the proof of any conspiracy."

Mclean looked to the window, where the skies now looked threatening. "Very well, a brief inspection," he agreed uneasily. "But if it's not him. . ."

"It is, I'm certain."

"Then we'd better go see," he sighed, and for the second time that day he reluctantly extinguished his pipe.

When she heard her cousins' voices Claudia had to bite her lip to stop herself calling for help. She even considered bolting past the woman while the door stood open. Her heart seemed to think it was a good idea, indeed it felt to leap from her chest in a bid to run off first. No, she must not move, she told herself.

The woman dismissed the boys and closed the door and to Claudia's horror she bolted it. She crossed the room and out of sight, saying something about 'lighting the fire' and 'being chilly'. *She doesn't know!* Claudia swooned with relief. *Thank the stars, she doesn't know I'm here!* A few moments passed and her heart was just beginning to slow when suddenly the wardrobe door was thrown open. She was so startled that she forgot to scream, even when the woman reached in and hauled her out, that is until she saw the three little devils sitting on the bed leering at her, and then she simply fainted in terror.

Mclean took two men from the Guard Room. "When we get to the landing wait by the stair until I call you." He turned to Skulle. "Do you think he's a threat?"

Skulle took his elbow and directed him a distance away from the guardsmen. "The Knight Superior died in battle. He suffered many injuries but no man survives a bullet to the head."

"A bullet?" He rolled his eyes to the ceiling, now wondering. "You think he—"

"Yes, I do," Skulle finished gravely.

"But surely it was one of the coven brutes who found a rifle or such like?"

He adjusted his thick glasses. "It was assumed so, but keep in mind that many bodies were not recovered. It was likewise assumed Bertrand Hathwell had also died. What other 'assumptions' were wrong I wonder?"

Mclean felt clammy, and it wasn't just the change in the weather. "You think Hathwell murdered him?"

"Perhaps. And now he's aiding a rival bloodline. Perhaps he was even paid to kill the Knight Superior."

Mclean swayed a little. "We don't know whether it's him or not yet, and even if it is, we'll have to evacuate the guests first before we arrest him."

"Try to take him alive," Skulle advised. "And remember who initiated this action when you make your report."

Mclean gave a brittle smile and drew a revolver from his jacket. "And I'll remember who might be sending us off on a wild goose chase too. You two!" he called the guards, and swept past the older man. Skulle scuttled along at the rear, already anticipating his reunion with Mr Hathwell.

At first she believed she was back in her room. Not the one here in this horrible castle, but rather back in Cambridge, with Saara, her nanny, and the gardens lined with apples trees where she loved to sit and read. It felt so real that she smiled to herself about her silly nightmare, but when her eyes fluttered open her stunned mind wasn't sure what was real and what wasn't. Now Cambridge was just a dream and the black witch was real. In fact she was sitting at her bedside watching her. Claudia gasped, and wriggled backwards, thudding her head against the wall as she did. Hilda shuffled closer, and for a moment Claudia saw just a woman, and a concerned woman at that.

"You fainted," Hilda explained.

Claudia's wild eyes rolled, taking in the room, and then she saw them; the three devils, but now she was closer she saw that they looked more like magnificent hawks with arms and legs and blue feathers. Fear and fascination robbed her voice.

"Nobody in this room will harm you," Hilda promised.

Claudia noted how the shadows had deepened and she was stunned to see delicate snowflakes swirling outside. The other woman was sitting under the window, facing away from her. She didn't even seem to sense that Claudia was there. "It's snowing," she stated simply.

Hilda smiled. "You know who and what we are?" she prompted.

The girl nodded faintly.

"And you know the terrible things we are rumoured to do?"

Another nod.

"And if they were true, why would I have picked you up and laid you upon this bed? Why didn't I kill you as you lay unconscious?" Hilda studied the girl closely. She wore a white apron over a black dress that reached to her calves and black woollen stockings. Her slender face was framed by her plaited, mousy-brown hair. "Well?" she asked.

She had no answer for this simple premise. "You're witches?" she swallowed.

"Yes," Hilda said proudly. "And these noble creatures are thunder-sprites, our allies," she gestured to Skald and the others. "Consider yourself lucky. Few outside a coven have ever seen such beings."

"Lucky indeed," Skald puffed out his chest.

"You're witches." Now it was sinking in.

"Witches," Hilda affirmed.

"But witches –,"

"No," she interrupted. "Witches do not. Whatever you have been told, it is untrue, and in no time at all we'll be gone and you can go about your game."

"I was playing." It sounded unreal to her now.

"I know. And were you having fun?" Hilda's smile had a hint of sadness about it.

Claudia shook her head, while one of the devils ruffled its blue feathers and watched her closely.

"I see," Hilda sighed and her gaze fell upon her misshapen hand.

Claudia saw her interest and instinctively curled her hand out of sight.

"I think I know why you play games you don't like." She slid her own hand gently over the girl's, who tried to pull away, but she held her steady. "And no child, whether Illuminata-born or coven-born ever wants to feel left out." She held her gaze and began to hum softly, all the while caressing her hand as the snow continued to swirl outside.

A sizeable part of Claudia's mind told her to run, but it seemed silly compared with the voice telling her to listen. Suddenly her eyes sparkled with tears. "I just want to go home," she heard herself say.

"And read under the apple trees," Hilda finished, prompting a tiny smile.

A groan made both turn. The young woman by the window was beginning to stir. "That's all. I can't ask for more. The storm will have to mature by itself," Kolfinnia stretched and climbed to her feet. Claudia saw that she was wearing a gorgeous satin dress and clearly she was very beautiful. The idea that she was also a witch seemed absurd. Kolfinnia rubbed her stiff hips and turned away from the storm outside. She at last saw the child, and blinked and her mouth fell open.

"We have a guest," Hilda announced before she could speak.

"She knows? But this is –,"

A sudden knock at the door silenced them both. Hilda saw Claudia's hopeful expression. "Sorry my dear, your rescue will come a while later yet." She turned to Kolfinnia. "Catherine. Be so good as to let your father in would you?"

"Yes, mother." Confused, she lifted her dress and glided across to the door, all the while keeping the girl in view.

It was indeed Hathwell and she almost wilted with relief at the sight of Clovis. She waved them inside and Clovis pulled down his mask, about to speak, when he caught sight of the girl and let out an involuntary hiss, making her cringe. "What in Oak's name!"

"An unexpected guest. She was hidden even before we entered," Hilda explained. She still held Claudia's hand, and she could feel the girl's tremors like a frantic telegraph message.

Hathwell bolted the door and now the room seemed awfully full, while outside the wind was driving the snow against the windows and howling across the chimney pots. The three of them all stared at the terrified girl, lost for words and from the thunderous look on Clovis's face, Kolfinnia half feared he might strike her dead just to protect their plans.

It was Hilda who broke the heavy silence. "Did you find him?"

Hathwell wiped his brow. First summer heat, then winter cold and now this disaster. No wonder he felt ill. "Yes, Games Room," he panted.

"Games Room?" Now Kolfinnia understood Clovis's dark mood. The Therion adorned a play-den for rich men. "I'm sorry," she touched his arm, but he shrugged her off.

"It's no matter. All eyes in the castle are on the snowstorm. We have to go now."

"But what about the girl? She's seen us now, what do we do?" Kolfinnia asked.

"She'll have to come, won't she?" Hathwell suggested.

"We'll never get to the door with a screaming child in-tow, let alone downstairs," Clovis growled, glaring at her.

Only Hilda looked composed. "She can stay here. She won't tell anyone."

"Hil—" Hathwell stopped just in time. "Mrs Saxon, why in God's name will this child keep her peace?"

"Because she knows how it feels to be left out." At that she released her hand and immediately Claudia clutched it to her chest, protecting her shame. "There's no need for that," she said with maddening calm and then stood and smoothed the creases from her dress. "Now, gather only what you'll need. We're leaving Helthorn," she announced.

Sprites vanished into staffs, briefly illuminating the ever-darkening room. Hathwell was already at the door, sliding the bolt and turning the handle. The party went from stealth to speed and witches shone through their disguises, even though they shed not a stitch. "It's clear!" he signalled.

Clovis shouldered his bag, the all-important one containing Janus, and glanced at the girl cowering on the bed. He knew he must seem like a monster to her. "You recognise my kind girl?" he imagined the travesty standing in full view in the Games Room.

She nodded mutely.

"Answer!" he barked.

"Yes!" she pleaded.

"Clovis, please!" Kolfinnia couldn't stand her terrified expression.

He simmered down. "This is your responsibility Mrs Saxon, I hope you know what you're doing," he warned.

"She won't speak," Hilda shot back angrily. "Now the storm's building, let's not waste it." She grabbed her things, bustled past them all, now carrying her staff, and out into the corridor where the lights already flickered under the storm's fury. Clovis came next, followed by Hathwell and last to leave was Kolfinnia. They had spent less than an hour in their appointed rooms.

As Kolfinnia closed the door, she took a last look at the girl. She was sitting on the bed with her hands in her lap, staring at them in mute wonder, but in particular her right hand. Kolfinnia had no idea what miracle the girl saw there, but clearly a miracle it was. Tears were flowing down her face, and she didn't appear in the least bit interested in them. All Kolfinnia saw was a child staring at a pair of perfectly normal hands. *Whatever you did Hilly I hope you're right.* The thought was chased from her mind by more immediate worries, and she closed the door on the unknown girl.

Again, they trod the Picture Staircase, but now clattering down in haste, hoping guests and staff were absorbed with debating the weather. "That's him," Hilda flicked her eyes towards one of the portraits, that of a hard-faced man with pale eyes and a naked scalp.

"Krast," Kolfinnia understood. In the brief instant the painting occupied her vision, she hunted for something behind the face that would explain how a boy could grow into a monster. But the brushstrokes kept their secret and the image of Krast flashed by and was gone. "Now I understand why Sunday burned Thorpe Hall to the ground," she seethed.

"Allow me," Skald offered.

Although sorely tempted, she instead chased after Clovis, who was now hell-bent on reaching the Games Room before they were caught.

As soon as he knocked, Skulle knew he wouldn't get a reply and he tried the handle instead.

"I say, that's not permitted!" Mclean protested.

"I suspect the room's already empty." He was half right. He pushed the door open to find a girl sitting on the bed with her arms outstretched before her like a statue.

Mclean pushed past him and recognised her at once. "Miss Claudia?" The daughter of Earl Spennyforth was the last person he expected to see. "Miss Claudia, what are you doing in this room?" he asked warily, dreading the answer.

Her head wobbled around to face them. She had been crying but her smile was angelic. "Sir?" she asked faintly.

The swirling snow outside finally caught his eye. "Miss Claudia," he raced, "what became of the people in this room?"

She didn't register the question. Instead she continued to stare at her right hand, stroking it and flexing it to make sure it was real. "I was playing," she mumbled.

"Miss Claudia!" he barked, angered by his own fear. "Where did they go?"*And what did they do to you?* he dreaded quietly.

"Mclean, wait!" In many ways Skulle would have made a superb detective. He noticed small details, he was a copyist after all, and he knew all the guests by sight. He also had an excellent visual memory.

Because of this he saw Claudia's miracle instantly and came to an electrifying conclusion. "Witchcraft!" the forbidden word shot from his mouth.

"What?" Mclean reached for his gun.

"The girl's healing, this unnatural storm. Don't you see? Hathwell's not aligned with rival bloodlines, he's aligned with witches!" He bolted back into the corridor, already on their trail.

"Skulle, wait!" Mclean was none the wiser, but he *was* sufficiently convinced that something sinister was loose in Helthorn Castle. "Miss Claudia, do not leave this room, understand?" He didn't wait for a reply, but instead dashed off after Skulle, who was now just a scuttling shape further down the corridor. As he sprinted across the red carpet the wall lights buzzed and flickered as Kolfinnia's storm began to bite.

Claudia listened to them go and then slid from the bed feeling dazed, but filled with a strange sense of potential. She cradled her restored hand and let out a sigh that had festered for ten years. After a lingering look at the wardrobe she walked out into the corridor closing the door behind her, knowing she need not play with her selfish cousins ever again.

Kolfinnia's storm had done its work. As they bustled along the ground floor lobby, Kolfinnia snatched a glance into one imposing room after another. Sure enough people were standing at the windows, admiring or quailing at the sudden onset of winter.

"It's the old man himself," one laughed. "Krast disapproves of the idea of the Crayford's taking the place!"

All along the corridor towards the Games Room, she heard the same bluff comments and tense laughter, and those guests that crossed their path never even looked at them. She passed a large woman in a black dress adorned with peacock feathers, and carrying a small whimpering dog under a doughy arm. A young man wearing a flat cap and tweeds rushed past carrying a lantern and looking like he had an urgent message. A giggling young woman hurtled out of one room and into the next, leading a bearded old man who was clearly not her father. "What an adventure, imagine being snowed in with Thomas in the very next room, such delicious scandal!" She sounded delighted, while her companion just laughed drunkenly. Kolfinnia noticed his collar was unbuttoned.

They passed a servant girl carrying an armful of folded towels. She stepped aside and directed her gaze to the carpet. "M' Lord," she mumbled, and only continued on her way once they had passed.

This might work, Kolfinnia told herself, even though her heart beat so hard her throat pulsed. The red carpet seemed to go on forever, like a huge limp tongue, and the walls above the oak panels again bristled with antlers. "How long is this bloody corridor?" she complained under her breath.

"Almost there," Hathwell could see the Games Room up ahead.

A sudden clatter made her jump and she turned and caught sight of a room lined with decorative china plates. A cluster of elegantly dressed women was gathered around a window where hail and snow were pelting the glass. All of them were tittering and chattering nervously. "Will Richard's party be safe do you think? They've been gone since lunch," one fretted.

"Calm yourself Tatiana, no doubt he's already snug in some tavern wench's bed by now," the other sniped.

Kolfinnia heard woeful sobbing, followed by peals of cruel laughter and then the room was gone.

"On the right," Hathwell hissed.

"Wait." Clovis halted outside the Games Room. He listened a moment, and once satisfied he slipped inside. After a look back, Kolfinnia disappeared after him.

Clovis heard someone's wheezy breathing and detected the tang of alcohol. There was an elderly man slumped in the armchair by the fireplace, sleeping off one too many brandies and with a cigar stub smouldering between his knuckles. Other than that, the Games Room was empty. "Ignore him," Clovis grunted. "Hathwell, bar the door." As he went to work he took his sword from under his long coat.

Hathwell swept off his hat and glasses, pulled the huge doors closed and bolted them, meanwhile Hilda and Kolfinnia looked around aghast. She naively expected billiard tables and such like. Instead what she saw was a huge altar-like fireplace, and lying meekly before it was a stuffed stag. The walls again were lined with hundreds of rifles, claymores, shields, tartans and stuffed animals, and the only real game she saw was a lone card table. The room was oak lined almost all the way to the ceiling.

The windows were high and offered little view of the storm outside, hence most of the guests had gone for the moment. "The door's the only way in and out," she noted darkly. Clovis was already pacing across the room to a glass cabinet in the far corner, and now she could see why. "The Therion!" She went to help him.

"I can manage," he dismissed her.

"Clovis?"

He turned, and his eyes were hard. "Keep watch by the door, tell me if that old fool wakes up and if possible keep the storm-spell alive."

She glanced at the stuffed Therion behind the glass. He was stunning, which made his entombment and desecration all the more vile. "Clovis I only wanted to help."

"Then do as I ask."

"Very well," she complied and left without another word.

He placed his hands on the glass and peered through. It was the first time he'd seen one of his own in almost a year. The fur was desert red dappled with ochre patches and the Therion's build was slender, the face narrower, but they were of the same blood. "How could they?" he whispered. At that moment, to his shame, he detested all humans, even his friends.

"He led the forces at Solvgarad," Hathwell's unexpected voice came.

"*She*," Clovis corrected, still gazing into her emerald eyes. "This is a 'she'." Hathwell reeled. "I'm sorry, I didn't –,"

"Leave me," he interrupted. "Go watch the door." A moment later he heard Hathwell's shoes squeak across the carpet, but didn't look round. A few hailstones found their way down the chimney and sizzled in the grate, while the old man groaned in his sleep. He turned back to the Therion. This pure soul had crossed from the faded-realm, and he had no idea why. Once here, she had found herself allied to a coven and waging a desperate fight against the Illuminata. He thought the parallels were significant. Now she was conquered and desecrated, and he fought to control his anger.

He had a job to do and anger would only confound that job. He studied her corpse again, but without emotion this time, looking for the pact-of-grace. If she didn't have it, then they must escape Helthorn immediately. The storm wouldn't last much longer. Snow beat against the windows in answer and then Clovis saw it: a small lead locket around her neck. He took his sword and pressed the tip against the glass. It would be too noisy to smash it. Instead, he had to be careful and precise. He pressed gently, and the incredible blade sank into the glass without cracking it. He held his breath, steadied his hand and began to slice a crude opening. Glass squeaked faintly against steel but it didn't break, such was the edge of his sword. "If only we could take you home with us," he whispered longingly. The hero of Solvgarad, that the Illuminata in their ignorance had long assumed must be male, stared back at him. Those eyes were just glass replicas, but for a moment he was sure he saw approval in them. "Part of you goes home today at least, my Lady," he promised.

"I hear footsteps," Hathwell dropped to one knee to spy through the keyhole.

"What do you see?" Kolfinnia huddled close.

"Your storm was too good. Lights are dead out there. Can't see much."

Just then the old man in the chair groaned and ash drizzled down from his neglected cigar. Hilda noted a half empty decanter of brandy on the table. "He'll be out for a while yet."

"Do you think the girl will go tell anyone?" Kolfinnia asked.

Hilda just shook her head.

"Wait!" Hathwell interjected. "I see a lantern. Someone's going room to room."

"Searching?" Hilda dropped to his side.

"For us?" Kolfinnia feared.

"Shhh!" he flapped a hand, telling them to pipe down. Moments dragged by and nothing happened. Kolfinnia bit her tongue and listened to the crackling fire and the howling wind outside. Hathwell suddenly stood. "They're coming this way."

"They?" Hilda said ominously.

"Soldiers," Kolfinnia knew. "They've found us."

The ragged plate of glass came free and Clovis laid it aside. He flexed his fingers and then eased a hand through the opening and took hold of the locket. A *pact-of-grace*, he praised their luck. Their wild gamble had paid off, now all they had to do was get out. "I have it!" he growled and turned to the others wearing a triumphant, but short-lived smile.

"Outside!" Kolfinnia hissed. "Soldiers!"

He stuffed the precious artefact into his clothes and went to see for himself. "Let me."

Hathwell stood aside. "See anything?"

His eyesight was far superior and he did indeed see something, and he straightened, wearing a stern expression. "Get ready to fight," he warned.

The party stood back facing the door. It was their only exit, but how many enemies now lay beyond it? Hathwell searched about and seized a rifle off the wall. The antique wouldn't fire but it made a good club. They were readying to fight, and so all of them jumped in surprise when there came a polite knock at the door.

"Mr Saxon?" a reasonable voice called. "Mr Saxon are you in there?"

"Shhh," Clovis warned.

"Mr Saxon the storm appears to be getting worse and we're anxious that our guests are safe."

Hathwell recognised it. "It's Mclean."

"Tell him you're fine, he might go away," Kolfinnia breathed.

Clovis twitched his nose and sniffed. "It's a ruse."

"I agree," said Hilda.

"Mr Saxon, I know your party is in there. Please, allow me to escort you out. This part of the castle can be hazardous in bad weather."

Clovis regarded the stout walls and roaring fire. "And not a very good ruse," he muttered. The four of them waited and listened. There were muffled voices and strange metallic clicks.

"Firing pins!" Hathwell warned. "Everyone back!"

In the next moment he was proved right as a volley pelted the doors. The hall echoed to gunfire and the doors rattled, but they didn't yield. Kolfinnia yelled in alarm and jumped back, while the old man by the fire stirred and grumbled in his sleep.

"At least the act's over," Clovis sighed.

Hathwell shuffled back a step and raised his makeshift club. "Bastards have us cornered!"

Strangely, Kolfinnia relaxed. The waiting was over. She took her staff and on impulse she began tearing at the buttons on her dress.

"Kolfinnia?" Hilda was startled.

"If I'm going to fight I need to be able to move and if I'm going to die I want to die as a witch, not some painted duchess."

After a moment Hilda smiled defiantly and loosened her hair, letting it fall in streams. Already Hathwell was unbuttoning his stiff collar. "Thank God. I thought I'd choke in that thing."

Clovis ripped his scarf free and tossed it away, and with a powerful flex of his shoulders, the black frock coat split along the seams and he growled in relief. "Baron be damned."

"Hathwell," another voice came, and this one was stony. "We know you're in there. Come out and surrender. There are questions to be answered regarding the death of the Knight Superior."

"An old friend?" Hilda guessed.

He shook his head, "Don't know?"

There was a long silence like a bated breath, and then suddenly there came a second volley. The noise was terrifying and the doors groaned again and this time little clouds of masonry dust drifted down. "There's no other exit Hathwell, come out now and we'll consider terms," the voice offered when the gunfire faded.

"I'll go," Hathwell volunteered. "You use those staffs of yours to get out." He jerked his head towards the high windows.

"No!" Hilda argued.

Clovis gave him an appreciative look. "A noble offer, but the windows are too narrow. And besides, we couldn't let you."

"Then let me go bargain your release, they'll take you as Illuminata rivals, not witches!" Hathwell plotted.

Someone banged furiously on the doors. "Hathwell! Come out, you and your Jik scum!" Mclean was losing patience.

"A nice plan, but a touch too late," Kolfinnia observed coolly.

"Quick, make a barricade at least!" Clovis began hurling chairs and tables with incredible strength against the doors and the others followed suit. Together he and Hathwell dragged a heavy sideboard across, its wooden legs screamed against flags and the bronze figurines on its top tumbled down almost musically.

"There has to be another way out?" Kolfinnia implored.

"There's isn't!" Hathwell mopped sweat from his face.

"You're sure, no priest-hole or concealed passage way?" Clovis ripped his coat free and began unbuttoning his shirt, glad to be rid of it.

"They'd have used it if there was."

Even as they barricaded the door, more gunfire sounded and the stack of furniture rocked. They were racing through their options when the situation instantly became worse. "HELP!" a reedy voice cried. "Help I'm trapped in here!" Everyone wheeled around to see the old man now standing by the fireplace, and his face was pale with horror. "Witches, fiends, devils!" he babbled and then began to sob. In response the door rocked under a mighty blow.

"Lord Grover? Is that you?" Mclean called.

"It is!" he screamed. "Help me I'm hostage!"

"Damn it!" Kolfinnia flew at him and shoved him back into the chair. "Stay quiet old man or there won't be just a stuffed deer lazing by this fire before the day's out, understand?" she pushed her face into his.

Grover made a whimpering sound. "Please, spare me. I have money, plenty of money if that's your aim?" Another barrage hit the door, men not rifles this time, and on this occasion they all heard the gut-wrenching sound of splintering wood.

"Keep your mouth shut!" she jabbed a warning finger into his face, backed away and finished ripping off her clothes. Suddenly his elderly features came alive, but sadly for him the elegant dress fell away to reveal short trousers and a vest. "Not a word!" She stepped out of her disguise, scowled at him a last time and then went and stood alongside the others, staff at the ready.

The doors were hit again and now one of the lower panels actually caved in and a zigzag mouth of splinters appeared. "Hathwell, you'll dance on a rope for this day's work!" Skulle blared.

"There's no way out," Hilda said bleakly.

A single gunshot ripped through the air as someone fired through the breach in the door, forcing them to scurry deeper into the room for cover. Kolfinnia dropped behind a leather sofa as more bullets zipped overhead, shattering wood, glass and plaster.

A cry came from the corridor, "HEAVE!" The doors bulged and the furniture shunted. To make sure, another spray of gunfire peppered the room.

Kolfinnia cried out as the sofa was hit and tufts of horsehair drifted down.

"Kolfinnia, speak to me!" someone demanded. It was Hilda.

"I'm fine, I'm fine!" She dared look out just as the barricade shuddered again, and ducked behind cover just before the next round of gunfire. She heard bullets ring against the suits of armour, and the Therion's glass case shatter. Banners fluttered down and claymores clattered to the floor.

"Hold your fire!" Grover staggered drunkenly towards the doorway, still holding a brandy glass in one hand and with his cigar stuffed between the knuckles of the other. "Hold your fire! I'm their captive, I'm Lord Grover!" Clearly this didn't fully register with the alarmed troops and Kolfinnia swallowed a scream when she heard guns roar again. Grover jerked in time with the blazing rifles and his jacket fluttered as bullets ripped through him. Even his cigar was hit and it exploded in sparks, and then the shooting stopped and he flopped sideways and hit the floor. Amazingly the brandy glass rolled away intact.

"Last orders," Hathwell grimaced blackly.

"Cease fire! For God's sake cease fire!" Mclean's panicked voice came.

There was brief lull, and Kolfinnia saw Hilda curled behind a table clutching her staff, and Hathwell trying to wrench a sword from the wall. Both of them looked desperate. "There's no way out," it truly began to dawn on her, "no way. . ."

"There is," a powerful voice came, "if you dare take it."

She looked around into Clovis's face. He crouched beside her cradling Janus and for a moment she thought he meant the god of doorways. "How?" she repeated. Before he could answer, the doors were barged again and this time she heard a heavy chair topple and crash to the floor. They were almost inside.

"Hathwell, Hilda! To me now!" Clovis called.

Hathwell finally loosened a sword from the wall, grabbed Hilda's arm and ran to join them, prompting more gunfire. "Reckon I can do plenty of damage with this!" he brandished the antique.

The doors were rammed yet again, and this time the furniture came thundering down and the air filled with the roar of guns. Kolfinnia covered her ears as bullets whipped overhead and the sofa rocked and glass decanters and picture frames shattered. "Take this!" Clovis thrust his bag into her arms.

"What do I do?" she screamed over the gunfire.

"Hold it with all your life!" He rummaged in his tattered shirt and drew out the pact-of-grace. "Now all of you, hold onto me and don't let go."

"Clovis you can't –," Hilda began.

"I must! Just take hold!"

"CHARGE!" Mclean bellowed and the last push cleared the doors and the troops rushed in, many of them firing already.

One way out, but only for the bold, Clovis thought. He looked into Kolfinnia's bewildered but beautiful eyes, already knowing she was bold enough. He just hoped the others were too. With that in mind he sprang the catch on the locket.

"Clovis!" Now she understood and she threw her arms around him, terrified but gladdened. Hilda and Hathwell pressed in. All of them were taking that one and only way out: a dream within a dream. They were going to the faded-realm.

Mclean saw his chance for absolution. "They murdered Lord Grover!" he screamed in accusation. "CHARGE!" Soldiers ran at the shattered doors, shoved them aside and stampeded into the Games Room, leaping over Grover's body and blasting everything in sight. By the time it dawned on them that the room was empty there wasn't a great deal of it left. "Cease fire, cease fire!" Mclean stumbled after them, coughing and waving clouds of smoke from his face. He stepped delicately around Grover's body and surveyed the catastrophe. "It's a disaster," he whimpered, "a bloody disaster."

Skulle appeared silently at his side. "They appear to have departed," he commented blandly after a glance around.

"It's a bloody disaster!" He couldn't think of any other words. The Games Room and its priceless collection were wrecked, and Lord Grover lay dead.

"Sir, over here!" One of the soldiers stood by a sofa riddled with bullet holes.

Mclean hurried over hoping to find a heap of dead witches behind it. What he saw instead was a heap of discarded clothes; a woman's dress, a frock coat, a ripped shirt, a lady's fan, hats and gloves, but nothing else.

He turned full circle, wondering how the hell they'd escaped so completely from a sealed room. The stuffed Therion caught his eye. It leaned crookedly in its shattered case, leering at him scornfully. Its head was split and stuffing hung from it in fluffy clots like spilled thoughts. "A bloody disaster," he said quietly.

Skulle surveyed the room wearing a sullen pout. Hathwell and his allies seemed to have eluded them. It was a pity he thought, but he was a practical man and saw no use in crying over spilled milk, besides he now had pressing clerical duties to see to. For one thing Lord Grover had checked-out early and there was a final bill to prepare for his family. "One less claimant on Helthorn," he made a note to himself. No doubt the rest of the bloodlines would be rubbing their hands with glee. He clasped his hands behind his back and ambled slowly back into the corridor, thinking of the all the paperwork this mess would entail.

CHAPTER FIFTEEN

A dream within a dream

'Between every breath and every heartbeat there lies another world.'
Morton Stocks - Ward of Tumble Hill-coven, Dartmoor

Marsh willows grew all along this stretch of the river, and Captain Taal and his small party elected to shade from the heat under their trailing branches. He broke a loaf of bread and idly began chewing, as the rest of his patrol found places to rest.

"A hot day," Peri observed.

Taal swallowed before speaking. "The seasons drift. A hot summer, just like the last and the one before that."

"At least the crops will be strong," she added hopefully.

"Not if it doesn't rain soon." He was worried, many were. The summer was dry and punishing. Hardly a drop of rain had fallen since midsummer and today was August 1st. How long could the heat last they all wondered? Even the fairies were tormented by it. Taal watched a flock of willow-fairies spiral lazily through the branches, going about their work with uncharacteristic lethargy. "A mean summer," he brooded and thought back to his grandfather's favourite saying: *'the fuller the world gets, the hotter it gets.'* As a young Therion he'd learned to ignore most of his grandfather's babblings, but now they were ominously prophetic. The world was filling up and speeding up too. That's why his ancestors had been forced to come here, a heartbeat away to the faded-realm, but what happened in the world found an echo here, sometimes even more so.

Peri set down her staff and stretched gratefully, arching her back as she did. Taal envied her supple build. She was lion-like, slender, blessed with golden fur and innate grace, while he was a Caprian and blessed with bad breath, goat-like horns, a thick beard and a woolly coat. Fine for mountain life, but not a summer such as this. He wore short trousers and his lower legs were shaggy and his hoofed feet were bare. There was a dragon emblem stitched to his ragged waistcoat, and while the party might call themselves soldiers, their weapons were old and ill suited. Their ancestors had come here looking for refuge, not battle, but in recent years conflict had come looking for them. He wasn't even a real Captain, but he kept his sword sharp and he was the best his encampment had.

Peri sighed, drawing her knees to her chest and sitting with casual elegance. "Do you think the heat is somehow connected to the Magnon?"

He shrugged, "The world changes, who can say?"

"Have you ever seen one?"

"You ask me that five times a day, and the answer is still no."

She smiled bashfully. "I suppose at least that proves the infection hasn't got this far."

"But infections spread Peri, that's what they do. If it continues then the Magnon will overrun this place as they have further south. And most of our bravest are off defending against trollen from across the seas." The faded-realm's state of peace was breaking down. Therions were now defending their borders against other Therions, in this case trollen incursions from across the Northern Sea. Taal checked himself. He hated how most of what he said these days was dour. "But you're right, no Magnon here yet," he laboured a smile, until she wiped it away.

"And now there is this plague affecting the iron-fays. Has anyone an explanation for it yet?"

He finished his bread. "Our best witches are putting their minds to it, I know they'll devise a remedy soon." But he didn't know, and in their small encampment the only witch they had left was an old Hortar, who could manage a few conjuring tricks and little more. They had few weapons, no training and even magic seemed to be flagging in the heat. The faded-realm was just that: fading.

A scout navigated his way through the willow branches, some of which tangled in his horns, and dropped to his side. "Captain, there's something you ought to see."

"Trouble?" His hand went to his sword.

"I think not, come see for yourself." The scout, named Keel, was away, indicating for him to follow.

Taal eyed the rest of his band. "Wait here," he ordered, but Peri stood up. "Strength in numbers," she argued.

As always he couldn't resist her smile. "Come on then." The pair disappeared after the scout and out into the heat to see what the problem might be.

"There," Keel pointed to the hills opposite.

Right away Taal saw it, and this time his smile was genuine. "Rain?"

Peri saw it too. The sky was dark and threatening. "Really? Rain's coming?"

The three of them watched as the cloud steadily darkened. "Shall we go see?" Keel suggested.

Taal took in the steep valley, knowing it would be a tough slog up the hill. "Gather the rest Keel, we'll go see what's what." Keel went to fetch the others while Taal continued to watch the churning cloudbank. He imagined a giant cauldron hidden behind the hills, brewing hail and thunder.

"Rain at last." Peri fixed her golden mane into a ponytail.

"Aye, rain at last." He stroked his great beard and allowed himself a moment's optimism.

As it turned out, both of them were wrong.

"Charge!"

Kolfinnia distinctly heard Mclean's last order, followed by the crash of falling furniture. Then everything had gone silent, as if a blanket had been thrown over the world. She lay with her head buried against Clovis's shoulder, breathing rapidly and expecting a bayonet thrust any second, until eventually he spoke, "I think it's safe now." And he gently eased her away, and looked around.

She raised her head from his fur. "Clovis?"

"Where are we?" Hathwell realised the light had subtly changed, although he saw from the narrow windows that it was still snowing outside.

Clovis climbed to his feet. The soldiers were gone, and even Grover's body had vanished. "We did it," he informed them. "We crossed over." He looked down at the pact-of-grace in his hand. The locket hung open and inside was the body of a tiny fairy. This is why pacts were so rare, because each held the remains of a great Burning Heart, a fairy Lord or Lady.

"Clovis, we're really here, in the faded-realm?" Kolfinnia looked about. He nodded once.

"A dream within a dream," Hilda said respectfully.

To Kolfinnia, the room looked like a jumble of memories. Parts of it looked the same, other were drastically different. For one thing it looked to have been empty for years. The furniture was green with mould, the fire was cold and dark, and there was the distinct smell of decay and dereliction. Slowly the four of them found their feet and spread through the Games Room, looking around with childish wonder, although it was no longer the Games Room of Helthorn Castle, but of some strange twin that was familiar yet unique. *A dream within a dream,* Kolfinnia understood now.

"The faded-realm." Hilda took a serving of pristine air, and suddenly a thought dawned on her, "Clovis, are the soldiers still around us?"

"Yes, right beside us, but a breath away."

Kolfinnia shivered. "Then hadn't we better go?"

"We're as far from them as the moon." He spoke quietly despite this.

"We're ghosts," Hathwell realised.

They all turned his way. "Yes, to them we might be," Clovis agreed solemnly.

Hathwell stooped and collected his baggage, while Hilda discarded the last of her disguise, and let it drop to the rotten carpet. She stepped away from Mrs Saxon's stylish black dress, which was now torn and dusty, seeming not to feel the cold and damp of this strange new Helthorn.

Kolfinnia noted the contents of the pact just before Clovis sealed it again. "Clovis?"

He looked from her astonished face to the artefact in his hand. "Every pact is a tomb for some former great fairy. They are only given to the trusted." He thought of the trophy Therion and looked about for her, but of course she wasn't here in this Helthorn.

"Did you know that?" The sight of the tiny body had upset her.

"Yes."

She wiped her eyes, smudging her complexion, and then handed back the Janus vessel. "Here, I get nervous just holding this, I'm afraid I'll drop it."

He took it gladly. "Nothing so mundane can open this vessel I promise you." He mustered a smile as he began to wrestle with his new problem. He had delivered Janus to the faded-realm, but he'd also brought others. *One problem at a time,* he concluded. "First we find somewhere to rest, then we find a local."

"I think we just have," Hathwell pointed to the crumbling wall panels.

An oak-fairy was perched on the picture rail watching them. He'd been there all along, and he snapped his wings once before he spoke. "Where is Leenyssa?"

Clovis stepped forwards. "Greetings –,"

"Leenyssa?" he interrupted. "Where is she?"

"Pegalia is spoken by three of us alone, and as you see there is a fourth," Clovis negotiated. "Will you grace us by speaking the language used by those a heartbeat away?"

The fairy growled something rude and started again, now in fractured English. "Where is she? What have you done with Leenyssa?" He spoke with great force for such a small being.

"Leenyssa. Who's she?" Kolfinnia wondered.

"Of course." Now Hathwell understood and now he had another memory to torment him. Not only was Solvgarad's mysterious Therion female, but he had a name to put to her too. "Leenyssa was Krast's trophy."

"Is it so long since I saw rain that I've forgotten how it looks?" Taal asked, stupefied. They were now gathered at the top of the ridge, sweating and panting, and watching a storm rage over the plain below. But there wasn't a drop of rain.

"You haven't forgotten Captain," Keel agreed faintly.

They continued to watch, and Taal became aware of Peri by his side. She shielded her eyes against the baking sun, for it was still very much high summer where they stood. "Have you ever seen such a thing?" she whispered.

"Snow in August, and so localised. No, I've never seen such a thing."

"Some magic at work?" Keel suggested.

"Where there's magic there are witches," Taal pondered.

"Didn't you say witches might cure the iron-fairies?" Peri brightened. "Shouldn't we go see?"

Taal gave her a disparaging look. He was very fond of her, but she literally waltzed into danger without a care, which made him feel old and feeble, although on this occasion she had a point.

"The storm seems to be fixed over Helthor Castle," Keel observed.

"Helthor's a haunted place Captain," Brisk, a Caprian like himself, reminded them and the rest muttered in agreement.

Taal watched the snow swirl in sparkling curtains. Helthor Castle lay at the heart of that blackness. Fairies that came and went claimed that on the other side Helthor was a dangerous place, while at least here it was just a sickly ruin.

"Captain?" Peri prompted.

He thought of the vile Magnon seeds that were spreading through the faded-realm, and the strange and terrifying infection afflicting the iron-fairies. If there was magic at Helthor they needed it badly. "We go," he said finally.

"Where is Leenyssa?" the oak-fairy demanded again.

Clovis held up the pact. "I claim protection in these lands."

"Thieves!" he shrieked.

"No!" he boomed. "Leenyssa no longer needs it, for she'll not be coming home."

Hathwell squirmed at this.

The oak-fairy stilled. "Leenyssa is dead?" Clovis nodded once, while Kolfinnia diverted her eyes to the floor. The fairy fluttered down onto the remnants of an armchair, where the velvet was smothered with fungi. "Leenyssa is dead?" he repeated, looking confused.

"I'm sorry," Clovis felt for him.

"But my task was to await her return." Now he sounded lost. "How did she die?"

Hathwell's heart clenched again. This tiny creature had waited over twenty years, not knowing that just a whisker away her corpse stood in a glass case. *Krast you bastard,* he thought, and this time when he remembered that single gunshot he felt satisfied.

"There was a battle," Clovis said tactfully. "She fought well. Witches owe her a great deal."

Now the oak-fairy turned his attention to the humans and his green eyes narrowed. "Many years since such beings walked this way. . ."

"These are my friends," Clovis announced. "They share my protection."

The fairy shot the locket a curious look, as if he resented its authority. "Protection," he agreed reluctantly.

Kolfinnia coughed politely. "May we ask your name good fairy?"

"A name for a name young witch. You first."

"My name is Kolfinnia Algra, I am mother of Stormwood-coven. This is Swanhilda Saxon, my Ward and friend and this is Mr Bertrand Hathwell, our guide."

"Not a witch?"

"He's learning our ways," Hilda defended him.

"And you?" The fairy spun around to Clovis.

"I am Clovis Augmentrum, coven-father." He drew the cloth aside and gave the fairy his first glimpse of the Janus vessel. "And I came here on a mission of star-wide importance."

The fairy scuttled back. "Another visitor under your protection?"

"For now, but once he's freed then no soul in this realm or any other will need protection again."

The fairy's hostility thawed a little, "Truly?"

He smiled, "Truly."

They descended through thick pine forest, and it wasn't until Taal's patrol had reached the plain below that they noticed the sky was lighter and the storm was waning. Even the craggy profile of Helthor itself was visible again, although now frosted with snow.

"What if it's the Magnon's doing?" Keel wondered aloud.

"Magnons don't know magic," Taal grunted.

They forded the river, which was shallow indeed for this time of year, and moved out over the flood plain beyond until at last they reached the first snows.

"It already melts," Peri noted sadly.

Taal advanced cautiously. Here it was less than an inch deep, and heather and bilberry were still visible, but further on the ground was covered. "It seems like plain old snow?" This only puzzled him further.

The sun was claiming back what the storm had briefly taken, and the dark skies were almost blue again. Steam was rising from the melting snow, and the lovely smell of wet earth came with it. Overhead, Peri could hear birds singing again, and even a few dormant frost-fairies had been drawn out of hibernation and were flitting over the gleaming crystals. "Poor frosties, they look so confused."

"Aren't we all," Taal huffed. As they drew closer to Helthor the flood plain grew thicker with dead trees, although they were not dead in the usual sense. They had been petrified and even the stone-fairies wouldn't go near them for they were soulless. The faded-realm was covered in thousands of square miles of such devastation. Where humans stripped native forest for grazing in their own world, the trees lingered here as stony relics, and every year the rate had accelerated. "Eyes quick. It's said Magnon are often found near stone-woods," he reminded them.

The sense of caution grew heavier and now they crept forwards in silence, unsure if this unusual snowfall was as innocent as it seemed.

"Good fairy, we have yet to learn your own name," Kolfinnia asked tartly.

"Posit," he said – but begrudgingly.

"And you're the only one of your kind here?" She looked around the forgotten room, noting the lack of fairies.

"Fay's don't come within Helthor."

Helthor. They all caught the slight difference in the name. "But not you?" Clovis clarified.

"I have my duty. Wait for Leenyssa, return pact to proper place when it comes home."

"And you tracked it here and waited?"

He grunted and shook his wings in reply.

"A lonely duty, and a stoic one," Clovis was moved.

"Posit, why do fairies avoid this place?" Hilda finished buttoning up her Flower-Forth dress as she spoke.

"Helthor is soulless witch-Hilda. No need for fairies to find souls here. More and more such places as years go by."

Clovis thought for a while. "Posit, if you'll help us, then I'll return the pact-of-grace to you once my task is done, and my friends are safely home."

"Help?"

"Therions, there must be many of them here? I need their help to find the right place for this," he tapped Janus's vessel, now hidden under his cloak.

"Therions a plenty, and many like you witch-Clovis, but none like them." He regarded the others with veiled distaste. Seemingly, even witches were less than welcome, and Kolfinnia resisted the urge to answer back.

"Come then, I think our stay at Helthorn's been long enough." Clovis shouldered his staff and led the way. There was no barricade here, damaged or otherwise, and the door swung open with a groan of rusted hinges. Posit flew ahead, perhaps leaving this chamber for the first time in years, and they left the Games Room behind.

A ghostly whisper made Kolfinnia stop and take a final look back and she imagined soldiers searching just a skin's thickness away. "I'm sorry Leenyssa," she whispered and drew the doors closed again. . . just in case.

This Helthor might be just a ruined shadow of its counterpart, but what it lacked in splendour it made up for in presence. Captain Taal and his companions advanced silently through the ornamental gardens, although here the stone urns were cracked with creeping roots, and the trees were wild and grasping. Therions and fairies feared the place. Tales of its supernatural nature were as common as molehills and Taal hadn't been here since he was a boy. Something bad lurked just on the other side of Helthor and found an echo here. He half expected his advancing years to banish those childhood fears, but as he approached he started to feel like a scared infant again. They halted fifty yards from the castle, where the doors were long fallen in and the archway resembled a huge toothless mouth.

"Do we go in Captain?" Keel swapped his walking staff for his sword now.

He was about to answer when snow tumbled from one of the turrets, making them all jump.

Peri drew close. "You think this snow is from the *other* side?"

He sniffed again, but nothing smelled untoward. "No, whatever made it wasn't malign."

"Behind Helthor lies a bad place, or least I've always been told."

"Aye, so have I." That open gateway seemed to challenge him. If Peri hadn't have been there he would have ordered them back. Nothing smelled bad, and as the snow was melting now there was no need to linger, but she regarded him as a father and he didn't want to tarnish that. "Wait here, I'll go see."

He took a step forwards but suddenly Keel stopped him. "Captain listen!"

He stopped, feeling grateful, and listened. Yes, now he could hear voices. "Everyone back, find cover!" They scattered and vanished behind tumbled walls and overgrown hedges, and watched and waited. The voices grew more distinct. Someone was coming out of the castle.

"It's the same but different." Kolfinnia found herself wandering corridors that only twenty minutes ago had been carpeted and brightly lit. Now there were grasses and fungi growing on windowsills beneath broken panes, and the carpets were just rotten mats. She glanced into the China Room perplexed as to why all those delicate plates were neatly stacked in one precarious pile almost reaching to the ceiling. *Everything's a mystery here.* The strangeness disorientated her. They had to pick their way through mounds of plaster that had sloughed from the roof and walls. The collection of trophies had changed too. Now they appeared to be of monstrous stags never before seen on Earth, with antlers so broad that they spanned the corridor and were hung with cobwebs as thick as dust sheets. Right now she felt more incredulous than afraid. "Is that what you expected?" she tested Clovis.

"Each world has its own shady counterpart," he guessed, still pondering how to get them home.

Hathwell was in for a shock too. It wasn't just the decay that marked Helthor as different. There were other tantalising changes. For starters, the heraldic beasts were altered slightly. It was as though the snarling stone dragons, serpents and lions had conspired to move when nobody was looking. "That eagle should face right, I swear it," he muttered.

They arrived back at the main entrance, and Kolfinnia saw how the huge doors had long ago toppled inwards and gathered mounds of windblown leaves like cradles. To her great satisfaction there were even oak saplings sprouting out of them. "I think I prefer this Helthorn to the other one."

"Helthor," Posit corrected. He floated across the decaying doors and out into the wider world.

"I don't think he likes us," she said privately.

Clovis turned to address them equally privately. "Listen, it wasn't my intention that you should come here and as soon as I can I shall send you back, but for now I'd ask you all to be vigilant and remember this is not your world any longer."

"Are we intruders?" Hathwell clarified.

"No, the pact-of-grace is our authority here, it cannot be denied. But remember, your welcome might be under sufferance."

"Therions came here because of mankind," Kolfinnia remembered sadly. "And we're mankind."

Hilda huffed in amusement, "No, you and I are *women* dearest, don't forget."

"Hold on a moment!" Hathwell protested.

"Shh!" Clovis growled. "Just watch what you say." He clambered over Helthor's doors and out into the sunlight after Posit. The rest strung along behind and Hilda gladly accepted Hathwell's steadying hand as she negotiated the doors.

Once outside it was Hathwell who noticed first. "I keep seeing movement in the corner of my eye." Each time he looked it was gone and there were so many flickers that the air looked to be packed with tiny shooting stars. "Am I going mad?"

"Fairies," Hilda explained. "You don't need spells to see them here. Your eyes will adjust soon."

"Oh, I see." He wasn't sure that proved his sanity.

Kolfinnia rejoiced at the brilliant sunshine and the dazzling snow. "We did it," she realised, "we escaped Helthorn." She indulged herself with a grin and collected a handful of snow and began scrubbing at her painted face, anxious to be just a witch again. Her face emerged once more along with that most special scar and her worries seemed to melt just as easily. They had escaped, she was a witch and Clovis was still by her side. She pulled her elegant hairstyle free until her dark hair was tangled and wild, and she loved it. The last of her trappings she discarded and began rummaging in her baggage for her real possessions. It was only after she'd retrieved her tatty Flower-Forth dress, now just a mess of creases, and pulled it over her head that she realised the rest had stopped still.

"Kolfinnia!" Hilda cautioned.

"What?" She finished fastening hrafn-dimmu back where it belonged and turned around.

"We have guests." Or more accurately *they* were the guests, and their hosts were watching them from just a few yards away.

Kolfinnia's hands flopped to her side and she took a sharp breath. Standing opposite, regarding them with utter amazement, were more Therions than she'd ever seen in her life.

Curiously, Vega's two opposing warriors found themselves at opposite ends of the country, but only one of them commanded their own army.

Sef wiped the blood from his sword and now the battle was over he took a moment to look around. He saw how the village was little more than a shanty town, straddling the river on wooden piers and bridges. The place was sprawling, ramshackle and damp-smelling. He'd never had much regard for Lutra, thinking them vermin amongst Therions and killing them had been highly satisfying. One of them was still alive, crawling on his belly towards the river, which now glistened with a film of blood. Sef polished his sword to a shine and stalked over to him.

Geris hauled himself away from the ruins of his village with no plan or purpose. He and Mana hadn't been fast enough. They got back to find the black Therion already there and with it came a swarm of flesh-hungry demons. A shadow fell over him and he knew what would happen next, but he no longer cared. Mana was dead and soon he would join him. He rolled over, determined to face his killer.

Sef looked down at the wretch. His fur was bloody and his eyes were swollen almost closed from countless bites. He planted his foot on his chest and leaned hard, prompting coughs and gurgles. "I came looking for clues, not a fight, yet you opposed me. And so I ask again Lutra: where in the faded-realm can I find the place of ascension?" Clovis *had* to be heading there.

"Go to Nevermore!" he croaked.

Sef dug in his heel. "I'll raze village after village to find out what I want. Spare them your fate and simply tell me, then I shall leave this realm in peace."

For an instant he considered.

Sef saw him waver. "Yes boy, tell me and I'll leave." To prove it he sheathed his sword and took a step back.

"North," he gasped.

"You swear?"

"Somewhere in the northern isles, all I know."

Sef considered. The information was far too vague, but it was a start. "Then I shall go. Farewell Lutra." He made a mocking bow and turned. He was twenty yards away when Geris shouted after him.

"When the dragon comes back, the days of your kind are ended!"

Sef halted. *Dragon?* For some reason he clutched his garments where the dragon's egg lay, and then turned and squelched back across the boggy ground. "Dragon? What dragon?"

He struggled for breath. "She'll come back and when she does the faded-realm will be renewed, and filth like you will never set foot here again!"

"Desperate talk from a dying coward."

"You're one of us," he coughed. "Yet you behave like man."

Sef sneered. "I am Therion yes, but not one of *you*, river scum." He surveyed the burning village, littered with bodies and feeding fairies. One building caught his eye. It was a wooden hall with a thatched roof and a carved dragon gable. "Dragons," he muttered, thinking now. "What is yonder hall?"

"She'll come back one day. She promised, she. . ." His words collapsed and his head flopped back into the mud.

"What is that hall?" he kicked the youth.

"Promised," he uttered.

"Useless!" The fool wasn't worth soiling his sword with. He left him to his torment, and padded over to the hall, in thrall to his intuition, which told him there was something here that could profit his cause. It was some kind of temple, and he assumed the carved dragon alluded to the sleeping twins.

"What do you expect to find here? Salvation?" Iso mocked.

"I don't know yet." He held his staff ready, and slowly pushed the slatted door open with his foot. There were no windows and it was dark inside.

"Is it my turn to die?" a weary voice asked.

Sef backed away and lowered his staff. "Come out witch."

Shuffling and grunting sounds floated towards him, and a witch emerged into the daylight. Sef saw he was not a Lutra like the rest, but rather he was a Caprian, and a very old one. The thick horns that curled either side of his flat face were deeply crinkled, and the tip of one was broken off. Milky eyes peered out at him, and the left one was runny and sore. His slit nostrils were pink and fleshy, and they wrinkled as he scented his foe and his lips peeled back in a defiant sneer, revealing teeth that were brown and worn. His beard hung to his waist and was dirty grey like the rest of him. "Well, kill me then."

Sef smirked, "Kill you? But I've just cleaned my blade."

"Isn't that why you came?" The witch struggled forwards, clutching the doorframe for support. In his other hand he held a staff tipped with a garland of oak and holly leaves. He wore shabby robes, and there was a gnarled wand in his belt. Now he rested a knotty hand against its hilt, ready to use it.

"I wouldn't recommend that," Sef warned.

The witch looked about at his devastated home. "Oh? What more can you do to me?"

"Plenty," he promised. "But words, not wounds, are all I want from you."

The Caprian stood proud and jutted out his chin. "I am Astar. A witch. This is the temple of Hethra and Halla."

"Yes I gathered that," Sef said blandly. "But the sleeping twins are not the only dragons are they? Tell me who *'she'* is."

Astar's eyes narrowed. "You seek to insult me before you murder me? All Therions know who *she* is," he rebuked him.

"Not this one."

"Then you're a simpleton as well as a devil."

Sef flexed his shoulders and listened to bones crack. He was weary and battle had drained him. "I am a stranger. I came from afar, across the star-sea you might say."

A look of realisation dawned on his face and he smiled faintly. "Then all is well."

Sef snorted, "Well? Your village burns and the fairy-nations are powerless to stop me."

Astar sighed contentedly, "But when you came and the killing began, I thought for a terrible moment that one of us had finally committed the worst possible treason."

Sef was affronted. "I am no traitor," he growled.

"I'm sure you're loyal to your own desires, oh yes," he agreed sadly, "rather, I meant that one of us in the blessed faded-realm had sided with the human world and brought death here in their name. Blessed be the twins that I was wrong."

"You can trust me to bring death if you do not tell me who *she* is," he pointed to the carved dragon above the hall. Clearly it was neither Hethra nor his sister Halla.

Astar regarded him pitifully. "How little you know."

"Then enlighten me, else I'll dull my blade a second time today," he tapped his sword hilt.

The old witch directed his gaze to the dragon's noble face. Any human child would recognise it as the archetypal dragon, blessed with horns and scales, flaring nostrils and fanned ears. It was the dragon that haunted countless human tales, the dragon Saint George had slain, the dragon in the garden who first tempted Eve, the dragon who had brought mighty Beowulf to his knees. And yet she was none of them. Now Astar's eyes brimmed with tears. "She never found sanctuary here, she lingered too long across the veil and left it too late, and the faded-realm is condemned to slow decay without her. Oblivion awaits us all."

Some great secret was just waiting to be seized. Sef could almost taste it.

"There are no dragons here in the faded-realm." He understood now. "They're extinct?"

Astar hung his head.

"Answer me."

"She will come back!" he shouted, finding his fire again. "And when she does the land will be renewed!"

Sef had what he wanted. "Once the door to extinction closes it never opens again."

Astar slouched against the doorway again, drained and beaten. "Just get on with it," he grunted. "Kill me."

"I'll let Time have that particular pleasure." Sef turned to leave, now harbouring an incredible notion. "Chentek! Where are you, you blood-sucking louse?" The war-fairy appeared almost at once, hovering by his shoulder. "Are your legions well fed?"

Chentek turned his burning eyes on the witch. "One still lives."

Sef looked back. "He's old and bony, let him wallow in his misery."

"Therion!" Astar stumbled after him. "She *will* come back!"

Sef halted, turned and faced him. He made a display of curling his muzzle and scenting the air before shaking his head disdainfully. "I smell false hope, witch."

"She will!" he gave an involuntary stamp of his hoofed foot.

"Maybe in the end that's why she never came," he continued. "Because you gave up hoping long ago." He could hardly have inflicted more damage with his sword. Sef left him to his shame, now drawn northwards to find Clovis. The coven-father had a good lead on him, but Sef was fast, and armed with Chentek's plague nothing could stop him. He broke into a run, grasped his staff and flew.

Astar listened to millions of wings take flight and follow, and then he dropped to his knees as ash continued to rain gently down. His village was gone, but worst still, so was his faith. He hung his head and stared at the dragon's murky reflection in the puddles, now ruddy with blood. "She will come back one day," he recited the long-held promise, but just like Sef he smelled the stench of false hope.

Captain Taal hadn't heard of humans walking the faded-realm for many years, but he recognised them as witches right away. "Wait here," he cautioned and started forwards, sword at the ready.

"Be careful," Peri whispered.

Kolfinnia saw one of the Therions begin forwards and she drew closer to Clovis. "I'll go."

"Not this time, it's my fault you're here. Wait here." Like Taal, he started towards his opposite.

"Be careful!" she urged.

Taal saw the lion Therion approaching, and from his look he was clearly someone of rank. His companions held back and Taal was glad of that. He hadn't shared words with humans in a long time and considering the realm's plight he wasn't sure he wanted to. As they drew closer, both held up empty hands to show their good intent until at last they met across a broken stone table in Helthor's derelict garden.

"Brother," Clovis greeted him.

"Brother," Taal agreed uncertainly.

"My name is Clovis, I have arrived with companions."

Taal wasn't sure what to say. He was a carpenter masquerading as a Captain, not a diplomat. "Erm, then welcome Clovis. My name is Harak Taal. I'm the Captain of my encampment." He looked past him. "Your companions, they're. . ."

"Human, yes."

"From across the veil?"

"Yes."

He wasn't sure what to say next. Certainly the lack of outraged fairies could mean only one thing. "You possess a pact-of-grace?"

"Yes Captain," Clovis presented it ceremonially. "It is genuine."

Taal wouldn't know a pact from a pancake, but the artefact looked suitably old and venerable. He took it and made a show of examining it, but it was no use pretending. "Forgive me Clovis," he sighed. "I am no dignitary, not even a real Captain."

Clovis felt for him and smiled warmly. "The pact is real I assure you."

"Indeed it is," a tiny voice whistled. Both turned to see Posit hovering close by.

"You vouch for these travellers?" Taal asked.

"Not just travellers – witches," Posit remarked.

Taal reappraised the humans a distance away. By Oak his people could do with their skills right now, but could he bear to do business with such creatures?

Clovis read his thoughts easily. "Captain, my friends did not come here by choice. We were in a desperate situation. Very soon I intend to send them back. Can't you welcome them for just a little while? I too am a witch, and whatever help you seek I can provide."

He returned the pact, swallowed his pride and stood a little taller. "Then welcome, all of you."

"Who's that?" Kolfinnia whispered, watching the exchange.

"No idea," Hilda said, "but he's a Caprian."

"They're supposed to be stoic and hard working aren't they?"

"You mean the goaty one?" Hathwell interrupted.

"Best not use that word," she advised.

"I see." And he did see. Lately he had seen sprites, fairies and other 'impossible' things, not to mention Clovis himself. He thought he could easily take a goat-headed man in his stride. "Caprian," he practised. As a squire, he'd spent years around horses. The beings opposite, although exotic to the point of fantasy, exuded the same raw, animal honesty, and the same scent of body-warmth and life.

Kolfinnia meanwhile counted three other Caprians and a being similar to the tragic Leenyssa. *She's one of Clovis's kind, and female too,* she thought with vague unease. Just then, Clovis looked over his shoulder and gave them a nod.

"Here we go," Hathwell took a deep breath.

"Promise me you won't say 'goaty'!" Hilda hissed.

"I promise."

The three set off shoulder-to-shoulder, dimly aware that here, they were the fantastic ones.

Clovis waved them forward and introduced them, "Friends, I give you Captain Taal." He put the emphasis on 'Captain.'

They offered their names and Taal greeted each in turn, but did not shake their hands. "It has been some time indeed since witches crossed the veil and walked here."

"We shall be happy to offer whatever help a witch can." Kolfinnia tried not to stare. Taal's clothes might be threadbare, but he was impressive. Huge horns curled gracefully back from his brow, a plaited beard of silvery grey hung from his chin and rectangular pupils floated in his sulphur yellow eyes. She had no idea how old he was but she got the impression of a world-weary soul.

Hilda muttered a translation for Hathwell and Taal pricked his ears. "Your friend has trouble hearing?" he enquired politely.

"My friend speaks no Pegalia, although he is learning," Hilda excused him.

"He is not a witch then?" He shuffled back a step.

"He's come late in life to witchcraft, but I am schooling him in our ways."

Taal's mouth crumpled into a worried smile. "If only more would."

"You live close by?" Kolfinnia asked, changing the subject.

"Our encampment is just a few miles from here."

"Rest would be most welcome," Clovis suggested. "And once rested I shall gladly explain why we made the hazardous journey here."

A polite cough made everyone turn. Taal's companions watched from little way off. "Are we an embarrassment, Captain?" Peri smirked.

Taal groaned quietly, "Oak's-Oath! She won't let me forget this one."

Clovis saw that his band consisted of three grizzled-looking Caprians, but it was the young female who caught his attention and he was overjoyed to see one of his own again.

"Please," Taal encouraged them forwards.

The two parties met and names were exchanged. Suddenly Hathwell was surrounded by fantastic creatures and incomprehensible words, and wished he were back in Edinburgh, while Hilda was kept busy translating and acting as witchcraft's good ambassador, but Kolfinnia was curiously silent. She was watching Peri closely.

"Clovis," Peri tried his name.

He struggled to hide his interest, and his smile was as wide as his eyes.

"Something wrong?" she asked.

He coughed nervously. "No, just that I've spent almost a whole year without seeing one of my own."

She smiled, pleased for him, and tried to conceal her own interest. He was steel-grey, and his amber eyes had clearly seen more than she would in twenty lifetimes. His attire and sword were fittingly splendid, and she noted with relief his emblems of magic. If this warrior was as skilled as he was handsome then they had nothing to fear from the Magnon.

"Peri?" he enquired.

"Forgive me." She dipped her head in embarrassment. *Peri you rock-head, he's a witch remember! What if he read your thoughts?*

While her eyes were averted, he admired her golden mane and slender build. She reminded him strongly of home, but she stirred other feelings also, powerful and confusing feelings. She looked up suddenly, and Clovis quickly pretended he hadn't been staring.

"Our encampment is less than nine miles distant," she said humbly. "You will be our guests?"

"And once there you can tell us why I found four witches strolling out of a snowbound Helthor today." Taal's expression was a blend of optimism and apprehension.

Clovis took in their old weapons and dishevelled clothes and silently swore he would do all he could to help them. "What I have to tell you will change your world forever."

Hilda unrolled her battered hat and pressed it onto her head. It was crooked and crumpled but she felt herself again. "I'll teach you a little Pegalia as we go."

"Yes, I think I'll be needing it," Hathwell said gloomily. The party was moving off now with Taal and Clovis in the lead. Peri lingered discreetly by the Captain's side, but not for the sake of his company alone. "Miss Kolfinnia?" Hathwell hauled his bag over his shoulder. "You don't want to stay here do you?"

She looked around, only just hearing. "Sorry, what?"

"We're off."

"Yes. I'm coming." A moment ago she was delighted to be here with Clovis, so why was there a dark cloud over her now she wondered? She took a last look at the derelict castle, thinking of the people a whisper away in her real home, both friends and enemies. After a while she shouldered her things and followed the others, but lingering at the back.

Right now she just wanted a little privacy to think and it wasn't long before she found herself thinking of Peri's shining mane and dazzling eyes.

"Ah-lem," Hilda pointed to a buttercup.

"Ah-lem," Hathwell repeated.

"Desa." Now she gestured to the sky through the trees.

"Desa," he practised. "Does that mean sky or blue?"

"Neither, it means up," she chuckled.

The lesson continued and Kolfinnia listened with half an ear. They were following a river that navigated a narrow valley. It was shady and pleasant and for the first time since leaving Stormwood they had allies of sorts, but her mind kept drifting back to Peri. A rustle in the trees snagged her attention. She turned to see a young foal prance nervously back to its mother's side, and wonder of wonders she saw the foal was blessed with a stubby horn on its brow. "A unicorn!" The branches thinned and she saw them clearly. The mare's coat was shaggy and unkempt, and her mane reached almost to her hooves and was clumped and knotty. She watched silently as the party passed. Her horn must have been almost a yard long, but it wasn't the slender spike she would have expected. Instead, it was whorled and yellowed, like a narwhal tusk and it looked fragile. The mare turned and ambled up the hill, and Kolfinnia saw she was limping. Her foal trotted after her and within seconds the pair vanished into the greenery.

The first real shock came as they ascended the valley. The trees changed abruptly and within just a few yards they went from healthy to dead hulks with bare branches. "What in Halla's name?" Sunlight flooded through the naked forest revealing the devastation in stark detail. Now she saw that the trees weren't just dead, they were petrified. She reached out and touched one, finding it as cold as marble. "Stone," she whispered, horrified. "What caused this?"

Taal waited for them to catch up. "Is the going too heavy?" He seemed oblivious to the spectacle.

"The trees, they're all petrified!" she exclaimed.

He looked around sadly. "One gets so used to them it's easy to forget."

"You mean there are more?"

"In places they go on for miles. Dead forest with not a bird or fay in sight. This one is but a baby, we'll be clear of it soon."

"But what did this?"

"Nobody is certain but many suspect that this," he patted a stony trunk, "is a consequence of events across the veil."

Kolfinnia felt accusing glances as sure as prodding fingers, including Peri's. "You suggest this destruction is caused by humankind. . ."

"But certainly not witches," Clovis interrupted. "The Captain was just telling me so, weren't you?"

"Er, yes," Taal agreed diplomatically.

For the first time, she wasn't sure whether to believe Clovis. "If I could change the world I would, believe me. But I'm only a single witch."

Taal was keen to exploit their skills. Offending them wouldn't help. "It's a matter best discussed later. For now we press on."

Almost instantly a call from further up alerted them and Keel ran back looking mortified. "Captain, Captain, I think it's one of *them!*"

"Them?"

He bared his yellow teeth. "Magnon!"

Magnon. The word was a knife.

"What's your scout seen?" Clovis questioned.

"We call them Magnon." He swallowed and turned in Keel's direction. "W-where?" he gulped.

"Just further along. In a little glen. It's down there. . . feeding."

"You mean it's already grown!" This was far worse than he thought. Taal raced for a plan and finally did the only thing he could do. He turned to his new guests, already feeling inadequate. "That offer of help still stand?" he asked humbly, and Clovis's steady gaze said it all.

As they moved silently into position, the burning question in Kolfinnia's mind was 'what are Magnon?' The petrified wood changed to living trees once more, and the party came to a steep incline. "It's over this rise," Keel warned.

"Stay here," Taal began up it and crouched at the top and scanned the secluded valley below. It was carpeted with spindly sycamores, bisected by a small brook and filled with the aroma of wild garlic, but it wasn't deserted.

He sank down again, and returned to the others looking shaken and with one of his ears twitching nervously. "It really is – it's a Magnon," he confirmed.

"How in the twins' name did it get here, so close to us!" Keel made to have another look.

"No, don't," Taal restrained him, "don't. How it got here doesn't matter. We have to kill it right now."

Kill it. The words seemed so final Kolfinnia thought. "Must we? Are they so dangerous?"

"More than you know. They're slow but tough as stone and their touch is lethal." He regarded Clovis. "Still want to help?"

He just nodded.

"Then take a look, tell me what you see." *Because I've no idea what to do,* he worried.

Clovis slithered up the bank and peered over. The scent of blood caught his attention, and there he saw it. The creature was kneeling by the brook, hunched over a deer, amid a swathe of trampled garlic. *'Feeding,'* Keel had said, and so it was. From here, all he could see was a lumpy, human-shaped thing devoid of clothes, or even fur, hair, skin or feathers. It was a uniform reddish-grey and slick all over, and Clovis had the unsettling impression of raw clay come alive. He silently crawled backwards to the others. "I see a creature by the brook, it looks 'made' not living."

"Magnon." Keel was adamant.

"Well, Captain, your orders?"

Taal thought hard, but nothing came. He ground his jaw and nibbled his lip, and still his mind was blank.

"You ever encounter one before?" Clovis ascertained.

He looked to his hoofed feet. "No."

Instantly Kolfinnia was afraid and angry. "Clovis, they've never even *seen* one before? Then how do we stop it?"

"You don't. I do." He was already moving.

"Clovis!"

"I brought you here," he stopped her. "This is *my* responsibility. And this is *yours*." He pushed the bag containing Janus into her arms. "Captain, lead on."

Kolfinnia issued some protest, but Hilda hushed her. "He knows what he's doing."

She watched anxiously as Taal and Clovis clambered up and over the banking, joined by a Caprian called Hadd, and they vanished from sight. Immediately the rest crawled forwards to watch what happened next, and soon, many would wish they hadn't.

The three crept down the slope and hid behind a tree. Taal looked out and saw the Magnon still feeding. At his signal, Clovis and Hadd dropped closer still and hid again, while he edged along the incline aiming to get on the creature's far side.

Clovis waited and watched him stalk through the trees. Inevitably he heard leaves rustle and twigs snap and he winced, but when he looked the Magnon hadn't shifted. Its apparent disregard was chilling. *It has no fear,* he realised.

"*It has little of anything,*" Tempest added from his lightning-staff. "*Clovis, something's wrong here.*"

"*So I see.*"

"*No, not just the creature. This whole place feels under siege.*"

"*You're right, but one enemy at a time Tempest.*" At last he spotted Taal's signal from the trees opposite, and he angled around to Hadd, who dipped his horned head in understanding. He was tempted to look back at the ridge, but seeing Kolfinnia's worried face wouldn't help. "Come on," he prepared Tempest, "let's see if these Magnon are as tough as they say. . ."

Kolfinnia watched him emerge and close in on the creature. Beside her, Hilda watched just as closely. She wanted some reassurance from the older woman, as she had when she was just a pip-staff, but she was coven-mother now and must appear in charge. Instead, she sent her worries inwards. "*Skald – if he needs backup. . .*" she thought to him.

"*Understood,*" he agreed, and the staff buzzed in her hands.

Now he was closer, Clovis saw that the thing didn't just look like clay – it was clay. He thought of the amalga and for a horrible moment wondered if Sef had beaten him here. The Magnon remained static, bent over a deer carcass with its malformed fists planted on the animal's chest. *What in the twins' name is it doing?* he wondered. Maybe the creature wasn't completely insensible, because just then it turned and shambled upright, giving Clovis his first good look at it, and he swallowed his revulsion.

It was bulky and distorted, and glistened head to foot. The crooked arms were differing lengths and the digits on its hands were not equally shared nor even shaped like fingers, but more like melted candles. It looked like the clumsy product of a sculptor who despised their craft, but its face was most disturbing. Clovis saw a domed head studded with growths and nodules, with no apparent neck, and blank bulbous eyes above a wide frog-like mouth.

"Whatever it is, it has no rightful place in this world," Tempest understood.

"Or any other." Clovis was about to signal the others when someone hurtled past him, just like Tiber all over again.

"OAK ENDURES!" For Hadd there was much at stake. There were humans watching, and witches or not he had to show them who ruled this realm. Ignoring the others, he bolted past Clovis and right towards the Magnon, bellowing a war cry. "OAK ENDURES!"

"No! Hadd! Come back!" Clovis exploded from cover. He was only yards behind when the foolhardy Caprian reached the creature, and what he saw next haunted him for the rest of his days.

The Magnon slowly turned as Hadd leapt at it, whirling his old sword. The blade landed in its chest with a dull thud and simply wedged there. The creature swung around, and Hadd, still gripping the sword, was wheeled around with it. Its strength was monstrous and Hadd's furious scream became an agonised screech as the thing swung an arm and clamped a hand like a bear-trap over his head, engulfing it. Fingers clenched, bones crunched and Hadd's scream became a smothered gurgle. But that wasn't the worst. His entire body was instantly sucked empty. Clovis, still charging towards it, saw it happen in damning detail. One moment Hadd was whole, the next there came a wet popping sound like boiling mud, and he was just dangling skin and empty clothes. *'Don't let them touch you,'* he remembered. Now he knew why. The Magnon guzzled down his blood, bones and organs in an instant, and as it did it swelled in size, its eyes bulged like overfilled balloons and the whole thing bloated with added bulk and menace.

"Don't let it touch you!" Tempest screamed.

With no time to answer, Clovis swung his staff and roared.

Taal came crashing through the trees and vaulted the little brook. Ahead he saw the Magnon drop what he assumed was the deer's flayed skin, not knowing it was the remains of his friend. "Clovis! I'm coming!" He landed hard on the banking, skidded in the slimy leaves, righted himself, and raised his sword just as lightning flashed and the world became a haze of brilliant blue.

'Don't let it touch you.' Clovis thought of nothing else as he attacked. Tempest stung it with all he had. Lightning blazed, thunder boomed and the Magnon was spun through the air and dashed against a tree. Clovis didn't wait for a second chance. He leapt Hadd's steaming remains, heading straight for the Magnon, now jammed prone against a tree and jerking like a broken clockwork toy. Its hands opened and clenched in spasm, and Clovis saw tufts of Hadd's fur still clinging to them. Its expressionless head slithered around to face him, squelching like wet mud as it went, and with icy precision Clovis delivered a second and final blow. The staff impacted right between its eyes and Tempest fired again. Thunder ripped through him, scorched debris pelted his face and the world became a void of light, and then he wrenched his staff free and stepped back with a snarl.

A moment later Taal was with him, and both of them stared down at the charred thing. Its head was split open and Clovis was bewildered to see that the creature was hollow. "In all my years, I never saw such a thing," he said softly.

"Where's Hadd?" Taal chased his breath.

Clovis leaned across the Magnon's body and peered down into that dark cavity. There was the dull glimmer of some thick, red liquid in there, like congealed offal in a half-empty bottle. *That's all that's left of Hadd.* The thought was terrifying.

"Clovis?"

His heart was thudding and his ears still rang with thunder. "He fought bravely," he said evasively.

Taal's next words were cut off as the others came crashing down the slope. "Clovis!" Kolfinnia ran to him at once, closely followed by the rest.

"I'm fine," he assured them.

"Taal?" Peri flattened her ears and stared about the brook. "Where's Hadd?"

He was still struggling for words when Clovis gave them the hard truth. "The creature killed him Peri, I'm sorry." He averted his eyes from her dismay, and the bloody skin and clothes lying in the grass.

"It would have killed me too if not for Clovis," Taal added shamefully. "I never saw anything like that."

Clovis regarded the circle of stunned faces. Humans and Therions looked like scared children. "We should make speed for this encampment of yours," he proposed firmly.

Taal reached down, dragged Hadd's sword free of the creature's chest and regarded the weapon trembling in his grasp. "And when we get there, I'll sharpen these blades."

The others didn't see the realisation in his yellow eyes, but Clovis did. Like it or not, the faded-realm was failing.

CHAPTER SIXTEEN

The world-seed

'All that man creates shall be destroyed,
while all he destroys shall testify forever.'
Senna Deens - Caprian witch of the faded-realm

More trouble awaited them just further along the brook. "This must be where it came from." Taal pointed to a shrub growing by the water's edge.

At first Clovis didn't see the connection but as he approached, its fruits became all too apparent. "It grew here?" he gathered.

"Clovis?" Hilda peered out from behind him. The others fanned out and stood around the shrub. It was stunted and wiry and its narrow leaves were dark and glossy, but it was the fruits that horrified them all. Each was a tiny clay figure, a Magnon, and there were at least a dozen hanging from it.

"What is this monstrosity?" Kolfinnia shivered.

Clovis surveyed the woods, alert now. *How many more fell and grew?*

"Peri, hand me your flint and knife." Taal was making ready to burn it.

"No need." Clovis stepped back and the instant he touched his staff to the shrub it was alight. "Keep back, everyone."

They retreated, but remained powerless to watch as the flames first curled and blistered the leaves, and then roasted and cracked the Magnon pods. Kolfinnia almost expected them to scream or writhe but they died silently staring back at them, which was somehow even more disturbing.

Clovis moved away, wary of the noxious smoke, as did the rest. Very quickly he'd become the leader of this little expedition and Taal for one looked relieved. "Be watchful. Others might have germinated," he warned.

"Best keep going," Hilda pressured.

"Poor Hadd." Peri clasped her hands to her mouth in prayer.

Clovis resisted the urge to comfort her. "Come on, daylight's wasting."

Roused by the threat of darkness, Taal's group deferred their worries and mistrust of humans and set off again, now bonded by fear, and an awful sense of being watched.

Lisal expected her husband's party back very soon, and so she had a large pot of vegetable broth simmering. The encampment wouldn't eat until everyone returned, one because it was more economical and two because it was a way of thanking Hethra and Halla for safe homecomings. Taal patrolled most days and always Lisal worried about him. Magnon were chief amongst her worries, but so far they hadn't been seen this far north and she prayed it would stay that way. She caught movement from the corner of her eye. Little Nonni was standing with a crust of bread, mesmerised by the pot. "Nobody dips their bread 'til the rest get home, you know the rule," she said cheerfully.

Nonni was a Caprian like her, except his horns still hadn't budded despite him being eight years old. This afforded him a bit of teasing from the other children, but conversely a lot of favouritism from her. He watched her stir the pot and his belly rumbled at the delicious smell. Suddenly, he smiled, "No more waiting, they're back!"

"Thank the twins." She wiped her hands and turned about. Her smile quickly wilted when she saw her husband returning with strangers, and it disappeared all together when she saw what they were. "Nonni, go find Hortar, quickly now," she shooed him. He scurried off, still clutching his bread, leaving Lisal to greet unexpected, not to mention unwelcome, guests.

Kolfinnia hadn't expected much, but even 'village' was too grand to describe Taal's temporary camp. She saw a collection of tee-pees erected by a river, and comprising twenty Therions of differing races: eight adults and twelve children. She later learned they lived in such camps during the summer, seeking out the best forage.

They approached through meadows cloudy with cotton grass, while the river seemed to shirk the drought and run deep and fast. The encampment was surrounded by gentle hills carpeted in heather and crowned with sturdy pines. It was an idyllic setting, although their arrival was less so.

Rising steam caught Kolfinnia's eye and she saw a Therion-woman tending a large cook pot. *Lisal,* she guessed from what Taal had said. Lisal stopped, and watched them approach, while a youngster scampered off at once. *News will spread,* she steeled herself, feeling more like an invading army than an invited guest.

Lisal shielded her eyes against the sun, which was now low in the sky and Kolfinnia saw she wore a long blue dress and white apron, and without horns she looked eerily human. Her hair was tied under a headscarf, and her large brown eyes, which were set in a slender face stippled with creamy white fur, heightened her solemn expression. Her beauty was fittingly unearthly.

The party advanced with no fanfare and no talk. One of their number was dead and a mother's son wasn't coming home tonight. "Let me, the rest of you wait here." Taal went ahead to speak with his wife.

Peri watched from Clovis's side. "Poor Captain. He'll have to go and find Hadd's mother."

Clovis sighed heavily, "A task I've done more than I care for. I'll go with him when the times comes, if you like."

"Thank you," she accepted readily.

Clovis watched the conversation between Taal and his wife, guessing what his ears couldn't hear. Every now and again she looked their way and her expression was fearful. Inevitably more villagers drifted over and soon there was a crowd. Clovis didn't see a single kindly face, but an aged Caprian with a staff, hobbled over and Clovis guessed he was a witch.

"Tempest?"

"I hear you."

"He's the one. We need to speak with him about finding the place of ascension."

"That's if anyone even knows. This realm is in a state of senile decay."

"Clovis?" Kolfinnia roused him from his silent debate. "We're not welcome here – are we."

Peri looked at the grass, feeling uneasy.

He watched a moment longer. Now Taal was hugging his wife, perhaps comforting her. "No," he admitted, "not welcome, but not enemies either."

Kolfinnia saw Peri afford him a grateful look, and again that peculiar feeling swept over her. "You're welcome though," she noted, and instantly realised her mistake.

He flashed her an angry look, reading jealousy where none was meant.

"Clovis, all I meant was –," At that moment Taal called them over, interrupting her.

"I know what you meant." But his sharp tone suggested the direct opposite. "Now come on, there's a lot at stake."

Damn it! She hurried after him, eager for a quiet word, but Peri seemed glued to his side. Her quiet word would have to wait. *Damn it!* she fumed quietly.

Their welcome was cool, but civil. The young ones watched from behind their parents, as if the humans were Magnon themselves, while the adults clustered into a defensive pack. "Everyone," Taal began, "we have guests – four witches from across the veil."

Again, Kolfinnia could feel wary, even condemning, eyes on her.

"And Clovis is their leader," Taal placed a friendly hand on his arm.

Funny? she objected. *Nobody said outright that Clovis was in command. . .*

"Simmer down," Skald urged, catching her mood.

"And just as well we have such a strong witch join us today," Taal continued, "for we also found evil on our patrol." Now he faltered, and fortunately Hadd's mother was nowhere to be seen. He shook his head to clear it. "Today we found our first Magnon."

Kolfinnia suddenly imagined Sunday amid the horrors of Smithfield Market and the sounds of mournful bleating, crying and lowing. Taal's fellows reacted with similar cries. The sounds got under her skin and crawled in her head. *It's your fault!* they seemed to say.

Clovis turned about, letting them all see him. "Your Captain's right. Evil came here today, but I and my companions have pledged to stop it."

"Hilly?" Kolfinnia hissed, "I thought he simply had to open the vessel, why all this palaver as well?"

"Politics," Hilda answered.

She folded her arms huffily and listened to Clovis introduce them by name, all the while wondering what was the good of being coven-mother if she didn't have a fraction of Hilda's insights. She stole a glance at Hathwell's baffled face, and for once she knew just how he felt.

"But for now, I promise you that our skills are at your disposal," Clovis finished.

Peri was first to lead the applause and for a painful moment she was alone until the rest hesitantly joined in. Then as if on cue the crowd pressed in on Clovis, full of desperate questions.

Kolfinnia, Hilda and Hathwell stood a little way off. Nobody seemed to want their opinion. "Hilda, what did you mean?" Kolfinnia asked discreetly.

"Clovis's journey is still a long one. He'll need their help to find the place of ascension." She smiled politely at curious onlookers, but none approached.

"Of course," she groaned, "sorry, my wits seem asleep today."

"It's been a long day with a horrible end. You'll be better in the morning."

"This place isn't what you expected is it?"

"No. It seems what I told you of a 'magical realm' is a lost age now." Hilda surveyed the impoverished camp. "I'm sorry."

"No wonder they don't like us," she brooded.

"What's in the stew do you think?" Hathwell asked suddenly. "I'm famished."

The two women exchanged amused looks. "I'm glad some things here are just the way they are back home." Hilda took his hand and patted it, and just as he tried to hold onto her she pulled her hand away.

Yes, just the way they are back home, he thought with resignation.

The broth was good, and Kolfinnia realised that she hadn't eaten since Edinburgh that same morning. *A world away,* she reflected as she sat with Hilda, Hathwell, Peri and Taal. She chewed her bread and chewed over the day's events, while Taal made strained attempts at conversation and Hilda continued Hathwell's language lessons. Small family groups sat around in isolated pockets. She wondered if they always ate this way, or just because they were there. Clovis sat with Hortar, the encampment's witch and spiritual guide, and Kolfinnia didn't need magic to guess what they were talking about.

"You didn't come here to fight clay-men Clovis-witch." Hortar shovelled more broth into his mouth. He was old but he ate with gusto, and to match his temper he had not two, but four horns: an upright pair like spears, and a shorter downward pair. They were oily brown, like his coat. "But of course, if slaying Magnon is your life's aim then far be it from me to stop you." More broth vanished into his hairy mouth.

"I came here on a special undertaking." Clovis nibbled his bread, while Tempest sat by his side and watched them.

"Oh I know that! I have eyes," he chuckled. "That thing wrapped in your cloak. That's your 'undertaking'?"

Clovis was impressed. "Yes, but before I tell you, tell me of Magnon?"

Hortar instantly stopped eating. "Magnon," he steeled himself and swallowed loudly. "They first appeared in the southern regions about five years ago. Nobody knows where from."

"But you have an idea don't you."

He grunted and twitched his drooping ears. "Very astute."

Clovis considered. "My companions, I see the way you look at them. You think they're to blame."

He set down his bowl and stroked his wispy beard. "I see you have a wolf's eye and I shall have to shepherd my feelings from you," he complimented. "Magnon we called them and for good reason. We named them after yonder creatures." His gaze traced to Kolfinnia and the others and his voice became husky with dislike. "Cro-Magnon they are."

"They are witches, and good people," Clovis defended them. "If all their kind was as them then the world would be transformed."

"And you are right," he conceded. "But once a dog bites, a wise Therion avoids *all* dogs."

"They're not to blame," Clovis insisted. "A witch knows better."

"I only tell you what my heart feels," he retorted. "I never said I was proud of it."

Clovis waved an apologetic hand. "Forgive me, go on."

He scratched at his muzzle. "Like all witches in the faded-realm, I serve the spiritual needs of Hethra and Halla, and this camp," he jerked his head around to his own tee-pee where oak and holly symbols were painted on the canvas. "We suspect the Magnon are spawned from evils committed on the other side."

Clovis thought of what Sunday had said of places like Smithfield being a never-ending flow of blood and terror. "Seeds of the world," he said bleakly.

"It was only a matter of time before the Magnon found their way here," Hortar foretold.

Clovis scowled, "So what'll you do? There are youngsters and parents here. It's not safe."

"Move of course!"

"Another camp wouldn't be any more secure than this one."

"No, I mean our winter quarters, the city of Sterling is fortified. We'll end this summer's forage and go back."

"A wise choice."

"You should come too," Hortar invited.

"And why's that?"

"So you can finish this 'quest' of yours." He tapped his spoon against Clovis's bundled cloak, leaving dribbles of broth. "Wiser witches than me in Sterling, they'll help you find your path." He went back to eating, considering the matter closed.

Clovis stretched, and finally asked what had been on his mind from the start. "That dragon on your tunic, it is neither Hethra nor Halla I believe?"

Hortar's spoon stopped halfway to his mouth, and the light in his eyes dimmed. He took a breath, clicked his yellowing teeth, and said, "She is but a lost hope now, witch-Clovis."

"Forgive me, I didn't mean to pry."

He gently set aside his bowl and clasped his hands reverentially. "You are not a Therion of Earth are you? Else you'd know."

"I came from Vega-the-Blessed."

He bleated softly, "Ah, royalty amongst us I see!"

Clovis just smiled. "Alas, Vega is not all it was either."

"There we have much in common." He gently touched the embroidered dragon symbol, remembering something important.

"Who is she?" he asked gently.

"When our kin first came here, we came as refugees and made pacts with the fairy-nations to live in unity. Some species held out a long time on Earth, some even still linger I'm told; water serpents that hide in the deepest lakes, ape-men that live high in the snowy mountains, and others relics too. But by and by, differing races migrated here until they were all present but one."

The symbol seemed to cry out to him now. "Dragons," he understood.

"Dragons were revered because they were held to be the kin of Hethra and Halla themselves, but in their pride they believed they could withstand man's onslaught, perhaps even change man for the better. They lingered too long across the veil, blind to the obvious scale of our defeat, and in the end they never came." His voice juddered, and ground to a stop.

"They were hunted to extinction?"

He stifled his upset, disguising it as a cough. "The time came when there was only one left, a female called Astriss. It was hoped she would find her way here, but she vanished and her fate was never learned."

"You hope she still may come?"

Hortar laughed bitterly, "I'm a kid no longer. Such hopes are just stories." He wrung his hands absently as he edged towards the truth. "But we hoped, yes, of course we did, and in time she *became* our hope. But it is a dangerous thing to hope. Especially here," he looked around warily, "the faded-realm is a strange place, hopes and fears become real here."

Clovis sat silently for a while, listening to subdued chatter and someone's gentle sobbing. It had been a grim duty to tell Hadd's mother the terrible news. Before long, he became aware of Tempest's gaze. *'Tell him,'* he appeared to say, and he couldn't agree more. "Hortar," he began thoughtfully. "What would you say if I were to tell you that my mission here would change all worlds forever, if completed?"

He was now drinking from a wooden cup. "Then I'd bless you with all my heart."

"You could perhaps even go home again."

He scowled, wondering if he was being toyed with. "Can one task so great be completed by a single witch?"

"I am just the instrument. The agent of change is here." He spread his hands above the bundled cloak and Hortar was left to imagine what incredible treasure was hidden inside. "All I have to do is find the place of ascension."

He drained his cup slowly, without breaking eye contact, appraising the warrior's truth and finding him honest. "Then it's all the more vital we move camp and head for Sterling. We'll go tomorrow."

"Thank you," Clovis sagged with relief, knowing they had been accepted.

Later that night, Clovis slipped out into the darkness with a gristly but essential task in mind. Kolfinnia was sleeping beside Hilda in a small tent, while Hathwell was bundled up, snoring by the entrance. Skilfully he exited without waking anyone, crept out of the camp and back into the woods. It never occurred to him to be afraid. It was simply something he had to do.

Night is always a time of mystery in any land, but here in the faded-realm night was a kingdom apart. He walked through the darkness accompanied by luminescent moon-fairies on their nightly migration, emerging from their daylight haunts and drifting miles into the blackness. He closed his eyes and stood amongst them for a while, feeling their ethereal bodies glide past like delicate jellyfish. *How lucky you are*, he thought. *To have a singular purpose and no need of politics.* Each expired moonbeam they harvested would relinquish its soul and the fairies would escort them to Evermore. "Is there a Clovis-fairy out there to guide my way there soon?" He tried to smile at the idea, but found no humour in it.

"Clovis, remember," Tempest advised.

"I know." He drew his staff from his shoulder just in case, and continued.

A few miles later he found himself back at the brook, now dark with shadow and silver with moonlight. The Magnon's scorched body lay just where they'd left it, and with his keen sense of smell it didn't take long to find what he'd come for. He opened his cloak and respectfully laid Hadd's remains within, and then he bundled them up and tied it firm, but the clay thing was like a magnet and he found himself turning to look at it. Its head was shattered, but the grotesque eyes stared back at him. "Magnon." Clovis even hated the word. *How many more might have seeded?* But all he heard were rustling leaves and the brook's constant song.

She was waiting for him when he got back. He set down the cloak and its harrowing cargo and went to her. "I know where you've been," Kolfinnia said.

"Foolhardy I know."

"No, it was noble. A mother can at least bury her son, and you gave them reason to trust us." At last she was catching up with Hilda.

"I'm sorry I was curt with you earlier. I misunderstood," he admitted.

She looked about at the strange midnight world and shivered faintly. "There's much here that can be misunderstood."

He looked at his feet shyly. "I know you're here by my doing, but I could see no other way out. I'm sorry. . . but also I'm glad."

Without thinking she slipped her arms around him and whispered, "So am I."

He returned her hug, but it wasn't Kolfinnia's earnest face he imagined as he embraced her. Like it or not, Peri had quickly found her way into his waking thoughts.

The sun still rested below the horizon but his emerald eyes saw mile after mile of stony forest streak past. The dead trees stretched on forever and Sef had a shrewd idea why. He swept northwards, thinking of Kolfinnia, and it pleased him to imagine Clovis's heartbreak as he first defiled her and then devoured her. With so many pleasurable delights ahead he wondered how he would fit it all in. As he flew he drew strips of rabbit flesh from his belt and chewed them.

"What lifts your spirits?" Iso's voice rang through his mind.

"I was just thinking!" he shouted above the wind, "thinking of concluding our business here and paying back all those slights against me."

"Ah, vengeance! There's no warmer daydream to sweep away the clouds." Iso felt they were finally getting somewhere. Once they located the place of ascension they would simply sit tight and wait for Clovis to come carrying Janus. The plan was very neat he had to admit. *"Where are we, do you think?"*

"Trust me, we head ever northwards."

"But as yet 'where' in the north remains a mystery."

"Not for long. Chentek's rabble will prise answers from the terrified mouths of whomever we choose."

"But many settlements we have passed already."

"Too small. I need a larger town with a real witch, not like that broken fool Astar." Sef scanned the landscape. It seemed to be mostly forest and deadwood. "There!" he said at last. "That will suit our purpose." He saw a moderate township nestling in a swathe of forest and that's where he would find his answers.

Tallpine was the settlement's name and Rishok was their resident witch, although at this early hour it was best to leave the irascible old bear sleeping. Rishok was a Bjoren, one of the bear-Therions, and true to his nature, he excelled in sleeping and sore-headed-ness. This morning was different however. This morning he had risen early because of a strange dream. He dreamed of starlings circling the village and filling the heavens with their rapid chatter. Unsettled, he dressed and went to sit vigil under the morning star, on an outcrop that rang to the sound of dripping water, even in this prolonged drought.

At the first touch of dawn, he heard the sound of starlings. His muzzle curled back and he growled softly in warning, but the sky was empty. Rishok shook off his weariness and stood. His fur was chocolate brown, except around his muzzle where time had polished it silver, and his chestnut eyes gleamed. He shook his head again, making his shell necklace rattle faintly and he retrieved his staff. He respectfully kissed the oak and holly leaves at its top. "Lend me your strength Lord and Lady, my ears tell me Tallpine will receive a dark guest today." After a last look at the pink sky, he ambled away from where he had been sitting and hurried back to the village.

The journey was less than a mile, but with each step the chatter of starlings grew louder until eventually he didn't need magic to hear it. All of a sudden it stopped, which in turn made him stop. He caught his breath and listened. Nothing. The silence concealed something cunning, he thought, and on impulse he broke into a shambling run. He prayed, although not to the sleeping dragons now, but another dragon: Astriss-the-Lost. Although he was known as Tallpine's crotchety witch, he had a romantic heart and he firmly believed she would defend them in their greatest need. Ominously, his heart told him today was that day. *Astriss, have you come home at last?*

He charged through the forest and over the stream, making the wooden bridge bounce under his weight, and into the village. On first inspection all looked normal. He saw the little huts built on stilts surrounding the pond, and geese paddling contentedly. He saw the dragon banners around the meetinghouse still waiting to be unfurled, and the baking ovens waiting to be fired and stacked with flat-breads. Last night's worship bonfire still smouldered. It was just an ordinary dawn in Tallpine, except that it wasn't, and then it hit him. *Where in the twin's name have all the fairies gone?* Usually they were as commonplace as the breeze, but today Tallpine was devoid of a single one.

Tallpine might have a foreboding absence of fairies, but the town's folk seemed not to notice because incredible news was spreading like a fever. Therions were dropping from their stilt-houses and running to the meetinghouse, some of them still pulling on their clothes or simply running in nightshirts. Adults ran with cubs and Rishok could hear their excited calls. *What goes on here?* he thought in bewilderment. *Damn it all, I'm the witch yet I'm bloody last to know anything! Naomi, her senses are sharp.* He thought of his young apprentice. Most of Tallpine's inhabitants were Marta, akin to martens or badgers, and Rishok found them agreeable but woefully naïve. Naomi was not like them, she was feline and her instincts were just as keen. *Naomi, got to find Naomi!*

He charged through the willow stockade and into the village proper, and finally joined the throng. That's when he saw a stranger approaching from the opposite direction: a black Therion with green eyes. But then the crowd pushed in and he saw nothing. "Let me through!" he demanded, hauling folks aside. Someone ran at his side, panting in anticipation.

"Rishok, thank the twins you're here! Have you heard the news? Meesa says a witch has come carrying an egg, a *dragon's* egg!" Lomali was young and impressionable. "Is it true? I mean it can't be can it? Can it? What it if is though!" he babbled.

"We'll know for sure when I'm permitted a view!" he snapped.

"Yes, yes! Stand aside for Rishok!" Lomali yapped. "Stand aside!" The villagers gradually parted and the black Therion was revealed again.

Careful Rishok, the old witch told himself, *I don't like this at all.*

"That's him, the one with the egg!" Lomali's tongue lolled in excitement.

Rishok recognised the stranger as a magic-worker at once, but that didn't necessarily make him a witch. He slowed to a walk and then a saunter, all the while looking out for Naomi, or even a lone fairy, and then he stopped, seeing neither.

"Greetings." The stranger lifted a gloved hand. In his other hand he held a lightning-staff.

Rishok ignored him and glanced at the deceptive skies, now turning from pink to blue. *Starlings. I heard enough to reach to the moon and back, so where are they?*

"Greetings on this fine morning," the stranger tried again patiently.

Rishok stood his staff upright and mustered the dignity his station demanded. "And twin's greetings on you stranger. You've come far?" *You must have because I don't recognise your scent or your garb*, he thought with suspicion. A circle of animated faces huddled around them, and Rishok didn't like the rapt way they regarded their visitor.

Sef smiled, "I have come further than you could guess, and with a purpose greater than anyone knows."

The crowd watched the exchange. Now their eyes rested on Rishok again, waiting to see what he would say. "I am Rishok, witch and spiritual guide to Tallpine." He angled his head in a begrudging bow.

"Greetings Rishok, and I am Sef, a witch also." In contrast he bowed deeply, earning a few approving 'oohs' and 'ahhs'.

"So noble!" Lomali gasped softly.

Dimwits! Rishok groaned. *They'd praise a flea if it leapt high enough.* He flattened his ears, careful not to display any warning signs. "Tallpine receives few visitors, and none at such an early hour and so richly prepared." He noted Sef's wand and staff.

"These are but the least of my treasures," he said humbly. "Yet I have something of far greater worth here." Now he pressed a hand to his belt.

A dragon's egg, could it be? Rishok resented the way his hopes were inflamed. He opened his mouth to speak when suddenly a disturbing noise swirled around him, and then it was gone. It was the faint chatter of starlings, and he pricked his ears, alerted now.

Sef's pretend smile flickered. *"He hears them. I know he does."*

"Then just get on with it," Iso instigated. *"Kill him."*

"I need to question him first."

"Then take his thick skull and let's be off!"

"No. I desire to see this work first." He curled his hand around the egg.

He's lying. Rishok knew this as clear as his own name. He just didn't know the nature of the lie yet. He felt a breeze ruffle his fur, as if a flock of birds had passed within inches. But the air was empty. *There's something here with us, something hiding beyond the veil.* Yes, now he thought about it he could almost see them. There was the blurred suggestion of movement, like the haze from a fierce fire. *Fairies, is that why they've gone: driven off by fear?*

The crowd waited in puzzlement. Not a word had been said for almost a minute, when a cool voice broke the tension, "Rishok, I've been looking all over for you."

He turned and beheld his finest pupil. Naomi.

Sef saw her too and he struggled to stop his already fat smile from widening further. She was beautiful.

Naomi eased her way through the crowds with sensuous grace. She was a Therion just like Peri; cat-like, finely boned and blessed with long snow-white hair, elfin ears and blue eyes. Her robes were white and emblazoned with the crest of oak and holly. She was Rishok's apprentice and a witch in training. "Rishok?" She came and stood beside him, instantly wary of Sef.

"Naomi, we have a guest. Sef has come from afar bearing great gifts." He made it sound sleazy. That strange breeze enveloped him again, and he wondered. *Starlings?*

Naomi's jaw parted slightly and she sampled the air and found it wrong. *He's lying,* she thought.

Rishok eased a powerful arm around her shoulders and felt her unease.

"Welcome Sef," she said flatly. Around her the Marta appeared to be under some kind of sedation, all wide-eyed and compliant. *Can't they feel it?* she thought worriedly.

"My Lady." Sef gushed and bowed again, licking his lips as he did. "I am but a humble wanderer, but I bring an announcement of great joy."

He slowly drew out the egg, the one containing the dragon engineered to take him home, and presented it in the flat of his palm.

In the religious silence that followed, Rishok heard the sound of starlings louder than ever.

"Every one of you must know what I hold here in my hand." Sef sounded even more confident in the adoring silence. "The salvation you have long dreamed of, the one taken from you by Man's cruel hand. She has at last come home."

Someone began to cry while others whispered, gasped or whimpered.

"She?" Rishok tested.

"Astriss!" Lomali blurted.

Dunderhead! Rishok cursed silently. He was convinced this 'Sef' was playing them for fools.

"Yes, Astriss!" Sef proclaimed and the crowd erupted with delighted cries.

Naomi clutched Rishok's arm and hissed, "What's going on here, why's this stranger insulting the great Lady's name? And where have all the fairies fled to?"

"We'll soon find out," he growled. "SEF!" He rammed his staff into the dirt and a hush fell at once. "Maybe my eyes are obscured by the sands of time, but the Lady Astriss appears somewhat more youthful that I remember?" He pointed at the egg. "She was fully grown when last she was rumoured to have walked the world. Is your magic so great that you're able to squeeze her back into her shell?"

There was a threatening silence and the very air felt to tingle.

"That's right, it can't be her," someone realised.

Lomali shambled forwards and sniffed. "Not a dragon?"

"Not a dragon." Rishok turned full circle, making sure they understood. "Not a dragon. Not Astriss!"

"But why, why say it was?" He couldn't grasp why anyone would offer false salvation.

Poor Lomali, Rishok thought. "Come hither Lomali, the stranger's nothing to offer you, *any* of you." He faced Sef and emitted a rumbling growl, while Naomi hissed faintly. The crowd edged away, moaning softly, while some stamped, or scraped the ground with their clawed feet.

Sef knew desire for hope would sweeten his lies, but his well of honey seemed to have run dry. *"A pity. The deception was going so well."* He saw waking eyes around him and knew the spell was fading.

"I told you so," Iso said smugly.

He shrugged, smiled affably and slipped the egg back into his belt. "Well, I tried at least. Now we must do this the hard way." His sense of regret was almost genuine.

"You lied!" Lomali shuffled forwards. He wasn't naturally brave, but he was offended to the point of fury.

"Yes, lied!" a few of the others heckled.

"How much you have to learn 'Lomali', and yet no more time to learn it," Sef shook his head, while inside his staff Iso laughed quietly.

Lomali's stubby tail quivered, and he let out a guttural cry, "LIAR!"

"Come hither Lomali, right now!" Rishok boomed.

"Brave little rat," Sef chuckled. "But you ought to have stayed curled in your nest today, suckling your mother's teat while she plucks your droppings from the straw. No wonder men loathe you so much."

Outraged, Lomali drew his knife and leapt.

"CHENTEK!" Sef roared at last.

"NO!" Rishok started forwards just as a hundred million starlings all screamed at once.

They had been hiding across the veil waiting for Sef's signal, and now they came. Lomali was within striking distance when the iron-fays materialised and fell on him. They poured down his throat, strangling his screams, through his eyes and down his ears. He was eaten from both inside and out, so fast that when his body hit the ground it was nothing but a necklace of bloody bones sewn with tatters of flesh. His small knife thudded into the bone-dry dust. There was nothing to moisten it with, not even blood. They had taken every last drop.

In the next breath they were gone, leaving a gust of wind, a skeleton and a blunt knife that never got close to striking its target. Therions fell over one another and screamed in horror as they bucked and backed away, but they did not flee, and neither did Rishok. He was trembling with shock, and he could hear Naomi's rapid panting and smell her panic. "Get behind me!" His fur bristled and he looked twice as large.

"Behind you, no. Beside you, yes." She pressed to his side, wand at the ready. Their coats touched and static crackled.

Praise the twins I have you, he thought proudly.

Sef held out his hands apologetically and took a step closer, making the crowds flinch and wail. "You wish to kill me I know. Well?" he goaded them. "Will nobody try?" In answer they spat and cursed at him but no more, making him laugh.

Rishok dug his claws into the dirt, ready to pounce.

"Please no!" Naomi pleaded. "He'll kill you."

"Oh on the contrary. Please Rishok, try." Sef singled him out with his staff, but the great bear didn't move.

He's after something, that's the only reason any of us still draw breath. Rishok's heart pounded so hard that his vision pulsed red.

The two witches locked eyes.

"No?" Sef bared his fangs. "Then you're wiser than you look, old witch." He lowered his staff and turned to address the crowd. "If Rishok gives me what I desire, I shall leave this township and never be seen again." He spoke levelly, like a politician. "It is your desire to live today, is it not?" He raised his hands in question and turned in a circle. Hundreds of terrified eyes darted between him and their faithful witch.

"Bargain not with innocent souls. State your price Sef!" Rishok brandished his staff and ominously a stray oak leaf drifted down from its tip. *Today will be bad,* he thought.

"Rishok, you can't!" Naomi stepped in front of him.

He pushed her aside with fatherly concern. "This isn't *your* duty." He was afraid for her. Something in Sef's gaze made his stomach churn. *If he dares hurt her. . .*

Sef's expression hardened. "Words witch, all I want are words."

"Oh I have choice words for a devil like you!"

Sef laughed, "Tell me what I desire and no more souls need die." He prodded Lomali's pathetic remains with his staff.

"Nothing you desire can serve us well."

"Then it's well I serve another, and not you." He lay the staff across his shoulders. "The place of ascension: tell me where it is."

For a moment Rishok wasn't sure he'd heard right. The demand was so obscure. "What game is this?" he growled.

"No game. I told you, I came from afar. Your realm is a mystery to me, and I seek the place of ascension." He shrugged casually. "That's all. Surely such a harmless request doesn't merit further death?"

Rishok looked around at desperately hopeful faces. *'Tell him!'* they begged.

"Don't tell him." Naomi sensed terrible consequences.

He looked from Lomali's bare bones to the cubs and kittens surrounding him and swallowed.

Naomi heard rasping breath and grinding teeth as he deliberated. "Please don't!" she implored.

"I must." He manoeuvred in front of her. "I tell you, you leave?"

"You have my word."

He bared his fangs. "Then the place of ascension is Ultima Thule."

"Location?"

"Many days travel to the northern isles, and Thule is the northern most headland of the northern most island. In the man-lands it is called Unst-of-Shetland."

"You speak the truth?"

"You wouldn't recognise the truth! Now I have spoken, get your stinking visage out of my sight!"

Sef considered and then remembered who he served. 'Self.' And now was the time to honour his god by taking something purely because he could. His eyes fell on Naomi and the pupils narrowed to slits. "There is one more thing I desire: or this village dies."

In his heart Rishok knew. "You can't!"

Naomi knew it too. She also knew what would happen if she refused, and she took her first unwilling step towards him. "I will return shortly Rishok," she growled.

"Naomi, I forbid it!" He lowered his staff, trying to bar her way.

"This isn't *your* duty," she smiled as best she could.

His words wouldn't come, only a strangled groan. She laid her hands on the staff, lowered it gently and stepped past him. "You can't!" He stumbled forwards, blinded by tears of rage and clasped her arm in one of his great paws.

She looked into his face and spoke with resolve beyond her years, "I shall survive. Tallpine will endure. No more will die. And the beast will leave us."

Her logic was so ruthless and faultless that his great hand reluctantly slid from her arm. "You can't," he stammered.

"We have many years ahead of us, much I want to learn from you. This is but one day." She kissed him respectfully, and in reply his pushed his great head against hers, mingling their scents.

"Twin's blessings on you," he said in a cracked voice.

The crowd watched in silence and shame as Rishok's young apprentice walked towards Sef with solemn dignity. At last she stood before him, and he drew a lungful of air and savoured her scent. "I will not harm you," he promised.

"No. You will not." Her conviction was total.

"Come." He took her arm and started away, to find a quiet place where they could be alone.

Not long after Sef watched her slip her robe over her head and walk away.

Something inside him was out of balance. He took possessions for pleasure, but on this occasion it paid him back in uncertainty. Just like murdering the two milking maids, he felt less in light of his conquest, not more. *Is this all there is?* he wondered heretically. *How is it that the vermin I killed today can remain coupled for life, yet. . .* He dare not finish that thought. "Naomi!" he called, unaware he was going to speak.

She turned and regarded him with peculiar pity.

He hesitated. "I gave you my word you would not be harmed did I not?" He was master of this world, and so it tormented him that he needed anything from her.

She straightened her robe and smoothed her mane, anxious to bathe in the river. "Sef," she began coldly, "if that is your name, I will say this: that of all the souls I have ever met, yours is the most *human*." She left him with her last word buried in his heart like a cleaver.

He climbed to his feet and groped for his own robes as he watched her lithe figure vanish through the trees. Around him in the ether he heard

Chentek's slaves buzz and groan in hunger. He had what he wanted; the location where Clovis was heading, a dragon's egg that could beguile, and he plotted to take Janus and murder Acola with Self's blessing. Everything he wanted was his, but that which he unconsciously missed. Naomi's shimmering figure finally disappeared from sight and he was left with all the toys in the world but nobody to share them with, and yet the real tragedy lay in his ignorance of it.

Hathwell watched perplexed as Taal threw another pinecone on the fire. Everything was strange here. Fairies piloted the skies, Taal looked like a goat and the pinecones were as large as his head. As he was pondering this, Taal said something and to his delight he partially understood. "Yes, I think I see: fire opens the cones, yes?" He gestured to the flames but Taal didn't understand. He started again, this time in Pegalia. "Fire. Open." He made a fountain gesture with his hands, but resisted the urge to make a 'whoosh' sound.

The smouldering cones gave a loud 'crack', interrupting Taal's smile, and he raked them out of the fire. "Here." He shared one.

"Thank you." Hathwell wasn't blessed with thick skin and a tough coat, but he had the next best thing. He tugged his handkerchief from his coat, and then with his penknife he prised the pine nuts out of hiding and found they were delicious. "By heavens, you could earn a few bob selling these in London!" But he wasn't the only devotee of pine nuts. A moment later a pine-fairy landed on the cone in his hand and began eating. Hathwell yelled, dropped the cone and tumbled back off the log, while the fairy buzzed away, spitting insults and Taal let out a gruff laugh. Shamefaced, but unhurt, he patted the dust from his clothes, sat back down and continued as if nothing had happened. Taal said something he didn't grasp, but guessed from his smile that it wasn't too scathing.

He recognised her soap even before he saw her, and Hilda was beside him with a satisfied sigh. "Making friends with fairies I see?"

He smiled at his own humiliation. "It didn't seem friendly. It was like a bloody huge wasp."

She covered her own smile. "A good sign though."

"Good that it deemed to annoy me in person?"

"Take it as a compliment. Are the nuts pleasant?"

"Delicious."

"Pity they don't grow so big on our side of the veil." She took a stick and rolled a cone from the fire. "May I?"

"Cones are always plentiful." Taal uncorked a bottle and took some water. "After breakfast we pack the camp and begin back to Sterling."

"How far?" She savoured one of the nuts, which were rich and smoky.

"Ten miles. But there's a lot to transport." *And possibly Magnon to run away from,* he fretted silently. He got to his feet, which Hathwell again noted were cloven and bare. "I'll leave you to your breakfast." He bowed, a little self-consciously, and left them.

"He seems a bit friendlier today," Hathwell remarked once he was gone.

She leaned closer to speak. "Last night, Clovis went back to where we found that disgusting creature. He brought Hadd's remains back for burial."

Hathwell's next nut went uneaten. "Hilda," he began, "this place isn't what I expected. Not that I expected to come here at all, but for a magical realm it seems there's a lack of. . . well, magic."

She looked long at him. "You've noticed too?" She prodded the small fire and thought hard. "No, the faded-realm is not what I expected either. It seems the outer world is changing too fast for it to keep apace."

"There's that guilt again," he grunted. "Like I'm the one responsible."

"We're *all* responsible. Whenever we deny our conscience this world suffers."

Daunted by the enormity of it all, he found relief in the familiar. "Pine nut?" he offered. She took it and paid him with a smile. After a while he asked her something. "Taal said something about me in Pegalia."

"What did he say?" she asked, and he told her as best he could remember. "Really?" she raised her eyebrows.

"So, what does it mean?"

She smirked and ate another nut. "Never mind, but let's just say I agree wholeheartedly."

After eating, Taal found himself in Kolfinnia's company, albeit briefly. "Thank you for lending me a blanket." She handed it back regretfully. It was woolly and superbly warm.

"It was good yes?" He draped it over his pack.

"Wonderful."

"It took a long time to make."

"You made it?" She was impressed.

"Lisal wove it, but it's my, erm," he struggled, "coat," he said at last.

A quick glance told her what should have been obvious: Taal and the blanket were exactly the same colour. "You mean. . ."

"Yes. Each spring I cut the winter's growth." He smiled at her amazement and tugged at the creamy mane under his neck.

"And save it for weaving! I wish we could do the same."

He regarded her clear skin and shiny hair. "Not enough to make socks for a flea," he joked.

"A good thing too." She smoothed her chin and laughed. The brevity passed and she sensed he was anxious to get ready. "Thank you again."

"My pleasure." As he dipped his head respectfully his horns glinted in the sun and his yellow eyes regarded her fully, and then he returned to his packing.

Ten miles. It might have been a pleasurable hike if not for the spectre of Magnon. *'The poison plants are rumoured to grow near water,'* Taal reminded them and so by Clovis's recommendation they followed the waterways where they could.

'If you find anything that looks unusual or wrong, burn it.' His extreme command became everyone's watchword.

Burn it, Kolfinnia thought in dismay. Here they were in the fabled realm of fairies and mythical creatures, and already war had followed them. Perhaps the Therions were right to be wary.

They moved like soldiers now, keeping the young and the old in the centre, and the strong on the perimeter. Clovis walked at the front, with Kolfinnia on the left flank and Hilda on the right. In this way they had three lightning-staffs to protect them as well as Hathwell at the rear with a borrowed sword. The strongest Caprians walked with swords, knives and wood axes ready.

"Did you and Valonia ever see anything like the Magnon before?" Kolfinnia kept her conversation with Skald private.

"Monsters are more plentiful than fish in Iceland, but things like these Magnon, no."

"Tempest finished it easily enough I'm glad to say." A snapping twig made her freeze. *"Skald?"*

"Just a squirrel," he calmed her. *"A funny turn of events though, yes?"*

"How do you mean?"

"Yesterday, they were undecided about you, now you're providing them an armed escort."

"Yes," she sighed. "But there's better ways of making friends."

"Kolfinnia?" someone enquired, and she turned to see Peri's concerned face. "You spoke?" In her small hands she carried a hatchet.

She curbed her mistrust. After all, she'd done nothing wrong. "I was just talking to myself." She disregarded the matter and turned her attention back to the woods.

"I should thank you, we all should," Peri continued.

In truth Kolfinnia just wanted to tell her to 'shut up'. She needed to remain alert. "You owe us nothing, I promise."

She appeared to consider this. "How long have you known Clovis?" she asked unexpectedly.

Kolfinnia bristled and even Skald felt her resentment. "A year next month," she said coolly.

"He is here with a great purpose I'm told."

"Hortar told you that?"

"He merely said Clovis would divulge his secret once we get to Sterling."

"And I'm sure he will."

"He also forged a coven called Kittiwake I'm told?"

You've been told a lot, she thought peevishly. *"We* made a coven, Clovis and I," she corrected.

Peri looked away and struggled for something further to say. "Witches are rare in the faded-realm these days, and a witch like Clovis is rarer still. You're fortunate to –,"

"Peri!" she interrupted, "Please, I need to concentrate on the woods."

"Of course," she submitted.

Kolfinnia turned away. Not vigilant for Magnon, but to hide her burning face. You might say 'Self' had got the best of her. They walked in silence until she couldn't stand it any longer. *"Skald?"* she asked timidly.

"Yes?"

She readied herself. *"Sometimes I think I don't deserve Valonia's wand."*

"Funny, sometimes Raven's wand didn't think it deserved Valonia."

She smiled gratefully. "Peri," she began sheepishly. "When we get to Sterling, ask Clovis to tell you how he saved Kittiwake."

"I'm sure he will be so busy that I shan't see him again."

Gladness and regret fluttered in her chest. "Oh I think you will," she forecast, "I think you will."

The river forked and the main channel detoured away, and so they were forced to follow a tributary. Clovis scanned the dense forest.

"See anything?" Taal asked quietly.

His sensed an assortment of fairies in hiding, but nothing evil. "No. But fays are nervous though."

"Hmm, there's word of a plague affecting the iron-fairies further south." Taal saw Clovis open his mouth to speak but stopped him. "I can't say more because that's all I know. There might be fresh news in Sterling. We haven't been there for eight weeks."

Clovis considered this. "So, how lies the land after this?"

"The going's easy, but the forest soon ebbs."

"Ebbs?"

"You'll see," he warned and set off again, taking the lead now.

Not long after, they all saw. Living trees became petrified hulks in the space of a single stride and before them was a sea of stone. "Halla's Claws! More of them?" Kolfinnia's heart sank.

"This is no place for a tree-loving sprite," Skald agreed.

"This is awful," Hilda whispered.

At the back, Hathwell pivoted this way and that as he stumbled on, taking in the impossible spectacle. "Faded is the right word," he said to no one.

"Better light though!" Clovis called back. It was harsh but true. Leaf-less branches didn't block the sunlight. At least they could see further into the forest, although that was a mixed blessing.

They continued in near silence, except for the sound of their tramping feet, swaying baggage and the little ones wriggling restlessly against their mothers. Somewhere out of sight a branch crashed down, sounding like a landslide, and Kolfinnia jerked, ready for action. "It's nothing," Taal assured her. "One too many winter frosts. Even stone trees break in the end."

The ground nurtured only sickly grass and scruffy moss, but to Kolfinnia's surprise a pine-fairy drifted alongside for a while. Glad to see a little life, she reached into her satchel and drew out a nut. "Looking for this?" she held it out. He landed without a care, and she earned a closer look at him. He was covered in emerald needles like spines and his curling arms and legs resembled roots. His abdomen was studded like a pinecone, and his eyes were orange and glistening like resin-drops. After a quick sniff at the nut he snatched it and buzzed away. "Eat well," she wished him.

For a while she walked on with renewed hope, but before long the dead wood's pessimism invaded her bones again. When she heard shattering stone once more she imagined a falling branch, what she didn't expect was an immense stag watching them from a higher slope. Nothing like it lived on Earth now. His antlers were vast, just like the trophy skulls in Helthor. They looked impossibly heavy, and he staggered through the trees with its head hung low, demolishing branches as he went. Rubble and dust rained down across his matted coat and at last she couldn't stand it. "Captain, that stag!"

Taal was all too aware of it. "He'll not harm us."

"But he's lost. Shouldn't we help him?"

He wore a strange expression of sympathy and resignation. "He'll have to find his own way out."

"Can't we do anything?"

He directed his sight up the hill towards the huge animal, now ploughing on as best it could. "If we chase he'll bolt and perhaps break a leg, or injure one of us. No, he must find his own way."

He was right she knew, and just like the great stag they had their own obstacles to face and they must do so alone. She forced back her worries, turned away, and walked on.

CHAPTER SEVENTEEN

Walls of Hope

'The Therion races were degradations of man's divine form.
They had no soul like man and no place in the creator's heart.
Their purpose was to toil for man or provide him sustenance.
They failed in these simple tasks, and justly paid with extinction.'
Solomon Barnet - chief deviser to the Williamson Illuminata bloodline,
Canterbury 1421

"So, you haven't said much of Sterling. What's it like?" Kolfinnia wondered if it was similar to its namesake across the veil, not that she'd visited there either.

"Hope's fortified." Taal went back to rummaging in his pack.

"Hope?"

"Oh," he realised. "Hope is the city's other name. *Our* name."

"I like it."

"You'll like it more when you see it." He drew two apples from his pack, offered her one and then sat back on the log and looked thoughtful. "As more families move there from fear of the Magnon, the more the city's name fits." He crunched his apple, whole and in one mouthful, seeming to forget the matter.

"How far now?" she said between mouthfuls.

He pointed through the trees, which thankfully were now healthy again. "Close. You can often see chimney smoke from the brow of that rise there, smell the river too."

She looked to where he was pointing. The rest were standing amid the trees looking northwards, and the young ones were chattering excitedly. Now she knew why. "They see Hope."

"Aye." He liked the way she used their name for it. "No fear from Magnon in Hope." As he spoke an apple-fairy landed on the tip of his horn. Kolfinnia thought he was just lurking for scraps, but to her surprise the pair knew one another.

"Taal!" the fairy chirped.

He twisted around to see, making him buzz back into the air. "Bikwell. A fair day to you." He broke an apple with his strong hands and held up a chunk.

"Good news, the fleet has come home!" Bikwell snatched at the fruit.

"At last! And all's well?"

"All hands home safe." Bikwell alighted on his shoulder clutching his meal and finally noticed Kolfinnia's curious stare. "I don't know you," he said bluntly.

"Sorry." It was hard not to stare. In the last two days she'd seen more fairies than she could count, and still their variety and beauty dazzled her. "I'm Kolfinnia," she introduced herself.

"A witch," Taal added approvingly.

"Of course a witch," Bikwell scoffed. "Who else would come here?" Kolfinnia thought of Hathwell but said nothing.

"So!" Taal slapped his hands down on his knees. "Tell me all about the fleet's homecoming!"

"I just did." He sniffed at the apple core. "You're going to eat that?"

He rolled his eyes and put it on the log for him and stood up. "Eat well." Taal and Kolfinnia gathered their things and went to join the rest. "Too many sour apples in that one I think."

"What did you mean about the fleet?" she asked.

They were almost at the top of the bank and he was about to answer when Peri shouted down, "Taal, the fleet's home!"

"I know!" He offered Kolfinnia a hand up. "Come see for yourself."

She clasped it and felt his rough pads and wiry coat against her palm, and when at last she stood with the others she saw what he meant. "Hope!" she gasped, and knew the name was perfect.

Just minutes later, the Therions began trooping through the woods towards the city, looking like a straggle of refugees. Kolfinnia however just stood and took in the view of an expansive floodplain, dotted with windmills and with a hulking castle sat right in the centre of it. The River Forth, if indeed it shared the same name here, looped around the castle protectively before snaking westwards towards the North Sea. She fancied the morning sun had painted it silver just for her benefit. Just then, a passing cloud muted its brilliance and she saw a fleet of vessels with red and white sails moored along the river near the castle. The fleet had come home. Kolfinnia had no idea where they'd been, who crewed them or what dangers they'd faced, but she found herself glad for them. "Hope."

"A splendid name wouldn't you say?" Hilda joined her.

"I don't know why I never thought of it for a coven." She dabbed her eyes. The sight was strangely moving.

"Enjoy it while you may." Clovis looked preoccupied.

"Because. . ?" Hilda lay her staff across her shoulder.

"Because now I think we're far enough away from Helthorn for me to send you home." He kept walking, following the rest, and determined not to look their way.

The more he delved into Barda's knowledge the more treasures he kept finding. Sef was gratified to discover that Barda's mental map of Britain was sufficient for him to locate the remote island known as Unst. Barda might have glimpsed it on a map for less than a second, but the subconscious recorded everything. Sef found the relevant scrap of information and set off at speed now. *To Ultima Thule*, he reminded himself, as mile after mile of the faded-realm sailed past him below, *the furthest north of Britain, and the place of ascension.*

Even Iso recognised the need for haste. He seldom spoke and curtailed his complaints, although Sef detected his reservations throbbing away like a grumbling tooth. Considering they were racing against time, Sef almost overlooked the spectacle below.

They were traversing a huge bay, that across the veil he identified as Morecambe. It was hemmed in by mountains to the north, moors to the east and deadwood to the south. There was a long sandy island like a bent sword at the bay's western edge, and a minuscule scrap of land off it, like the sword's tip had broken off. It was this speck of land that caught his attention. From an altitude of three hundred feet, he saw a lone tower in the island's centre, but it was the crowds surrounding it that caused him to stop and think.

"Sef, keep your eye on the goal. I can't fly straight if you don't think straight!" Iso complained.

"We're going to make landfall." He'd already decided, and was guiding the staff downwards.

"What for? Nothing of worth there."

"That's because Lord Self does not speak to you, but me."

The sprite bit his tongue and instead monitored their flight as the island loomed closer. A few wispy clouds flashed past. He smelled the sea, sand and wet mud, but something else also: clay. And then he saw the figures. *"There's a gathering,"* he warned, *"have we need to visit another village?"*

Sef didn't answer. The island was too small to support a village and the tower looked like a ruin, and so why were there hundreds of figures clustered around it, he wondered?

He dropped low enough to skim over the bay's calm waters. As he approached the island he slowed to a crawl, suddenly cautious. There was a muffled clicking noise, not regular like a clock, but random and chaotic. It wasn't what he was hearing that troubled him however, but what he was seeing. The shore was lined with row upon row of huge clay figures. All of them had thick limbs, barrel-like chests, massive hands and domed heads, without any discernible neck, and disturbingly, all of them were facing Sef as if they'd sensed his approach. No two faces were alike, yet all of them looked to have been made by the same unbalanced mind.

"What are they?" Iso shivered.

"I do not know," was all Sef could say. On his shoulder Chentek was passive and silent. "But they are living, whatever they are."

"That noise – are they speaking?"

Sef listened and allowed that sinister ticking and tapping into his head. Both he and Chentek might have come from other spheres, yet this was completely alien: *Fast. Slow. Urgent. Frantic. Forever. Never. Ponderous. Point.*

Counterpoint. Do. Do-Not. This. No. Yes. That. It. I. I. I. I. The rhythms were painfully abstract. Before long he knew without doubt, and winced at the discomfort. "Yes, they're speaking." He clutched his wand, all senses on alert.

"What do they speak of?"

For once he didn't have a scathing retort. "I do not know, nor would I ever wish to."

Chentek whined something and retreated further into Sef's robes.

"Lord Self guided you here?" Iso said in disbelief.

Sef wondered now. "We shall see. Forwards." Iso began at a crawl towards the shore, now less than seventy yards distant, while Sef directed the staff a little higher. And that's when he noticed. As they drew higher, it became clear that the whole island was covered in them, hundreds, possibly thousands, and one by one they turned their empty faces.

Sef watched with rare humility, as the sea of lumbering figures jostled and bumped against one another to turn and watch them, and in response that eerie ticking became overwhelming. *They're talking about us*, he deduced. Within minutes, the whole colony had moved to face them, but despite his immediate concerns Sef was intrigued by the object they had all been staring at. The tower.

They moved at a considered pace, gliding just twenty feet above the creatures. Hundreds of misshapen, hollow eye-sockets tracked their passage and Sef heard the slurp of shifting clay between the endless clicking. Some of the creatures tried to stumble after them, but managed only to lumber into their fellows. The noise had a needy sound to it, but needy for what, he wondered?

Closer to the tower now, Sef saw it was perhaps a remnant from a larger structure like a castle, because it was round, three floors high, lined with narrow windows and lacking any visible entry on the ground floor. The creatures around it were packed so thick that the ground wasn't visible, and those closest the tower were pressed up against the stonework, leaving ruddy smears of clay. The noise here was constant, raucous and mindless. *What thing inside the tower could madden them so?* he thought. A moment later he had his answer.

"Help us!" someone cried.

Sef looked and saw a stricken face appear at one of the windows.

"Help us, please!" The cry became a scream, and a small hand appeared, waving a rag. "Please!"

"I think we've just learned the creature's apparent interest," Sef observed, and began forwards.

"Merciful rescues are not your profession," Iso jeered.

"Who said anything about rescue?" He saw the tower's prisoner better now: some young Caprian woman. To her, he must have seemed like a witch in shining armour.

"Please!" she bleated again.

The windows were too narrow to pass through, and so Sef indicated the roof. She nodded fervently and vanished from sight. Outside, he elevated the staff up onto the tower's pinnacle roof. There was a narrow walkway between the battlements and the roof, and even before he'd landed, the small door was flung open and she barged through it. "Thank the twins!" she sobbed, and not waiting for an answer she grabbed his arm and dragged him through. Bemused, he allowed himself to be led. Once through the door she shoved him aside, sobbing all the while, and roughly slammed it shut, before seizing his wrist and hauling him after her down the stairs. "Thank the twins!" she babbled over and over. Sef stumbled down the stone spiral behind her, which echoed to those hungry clicking noises from outside.

It was almost wholly dark inside. The windows had been stuffed with rocks and rags, anything to keep the hideous noise out. He listened harder, and discerned the faint sound of clay hands slapping and groping at the stonework outside. It sounded moist and relentless, like the sea or a searching tongue. She hurried down through the dark, heedless of injury and reeking of panic and filth. How long had she been here he wondered? Eventually, she stopped at a small landing area and banged on a hefty oak door. "Bersik, it's me, let me in!" she panted, all the while maintaining her iron grip on him. Bolts were drawn and instantly she was shoving the door open and dragging him through.

He found himself in a circular room with slot windows on three aspects, two of which were sealed with rubble and debris. The floor was covered with filthy straw, which had a farmyard stink, and two young Caprians, a boy and girl, huddled beneath the window. *"They've been soiling this room, too fearful to leave it,"* Sef deduced.

"Savages!" Iso snorted.

He heard bolts scrape back into place, and before he could even look around, the woman had thrown herself at him and was sobbing against his chest. "Thank the twins!" It seemed all she could say for now.

Sef tolerated her embrace for a while and then held her at arm's length. "What's your name?"

She took a moment to think, swallowed and then said, "Jenilla sir, my name's Jenilla. And these are my young, Bersik and Deeya." She gestured to the boy and girl in turn.

Sef saw two frightened faces regard him with awe and hope. They were dirty, and their coats were brown and white like their distraught mother's. "I am Sef," he replied.

"You're a witch aren't you?" she pleaded.

"I am," he smiled and let his hands drop from her shoulders.

"Thank you!" Her eyes swam with tears and now she clutched her hands under her chin. Sef saw she was dishevelled but otherwise attractive. Her face was white, while her ears, neck and shoulders were chocolate brown. She bore no horns but her mane was elegantly plaited, or at least had been. Now it was scruffy, but there were shells and beads still woven into her soft hair. She wore a long blue smock and a woven grey shawl.

"Jenilla, how did you come to be here, surrounded by such monstrosities?" He took her hand and bid her sit where the straw wasn't so dirty. As soon as she sat down her young scurried over to her side. Three anguished faces watched him, and Sef felt something terrible stir within him.

"Three days ago," she began, and took Bersik's and Deeya's hands in hers. "Our boat ran aground and we were trapped in the sands. I'm a stranger to this coast. We all are. There were four of us to start with." Fresh grief overcame her and she stopped. Without realising, Sef reached out and laid his hand over hers. The young shuffled closer and again that awful serpent writhed in his chest, while Iso growled faintly from inside his staff. "My mate, Haskar. We were trapped on the sands." She spoke slowly now, struggling against her feelings. "We soon found them treacherous and soft, but we managed to find a safe way through at first. Our boat was damaged and we had to leave it." She swallowed again.

"Take your time," he comforted her.

She offered him a weak smile. "Soon the tide began to run in. Never have I seen such a fast tide. In minutes we were ankle deep, then knee deep. We saw this island and headed for it. That's when they came."

Sef directed his ears to the commotion outside. "Them?"

"Yes." The young pressed even closer to her. "Haskar tried to fight them off, but. . . but you mustn't let them touch you. Mustn't. . . because, they — they —," her words sank into heaving sobs.

"I can guess," he finished for her. "And you fled here to this tower?"

She nodded without looking up.

"Can you help us sir?" Bersik was shaking. Perhaps they hadn't eaten in days. Now his mother looked up too. Her face was equally beseeching.

He sighed evasively, "What are those beasts outside?"

She smiled cynically. "Truly sir you come from a happier land than this. They are Magnon. But I've never seen so many. At first we were attacked by just a handful of them. They rose up out of the very mud. But after we hid here, they began to seed."

"Seed?" Plots were already whirring through his mind.

"Their numbers multiplied, without end it seemed." She cupped her mouth. "They cover this whole little island now. We were trapped — until you came." She took his strong hands gratefully, ignorant of all the misery they had inflicted. "Thank you good witch."

Sef only partially heard her. He was thinking of these Magnon creatures.

"You can help us can't you?" she repeated.

"I can help," he replied truthfully, but that didn't mean he would. "But tell me more of these Magnon."

She shrugged hopelessly. "Sir, I cannot."

"Anything might help." She didn't detect his ulterior interest.

She thought hard. "Some ten years ago the tales began of the clay-men. Just tales they were, until five or six years ago the first Magnon was found growing in the south."

"South of these isles?"

"Yes, but I do not know the place. Since then they have spread like strangle-weed. They are dumb but destructive. They kill any and all things, seemingly without care or reason."

The perfect warriors, he thought.

"That's all I can tell you good witch." *'Now please, just get us out of here!'* her eyes appealed.

"You are a good and brave mother Jenilla," Sef praised her. He stood and right away they jumped to their feet in a panic.

"You're leaving?" Choking fear rolled over her again.

"You asked me to help you did you not?" He made sure never to say anything binding, and let others hear what they wanted in his words. It was the art of Sef.

"You'll return with help? Perhaps carry us away with that magical flying staff of yours?" she laughed nervously.

"I can pass easily over these Magnon Jenilla, have no fear." And he meant it.

"Thank the twins." She sagged with relief, and then wrapped her arms around his neck and held him tight.

Sef wore a practised smile, but inside him that worm wriggled in his gut again.

"Sef, what are you thinking?" Iso chastised. *"Has the Naomi-witch softened your heart?"* Right then, Sef could have cheerfully ripped him in two, but of course he said nothing.

A small body pressed against his leg. It was Deeya, the girl. "Thank you, sir." Her voice was just a whisper.

Troubled and frightened, he stepped away from both her and her mother. "I must go."

"Yes, of course." She sounded apologetic for having detained him. "We shall await your return witch-Sef." Her young again clustered around her and she held them close.

Darkness all around them, yet the darkness in my heart is deeper still. The thought hit Sef hard enough for Iso to hear it too.

"Be warned 'good-witch', all that happens here Acola shall see."

"Sef?" Jenilla asked gently. "Is all well?"

Her concern for him was the tipping point. "The day is wasting, I must go."

She was past him in a flash, pulling the bolts free. "A safe journey, and twin's blessing on you Sef."

From his shoulder he heard the hidden Chentek chuckle softly, "Meat for Magnon."

"And blessings on you," Sef returned. There came more quiet laughter from Chentek, while the lightning-staff was frosty with Iso's disapproval. He took to the spiral again, heading back towards the roof. Behind him he could hear Jenilla's soft footfalls and he tried to outrun them. At the roof he kicked the door open and was up on the battlements and mounting his staff as she caught him up.

"Blessings on you good Sef!" she called after him.

Sef never looked back. He streaked over the Magnon army below, leaving her hopeful words behind, along with the terrible feelings she'd awoken. By the time he reached the island's shore, the tower was out of sight and he was composed enough to find a relatively safe spot and collect a dozen Magnon pods and slip them into the gelding-sack. They would remain dormant there until he needed them.

"That's better," Iso warned.

Sef was just finishing, when the first Magnon came plodding towards him, and he was airborne and sailing over their heads before they even got close.

As they approached Hope, Kolfinnia found herself passing cultivated gardens, orchards and cereal crops. The effect was like walking into Stormwood and a sudden wave of homesickness washed over her.

"Kolfinnia?" It was Clovis.

"Thinking of home. That's all."

"I promise you'll be there soon," he smiled.

"They appear happily self-sufficient." She avoided the issue, and instead appraised the acres of produce.

"Treaties of non-aggression, underpinned by a plant diet. Grazers and hunters can live side by side," he explained with some admiration.

"Is it like that on Vega?"

"Largely." His expression was wistful.

"I know you must miss your home, but you'll be there soon too," she smiled for him, but if there was any cheer in the idea for her she couldn't find it.

"First I have a promise to Janus." He patted the bulge under his cloak.

"We could always delay our return, you know, to help you?"

With Sef on the loose and the Janus vessel filled with poison? I think not Kolfinnia. He stroked his hairy chin. "A touching offer, but from Hope I go on alone. It's too dangerous and only I know the ritual."

"Oh." Lost for anything further to say she hefted her staff to her other shoulder and they plodded on after Taal's band.

Before long she noticed how Therions were slowly gathering from the surrounding fields to see Hope's new visitors. She wasn't sure if they were going to pelt them with vegetables or kneel in worship. As it turned out they watched from a safe distance, and while Kolfinnia couldn't guess their mood, the cubs, kittens and pups gave it away: a sense of intrigue over unease. They peeped out from behind the adults, hid behind carts, barrels, hurdles and walls. All of them were fascinated, but fearful enough to keep a distance. Their garments were poor and ragged, but each glance, smile or titter had the same meaning: *'Human witches are coming to Hope,'* they seemed to proclaim.

Hathwell caught her up. "I half expected a shower of arrows and spears."

"I think without Clovis we might have faced just that." Feeling bolder, she waved to a young Therion, who was almost impossibly endearing. He blinked his large eyes, twitched those fluffy ears and backed away. *Bjoren,* she told herself, remembering Hilda's account. *The bear-like are called Bjoren.*

"And those dragons, that must be Hethra and Halla?" Hathwell pointed out, keen to show off what he'd learned.

"Dragons?" Now she noticed too. The flags fluttering from the city walls all carried the image of a dragon, but she didn't recognise it as either of the twins.

"And there too," he twitched his head discreetly.

She looked and saw a tall Therion with antlers and soulful eyes watching them from where he'd been cutting wheat. His ragged tunic was decorated with the same image. "Maybe there are more dragons in the world than we knew," she wondered aloud.

Hathwell took heart. Her not knowing made him feel less adrift. "I hope so."

Further up, Kolfinnia could see Clovis deep in conversation with Peri. She must have said just the right thing because she heard his rumbling laughter. *Hope,* she thought, and suddenly there was just one thing she hoped for, but it seemed to be slipping further and further away from her.

The city was walled and the gates fortified. A heavy portcullis stood between stone towers, each decorated with gargoyles and topped with battlements. 'Hope'. It wasn't just a name. As soon as she was inside, Kolfinnia felt a change and realised that outside she'd felt a vague but constant sense of menace. Once through the gates, it vanished and despite everything she savoured her first genuine smile in many days.

"This is the faded-realm as it ought to be," Skald approved, and she couldn't agree more.

The track stopped abruptly, giving way to a cobbled street lined with crooked little houses. A great castle lay at the city's heart, surmounting a hilltop and dominating the view. A quick look at her feet delighted her also. The cobbles were all shaped like overlapping scales and the effect was like walking across the flanks of a huge fish, or more aptly a dragon. A fast flowing stream ran either side of the street, through purpose-built stone channels. Its constant music made her smile, and wonder about the water's source.

Faces young and old, from endless species, all looked out from windows, doors, alleys and rooftops. The word was out. Today, witches from across the veil walked in Hope. Kolfinnia smelled sweet hay and fresh bread, tangy berries, stewing apples and roasting corn. She heard Pegalia all around, spoke in accents too numerous to name and rolling off tongues so non-human that the language seemed new all over again. Weather-beaten pennants fluttered from houses, taverns, trading posts and artisans' shops. All of them showed the same mysterious dragon with wings spread and jaws wide, not in hostility it seemed to her, but song. She smiled at the unknown dragon, just as she smiled at the sunflowers, daisies, tomatoes, peppers and beans growing rampant in window boxes and troughs. Petal-bats and keddy-pots were roosting the day away under the eaves, oblivious to the bustle below. Fixed to those bowed and crooked walls, she saw miniature wooden houses and for a moment she couldn't fathom their purpose. That is until a fairy sailed out through a tiny doorway. "Fairy boxes?" she grinned. There were offerings of apples hanging from some, pinecones from others, and feathers, chestnuts and flowers from yet more. Fairies swirled overhead along with an incredible number of bumble bees.

Traders and craft-workers had set up their stalls under brightly painted tents, shaping metal, wood, weaving yarn or even working glass and pottery. No money passed hands, just goods for other goods, but trade stopped as their band passed by. She felt their intense curiosity, and saw Therions of types she'd never dreamed of and others so strikingly familiar she felt she knew them. For a strange instant she saw Clovis amongst the crowds. He had the same steel-grey fur and stern look about him, but an instant later the look-a-like melted away to be replaced by another exotic stranger.

Ahead, she heard Taal greet old friends. His bleating laughter rolled along the narrow streets followed by shouted welcomes in every conceivable voice: baying, barking, whistling, grunting growling and cawing. Every sound she heard reminded her this was not Earth. "The faded-realm." She shook her head in amazement. It seemed more ethereal and unreal than ever, and she couldn't help but grin. She was still grinning when she almost tripped over something and she looked down to see a black cat tear off into an alley, and now as they entered a market square she was in for the biggest surprise of all. "Cats!"

There were hundreds of them, strolling, stalking and meandering around the square. She saw black cats, white cats, tabbies and tortoiseshells, cats with stumpy tails or extra toes, nursing cats trailing kittens, and scruffy ginger bruisers on the lookout for a scrap. She saw cats with chewed ears, silky coats, bent tails, round bellies or spindly legs. Cats were everywhere and soon she realised why. There were pots and pots of catnip in full bloom around the square. She saw other plants too: medicinal ones. She saw cat-sage, bright-sail, dewberry-claw, yarl's-beacon and whittle-way. "It's a cat hospital!" she laughed.

"And why not?" Suddenly Hilda was beside her.

"But cats!" she exclaimed, remembering a fairytale she'd once heard at Wildwood, all about cats and fairies. It seemed it was true after all.

"Of course. Ask anyone who's spent time with cats and they'll tell you cats have a knack for seeing the uncanny."

"And they vanish for weeks on end too."

Hilda waved a hand at the square, "And now you know where they vanish to."

Kolfinnia dodged a kitten as it scampered across her path. "So cats come and go to the faded-realm when they please!"

"I think the proof's all around us."

She laughed again. "It's just one mystery after another." Hilda said something in reply, but it was lost amid all the commotion in the square. "Where's Taal taking us?"

"To the castle. He wants to introduce Clovis to the witches who govern the city."

"To recruit their help?"

"I expect so."

Now she felt sombre again. "Well I hope it's soon. Best to get it over with."

"Once the city finds out about the Magnon they might need some extra witching skills," Hilda added tactfully.

"You mean they might like us to stay?"

"It's possible."

She swallowed a lump. Her life must be topsy-turvy indeed if she would rather stay and fight Magnon than leave Clovis.

After passing through a twisting honeycomb of lanes, some of which were only one house long yet still had their own names, they arrived at the castle gates. Kolfinnia took stock and looked about. She was surprised to see a crowd had followed them up the hill. Behind her, stood scores of Therions. Some must have abandoned their jobs to come and see, because she saw a hulking bear-Therion wearing an apron and carrying a blacksmith hammer, and slender Therions just like Peri carrying baskets of plums, woven rugs or garden tools. Everywhere, she saw shy smiles and bobbing heads as they jostled for a view.

"Kolfinnia." Clovis jerked her back to her senses. "Taal says Hope-coven will meet with us right away."

"That's excellent," she pretended.

"Quite so," he agreed, oblivious to her worries.

Taal stood to one side now. Of the group they'd arrived with, all the others had drifted off and now only Taal and Peri remained. "This way," Taal instructed.

They followed him towards the castle. Its main gate was robust and ancient, and through it Kolfinnia could see green lawns and rowan trees. Taal, Clovis and Peri led the way, with Kolfinnia, Hilda and Hathwell making a small group of their own behind. Humans and Therions separate. Inside the castle keep the atmosphere was more tranquil and there were those same dragon banners everywhere, but again they were tattered and sun-bleached. There was a magnificent fountain in the courtyard, and the source of the streams that flowed through the streets. A stone dragon reared up out of a sparkling pool, and water poured from its mouth, through sluices and into stone gullies. The question was, Kolfinnia wondered: how did the water get up here in the first place? She felt a touch reverential once inside, and when she spoke she did so quietly. "How many witches govern the city?"

"A dozen, I'm told," Clovis whispered back.

Peri offered her a friendly smile, and Kolfinnia paid her back with a slightly wooden one. "Nobody from across the veil has ever walked here in my lifetime," she complimented.

"And how old are you, if you don't mind my asking?"

"Next spring I shall be one-score years in this realm," she said proudly.

We're the same age, Kolfinnia thought, surprised.

"You're still but a young one," Clovis chuckled.

Peri smiled bashfully, but Kolfinnia wondered if he regarded her that way too. "Captain Taal, you said the fleet was home, where had they been?" she changed the subject.

He cleared his throat. "Not all Therions live in peace witch-Kolfinnia."

She thought he was going to say more, but the seconds drew out and he seemed reticent. They were approaching the main tower now, and the heavy doors were being hauled back to reveal their hosts. Kolfinnia could hear clanking chains and creaking gears.

Hilda stood with her staff upright and her chin tilted high.

"Here we go." Hathwell smoothed his hair.

"Don't say 'goaty'!" she reminded him.

"I wish Valonia was here," Kolfinnia added silently.

"Her wand is, so she is." Skald's faith made her smile.

Clovis watched the doors open up, with his ears pricked forwards. *Soon Janus,* he promised and clutched the bundle under his arm even closer.

Taal kept his head bowed, wondering how to reveal the awful news about the Magnon, while lastly Peri paid due respect to the approaching dignitaries, but also stole furtive looks at Clovis.

There was no fanfare and no proclamation, and the first thing to exit the tower was a cat. The black and white tom swaggered through the gates and veered off towards the sparrows under the trees, which fluttered away easily. Kolfinnia stifled a smile, wondering if he was the coven-father. After all, stranger things had happened, but she quickly swallowed her fun when she saw two figures approaching. *Dogs?* was her first thought. But she was wrong. Neither of them were such. Kolfinnia was about to meet Hope's coven-father, as well as her first werewolf.

It was time again for Chentek's followers to feed, and for Sef to boost his ranks. His intention now was to head directly to Thule. He had almost four hundred miles to go and he must cover them as fast as possible, which was no mean feat even for a thunder-sprite. Also, he had no idea what forces he might encounter there. Would Thule be heavily defended? What he'd seen so far suggested that it wouldn't be. The Therion's realm was in decline, and he judged they had better things to worry about than protecting some obscure ceremonial site; things such as the Magnon.

The creatures fascinated and troubled him. The pods he'd taken remained in the gelding-sack, alive yet unchanging. They could languish there until judgment day without altering. The gelding-sack's power lay in the fact that the interior was a point outside of time, a separate universe in its own right. Perhaps he wouldn't need the Magnon pods when he got to Thule, or perhaps he would just seed them for the devilry of it. He thought of nothing else, or at least he *tried* to think of nothing else. Twice in two days he'd caught himself off guard and not liked what he'd seen. If the faded-realm was truly a mirror of sorts he wasn't enjoying the reflection. He sought altitude and flew hard, perversely enjoying the harsh conditions, imagining they could scrub away the memories of Naomi and Jenilla.

"Chentek hungry," the war-fairy stirred against his shoulder.

"No foundries here. Little iron, little blood, little of anything. We must go further." There was little below except for forest, both living and petrified.

"Hungry!" Chentek hissed again.

"You must wait." The wind was cold and he huddled further into his collar.

There was a weighty silence and then without warning Chentek scuttled forwards and scratched at his neck. "Hungry!"

Sef twisted around and snapped at him. "Bother me again blood-tick and you'll feel your limbs plucked off one by one!"

"Ha! Sef needs me."

Sef listened to the whoosh of wings around him. They had served him well so far, but the infection was virulent and they died after a few days. He constantly needed a fresh supply of victims to infect. "Your host have deep bellies, it slows me having to tend their appetites."

"You'll feed us, all of us. Now," Chentek grated.

Iso listened with rising impatience. *"Just kill it Sef,"* he provoked silently. Chentek shook his wings in anger. "Hungry!"

"My blood revived you. You eat when I say so. Now no more of this."

Chentek wore a sly smile. "And when Sef is no more, Chentek goes where he pleases. And who is to say when Sef will breathe his last?"

"Such insolence!" Iso gasped.

Outwardly, Sef remained calm, but Chentek had unknowingly earned himself a punishment. "The faded-realm has little manufactured iron. We must cross the veil, back to Earth. Only then will you and your followers feed." He left it at that, and Chentek's grumbles were silenced, for now.

Mavis Downs looked at the clock on the mantel, feeling apprehensive. She told herself this time she would go through with it. Likewise, when she pressed a finger to her bruised eye, she told herself that yes, this time she would. When she remembered how her husband had kept her housebound while that bruise faded, she told herself she'd see it through this time. In fact, when she finally decided to stand up to her husband's bullying she swore she'd stand firm, but as the seconds ticked away to midday she began to waver. Matthew Downs was often as tender with his hands as he was rough. She reasoned he was no different to any other husband in town. Almost all of them worked in the shipyard, and men who beat iron were bound to sometimes beat their wives. But she wondered. She never saw Margaret Bell or Susan Hartley with bruises, or mysteriously hide indoors for days at a time. She would go through with it she decided, but each click of the second hand whittled away her resolve. Finally, when she heard the yard whistle at midday, her heart sank and she realised without being aware, that when he came through that door at three minutes past twelve nothing would change.

At two minutes past twelve, Mavis dutifully slipped her husband's dinner of rabbit and salted onions out of the range, and put it on the table. She heard the door to the outhouse slam shut. Matthew kept ice in there from the fish dock. That meant he must have suffered another burn. Last year, a rivet had burned his neck, and his temper had been likewise hot. She'd stayed indoors for two weeks that time.

At three minutes past twelve, Matthew Downs came into the kitchen with his hand wrapped in dirty cloth and wearing a black scowl. His eyes went to the clock, then to the dinner on the table. His scowl didn't fade though. He sat without speaking and she glided past him to take the kettle off the boil and brew a pot of tea. She cast a surreptitious look over her shoulder, at the top of her husband's head. She could see tiny cinder burns against his scalp through his red hair, and he ate while still clutching that soothing piece of ice. The burn must be a nasty one, she worried.

She poured a mug of tea without being asked or thanked, and then sat and began her own dinner, which comprised warmed stew from the previous night. She ate without tasting the food, and listened to the harsh clack of his knife and fork. Nothing was said until he'd consumed his meal, whereupon he drained his tea in one swallow and then sat back and scrutinised her face. "Chapel meeting tonight Mave?"

She coughed to conceal her relief. "Yes, seven o'clock." He'd just given her permission to go, which meant he judged her face sufficiently healed. "Is it so bad dear?" her gaze fell on his hand, where droplets from the melted ice dribbled down his waistcoat and sparkled next to his watch chain.

He held his hand out petulantly, desiring her fuss but not wishing to look soft. She gently unwrapped the handkerchief, now both black with soot and moist with serum. The wound was on the inside of his index finger. The blister was white and shiny and shaped like an undulating river. "You're usually so careful." She knew it was wisest to divert the blame.

"Smith has a new foreman. Fool weren't doing his job, a job he's mightily well paid for I'll add."

"Thirty years you've put into that yard. It isn't right that Mr Smith's overlooked you so long." She was already smearing a knob of butter across his wounded finger.

He pulled his hand free and began bandaging it once more. He would cast it off before he got back to the yard though. "You're only speaking what's long been on my mind." He disliked admitting that she was right. "I've a mind to speak with Smith this afternoon." He scowled at his burned finger. Now the pain was as much to do with being overlooked as it was about burns. "Aye, reckon I'll do that. I'm going to head back there and pull Smith from his cosy hidey-hole and have it out with him."

Mavis saw his temper was waking, and she slowly leaned back in her chair, out of range. "You've every right. But remember as to tell him even-handedly. Mr Smith'll heed harder if your words are softer, if you take my meaning." She didn't want him losing his job by punching the manager, although a tiny part of her knew her husband was a coward and picked his fights accordingly.

He squinted suspiciously at her, before deciding she hadn't belittled his manhood. "Aye, well that's as maybe. But I tell you: if Smith thinks I'll take orders from his new foreman like a darkie potboy, then he's got another thing coming. Mark my words." His cheeks had reddened and he jabbed his finger at her to emphasise his point – his good finger. "You hear me?"

She heard him all too well, and shrank back a little further. "He respects you too well for that," she said meekly.

"Does he now? And you knows him well enough to say so?" Again, that finger was shoved her way.

Suddenly, she had a horrible feeling that she might not be going to this evening's chapel meeting after all.

"Meddlesome, that's your trouble. Meddlesome!" He propped an elbow on the table, leaned closer and thrust the finger just inches from her nose. "And I'll tell you something else for free –" That finger was about to jab her cheek, but this time there was a soft 'puff' sound and something wet sprayed across her face.

She was still staring at his accusing finger, only now it had vanished, and the finger ended at the knuckle. The rest had gone, leaving a bloody stump with a neat circle of bone in the centre, which was soon swamped by a rising flow of blood. "M-Matthew?" she uttered.

Dumbfounded, he stared at his severed digit. He continued to stare, even as the first heavy drops began to plop down on the tablecloth, and he had the absurd idea that she'd tricked him somehow. "What have you done woman?" he rasped.

Me? Had she heard him right? Outside, the foundry whistle blew. It was twelve thirty. The clock on the mantel joined in and chimed half past the hour. And then her husband exploded.

"You bloody whore!" He jumped to his feet, throwing the chair across the room. "What witchery is THIS?" He waved his severed finger, showering blood across the dinner things.

"Matthew!" She tried to get up, but banged her knees on the table's underside and she slumped back into her chair. "Matthew, I —"

"WITCH!" He balled his hands into fists, heedless of burns and blood and flew across the table at her.

He would kill her this time she knew. She shrieked and shoved herself away, but the chair just rocked on its stubborn legs and threw her backwards. There was a rush as she fell, then her head hit the flags with a hefty crack. Pain scattered her vision, but through it she saw her husband bearing down on her. "Matthew, please," she groaned.

"EVIL WITCH!" He seized her apron-front and heaved her to her feet.

She heard fabric rip, and chair-legs scrape over the flags and something else. It sounded like chattering starlings. "Matthew, no!" she pleaded.

He held her square and steady, and pulled back his fist to land a crushing blow. She saw blood flowing copiously from the fist ready to drive into her face, and knew there would be no black eyes this time, just a trip to the undertakers. The worst of it was his expression. His eyes blazed with satisfaction, but just before he unleashed his retribution his eye exploded.

The fist stopped. Mavis forgot how to breathe and the shrill whistle outside finally ran out of steam. Silence returned, broken only by his murderous panting and the distant sound of starlings. The hand holding her captive loosened and flopped down to his side again. Mavis staggered back horrified by the sight. Blood flowed down his face, and his right eye was just a dark bowl. His lips twitched and trembled as if a word was trying to force its way up his throat, and when it came she knew he was just as dangerous as ever. "WITCH!" he exploded and snatched the bread knife from the table and lunged at her.

He was just yards away, but Matthew Downs never completed that short journey. Suddenly, huge craters exploded across his whole body. Bite sized chunks were torn away by invisible jaws. He raised the knife, possessed by the idea of murder and stumbled forwards. More wounds appeared from nowhere and more blood flowed. The sound of chattering birds filled the room and she saw fleeting traces shoot back and forth across her vision, like tiny sparks. Each time they passed, more of her husband was consumed. His remaining eye was eaten in a wink. He howled in bloodlust and swiped the bread knife through the air, determined to slice her to pieces come what may. Gibbering in terror, she flailed at the kitchen door until she hit the latch and it flew open, and she fled into the backyard.

The sun had gone in. That was her overriding thought because suddenly it was dark outside, and the sound of birds was so intense that she couldn't even detect her own screams. She pulled the washing line down in a panicked stampede, and half fell, half vaulted the garden gate trailing clean tea towels as she went, and the next thing she knew she was pulling madly on the door to the ice house, not remembering how she came to be there. Still screaming, she threw herself through, battered the door closed and grabbed one of the cargo hooks as a weapon. Outside, the sky was black and now there came the sound of hail against the tin roof. She covered her ears to the abominable noise and collapsed to the floor, covered with icy water and slush. The reek of fish was all around her, the noise pummelled her head and her throat bulged from screaming.

At first she didn't register the pain, but when she looked she saw what she took to be an oversized insect. It had bitten right through her woollen stockings, and was chewing at her ankle. For a dazed moment she watched it, stupefied, until at last she understood that it was eating her, and she screamed and swept it away. It landed harmlessly in the icy water, and blubbering and shaking, she crawled away and watched the creature's struggles grow weaker until finally it stopped all together.

Mavis Downs huddled against a stack of fish crates, oblivious to the cold, the water and even the hail of death outside. She sat that way until finally a despairing sleep overcame her and when she finally awoke the darkness was merely night, and the horror that had been visited upon her town had gone.

Sef watched from the hills above the town with irritation and boredom. He had crossed back to Earth looking for a suitable place to feed his army. He didn't know the town's name, but he'd seen the shipyard and guessed iron would be abundant. The town wasn't large, but he was right about the iron. When he'd first discovered them, the diseased iron-fairies had awed him, but now they were just fodder and feeding them was proving to be a chore. The dark flock above Workhaven tumbled and rolled in an impressive formation. They should be well sated by now, he calculated. In fact the distant screams had dwindled to nothing, and the fays' incessant chattering had finally abated. Sef recognised the silence as the contentment that comes after a good meal. "At last!" he grumbled. This was taking too long.

Iso floated up onto his shoulder. "What are you going to do about Chentek?" he asked quietly.

Sef yawned. Killing just didn't have the same thrill as it did when he was younger. "I've a mind to introduce him to some of my other companions."

"Companions?"

"You'll see," he purred. The pair watched the last moments of doomed Workhaven play out. Before long Chentek buzzed down and landed in the grass, glistening with blood. "Well fed now?" Sef enquired politely. Chentek just cackled some insult and got on with licking his claws clean. He made a show of looking across the ruined town. "A whole town must take a lot of digesting, you'll be wanting to rest I expect?"

Chentek was too gorged to note his sarcasm. "Rest now, fly later," he agreed.

"Oh you'll rest I promise you," he growled softly and Iso smirked. Behind his back Sef manipulated the gelding-sack open, making sure the Magnon pods didn't fall out. "A long rest will do you good." He crouched down slowly. The war-fairy was still cleaning up. Sef saw his armoured tongue flash in and out, looking like a tiny silver fish.

"Mmm, rest." Chentek wasn't even looking at him.

Sef watched him with amusement, wondering why he hadn't thought of this before. "Bedtime little fairy," he sang, and reached out and grabbed him. It all happened with incredible speed. Chentek barely had time to squeak before he was dropped into the gelding-sack and Sef had drawn it closed. And it was done. The bag didn't move and no sounds came from within. "Alive without changing," he gloated.

Iso chuckled, "He'll spite you once you let him out again."

"He can spite all he wants. My blood controls him, and therefore the swarm. Once Clovis is dead we shan't need Chentek any longer."

"Then you'll put him under your boot and crunch the imp?" Iso incited.

Sef yawned, revealing huge teeth. "You really think me so cruel? No, I shall let Chentek loose upon the faded-realm. Him and his filth may eat their way through it for all I care. We shall be long gone." He imagined the likes of the beautiful Naomi being eaten alive. Strangely it didn't cheer him.

Iso hopped over to his staff. "North then."

"North. And we cross only to the faded-realm once we get to Thule. I wish our arrival to be unannounced." He held the sack up and gave it a little shake. "I trust you'll find your new companions to your liking Chentek?" He pretended to listen, and cast Iso an amused glance. "Nothing to say. He must be resting indeed."

The pair laughed, and Sef took his staff and mounted. They lifted off and were soon tearing across the sky, leading their newly boosted host behind them. They had a long journey ahead and the next stop would be Thule, and when Sef got there he had some special seeds to plant.

Kolfinnia drew a sharp breath. One of the Therions was tall and broad. He moved like a fighter and was clearly more wolf than man. *Werewolf.*

She thought the name fitting despite its muddled meaning. His muzzle was short and blunt and his nose was a black 'V' shape, while his ears were pointed and set high on his head. He had a thick coat, this time of sandy grey, with a dark mask across his eyes: and those eyes were silvery and judgemental. He made no secret of his mistrust and for the first time Kolfinnia felt genuine hostility from a Therion. His dress put her in mind of a Viking pirate. He wore an open-necked shirt, a waistcoat of chain mail, and a well-used sword sat in a heavy belt by his hand. He folded his arms and regarded them coldly.

The other was smaller, not just smaller than his wolfen companion, but smaller than her. His furred face was long and slender and if it hadn't been greyed with age it would have been rust red for he was a fox-Therion. His eyes were a milky green colour and the fur below his chin and down his neck was white, while his ears were tipped with black. He wore a dark blue tunic, short trousers, and bare feet. Tellingly, he carried a staff and wore a necklace of carved oak leaves. There was a satchel over his shoulder, and a wand-sheath around his waist. He was a witch, but he carried himself with a dignity that poor old Hortar had lost. Both of them spared Kolfinnia's band a doubtful glance, lost interest and finally gestured for Taal and Peri to approach. Kolfinnia noted how they at least smiled at their own kind.

Taal and Peri dipped their heads respectfully and began forwards, while Clovis waited alone, leaving Kolfinnia and the others standing as a distinctly separate group behind. She saw a brief flash from the corner of her eye and instantly Skald was perched on his staff, watching fixedly. A second later Five also appeared and the witches, along with Hathwell, felt grateful for their support.

"Friendly sort," Hathwell muttered. "Will they let us stay?"

Unusually, it was Skald who answered. "Maybe. And if they do tell us to pack up and get out we're none the worse off."

Kolfinnia caught her breath. "No, they can't do that!"

"Oh they could," Hilda added soberly. "Our task was to get Clovis to the faded-realm."

"And we've done that," Skald reminded them. "And more besides."

They were right, she knew. Just ahead she saw Clovis twitch an ear. He must have heard their little conversation.

"*She's right,*" Tempest agreed.

Clovis gripped his lightning-staff for comfort. "*Even if they're denied and must go back, they're well clear of Helthorn.*" He watched Taal, and Peri in particular, as Hope's coven-father received them, but he could smell animosity on the tall wolf-Therion. "All that matters is Janus," he muttered under his breath, wishing he could think of nothing else.

"Coven-father Bru, Captain Ulfar," Taal bowed to the old fox and the wolf in turn.

"So Captain Taal. How is Lisal?" Bru asked warmly.

Taal was bursting to speak of humans and Magnon, not his wife, no matter how he adored her. "Erm, she is well coven-father, but as you see I have news of some weight."

"Oh I already know." He twitched his nose and looked over Taal's shoulder to Kolfinnia's band, which was no mean feat considering how much shorter he was. "But Lisal, she is over her bout of cedar-cough, yes?"

He was touched that he remembered. "With your help, yes coven-father."

"Good, good," he smiled serenely, closed his eyes and seemed to drift off. "That's good."

"Tell him!" Peri hissed.

Taal coughed nervously. "But coven-father, just yesterday we –,"

"I know, I know," the old witch sighed and his eyes slid open again. "Humans and Magnon within our borders."

"Truly you see all, coven-father," Peri bowed.

"No not really Peri. I just listen to all the fairy gossip." He peered around at Clovis and the others. "This witch has a tale to tell," he smiled cannily.

"And explaining to do," Ulfar rumbled. "Bringing *them* here!" He shook his head in distaste.

"Three months at sea has made you grumpy," Bru added.

"It's good to see you home Captain," Taal said sincerely.

Ulfar twitched a rusty but genuine smile. "The fleet's glad to be home, brother."

"Taal, have them come in before it rains." Bru turned and wandered back into his crumbling castle.

Peri looked up. The sky was clear. "How does he know it's —"

"Fairy gossip!" Bru shouted back. "Now come along, my dinner grows cold." Behind him he heard muffled conversations and footfalls. They were following, bemused, perhaps even affronted, but that didn't matter. After months of drought two storms were coming. One would bring rain to the land, the other would bring rain to hearts and minds, and Bru was deeply glad of both.

CHAPTER EIGHTEEN

Father fox, brother wolf

*'I remember when times were better, but I wonder if those
better times ever remember us.'*
Janek Bru - coven-father, Hope-coven

Skald was in his element. In fact all the thunder-sprites were. Outside
Sterling Castle, or rather Hope-coven, thunder rumbled and lightning
flashed. Skald, Five and Tempest each sat happily on their respective
witch's shoulder enjoying the storm as much as children enjoy the snow.
It was perfect. What wasn't so perfect however was the state of the castle
itself. It looked imposing but large portions of it were roofless ruins.

The fearsome Captain Ulfar had taken Taal and Peri to the river to welcome
the fleet. Kolfinnia still wanted to ask about the fleet's purpose, but coven-
father Bru had others ideas. He escorted them through the rambling castle
towards the coven's headquarters, which he cheerfully assured them not only
had a roof and a fire, but *two* glass windows. He sounded very proud of this.

Along the way, Clovis and Bru chatted like old friends. "I must say it's
long been an ambition of mine to see a thunder-sprite," Bru revealed.

"I was curious," Clovis said delicately, "witches here don't use
lightning-staffs."

"No. Not anymore." His tufted ears flattened sadly. "Much wisdom has
been lost down the years."

They passed through a grand hall, except that it wasn't grand. Rain poured
through gaping arches once occupied by stained glass. For a split second,

lightning cast stark shadows on the walls to the symphony of thunder. They stepped through puddles and dodged cascades of water. Everywhere was the smell of damp wood and wet stone. Bru loved it however. "The storm can rage all it likes, but no thunder-sprites descend these days." He lifted his face to let water run down his fur and smiled. "But the rain is a welcome guest."

"I have someone with me coven-father," Clovis revealed. "Someone who can reverse this malaise, and I brought him here to be set free."

"Oh I know." They passed a waterfall pouring through the ceiling and had to shout to be heard. "It's 'Bru' by the way. Life's too short to be spluttering 'coven-father' all over the place. Never liked the title anyway." He shook water from his fur, skipped nimbly over fallen masonry and veered unexpectedly down a corridor.

"Not a conventional witch." Tempest watched the old fox vanish.

Clovis shook his wet mane. "Just as well for us."

They continued through a gallery lined with scented candles. The floor was gritty, the ceiling low and their echoes muffled. It was like entering a burrow and even the rumble of thunder was diminished. "This is Hope's great coven?" Kolfinnia whispered uncertainly.

"Shh! He'll hear you." Hilda mopped her face dry.

"He doesn't speak English."

"Not far now," Bru's voice drifted back to them – in perfect English.

"He's a quick learner," Hathwell quipped.

There was an archway ahead, this time with a stout oak door and Bru waited for them to catch up. "Make sure this door stays closed at all times," he said gravely. "It must not be left open."

"A coven secret?" Kolfinnia ventured.

He squinted at her mysteriously. "No. Rolo has cat flu. I don't want him getting out." With that, he tipped the catch and slipped inside.

Her mouth tightened around an embarrassed smile and she followed. Finally when the last one passed through, the door was closed and bolted.

It turned out that the castle was just a shell protecting the precious contents within. This one room was Hope-coven and just as Bru had promised they did indeed like it.

It was an octagonal room with a window facing east, and one west. The walls were so thick and the windows so deep that the recesses were almost separate rooms in their own right, while the windows comprised countless squares of rippled glass fixed with lead strips. In one recess Kolfinnia saw a little stool and an easel with a half finished watercolour. Bru was a painter it seemed. Books and rolled charts jostled for space. There was a telescope and a beautifully painted star chart. Accurate brass models of the spheres hung in the windows and glittered with each lightning-bolt. The rain battered the glass, but the room was snug, thanks to a fire roaring away in the largest fireplace Kolfinnia had ever seen. *You could fit all of Crow-top in there!* The thought made her smile. The fire, while large enough to heat the chamber, looked comically small for the hearth. There were sweet-smelling cakes steaming away on a griddle, and kindling stacked either side of the grate. There was even a little armchair in there, and a cupboard packed with bottled oils and dried leaf ingredients.

Heavy beams supported a ceiling where bouquets of herbs hung like an upside-down forest. But it was the walls themselves that made her catch her breath. If Bru was the artist he was an exceptional one. The walls were painted with that same dragon, the one she'd seen all over Hope. She, for Kolfinnia had the overwhelming impression of femininity, rolled and swirled across the walls, depicted dozens of times over, each painting lovingly wrought and showing her in differing guises. In some she appeared wrathful, breathing fire over blighted crops, while in others rain seemed to fall from her wings, refreshing the land. In the paintings, Therions tended her and she in turn tended them. In some she seemed to shelter them under her broad wings. Her throat tightened, but she couldn't say why. "She's beautiful."

"Astriss," Clovis said quietly.

Bru took a stool by the fire. "Yes, Astriss," he sighed, and leaned his head against his staff.

Kolfinnia saw him scan the walls, reading a hundred different stories there. She came and joined him. "I don't believe we've introduced ourselves properly." He looked her way and smiled just as a peal of thunder boomed in the cavernous chimney, and it dawned on her. "Ah, let me guess, fairies told you?"

"Welcome coven-mother Kolfinnia." He slipped the satchel off his shoulder, reached around and took a wooden box from the fireside. She saw a blanket in there, but little else. "And welcome too to Hilda, and Hathwell half-witch." He slipped a hand under the blanket, lifted the whole bundle out and cradled it carefully. "Won't you sit?" He looked around the group, perhaps wondering why they were all just standing there.

Kolfinnia searched about, removed a stack of books from a nearby chair and sat beside him. The others found what they could and soon everyone was huddled around the fire. The thunder-sprites flapped off and sat by the window, irresistibly drawn to the lightning, but Bru watched them with fascination. "After all these years of wanting to see one, and three come together." He rocked with husky laughter, seeming to find this delightful and wrinkled his muzzle in a macabre smile, showing his sharp little teeth.

Kolfinnia frowned. "There are no sprites here?"

"Alas no, as I was only saying to Clovis." He stroked something hidden in the blanket as he spoke. His English was good, but his long jaws gave the words a vaguely mournful lilt.

"And I was saying how that might change," Clovis reminded him.

"Which brings us to the reason we came here," Kolfinnia said neatly.

Without forsaking the blanket, Bru reached down and took one of the cakes from the griddle. "Barley and rose-petal cake anyone?" He saw heads shake in reply, even though they were all hungry. Undaunted, he ate. "When first I heard that witches had come I was astounded. When I heard that they carried the pact belonging to Leenyssa I grieved. But when I heard that one of them was looking for the place of ascension I prayed."

"Mmm. I'd better watch what I say," Clovis realised.

Bru gave him a cunning smile. "Fairies everywhere. I keep watchers in the woods and surrounding land. They report back for the price of an apple-tart, or such. Fairies always had a sweet tooth."

"So you know?" Clovis spread his hands.

"Only what was overheard."

"Overheard?" Kolfinnia thought this rather sneaky, and he deduced as much from her tone.

"Not proper? Perhaps. But much news comes my way in this fashion, and just as well. Since the Magnon came, much of that news has been bad, but forewarned is forearmed." He gently shuffled the blanket on his lap into a better position. "Besides, you can't truly think four witches can cross the veil and not start a landslide of gossip can you?"

"I'm sorry," she retracted, but she also couldn't resist asking, "What *have* you got there coven-father?"

"It's 'Bru' as I said, and this," he teased down a corner of the blanket, "is Rolo."

Wrapped inside, she saw the tiniest kitten possible. He was creamy white with a pink nose, but his eyes were runny and his nose scabby. He just lay there snuffling weakly. "The poor thing!" she mourned.

"He's very sickly, but we do our best for him." Bru smiled down at the ailing kitten.

"Will he be alright?" But Hilda had seen severe cases before, and knew 'alright' was unlikely.

He licked his muzzle thoughtfully. "All we have are guesses witch-Hilda. Just guesses." He wrapped Rolo back up again.

Clovis cleared his throat impatiently. "I met a witch called Hortar, he told me the council here could show me how to reach the place of ascension."

"Ah, the council, yes. . ." Bru considered.

"Would it be a serious undertaking to gather them? My mission is of some urgency."

Bru sighed, "You *have* met them."

They swapped mystified looks. "Did we?" Hathwell said bluntly. By now he'd helped himself to one of the cakes, which Hilda thought rude even though they smelled delicious. "I don't remember meeting a council?"

"Hathwell!" Clovis hissed.

"No. He's right," Bru regarded the former squire. "Half witch, but all right. You have met the council." He took a deep breath. "The coven of Hope, that which many believe constitutes a dozen witches and serves the wellbeing of this city, is in truth myself and Hortar."

Just then thunder boomed, the windows rattled and Bru looked to have aged another twenty years. Hope, it seemed, was a fragile illusion.

'May the wind be always at your back,' is a common blessing in many cultures, and Sef was fortunate enough to enjoy a prevailing wind that pushed him on. He raced over the mountains of Cumberland, and never even set foot in Dumfries and Galloway. All day he had harboured a hazardous idea, but he needed just the right place to test it out, and just between West Kilbride and the southern tip of Bute he found it, on the small island of Little Cumbrae.

"Get this over with before dark," Iso fussed.

"Why, afraid?" Sef pretended he wasn't.

"It's wise to be cautious. Remember how quickly the female said they seeded?"

Jenilla. He felt a twinge, shoved the memory away and carried on. "We have the iron-fairies. They can easily kill a Magnon."

"That's an assumption." Iso looked glumly over the sea. He was tired from his hard flight and rest is what he craved, not dark magic and clay monsters. "Just get on with it."

Sef reached into the gelding-sack. His claws tapped against Chentek's helpless body, but it wasn't the war-fairy he wanted. Instead he carefully drew out one of the Magnon pods and closed the sack again. He held it up and examined it. It looked so inert. It was just a crude humanoid shape with legs moulded into one thick stem. The face had an un-born look that Sef found unsettling. "Today you are born, and today you die," he informed the pod. With one swipe of his claws he scooped out a hollow in the sandy soil, covered the Magnon over and stood back.

Sef went and sat in the grass overlooking the shore. Behind him in the marshlands, he heard a curlew's lonely piping. The light was failing now and from the smell of it, a storm was on the advance. The air had a coppery edge to it. He checked the dragon egg, and was reaching for his sword intending to clean it, when suddenly the soil heaved. "Impossible!" he gulped.

Iso scurried closer. "It moved!"

Sef watched without replying. Now it looked dormant, waiting. *It's listening?*

"Sef?"

"Shh!" He eased his blade from its scabbard with no intention of cleaning it now. "Iso, staff, now."

The sprite vanished, while Sef turned an ear to the sky and detected the faint whirr of wings. The iron-fairies would kill the thing if it grew too strong, or so he hoped. The earth bulged again as something began to germinate. *Nothing can grow so fast,* he worried silently.

Inside the staff, Iso heard the approaching thunder. He also heard the earth pulsing as a newly born heart began to thud. The Magnon was alive. He had no regard for either Earth or the faded-realm, but no world deserved this pestilence. Above him, circling in the sky, he detected the mindless hunger of the iron-fairies and for once he was glad of them. *They'll rip it to pieces,* he thought, but he remembered what doomed Jenilla had told them: *'You mustn't let them touch you.'* What if the thing could swallow down a thousand iron-fairies without even a hiccup? They would soon see, he was certain of that.

There was a creaking sound and the earth was pushed aside by the first glossy black leaves. Sef's eyes widened as he watched the shrub begin to snake up out of the ground, flexing and twitching its spindly branches, seeking out light like a louse seeks blood. The first rumble of thunder charged across the sea and a flurry of wings announced the curlews' departure. A trio of them soared overhead, crying in alarm.

The sinister plant juddered skywards, reaching a height of three feet in just a few seconds and crackling with new leaves. Sef backed away, staff at the ready. He felt a spot of rain against his neck, just as the first Magnon pods began to swell on the branch tips. Within seconds, the evil-looking plant was laden with them. The branches drooped, making a revolting sighing sound and he realised what was going to happen. Very soon the first fruits would touch the soil. He had to be quick.

A wind tugged at his robes, flapping them as it strengthened. With only inches left to spare, he flicked his sword and cut the first pod free just before it touched down. He sent it spinning away, and then without looking to see where it landed, he thrust his staff into the tangled branches and Iso set it alight. Blue fire blazed and a crown of smoke whipped up and was stolen by the wind. Fire crackled, and confident the plant was as good as dead he turned back to the pod and saw with amazement, and trepidation, that it was already germinating.

"They're too fast to control, this is a bad idea Sef!" For once Iso's fears were well founded, he thought.

The pod had buried its base in the soil and was wobbling like a top, trying to stand upright. Sef watched mesmerised. He didn't smell the burning bush or see the distant lightning flash across the sea. The newborn Magnon captivated his will. He stood before it and watched it grow.

It sucked the goodness right out of the ground. The grass yellowed and even the stones lost their colour. It began to pulse and fill like a balloon, swelling from the legs up, all the while draining more nutrients from the soil. Sef smelled ammonia and methane. Already it was synthesising waste by-products. "Incredible," he uttered, "incredible!"

Ashes from its incinerated parent drifted past, and now the Magnon was over eighteen inches tall. The limbs thickened, and they throbbed with raw strength, while its stout hands began to flex and grope. Its head boiled up from its trunk and as soon as it rose into view a gaping mouth opened up like a funnel, followed by bowl-like eyes. *"You've seen all you must, kill it Sef."* Iso saw no reason to continue this madness.

Sef heard, but he was compelled to see the thing fully born. Fat raindrops now splashed against its slimy flanks and ran down in trickles. Its hide took on the sheen of wet clay and it finally wrenched its arms free from its torso with a moist sucking sound and reached out, driven to consume. When it had grown to five feet high, and was struggling to take its first steps, Sef decided he had had enough of fatherhood. It was time to kill his monstrous child, but he was inexplicably reluctant. It was ghastly but impressive. Now it stood five and half feet, and still it continued to build.

"Sef!" Iso spluttered.

"Magnon," Sef said in dreadful wonderment. In reply the thing emitted a deep rattling sound and Sef at last seemed to come fully awake.

"Kill it!" Iso pleaded.

"Wait. There is something I have to know." He backed away as the thing heaved a step towards him. "What is your dearest desire?" He looked into those nowhere holes that constituted its eyes. "Desire. Tell me." The Magnon didn't speak but Sef saw his answer. The Magnon were empty vessels looking to fill themselves and they knew no other way than to consume, any and all things. They would consume the world but they would never be filled.

As the thing reached out the clicking reached a crescendo, and just inches before its groping fingers latched onto him Sef swung his sword. The steel made a slithering sound as it sliced through clay. A second later the Magnon waved its shoulder stumps impotently, unaware that its arms were now lying in the dirt, and Sef saw the creature was just like its desires: hollow. It lumbered forwards, and that noise clattered away in its guts sounding like an angry engine. '*I. I. I. I. I. I.*' The assertion came over and over and he realised it was all the Magnon understood.

"Finish it," he ordered, and lunged.

"With pleasure," the thunder-sprite obliged and the Magnon was sent hurtling backwards, billowing smoke.

Rain was falling heavily now, and the air felt raw and sultry. After a last look at the smouldering bush, Sef went and stood above the dead creature. Rivulets were streaming down its expressionless face like tears. He prodded it with the staff again to be sure, but it just lay still. He guessed it was too primitive to feign death, but to be sure he stabbed it between its eyes and Iso split the head open. "Hollow," Sef said blandly. The charred embers were quickly subdued by rain and soon the Magnon would dissolve back into the earth it had stolen life from.

The silence was painful but it seemed only proper to wait. Bru sat stroking Rolo, staring up at the walls where images of Astriss stared back at them all. The storm rumbled on, sporadic and diffused now, while the chamber was quiet but for Rolo's clogged breathing and the fire crackling in the grate. At last Bru sighed deeply and closed his eyes. Now, in the privacy of his own darkness he saw the past and began to tell them how the faded-realm had first been their refuge, before turning into their prison.

When the world was younger, before men and women embarked on their great culture of enslaving animals, Therions abounded in the world. There were more species then than I can speak of, many of which have passed through the gates of un-being and into the netherworld of extinction. But at this time Therions and humans saw no distinction between their respective species. They were all simply creatures of Hethra and Halla's dream. The balance was perfect. So how did it go astray?

It only requires a tiny nudge for a soul to leave its true path, but as time goes by the path diverges even more. Others around them suffer because of it, but by now the lost are protective of their new-found course, and desire to hold to it. My ancestors saw this change in humankind. They were much wiser than I and even they couldn't say how this corruption took a hold, but afraid for their own futures the Therions grew. At this time our remaining human allies were witches. We shared our understanding of magic, we respected the sleeping twins together and we honoured their dream. But the corruption continued to spread, until humans saw the world as their birthright and the creatures on it theirs to commodify. They invented and worshipped new gods, all of which approved of humanity's subjugation of living creatures. These gods quickly began to approve of other things too; the killing of those who worshipped rivals, the blood sacrifice of animals and the dominance of one sex over the other.

The Therion nations watched in fear as this new mindset swept across the Earth and when the first human armies marched into Therion lands and committed war against them we knew the hour had come. Witches suffered also. It was at this time that the new gods told their followers to burn and kill all who held to the witches' path, but it was not the voice of god that compelled these crimes, rather it was a deeply buried guilt. Man, for now men and women were split and man was dominant, declared war against the whole Earth to silence that quiet voice of regret, believing that sin would silence sin. That tiny nudge had become a gaping chasm. Duplicitous man slaughtered the Therions even as he raised them up in his myths and legends. But there was one last chance of salvation.

A dream within a dream: the realm where fairy kind live as they always have, harvesting souls and turning the wheel of life ever onwards. With great magic, and with great help from our dwindling human allies, we crossed over to this hidden dream. We listened, as if from behind a curtain, to the screams of the Earth and the Therions who stubbornly stayed upon it. We listened to them die and listened for traces of survivors. They came in dribs and drabs, all but one; the very greatest of our kind, the Sleeping-Children, the dragons, considered hallowed manifestations of Hethra and Halla's will.

The survivors all came with the same incredible news: that the dragon races were engaged in one last bitter struggle. At first they used wisdom and reason to try and close that destructive chasm that had opened up in man's heart, but man fought back, not with steel but with lies. It became a 'truth' that the great worker of evil in all new religions was a dragon. All of the Sleeping-Children were vilified and hunted down.

The lie that dragons were creatures of sin sank deep into man's bones, until in the end
he even believed this himself. Yet still the dragons refused to cross to the safety of the
faded-realm.

The last of the Sleeping-Children was Astriss. Too weak to cross the veil unaided,
and cornered by her enemies, she was rescued by a coven called the Ragged-Brothers,
who hid her from harm. Coven-master Abraham sent word across the veil, and an
attempt was made to smuggle Astriss to the safety of the faded-realm. Therions
went to her aid, but when they arrived at the appointed place there was only ash
and destruction. Man had got there first. Angels, emperors, and kings had banded
together to cast out this 'last evil serpent'. The Ragged-Brothers numbered just a
handful, yet they faced a vast army. The battle must have been stupendous, for the
Therions found many tens of thousands of slain enemies strewn across the sky, piled
on the earth and under it also. Amid the carnage they located the Ragged-Brothers,
including coven-master Abraham, and carried their bodies to the faded-realm for
burial with honour, but they never found Astriss. Astriss the Lost she became, and
Astriss the Lost she stays.

"I'm sorry," Kolfinnia sniffed. Right then she was sorry for Bru, sorry
for Therions and sorry for being human.

"We're all sorry," Hilda swallowed.

Clovis sat with his hand pressed to his eyes, as if nursing a headache, but
she saw tears glisten on his knuckles, while Hathwell was mopping at his
face with a handkerchief.

"Astriss the Lost," Kolfinnia regarded the wall paintings anew. "She is
beautiful."

"She is," Bru agreed, "but she also became our burden."

Clovis looked to the window to hide his upset. Outside the sky was
clearing. "Burden?"

Bru set Rolo down closer to the fire and tossed another log into the
flames. "We hoped she would come," he smiled apologetically. "Easy to
forgive us that indulgence. She was never found after all, and some hope
was better than none. But the faded-realm can be a strange place." He
climbed to his feet, leaning on his staff. "It is often more dream than real,
and over time hopes and desires can shape the world. Sometimes I wonder
if the Magnon's coming is our fault."

"Impossible!" Clovis argued.

"Oh, don't be too sure. If you hope for endless centuries as we did, you risk building a tower of disappointment that must come crashing down one day. I think over the last few decades that tower has begun to crumble. There is a forlorn song on the wind and the Magnon followed it here."

"You stopped hoping," Clovis concluded.

Bru's expression didn't change but his voice grew hard. "Brand us weak if you must."

"I didn't say that."

"No. But the comparison is unavoidable."

"But you kept looking didn't you?" Kolfinnia interjected softly.

He turned her way, curious. "Really coven-mother?"

She dried her palms, and addressed them all, "Therions kept looking for her. They crossed the veil, contacted the remaining covens and searched didn't they?"

He suppressed a faint smile.

"Yes," she answered for him. "Even recently. Leenyssa, whose pact we used to get here: she went to Solvgarad to help witches look for Astriss didn't she?"

Bru's smiled faded and the tip of his long tongue played between his dark lips. He shuffled back to his chair and sank back into it. "She was my finest student," he said at last.

But she didn't find dragons, she found Knights instead, Hathwell deflated, wondering if the past would always gnaw at him. He felt a friendly hand on his shoulder and looked up to see Hilda.

Clovis went and stepped up into that huge window space and rested his hands against the glass. Outside he saw bedraggled banners flop lazily in the wind. They were worn and soaking wet. "You can't give up hope Bru."

He sighed. "Choice is not involved. Giving up is just something that happens over time, like getting old and losing one's teeth."

"Can you still practise magic?"

He looked uncomfortable. "A little. But without hope there is no magic."

"But I have something here that can change that, as I said."

Bru looked unimpressed, "Hortar tells me you're looking for the place of ascension." He hooked his thumbs into his belt. "A wild scheme."

"Hortar had twice your faith in the plan."

"Hortar is half my age and has only half my cynicism," Bru sneered. "Finding the place is easy. Three or four days' sail up the coast and there you are. But what when you get there Clovis?"

He caught Kolfinnia's eye. "Could you please?"

Obliging, she carefully unravelled his cloak and withdrew the priceless contents. "Janus, god of doorways," she proclaimed.

Clovis stepped down, went and took the vessel. "If this vessel is opened in the right place then that chasm you spoke of will one day close again."

Bru frowned and studied the glass jar. Inside he saw a small figure floating in the iridescent liquid. "Janus?"

"The reason souls listen to Self so readily is because Janus was betrayed, the third eye closed and conscience became but a whisper. He can open it again. That whisper can become a shout."

Bru stifled a growl of shock. Everything he'd ever hoped for was there for the taking, but he feared the bitterness of failure also. He approached warily and peered at Janus. "Truthfully?"

It wasn't Clovis who answered however. The figure in the vessel turned slowly. The fluid swirled and bubbles glittered. "Truthfully," Janus promised.

A while later, when Bru had calmed down and prepared them all tea, they sat by the fire once more. "Ultima Thule, the place of ascension," he pondered. "They say that Thule is closer to Hethra and Halla's waking mind than any other place in either world. Words spoken there are heard in their very ears."

"Witches have told tales of Thule for generations," Hilda added. "Many of them dark."

"Just so. Charts of the world beyond Thule are empty. Nobody goes there. Nobody wants to. It is a dread place," Bru stated.

"Could Captain Ulfar take me there?" Clovis pressed, undaunted.

Take us there you mean, Kolfinnia corrected silently.

"The waters as far as Thule are relatively safe, yes."

"The fleet, has it been far?"

Bru grimaced at the question. "Just south to the land North-of-Umber."

"A fighting expedition?" Clovis guessed.

"Magnon and diseased iron-fairies aren't the only foes we face here. Trollen raiders now come from across the sea. Even the long held pacts of peace between Therions are showing the strain."

Clovis pricked his ears, "Diseased iron-fairies?"

"An unknown malaise that began in the south just a few weeks ago. Reports are scant, but clearly it's spreading northwards," he elaborated.

"Clovis?" Kolfinnia saw his scheming look. "Is it Sef?"

"Too vague to be sure," he brooded.

"And who is Sef?" Bru poured a second cup of tea for them all.

"A foe that wishes to see Janus stay where he is."

"Huh! What human wouldn't?" he scoffed, and then offered the others a pained smile. "Forgive me."

"Forgiven," Hilda said smoothly.

Clovis rubbed at his brow as he thought. "That's the worst of it, Sef is a Therion."

Bru's mouth twisted in revulsion. "Have you any good news today?"

"This fleet. All summer it has protected the coast. How soon could Ulfar sail again?" Clovis even looked to the window to check the weather.

"He might spare you a single ship, but the whole fleet? That would leave us unprotected."

"Give me one ship, that's all I ask."

Bru looked around at the others and asked that most painful question, "And your friends, will you take them also?"

"No."

Not a word of protest was said but Bru sensed heartbreak. "I'll speak with Captain Ulfar," he promised.

Kolfinnia concealed her sorrows and watched Rolo's laboured breathing, and felt time slipping away for all of them.

Taal had good reason to be happy. The fleet was home and so was his brother. Ulfar wasn't his real brother of course, but a widespread tradition in the faded-realm was for young ones to live with neighbouring families. That was why Taal and Peri were also so close. She was his 'daughter'. It strengthened bonds and reminded Therions of their common heritage, despite their differences. From the age of thirteen Taal had grown up in Ulfar's household, and he likewise.

"It was a big relief to see you back." Taal sat by the dock in the rain, watching Ulfar's sailors tend the ships. All of them were wolfen like Ulfar, and an intimidating fighting force they made.

"Now you don't have to be 'Captain' any longer. I know how much you felt the strain."

"And just as well. Yesterday we ran into a Magnon."

Ulfar flattened his ears and bared his teeth. "Here? So close to the castle?"

"It was a few miles back, towards the Helthor place."

"Ah, where our *human* visitors emerged from." He didn't even like the word in his mouth.

"But just as well they did." Taal shook raindrops from his mane and looked downcast. "Ulf, when I saw that thing. . . I didn't know what to do."

"Who would? Such mysterious foes, more earth than flesh," he consoled.

"In the end it was Clovis who killed it, but not before it'd killed Hadd."

Ulfar nodded solemnly. "I'm sorry."

"His bravery got the best of him."

"That happens all too often in battle."

Taal cast the horrible images from his head. "And how did the expedition go?"

He twitched an ear. "For the most part boring. The trollen ships were few and kept out to sea. I think our being there was enough to deter them."

"I'm glad. Boring is better than brutal."

He managed a rare smile. "So am I. I've no desire to die on the end of a trollen spear."

"Things must be bad across the sea. Are the trollen so plagued by Magnon that they risk warring against us? We've lived in relative peace from the start after all."

"They were ever a surly, secretive lot. If they've got Magnon sprouting in their gardens they wouldn't say a word about it." Ulfar looked grim. "Brother Therions they might be, but I'll not see our grain stores emptied just to keep them cosy through the winter. And worse, it's rumoured they have started taking flesh again."

For a while both watched the bustle on the dockside, with Ulfar shouting the occasional command to his crew. Plenty of relatives had come to welcome the fleet back and there was a festive atmosphere despite the rain. Eventually the sun parted the clouds and Ulfar spoke. "This Clovis, you know what his band want?"

Taal shrugged. "They spoke to Hortar the witch, and now they're speaking with Bru. Probably discussing the Magnon."

"You think this Clovis came here to help fight them?" Ulfar posed, shaking his head slowly. "No, there's more going on."

"Maybe." He watched a gull peck at scraps on the quayside. "Either way, it's good to have some witches here." He almost said *real* witches.

Ulfar couldn't dispute this, despite their race. "It's cheered Peri up, I'll say that."

"Peri? How?"

He shook his head in pretend exasperation. "Taal, if you'd been born with a wolf's nose and not a goat's thick skull you'd smell it. She practically glows."

"With what?"

He chuckled, "Never mind 'Captain', now come on, give me a hand with the rigging while it's dry."

The evening had a refreshing feel to it absent for many weeks and a sky the colour of rose petals. The storm had swept away the sultry air and behind it came a warm breeze heavily scented with flowers and renewed earth. It was in short, a beautiful evening.

Bru had appointed them sleeping quarters within the castle. The rooms were small but cosy, and at least the slates didn't leak. Soon Kolfinnia would take to her bed, but first she wandered the gardens, and in particular the blossom gardens. When Bru had shown her the place earlier, she had been struck speechless. It was an acre of cherry trees, and thanks to his magical talents he'd asked them all to flower just for his guests.

She wandered under the pink sky as pink blossom rained down gently around her. For a while she was able to box away her worries and just be. She removed her boots and walked through the wet grass, stroking those polished trunks as she went. It was so peaceful that she didn't hear her visitor until he spoke. "We had a garden much like this back home."

Her eyes fluttered open to see Clovis near by. "Cherry blossom, on Vega?"

He looked about. "Not as vivid as these perhaps, but a sight I loved."

"You'll see it again soon, won't you?"

"I will," he lied.

"But first there's much to do." She pushed a lock of hair back behind her ear. "And foes to face."

He shrugged evasively.

"Foes like Sef," she continued.

"Which is why you can't come." The matter it seemed refused to be resolved.

"Which is why it's all the more vital we do. Clovis, if the witches of the faded-realm are weak in magic then who better to fight by your side?"

"It might not come to a fight," he said evenly.

"You know it will."

He narrowed his eyes and looked elsewhere. She was right. "I can deal with Sef alone."

"But what if he's not alone? What if he's stirring up the iron-fairies? You heard what Bru said." Suddenly her old fears escaped their box again.

"Tempest and I, and perhaps Ulfar's crew can deal with things."

"So you'll take a sea Captain you've only just met rather than us? Remember how we stood together at Kittiwake? We can do that again."

"This is different."

"Different how?" she asked, but he just stared at her, and perhaps the faded-realm was a mysterious place indeed because she saw something in him she'd never seen before. "Clovis, what are you hiding?"

"Nothing." He backed away.

"There's something you're not telling me." She started towards him, but he rebuffed her by holding his hands up.

"Stop! You're not coming, because –, " It was on the tip of his tongue. *The Janus vessel is poisoned.*

"Because?" She waited, mouth open, eyes wanting. "Because?"

He resorted to logic, "Because Stormwood needs you, Rowan needs you, because if I die in Thule it might not be possible to send you all home again, and even if I live to free Janus, then my next journey will be back to Vega. Having come so far, could you turn back then. . . could you really leave it all behind?"

"Yes – I'd go with you!" The words exploded from her.

There was a hard silence and she felt her cheeks grow hot.

He coughed uneasily. Her affection was a blessing, but it ran too deep for his liking right now. "I hadn't realised how committed you had become," he said tactfully.

She looked at the grass, humiliated, and folded her arms defensively, covering her battered heart. "Good night Clovis." She didn't look up. After a moment, during which she hoped he would say something kind, he wandered away without a word and she was left standing in the soft pink rain under a perfect sky, but feeling like the colour had drained from the world.

"Again you've come away without engaging war." Bru was profoundly satisfied.

Captain Ulfar prodded the dying fire. "It's just a question of time father-Bru, you know that."

"Ah, but not this year."

"And perhaps not the next, or the one after, but finally the trollen will be desperate enough to land on our shores." He reached into the basket and stroked Rolo's head, but the kitten just lay still.

Bru idly stroked the oak leaves around his neck. "I know," he sighed at last.

They sat listening to the crackling fire and the city-clock chime midnight. Ulfar tugged at some clots on his furred arms as he thought.

"It's rumoured they have begun to eat flesh once more," Bru continued.

Ulfar growled, "Not just rumour."

"Oh?"

"We found a row boat adrift in the watery wastes. The artefacts were trollen, but the bones weren't."

Bru considered this. "Bad news indeed. Which is why we should try another attempt at peace before war breaks out."

"If we went there, they would likely have a pot waiting for us."

"Maybe, maybe not." He smoothed a hand across his furry scalp.

Ulfar flashed his long canines. "And how long before we too slide back into the old ways?"

Bru shivered. "Don't speak of those days. We can't let that happen."

"A voyage to the trollen lands might even provoke war rather than prevent it," Ulfar calculated.

"Then perhaps we must address the decline of our realm. If we can reverse it they'll have no need to plunder our lands."

He growled a cynical laugh. "Is that all coven-father? I'll add it to tomorrow's job-list."

"It's not so far-fetched. There is a way."

He peered at him and those silvery eyes contracted. "You're serious aren't you? Would this have anything to do with Clovis?"

"He carries a great artefact."

"He must do to risk bringing human-folk here."

"Ah, but you don't know what it is."

Ulfar leaned back. "And are you going to tell me?"

He paused, choosing his words. "An imprisoned god."

The wolf Captain licked his jaws and smiled. "A jest!"

Bru merely shook his head.

Now he leaned forwards. "And what purpose does this imprisoned god serve?"

"A cosmic one." Bru felt tearful just speaking of it. "This Janus will revive the third-eye."

To Ulfar this was both glorious and unsettling. "You mean on Earth?"

Again, Bru shook his head. "I said his purpose was cosmic, and the effects will be equally so."

Ulfar wrinkled his muzzle and leaned back, suspicious.

"I give you my word as a witch," Bru added softly.

Suddenly Ulfar felt like a pup again, and he rubbed at his eyes to deny any risk of tears. Tough sea Captains weren't supposed to show feelings. He tried to speak but found he couldn't.

"Ulfar?"

"I'm fine," he growled, without looking up.

After a moment Bru sighed, "And so, I must ask you the question I called you here for. Will you take Clovis to Ultima Thule?"

"And his 'friends'?" He quickly brushed his eyes dry, and glanced at Rolo. The kitten's chest trembled and wheezed. *He's dying,* he thought, *just like us.*

"Perhaps them too, yes."

Humans on my ship, he thought and shuddered.

"Ulfar?"

He looked up. "Yes, I'll take them."

Bru silently marked the day and the hour for this moment was auspicious. Today the seeds of hope had been sown.

The storm had scrubbed the heavens clean, leaving a bright canvas encrusted with stars. "Can we fly further?" Sef was anxious to push on.

"One more hour," Iso resisted. *"That's all."*

He grimaced. "Very well. One hour."

There was little to see below or above. Now and again the moon glinted off a river or lake, but it was only the tearing wind that proved to Sef he was moving at all. His supreme senses told him his course was true, but in the void of night, with little to occupy him, that minuscule scratching at the corner of his mind grew more and more insidious. *"Open the gelding-sack and release us."* The idea was delightfully destructive. He could toss a few Magnon pods down into the blackness and let chaos seed them. Would Britain be consumed, or would Victoria's iron empire prevail? Not caring was intoxicating. *"Set us free Sef and watch us grow. We are hollow vessels that hunger to be filled. Free us!"* He could picture Britain's pastoral fields erupting with Magnons. What being devised them and for what purpose? They scared and inspired him. *"Release us!"* they pleaded.

"I'd advise against it," Iso cut in, startling him.

Sef couldn't hide his anger. "Something else you intend to take back to Acola, little spy?"

"When one's thoughts boom like cannons, it's hardly possible not to hear. The Magnon are more than they appear."

"Nonsense!"

"You were thinking about them."

"So?"

"Was it your will to think about them or was it theirs?"

"Nothing escapes the gelding-sack, not even a thought." Just in case, he reached around to check it was tightly fastened. "Nothing!"

"Perhaps they'd already planted a seed in your mind before you locked them away."

"Perhaps we'd make better progress if your wings flapped more than your mouth."

They continued in sullen silence. Sef's mind returned to the Magnon, and something that ought to have been clear from the outset finally struck him. Their only desire was their fulfilment. *Themselves.* They truly were the children of Lord Self. A contented smile parted his muzzle. Now he understood why he had been led to them. *"Thank you Lord Self."*

Iso sensed his conviction. *"Something pleases you?"*

Something had pleased him very much, and for a while he could even forget about Naomi and Jenilla. "Yes, I am pleased." Lord Self was guiding his way so completely that he fancied the staff might pilot its own way to Thule. The outcome was so certain that he pitied Clovis.

But if Lord Self did indeed light his way then he had a peculiar sense of irony, for although neither sensed the other, just then, Sef was passing within ten miles of where Clovis slept just across the veil. Next time, the two warriors would meet much closer, and one of them would sleep forever.

Chapter Nineteen

Furthest north

'Ultima Thule. Where gods listen and answer.'
Traditional saying

The riverside was busy even at this early hour, and the faded-realm might be bereft of dragons but here on the dock there were at least twenty of them. The fleet of dragon ships hadn't fired a single angry shot all summer, but that didn't make their upkeep anything less than constant. Ulfar's ship was named The Hornet, and proudly sported a dragonhead carved to resemble Astriss, with her jaws agape and jagged fins down her neck. As flagship, The Hornet was also the largest, but right now it looked far from imposing as Therions strained to drag her up the jetty. The Hornet's hull had suffered a summer at sea, and she needed her backside scraping.

Ulfar roared encouragement. The Hornet's crew was forty, but this morning more than twice that number were hauling her out of the water, including Taal and Peri. "Heave!" Ulfar pulled for all his worth, as did a hundred other pairs of hands, and The Hornet inched forwards. There was a lull, followed by the next inevitable, "Heave!" Tree trunks rumbled again as the ship crept forwards. "Heave! Drag this fat maiden out of her bath!" Behind him, Ulfar felt a fresh volunteer clutch the rope and take up the challenge. "Don't crowd me!" he barked without turning.

"Aye sir," came the reply.

"Heave!" he brayed. Grunts, bellows and curses filled the air again, and The Hornet left the water behind. Now all they had to do was drag her up the jetty and onto the level.

Fifteen exhausting minutes later, The Hornet was landward and the crew was busy hammering props in place to keep her upright. Ulfar looked down at his raw palms, panting and hot. "A good morning's work sailor," he said without turning.

"Sorry Captain, I'm no sailor. I know little of ships."

He turned and saw Clovis staring back at him. "Ah, Clovis," he began uncertainly. "My thanks."

Clovis rubbed at a shoulder. "My pleasure. Bru asked us to be useful."

"Had you a spell to make The Hornet fly from the water, I'd have owed you the rest of my days." He wasn't good at small talk.

"Had I such power I might not have been forced to bring my friends here. I'm sorry their presence disturbs you so."

His point was refreshingly direct. Ulfar was about to reply when a potent and distracting scent caught his attention. He turned and saw Peri watching them closely. *She's different,* he thought, and he knew why. "My thanks Peri. You haul as well as any brute I ever sailed with," he complimented roughly.

She swept her mane from her eyes. "Erm, thank you, least we can do Captain for keeping our shores safe." She offered Clovis a shy smile, excused herself and vanished into the crowds.

She's bitten bad, Ulfar sighed, and when he looked Clovis's way again he saw she wasn't the only one. "Clovis?"

He floundered for a moment. "Ah, yes. As I said, I'm no sailor."

"You will be soon."

He wiped the grit from his hands. "So I hear, Bru told me this morning. And I thank you deeply on behalf of Janus."

Ulfar nodded absently as he watched his crew clambering over the ship. "Which is why we must make her seaworthy again soon."

"Is there much to do?" It was a polite way of asking 'when can we go?'

"Two or three days. The hull needs some caulking."

"I'd be pleased to help."

"If you can haul ropes and scrub decks, then yes you can help."

"We'll do all we can," he promised.

For a moment Ulfar imagined three humans aboard his cherished ship. They might be witches but in all her years The Hornet had never carried such passengers. "This way," he said at last and led Clovis off to begin work.

Kolfinnia was working in the gardens. A dozen Therions were scattered around, digging or weeding, but despite their curiosity they respected her privacy. She had risen early to avoid Clovis, mostly because she felt awkward, but soon enough he'd also broach the matter of sending them home. Skald watched her turn the ground ready for seeding. "Looks like you're getting settled in," he commented.

She was unsure if he was chastising or chatting. "Just keeping busy."

"So I see. Clovis went to the port you know."

She stung a little at that. "Did he say what for?"

"No. Just saw him leaving first thing."

She straightened and rubbed at her back. "Bru and Clovis were talking earlier this morning."

Skald noted the sun, which had only just cleared the horizon. "Any earlier, and this morning would be last night."

"I couldn't sleep," she explained. "So I took a walk and saw them." She caught his expression. "I wasn't spying!"

"Never thought it for a moment."

"Anyway," she brooded. "I'm sure he's persuaded Bru to take him to the furthest north."

Skald stretched a wing. "But that was the whole purpose of our mission."

"Was?"

"Our part looks to be coming to an end."

"I know," she grumbled. "But I thought Clovis might keep us informed."

"Maybe he's just trying to distance himself."

"Ready for leaving us behind," she muttered under her breath.

"That was always the condition." He sounded hard now.

She leaned on her spade. "Did Valonia never have anything similar to deal with?" At all costs she avoided saying 'been in love', but he understood.

"She left many dear things behind in her life, but something good always came to fill the void." He thought of a certain someone who'd meant a lot to Valonia, but who'd vanished without trace. 'Thomas Hobby' was a name *never* spoken around Wildwood.

"I suppose," she sighed, watching a robin flit around the newly dug earth. "But I'd feel much better if he took us north with him."

"Has he said why he doesn't approve?"

'Yes, I'd go with you!' she remembered and cringed. "I suppose he doesn't want to delay the inevitable goodbyes any more than he has to."

"Makes sense," he nodded thoughtfully.

"But still," she worried, "these Magnon things, and this mysterious iron-fairy disease. What if he needs help?"

"Clovis and a ship full of brutes like Ulfar could fight them all."

"Could they? Could anyone? Witches can help. Hilda and I could make all the difference."

"And what of Mr Hathwell?"

"Oh, well, yes he should come too," she added hastily.

He flapped over and landed by her feet, scaring the robin away in the process. "Has Clovis said how the ritual is to be completed?"

She paused and frowned. "No, come to think of it he hasn't." Skald seemed to forget the matter, but it left her wondering, *How do you set free a god?*

She was still thinking about this when Hilda came charging up, and she was so breathless with worry that she didn't even use her full name "Kol! Come at once!" She grabbed her sleeve and started off.

The spade fell with a thud and Kolfinnia was running by her side. "What's the matter?" Already she imagined clay men marching through the city gates.

"Matter of life and death. Bru needs our help!"

Around the gardens Therions were peacefully tending their plots. It didn't look like an impending invasion. "What's wrong, are Magnon coming?" she panted.

"No, worse – babies are coming, hurry up!"

Hathwell woke the following morning to find everyone gone but him and couldn't help but feel a little dejected. He wandered the castle's derelict corridors looking for anyone he knew, until he chanced upon Bru's study.

It was empty, but for Rolo in his basket. The kitten looked beaten and fought for each breath. "Poor little bugger." He rubbed a finger across his brow, but the kitten didn't respond. "Bru? Anyone home?" he called. When he didn't get a reply he left, making sure to bolt the door, and feeling like a burglar.

Finally he met Bru at the gates coming the other way. He walked with a purpose and looked perturbed. "Erm, father-Bru, good morning," Hathwell greeted him.

Bru stopped and raised his muzzle to look up at the squire. "That remains to be seen Berand."

Berand? He smiled when he realised it was the closest Bru could get to pronouncing his name. "Is there something wrong?"

"Maybe, maybe not," he grunted. "It all depends on your Hilda."

He liked the phrase *'your Hilda'*. "Why, what's she doing?"

"Difficult birth."

"And she can help?"

"Beyond my skills," he admitted reluctantly.

"Well, Oak bless them." He had no idea where the phrase sprang from, but Bru's reply stunned him.

"Bless them indeed, fellow witch."

He felt a lump in his throat, while Bru suddenly started away without any goodbye. "Wait, coven-father!"

He turned expectantly; ears pricked, nose raised.

At a loss he thrust his hands in his pockets. "I just wanted to say, if there's anything I can do to help around here."

He smacked his lips and considered. "Extra hands always needed to keep the walls in repair. Hope doesn't mend itself you know."

"Defences are vital," he agreed.

"More so now with Magnon so close." Bru's shoulders melted an inch.

"I can repair walls," he tried to hearten him. "And a ditch wouldn't go amiss."

His nose twitched and his eyes glinted. "A ditch?"

"Aye a ditch around the city, stocked with firewood and oil. It'd make a good defence against Magnon."

"If they ever came in huge numbers," Bru pondered, finding merit in his idea.

"I'm sure they wouldn't!" he laughed, but Bru's expression said otherwise.

"We must be ready for the worst Berand." He leaned on his staff. "Can you explain this idea to the city's chiefs?"

"Yes." The reply came before he had chance to even think.

"Good, I'll gather the generals and we'll meet here in an hour."

Generals? he thought nervously. In the Illuminata he'd been forbidden to even look at such men, let alone speak to them.

Bru saw his consternation. "Don't fret Berand," he gave his belly a friendly jab. "They're not real generals."

Hathwell smirked. "One hour." He watched him hurry away, as sleek and as determined as any fox. "One hour," he worried, already working on his speech, because there were lots of other ideas he had for Hope.

She might be coven-mother, and fought krakens and barghests, but there was one skill Kolfinnia couldn't yet boast. She got her first lesson in midwifery from Hilda, in a hut nestling on the slopes outside the castle.

The babies were twins lying breach in the womb, and the mother was a Caprian named Sedna. By the time Hilda finally cradled the pair of boys, it was noon and Kolfinnia had lived through one of the hardest mornings of her life. How Sedna felt about the morning was anyone's guess, but as she finally held the infants, who'd almost died and killed her too, Kolfinnia watched with a huge sense of accomplishment.

The witches stepped out into the midday sun, bedraggled and weary, but greatly satisfied. "Well that was a first. Never delivered Therions before." Hilda pulled her headscarf free and tussled her hair.

Kolfinnia cupped water from the rain barrel and doused her face. "You were incredible," she praised.

She smiled broadly, and with good reason. "I thought for a while we'd lose them all."

"Like I say, incredible." From inside the hut they could hear Sedna and her family crying happily, and the sound of babies murmuring.

Hilda splashed water over her own face. "You know that was quite something."

"Oh I know," Kolfinnia passed her a towel, full of admiration.

"Not the birth."

"What then?"

Hilda looked about. There were Therions watching from huts and others wandering over to see Hope's newest arrivals. She took her elbow and gently directed her away. "Without Bru's intervention they wouldn't have let us anywhere near a mother-to-be, let alone deliver the babies."

"Even though it was so difficult?"

"Even then."

Kolfinnia lost a little of her elation. "They hate us that much?"

"Not hate," she clarified. "Cautious perhaps. It was quite a thing for Sedna and her family to agree."

"The poor lass was in too much pain to say no."

Hilda wiped a handkerchief over her face. "Come on, we'll leave them to their celebrations."

"Are all births so difficult?" Kolfinnia wondered.

"Most are just bloody painful, not dangerous," Hilda laughed.

"Sounds like the same thing to me."

"Not so. Flora for instance, now she came like a dream."

Kolfinnia rocked on her feet, "What!"

"Oh yes," she revealed. "I delivered a screaming little Flora into the world." She looked back at the crowd gathering around the hut. One or two cats were sat outside too. "Come on, we'll find some lunch and I'll tell you all," she promised, and led the astounded Kolfinnia away from where two new lives had joined Hethra and Halla's dream.

By evening time Kolfinnia found enough courage to go and find Clovis. Their paths had crossed earlier when they glanced one another across the gardens, but each was off doing different things and a brief wave was all they shared. However, it broke the ice and for the rest of the day she could get on, without feeling too preoccupied.

She learned that Clovis was still at the docks and she wanted to speak to him, feeling she couldn't wait any longer. As chance had it, she met him wandering back towards the city. He looked oddly youthful in his work clothes; a tatty shirt and cotton trousers, both now daubed with fresh tar. He looked up, saw her and forced a tired smile. "Kolfinnia."

"How goes the ship work?" she asked coolly.

"Well. Ulfar tells me to fasten that and scrub this, or tar the other. I don't know what they are but I do it and he looks pleased."

"And he's sailing north as soon as you're ready?"

He merely nodded, before changing the subject. "I hear Kolty and Hilda are doing well."

Her mouth twisted as she thought. "And who are they?"

"The twins you delivered this morning," he chuckled.

"Kolty and Hilda?"

"Yes, they named them for you."

She stifled a laugh. "But those are women's names!"

"Not here they're not," he reminded her. For a moment they laughed together and when the frivolity faded he gave her a sideways glance. "It was great skill that saved them, and cemented our acceptance."

They set off walking again and she swung her arms as she ambled along, wanting so much to take his hand. "Is that why Ulfar agreed to take you?"

He shrugged. "I'd like to say so, but it was the promise of Janus that won him over."

She picked at a blister on her palm as she thought. "Clovis?"

He stopped. "You can't come Kolfinnia."

"That's not what I was going to ask," she said frostily.

"Forgive me, go on."

"I was going to ask how the Janus vessel must be opened."

"It must be taken to Thule and opened there." He repeated what she already knew, and then set off again, hoping the matter closed.

She caught him up. "I know the where, but what of the how? How's it done."

This topic was shaky ground. "It takes a witch to open the vessel, and in the appointed place," he waffled.

"Clovis." She took his arm and both of them stopped again. "You're not telling me something."

He opened his mouth to speak.

"I know I can't come!" she cut in before he could say so again. "But when I ask how Janus will be freed you keep giving me the same non-answer."

"I do not!"

Again, he looked different to her and again she knew why. *He's concealing something,* she thought. "Is there a spell involved?" she asked reasonably.

He sighed, knowing he must indulge her a little. "The vessel was made long ago, and built into it is an intelligence. The vessel will know."

"Know what?" Fascination overcame her worries.

"Know that a witch with pure intent desires to break the glass and release Janus. Providing the location is correct the glass will break. Otherwise, the vessel is quite indestructible."

"So just the right will and the right place are required?"

"Yes, merely that and nothing more."

She made no secret of scrutinising his face.

"Kolfinnia I assure you," he vowed.

"And if this Sef got Janus, would the vessel open for him?"

Suddenly he was wary. "There are safeguards. They couldn't open it without care."

"Only the worthy can open it then?" she guessed wrongly.

"Yes," he lied easily, and hated himself for it.

"I see." She looked at her tatty boots and noticed a few spots of rain land in the dust. "We'd better be getting back I suppose."

He took her arm, wishing he could tell her. "Ulfar won't be ready for perhaps two days. Will you stay until I leave?" he asked tenderly.

She felt a splash of rain against her neck. It was cold and comfortless, despite recent droughts. "You know I will." He looked satisfied, but she wasn't done. "And on the morning you sail north Hilda, Hathwell and I cross the veil and go home."

"Yes." It was all he could say. The rain began to fall in earnest now and he pulled his cloak from his pack and threw it around her shoulders. "Cheer up, you have a healthy young boy named after you."

She couldn't help but laugh and together they continued, now at a hurry, back to the castle as the rain began to batter down.

The four found themselves once again eating supper in Bru's study. Kolfinnia gulped down stew and dumplings like a navvy. The hard work had both refreshed and tired her. The thunder-sprites sat by the window and watched the rain, which although heavy was not stormy. Bru served them another helping and listened to their day's events. At last, when all was said Hilda turned to Hathwell. "You're quiet, how did you spend your day?"

He looked up with the spoon halfway to his mouth.

"Berand has been discussing the city defences with the generals," Bru surprised them.

All heads turned his way. "Just a suggestion here and there," he said modestly.

"But good suggestions," Bru agreed.

"Berand?" Hilda asked quietly.

"Like I say to many I meet, 'call me Bertrand'. Hardly any do though, but Berand's near enough," he smiled.

Her face slipped and she felt an unexpected guilty pang. "I like it, Berand," she added quickly.

He raised his spoon in salute and continued eating, seeming not to notice her flattery.

"Berand has the skill to make catipuls," Bru revealed proudly.

The rest looked confused and Hathwell swallowed his stew. "Catapults," he clarified.

"Why would Hope need siege engines?" Kolfinnia scowled.

"In case the Magnon come in force," Clovis said gravely, guessing the city's worries.

An uneasy hush settled, which Bru eventually broke, "Yes, fire is our defence against them."

"A catapult could shoot fire over the wall," Hathwell explained.

"There'd have to be a few thousand Magnon outside to warrant such dire action," Clovis cautioned. He didn't like the idea of war machines here either.

"A few thousand it might come to," Bru warned. "We would rather build machines we never needed than not have them at all."

"You're right, I'm sorry," he retracted.

"Yes, well, I can draw up some plans how to make them, they need only be short range things." Hathwell resented the unspoken accusation of warmongering.

"The city generals took the plan to heart," Bru defended him. "We can't rely on magic alone to repel the Magnon, and who knows what else might come along as the world continues to change."

"There are others ways too," Hathwell placated. "A protective ditch, a palisade, manned lookout posts linking scattered towns. It needn't be about weapons alone." He found the challenge perfect for his skills and at last felt useful.

"General Hathwell," Kolfinnia smiled at him.

"No," he laughed. "I'm just an old squire looking forward to getting home. I hope Rowan's watering that plum tree for me."

As always, mention of going home split Kolfinnia's heart down the middle.

"The day after tomorrow, Ulfar will be ready to sail," Bru concluded. "A three day journey to the north, if the weather holds, and then. . ."

"And then Janus shall be released into the universe." Clovis met his gaze steadily.

Bru didn't dare ask what would happen, or how long it would take. He just hoped, as he had for years.

Later, when the chat and food were done, Clovis sat alone on his rough cot and toyed with the small silver box Kolfinnia had given him. It was intended as a parting gift, but here she was still by his side. He stroked the engraved lid and thought of all those slivers of wands and staffs within. But he wasn't going back to Vega. "She's beginning to suspect." He pressed the silver box to his cheek.

"Two more days and it won't matter," Tempest consoled.

Clovis looked to the corner where the Janus vessel was safely hidden. "God of doorways he is, so why isn't there a happy doorway out of this infernal situation?"

"We have to hope," he said, but without faith.

The silver box continued to turn idly between Clovis's fingers. He thought of her gift of love inside, and how much he wanted to return it. "She wanted me to open this treasure on Vega."

"We must hope," Tempest repeated, wishing the small word wasn't such a huge challenge.

With that in mind, Clovis retired and found escape in sleep.

Birdsong roused him from sleep just a few hours later, and he rolled out of his cot with a grunt and reached for his boots. Last night, while lying awake he had stumbled across an idea and he was so taken by it that he almost leapt out of bed and went right then. He looked to the Janus vessel again, knowing he would need to liaise with the sleeping god first. Before he even finished dressing, he uncovered the vessel, bowed his head and reached for Janus within, while outside Hope began a new day.

After breakfast, Kolfinnia and Hilda headed for the gardens while Hathwell went to find paper and pencil and begin making plans for the city defences.

The day was overcast and the gardens muddy, but Hilda and Kolfinnia found the day brighter than any so far. Therions spoke freely with them for the first time. Some even brought gifts of gratitude. Indeed, they were so popular that they spent most of the morning 'gabbin not gardenin' as Ada Crabbe would have said. Sedna's mother even came to find them, with a gift of cherry-loaf and invited them to see the twins later when they had a moment, something they gladly accepted.

While Hilda and Kolfinnia played witchdom's good ambassadors, Clovis went to execute his plan. He had spoken briefly to Janus and now he was ready. Taal directed him to the right place, pleased that he'd decided to go, thinking that kind words and comfort were his aim, but not realising the incredible truth.

She lived on the busy main street below the castle, a narrow cottage sandwiched between others like it, and when he saw the sign above the door he understood she was a seamstress. Golda had one son: 'had' being the correct tense. Three days ago a Magnon killed Hadd, and Clovis had promised himself to check and see how she was. Shamed to have taken so long he knocked at the shop door, surprised to see it closed on a busy market day. He stood there for some time, becoming the spectacle of many passers-by and in the end he tried the latch. The door creaked open, and he ducked under the low lintel and slipped inside.

"Golda?" he called. There came a creak of floorboards as somebody upstairs moved. He followed the sound, finding a narrow flight of stairs and making his way up them. "Golda it's Clovis." No reply came, but he detected soft crying.

At the top of the stairs there was a tiny landing area with a door either side. Both were closed. He rapped softly on the door where his ears told him a grieving mother sat in solitude, but no answer came. "Golda, it's me

Clovis, may I enter?" he tried again. The crying behind the door became sobbing, and feeling nervous but determined, he thumbed the latch and let himself inside.

The windows were tiny and the room was further darkened by red drapes, which made the light appear rusty. Golda sat in a chair by the window with her head in her hands. "Golda." He quietly closed the door and went and knelt beside her.

She rocked gently, seemingly oblivious of him, and occasionally her chest heaved and fresh tears ran between her cupped hands and gleamed in her coat. "What day is it?" she croaked.

He reached up, clasped her wrists and gently uncovered her face. She was old. Her coat was grey and coarse and her eyes were raw globes of grief. "Golda, it's Clovis," he tried again.

"Clovis?" She looked past him to the room's dark corner. "What day is it Clovis?" she asked incoherently.

He saw she was in deep shock, and cursed himself for not coming sooner. "It is Wednesday August 3rd, Golda I came about Hadd."

"Hadd?" The name elicited a dreamy smile. "He's not here."

"No," he swallowed, "no he's not, but I came to show you where he's gone."

"He's gone far away," she whispered and then her smile wilted and she slumped again.

He eased her back into the chair. She was breathing fast and shallow and he realised her own death was close, maybe weeks or months from now, but it was surely coming. *The Magnon killed two souls that day,* he cursed silently. "Golda, I have something for you."

"No you haven't." Her head sagged to her chest. "Nothing for me."

"Golda!" She was far worse than he'd realised. "Golda, Hadd is here with you right now." He clasped her hands and did what he'd come here for. *Wish me luck Tempest,* he asked silently. If this didn't work Golda would go to her grave early, stricken by madness. He held her hands firmly and delivered his miracle.

She was standing on a spiral of stone steps that wound upwards forever. The air was so pure that it washed away her despair, and for the first time in days she stood proud and remembered her name. Golda saw spectral souls drift past her in untold numbers, and doors of types without end lined the walls around her. Above her, clouds rolled in stellar colours and stars twinkled from the edges of the universe. Evermore. There was no fear here because there was no death.

She climbed the steps without moving and looked down to see that she was just a spirit also. Somewhere in this multitude her son now drifted with the others, or perhaps he'd already chosen a door and gone to start again. She longed to see him, and began to spiral upwards faster and faster.

How she was drawn there, even Clovis and Janus couldn't say, but perhaps the bond of union is too strong for mere things like death and reality to conquer. Then she saw him, rising in the company of humans and Therions alike. Hadd, her son. She didn't need to call to him and couldn't have done so anyway. But he knew. He turned, saw her, and all was well with creation. The two met, and the Magnon's evil was undone.

Clovis let out a huge groan. "The vision fades," he gasped. At last he was forced to stop, feeling defeated and dizzy. "Golda I'm sorry!" he looked up but it wasn't Golda looking back at him, at least not the Golda he found crumpled and dying in her tiny house. "You saw?" he asked with trepidation.

She looked around the dingy room, newly awakened to its despair, and finding it suffocating. Compared to her vision this was a living hell. "I saw," she confirmed. Slowly she rose from her chair. The blanket dropped from her shoulders and Clovis got to his feet, still clutching her hands until the two were stood face to face.

"You saw," he said with relief.

She gripped his hands tight. "Promise me it was no lie," she said fiercely.

"Evermore is real. I know because I've walked there."

"Evermore." She let out a shuddering breath, wiped her eyes and went and swept the curtains aside. Light flooded in and Clovis watched her busily flit about the room, tending and tidying all she'd neglected during her darkness. Finally, she stopped and when she looked his way again he saw a mother burdened by loss, but lifted by hope. "Would you like me to put the kettle on?" she asked pleasantly.

He felt wrung out but contented. "Yes, that would be nice."

She nodded demurely, as if he'd been the one to suggest it, and then she hurried downstairs to draw a kettle of water, telling herself all the while it was high time she opened the shop.

Clovis listened to her feet on the stairs and realised she wasn't the only one who felt better. Evermore. When the Janus vessel broke he would go there. No more Clovis, no more coven-father. But that wasn't the end. He collected her discarded blanket from the floor and gently set it across the chair, and then on impulse he opened the window a crack. Fresh air and life from the busy streets drifted in and the madness was expelled. "Thank you Janus," he said quietly, before heading downstairs wearing a satisfied smile, to where the kettle was already whistling.

The commotion in the gardens was largely due to Skald. He sat watching Kolfinnia and Hilda dig and weed, as was usual, but word soon spread, and it seemed most of the city was huddled at the garden's edge. It wasn't just Bru who had long desired to see a thunder-sprite. Tempest and Five joined him, clearly revelling in the attention.

"Shameless!" Kolfinnia tutted.

"Can I help it if I'm so magnificent?" He puffed out his feathers for his audience.

She was still laughing when she saw Clovis wandering through the gardens towards them. She wasn't laughing a moment later when she saw Peri intercept him. *Let it go Kolfinnia,* she told herself. She bent to carry on working, but stole furtive glances their way, wondering what they were talking about.

"I just don't know what to say," Peri stammered. "Taal told me you were off to speak with Hadd's poor mother, but the change in her! What did you say?"

"She didn't tell you?" Clovis rejoiced in her delight.

"No?"

"Then perhaps that is for Golda alone."

"I understand." And to his pleasure, clearly she did. "Thank you again." She struggled for something further to say, just as he struggled for an innocent reason to stop her leaving. In the end both spoke together, got tangled in words, and finished with bashful smiles.

"Sorry, you first," he invited.

She started again, but now sounding worried. "I hear Ulfar is taking you northwards. Is that so?"

"Yes. Perhaps two days' time."

"And have you selected a crew?" she asked hopefully.

He raised eyebrows in apology. "Ulfar's ship, he decides the crew."

"And he's not a Captain to argue with." She fidgeted as she spoke.

"Indeed." His smile quickly faded and that same awkward longing descended. He stared at her longer than he should. *What the hell's wrong with you?* he bashed himself.

"Well," she began nervously. "I shall not detain you, but once again thank you." She was already moving off.

"You're welcome," he said meekly.

"Goodbye." A second later she turned from him and disappeared through the gardens.

He watched her go and suddenly he found his legs were shaking. "Damn it!" he cursed. All this time he'd warned Kolfinnia how Sef could manipulate desires and here he was succumbing to his own. For her sake he had to withdraw. If his plan went well then in a few days he would be opening the Janus vessel and die of its poisons. . . if it went well. Already brooding, he boxed away his desires, set his mind to the task ahead, and went and joined the others, already trying to forget the name 'Peri'.

After strenuous and almost unceasing flight, and while Clovis and his Lions languished in Hope, Sef reached the northern coast of Britain.

It was August 4th, and now he once again crossed to the faded-realm, sensing his journey's end was close. He left the Orcadeas behind, the last group of islands before Shorland. These were their names in the faded-realm, while across the veil they were known otherwise. Thule was the furthest of the Shorland islands. The world extended beyond it of course, but to Therions it was a mystery. Their maps and charts all ended there, as did their history of the world. Beyond it there was only a mysterious region they named Hyper Thule, and what might be found there was sheer, and often fearful, speculation.

At first Shorland appeared as a tiny island on the horizon, but before long it was joined by others until they merged in to a wall of towering stacks and headlands. "Keep us steady!" Sef commanded.

"I have been flying since dawn!" Iso complained. *"You have merely been sitting!"*

Sef disregarded him.

"I must rest," he persisted.

"You think I would stop when we're this close! No, we keep going until Thule itself."

"Then you'll fight alone when we get there, my reserves reach only so deep."

"I'll not fight at all!" he laughed, and patted the dragon's egg. If his theory proved correct, then Thule's custodians would welcome him with open arms.

He raced across the waves following Shorland's eastern coast. The mainland stretched north like an undulating spine, but from this distance all he could see through the haze were brown summits and a crinkled coast. There might be settlements, but he had no interest in them. He was perhaps only forty miles from his destination and his sense of victory grew with every mile.

Another feeling that grew with every mile was the sense of strangeness and a feeling of 'reaching the edge'. Sef told himself the Therions of the faded-realm were superstitious and backwards, and if one were to continue north then eventually one would merely be travelling south again. It was logic, not magic. But this was no ordinary sphere like Earth or Vega. This was a dream inside a dream, and deeper things than science and even magic governed here.

Thule.

Sef wiped the snot from his nose and the tears from his eyes. Flying was fast and cold. The sea was a living mystery of glossy black below him, while the sky was leaden and ancient-looking.

Thule.

The word came again and he shivered. Resenting his own fears, he leaned into the staff and called more speed from his tired sprite. They accelerated and now the sea streaked past. Sometimes large waves reached up and raked at him with foamy fingers. He saw silvery Merlins, or mermaids as humans had them, flash by in the depths. They never broke the surface and were gone before he could see clearly. Were they toying with him he wondered?

"Sef, your mind drifts, keep us on course!" Iso protested.

"I know!" he snapped.

They continued for the best part of an hour and the islands became more sprawling and fractured. Someone without a keen sense of direction might have lost their way, but not Sef. The north drew him as much as it mystified him, and finally he saw a low-lying island little different to the rest and he knew. "This is it!"

"Thule?" Iso took a sharp breath.

"Not quite, the headland at the north of this island. Only six or seven miles now." Without knowing he slowed the staff to a moderate pace and watched the scrubby tundra roll by below. It was brown, malnourished and rocky. To his amazement he saw snow nestling in the deepest valleys, and as they flew parallel to the coast he noticed how it became hillier and the cliffs steeper and more dangerous the further they went. It was almost as if the island's northern half was reaching into some unknown influence and belonged to that of another world.

Thule.

Sef slowed. That wasn't his imagination. Some outer voice had spoken to him. "Iso?"

"What?"

"Never mind," he growled. The temperature dropped by degrees and he slowed to a stop. Ahead he could see the island sweep upwards to form towering cliffs split down the middle by a deep inlet. How, he couldn't say, but he knew Thule occupied the hills on the western side of that inlet. He looked and listened harder and what he had taken for a bank of grey mist became clear. There was a huge fortress built on the tip of that headland. "Thule," he whispered.

Thule. This time it really was a voice.

"Iso! Didn't you hear that?"

"Lack of sleep has maddened you, and tried me," he grumbled.

He pulled down his hood and listened hard. An idea settled upon him that was both chilling and beautiful. The world had been connected to the universe when creation was young. This connection was Thule. Was Lord Self whispering to his chosen son through that ancient conduit, perhaps even watching from beyond? Sef bowed, believing it was, "I will not fail you."

"Fail who?" Iso worried.

Sef turned his gaze upwards to those primordial clouds. "Lord Self?"

"Sef, for Vega's sake get a move on. We're so close!"

His eyes narrowed and he perceived that distant fortress better. It was huge and clearly hewn by beings other that feeble Therions. The terraces and levels all climbed higher, until at last they created a platform for a towering lighthouse, but it was for no earthly ship. "Fools!" he scoffed. "They think Astriss will be guided home by a mere light."

Ultima Thule was a lighthouse at the end of the world, built under the auspicious gaze of the cosmos and intended to bring home a dragon that had died generations ago.

There were only a few miles left now and Sef devoured them. The landscape seemed to age before his eyes, growing ever more rocky and ancient. The island's mythical reputation was further enhanced when he saw huge beasts wandering the hills below. They were elephantine and bore huge curved tusks. Their coats were shaggy and dark in colour, and he recalled a memory of Barda's, of standing in the Natural History Museum some years before and admiring a mammoth skeleton. Now he was seeing the real thing. Here were more relics from across the veil that had found a desperate toehold here.

He flew across them, towards Thule lighthouse. Closer still and he saw the stonework was grey and uniform, as if made from precisely engineered blocks, but of colossal size, and the ledges were thick with nesting sea birds. Rivers of white guano ran down the fortress and birds swirled around it like smoke. The lighthouse itself was a marvel. Its hexagonal tower reached half a mile into the sky from its foundations to its crown, while galleries and windows dotted its walls, and a palace of crystal sat at its summit.

Less than two hundred yards now, and Sef saw the tower's light was a building in its own right: a building made almost wholly of glass. Stone pillars supported a domed roof capped with green copper, and in between those pillars were huge sheets of ancient-looking glass. He saw complex machinery within, dominated by a massive lens. But the light was cold and the machinery dead. *They have given up hope,* he thought with satisfaction.

With this in mind and a smile on his lips, Sef touched down on the lighthouse of Ultima Thule.

He took a moment to survey his location as the wind whistled around him. The light was indeed fabulous and its construction supreme. The glass was old and rippled, but clear and hardened by time. The sheets were bolted together with an alloy he didn't recognise. It looked strong, but the elements had dulled the metal and eaten tiny holes in it. He craned and looked up. The structure must have been over eighty feet tall, and the lens inside was almost equal in height. The great disc sat looking magnificent but forlorn and useless, like a jilted bride. The light source was again some mechanism he didn't recognise. There was machinery and technology like nothing he'd ever seen and he understood the lighthouse's creators must have been highly accomplished. He looked out to sea, drawn to face north, to Hyper Thule and the mystery beyond, but all he could see was a dense fog bank that reached from sea to sky. A few fog-fairies and rain-fairies circled the tower, but there seemed precious few of them overall.

"What lies beyond do you think?" Iso gazed northwards from the balustrade.

Sef shook his head. "Nothing we need concern ourselves with." The wind whipped at his robes and he felt cold.

Iso watched gulls sail by, casting them a suspicious eye. "This place is empty."

"No it is not." He reached for the gelding-sack as he spoke.

"Look around you, there's nothing. The light is dead and the island's barren!"

"I did not come to see the sights Iso," he grunted as he opened the sack.

"Even if Clovis comes, and I'm still uncertain he will, then the ascension can't succeed. This place is dead and forgotten."

Sef snorted in amusement, "I don't want the ascension to succeed, and you're wrong; there *are* Therions here and Clovis *is* on his way."

"How do you know?"

Sef pointed to the grand doors built into the glasswork. The brass knobs were shiny. "Brass doesn't smooth itself. Someone comes here regularly."

"Huh," Iso conceded. "And what of Clovis?"

He took a greedy breath and looked skywards. "Oh he's coming."

"A hunch isn't proof."

Sef looked through the clouds to the cosmic connection above, thinking of Lord Self. *I am here to act as your will,* he acquiesced.

Thule, the voice came.

My Lord.

"Sef?" Iso barked, "you're not listening!"

"Clovis will come. Lord Self has promised," he bowed his head.

Iso looked about. A more foreboding spot would be hard to find, but he certainly didn't feel the presence of Lord Self. "You're certain?"

"Neither he nor Kolfinnia were at Stormwood – they are coming here, be certain." He smiled and reached into the gelding-sack. "We need to prepare for his arrival." Inside, his fingers wrapped around the helpless Chentek.

"He will be angry," Iso warned.

"Once free of the gelding-sack the days of hunger will catch up with him. He'll be weak and compliant."

His fist emerged from the gelding-sack, where the sinister Magnon also lay inert, and he uncurled his fingers to reveal a furious but half-starved Chentek. "Sef betray me!" he gargled.

Sef held him meaningfully above the open sack. "Be polite, or the sack will become your permanent abode."

Chentek glowered up at him and pawed feebly with his legs. "Sef betray me," he growled again, but now with a snivelling tone.

"You must be hungry Chentek, good. Will you obey, or do you prefer to go back with your Magnon fellows?"

Chentek looked frightened. "No! No, not back there. Magnon whisper madness, always madness!"

Sef smiled, "Then we are ready." He helped the war-fairy on to his shoulder. "Stay hidden, and when I give the order you may feed, but not before."

Chentek clung weakly and hissed in acknowledgement.

"See," Sef turned to his doubting sprite, "the creature *can* be reasonable."

Iso just snorted, while Chentek plotted the awful things he'd like to do to Sef.

"Good, then let us ready Clovis's arrival!" Sef declared grandly, and set off following flags smoothed by passing feet, that led below to the heart of Ultima Thule. He had beaten Clovis in the race, now all he had to do was sit tight and claim the prize.

CHAPTER TWENTY

The light at the end of the world

'They turn our hopes into baited traps, and make us fight ourselves.'
'The Saga of the Ragged Oak', 12th century
Author unknown

The stone stairs wound downwards in a broad spiral. Narrow windows allowed some light, as well as drizzle, from outside. To start with, Sef saw numerous chambers and rooms, probably intended for the light's keepers, but they were empty and the machinery looked forgotten. Every so often he would pass a doorway leading out onto a balcony. He braved the elements and checked one. Agitated sea birds hissed and squawked at him, and the stink was powerful, but he saw the courtyards and buildings below growing closer. Soon they would be at the tower's base, and presumably into the fortress complex itself.

They moved in silence and finally Sef's theory proved right when they emerged from the spiral to find a grand hall. It was again carved from huge blocks that blended seamlessly with the bedrock, and many pillars supported the cathedral-like roof. The architecture was stark and plain and the only things to soften the austerity were statues of grim-looking Therions, and they were much like the fortress: immense. Thule looked to have been built by giants.

"How were such blocks moved?" Iso ventured.

"Magic," he whispered.

"I sense abandonment here."

Sef stopped and listened. He could hear dripping water, the clamour of sea birds and the distant waves. The windows were all broken and caved in. "They've abandoned hope yes, but not completely."

"How so?"

"Signs of occupation," he reminded him. A breeze tempted his nose and he took a draft of air and sampled it. "This way." He crossed the hall in long strides, aiming for a stairwell running downwards. The floor was mossy and he saw bird droppings splattered against the flags like white explosions. He crunched over a few discarded eggshells and crab-claws, and sea-slaters scuttled out of his path. Somewhere down those steps he could smell living creatures and hear them too. It was time to meet Thule's keepers.

Sisi looked up, suddenly alert.

"Mother?" a concerned voice turned her.

Coven-mother Sisi looked to her Captain, a hulking Therion like a musk ox, named Umbra. She listened carefully, while Umbra watched with growing concern. *Steps on the spiral?* she thought uneasily.

"Coven-mother, you hear something?" Umbra stood from where he was sitting by the fire.

"Wait." Sisi raised her slender muzzle and sniffed. She was much like Bru, slight of build and distinctly fox-like, except her fur was snowy white and her nose and almond-shaped eyes were dark. She licked her nose and twitched her short ears. "Someone is here," she concluded.

Agitated, he collected his great sword and was already marching to summon his scant guards.

"No!" she stopped him. "Gather them with stealth."

"At once." He dipped his shaggy head and stalked from the room.

She diverted her gaze to where a pair of huge doors stood in a stone arch. Beyond it was the path that climbed to the light, which was no metaphor. The light was the Beacon, the glass reflector-housing above, and the spiral was the same one Sef was walking that very moment. "Whoever comes so far can only bring hope surely?" she said to herself, and wondered, if so then why was she suddenly tense? She focused her mind and listened.

The hint of footsteps was unmistakable, and something else almost out of range: the chatter of birds, sounding eerily like thousands of starlings. She touched her wand and straightened, all the while staring at the doors, certain either death or hope would come through them any moment.

The stairs ended in an open courtyard. Sef could smell the outdoors even before he exited. He stepped from under the arch and a drizzle of guano just missed him. A bird cackled overhead and he wrinkled his muzzle in disgust. The courtyard was square and lined with niches each bearing a bronze vessel. From the melted wax he assumed each was meant to hold a torch, but just like the light, they were dead and cold.

He saw a pair of doors on the courtyard's opposite wall. The wood was recently tarred and the pathway swept, and while the courtyard bristled with weeds, the flags around the doors were clear. "In there," he warned Iso.

"I told you: too much flight means less fight."

"I shan't need you," he scoffed. "But watch. Be extra eyes for me. You too Chentek."

The war-fairy growled some rude reply and buried himself deeper, out of sight.

Sef flexed his hands, making bones crack. He touched the dragon egg a last time, and then under Lord Self's watchful gaze he walked across the courtyard towards the doors, gripped the handles and shoved. The lock turned and the doors parted silently. Someone had kept them oiled and in good order, and when the doors swung wide Sef at last saw that someone.

She was white and fox-like. Her robes were also white and he immediately understood she was a magical practitioner. As for her guards, they were much like the mammoth, shaggy and prehistoric-looking. A dozen of them stood flanking her. They all had long dark fur, huge horns curving down from their broad heads, and their wet noses were flat and almost bovine. They exuded strength, and stood over seven feet tall. Sef noted broadswords buckled around their waists and already he was calculating methods of attack. The hall was grand but again austere. A fire blazed in a cavernous chimney and banners hung on the walls, and all of them depicting the same white dragon. The highest windows were broken and a few kittiwakes circled above while others nestled on window ledges, watching everything with a keen eye.

The white fox stepped forwards. "Visitors are few here." Her nose twitched as she appraised him. "But all are welcome," she added reservedly.

"Coven-mother," he guessed and bowed. "My name is Sef."

"Sef?" Her ears twitched. Had she heard that name before she wondered? She couldn't be sure, perhaps it was just his unexpected arrival that put her on edge. "Welcome to Thule, Sef," she said graciously, but didn't return his bow. "I am coven-mother Sisi, and this is Umbra, Captain of my guard."

Sef looked his way. "Blessings on you for keeping the good lady safe."

Umbra studied him before twitching his head in reply.

"My lady," Sef continued. "I have come far and braved much to bring you incredible news."

She raised a cynical eyebrow. "Forgive us Sef. Our duty here has been a long one and incredible news has yet to visit us in person."

"But I assure you I have." He took a step forwards and saw Umbra's hand go to his sword.

"Let him approach," she ordered softly.

"My thanks great coven-mother," he acted.

"You're overdoing it," Iso crackled.

"Be silent!" he shot back.

Sisi detected an interchange of sorts, and her eyes darted to the staff around his shoulders. "Am I to believe you are a witch Sef?"

At last she sounded animated, Sef thought, and he laughed politely. "I am, but alas good lady my thunder-sprite is equally honoured to be in your presence. He chatters like a thrush to me, singing your praises."

Or a starling, she thought uneasily.

At the mention of thunder-sprite, Umbra looked startled. "This stranger is a witch?"

"It appears so." Her tone was equal parts hope and doubt. "Forgive me Sef, but a witch with a flying staff is all but unheard of here." She cocked her head, awaiting an explanation.

"Coven-mother —," he began, when suddenly a kittiwake screamed from high up. Sisi and her guards seemed not to notice. Its shriek rang around the hall and finally died away. "Coven-mother," he started again, scowling at the bird.

"The birds come and go, Sef," she interjected. "It is a tradition here. Please continue." She clasped her hands, still waiting for an answer.

He smiled humbly. He didn't like the birds but couldn't say why. "I came here as fast as I could with great news."

"The only news we seek here is of Astriss." She looked pensive. "Have you such news?" Around her the guards unconsciously leaned closer.

Sef had learned from Tallpine, and his story had a new twist. "The lady Astriss is indeed lost coven-mother. She cannot return because she has left this world."

Her eyes were stony, but rapt. "Go on."

"But she did not go to the nether world without first leaving a great treasure behind." Somewhere above a kittiwake screamed again. Its shrill call echoed around the hall and he frowned in annoyance. It was ruining his moment.

"Treasure?" Sisi ought to know better, but she couldn't help herself. "What treasure?"

"Astriss has blessed us." He reached into his robes, making Umbra reach for his sword in reply, but everyone froze when he withdrew the egg. "Astriss is gone but her descendants live on."

Sisi heard a beating heart within and her eyes widened. "Offspring!"

Sef smiled. They were his he knew. It was all so easy.

Kittiwakes looked down from the heights above, where balconies and ledges played host to nests and guano. Thule was defended by more than just aged witches. Sisi wouldn't know until her time came, but each bird was a reincarnated witch who had guarded this lonely outpost just as she did now, and they saw with clear eyes and cool hearts, unburdened by desire. The stranger was lying.

Sisi shuffled forwards. "Astriss gave birth?" she uttered.

"She gave birth and gave us hope!" Sef announced. "Hope to rekindle the light at the end of the world." Iso chuckled again and even Chentek managed a smirk.

"Oh Astriss!" Sisi's caution was smothered by desire.

Sef smiled warmly, even as he pondered her death. *Should I let Chentek eat the white-bitch? Lop off her head for the gelding-sack? Or should I keep her hostage? Tender-hearted Clovis would risk all to save a stranger.* All of the options sounded pleasurable. "Yes coven-mother, Astriss wanted her offspring to be born here in Thule." He held out the egg like bait for a starving animal. "And I fulfil her last wish now."

Sisi was trembling. Her dainty paw reached out for the egg, which was a delicate sky blue colour, speckled and slightly tapered at one end. Inside was everything she'd ever desired, for her people and her realm. Inside was hope incarnate. "Astriss be blessed," she whispered and tears glinted in her eye.

Just as her fingers brushed against the egg, something white, noisy and very angry crashed into Sef's head and was gone before he could react. Another followed it just as swiftly and splattered guano across his head. The screaming birds dive bombed him and sank his glamour without trace. "KAAA! KAAA!" they screamed.

Sef recoiled with a snarl, and Sisi looked again and saw what desire had concealed. This was no real witch and whatever lay unborn in that egg was no kin of Astriss. "DECEIVER!" she howled in warning.

"Always the hard way!" Sef gave a savage laugh, grabbed her neck and hurled her down even as Umbra and his guards charged into the fight.

It was Umbra who came at him first, and consequently fell first. Sef whipped his sword free and struck with cold precision. The gravantium blade ran him through and stopped his charge, as well as his heart. Umbra fell and his sword rang against the flags.

The battle was short but bloody. Umbra's guard were devoted and well trained, but Sef's guardian was Lord Self. Nothing could stop him. Two minutes later, the twelve Therions lay dead and dying around the great hall and Sef stood panting but impassive. He checked each in turn to ensure the dying were swiftly sent to Evermore, before turning back to Sisi.

She lay in a heap, nursing a fractured wrist, and blood matted her brow. As he approached she hissed in pain and tried to draw her wand. "Deceiver!" she groaned. Kittiwakes took well-aimed swoops at him and cried over and over, but they couldn't stop the inevitable. To prove his case he spun around and sliced one from the air as it whooshed past. It landed in two halves with its wings twitching madly.

"Birds and brutes? Is this all you have to guard your holy of holies?" he sneered.

She groaned again, and managed to pull her wand free.

He cleaned his blade and swung the sword through the air, making a whistling sound. "Why must it always be the hard way?"

She raised her wand and cursed him, "Back, in the name of Astriss back!"

He towered over her and kicked her hand aside, hardly noticing the spell. The wand clattered down, and she tried to snatch it back only to find his hand crunch down on her paw and break it. She screamed again, and flailed with her arm, forgetting her broken wrist, and fresh agony surged through her. "Care to try again witch?" he goaded, and stepped away.

Defiantly she extended a trembling and broken paw towards her wand, only for him to bring his foot down again, this time on the wand itself. The slender shaft broke in two with a loud pop. "No!"

"Always the hard way," he shook his head. "When will you learn? Self is in us all."

She lay sobbing and defeated, undone by her desires. "Chentek," Sef ordered. "Clean this mess up." he gestured to the bodies around the hall. "They ought to prove a worthy snack. And then kill every fairy you find but one, and bring it to me. I need a messenger." Chentek cackled hungrily and took to the air and within seconds the rattle of iron wings filled the hall as his minions invaded the faded-realm. "Now, coven-slut you will tell me all that's involved in the ritual of ascension," Sef shouted over the racket, and reached down and grabbed her ear and dragged her to her feet.

"Never!"

"You'll tell me," he sighed, tired of hearing the same pointless resistance. To prove it he took her broken wrist and twisted.

"NEVER!" she gave an animal scream. Above her, the hall darkened as the swarm of iron-fays congealed and the sea bird's cries became frantic. Sef twisted again. "NEVER!"

"Never?" He released the pressure and listened to her pitiful moaning. "We shall see." He licked his lips and smiled. It might be weeks before Clovis arrived. There was plenty of time for him to persuade her otherwise, and even if he didn't get his answers, torturing her would stave off the boredom.

Word of Clovis's miracle had spread and he took comfort in knowing that joy not gossip was the engine of dispersal. The idea that Janus was going to restore conscience was infectious, and in consequence all of Hope seemed determined to get him to Thule. Clovis threw himself into the work, even though he sometimes saw parallels with making his own coffin. Over the last few days he'd repaired rigging, tarred and caulked timbers, and learned to mend sails. They had waited three days for Ulfar to make his ships seaworthy again, and it was looking certain that tomorrow he would sail with the morning tide. As the sun rose on the morning of Friday August 5th, Clovis understood that he was enjoying his last day in the company of Kolfinnia and his faithful Lions. He wanted it to be joyous but the melancholy was never far away.

Each time Hope's clock chimed, Kolfinnia heard it no matter where she was in the city and knew Clovis was another hour closer to leaving. "Tomorrow," she sighed, stopped working and looked up.

Hilda cast her a worried look. "Tomorrow we go home too, now isn't that a good thing? And Clovis has been away from his home for almost a year."

She took her knife and began chopping herbs again. They were making curatives for Bru's apothecary. "It's not merely 'going home', he's not telling all."

"He has to complete a mission that's as old as the stars. Surely even he can't know all involved?"

She worked the knife, watching the blade glint and flash. "Intuition tells me otherwise," she said glumly.

Hilda understood the power of intuition. "Why would he lie to you?"

"Only to protect us." She was surprised at her own answer. Within it, she found an explanation of sorts. *Yes, he would lie to protect us.*

"Kolfinnia?"

"Nothing. You're right. I should make the most of the day."

She relaxed a little. "Bru's preparing a feast this evening. My advice is to enjoy it now and grieve later."

"Fifty years later suits me. You're right though. It'll be good to get back to Stormwood."

"Stormwood," she echoed. "I didn't spend long at your wonderful coven, but I'm looking forward to living the rest of my days there."

"I hope it's just as we left it."

"It will be," Hilda said certainly. "It will be."

Bru prepared a feast in gardens where cherry blossom lay as thick as snow. They had a pavilion and a table heaped with delicious food. Hathwell recounted his last day, explaining how he had drawn instructions for city defences and suggested suitable locations. Hilda and Kolfinnia had left the apothecary stuffed to bursting with remedies, and once again visited Sedna's twins. The idea of two boys growing up called Kolty and Hilda didn't seem so strange now.

Taal and Peri came to join them and Kolfinnia unexpectedly found Peri's sadness made her feel less alone, and for a while they were sisters united by loss. The thunder-sprites sat perched around the gardens nibbling on pinecones, while an endless stream of fairies flitted around the trees going about their business, oblivious to them all.

It was a picture-perfect summer banquet, yet it wasn't. Clovis forced every smile and ate without enjoyment, morbidly wondering why he bothered to eat at all. In a few days he'd be dead after all. Despite his overwhelming burden he did his best to show an optimistic face, knowing genuine love demanded it. Several times he caught Kolfinnia studying him over the rim of her wine glass, or between mouthfuls. He smiled warmly, belaying her fears until the next time he caught her, and her gaze always said the same: *'What are you hiding Clovis?'*

When the time came for the gathering to break up and find their beds, the rest helped Bru clear the table while Peri took Clovis to one side to say a private farewell. "So Clovis, you're leaving." She hoped the bland statement would open up other avenues.

He watched petals drift down around her, wishing he could hold her. "What happens from here on is not my will, merely my duty. If I could I'd stay."

"I know." She reached for him, but he withdrew and the hurt in her eyes was unmistakable.

"I shall not come back Peri," he said flatly. "Get used to that."

She swallowed her shock, wondering how she'd offended him. "Erm," she hesitated, "then twins' blessing on your journey coven-father." She struggled to keep her voice even. In her dress pocket she had a gift for him, but now she felt foolish, and left the little token where it was. "Good night," she finished awkwardly and left.

"Good night." He watched her go and his expression was blacker than the tar staining his work clothes. *Is that how you'll farewell Kolfinnia tomorrow?* his conscience asked. Sef preyed on desire, and Clovis was determined all his desires should lie dead before he stepped foot on Thule. *Will you?* conscience persisted. "Yes," he whispered. "Yes I must."

His name was Jaskar and he was a moss-fairy. His nation was Thule and just yesterday his family had numbered millions. Now they were all dead. Jaskar had been brought before the black Therion and told to deliver a message. As the Therion spoke, he took one of Jaskar's wounded kin and plucked his wings off, and then his arms and legs, before silencing his agonised howls for good. "I am Sef," he had said, "and this is my message to Clovis and all of the faded-realm."

Sef had told him to repeat the message, and then he had been chased from the fortress by the war-fairy and jeered and gnashed at as he fled in terror. He must find this 'Clovis', but no matter how fast he flew the sound of breaking bones and Sisi's crying followed like a shadow.

Kolfinnia was already awake and packed, when she heard the clock strike five the following morning. She was sitting on her bunk, idly tracing the serpent tattoos on her forearms. "Let's get this over with," she muttered to nobody. She donned her cloak and collected her few things. Once she had her staff in hand and listened to Skald's gruff advice about this and that, she felt strong enough to get on with things. She descended to Bru's study, not at all surprised to see the others already gathered.

Bru could smell sorrow like overripe fruit and so kept his chatter light and airy. "The remedy you made for Rolo worked!"

Kolfinnia noted the kitten now sitting up. "He'll be fine now," she said, genuinely relieved.

Bru gave him a friendly scratch behind the ear. "Now, if you're like me, the idea of food at this hour sets me aquiver, so I've packed a few provisions you can eat later." He handed over bundles of linen tied with string. Tellingly, there wasn't one for Clovis.

"Our thanks coven-father," Hilda accepted.

"And our thanks for all of your understanding and hospitality," Kolfinnia added.

"If the old ways still held then I would ask you to come back again soon coven-mother," Bru smiled wanly. "But the world changes and the faded-realm ever fades."

"Perhaps not for long," Clovis added.

Bru thought of the incredible task ahead, and grew serious. "I shall see you at the dock later this morning Clovis."

He nodded briskly and then turned to his Lions, who'd come so far but cruelly couldn't join him on the last mile. "Are we ready?"

"Ready." Kolfinnia stood tall.

"Ready," Hilda and Hathwell agreed together.

"Until later Bru," Clovis acknowledged.

Bru stepped back, knowing this wasn't his moment. Kolfinnia passed her staff to Hilda and went and hugged him. Bru only reached her shoulder but his embrace was strong. She felt his coppery fur against her cheek and his whiskers tickle her chin. "Twin's blessings on you."

"And you coven-mother, Stormwood must be a lucky place." He wrinkled his nose, determined not to cry.

No sooner had Kolfinnia released him, than Hilda came next. "Goodbye Bru."

"I'll keep an eye on little Hilda, and little Kolty. Twin's blessings on you."

Hathwell shuffled forwards. He had rehearsed his lines in Pegalia. "Good bye coven-father. It has been an honour to come here." All in all he managed well.

Bru understood and regarded him fondly. "Few squires join covens, fewer still journey to the faded-realm. Farewell witch-Berand." Bru couldn't have pleased him more.

Clovis blew out a long breath. "We should be going. The morning tide won't wait." He saw three sad faces and the urge to comfort them overwhelmed him. *Kill your desires,* a voice commanded, and he did. "Follow me." He swept past them all and out of Bru's study. It was time they left and time he finished what he came here for.

As they journeyed through the woods west of the city, Hilda and Hathwell chatted amiably, mostly to fill the silence, while Kolfinnia walked beside Clovis and felt every passing minute like a knife. *Tell him. What's there to lose now?* The thought left her chilly with dread but it had a reckless merit. *Tell him you love him as you'll never love any other man.* It would be a fitting farewell, but would it do any good? He'd changed these last few days, and when she spied a tearful Peri leaving the gardens last night she guessed he'd been hard with her. She wanted to say it, but now she dreaded his reaction. He might even sneer or laugh. Days ago she'd have scoffed at the idea, but something was wrong inside their beloved coven-father, and she didn't know what.

"I should thank you," he said from nowhere, startling her.

"Thank me?"

"Remember how you saved my sword?"

She smiled dreamily, "I remember. It was lying in the heather, too heavy to lift."

He smiled too, and remembered her marching through the heather towards him, and how elated and beautiful she looked. "Odd isn't it. . . those were happier days."

"In some ways. And will you need that sword again soon?"

"I cannot say." His smiled faded.

She tried to rekindle it. "You still have that silver box I gave you?"

"Of course."

"When I look up at Vega I'll know you're there, and me too, and all of Stormwood."

"It was a very moving gesture," he said sincerely.

"When you get home, will you set about reclaiming your coven?" She kept her conversation practical.

"A good question. I hope in my absence, my sister Neeri has rallied survivors."

She grinned despite herself. "You have a sister?"

"Hmm. Two sisters to be exact."

She shook her head in amazement. There was so much she didn't know about him, and so much she wanted to discover. *I love you Clovis.* She almost said it.

"This way," he directed her, and the words went unsaid.

He took them to where the trees were oldest, hoping that across the veil they were equally old and undisturbed. They could appear without being seen.

Now the moment had come she felt oddly calm. Later she might cry, but this was the testing hour and she was determined to be dignified. Before she knew it, Skald sat on her shoulder and it was like having Valonia close by. *Thank you,* she thought gratefully.

Clovis went and stood a little way from them. Tempest appeared from his staff and sat on his shoulder, looking equally sombre. Clovis forced a smile. "So, my dear Lions, here is where our paths diverge." He drew the pact-of-grace and regarded each of them in turn, lingering on Kolfinnia. *I love you.* He desperately wanted to say it, but to even think it might give Sef a weapon.

Tell him! Kolfinnia's throat tightened and she took a deep breath. "Kittiwake-coven wouldn't have lasted a day without you. All of us owe you so much."

"Blessed be," Hilda agreed.

"Aye," Hathwell added.

"This is only the beginning," he imparted. "Janus couldn't have awoken without you, or a hundred other small things that conspired to bring us together." Again, he thought of the mysterious ROWAN door on Evermore.

"What will happen next?" Kolfinnia asked softly.

"It might take many generations for Janus's song to spread through the cosmos. . . but when it does!" he growled, and for a moment he was the Clovis of old.

She took heart, found what strength she needed, and spoke those awful words, "Goodbye Clovis," she smiled bravely. "We all love you." *I love you.*

"Indeed we do," Hilda sniffed.

"My love goes with you all," he said, lingering on Kolfinnia's beautiful face, "I won't fail you." He pressed a thumb to the pact-of-grace. When the locket opened they would be gone. Such a tiny gesture he thought, yet such a void it would leave. He offered them a last smile, looked deep into Kolfinnia's eyes, and squeezed the catch.

"Wait!" Tempest shouted.

Clovis froze, with his thumb hovering over the lock.

Tempest heard it again. Someone was shouting their name. "Someone comes!" he revealed, and flapped into the tree. "It's Bru!"

"Bru?" Clovis almost cursed. *What the hell's he thinking?* He swallowed his fury and slipped the pact back into his cloak. "Damn it!" he hissed.

"Clovis wait!" Bru came stumbling towards them.

Kolfinnia caught his arm, "Bru, what is it?"

He stood chasing his breath. "Clovis!" he gasped, baring long teeth and a flapping tongue. "Word from Thule – be warned, this enemy of yours has beaten you to it!"

"Sef!" Kolfinnia exclaimed.

Clovis felt chill. "Sef knows we're coming?"

He wiped the froth from his muzzle. "Aye, he sent a messenger, a lone fairy. Only survivor of his attack."

"He knows I'm here?" Clovis cursed himself for not guessing sooner.

"This blasted foe of yours gloats," Bru snarled. "He defies you to face him!"

"Just tell me what he said."

"He awaits in the north, and he says," he hesitated and shot Kolfinnia a mortified look.

"Bru! What did he say?"

"He says bring Kolfinnia, or coven-mother Sisi will die."

Kolfinnia took a sharp breath. "Clovis that seals it, we're coming with you!"

"You *can't* come!" he retorted.

"We must!" Hilda argued. "You need witches, and you have two willing ones here."

"Three." Hathwell stepped closer.

Aghast, Clovis looked from Bru's stricken face to his Lions. *A moment later and they'd be gone. Damn fate forever!* he cursed.

"Clovis?" Kolfinnia searched his face.

"Curse this day," he uttered. Like it or not they were coming, even though they were all walking into a trap.

They arrived back to find Hope in uproar. There was a large crowd at the gates and Bru had to push his way through, battered by questions. News of Sef's attack was spreading fast.

"Clovis, Bru, this way!" Ulfar pulled them to one side. The rest followed and he directed them back up along the main streets towards the castle, snapping and snarling at townsfolk who tried to prise answers out of them. *Has Thule really been invaded? What's this we hear of a ravenous swarm and the fortress guards killed? Is coven-mother Sisi a hostage, I heard she was dead?*

"Stand aside!" Ulfar shoved through a wall of spectators clustered around the castle gates. He ushered Clovis and the rest inside and swung the gates closed and listened to the anxious shouts from outside.

"Is it true Captain, has Sef really taken control of Thule?" Kolfinnia demanded.

"Aye. It's true, that's why I can't take you as planned." Ulfar flattened his ears and bared his fangs.

"But I must get there!" Clovis spluttered. "By all Halla's scales, I'll fly there alone if I have to."

"Let me finish!" he argued. "I can't take you alone is what I mean. One ship against this Sef and his swarm wouldn't even reach the shore."

Clovis shook his head in bewilderment. "What are you saying?"

Ulfar was already heading back to the docks. He turned, looking implacable. "Wolf-kind live as a pack. One ship will not sail to Thule, but one fleet will. Every ship in Hope is going with you."

Clovis was still digesting this as Bru hurried them back to his study, where he had another revelation. When Clovis saw the familiar room again he had the feeling of running but not getting anywhere. "There's someone you must meet." Bru waved them towards a table where an assorted throng of fairies was gathered. "Good fays, make room," he said impatiently.

"But he's wounded," one pleaded.

"He'll come round." Bru gently pushed them away with a paw and the rest gathered around to see. A wounded fairy was lying on the table. His breathing was wheezy and his wings tatty. Kolfinnia didn't recognise the species, but his skin was velvety and green and his eyes were like jewelled droplets. "This is Jaskar, a moss-fairy from the far north," Bru announced.

"From Thule?" Clovis realised.

Bru nodded once. "Jaskar, tell these folks what you told me."

The small creature looked up at the sound of his voice. He struggled onto all fours, winced in pain and began. "A black Therion came with iron-fairies, more than I've ever seen, and all of them diseased."

Clovis knelt level with him. "Diseased?"

"The lust for blood, the food of the old times," Jaskar shuddered. "Flown all night to get here, the black Therion killed all my nation."

"Genocide?" Clovis asked horrified, and heard Kolfinnia gasp softly.

"Fed them to his swarm," he accused in a trembling voice, making the other fairies hiss and spit.

"See!" Bru said, "Sef's taken Thule and has an army ready to face you! Ulfar's right, you can't go alone."

Clovis thought for a moment. "What of this coven-mother Sisi?"

"She's Thule's custodian," Bru explained. "I've known her all my days."

"What did he do to her?" he asked, turning back to the fairy.

Jaskar hung his head. "Took her captive, killed the guards. Will kill her too if you don't come."

"He knows I *have* to go there to release Janus!" Clovis ground his teeth.

"But not alone. Must bring one called 'Kol-finnia'." Jaskar looked around, wondering who the unlucky witch was, while Kolfinnia felt violated to think that Sef knew of her at all. Beside her, Hilda took her hand.

"And how on Vega does he know Kolfinnia's with me?" Clovis fumed.

Jaskar coughed and slumped to one side. "Don't know, don't know, so tired."

Bru cut the debate short, "Clovis, I must treat Jaskar's wounds at once."

"Understood. Meanwhile our priority is readying the fleet." He caught Hathwell's eye, "You ever sailed before."

"A few times."

"Good, follow me down to the docks, there's a lot to get done. Kolfinnia, Hilda."

"Yes?"

"Gather me as much bistort as you can find. Make preparations of it."

Kolfinnia already guessed his logic. "It staunches bleeding."

His eyes narrowed dangerously. "Yes it does, and make as much as you can. We're going to need it."

So began one of the most turbulent days of Kolfinnia's life. Selfish or not, she couldn't deny feeling grateful to still have Clovis. Ulfar decreed they would sail tomorrow, to allow time to gather fighters from surrounding districts and supply the ships. It had taken Ulfar three days' careful work to get The Hornet ready, now he had to do the same for twenty ships in only one day.

"There's really no rush," Clovis said bleakly as he helped with the rigging. "Sef's already there waiting for us."

"We take advantage of the up-swell," Ulfar recommended. "If we wait, then more of the willing will get nervy and change their minds."

"And the journey?"

"Perhaps three days. Bru has sent word to the settlements further north. We'll gather more ships as we go."

Clovis tied a knot and moved onto the next. "Many Therions face death in this attack, you know that don't you?"

His silver eyes glittered. "What you have in that vessel of yours is worth it to them. They'd die to see this realm restored. As would I."

"Forgive me."

"Don't let us down," he scowled. "And your friends – it'd settle my lads to think witches were coming."

"They're coming," Clovis said regretfully.

"Good," Ulfar slapped his shoulder. "That's good."

Is it? he wondered. *This is just what Sef wanted.* He looked to Hope Castle, some half mile distant. The turrets were ablaze with colour. Bru had hoisted all the dragon banners, and the city was alive with speculation and determination. "Don't let them down Clovis," he told himself and got on with his work.

The day passed with anxious speed. Several times Clovis saw Peri around the dock but he avoided her. She even came looking for him, but he told Ulfar to send her away saying he didn't know where he was. He caught sight of her golden mane as she left the ship looking despondent, before crawling shamefully out of his hiding place. *Oh Tiber, if you could see me now,* he lamented, *hiding from my own desires.*

Taal came to join them, with scores of willing fighters. A hasty dockside workshop was established turning planks into shields, while outside the smithy, long queues gathered to have their weapons sharpened. Hammers rang out across Hope all that day. Clovis watched Taal's fighters training to make shield walls and thrust their spears. He wondered how such tactics would help them against diseased iron-fairies, but said nothing. The fact that they were coming was enough. In the end, it might take such a force just to kill Sef if anything happened to Clovis.

If anything happened to me? he thought bleakly. If it did then Janus would be imprisoned indefinitely. It occurred to him that he should tutor the Lions about the ritual, just in case, but couldn't see a way of doing so without revealing the vessel's deadly nature.

The city worked ceaselessly, and the fleet looked more steadfast with each passing hour. Ulfar conceded some ships would benefit from more work, but their planned expedition was going to be short and bloody.

By evening time Kolfinnia's hands were raw and stained from preparing bistort. She felt they had a mountain of the stuff, but if the battle went as Clovis implied then even a mountain might not be sufficient.

She wandered down to the docks under a glorious sunset, carrying her blanket and other possessions. Skald sat on her shoulder. He and the other sprites had done little today, but only because they would do much in the days ahead. "Have you thought any more about what I said?" he asked again.

"Bru has agreed to send word to Stormwood if we don't return," Kolfinnia confirmed. "At least they'll know what happened to us."

He grunted in satisfaction. "I'm sure it won't come to that though."

"Only time will tell." *Or the Timekeeper,* she thought, wishing ardently she could speak to him. She even touched her scarred cheek.

"Thinking of him?" Skald asked.

"You know me well," she smiled.

"And I like what I know." This was flowery talk for Skald, and her smile widened. "Don't let it go to your head," he grunted.

She was still smiling when she got to the ship. The meadows around the river were home to countless tents and campfires. Therions sat polishing weapons or cooking meals, checking their gear a last time or spending a few hours with their families. Campfire smoke drifted by as did subdued chatter and the faint sound of children's laughter, but for a garrison of many hundreds, the encampment was strangely hushed. Therions of widely differing races stopped and watched her pass and all acknowledged her with either a nod or a touch to the temple. Fighters they had aplenty, but witches were rare and if they faced magical enemies at Thule then Kolfinnia and her companions would be their only protection. "Blessin's on you witch-Kolfia," one rumbled.

She turned to a hulking bear-Therion wearing a blacksmith's apron. "Twins bless you," she replied.

"Blessing's good witch," a Caprian dipped his head. She saw his horns were huge and his mane plaited.

"Blessings sir." As she continued through the camp, more and more of them came to watch her pass until she walked through a corridor of them. She saw horns, tusks, fangs and fur, but each face was somehow more humane than any soul back home. Their dignity made her skin tingle and her throat tighten.

"Blessings good witch." The greeting came over and over, and each time it was spoken like a charm.

"Twins' blessings go with you." She felt her eyes prick and finally she was glad to see the ships' masts through the crowd.

At last she was through and ahead she saw The Hornet with its sails raised and oars ready. Tomorrow they must row many miles before reaching the open sea. She wasn't surprised to see Ulfar and Clovis already on deck. It occurred to her they hadn't left the ship all day. "Permission to come aboard." She waited on the riverbank.

Ulfar looked down and grinned, showing rows of teeth. He jerked his head, and that seemed to be all the invitation she was going to get.

"Grim fellow," Skald muttered.

"Just what we need." She set off up the narrow plank and dropped neatly to the deck and Skald flapped up into the rigging.

"Kolfinnia." Clovis greeted her with a reserved hug. "Spending the night aboard?"

"How did you know?"

He indicated two other bedrolls lain out on the deck.

"Hilda and Hathwell?" she asked.

"It's an early start, and why walk from the castle when we can begin right here." He looked very tired she thought.

Ulfar sniffed the air. "It'll be a dry night, bed down where you may." With that he cast Clovis a surly wave and bounded down the walkway and onto the riverbank.

Kolfinnia felt the ship rock gently under him. "How is he?" she asked when he was gone.

"Determined." Clovis took her bags.

"And the others?" she asked, noting the empty blankets.

"A few last farewells around the city." He looked up to where the castle walls were black against the evening afterglow. Torches blazed along the battlements, illuminating many of the dragon banners in the fleet's honour. "Bru," he smiled, "quite the sentimentalist."

"Is there anything wrong with that?" She edged closer.

"Only when it clouds judgement." He stepped aside, making an excuse of checking the rigging.

She concealed her irritation. "Have you given any thought to our tactics?"

He checked they were alone before speaking. "I've never fought such a foe," he confessed.

She frowned. "You haven't?"

"Sef I can deal with. It's this virulent swarm he's conjured." He shook his head, at a loss.

"We'll figure something out."

"I hope." He leaned on the gunwale and looked out over the dark river. "Would you think me cold if I told you most won't come back?" he asked without turning. "That I've calculated the fleet's value as a decoy?"

"It's alright," she tried to soothe him.

"But it's not." He turned, looking anguished. "While the fleet battles the iron-fays, you, Hilda and I must fly to the place of ascension and release Janus. It's the only way."

She swallowed. "But they're counting on us to protect them against this horrible swarm."

"I know, but we can't be in two places at once. The only other option is you let me tackle Sef alone."

The idea instantly horrified her, and she looked away, convinced her love for him was written all over her face. She looked down at the river's inky surface, thinking hard. "If only we could neutralise the swarm, then the three of us could unite against Sef."

"Yes, but as you say – only if we can think of a way to disarm the iron-fairies."

"And if we can't think of a way?"

"Then Ulfar's fleet will have to manage as best they can while we get on with Janus."

"That's terrible," she whispered.

"Aye, Ulfar thought so too. But he's willing."

She stared his way, taken aback. "They would willingly march ashore without us to protect them?"

"I told you, the Therions are putting their hopes in Janus, not us."

She was silent for a while. "That's what we came here for though isn't it."

He released a rumbling sigh, "Now you see the truth of it."

"And what if you're killed, and one of us has to open the vessel instead?"

The question caught him unprepared. "We'll discuss that on the way," he shrugged, pretending it wasn't important. "Now, we'll be rising in a few hours. Can you sleep?"

"No," she laughed. "Can you?"

"Try," he encouraged. "Let The Hornet rock you to sleep."

She set her blanket out under his watchful eye, wishing he'd rock her to sleep instead, and lay down and looked up at the first stars shining. Vega caught her eye and she thought of home and of Rowan and Sunday, her fated sisters. *Would my Dear Champion have brought me so far, only to let me fail?* It wasn't his to decide, but the temptation to hope was too great. From the riverbank she could hear fiddle music and smell smoke. Skald was just a silhouette in the rigging above, and The Hornet's banners rippled lazily in the night breeze. "Dear Champion," she whispered and closed her eyes.

Above unseen, Arinidia the spider twinkled in answer, but Kolfinnia had already drifted off to sleep and the star's secrets stayed secret.

Chapter Twenty-one

Hornet and Raven

'Before each battle the Kanzui warrior kills his heart.
Thus he kills his mercy and his fear.'
'Ways of War' - Parovian text, 1st century BC

In the early hours of Saturday August 6th, Kolfinnia awoke with a start.
The sky was still indigo but it had the sheen of approaching day, and
birdsong was beginning. *Dawn's coming. I must've slept after all?* she looked
about groggily. Hathwell and Hilda were just bundled blankets close by.
They must have arrived in the night, but she hadn't heard a thing. Soft
footfalls came, and she wriggled upright, blinking away the sleep as Clovis
knelt beside her.

"Time to go," he informed her.

"Did you sleep?" She rubbed her eyes.

"More than I ought," he exaggerated.

She stretched her aching neck and detected voices and the tangible sense
of excitement as the encampment came alive.

He looked across the riverbank. "The crews are getting ready, I'd better
go help."

"I'll help too." She tossed her blanket aside and got to her feet.

"You can help by rousing them," he waved a finger at the two sleepers on
the deck.

She reached down and gave Hilda a gentle shake. "Time to go," she said expectantly. "You too Mr Hathwell." She heard groaned replies and considered her task done, but when she turned to look for Clovis he had already vanished. "Time to go," she said again, this time to nobody.

The rallying happened incredibly fast. Hundreds of Therions simply awoke, grabbed their things, hugged their families, and set off, leaving the camp's dismantling to those staying behind. Within thirty minutes of waking, Kolfinnia was amazed, and a little unsettled, to see the first oars lowered and the first gangplanks stowed. "Where do I row?" she asked. All the benches seemed taken with fierce wolfen.

"You don't," Ulfar growled. "You save your strength for when we get there."

"But I want to help."

"Then help by saving your strength," he dismissed her, and stalked across the deck shouting orders, leaving her slightly breathless.

She joined Hilda and Hathwell standing at the bow. Looking towards the castle as the sky brightened, and filled with diurnal fairies. Huge crowds had gathered on the riverbank, many perhaps looking upon their loved ones a last time. "I feel like fragile cargo," she complained.

"They know what's best." Hilda stood stroking her wand thoughtfully.

"Doesn't seem right." Hathwell looked back, where Therions were manning the benches. "I'm no witch, I should be pulling an oar instead."

"I'm sure someone will swap once we've been at sea all day." Kolfinnia tied her hair back and scanned the riverbank, and waved when she saw Bru. "How's Rolo?" she shouted.

"Leaps and bounds Kolfinnia, leaps and bounds!"

She blew him a kiss. "Some good news to send us off with."

Hilda joined her and waved in Bru's direction. "Where's Clovis?" she asked eventually.

She searched the deck, and saw Clovis stood at the stern with Ulfar. "He's busy," she said simply.

Only minutes after, Kolfinnia heard Ulfar's first genuine command. He roared and the crew responded with a mighty heave. The ship surged and she grabbed the gunwale and heard water thrash and wood creak. Forty pairs of hands pulled at the oars, and The Hornet slid gracefully out into the river's dominion. *This is it,* she told herself. Each ship in turn echoed Ulfar's command, and now twenty ships, crewed to bursting point, howled in farewell. The Therions on the banks joined them and a cheer went up.

Kolfinnia raised a hand in salute, just as the sun broke the eastern rim. Gulls and crows, and the odd heron soared overhead. The sun glinted off the waters and she saw salmon and water-fairies dart away in the depths. It was hard to believe they were going to war. A brutal roar made her turn and she saw the following ship breaking away, with its crew hauling at the oars for all their worth. It was paying off too, because they were catching up.

"They're making a contest of it," Hathwell smiled. "You know I'd give anything for an oar of my own."

The ship behind, named Dawn-Star, was crewed wholly by Caprians, and Taal was amongst them. Kolfinnia saw a forest of horns rise and fall as rowers pulled at the oars. There were a good number of females amongst them too. So many had volunteered that there were plenty of disappointed ones left behind, and she hoped, not for the first time, that they all knew the risks.

"Faster!" Ulfar barked, relishing the contest. "You want to see bearded sheep lead the way?" His wolfen snarled and slobbered and oars were pulled with manic strength.

From nowhere, something whipped overhead and plopped into the river, making a sizzling sound. Kolfinnia looked up to see trails of fire streaking across the ship in reckless directions. "What in Oak's name?" Her mouth dropped wide as she watched archers on the riverbank, shooting fire arrows across their bow, and alarmingly, through the rigging and past the sails. "Are they mad?"

"Nay!" Ulfar stood close by, looking proud. "This is good luck!" More fire arrows whizzed overhead and the river was pelted, and a fine smoke rose up from the sunken shafts.

"What if they miss?" she shouted over the cheering crowds.

He looked affronted. "Have you ever missed with a spell?"

She shook her head meekly. "No."

"Well then!" he laughed dangerously, and turned to the bank, drew his sword and held it above his head. The cheers rose in volume and more arrows whistled past.

At the stern, Clovis clutched a rope and watched fire rain down. It wasn't long before he turned his attention to the crowded banks, looking for one face in particular, but as the river drew them seawards and the crowds thinned he didn't see her. The last arrows fell in a light scatter and he turned to watch the following ships each saluted in turn.

He slipped a hand into his satchel intending to check the pact-of-grace, but found something unexpected, and withdrew a small bundle of tied linen. At first he thought it was one of Kolfinnia's medicine bags, but the scent was unmistakable. "Peri," he realised, and opened the bag carefully. Inside was a stone pendant decorated with an etching of Astriss. It was the gift she'd wanted to give him two days ago when he'd rebuked her. She *had* found him yesterday, and hidden it without him knowing. "Peri, I'm sorry," he said, meaning it with all his heart and slipped the little stone around his neck, but understanding that regret changed nothing.

Kolfinnia smelled saltwater and noticed the changing fairy species, and knew the river was becoming the sea. Two hours after leaving Hope, the river widened into a huge estuary and beyond it lay a flat horizon sparkling in the sunshine. "The sea." Always it lifted her and once out there she had a surprise ready for haughty Captain Ulfar, something to prove that she wasn't just fragile cargo. She patted her wand-sheath. "We'll show them a thing or two hrafn-dimmu eh?" she promised.

Now the wind made its presence known, and it was time to lower the sails and rack the oars, and although the billowing dragon pennant showed an unfavourable wind, Kolfinnia couldn't have been happier. While Ulfar grumbled, she sat quietly in the shelter of the bows, drew hrafn-dimmu and felt for the serpent-twins. It was much easier than she anticipated, frighteningly easy in fact. Almost instantly she felt their drumming hearts and with just a few askings the wind began to sweep around from blowing easterly to southerly. *A dream within a dream,* she reminded herself, and perhaps that's why the effect had been almost instantaneous. She clutched Raven's wand, and heard Ulfar's frantic shouts as the crew made the most of the sudden change in their favour.

"Good spell work coven-mother," someone complimented.

She opened her eyes to see Clovis watching her. "Just doing my part."

"I thought you might try this, so I had Ulfar ready a surprise for you," he smiled secretly.

She clambered out of the bows, now swaying with the swells. "Surprise?"

"Watch."

"Sails!" Ulfar bellowed. Crews obeyed, knots were loosened, the sail dropped and Kolfinnia cupped a hand to her astonished mouth.

"Told you!" he beamed. The crew burst into applause and howls, even Ulfar smiled, and Kolfinnia was left speechless. The billowing sail had been decorated in her honour. A huge black raven with spread wings was painted across the canvas.

"Hrafn-dimmu guides our way!" Ulfar called.

"You told them?" she gasped.

"What better emblem for our flagship?" He smiled at her joy, and above them the black raven heaved in the wind, as if it wanted to fly free.

She gently slid Valonia's wand back home. Its former owner might have gone to Evermore, but Kolfinnia imagined her pride at seeing the wand do what it did best: to inspire and defend. "Dark raven leads us," she said, feeling like the very tip of the spear.

Hundreds of miles north, where the strange dream-like world of the faded-realm became stranger yet, a lone kittiwake patrolled the skies and looked down onto a drastically changed landscape.

The island of Thule looked out to the edge of the world. Its fortress lighthouse stood dark and untended, and its rocky shores were bare. The only life appeared to be the ever-circling sea birds, but there was new life on Thule. Its soil might be hard and stony, but this was no obstacle to determined seeds. The Magnon had spread with terrifying speed, sweeping across the island in just a few hours, and consuming what little life there was.

The kittiwake skimmed easily over the highest hills. Nowhere did she see any other life but the shambling hordes below. She witnessed the last of the grazing mammoth encircled and swamped. Even from this height and over the rush of the wind she could hear the animals' desperate trumpeting and the Magnons' mindless clatter: *'I, I, I, I, I.'* The litany never stopped.

A black Therion looked out from one of the lighthouse balconies. He didn't feel the tearing wind or hear the sea birds. He watched the Magnon multiply before his eyes, appalled and fascinated. It occurred to him this might be the beginning of the end for the faded-realm, but his guilt was small compared to his glee. Once he had what he wanted he would leave this world to its fate. He smiled at the thought and returned to the lighthouse. The waiting was dull, but he had a distraction and it would be impolite to keep her waiting.

The fleet raced northwards, following The Hornet and guided by the Raven. Kolfinnia's asking kept the wind at their back and their speed was impressive, but like all things, spells cost and she was tiring. "Hilda, would you take over for a while?"

"Of course." She drew her own wand, squeezed down beside her and began the asking. The wind gusted haphazardly before settling southerly again.

"Thank you." She flexed her tired hands, but Hilda was already sat clutching her wand, with her eyes closed and wearing a serious frown. Kolfinnia took a blanket, draped it around her shoulders and kissed her, although the older woman hardly noticed. "Thank you," she said again.

Hathwell watched in fascination. "Could you teach me that?"

She crossed the swaying deck and joined him. Now the wind was driving them, the crews had minimal duties. Many were rolling dice, eating, chatting or tending their gear. She pushed her hair from her face. "First thing you need Mr Hathwell is a wand."

"There's that 'Mr Hathwell' again," he pointed out.

"Sorry, Bertrand. Or do you prefer Berand?"

He just smiled modestly. "So how do I get a wand?"

"You don't get one, you make one."

"May I see yours?" he asked.

She hesitated. "Yes, of course." She drew hrafn-dimmu and handed it over.

He took it very carefully. "Valonia's wand." He turned the black shaft this way and that, perhaps looking for traces of her.

"And Sunday's too for a while." She watched him, strangely uneasy at seeing it in another's hands. "Bertrand?"

"Hmm?" he looked up.

"Hilda says you were the last to see Valonia."

His face slipped. "Yes, yes I was."

"Forgive me but," she paused, "what did she say?"

He looked out to sea and remembered that day, and when a faint smile surfaced he said, "She asked me to check on Hilly."

"I'm sorry."

"No, it's alright." He found he wanted to tell someone, and who better than Valonia's heir? "She also said something that stuck with me a long time. Even now I think of it a lot."

"Yes?" She leaned on the gunwale and peered at him.

"She said 'You don't need a wand to be a witch Mr Hathwell'."

She smiled longingly. "She didn't call you Bertrand either?"

He chuckled. "No doubt she had cause to call me many things, but Bertrand wasn't amongst them." He gazed down at her wand again. She was struggling for something to say when he spoke again. "So how do I make a wand?"

"You find a stick. Keep it and love it, and hold it when you make magic."

"And that's it?"

"The wand takes on a little of you. A very old wand has a life of its own."

"Like hrafn-dimmu," he understood, and handed it back.

She took it gratefully. "It's truthful to say a part of Valonia is still with us."

He planted his elbows on the rail and watched the waves roll by. "I think I'll have a go at making a wand when I get home."

'Home.' She liked the idea of his joining them. "I'd help you, but. . ."

"I know, it's one of those things I have to do alone."

She nodded. "Later I'll show you how to make the wind-spell."

He raised his eyebrows, "You will?"

"Of course, you've got to pull your weight Berand." She gave him a pretty smile and he was still chuckling to himself when she was halfway along the deck, looking for Clovis.

The Hornet had an open deck and was built for speed not comfort. Clovis had to clamber under the decking and into the narrow hold to check on Janus. He sat hunched over, listening to the sea batter the hull as he unwrapped the vessel. Once it was in his hands again, he thought of Tiber and how far he'd come. "Janus?" He set the vessel down. "Janus do you hear me?" The small figure rolled with the ship's pitch, but he was completely inert. Clovis rested his chin on his arms watching the helpless god. *The battle against all those lies must be tearing him apart, will he even last the journey?* The idea of Janus dying had never occurred to him, but seeing him now it felt horribly feasible. When he heard someone drop down into the hold he threw the blanket over the vessel. "Who goes there?" he demanded.

"Relax, it's me." Kolfinnia staggered towards him, minding her head on the spars. "How's Janus?"

"Hmm, causing me problems as always."

She regarded the blanket and the lump underneath. "You said he's fighting all the badness he's put into the vessel over the years."

"Aye, but I wonder if he's winning?"

"We'll be there in a few days, if we can keep this tail wind up."

"A few days might be all he has." He cast a last look at the precious cargo and then stood and squeezed past her. "Come on, nothing we can do down here."

"Clovis?" she caught his arm. "How do we open the vessel, you know 'just in case'?"

"As I said, the right will at the right place."

"Surely there's more?"

"Later," he delayed her. "When we make port." He pushed past without another word and vanished up through the hatch, leaving her alone with her annoyance.

Their speed was tremendous, and by the day's end they reached the busy port of Abberan, or Aberdeen as Hathwell guessed. Word had definitely gone ahead, because a huge number of vessels, small and large, were ready, bolstering the fleet to almost sixty. After some rough plotting, Kolfinnia guessed that tomorrow in the Orcadeas the fleet might top eighty ships.

After that there was only Thule and Sef. *Eighty ships. Will it be enough?* she worried, and she wasn't alone.

They slept under canvas strung over the deck, although many went ashore to trade, meet old friends and make merry while there was still a chance. Kolfinnia lay in her blanket, and listened to the Therions' exotic laughter and shouts from the dockside as light rain pattered on the canvas. The Hornet rolled gently with the swells, and she tried to sleep and ignore Hathwell's snoring, wondering how he remained so relaxed, forgetting he had marched to war many times. In the dim lantern light she saw movement amid the sleeping bodies, and a small iron-fairy crept into view. It sniffed at a few iron rivets embedded in the timbers, lost interest and flitted away into the darkness, leaving Kolfinnia thinking of the millions of infected ones and their taste for blood. After that she hardly slept at all.

The following day the skies were grey and the waves choppy, spray lashed the decks and the wind was cold. After maintaining the spell for a few hours Kolfinnia gladly changed over with Hilda, who'd slept little better than her. Their speed was still good but the cost was telling. Both witches were as tired as if they'd rowed all the way after all.

"Hard?" Hilda asked, noting her heavy eyes.

"The wind has a mind of its own today." She rubbed at her stiff hands.

"Two more days." Hilda took her wand, tucked herself into the bows and pulled her cloak higher.

"And then on to Thule."

"Thule." Hilda closed her eyes, let out a long puff and resumed the spell.

Kolfinnia left her to it, and staggered down the deck, under the raven sail and towards the hold, past sailors bundled in their cloaks, and holding the rigging for support. "I think I like the sea best from afar," she said to nobody. Just then they hit a wave hard and the ship reared up. She cursed, slipped on the wet planks and came down hard on her backside.

"Kolfinnia?" Clovis shouted from the stern.

"I'm fine!" she snapped, clambering up and wiping the wet from her rear.

"Very well." He took her at her word and enquired no further, and instead remained at the stern with Ulfar, helping steer the ship.

Yes, thanks for the concern Clovis, she thought tetchily. With her cheeks still burning and her buttocks still throbbing, she hauled the hatch open and dropped down into the cramped hold, hoping for a few hours sleep. She squeezed through the cargo, and found Hathwell just where she wanted to be. "Room for two?" she asked wearily.

He opened an eye and looked up. Without answering he shuffled over and she slumped down beside him, too tired to notice how close they sat. Down here the ship's movement seemed accentuated, and there was something comic about the way they rolled and flopped in tandem. She leaned back and bumped her head on a timber. "Damn it!"

"I did that too," he sympathised.

She pulled her blanket up and drew her knees to her chest. The ship rocked again and she was shoved cheek-to-cheek with him. "You need a shave," she muttered, slightly embarrassed.

"You sound tired. I'll gladly take over."

"I haven't taught you the wind-spell yet."

"How about now?"

She groaned inwardly. She wanted sleep, not study. "If you wish," she sighed and sat up as best she could, and took his hands. Sitting so close and hand-in-hand, they looked like sweethearts, and both tried to ignore the comparison. "Now. Just clear you mind to start with."

"Like the sleeping-spells?"

"Yes. Clear your mind and listen for the twins." He clasped her hands firmly and she was glad of the warmth. "Now when you feel the twins, imagine asking them to send us a southerly wind."

"Is that all?"

"Imagine yourself asking them, and the wind responding. Imagine it and make it feel real." She squeezed harder. "Don't let your mind wander."

"I'll try." He closed his eyes, and didn't see her smile at his expression.

"Try to be joyful." She advised, and when a pained smile surfaced on his lips she tried not to laugh. The ship rolled again, and she fell across him and almost kissed him. "Keep your mind clear," she repeated, more to steady her giggles.

"I'm trying," he grunted. He didn't see her amused expression, and instead focused all he had on her instructions. He was determined to show Hilda he meant business about learning magic. He tried to think of wind and dragons and asking for things, but another thought just popped into his head and right then it seemed more real than all the rest: there was Valonia, dying at Kittiwake-coven. *"You don't need a wand to be a witch Mr Hathwell."*

Kolfinnia jerked back with a hiss.

He opened his eyes to see her stunned expression. "What?"

"How'd you do that?" she uttered.

"Do what?" A tear plopped from her eye and now he was really worried. Had he cast a spell on her he wondered?

"Valonia, you were thinking of Valonia. It was so real."

"Yes I was. You saw?" he asked guiltily.

She closed her eyes and tried to gather her impressions before they were gone. There was Valonia lying in the wreckage of Krast's kraken. She was dying, and Hathwell had gone to release her. To see her again, so clear and so vivid was a gift, even if the circumstances were dire. "Valonia," she called, as the image faded.

"I'm sorry, it wasn't meant," he apologised.

"No," she squeezed his hand. "It was the best present you could've given me."

"Really?"

She covered her face to shield the tears and just nodded, and he slipped an arm around her and held her close.

"I miss her too," he said simply.

They sat like that for some time, nestling against one another and rocking with the waves and thinking of old friends, while the ship rode the seas northwards to Thule, driven by magical winds.

The Hornet led the fleet, now sixty-two ships strong, into the Orcadeas that same night. The islands were named for the killer whales that haunted their waters, although Kolfinnia saw not a single fin break the waves. The last few hours, they travelled in the dark with the crews hauling at the oars, giving the depleted witches a rest. Kolfinnia noted how Clovis managed to keep a distance from her, even on a relatively small ship. He liaised with Ulfar and manned the steer-board, or helped cook and advise on fighting tactics. When the darkness became total the fleet kept contact with lanterns and as Kolfinnia looked south, she saw a trail of bobbing lights illuminating countless dragonheads, and swarms of flame-fairies darting around them. The sky was clear and perhaps in recognition to their increased latitude she saw faint streams of aurora play between the stars.

She slept ashore that night in the Orcadeas, in one of the little turf huts along the waterfront intended for cargo. From the sounds outside, some poor souls spent the night loading not sleeping, and there was the constant clang of smithy hammers making last minute preparations. A little later, while the moon was still high, Hilda and Hathwell slipped in beside her and slumped down with a grunt and a crunch of straw. Kolfinnia pretended to be sleeping, too tired to even utter 'goodnight', and within a few minutes Hathwell was snoring again and Hilda was breathing peacefully.

"Skald?" She touched her lightning-staff.

"I envy you," he confessed.

"She was there before my eyes." She smiled at the memory of Valonia.

"How did he do it though?"

"He said it was just an accident."

"That's some powerful accident," he complimented, *"but how did he do it really?"*

She rolled over and regarded Hathwell in the dark. "I don't know," she whispered.

August 8th, and she awoke aching and feeling thirsty. Breakfast was porridge and apples. She downed two tankards of freshwater to soothe her headache, reminding herself to drink more frequently, and then she spent the next fifteen minutes looking for a private place to relieve herself. As she boarded The Hornet, a raven perched on the mast and rattled off a series of croaky calls. She raised her wand in salute and the huge bird flapped away, leaving only its canvas counterpart below. It was a good omen the crew decided.

When The Hornet finally cut the waters of Shapinsay Sound that morning, she was leading a fleet of ninety-one ships, gathered hastily from all across the north. Some were cargo vessels, traders or fighting ships like The Hornet herself. Most had only the faintest idea of Janus's purpose, but they were willing to risk their lives for the cause. This struck Kolfinnia as heartbreakingly noble and typically Therion.

"I'm uneasy," Clovis admitted as they set sail.

"Why so?" She stood on the bow admiring the sight of so many ships.

"Because they think Janus will solve their problems in the wink of an eye."

"They're very trusting," she observed.

"I spent most of the night explaining who and what Janus is," he rubbed at his brow. "And drinking too."

"Serves you right."

He smiled briefly. "Janus's song might take centuries to spread through creation."

"Centuries are still better than never. And when this song of his does spread?"

"Then the third-eye will be revived and this poison entity we know as Self will be halted."

"Not defeated?" she asked.

"There'll always be some souls ready to listen to its whispers."

She watched a flock of gulls pass overhead. "And so how *do* we set Janus free."

"Later."

"You've said that for the last two days." Her anger was rising, she could feel it.

"Tonight we should make the Shorland Islands, and tomorrow Thule itself. I'll tell you all tonight."

"Promise me."

"Of course, I've nothing to hide," he pretended to be hurt.

"Alright. Tonight it is then."

He offered her a faint smile before weaving along the deck and back to Ulfar's side. Surely he didn't like the gruff captain that much, she thought? *No, he's just avoiding you,* a voice told her. "Why Clovis?" she asked the wind. "What's so wrong?" The wind didn't answer but it didn't have to, because tonight she would make him explain.

When at last Clovis saw a brown hump on the horizon he knew they had reached Shorland and somewhere amongst its numerous islands Sef sat ready for them. He kept his mind busy, preparing food and taking a turn

on the oars. It took another two hours of rough seas before they reached
the southern tip of the mainland, which comprised jutting cliffs, white
with birds. They were approaching the edge of their world, and the crew
had withdrawn into a subdued hush. Clovis came and joined Ulfar at the
stern. The craggy Captain scrutinised the sea while the wind ruffled his
heavy fur. "How far?" Clovis asked.

"Thirty miles to Lievik. I went some years back. The town's but some
huts by a bay, but it'll do for tonight."

"Could we not go on to Thule itself?"

"And fight in the dark?" he huffed.

"I take your point. And how far from Lievik is Thule itself?"

"Another thirty miles."

Clovis looked disappointed.

"Patience coven-father, we'll get you there, if your friends can keep the
wind in our favour."

"They will."

"Then we've nothing to worry about." He nudged the rudder, and peered
across the dusky seas, looking pensive.

Clovis went and stood a little way off and watched the waves speed by.
Fulmars and gannets shadowed them constantly, and at first he thought
he was seeing the sun's dying light on the waves. Silvery flashes under the
surface teased him but vanished when he looked. He clutched the side and
leaned over, curious now.

"Merlins," Ulfar said from behind.

He looked over his shoulder. "You're sure?"

"They've been trailing us since dawn," he grinned mirthlessly. "There
might be many hundreds down there, and all at your command."

Clovis couldn't decide if he was being sarcastic. He ignored the remark
and looked again and now he knew what to look for he saw distinct shapes
swimming along in the depths. "More victims," he said under his breath.
The Merlins, or mermaids, were following to join them for the fight.
He should have been grateful but he saw only more innocents heading
towards Sef's trap.

He continued to watch as darkness slowly concealed the spectacle and
his mind turned to things best left alone. *Kolfinnia, soon I'll have to tell her*

the vessel is poisoned. He sighed hopelessly, but only the passing gulls seemed to notice his melancholy. *Kolfinnia*, he ruminated and glanced over his shoulder at her. She sat in the bows, her serious face framed by her dark hair. *She's beautiful, why couldn't things have been different? Why couldn't she have been mine?*

"KAAA!" At that moment a gull rushed past and screamed, making him jump.

Clovis shook his head clear. "Those weren't my thoughts?" he realised. He spun around and scanned the decks, but nobody seemed to have noticed, not even Ulfar. He looked skywards, to the veil of clouds. They were nearing Thule, where gods listen and answer. "Self," he growled.

Abandon Janus and turn back. Live out your years in comfort by her side at Stormwood. Perhaps magic might even overcome your differing natures. Imagine: you could be one, just as you longed for with Peri.

He pressed his hands to his ears, took a deep breath and held it. "Leave me."

I can give you these things Clovis.

He held on until his chest burned, and finally expelled it in a huge rush. "You give only false hope."

I merely direct souls to their desires. And you desire her.

"I desire only to see Janus freed," he said scornfully.

"Clovis?"

He looked around, trembling and disorientated.

It was Ulfar. "What's the matter?"

"Nothing," he lied.

"You were talking to yourself."

"No, I was talking to Self." He ran a hand through his mane and gulped down cool air.

"To who?"

"Never mind." He glanced Kolfinnia's way again, ashamed and confused. She sat chatting with Hathwell, unaware of his visitation. "We're getting closer to Thule."

"Oh? What makes you say so?"

"Because the gods speak through Thule," he answered mysteriously, and then went to get a drink of water.

Ulfar watched him shamble along the deck like an old man, and vanish into the hold. "Don't go to pieces now coven-father," he rumbled. "Not now." A gull raced past and Ulfar turned his gaze north again, to where gods speak and Sef waited.

The northern twilight seemed to last for hours, Kolfinnia felt. It was still half-light when The Hornet rowed into Lievik and for a moment she forgot looming war and managed to smile again.

The town was built around a rocky bay, quite literally. The cliffs were steep, if not huge, but it was the houses that were a marvel. Crooked huts were suspended from them with twisted roots and coarse ropes. One hut joined another with rope ladders and the lowest were propped up with stilts planted right into the sea. Countless birds nested on the sloping roofs, where luxuriant turf and thrift grew thick. Scores of narrow boats were tethered below, and they bobbed and knocked one another in the swells and the sound of clunking wood echoed around the bay. The settlement appeared empty, that is until she saw someone watching from one of those little huts: a bird-Therion. She waved, but the feathered head sank back into the shadows and the settlement once again looked deserted.

Ulfar had the crew row past the cliffs, towards a gently sloping bay fringed with a shingle beach. The huts here were stone and domed like beehives. Each had a single opening and no apparent window, but smoke drifted from their crowns and many glowed with candlelight within. The village was decorated with wicker dragons raised on poles, hung with dried seaweed and feathers, and surrounded by a scrubby forest of birch and willow. "Lievik welcomes you," Ulfar snorted, unimpressed.

"Will they help us?" Clovis gambled.

"Hard to say. The avians were ever a distant breed."

"Well, they seem to be expecting us." He noted figures watching on the shore. None of them appeared alarmed or surprised.

Ulfar shrugged. "You can't expect to sail through countless fairy-nations and not have news arrive before you do."

Clovis saw creatures unlike any Therions he'd encountered before, even on Vega, and in the twilight they looked somehow unreal, as if touched by

Thule's mystery. All of them were tall and lean and unmistakably bird-like, and like their auk and gull neighbours, their feathers were variations on black and white. "Avians you said?"

"Avians. Odd folk, odd language, odd place to live." He wrinkled his snout at the bleak surroundings. "I'll go ashore and speak with the village leaders. You make sure the ship is secure and the crews get rest, they'll need it."

"They will," he agreed. They'd need it a lot, because tomorrow they would fight.

This was the moment Clovis had dreaded. He was tired and ashamed of his constant lies. Tomorrow, while Therions battled for his cause, he would attempt to open the vessel, and Kolfinnia must know its dangers in full. It was time to tell all.

He finished helping the crew ready the ship for dark, and went ashore himself. Within a few hours of their arrival Lievik had become a huge encampment. He eventually found his Lions gathered in a small tent by the shore, surrounded by hundreds of others. Hathwell was sitting outside, warming porridge over a fire. By now it was dark and he looked like a vagabond in the campfire light. "Fog's coming up," he noted.

Clovis also noticed the mist drifting in, although it was light at present. "When you're done, come inside, there's much to discuss." He continued past and vanished through the tent flaps. Inside, Hilda and Kolfinnia were deep in debate.

"Clovis." Kolfinnia gestured for him to sit. "We were talking about this iron-fairy disease."

He threw his cloak on the ground and sat facing them. "Hmm, that's given me much concern too."

"Well, I saw a genuine iron-fairy earlier, poor thing was frightened witless. He says all the healthy ones have fled," she established.

"Apparently the affected revert to consuming living-iron. . . blood," Hilda added.

"Blood, something about the blood," Clovis pondered, aware of a solution hovering tantalizingly close.

Just then Hathwell entered with a pan of steaming porridge. "It's bland but it's hot," he apologised and started ladling dollops into their bowls. "And is it my imagination or are there more fairy folk around right now? I could have sworn I saw my first porridge-fairy." He'd got used to talking about them without feeling absurd.

"There are," Clovis confirmed, "many nations have suffered from this iron plague. Now they're massing in readiness to finally defeat them."

"But can they?" Hilda stirred her porridge.

"Only if we find the source of the infection and kill it."

They sat in silence and ate without enthusiasm, while Clovis quietly steeled himself. Outside, footsteps and voices never ceased and Kolfinnia heard avians talking, but their thick accents confounded her ear. She finally finished and set her bowl aside. "So, Clovis, the iron-fairies, how do we deal with them?"

Now was his moment he knew. He took a deep breath and began, "Tomorrow I want you three to stay with Ulfar's forces, do what you can to help the fairy-nations against Sef's swarm."

"And you?"

"I shall take Janus to the place of ascension, this fortress Bru told me of. I shall release him and no doubt fight Sef in the process."

She was about to counter, when Hathwell spoke. "We could go as four to fight this Sef. Once he's finished and Janus is free the job's done isn't it? Then we can all just bugger off and the iron-fairies won't be under his control anymore." He looked around at three rather astonished faces. "Well, can't we?"

"He's right you know." The more Hilda thought about it the more she liked it.

"It could work," Kolfinnia approved.

"It could," Clovis sighed, "but it won't."

"And why not?" she argued.

"Because I alone must open the vessel."

"Oh Clovis!" she groaned, "forgive me, but I'm weary of your stubborn desire to be the lone hero." She looked away, surprised by the force of her words.

There was an uncomfortable silence as the rest picked at their food.

Clovis stared at the earth and before he knew it he was speaking. "I alone must open the vessel Kolfinnia, because the liquid within is deadly poison. The vessel can only be opened by a witch willing to give their life to the undertaking." He continued to stare at the earth, but his sensitive ears detected her heart pounding in shock. The air around him felt to contract, and their mortified stares felt like needles against his skin. There was a long and painful gap before she spoke.

"I knew you were holding back," she accused in a harsh whisper. "No wonder all along you wanted rid of us."

"Kolfin –,"

"You *never* intended to go to Vega!" She was appalled by how easily she'd been fooled. "All this time!"

"Kolfinnia please," he winced.

"How *could* you?" she stammered.

"Kolfinnia, this isn't helping," Hilda offered.

"No! No, I refuse to accept this!" Her voice cracked.

He stared mutely at the floor, feeling ashamed and sad. "I'm sorry," was all he could manage.

"Sorry? Have you nothing more to say?" She pressed a hand to her throat, feeling she couldn't breathe.

He tried to lift his head but it felt like stone.

"Look at ME!" she yelled. But he neither looked nor spoke. "Liar!" she spat, and now hot tears rolled down her cheeks. "You lied to all of us!"

"Now Kolfinnia, listen!" Hilda commanded.

"No – I refuse this!" She jumped up and stormed out of the tent.

Hilda made to follow, but Clovis caught her arm, "Let her be for now." She stood undecided, before slumping back down, feeling dazed.

"Let her be for now," he repeated gently.

"You spoke the truth?" she asked forlornly.

"I did." He bowed his head and touched Peri's necklace under his chain mail. *Now both of them are gone,* he thought icily, *but tomorrow the grief will be too.*

Hilda and Hathwell joined hands, and the three sat in silence thinking of tomorrow, as outside the little campfire smouldered away forgotten, and finally burned to nothing.

CHAPTER TWENTY-TWO

Shores in flames

'Hate me not for speaking truthfully.'
Coven-mother Susan Kellen
Imprisoned during Exeter witch-trials, 1779

By dawn on Friday August 10th the mist had become a fog. Clovis was frantic. He'd been awake all night looking for Kolfinnia, aware that if the fleet believed she'd fled their resolve would crumble. Between them, Hilda, Hathwell and he had wandered the camp armed with lanterns, rendezvousing hourly only to find the tent still empty. In all his fevered imaginings he hadn't expected this. He plodded along the shingle beach, and wondered how he could have done things differently. Around him in the fog, Therions were marching to their ships surrounded by luminescent fog-fays. Again, he felt like the liar for letting them sail to battle knowing one of the witches they were counting on had vanished.

He came to the busy jetty and stopped and turned full circle, lantern raised. He saw fierce carved dragonheads, ships, fog, fairies, warriors, gulls and burning torches, and when he returned to his point of origin he came face to face with her. "Kolfinnia!"

She looked drawn and tired, but resigned to the inevitable. "Forgive me," she asked wearily. "I said terrible things."

He saw tear-fairies float around her and knew she must have cried most of the night. "And now they're said and out, they need not be said again."

He drew a line under it all, just overjoyed to see her again.

She slid her arms around him and he drew her close. "I'm so sorry," she murmured.

"What made you change your mind?" he asked, rocking her gently.

"I had a long chat with Skald."

"Sprite-sense. It always works in the end." He sensed her smile at that, but just as quickly her smile vanished.

"Is it true what you said, about the vessel?" she whispered into his mane.

"Forgive me – yes."

She held him tighter. "Clovis, I—"

"Don't say it!" he cautioned. "For my sake don't say it."

She nodded breathlessly against his mane and they held one another close, both feeling what they dare not think or say.

The sun arose veiled by fog and its glory went unseen. Ulfar tried to ignore the bad omen as The Hornet weighed anchor, dropped sails and put to sea. Behind him, a massed fleet of almost a hundred ships, many carrying more than they came with, followed in formation. Lanterns and torches were strung along The Hornet's rails and the ship cut a swathe through the fog surrounded by countless fairies. Despite the infamy of Chentek's swarm, many fairies had come to lend their weight to the cause. Many Burning Hearts had unified under one banner, a unique event in itself, and the air was so thick with fairies that they spread out on all sides, vanishing into the fog. Their help was unexpected and miraculous, but even so, Ulfar wondered if there would be enough. So far the iron-fays had swept aside all resistance, and now their vile nest was centred on Thule, just thirty miles distant.

He looked back and saw Dawn Star's profile in the fog. She too glowed with lanterns and her rigging sparkled with alighted fairies. She looked splendid he thought, so why was their departure so timid. "Crews are afraid," he growled.

"Hardly surprising," Clovis said gloomily.

Taal came and stood with them, pleased to sail aboard The Hornet with his brother. "There's a danger we'll be separated in the fog." He adjusted his chain mail as he spoke.

Clovis listened to the mournful wind and the oars chop at the waters. "This is no natural fog," he warned.

"Sef?" Taal guessed.

"Sef."

Ulfar felt it too. Not just the mist, but also a pervading sense of woe encircling them. "Cunning bastard," he snarled, revealing his fangs. "Can't he fight without cowardly magic?"

Clovis ignored the insult. "He tries to strike before we've even started." He shot a glance at the subdued wolfen pulling the oars. *And it looks like it's working.*

"This is no way to face a foe, like frightened thieves creeping around an empty house." Ulfar bounded down along the deck to where Kolfinnia and the rest were standing at the bows. He snatched a lantern and barged through them without a care and bounded up onto the dragonhead, holding the rigging for support. "Can you clear this blasted fog witch-lass?" he barked.

"Once out of the bay we can begin the wind-spell," she promised.

"Good. Then do so." Without warning he raised his lantern and let out a spine-chilling howl. Gulls screamed in answer and fairies darted away in fear.

Compelled by instinct the crew responded and forty wolfen added to the chorus. Kolfinnia clapped her hands over her ears and winced.

At the stern, Clovis felt the same primal urge and let out a fierce roar. Taal bellowed, and the rest of the crew, those without an oar but holding swords and spears, added their own savage cries. The waters churned as more willing Therions joined their ranks. The Merlins were making their presence known at last. Seemingly from nowhere, hundreds of silvery figures rose from the deep alongside the ships. "Mermaids!" Kolfinnia shouted over the racket.

Ulfar saw their latest reinforcements and his howl rose in pitch. He finished with a ferocious snarl and shook froth from his muzzle. The wolf howls echoed down the bay and each ship took up the call. Battle horns were blown to bursting point. Screams, roars and brays rolled around the cliffs and across the waves towards Thule, perhaps so loud they even rang in Sef's ears. *'The Lion of Evermore is coming to end your days,'* they promised.

The Hornet surged as arms found their strength and Kolfinnia could have sworn the fog thinned a little, for now the suggestion of gold lingered in the east. She turned to Ulfar, perched on the bow and howling like a lunatic once more. Beside him the thunder-sprites clung to the rigging, blazing and spitting sparks, and the wind tugged her hair as their momentum increased. "Keep the pace!" he roared to his crew. "Keep the pace you mongrel-rats."

"Now!" Hilda waved her wand.

Kolfinnia dropped beside her, clutched hrafn-dimmu to her chest and after a last look at the raven sail, closed her eyes and began the final spell. "Raven guide our way," she whispered remorsefully.

"Blessed be," Hilda added, and together they began.

The wind answered immediately and the raven billowed and flapped. "Keep it up!" someone shouted, but Kolfinnia blocked it out.

A dream within a dream, the deepest part of Hethra and Halla's realm, she told herself. If anywhere magic was strong it was here. She called the wind, and heard timbers groan. A cheer went up, but again she blocked it. Their speed increased. She could feel the deck flex and roll with the waves. Spray splashed her cheeks and her hair whipped her face. Sweat broke her brow as something outside resisted her will.

"You are hurrying Clovis to his death. Is that true love?" a voice whispered, and she wasn't sure if it was her mind or someone else's.

"Leave me alone," she commanded.

"And you will be alone. When he is dead and gone. You will be alone."

She blocked out everything and delivered the divine wind with greater force. The Hornet crashed through the first waves of the open sea and the fog began to dissolve, but Kolfinnia saw neither, as she concentrated on the spell, hurrying Clovis to his fate.

Sef watched the Magnon herds far below. Even from this height he could hear their constant clicking and rattling. Their numbers were so dense that they formed an unbroken plain around the fortress, right the way down to the shore, where incredibly many were wading stupidly into the sea. Would they drift away to seed elsewhere? Sef didn't know or care, but it was frightening to see how resilient they were. The fortress battlements and turrets glittered with resting iron-fairies. They clung to the tiles and the stones like metallic moths. Soon he would need them, and the metal swarm would take to the wing a last time. Just like the Magnon, what they did after today's battle was no concern of his. Just offshore lurked the fog he had spent the night conjuring. He could imagine Clovis struggling to find his way through it like a blindfolded man stumbling towards a cliff.

Six days had passed since his victory and he'd not been idle. He'd been busy making Thule fortress ready for Clovis and his friends, something he couldn't have done alone, but of course he wasn't alone. Thule, where gods speak and listen, and Lord Self was so very close, telling him everything his must do. He was thinking of these things when Chentek dropped down like stone and scuttled towards him.

"Any sign?"

"None." Chentek sounded glum.

"Patience little blood-tick." Sef leaned on the balcony and stared off northwards, to where greater mysteries lurked.

"But Chentek hungry!" he protested.

"Clovis will come with companions. You know the plan?"

"I know."

"Good. Eat your fill, but leave both him and his cherished Kolfinnia." He balled his fists and groaned longingly. Planning his torments had kept him warm these last few nights. "He's coming."

"So you say, but never how you know," Chentek bared his tiny teeth.

"Lord Self tells me." He looked at the leaden sky where his patron watched over him.

"Chentek hungry," he snivelled again.

"Go fishing then."

"Bastard Merlins too quick!" he snapped. "Old witch easy meat though."

"I've told you: coven-mother Sisi still has some value. She's not to be rendered, yet."

Chentek stared moodily down at the Magnon far below. "Clay men hungry too," he said with a shiver.

"Sustenance is on its way." Sef listened and smiled. "Just a few hours now and this long game will be over," he promised, and then drifted away from the balcony and back into the lighthouse, leaving Chentek with only the clattering Magnon and a rumbling belly for company.

Kolfinnia watched as the crews began breaking out their weapons and armour, and the Merlins alongside grew in number. *Soon we'll be there, and this nightmare will end for good or bad.* Now she just wanted it over with, regardless.

It was mid morning, but the wind had proved stubborn all along. "Something's resisting," Hilda disclosed as she and Kolfinnia took a quick break. Hathwell sat in the bows practising his first wind-spell. It was little more than a breeze, but Hilda was quietly impressed. "A few minutes more and I'll go back to it." She drank from a flask and ate some bread.

"The fog's thinning, look," Kolfinnia pointed to distant shapes that could be islands, while the sky now had a glow about it and the massed fairy army was slowly revealed. *There looks to be trillions of them,* she thought, mostly in woe.

"You're right, the fog's lifting." It was Clovis.

As soon as she saw him she felt sick.

"Kolfinnia?" he asked tenderly.

"I was just thinking."

He gave her shoulder a friendly pat. "Take it from me, at times like this it's best not to think."

"We're getting closer." She looked past him to the crews, now busy preparing.

"We are."

She swallowed a bellyful of fear. "Janus is ready?"

"Everyone's ready," he surmised.

"And our plan?"

"It hasn't changed."

"I see." She clenched her jaw to keep from trembling.

"Once at Thule I go on alone. You and the others must stop the iron-fays somehow."

"So once there, we part ways." She couldn't stop herself.

"You know we must."

Her body seemed frozen, while her mind scurried in pointless circles looking for a solution that just didn't exist. "Is there no other way?" she asked weakly.

Surprisingly, he smiled. "You were *meant* to stay at Stormwood," he chastised gently. "I ought to have said farewell weeks ago."

She returned his smile. "I had you a while longer at least didn't I?"

"Maybe we have him to thank for that," he touched the little hourglass scar on her cheek. "And before this is done there might be other reasons for thanks."

Absurdly she felt a flutter of hope. "You think?"

"I told you, don't think." He flashed her his familiar grin, full of teeth and fight, and for a wonderful moment her fears were banished.

When he saw the huge fortress in the distance Clovis felt a shiver of anticipation, and when he saw the huge lighthouse emerge from the mist he felt a sense of destiny. The island was a murky red-brown colour, seemingly devoid of greenery. It looked a foreboding place.

"Back to your posts!" Ulfar barked as crews hurried to the gunwales to see for themselves.

"Where shall we make landfall?" Clovis enquired.

Ulfar checked Bru's sketch map. "Suitable shores on the north headland under the lighthouse. We'll land right on the front door."

"Good." Clovis buckled his armour, tightened his belt and checked Janus.

Ulfar scanned the shore, now less than a mile distant and his hackles rose. Clovis heard him growl. "Problem?"

Without answering Ulfar took his telescope and inspected the island closer. After a weighty moment he whined, "Sweet friggin' Janus!"

"What!" He snatched the telescope and looked for himself.

"Tell me I don't see that," Ulfar pointed.

But he did, and Clovis saw it too. The island was a red-brown colour because it swarmed with Magnon. He swallowed. "There must be tens of thousands of them." He swept the telescope left and right, taking in the whole vista, but every inch was infected. "Rabid iron-fays and now this! By Halla's teeth how do we even get ashore?" It looked hopeless.

"You don't," Ulfar growled, "we do."

Clovis blinked at him.

"You can fly – can't you?" he demanded.

"Yes?"

"Good, then take your witches and fly right to the lighthouse, we'll deal with the Magnon."

"But you'll be –,"

"I KNOW what we'll be!" he snapped, "I don't need you to tell me." After a deep breath he calmed a little. "What are our options, should we turn and sail home instead?" he leered.

Clovis looked again at the vast Magnon herd, and back to Ulfar. He was right, but that meant putting the fleet in grave danger and taking Kolfinnia and Hilda the last mile, right into Sef's clutches. *Just as he planned,* he thought vengefully. "Then don't go ashore," he suggested.

Ulfar sneered, "To come all this way and have a fleet stood idle while you go into danger alone? What do you take me for – a man?"

For once his spite was welcome, and Clovis regarded him sadly. "Then we head for land Captain," he said simply.

"Very good coven-father." Ulfar went and started issuing orders while Clovis raced to the bows to speak with Kolfinnia.

"Kolfinnia!" he shook her, rousing her from the spell.

"What?" she asked, alarmed.

"Hilda, you too, and Hathwell," he beckoned them over.

The four knelt in a huddle, buffeted by wind and waves and Clovis looked stricken. "We must change our plan of attack."

"What's wrong?" Kolfinnia asked.

He glanced around before answering. Crews were busy but not panicked, yet. "Magnon," he whispered, "the island's overrun with them."

She understood instantly. "Then it's just us isn't it?"

"Yes. Those of us with staffs will have to fly to the tower and complete the ascension. Hathwell, my apologies and my farewell. Without a staff you'll have to stay with Ulfar."

He found saying goodbye to Clovis more upsetting than storming the beach. "I'll do as you say."

Clovis bowed his head. "Ulfar will fight his way to the lighthouse and offer what assistance he can. Until then it's just us." He looked purposefully at Hilda and Kolfinnia. "You accept?"

"Without question," they agreed.

Hathwell still couldn't quite grasp that Clovis was preparing for his last flight. "You'll be alright won't you?" It was stupid, but he couldn't stop himself.

"I'll be fine," he smiled stoically. "Now I don't know what we'll face inside, but we must not be separated understood, not on any account, nor surrender to our inner demons. We *must* stay together."

Kolfinnia's heart warmed at the prospect. "We'll be at your side all the way."

"Not all the way. At the very end you must not be anywhere near the Janus vessel. Promise me."

"I won't," she promised, but her mind was already suggesting other things. She would rather be the one to die than face a life without him.

"Promise me!" he warned, seeing something worrisome in her eyes.

"I *promise,* now let's get a move on!"

They broke their conclave and when Clovis stood he noticed how much closer the shores were and how hushed the crews had become. *They know, and they're terrified.* He was more beast than man, and he could smell their fear.

"Weapons at ready!" Ulfar roared, "haul sails and man the oars."

"Cap'n!" a wolfen called out, "shore's thick wi' Magnon. If we beach they'll be all over us!"

"And that Sirus is why today we must fight like the Black-Wolves of Nevermore, all of us!" He drew his sword and swept it across the decks where scores of frightened faces stared back at him. "Even you bearded sheep folk," he stabbed his sword towards Taal. "And you grass-munching doe-eyed dung-machines." Now the sword jabbed towards a bull-Therion, eliciting a few laughs. "Same goes for you feathered seed-peckers." Now the sword singled out their avian fellows, and more nervous laughter followed. "Today you're mine and whatever we find ashore we kill. Today you're WOLFEN!" His words burst out of him like arrows.

His wolfen accompanied him with howls and the rest threw in their support and the ship literally shook with their cheers. So many races united under the Raven and willing to die for Janus. Clovis watched and again asked why – why must the good lay down their lives to undo the work of the evil?

"Taal!" Ulfar barked. "Signal the fleet, tell them to follow and beach beside us."

"Aye sir!" Taal was away.

"Clovis, make ready to go."

But he had other ideas. "Wait, we'll stay until we beach, then at least we can try and push the Magnon back with magic first."

He hesitated. "Very well," he agreed. Now he looked to Kolfinnia and Hilda. "Never before have humans sailed aboard my ship. But The Hornet's blessed by your passing. Make us proud."

Kolfinnia was first. She put her arms around him and hugged him, even though she only reached to his chest. "Thank you Captain."

He coughed awkwardly. "Don't forget your duty girl."

Hilda took his hand, a great shaggy thing tipped with claws, and kissed it respectfully. "I shall praise the moon in your honour Captain."

"Blessed be, good lady witch," he concluded.

Hathwell stood uncertainly at the back, having grasped a good part of the conversation. Ulfar peered at him from under his brow. "It seems fate wishes you to be a wolf, not a witch, today Berand."

He understood, although he longed to stay at Hilda's side. He held his hands out and spoke faltering Pegalia. "Give me a weapon."

Ulfar then amazed them all by drawing his own sword and handing it over. "Keep it. I have more."

Captain and squire exchanged a last look and then he left them, shouting orders as he went.

As Thule loomed closer, they heard the Magnons' insane rattle drift across the water. Ulfar's crew pulled on the oars, heading right towards them. Clovis didn't need the telescope now, and what he saw appalled him. The creatures stood shoulder-to-shoulder, bumping and jostling with mindless hunger. They occupied the shore right up into the hills and their calls bored into him, rising and falling in a chaotic symphony. "Sef," he uttered, and looked to the towering lighthouse. Even he hadn't believed the Sef could unleash so much havoc for his cause, and there was the small matter of the iron-fairies to consider. He looked up through the rigging, and saw the skies thick with their own fairy allies. Now the

Therions would have to cut a path through the Magnon, while the allied fairies kept the iron-fays at bay. Would they be enough, or would there be shrivelled skins and countless tiny corpses before Sef was done with them? "I hope you're worth it Janus," he said aloud.

Wolfen bonds were strong and so Sirus, the wolfen who'd doubted his captain, worked the oars doubly hard to make amends. Ulfar had said they were going ashore and ashore they would go. Along the gunwale they'd already hung their shields, and through the curved gaps he saw the sea churn under their oars, and he saw something else too. A face rose briefly from the waves and sink again just as fast. At first he believed it might have been a Merlin, but the face was misshapen and brutish. He pulled at the oar, with one eye on his captain, the other on the waves, and there it came again. *Dear Luna's wolves!* he thought, *but that looked like one of them.* He relinquished the oar.

"Sirus!" his oar-mate growled, "Can't row alone."

"Wait, I see summat!" He leaned over the rolling waves below and bared his teeth. Something was down there.

"No time for sea-puke, grab the oar."

"Wait." There was a brownish shape drifting in the water, and it looked to be clinging to the hull like a giant leech. He was already turning to alert his captain when the thing hurtled out of the water right at him. "MAGNON!" he roared and reached for his sword, but too late.

The Magnon exploded in a spray of water and clamped a hand around his throat. Sirus was dragged forwards, and even before he hit the water it had drunk him empty. There was a revolting crunching sound, and his oar-mate turned to see him literally sucked from his very skin. One moment he was whole, the next he was a bloody dangling pelt. His sword splashed into the sea, and the empowered Magnon clambered up over the shields, rattling with hunger and dripping with blood.

A cry went up, and around The Hornet the seas boiled with hundreds of surfacing Magnon. They barrelled towards the ship, thudding against the timbers and clawing themselves up with heavy clay fingers. Oars were dropped and swords and spears were grabbed. "Magnon!" The cry was universal.

Clovis hurtled down the deck to where one was already half into the ship, aiming for a Caprian struggling to free herself from the oars.

"HELP!" she screamed, and Clovis did just that. His staff plunged into the top of its skull and lightning exploded. The Magnon was shot back into the water like a torpedo, trailing sparks and vanished beneath the waves with a hiss. Now they came in force, hanging from the shields and the ship itself, and their fellows crawled over the others, and the ship began to sway. Soon they would be pulled under and never even make landfall. Once in the water, the Magnon would easily pick them off.

"CLOVIS!" Ulfar roared, slashing at an invader slithering over the rail.

Clovis dragged the Caprian woman free, just as more shapeless hands appeared on the rail and staring clay faces loomed up, dripping and rattling. "Force them back!" He rammed a spear into her hands and shoved her forwards. She plunged the shaft into its eye socket and thrust it back below the waves with a scream.

Clovis bounded back to Ulfar's side, where Magnon were already flopping onto the deck and staggering upright. The Hornet, not to mention every other ship, was besieged. Kolfinnia and the rest were fighting at the bows and crews were up against the gunwale, thrusting and slashing. All around them the seas heaved with an endless tide of monsters and the air was filled with screams and roars and that constant, insane rattle.

"Don't let them aboard!" Ulfar slammed a shield into an enemy's face as it crawled up over the stern, and split its skull down the middle. "Don't let them aboard!"

A scream went up and the fighters on the port side collapsed backwards as a wave of Magnon literally crushed themselves in an attempt to storm the ship. Shields crumpled and swords wavered. Magnon fingers found flesh, and the screams of the dying chilled the blood of the living. "BASTARDS!" Ulfar threw himself into the carnage, skidding and slipping across the blood-soaked deck. He leapt empty clothes and ragged skins, to land in the deepest part of the fighting, battering at all and everything. A Magnon slumped down with its head sliced in a dozen places, but his blow left his sword embedded in its thick fibre and slipped from his grasp. "BASTARDS!" He snatched up a fallen axe and brought it down with savage fury. An arm thudded to the deck, still grasping a steaming wolf skin. Clovis, and now Hilda and Kolfinnia, were suddenly at his side. Lightning-staffs crackled and smoke rolled across the deck.

Kolfinnia screamed and stabbed at one misshapen face after another. Skulls exploded and fluids splashed across her. Magnon died in huge numbers but their bodies slumped across the ship and it began to tip alarmingly. "We'll go down!" she yelled.

Ulfar saw the sea boiling with enemies. They couldn't hope to repel them. They had moments left. The port side was sinking. "FLY!" he commanded.

Kolfinnia and Clovis exchanged mortified looks.

"Take Janus, leave us!" He swung the axe again. A Magnon neck split open and its rattling call became a wet gurgling. "Leave us!"

Callous as it was, Clovis knew they must. He took his staff ready to fly, knowing he must look back and see the fleet overrun and hear the crews' last screams.

"Look!" Tempest saw it first – a silvery flash in the water. There came another and another, and with each flash a Magnon was dragged below the surface.

"Merlins!" Hathwell was hanging from the rigging on the starboard side. "Merlins have come!"

Clovis staggered back and saw salvation.

The waters around Thule now swarmed with mermaids.

They had followed, duty-bound, but warily keeping their distance. Merlins were the most aloof of all Therions, and even their landed kin were a mystery to them. But now their own realm was violated and they rose up armed with glistening blades, hardened scales and cold wrath.

Ulfar had seldom seen a Merlin. The sea-folk were secretive and separate. It was miracle enough that they had come, but he was in for a bigger miracle yet. Great schools of them swept around the beleaguered ships, hacking at the Magnon with toothed blades like swordfish snouts. He saw male and female alike. Their tails were shark-like, while their bodies were the most human of all Therions, but plated with shining scales, and their hair trailed for yards behind them like algal-weed. They whistled and sang their strange language, and as they whisked by they lashed at the Magnon, and severed limbs and heads began to bubble to the surface.

But the Magnon were driven by a bottomless hunger that made them immune to fear or sensibility. The silvery beings in the water were just as enticing as the ones on deck, and they splashed and groped towards them. The Merlins were faster by far, but the Magnon's numbers were endless. Soon enough clay hands clutched at silvery tails and fins, and the Magnon tasted their first mermaid flesh.

Ulfar tore his gaze from the seaward battle, even as the first bloodied scales and skins began to surface. "OARS!" he commanded, and crews now dove for the benches again. They must make land before the Merlin attack lost momentum. "Clovis!" he raged, "Why in Evermore's name are you still here?"

"We'll be gone soon as you make landfall." He snatched at an oar and began to pull.

"No, go now!"

"We can push the Magnon back with spells," he panted. "Create a bridgehead."

Ulfar saw his point. "Agreed. Move over." And he dropped to his side and joined him. "Now row!"

A quick look back, and Clovis was horrified. The sea was a mass of thrashing crimson waves as Merlins fought Magnon. Humbled, he threw himself against the oar and together the crew pushed hard for shore through the raging waters.

Sef watched from the lighthouse summit. From up here the clamour of battle sounded faintly reassuring. He watched the fleet's flagship briefly stalled in the bay, surrounded by Magnon. Something about the raven painted on the sail disturbed him. "Clovis," he realised. The waters were choppy and he narrowed his eyes and looked closer. The sea was full of Merlins. "Bravo Clovis," he applauded.

Chentek twitched and chattered with agitation. "Feed now! Feed now!"

"A moment more. You know what to do?"

Chentek watched the distant ships. "Make sure witch-Clovis and others come unhurt."

"And the rest do as you please with."

The war-fairy cackled in anticipation and waited for the signal, which would come very soon now.

The Magnon blundered into the sea at sight of the approaching ships, trampling their fellows. Kolfinnia saw that their numbers formed an almost solid barrier along the shore. "Ulfar means to land right into their lap?" she asked, incredulous.

"Spells to drive them back," Clovis insisted, "you know any?"

She thought fast. Maybe she could ask the wind and waves to help them, but just then her eye fell upon the lanterns in the rigging and a more practical idea struck her. "Help me!" she scrambled up the ropes and snatched one down. "Empty the oil from the others into this one." She pried the lid up and Clovis began tipping lantern oil inside.

"Your plan?" he asked.

"Fight them with fire."

He grinned, "Then we'll need some fire arrows." He looked around for Ulfar. "Captain, fire arrows, now!"

Ulfar was strapping a shield to his arm. He looked from the oily lantern, to the Magnon and grasped their intentions. "Taal!" he exploded, "Get up here with a brand and arrows or I'll have your beard as my hearth rug."

Clovis took the lantern chain from her. "Let me. I can throw it further."

"Wait!" She took the lantern, now greasy with oil, and whispered against the glass.

"Will that help?"

"I sincerely hope so."

A shout went up, "Land!" They were moments from shore. Around her, she saw fighters crouching with spears ready, waiting to spring from the ship.

Clovis stood, now holding the lantern chain with both hands. "You ready?" he turned to Taal.

The Caprian strung his bow. Someone held a burning rag to its tip and the arrow immediately caught light. "I am now."

"Do it!" Ulfar ordered.

Clovis lifted the lantern and swung it wide, quickly bringing it over his head and spinning it very fast. When it reached its maximum speed he released with a roar and the projectile sailed through the air dragging its jangling chain. It flew across the open water and landed squarely in the Magnon horde.

Glass shattered and oil sprayed across them, glistening on their heads and shoulders, but they pressed on oblivious.

"Fire!" Ulfar barked.

Taal aimed and released.

Every soul held their breath and watched the arrow streak overhead like a pointing finger. It dropped into the Magnon ranks and vanished from sight. There was a crushing moment when nothing happened, and then suddenly an explosion rumbled across the bay. The crew shielded their eyes against the flash and a fireball rolled into the sky. Flames engulfed the Magnon and a hot wind rushed across the water and over the ships. A huge cheer went up and Kolfinnia saw the monsters lumbering blindly, consumed by flames and sizzling and popping as they burned. Many were sagging to their knees, but still they groped and made that awful rattling sound. The need to consume was so powerful that they ignored their own demise.

"More!" Ulfar liked what he saw. "More right now!"

Lanterns were cut down, oil was poured and arrows were readied, and all the while the oarsmen drove them still closer. Before they could fire again, one of the other ships took the initiative, and Clovis saw a fire arrow shoot from its deck. A second explosion rocked the shore, this one lacking Kolfinnia's special touch, but devastating nonetheless. Blackened Magnon barged their way forwards, heedless of the very flames that destroyed them. Their dead formed heaped bonfires belching filthy smoke, and now more oil bombs dropped into their ranks followed by more arrows. The shore became an inferno and with every second the fleet drew closer. *They're going to land right in the middle of that hell.* The thought left Clovis breathless.

"Almost there, last push!" Ulfar went and stood at the bows, ready to be first to land on Thule. He grinned when he saw that the foremost Magnon were now just crumbling corpses. The sea was dusted with ash, while embers swirled down around them. "Clovis, make ready!" He clattered his sword against his shield to rouse his troops.

Clovis took his staff. "Hilda, Kolfinnia?"

Both stood waiting. "Ready."

Next to them Hathwell was fumbling with a shield. "Good luck, and take care, all of you."

Hilda saw now that people could change after all, and she didn't just mean Hathwell. She had changed too. She went to him and took his hand. "This is our second battle this summer, Bertrand."

He smiled, despite everything. "Tongues will wag, Hilly."

"Let them." She leaned forwards and kissed him, and when she pulled back she saw he was more troubled than before.

"Now I've more reason than ever to want you back safe," he admitted.

It was Ulfar who interrupted them. "If you're going Clovis, go now!"

After a last look at their friends, Clovis and his two Lions ran to the rail and clambered part way up the rigging.

"Good luck!" Hathwell shouted again.

They raised their staffs in salute, and then flew, with Clovis leading the way, carrying all their hopes.

"Hornets ashore!" Ulfar roared and at that moment the bows crunched up the beach in an explosion of shingle and juddered to a halt. Ulfar jumped clear, howling in fury and behind he heard a mighty cheer as Therions charged across the deck and crashed down onto the sands. "Shields!" Their only chance was to make a shield wall and batter their enemies back, forging a clear path to the fortress. They found their feet and found their places, and within moments Ulfar stood on Thule, shoulder to shoulder with his crew, with Hathwell on one side, Taal on the other. They locked their shields, hefted their spears, and began to push up the beach aware of other ships now also crashing ashore.

Together they held tight and advanced over a carpet of dead Magnon. The stink of charred earth burned their eyes and nostrils, and the air was bitter with smoke. Ahead, stood a seemingly endless army of Magnon, even now shambling towards them over their charred fellows. Behind him, Hathwell felt other fighters huddle tight, ready to thrust their spears between the forward ranks, creating a double-pronged attack. He briefly glanced skywards, seeking any sign of his friends. For a moment he thought he saw three shapes racing through the skies towards that imposing lighthouse.

"Eyes front!" Ulfar ordered.

Hathwell turned back, but when he dared look again the smoke rolled in obscuring his vision. *Good luck,* he wished them, and in particular Hilda.

Things had changed between them, and he only hoped he lived long enough to rejoice with her.

Clovis and his Lions raced across the infested island, aiming for the Beacon at the summit of Thule lighthouse. The air around them grew thick with fairies of untold species, all of them waiting in dread for Sef's swarm to reveal itself.

Kolfinnia looked back and tried to pinpoint The Hornet, but all she saw were more explosions and shores in flames, and knew her friends were down there in that hell and failure was not an option.

CHAPTER TWENTY-THREE

Tower of echoes

*'If you don't know yourself, then how can you be sure
those thoughts in your head are really yours?'*
Author unknown

He had traversed star systems and crossed realities for this moment,
and now finally his opponent was coming. Sef watched three tiny figures
streak away from the fleet. "At last," he breathed.

Chentek ground his teeth. "Feed, feed!"

"Now is your hour, little war-tick, but remember your orders, or dark
prisons await." He patted the gelding-sack.

Chentek glowered at him, imagining his swarm eating Sef to the bone.
Instead, he simpered obediently and scuttled to the window and flew.

Sef watched him buzz away to a speck. "You were right Iso," he said
grudgingly.

Iso listened from within his staff. *"And what will you do?"*

"When I have Janus, I'll kill the treacherous mite."

"For the sake of this realm?"

"Ha!" he barked, "Have you gone soft? No I'll crush him under my heel
because it pleases me." He wanted to stay and watch the swarm attack the
fleet, it would be amusing, but his guests were coming and there was much
to do. Sef turned from the battle far below and bounded up the steps
towards the Beacon. The reception for Clovis must be perfect, just as Lord
Self had commanded.

She could see Clovis just ahead racing towards the Beacon. The tower was incredibly high and Kolfinnia looked down at the landscape almost half a mile below and wished she hadn't. The height was daunting enough, but seeing the sheer number of Magnon from up here she wondered how anything could stop them.

She curled low and kept in Clovis's wake, where the wind wasn't so fierce. The lighthouse stood at the centre of the fortress and she noticed its myriad sloping roofs were shiny like steel. She was about to look away, when unexpectedly all of them shimmered with movement. She looked again, confused. "Clovis!" she shouted, but he couldn't hear. "Clovis!" The shimmering dissipated and a vast cloud rose up as if the whole structure had come alive. She saw ancient stonework and battered roof slates beneath and understood the metallic cloud rising towards them really *was* alive.

"Iron-fairies!" Skald warned.

She was about to alert Clovis, when he shouted over his shoulder. "Iron-fays!"

"I know!"

"Faster!" To her left, Hilda accelerated. If they didn't reach the Beacon they would be devoured before even touching down.

Kolfinnia crouched lower, tearing through the air now. She risked a look below. The swarm was breaking up, with half heading to the fleet, the rest rising to attack them. "They're attacking!" she screamed. But she was only part right.

The iron-fays had their instructions. One half would rip the fleet apart while the others would drive Clovis into Sef's trap. This required a little manipulation from Chentek, and so while his other kin set about feasting he had duties to carry out. The sooner he was done the quicker he could join the frenzy below. "Bastard Sef!" he cursed as he flew. His belly groaned for blood, but here he was catching flies. "Bastard Therion!" Once they were done here it was about time he showed Sef who was really in charge. Eager to get this over with and feast, he spearheaded his swarm towards the lighthouse. Clovis would get inside all right, just not the way he thought.

"We won't make it!" Kolfinnia saw untold millions of fairies rising to block their way.

"Enter lower down!" Clovis shouted back. There were small windows dotted up the tower's flanks. The highest were his aim. To enter any lower would entail a lengthy climb. "That one," he jabbed a finger to his chosen target – a vacant balcony immediately below the Beacon. "Stay together," he reminded them, and then raced for his goal.

Kolfinnia and Hilda followed in close pursuit, even as the glittering swarm swirled towards them in a great funnel, blocking their way as if guessing their thoughts. To her horror it then split into three wedges and each drove directly for them, moving with hypnotic beauty and terrifying speed. As they closed in she heard the rasp of countless wings and their ravenous chattering. "Clovis!" she cried.

He veered right to avoid them, while the swarm surged between Kolfinnia and Hilda. They tore past close enough to slice through her hair and clothes. The light vanished and her ears filled with the sound of grinding blades. She screamed, expecting attack, but the vortex continued past without even touching her. Nevertheless, she was forced wide of her friends as the wedge split them apart. *"That's exactly what they want!"* Skald warned.

She shielded her face from the wings streaking past. It was like a sea of whirling knives and she couldn't see a thing through it. Somewhere on the other side of it Hilda was likewise lost and looking for her.

Clovis looked back and saw them both veer away. "No!" Their tactics were blindingly clear, but no less effective. He tried to keep course for the Beacon, but a wall of slicing jaws tore past. Sunlight briefly glinted off untold bodies and dazzled him. Momentarily blinded, he flew right into them and it was like being buffeted by flying shrapnel. The swarm engulfed him, shrieking in his ears and nipping at his face, but never attacking. Without thinking he dropped low, hand before his face.

"Where are the others?" Tempest clamoured.

How could he know? He wasn't even sure where he was. The black storm accelerated, driving him even further down. *'Stay together,'* he'd cautioned. How mocking that sounded now. With a furious roar he forced the staff back upwards, but fairies crashed against him, battering his muzzle and his mane.

He tried to plough through them, but they sliced and stabbed at him. Even if they didn't attack, at this rate they would still shred him alive. The swarm parted, almost deliberately, and he saw a small window in the tower's flank. Like it or not, he had to get inside. "Down!" he bellowed, and Tempest obeyed and together they raced for the opening, knowing it was likely Sef's dearest desire.

'Thrust and move, thrust and move.' The command was simple, but if he failed to obey it they'd die. Each fighter thrust their spear or pike at a Magnon, then rammed them with their shield and advanced over them, including Hathwell. The spearmen behind finished them off as they lay jerking on the ground. A third rank then came with axes and swords and smashed what was left. In this way a column of Therions slashed and battered their way through the Magnon horde.

Hathwell was dripping with sweat, his metal knee felt on fire and his shoulders groaned. Another mindless face shambled into view, emitting that piercing rattle. He stabbed the spear in time with Taal and Ulfar beside him, and then the whole line rammed their shields and dropped them. *Thrust and move, thrust and move,* he thought blindly.

Behind them, the fleet were securing a bridgehead on the shore. Meanwhile, in the bay, the Merlins had all but repelled the seaborne Magnon, and were forming a protective cordon around the ships.

"Keep time!" Ulfar growled in reasonable English.

"I'm bloody trying!" he shot back.

"Try harder!"

Beside him, Taal stumbled over something. A half-dead Magnon tried to claw at his ankle, but the fighters behind swung their axes and it moved no more. The fortress crept closer, but slowly. Hathwell saw its monumental architecture and thought the imposing mass was the loveliest thing he'd ever seen. Another explosion boomed somewhere behind, bringing more smoke, more burning monsters. Crushed beside his fellows, he was breathless and hot, and the less said about a Therion's battle-stink the better. He stumbled again and this time fell. A critical gap opened in the shield wall. He tried to scramble up and fill it but suddenly strong hands hauled him up, and a hulking bear-Therion shoved him aside and took his place.

"I can manage." Hathwell tried to squeeze back into line.

"Take a rest!" Ulfar commanded between thrusts.

Hathwell watched the huge brute occupying his place, now ramming with gusto. After mopping his face dry he got on with his job, squeezing back into line while the shield wall continued its slow advance. A sudden scream distracted him. A Magnon had reached through the overlapping shields, and a withered corpse splattered to the ground and a shield rolled away. The Magnon visibly swelled in size, glistening with blood, and attacked again. Fighters rushed to fill the gap and a dozen spear shafts skewered its head. Hathwell saw the vile thing sink down and axes swing. *By God, this might work.* That was his overriding thought right then. It might work, and they might get to the fortress after all. As they slowly edged up the slope, he looked back and saw a well-defended corridor reaching right the way back to the ships. It bristled with spears and around them fires raged in the Magnon ranks. If they could hold this corridor they might just do it.

He heard a shriek and thought nothing of it. But then came another and for a moment the shield wall wavered as fighters looked up. Hathwell cracked another head open, making sure it never got up again. There was another scream, followed by a despairing cry. The language was a mystery, but the terror was plain. He wiped sweat from his eyes, and saw the Therions around him all now staring skywards, and he risked a look, and saw them at once. A glittering cloud was falling like a blizzard, heading right towards them.

"Shields!" Ulfar refused to let a few iron-fairies distract them. "Shields! Thrust and move! Shift you dung-breath cattle."

"But the iron-fays?" Taal cried.

"The fairy-nations must deal with them. Keep moving!"

A terrible noise engulfed the battlefield, as billions of fays all screamed at once.

Hathwell daren't look up. He kept moving as Ulfar ordered, while above him in the sky, two impossibly vast armies met in ferocious combat.

Burning Hearts, those legendary heads of fairy-nations, had gathered the largest fairy force ever assembled on Earth. They outnumbered Chentek's fighters by almost twenty to one. Species of incredible diversity had come to stop the infection spreading, for iron was the most abundant element and if the plague wasn't sterilized, the entire world would be overrun. Almost nine hundred Burning Hearts from all major nations had kept their stations above, and watched helplessly as the Magnon first stormed the ships and then fought the Therions on the shore. It took much resolve not to break away and at least try to help, but soon enough the Burning Hearts would have a battle all their own, one that mere Therions couldn't hope to take a hand in. Soon iron would come.

Each Burning Heart stayed central to their nation, hovering far above the battlefield where the air was quiet and strangely peaceful. Smoke drifted up from below and sunlight finally burned away the last of the fog. The island of Ultima Thule materialised from the mist and the fairy-nations were shocked to see its shores burning with war. Here of all places, at the place where gods speak. It was unthinkable that war had come to the deepest part of Hethra and Halla's dream.

The nations waited, and the occasional scream drifted up from below. They waited, pondering their chances. Kercus and the entire nation of Tresslain Wood had been exterminated, would they stand any better chance despite their advantage? The Burning Hearts all listened. A distant crackling sound wafted towards them, and they turned to see the fortress shimmer under the blossoming sun. The iron-fays were on the move and heading for the beleaguered Therions. Now was their moment.

"OAK ENDURES!" the call went up.

With a roar, the nine hundred 'Hearts all plunged down to meet them. Vast flocks, entire nations on the move, raced after them as oak, ash, fire and flower once again faced the wrath of iron.

Kolfinnia shot through the window and rolled across the flags. She hit the wall and whirled around, ready for fairies to strike any moment, but they didn't. The sky outside darkened as the swarm hovered, but they just hung there. There was no glass, no shutters. They could pour in and kill her, but they didn't.

She clambered up, panting and scratched, and slumped against the wall. Somewhere out there Hilda and Clovis needed her help, but she was trapped here. She glanced around and saw a broad spiral of stone stairs. It was dark but for the window's meagre light. She risked a step towards it, but the swarm rattled in response. *I suppose I'm not meant to go that way,* she realised. It helped nothing to think she was doing just what Sef wanted. "Up," she decided, seeing the stairs. "To the top, that's where Clovis will go too."

"And Sef," Skald reminded her.

"Well we won't achieve anything staying here." She drew her wand and reluctantly began climbing the steps, leaving the angry swarm behind.

After a short while her caution faded, and she began to run. It was dark but someone had lit torches along the walls, which burned with an angry orange light and made the air dirty. She cupped her mouth as she passed one. It made her skin crawl to think someone had lit them for her benefit. *Clovis,* she thought, *I have to get to Clovis.* She was terrified that he'd face Sef alone, and terrified he'd open the vessel by himself. "He can't die alone, he needs us!" she heard herself say.

"Or you need him," someone replied.

She stopped and looked about. "Skald?"

"What! Just keep going."

"You didn't hear that?"

"Imagination, that's all."

She looked back down the spiral and waited, but nothing came. Cautiously she set off again, but the steps were like a cruel illusion. They kept winding on and on, and she was sure they weren't getting any higher. After a while she stopped to catch her breath. *Must get to the top,* she told herself, *must save Clovis.* Secretly, she planned on someone else opening the vessel.

Not for him though Kolfinnia. For you. So you don't have to be the one to go on alone.

This time the voice pulsed in harmony with her own thoughts, and she couldn't be sure if it was hers or not. It made sense though. "I'm doing this for Clovis," she gasped.

Not your Self?

She frowned and rubbed her temple. *Self?* The tower was having a strange effect on her.

"Kolfinnia?" It was Skald.

"Nothing," she lied, "let's keep going." She set off again. More steps wheeled past, more dirty torches. The air was smoky and dead and her footfalls echoed like mocking hand-claps. *Each step shortens his life.* She pressed on, troubled by the thoughts in her head, troubled that they might not be hers. "Just anxiety," she pretended.

Think about it Kolfinnia. What is Janus really — he is master of doorways, and what are doorways?

"Opportunities." She stopped and leaned on the wall, feeling faint. "Opportunities? Why did I just say that?" she asked vaguely.

"Kolfinnia?" Skald was worried now. *"Who are you talking to?"*

"I'm fine." She pressed a hand to her eyes.

And such amazing opportunities you're throwing away by opening the vessel.

She considered for a second, and her inflamed curiosity was enough for the voice to continue.

Whoever commands Janus commands all doorways, the spiritual and the physical. The voice took on a seductive tone. *Even flesh and blood.*

Flesh and blood?

Oh yes, the voice agreed.

I could use Janus to change myself, she realised.

Such a thing is child's play for a god. But what would you change? the voice tempted. *Surely you're young and beautiful enough aren't you?*

She staggered up a few more stairs. *Not for him, not for Clovis. He's a Therion. And what if you were too? Would he stay then?*

She flopped against the wall feeling confused. Just where did these ideas come, and more chillingly, why did they make sense?

"Kolfinnia! What's wrong?" Skald felt he was losing her.

"I'm fine!" she snarled. "I'm just thinking that's all, let me get on with it!" He fell into a worried silence, and her thoughts again turned to that dark but tantalizing possibility. *Janus could turn me into a Therion, like Peri, couldn't he?*

The voice declined to answer.

Well? she demanded. *Flesh and blood you said, isn't that just another kind of doorway?*

There was a long silence. *What would be the point if Clovis is lying dead?*

She saw a terrible picture of him choking on the vessel's poisons. *And even if Clovis lives, if Janus sails into the black then I'll be stuck as plain old Kolfinnia forever.* Suddenly she thought of Peri's luxurious coat, slender frame and brilliant eyes. No wonder Clovis desired her. *Desire,* she thought greedily, and with it came a pang of jealousy so strong that her gut clenched.

"Kolfinnia, what's wrong?" It was Skald again.

"Nothing." She wiped sweat from her face.

"Kolfinnia, you're not thinking straight," he warned.

"I'm fine," she insisted, but softer this time. "Just something odd about the tower, I'm alright."

"Good, then keep going."

Yes, she thought, *we've got to reach the top.*

The trouble was, now she had different reasons to get there and she couldn't separate that outside voice from her own. She took a deep breath and continued, unaware of the intruder in her head.

Hilda had a cut to her neck, but otherwise she was unhurt. Like Kolfinnia she'd been forced towards a 'safe' window and entered the tower. Once inside, she began climbing, with Five, her thunder-sprite, sat on her shoulder. "No," she concluded his earlier question. "This spiral's too narrow."

"So there are small separate spirals climbing the tower?" he realised.

"Yes, and we've to hope Kolfinnia and Clovis have found one also."

"Found one? Had one shoved down our throats more like."

"I like this no more than you." She tried not to make too much noise.

"What happens at the top?" he whispered.

"Clovis opens the vessel."

"No, I meant this Sef? Surely he's waiting."

"I don't doubt it," she agreed.

There was a weighty silence and she could almost hear him thinking.

"If he's anything like Clovis he'll be hard to fight."

She scowled. "What do you mean?"

"It might be best to let Clovis finish him."

"Five, we're in this together." He was normally so bold. This didn't sound right coming from him. "Now's not the time for the shakes."

"I'm not scared," he reasoned, "but we're only here because of him."

He had a point she conceded. They pressed further on, and by now the spiral was beginning to make her woozy. "I hope Kolfinnia's alright," she added fretfully.

"Of course. Why else would Valonia choose her for coven-mother."

Again, she first frowned at his words before finding they carried some plausibility.

"And passed hrafn-dimmu into her keeping too, a sign of great trust for one so young and inexperienced," he continued.

"Shh! Keep the chatter down," she urged.

He gripped her shoulder, and again there was a considered silence. "Of course it could've been you."

"Me what?"

"Could have been, *should* have been."

"Five," she huffed, "what in Oak's name are you rambling about?"

He leaned closer to her ear. "I'm very proud of you," he whispered.

Now she stopped, frightened. "Five, what's wrong with you?" She peered sideways at him.

"At Stormwood. I don't know how you kept your cool, what with coven-mother Kolfinnia ordering you around. By my word, she's young enough to be your granddaughter and she's the one in command. Mocking isn't it?" he chuckled lightly.

Suddenly she felt clammy.

"And now she's put us all in danger just so she can follow Clovis." He shook his head reproachfully. "Maybe Valonia was wrong."

She licked her lips and thought hard. "You're right," she pretended, "insolent girl jumped the ladder and suddenly she's Valonia's heir."

"Yes!" His eyes glinted. "Maybe all of Stormwood feels the same." Encouraged, he leaned closer and whispered treacherously, "Better for all if she didn't come back."

Then she knew.

"OFF ME!" she cried and hurled him away. She lost her balance, tripped and fell and Five landed close by, spitting and hissing.

"What's got into you!" he erupted.

"Stay back!" She levelled her wand at him.

He shook with exasperation, "Hilda, WHAT are you doing!"

"Who *are* you?" she demanded, wand still raised.

His beak fell open in astonishment. "What?"

"Where's Five? What have you done with him?" She scrambled upright. "Tell me or by Oak I'll split you in two!"

Stunned, he backed away. "Hilda, lower the wand. You're not yourself." *SELF.*

"Hilly, it's me." And he hopped a step higher, into the greasy torchlight, trying to prove it.

Her arm slowly wilted. "Five?"

He stared up at her, unsure. "You weren't yourself."

"*I* wasn't!" she pointed to herself. "What of all those terrible things *you* just said!"

He shook his head in denial.

"But you did!"

"No." His face was full of conviction. "Hilda I haven't spoken a word since we entered this tower."

She took a sharp breath, not sure whether to believe him. "Don't toy with me!"

"Hilly, neither of us has spoken a word until just now."

Suddenly she felt dizzy with realisation. "No you haven't." She regarded him shamefully. "But something did. Forgive me?"

"Consider it done."

She managed a weak smile and then both of them glanced at the beckoning stairs twisting away into the darkness. Wondering who or what was listening and waiting.

Clovis charged up the spiral, just as he had when fleeing Vega, which had set him on course to meeting Kolfinnia. *Kolfinnia.* He couldn't shake her from his mind. 'Don't get separated' he'd said, now he didn't even know where he was, let alone her.

If she reached the top before him, Sef would be waiting to kill her, or worse, and he had a nasty feeling she wanted to get there first. Somehow all their best intentions were tripping them up today. *Intentions or desires?* he thought vehemently. *Is there any difference?* As he ran, he slipped his pack free and elected to carry it in his arms. Inside was the most important thing in creation, and although afraid for his friends, he felt a sense of wonder that this day had been aeons in coming. "I won't let you down Janus, I swear," he panted. But just like thoughts of Kolfinnia, he couldn't escape the idea that Janus was close to death. So strong was his conviction that he even suffered the insane notion that the world was reshaping itself to suit this nightmare. That Janus *was* dying simply because *he* thought it. As he hurtled up the steps he pulled aside the cloth, needing to see the figure within. "Janus, do you hear me?"

Janus rocked and swayed, but there were no signs of life and even the fluid looked cloudy and cold.

"Janus if any part of you can hear me then please answer." He doubled his stride and took great bounds. His sword and armour clattered and he almost didn't hear him.

"Clovis? Is that you?"

Janus's voice drifted towards him from the glass and he could have wept with relief. He stopped and held the jar up to his face. "Janus, thank the stars, I thought you were past help."

"Where are we?"

"Thule, a place of ascension, just as you told me to find." He couldn't help but feel proud of his efforts.

"Then the time is close." His voice was faint. "After so long, Clovis, I'm afraid."

"There's no reason to be afraid, at last this is your freedom."

Janus rolled feebly in the liquid. "Is this the right thing though?"

"Janus, only your ascension can bring about change," he argued.

"Self is too established Clovis, too strong. For pity's sake let me be, let me rest. I died once, is that not enough? Would you cast me out to see Self kill me a second time?"

"I – I don't understand?" he stammered.

"I am old and weak Clovis. Leave me to dream. Leave this vessel intact, take Kolfinnia and go without shame. Tell them I commanded you and who can refuse a god? Tell them."

As he floundered for a reply he imagined himself at Stormwood. Wouldn't a small piece of him gladly live out his days there with Kolfinnia, free of guilt?

"You love her Clovis I know," Janus confided, "and who can blame you. But I'm afraid. Leave me to dream, and take her for yourself."

"Myself?" He saw his ghostly reflection staring back at him from the glass. "My Self."

"Both of us win what we desire," Janus said softly. "Is that so bad? Leave me and turn for home."

"Home." Without realising he began to turn, shuffling on the step until he faced down the spiral.

"Home," Janus lulled him.

But which home, Stormwood or Vega? he wondered. Vega; his real home, where Tiber had fought along with so many others to ensure Janus reached this pivotal moment. Vega; where his sister and loyal survivors were perhaps battling the Unitari right this moment. Vega; the living heart of witchdom that Self's foul scum had violated. "Vega is my home, and I cannot go there!" he snarled. Anger cleared his mind and when he looked, the vessel was clamped between his hands and misted with his breath. He brushed the moisture away and saw Janus floating lifeless inside. The broken god had never spoken at all. "Forgive me Janus," he stroked the glass, "I mistook you for another." Tenderly he covered the vessel again.

"Clovis?" It was Tempest.

"It's as I feared, Self is here and its strength is great."

"It spoke to you?"

He secured the vessel and pulled his lightning-staff from his shoulder, glad to hold it again. "Yes, it spoke to me. Its lies are skilful." He looked around, imagining duplicate spirals like this one, and insidious lies drifting down from the entity in the stars above.

"Lies? Oh no coven-father, merely echoes, echoes of your own desires," a voice came.

Clovis wrinkled his muzzle in a silent snarl, hefted his staff and started up the spiral once more.

Such huge numbers put the fairy-nations at a distinct advantage, and they dropped from the sky in armadas so dense that the Therions were convinced twilight was falling.

First to come were magma-fairies, their most ardent fighters. Such heat radiated from them that they were compelled to form their own unit, and all others kept a distance. Under leadership of Morgus, a Burning Heart with molten wings and searing breath, they first swirled under the iron-fairy cloud and then pierced the very heart of it. The whole manoeuvre was like a massive upper cut. Instantly thousands of iron-fays exploded in flames and a terrible scream went up. Melted fays tumbled from the sky in smoking trails, as the glowing dagger carried forwards into the cloud, seeking the source of the infection. "Hand him over!" Morgus grappled with an iron-fay, pumping heat through its body, torturing the answer out of it. "Where is Chentek? WHERE!" Red-hot fingers sank into its hide. "TELL ME!"

It hardly felt the pain, only the hunger. "Living-iron!" It snapped at his head and flailed at him.

"Useless!" Morgus spat and with a single twist he tore its head off and set about seeking another, and there were many to choose from. On and on Morgus crashed through the swarm, questioning and killing as he went. His vanguard surrounded him, keeping them at bay and protecting their Lord, but while the magma-fairies were few, iron was many. Savage and insensible they might be, but even the iron-fays grasped the threat. They broke away from fighting the lesser species, and the killing cloud steadily condensed around Morgus and his band.

"What the hell's that?" Hathwell saw a glowing wedge in the sky. It looked like a spear tip and it streaked right into the iron-fay swarm. Sparks filled the heavens and showered down, and for a moment it appeared as if the stars were falling.

Ulfar grasped his shock if not his words. "Lava-fairies!" he said between blows. "Now keep killing!"

Hathwell plunged his sword over and over, until a desperate scream froze him.

"Kill it, kill it!" someone howled.

He turned and saw a grossly bloated Magnon crash through the shield wall. It was so gorged that it looked pregnant. *How many has it killed to grow so big?* he thought in horror. A spear was lunged and he saw something very disturbing: the creature ducked to avoid the blow. So far they'd been blind to the danger. "They're learning," he realised, "Ulfar they're learning!" Judging from its size the one stomping towards him had learned very well indeed. Another Therion charged it, again with a spear, but the Magnon merely grabbed the shaft and hauled its bearer of his feet and right towards itself. "No!" Hathwell knew what would happen. The stunned Therion landed right in its arms, and it grabbed him and drank him dead in a heartbeat. There was a sickly 'pop' as his hide burst, and the Magnon groaned ecstatically as it further increased in size. *God save us, but there's something human about it!* The idea terrified him.

It veered Hathwell's way, battering fighters aside, and towered over him. "Ulfar!" he cried, but the captain was jammed in the shield wall, hacking away for all his worth. The Magnon literally fell towards him, intending to crush him, and Hathwell stumbled and landed hard on his back. He held his spear up, and without conscious thought the wind-spell burst out of his mouth.

The words Hilda taught him saved his life.

A brief but strong gust swept over him. The creature slowed and struggled against it, long enough for a gigantic bear-Therion to remove its head with a great hammer. There was a satisfying crack, like an expert cricket hit, and the ugly head shot across the shield wall and back into the mob to be trampled flat, while the body exploded an ocean of gore across all and everyone.

Hathwell lay in the mud, shaking and dripping with ooze. His eyes rolled up to see his rescuer was the blacksmith from Hope. The massive bear-Therion tipped him a casual nod and waded back into the fighting. He staggered to his feet, bewildered by his first real spell and the horror of it all. "They're learning. Ulfar, they're learning!" he warned. But Ulfar's English wasn't as good as his Pegalia and his warning went unheeded.

It was a brave attempt, but the magma-fairies were too few. At last the enemy overwhelmed the vanguard around Morgus and pounced in endless numbers. But still he fought on, leaving a trail of incinerated bodies as he carved a path through their ranks looking for their prime infector. "Chentek! Bring me Chentek!" The swarm landed in wave after wave, biting and stabbing, but he ripped them away and flew on heedless, protected by his tremendous heat. Any other foe would have fallen back, but the iron-fays were crazed and undaunted. More fell on him until he was at the centre of a huge mass, and unable to fly they fell like a stone from the sky.

Searing heat cascaded off him, cremating those clinging to his back, but others scrambled to take their place. Morgus spat curses and flames, he grappled and wrenched at them as they fell like a doomed comet, trailing dead and dying.

Above him, he saw the sky filled with war, and across the whole of Thule tiny bodies drifted down like snow. They had come so resolute, yet if he with all his earth-fire couldn't even find this Chentek, then what hope was there for the rest, he wondered? *Fire can't stop them,* he realised, *can anything?* Iron fingers ripped at his hide and iron teeth clamped around his neck. His assailants died instantly, but others took their place and the wounds grew deeper with each try. Morgus killed until he forgot his own purpose and when he looked through a tiny gap in his smothering foe and saw the earth looming close, he smiled in gratitude. "Oak Endures," he whispered.

A moment later they hit the ground and Morgus and his attackers exploded in flames.

Hathwell took up a fallen shield and barged back into line. "Ulfar, the Magnon, they're getting cleverer!"

Ulfar impaled one right through the mouth and snarled with pleasure.

"Ulfar!"

"Keep killing!" It appeared this was his favourite English phrase.

"But —," just then he stopped. A sound cut through the battle. Alien yet familiar. The Magnon's chant had changed and at once they suddenly and unexpectedly fell back. Ulfar and the rest jeered at them as they did, and only Hathwell felt a sense of unease. They shambled back, away from the spear tips and formed a dense wall of blank faces. Many were weapon-scored, and their hides glistened under the noon sun. Steam drifted up from the sheer bulk of their numbers, and Hathwell realised he was parched and needed water.

"Push on!" Ulfar made to go.

"Wait!" Hathwell shoved the shield into his ribs and stopped him. "They're getting cleverer."

"Don't know 'keverer', now push on!" he argued.

"Not keverer," he groaned and groped frantically for the right word, and when he found it he shouted it repeatedly and the whole shield wall seemed to flinch.

Ulfar began to see what he meant. It also dawned on him that the Magnon had fallen silent, and not just here on the front line. Right the way across Thule, the Magnon stood silent and still. "I like them more when they speak," Hathwell whispered.

"I like them more when they die," Ulfar corrected.

A Magnon stumbled forwards from the rest and the shields rattled as fighters locked again. "Wait!" Taal called.

The creature dipped its domed head and stared intently at the ground. The silence was terrible. Hathwell could hear screaming fairies high above, and a far off sound like starlings.

"What's the thing doing?" Ulfar grimaced with disgust.

"Learning," Hathwell realised.

"Keverer?" Ulfar was learning too.

"Yes, cleverer." He raised his shield a fraction higher. *Come on Clovis,* he pleaded.

The Magnon bent clumsily, stooped and pulled something from the mud and regarded it blankly. It was a broken spear. Suddenly it made a single booming sound deep in its chest and Hathwell jerked in surprise. One by one the horde took up the chant, like a slow war drum.

Boom - Boom - Boom - Boom.

Hathwell swallowed. It reminded him of a war-drum.

Boom - Boom - Boom - Boom.

The Magnon holding the broken spear, lifted its head and regarded them all. Its eyes were empty clay sockets, but Hathwell had no doubt that something inside was looking back at them. It came at them, not shambling now but walking. Spears were raised again and shields clattered. It walked right towards Ulfar. "Ha! Not so keverer after all!" Ulfar grinned and lunged.

Incredibly the Magnon ducked, avoiding the blow and stepped back. Its movements were still clumsy, but there was something undeniably human about its intent.

The Magnon swayed side to side, evaluating its foe. The thing with the pointed stick was preventing it from feasting. If it could get past the sticks and the blades it could fill its emptiness.

Boom - Boom - Boom - Boom. The sound rocked the earth.

It came again, expecting the same, but Ulfar gave a nod and it was Taal who caught it blind side and rammed a spear through its neck. "Ha! How keverer is that!" Ulfar cheered.

The Magnon collapsed and lay still and the booming stopped.

What now? Hathwell thought. "Dear God," he breathed when he saw.

As one, the Magnon bent and copied the first. Not just those here, but right across Thule, even those at the rear who hadn't even set eyes on the Therions yet. Tens of thousands of them were compelled to obey a race command. They bent and clawed at the earth, most grasping nothing, while others clutched mud, stones and bones, anything.

The things with the pointed sticks were preventing it from feasting. If they could get past the sticks and the blades they could fill their emptiness.

Right now this idea blazed in all of them. Get past the stick. Fill the emptiness. They learned by mimicry.

"They're going to throw mud at us?" Ulfar stood slack mouthed, unsure whether to be afraid or amused.

"It's not the mud that's dangerous," Hathwell said, "it's the idea."

The Magnon began that ominous booming again, and shields were raised. Once the sound was loud enough to make their ears throb, they came at them. The Magnon advanced, but kept their line this time.

"Forwards!" Ulfar roared.

The shield wall started forwards again, now bristling with more spears than ever. The first Magnon reached the lethal tips and Hathwell wasn't surprised when he saw it hesitate. Spears were thrust and it tried to bat them aside. The rest now surged forwards and snatched at spears and tried to drag their owners from the wall.

If they could get past the sticks and the blades they could fill their emptiness.

Their strength was horrendous and Hathwell saw a spear grabbed and lifted vertical, with its owner still clutching it for dear life. "Let go you fool!" he shouted. Too late. The spear flipped backwards and the Therion was catapulted into the Magnons and vanished from sight.

Clay hands scrambled for sustenance and there was a ghastly scream. "Clever!" Hathwell roared out his fears and thrust with desperate force. Around him the Therions finally began to understand their danger and closed ranks tighter, as a new and more deadly Magnon resumed their attack.

Fighters roared and shoved the wall forwards, but now the Magnon weren't such easy targets. The fighting became fierce and the column began to slow. Hathwell looked towards the fortress gates, so close, but not getting any closer. Therions screamed and brayed, the Magnon boomed, and in the chaos, nobody noticed the tiny fairy corpses that drifted down from the sky in greater and greater numbers. The iron-fairies were breaking through.

CHAPTER TWENTY-FOUR

Winter comes early

'An empty vessel already holds the most important thing of all: silence.
For it is only in silence that we realise we are not empty.
Author unknown

At last the spiral's end loomed. Kolfinnia emerged onto a large landing with a vaulted roof and a flagged floor. The only way out was a set of huge doors. Banners depicting Astriss hung on either side of the gateway. "That's the way to the Beacon, it has to be."

Before rushing up there, she went to the far wall, where a gallery of arches looked out across Thule. The wide ledge was plastered with bird droppings, and a few gulls waddled away as she approached. She looked down, and inhaled sharply when she saw the fighting far below. Ulfar's column was so close to the fortress, but it hardly looked to be moving.

"Look up," Skald warned.

She did, and saw the skies swirled with warring fairies. In the middle of them, something like a burning rock fell like a meteor. "Dear Oak," she gasped.

"All the more reason to press on. It's the only way we can help them," Skald judged.

She backed away from the gallery, and back to her own problem. "The doors won't be locked. You know that don't you?"

"I know."

"He's just waiting for us." She ached for someone to make this decision for her, but choice was an illusion. She must go up there, even though Sef was waiting, even though she would see Clovis die.

"You're in pain my girl," a voice came.

She whirled around and saw a shadowy figure watching from the corner.

"Perhaps I can help?" it said again.

She knew the voice, and from the burning in her staff she guessed Skald did too. "Valonia?"

She came forwards, and she was all she ever had been. The same blue dress, the same glittering eyes and steely hair.

Kolfinnia stepped away. "Another trick?"

She spread her hands. "You've seen Evermore with your own eyes, is it really so incredible for a soul to come back when their loved ones need them most?"

Tears blurred her eyes and her throat bulged. "I want to believe it's you," she sobbed.

"Then do so," the old woman smiled.

"It is her!" Skald trilled.

"Valonia what do I do?" her shoulders slumped. "I don't know what to do."

"Yes you do. You desire to save Clovis. Always follow your heart's desire Kolfinnia." She clenched her fists. "Always!"

Inside his staff Skald listened wholeheartedly.

Kolfinnia stood tall. "Save Clovis."

"Clovis is obsessed with the vessel," she preached. "Take it from him, save him from himself. Don't let him open it. Keep for yourself."

"And then everything will be alright!" She pictured herself as elegant as Peri, and Clovis thanking her for saving him from his madness.

Valonia beamed at her, "Very well done my girl."

Kolfinnia's heart raced in rapture. She knew what to do, and she had no fear. "Blessings on you Valonia," she blew her a kiss, spun around and ran for the doors. Everything was clear now and even Skald buzzed happily, blessed to have seen his wonderful Valonia again.

A gull sitting on the ledge watched them go. All it had seen saw was a young woman enter the chamber, talk briefly to thin air and dash out again. It yawned unconcerned, tucked its head beneath its wing and went back to sleep.

Now they weren't making ground at all. The Magnon were grasping at the spears or swivelling away from the blows, and it was all they could do just to keep them back. He knew eventually the column would be forced to retreat, but would they make it to the ships at all?

Taal bleated as a Magnon reached through the shields and snatched at his mail shirt, and Hathwell almost wrenched his shoulder from its socket in a bid to hack at the arm. He chopped away with mad fury and the arm pulled back, now in concertina slices, and Taal bellowed something in way of thanks.

Hathwell glanced longingly at the fortress gates, less than a hundred yards away. But their column had ground to a halt. He was still half looking at them when something curious buzzed into view, landed on Taal's shoulder and began to bite. The battle-weary Caprian didn't notice at first, and then he yelled and smacked a hand to the pain. The iron-fairy scuttled away, around his back and delved into his thick mane and resumed gnashing. "What the hell goes on here?" he spluttered, trying to reach around.

"Stay still!" Hathwell seized the wriggling thing and tore it free.

"Damn it!" A good clump of his fur came with it.

It thrashed in his grip, squeaking and spitting, and set about chewing his fingers off. "Shit!" Hathwell screamed and flung it to the floor, but it sank its teeth into his thumb and just hung there. "Bloody shit!" He jerked violently and the thing shot off and splattered into the mud. Without thinking he stamped on it.

"Iron-fairy!" Taal looked up. The first of them were slipping through, and that meant the fairy-nations were losing the battle.

"Does this blasted day get any better?" Hathwell clenched his fingers around his wounded thumb. To his horror a second one dropped down. It glanced off Taal's shield and tumbled to the ground. He saw it scuttle away and vanish before he could snatch at it.

"They're coming now!" Taal shouted warning to anyone who would hear. "Iron-fays!"

"Iron-fays?" Ulfar whirled around. His tongue was red and his jaws were dripping. "Where?"

"Iron!" someone shouted, and a similar chorus swept through the ranks. All around them stray iron-fairies were landing to feed. They tumbled down, breathless and weak from battle, and so easily dealt with, but just like the Magnon soon they would come in force and then their problems would really begin.

Hathwell's gaze went again to the fortress. Hilly was in danger and they were trapped here. Booming Magnon surrounded them, blood-hungry fays began to fall from the sky and just then something huge rocked the shield wall and the line was pushed back an inch. The rout of the Therions had begun.

In the skies above, the fairy-nations were ragged and bloody. They still outnumbered their foes but far less now. They simply weren't strong enough to fight iron, and no matter how the Burning Hearts hunted for the elusive Chentek, there was no sign of him. The magma-fairies had killed huge numbers, but finally their force had been overwhelmed. The fairy-nations did what they could to protect their allies below, driving massive blocks at each attempt, but each counter-charge cost them dear and their numbers and resolve were being steadily eroded.

With both Magnon and fays to contend with, it looked certain the Therions would be finished. The battle for Ultima Thule would be remembered as the beginning of the end for the faded-realm.

"See anything?" Five asked quietly.

Hilda peered around the column again, and into a chamber identical to the one Kolfinnia had just entered. "Just a curved chamber with a gateway at the end."

"The way upstairs."

She let out a long breath. "The way upstairs," she agreed.

"This Sef will be waiting."

She rapped knuckles against her wand. "Good." Outside she could hear distant screaming and crying gulls. She stepped silently into the chamber. "Staff please," she whispered.

He vanished without a sound, and the staff in her hands became a weapon again.

She took in the whole room, wary of illusion and echoes. After touching her wand for luck she padded quietly into the chamber and towards the last set of doors.

Clovis rested his hands on the wood and listened for sounds beyond. He'd not only found the chamber at the top of the spiral, he'd climbed that last set of steps. The door at the end was the only barrier now between him and the Beacon. "I'm here Tiber," he whispered, "and what I do I do for you and all of Vega." No echo or retort came back, but he knew for certain Self was watching through that cosmic connection, like an eye at a keyhole. "And soon Janus is going to ascend through that connection and blind that eye." He smiled grimly and pushed the handle, but the door wouldn't budge. It was locked fast, and as implacable as stone.

Kolfinnia had no such trouble, and she listened, just as Clovis did. Beyond the door she sensed the Beacon. "Sef's in there."

"Clovis?" Skald asked.

She pressed harder, trying for him. "I don't think so." Her fingers curled around the handle. It was a huge iron affair shaped like a dragon, and already she knew it wouldn't be locked. Her thumb rested on the latch as she waited for her mind to settle. Outside, fairies and Therions were dying for this moment. She took a deep breath, raised her staff, thumbed the latch and pushed the door open.

"Bastard!" Hathwell slapped at his neck, ripped it free and threw the iron-fay down, and again put his boot to good use. Around him, Therions were trying to swat them out of the air and keep the Magnon at bay, but it was a battle slowly becoming a defeat. So far the iron-fays were a painful distraction, soon they would be a murderous swarm. "Ulfar, we must make a last push for the fortress. Once inside we'll be safe!"

Ulfar thought the same and certainly didn't need anyone to tell him so. The gateway was a mere forty yards away. Forty bloody and deadly yards stood between them and annihilation. Something in his head clicked and he decided that despite the odds, they were going to reach that gate. "FOLLOW ME!" he howled, broke the wall and battered away at the Magnon blocking his path. It crumpled to the ground and he laughed like a savage as he hacked it to pieces.

"Do or die!" Hathwell had never been more literal, and he joined Ulfar's insane stampede.

Hack - Slash - Batter. Hack - Slash - Batter. Weapons bit and Therions screamed.

Ulfar roared and raved, swinging his sword left and right chopping and killing anything in his way. Behind him the Therions charged into the fight, and surrendering themselves to the onslaught they became as mindless as Magnon. On and on they fought, heedless of death or defeat. Magnon fell in pieces, Therions screamed and died, madness engulfed them and Hathwell remembered the incredible berserks of Wellesley Hall and became like them in spirit.

Thirty yards now.

Hack - Slash - Batter. Hack - Slash - Batter. Magnon boomed and dead fairies continued to rain down.

At his back he felt hot and stinking Therions ram home their attack. Blades gleamed and he was overcome with the wild ecstasy of war and death. The Magnon saw something had changed and tried to press them back and two opposing forces piled up against each other like mountain ranges.

Twenty-five yards now.

"ON! ON! ON!" Ulfar slavered and whirled his sword like a windmill. If they didn't get to the gateway they would die. Hope's blacksmith shattered heads with that great war-hammer. Magnon were split open from groin to chin. Swords stabbed, raked and hacked. "ONWARDS!"

Twenty yards.

They were just twenty stubborn yards from the gate when the Magnon finally summoned enough strength to halt their charge. The shield wall reached its limit and stopped, and Hathwell felt fury drain from a hundred hearts and strength pour from tired arms. Magnon flocked around them, booming and clicking in triumph and the sky began to darken as the iron-plague descended to feed. "Sorry Hilly," his chest burned and he chased his breath, "God knows we tried." He heard shouts of dismay as iron-fays dropped on them like burning coals and began to bite. Beside him, he heard Ulfar panting and muttering in some unknown language: a final prayer perhaps? The sound of chattering starlings rose up around them like drowning waters, and Hathwell raised his crumpled sword and looked with longing at the gate. Hilda was in there, she might need him but he couldn't reach her. Instead he was trapped out here and soon they would all die. They were beaten.

Who can care about the weather when all the earth falls into war? No sensible Therion, or man, would think to even look. The sky was filled with fairies, both friend and foe, and whether there be snow, hail or sun up there as well was immaterial. But not today. Today the weather was vital.

High above Thule, a cold front of air finally rolled across the island. It had come a long way and taken many days. Nobody looked. Not the beleaguered fairy-nations hunting Chentek. Not the Therions fighting through mud and monsters to reach the lighthouse. Not Hathwell the lone human in their ranks. Not the Magnon, who were too mindless, or the iron-fays too consumed with hunger. The only creature to notice this anomaly was a soaring eagle.

It navigated the air currents above Thule, and saw a great bank of cloud prowling across the sky. It was the colour of tarnished pewter and it towered impossibly high. The eagle recognised them as snow clouds at once. Odd for this time of year perhaps, but nature was nature. It lost interest and pursued the now shifting thermals, as the cold air advanced, pushing everything else aside.

The eagle was just a speck heading westwards when the cloud finally reached Thule, and no living thing, eagle or fairy, man or Therion, noticed the first snowflakes begin to fall. The only army that could possibly stand against Chentek's plague had at last arrived.

Kolfinnia cleared the last steps and at last arrived in the Beacon. She had expected Sef to pounce on her and a hundred other things, but what she hadn't expected was to be awed. The structure was magnificent. *It's tall enough to hold a kraken!* she wondered. The room's diameter must have exceeded one hundred yards and the glass walls were held upright by thick stone pillars supporting a vaulted roof. It was more like a cathedral than a lighthouse, and the reflector at its heart was nothing more than a shrine. The disc was a crystal lens of unimaginable beauty. The sheer complexity of its polished surfaces was staggering, but the one thing it lacked was a light source. Something was lying at the foot of the lens, something wrapped in white: a small crumpled figure. Suddenly Kolfinnia was brought her back to her mission. "Coven-mother Sisi!"

She abandoned caution and ran to her. The reflector stood on a circular stone dais. Kolfinnia bounded up onto it and over to her side. "Coven-mother!" She gently turned her on to her back. "Sisi?"

The old vixen was bound at the wrists and ankles. Her fur was snow white, or had been. Brown rivers trailed from her sore eyes and her neck was crusted with old bloodstains. Her muzzle twitched and her eyes opened.

Kolfinnia looked into her pained eyes. "Coven-mother, we've come to your aid."

Sisi looked up at this mythical creature and wondered if she'd died. "A human?"

"A witch," she promised. "We have to get you away. Where's Sef?"

Her eyes widened as memories connected. "A trap!" she croaked.

Kolfinnia stiffened. Movement in the crystal's endless facets caught her eye, and her heart leapt. She briefly saw something black and very fast. Even before she was on her feet she knew she wasn't quick enough. "Stormwood!" she screamed and turned to see a leering black muzzle fill the world.

Sef brutally flung her staff aside, and wrenched her arm into an impossible angle. She screamed, and heard bone break. He hurled her to the floor and twisted again, filling her whole body with pain. She screamed again, and Sef laughed.

"Push again!" Ulfar screamed, but it was futile and even he knew it. They were just twenty yards from the rest of their lives. Around him, he sensed his fighters stumbling and sliding just to keep themselves upright. They couldn't storm again. "Keverer," Ulfar groaned, defeated.

"What do we do?" Hathwell panted. More iron-fairies descended and the bites were growing more numerous.

"Die well. That's what." Ulfar struck again, even as an iron-fairy landed on his skull and started shredding at his fur. "Damn it!" he raked the vicious thing off, raised his sword and slashed at another Magnon and hoped now they would just die quickly, well or otherwise. Beside him Taal and Hathwell both laboured for breath. The sun was hot, the battlefield stank and they were exhausted and beaten.

Or at least the sun *had* been hot.

A chill wind rolled over them from nowhere. At first Hathwell thought it was just windblown ash from the fires, but in the next instant he was stunned to find snow swirling around them. The sun's warmth perished and the landscape darkened. More snow pelted them, harder this time and Hathwell looked up to see the sky was shrouded with falling snow. "Winter comes early," he uttered, believing he must be delirious.

Only fairies hardened by centuries of civil war could stand against Chentek's abominations, and now they came, drawn from afar to pay their debt to the witch who'd freed them. They had lived under terror of cursed berserks, along a coast blighted by Valgard. Life had been savage and short, but Sunday had changed that.

They had been long in coming, but at last the frost-fairies of the Cold Coast now stormed down from the sky, and their leader streaked ahead of them still wearing a lock of golden hair as her symbol of trust. Neet screamed in victory and the island of Thule was engulfed by an army of frost-fairies more numerous than snowflakes in a blizzard.

The iron-fays pressed their attack against the fairy-nations, but now the defenders were little more than a distraction. Their huge swarms had been reduced to patchy flocks and they couldn't stop greater and greater numbers of iron-fays penetrating their shield.

Yosari, one of the last Burning Hearts, raced for her life. She was a dragonfly-fairy and so nimble and quick, but her reserves were failing. A pack of iron-fays nipped at her heels. Already she'd seen her companions ravaged and eaten, and she would be next. Terror kept her going, and if her heart beat any quicker it would burst. She dodged and weaved but they kept right on her trail, only inches away, twisting and turning just as she did. A desperate sob escaped her throat. She glanced back and saw them within striking distance. She screamed and turned front again, only to find herself flying right into a pack of fairies she didn't expect, and was that snow now falling from the sky?

The iron-fays crashed straight into them and without warning boiling thirst met freezing fury. The frost-fairies snatched them from the air and ran them through with their pointed limbs. Their diseased blood froze and the lust for living-iron finally died along with them. Dead iron-fays tumbled down and the blizzard gained in strength. It was the cold that had saved Marcus Rowley and Mavis Downs alike, and now the frost-fairies were going to bring winter early to the whole of Thule.

Something shot past Hathwell, some kind of fairy he'd never seen before. It was hard to tell in the thickening blizzard. It looked silvery grey and its limbs were pointy like stabbing needles, while jagged blades swept back from its bulbous head. 'Ugly' didn't describe it, but when he saw it attack an iron-fairy crawling on Taal's back it became the most beautiful thing he'd seen all day.

He heard a new sound all around him, like creaking ice, and snow began to fall fast and thick, and for every snowflake there came two frost-fairies. They blasted across the Magnon, landing in huge numbers like locusts and stabbing and freezing. Their clay hides cracked and shrank. The Magnon tried to sweep them off, only to find frozen limbs break and fall useless, and their shambling movements grew steadily slower.

"Press on!" Ulfar saw their sudden advantage. "Press ON!" His sword arm found new life and started hacking away once more, but now it was like hitting fragile pottery, not wet clay, and Magnon shattered with each blow. A howl went up through the Therion ranks and Hathwell felt a sudden surge at his back. Helplessly he joined the victory scream and the column burst forwards, no longer chopping at their foes but smashing them.

Ten yards.

The gate was less than ten yards away, which was now almost invisible in the blizzard. They had gone from certain death to dizzying hope. The Magnon's booming call had slowed to a dry tick, and their groping hands pawed at them feebly. Hathwell barged one aside, no longer worried. More came after him and feet trampled the dead Magnon crushing them to broken shells.

Five yards. Three. One.

Finally, after the hardest battle of his life, Hathwell reached the fortress gates. Before he even had time to wonder if they were locked, a now familiar bear wielding a war-hammer swung a mighty blow at the doors. Wood splintered and iron snapped. The doors were swept aside and the Therions finally entered the lighthouse of Ultima Thule, and the first in was Hathwell.

"Berand!" Ulfar saw him dart through the broken doors as nimble as a stoat. "Taal, go after him!"

"What of you?"

Ulfar shook snow from his mane. "I need sword practice."

"Oak endures!" Taal wished him.

Ulfar gave him a curt nod and got on with his practice. A Magnon head rolled, cracking in two. "Not so keverer now eh?" he leered.

Taal hastily gathered as many fighters as he could and set off after Hathwell. He charged through the doors and took the lead, with a huge hammer-wielding bear lumbering after him. Behind them came a score of wolfen and Caprians, all filthy, sweating and howling madly, still amazed that they had somehow survived, and determined to make somebody pay for this day's work.

He might have been an aging squire with a bad knee but Hathwell tore up the lighthouse like a scalded cat. The tower was incredibly high, his metal knee stung with every step and he was exhausted from battle, but one thing drove him on. Hilly was up there and after the horrors he'd witnessed this morning he would gladly smash that bloody vessel himself if it stopped evil bastards like Sef. He raced up step after step, teeth bared, heart hammering, knowing he couldn't waste a second. He could hear the faint clatter of armour and feet behind him and Taal's voice drifted up, *"Berand! Berand!"* But he had other names on his mind. Clovis, Kolfinnia and Hilda.

Skald wasted no time, and raced to Kolfinnia's aid, but Sef had allies of his own. Iso pounced from nowhere, landing on his back and sinking claws into his shoulders. Skald roared and crackled with power, bucked his opponent off, flipped himself upright and came face to face with the impossible. "A sprite?" His moment's disbelief cost him.

"Unitari!" Iso raked at him with his talons.

"TRAITOR!" Skald lifted into the air to match him, but he was suddenly surrounded by Sef's *other* allies. The iron-fays hadn't just been busy outside.

Hundreds of them swarmed over him and he was buried under a mountain of teeth and claws, and his cries became muffled.

Iso sneered and hopped away, wishing they had orders to kill, not just disable. Skald roared and struggled, but he was rendered powerless. Hot breath rasped in his ears and many slavering jaws clamped around his neck, and any second they might clench and finish him. He lay still and listened to voices.

"Calm yourself little sprite, we might have need of you still." Sef turned to Iso, "Keep an eye on him."

Kolfinnia tried to reach out to him, but Sef gave her wrist the tiniest squeeze, and agony ripped through her. She screamed again and he relinquished a fraction. "Save your screams for Clovis." He knelt beside her and peered closely at her, still gripping her tight. She fascinated him. *So this is the girl Clovis would die for?* A brief but disturbing image of Naomi flashed through his mind.

She turned to meet his gaze. Sweat dripped from her nose and she saw that outside the Beacon it was snowing. *Dear champion?* she wondered desperately. "So you're him – Sef the murderer!" she spat.

He smiled, "And you're the witch who's captured Clovis's heart. I should thank you."

"You'll get nothing from me."

"Really?" He twisted again and bone ground against bone.

"NO!" she screamed.

He relaxed and listened to her shuddering breath. "I should thank you," he resumed, "Clovis can't open the vessel because of you."

Shamefully she felt a spark of gratitude.

He sensed it, and smiled. "Your desires brought you here. His desires will undo him."

"Liar!" This time she spat in his face, and her spittle glistened across his muzzle.

"You will see," he said calmly, before his tongue slithered out and he licked the spittle away. "Lord Self sees all desires."

"My only desire is to see you dead!" She looked around for help. Skald was just a struggling mass and Sisi hardly had the strength to move. *Hrafn-dimmu,* she thought, *must get my wand.*

"I tasted your desires earlier," he went on, "Kolfinnia-Therion."

Her whole body suddenly felt cold. *How did he know?*

"A sweet idea. Clovis would stay if you were such, wouldn't he?"

She felt shame and embarrassment. Ignoring it, she inched her free hand around to her wand-sheath.

He gave a tiny tug and agony engulfed her. "I wouldn't try it," he leaned closer, "Kolfinnia-Therion."

"Liar!" she denied.

"Lord Self can grant these things, simply desire it and it shall be so."

Against her wishes and her honour, she couldn't stop herself imagining a different future.

"Yes!" he crooned. The damage was done.

"No I don't want that!" But although her desire was tiny, it was heard. Thule, where gods listen. Lord Self listened, and liked what it heard.

Kolfinnia struggled again and felt a change sweeping through her. Sef watched fascinated as the transformation began. Kolfinnia-Therion. She tried to break free, despite the pain, grimacing and snarling, and Sef noticed the tips of her teeth growing sharper and her eyes turning amber. He shuffled close and slid an arm around her, making her convulse with loathing, and purred into her ear, "Desire will undo him."

Clovis didn't have time for subtleties. He simply cut the whole door from its frame. The door groaned and buckled and he grabbed the handle and heaved it free, sending it booming down the steps behind, but the passageway was useless. "No!" Before him was a wall of broken rock. Sef had filled the entire corridor with rubble. He'd wasted precious time on a diversion. "Damn it!"

"What now?" Tempest flapped.

He was already turning back. "Only thing we can do: fly."

"But the iron-fairies?"

"We'll have to risk it." Intuition told him they probably didn't matter. Sef wanted him in the Beacon one way or another. "Now fly!" He dropped onto his staff and they streaked down the dark staircase, heading back to the gallery. Now he was angrier than he could remember, and killing Sef was his only desire.

He watched now with a burgeoning desire of his own. Kolfinnia's eyes glittered amber and a fine golden hair dusted her cheeks. Her ears became delicately pointed and her hair also changed, going from dark to golden, just like Peri's. Sef felt other changes too. Her body wanted to rise above her meek human form, but she was fighting it. "Give in!" he encouraged, "seize your desires."

As he admired her transformation she tried again to reach her wand, but the sight of her own hand terrified her. *No! It can't be!* Her skin was covered in fine fur and her fingernails were becoming hooked and sharp. *Claws?* she thought with horror.

Sef held her tight. The transformation was proof of Self's divine power, but she was resisting. "I seek to help you," he argued, "if Clovis desires you, you can have him for always."

"LIAR!" she screamed. Her fingers – claws – touched hrafn-dimmu at last. She had to kill him, for all their sakes.

"Give in!" he growled impatiently.

"LIAR!" she hissed, revealing her fangs. Sef smiled in satisfaction, but other changes were afoot that perhaps he wasn't so approving of. Kolfinnia felt a new strength in her limbs superior to anything she'd known before. "Clovis will kill you!"

"Give in!" he bellowed, but now he had to twist harder to earn the scream he wanted.

She writhed in his grip, and at last her fingers wrapped around her wand. *Now my turn, you filth,* she promised.

"GIVE IN!" he repeated.

"NEVER!" someone shouted. Only it wasn't Kolfinnia.

Sef jerked around and saw Hilda emerge from the stairwell and hurtle towards him. Her hair fanned out behind her and her eyes blazed. "LET GO OF HER!" Her staff was ready to strike. Her atheme was ready to plunge and stab. After a last vicious twist of her arm, he threw Kolfinnia aside and reached for his sword, as she landed on her broken limb and wailed in agony. Groaning she scrabbled at Raven's wand and pulled it free. Sef's blade whispered from its scabbard in a deadly thrust, while Hilda saw her target, the soft flesh at the base of his throat and powered her staff towards it. But Sef disliked fighting on even terms. His distraction was fleeting but effective.

Hilda saw Valonia clear as day. *"How could you disgrace us Hilly?"* she accused. *"How could you love Hathwell?"*

"Valonia?" Guilt blinded her.

Sef took advantage, and lunged.

Kolfinnia snatched Raven's wand free, aimed and released.

'The devil looks after his own,' they say. And perhaps such a being watched over Sef right then because one of the circling iron-fays swept into view and Kolfinnia's spell hit it rather than him. The small creature fell dead, and Sef's blade continued its inevitable course. "HILLY!" Kolfinnia screamed.

The blade hit her chest and continued out the other side. Momentum carried Hilda forwards and she slumped against her killer. They came face to face, but mercifully the last thing she saw was not his cruel grin, but the great reflector and she remembered their grand purpose. *Hope,* she thought, then she was gone. Sef held her a moment, almost tenderly, then pulled his sword free and let her fall. Her atheme clattered to the flags and she dropped like a stone, followed by a burst of light from her staff as Five rocketed towards the thunder-heights. The last of Valonia's Wards had gone to Evermore.

She forgot to breathe. She even forgot her broken arm. Kolfinnia forgot everything but hate. She raised her wand again, ready to use the most forbidden curses. Her eyes swam with tears and her hand quaked with fury. "DIE!" The curse shot from her, taking all her strength. There wouldn't be enough for another try. Sef expertly swung his blade and sent her curse aside with a roar of triumph, and there followed a condemning silence. He stood there panting and now both regarded the other, knowing the fight was over. He pounced and landed astride her, and swiped Raven's wand away. "You won't be needing that anymore." He took a fistful of her hair, which was now a golden mane, and dragged her across the floor.

"BASTARD!" she screamed.

He threw her down and took her broken arm again, and twisted hard. Bile rushed up her throat and stifled her scream and she almost lost consciousness. "You have other bones girl. I can break them too." At this point it dawned on him that snow was lashing against the glass and his ears twitched and his eyes narrowed. Something was wrong.

Kolfinnia's newly charged senses detected it too. Her eyes narrowed to slits and she growled in anticipation. The frost-fairies had come to fight iron, but maybe Neet's blizzard saved another life, because it concealed his approach. Sef was still staring at the glass when the windows behind him exploded. Broken glass and snow roared in, and so too did Clovis on his lightning-staff.

He dropped without slowing, carried forward by incredible fury. He saw Hilda's body, and Kolfinnia's torment. He saw his foe at last, and understood the gravity of his advantage. Clovis charged forwards, ripping iron-fay from his clothes and mane, staff and sword ready. He looked the total antithesis of Sef now, for his face and mane were crusted with snow, while amber eyes blazed in his white mask like terrible stars.

"Far enough coven-father." Sef yanked her head back and tapped his blade to her throat.

Anger tipped him forward one more step, and then he skidded to a halt, shoulders heaving, tongue lolling and snow dripping from him.

"Relinquish what you stole!" Sef commanded.

His eyes went to Kolfinnia, and what they saw wounded his heart. She was not only captive, but Self had transformed her into a weapon against him.

Sef saw his anguish. "The vessel is useless to you now. Surrender it!" The blade waved meaningfully.

"Forget me, do it for Hilly!" Kolfinnia cried.

Sef never took his eyes off him. "He can't," he said evenly.

Clovis stood torn by his feelings. His sword trembled and his ears flattened against his skull.

"Clovis!" she tried again.

"Tell me in all truth coven-father," Sef challenged. "What is your dearest desire? To release Janus, or save her?" He yanked her hair again, giving him a good look at her half-Therion form.

"Just smash it Clovis, for Oak's sake!" she pleaded.

Sef leaned closer. "I know the ritual as well as he. Only pure intent can break the vessel."

The realisation dawned on her. He couldn't smash the glass without giving up every shred of desire to save her. Sef forced her ruined arm further up her back. She fought to hide her agony, but it was hopeless and a terrible wail escaped her lips. Clovis flinched and stepped forward, irresistibly drawn to her.

"Enough! The vessel!" Sef could taste victory so close.

Clovis trembled with fury, unaware that his hand was moving to slip the pack from his shoulder.

"Clovis don't!" she begged.

"He must. Desire undoes us all in the end," Sef promised. "Now take out the vessel, place it before you and step away."

Kolfinnia watched through teary eyes as Clovis lowered the vessel to the flags for her sake. Glass chimed against stone and he stepped back.

"Desire undoes us all," Sef preached, and allowed himself a tiny smile.

CHAPTER TWENTY-FIVE

Undone by desire

'I came so far, always believing I knew my course,
yet in the end I found I had never left.'
'Essays on the Nature of the Soul' - Robert Howson-Jefferies, 1736

Having evolved as a consequence of a war-loving culture, Chentek
was a natural coward. All across Thule his iron-fays were falling in
huge numbers as the snowstorm continued to batter the island. Without
them, he was literally nothing, and much as he disliked Sef he needed
his protection. He weaved and fluttered through one savage fight after
another. Ice killed the thirst for living-iron and of course he didn't stop
to help his kin. If he could escape, he could begin the infection elsewhere
and put this rout behind him, but he needed Sef to get him away.

He whisked ahead of the Therions charging up the lighthouse spiral,
thinking inside would be safer than out, and he was almost right. He
didn't know it, but he'd been seen and followed.

One frost-fairy buzzed after him. He was different to the rest because
he wore a twist of blonde hair around his neck, which to him was more
valuable than life itself. "Neet! Neet!" he chattered as he flew. The enemy's
scent was strong, in fact it glowed like a red highway. Soon he would hunt
Chentek down and then he would plunge those limbs into his venomous
heart and freeze it stone dead. "Neet! Neet!" he gnashed his teeth and
flew faster.

Chentek hurried on, like the thief leaving the burning house, and guessed he was almost at the gallery leading to the Beacon. He allowed himself a satisfied chuckle. His pleasure soon vanished though, when something dropped on him from nowhere.

"NEET!" someone screamed and an icy blast surrounded him. Chentek scrambled and flapped, and although his hide was like armour, there was soft flesh between the joints and Neet's arms were the perfect weapons to slide through them. Chentek howled and fell onto his back as Neet rained blows down on him. It was like being attacked by a swarm of needles.

"Sef, Sef!" he cried.

"Neet not Sef's. Neet not anyone's!" he spat, and punctured Chentek's throat, and the war-fairy screamed.

"Better," Sef complimented. "Now, further back."

Clovis shuffled back, while his eyes bored into him.

"Good, good." Sef couldn't help but admire the Janus vessel. He'd never seen it before, and the journey to retrieve it had been cosmic.

"Let her go," Clovis growled.

"She means something to you I gather?"

Clovis sneered, "You couldn't know such values."

Sef regarded her approvingly. "She is desirable now is she not? Perhaps I'll take her home for myself."

Clovis bared his fangs, hissed and risked a step forwards. "Release her or I swear I'll destroy us all."

Sef pretended to look around. "I see no army to aid your boast?"

He smiled dangerously. If whispering the name of the Lady could cause a landslide, what if he *shouted* it? "With one word I could send this island into the waves. All would be lost, even Janus."

"You're lying."

"The Lady's name will finish us all."

Kolfinnia heard Sef's gasp. *He's frightened,* she realised.

"You're not –,"

"I AM!" Clovis declared. "One name, and all of us die. Is that your 'dearest desire'?"

After a moment's indecision, Sef growled, "Then do so. I'm fast enough to claim the vessel *and* take my trophy too." He jerked her arm to make his point, eliciting another pained groan.

Kolfinnia listened with half an ear. Her transformation had gone only so far, but something had changed that Sef hadn't counted on. She felt stronger and faster, broken arm or not. Sef was speaking but she wasn't listening. She looked up at him from where she knelt, and calculated her chances. Human-Kolfinnia couldn't have done it, even with two arms, but Therion-Kolfinnia might stand a chance. She swallowed, and ran a tongue over her canines. Yes, they felt deadly enough now. Her eyes narrowed and she assessed her target, already bunching her muscles ready to pounce.

Clovis heard something. Sef heard it too. Kolfinnia was too preoccupied. There were footsteps on the stairs. Someone was coming in a hurry. "I shan't warn you again, step back from the vessel!" Sef hauled Kolfinnia up an inch, ready to snatch the prize and be away.

Clovis lowered his hand slowly towards his sword.

"Do it!" Sef blasted.

The footsteps grew louder, and suddenly Hathwell raced up the steps and staggered to a halt, panting and dripping sweat. When he saw the crumpled body lying on the dais a strangled groan escaped his lips. "Hilly!" In no time at all he saw his option and made his choice. His pure intent was to see this monster finished, and he charged.

"Hathwell, no!" Clovis roared, guessing his aim.

At that moment Sef looked around – and Kolfinnia struck.

'Desire will undo him.' How true he was. She exploded from the floor, catching him unprepared, and clamped her jaws around his throat. She sank her canines deep and tasted hot blood. Sef screamed and tore back with his neck flapping open.

Clovis charged with a roar, while Sef dropped his hostage and raised his sword, and despite his wound he was still impossibly fast.

Hathwell continued past them all, with a bigger goal in mind. *'You don't need a wand to be a witch Mr Hathwell.'* He hoped it was true now. *For Hilly!* he thought, and landed with his metal knee crashing down on the Janus Vessel.

Clovis powered his blade at Sef's wounded throat, who raised his sword to counter it, but while it might have saved his life a moment ago deflecting

Kolfinnia's curse, now the debt must be paid. The curse had weakened the alloy and Clovis's blade shattered it easily and carried on towards his neck. Sef was left with a broken hilt and no more, and his eyes went wide in understanding. *Desire undoes us all*, he thought.

"FOR HILDA!" Clovis roared, and the coven-father's steel parted bone and Sef's head left his body.

For Hilda, Hathwell thought gladly, welcoming the poison. Better that than a lifetime of grief, or seeing beasts like Sef reign supreme. The glass recognised his pure intent and shattered. The fluid gushed out across him, and he laughed.

Meanwhile, in the gallery below, Chentek screamed a last time as Neet shoved his arm deeper. The war-fairy's heart crackled with ice and trembled to a stop. A dead stop. "Oak Endures!" Neet hissed into his dying ear. Chentek gurgled, twitched and lay still, and the curse of living-iron was ended.

In the Beacon above, the iron-fairies wilted and dropped away. Skald instantly exploded from under them and landed on Iso, talons ripping and beak stabbing. Iso shrieked, first at the sight of his doomed master and then as Skald's hooked beak found his throat. Valonia's thunder-sprite made short work of his opposite, and unlike natural sprites Iso had no thunder-heights to go to. Dead was dead.

Sef's head rolled across the dais and there was enough life left in it to witness the incredible. He saw the vessel break and Janus ascend. A terrified howl rang through the universe as Lord Self realised its danger.

Janus had waited for this moment, not just the preceding aeons, but since the Flowering had restored him. All his former deceits had plagued him since that day and resisting them was like holding his breath. Now he expelled that breath and streaked upwards, ablaze with new strength. Above, Self waited to kill him, but Janus wouldn't be caught a second time and he knew exactly how to defeat his old enemy. Self raced to counter him, terrified of what would happen if he achieved his grand purpose, but Janus had seen a magnificent Flower and his fate was his own to command. *"I am free,"* he said simply.

His will changed the universe and nothing could stop it. Janus tore through Self's dark shroud, ripping a hole in it as surely as a bullet. The entity that had plagued creation since the start, wailed and fell away in failure. Janus was free and Self flowed to the edges of creation in defeat to hide from his terrible light.

His first concern wasn't a god, but a young woman. Clovis dropped to Kolfinnia's side. "Speak to me!" Gently, he turned her over and saw her pale face and glassy eyes. Therion-Kolfinnia was gone and she was restored. He wiped Sef's blood from her mouth and his heart jumped when she looked his way.

"Are we leaving coven-father?" she asked weakly.

He gasped and gave exhausted smile. "Bless you."

She reached up and stroked his face, and he held her close.

"Clovis," someone whispered. It was Skald.

He turned to see Hathwell kneeling motionless in a pool of liquid and broken glass, as snow continued to swirl around them. The squire stared at the floor and his arms hung limp at his sides. Clovis helped Kolfinnia to her feet and she leaned on him as they hobbled closer. "Bertrand?" Clovis tried.

Hathwell's head hung limp, looking down at the shattered glass. His expression was blank, as if he'd died and simply not fallen over.

"Is he?" Kolfinnia whispered, and untangled herself from Clovis and limped over, nursing her ruined arm.

"Bertrand?" Clovis took his arm and knelt beside him. He didn't respond.

"Please, don't let him be. . ." She reached out a tentative hand.

"I'm still alive?" he mumbled, sounding dazed.

"Bertrand!" she sobbed in relief.

"Thank the twins," Skald sighed. Enough friends had died today.

Clovis regarded the pool of poison and finally understood. All along it had been just another safeguard. There was no poison, but that didn't change what Hathwell had just done. "We should go," he said softly.

Hathwell looked around at Hilda's body, too numb to cry. "What happened?"

Before Kolfinnia could answer, tears overcame her.

Clovis put an arm around each of them. "It seems you're a witch after all

Mr Hathwell." He helped both to their feet, and they and their battered thunder-sprites huddled together in sorrow as snow drifted in from outside.

Noise from the stairs made them turn. Taal barged into the Beacon, followed by a huge bear carrying a hammer, and behind them came many more. One of them was already freeing coven-mother Sisi. "Berand!" Taal dashed over. "Berand why did you run off?"

"Taal, I. . ." he tried to answer, lost his words and gave up. Instead he clasped his arm briefly as he passed, heading to Hilda's side.

Taal followed his gaze, and saw the tragedy. "Berand, I'm sorry."

Kolfinnia went after him and Clovis was left standing amid the broken glass and dead fairies. Something at his feet caught his attention and bent to collect it. It was Janus, or at least the carved figure that had so long occupied the vessel. He looked up at the roof and imagined the real Janus out there between the stars. Was he already singing the song of freedom he wondered? "Blessings on you Janus, make us proud." He curled his fist around the relic and felt a tiny vibration within. Janus had left something behind. Touched, he felt a tear fall. "Thank you," he bowed his head. Despite everything, Janus hadn't forgotten him.

Hathwell gazed upon her a last time, and then taking her cloak, he covered her over. Kolfinnia knelt close and took his hand. "We should tend your arm," he said faintly.

"And your leg." She saw how blood from his knee had stained the snow, and she remembered Rowan's peculiar dream.

He clasped her hand tighter and took a deep breath. "Sef killed her?" He needed to hear it.

"Yes."

He looked over to Sef's corpse, and saw a dark lump in the shadows under the reflector. *His head,* he thought hatefully. If he could, he'd take it and hurt it all over again.

"Come on," she tugged his hand, "Sef's taken enough from us already." She led him aside, where both of them could cry in private.

Ulfar watched as sunlight returned and the storm abated. He trudged through snow so deep that the dead Magnon were all but covered. Around him

Therions were gathering their wounded and their dead. He bent, scooped some snow and rubbed his muzzle to refresh himself. After a last look around the battlefield, he gave his sword a friendly pat and slid it home into its sheath. "Until next time my lovely."

He plodded wearily towards the fortress gates, through a gentle drift of fairies, many searching for their own wounded. The fairy-nations had suffered terrible losses.

"Cap'n, we sail home na?" A bloodied but hopeful avian stared back at him.

"Not yet, dead to tend," he said soberly.

He pushed through the broken doors into the lighthouse, and heard voices approaching. He leaned against the wall and waited, and soon enough a tired band of fighters came limping down. His smiled faded when he saw they carried a body wrapped in a cloak. Berand and Clovis carried her between them, while Kolfinnia came clutching her useless arm and looking close to exhaustion. "Dead to tend," he repeated quietly, adding another name to the list.

The fleet remained one night, long enough to gather the fallen and tend the wounded. The snow melted, and by nightfall both it and the fires were gone. Shattered Magnon were strewn across the whole of Thule like broken vessels, and the last of the frost-fairies departed. The fortress was cleared of Sef's occupation, coven-mother Sisi was treated for her wounds, and the bistort Hilda and Kolfinnia had prepared now came into its own.

Clovis watched the activity from The Hornet. After a while he took a lantern and went below to see Kolfinnia. At first he thought she was sleeping, and quietly turned to leave.

"Clovis?" she stirred.

He went and sat beside her. Her arm was heavily splinted, and he'd given her a strong draught for the pain. As soon as he sat down, she slipped her hand into his. "You feel any better?" he asked softly.

She opened her eyes, and he saw she'd been crying. "I dreamed of Hilly."

He smiled sadly. "What was she doing?"

"She was waiting on Evermore with the others. She was at peace."

"Then it was a good dream."

They sat bonded by silence and lulled by the ship's gentle swaying. At last, she spoke again. "Did you know?"

He frowned. "Know?"

"The vessel – it wasn't poison after all."

"No," he sighed. "No I didn't."

"But still you'd have opened it."

"Yes, just as Berand did."

She smiled at his use of the name. "But you can't go home." Just yesterday this would have thrilled her. After today's events though, it shamed her.

He gently squeezed her hand. "Janus left something behind."

"For you?"

He opened his hand and there was the carved little figure of Janus. "The relic has enough power to make one last trip through Evermore."

She was glad for him. "So you *can* go home."

He almost asked her to go with him.

She saw wheels turning, and grasped the wrong idea. "Do you hate me?"

His heart rolled in his chest. "Kolfy, what a terrible idea! Why would you think so?"

"Today, you saw my desires." Her words trailed off. *Kolfinnia Therion,* she thought remorsefully.

"Without those desires you couldn't have turned on Sef like that," he praised her.

"I only wanted to save you, not for me, just save you. . . that's all." It was important to her that he understood.

"I know," he said truthfully.

"You don't hate me then?" She tried to sit up and winced.

"Rest!" he eased her back down. "And no, not at all. Besides, I told you once – I like my women with longer whiskers."

She blushed and grinned despite herself, and he joined her. After a moment her expression darkened. "Did you know him, Sef I mean?"

He adjusted her blanket and considered. "For a moment I thought I did."

She chose not to ask further. "And how's poor Mr Hathwell?"

"Berand is quiet. He has been helping clear the Beacon."

"But his knee?"

He shook his head, looking concerned. "He refuses to take rest."

"Will he be alright do you think?" her eyes felt heavy again.

"He has good souls to look after him. Yes, I think in the end he will be. Now sleep." He bent and kissed her forehead. "Tomorrow we sail home."

He took the lantern and left her, but sleep wouldn't come. She lay there, watching memories flit through her head, replaying the day's horrors over and over. At last, she sensed she was being watched and she lifted her head to see a fairy sitting on her chest. She'd never seen his kind before, but he apparently had seen someone very much like her.

"Sisters," he observed.

"Pardon?" she said groggily.

"Little scar," he waved a pointed arm at the hourglass scar. "Seen its like before."

Her head was crammed and foggy, and it took a moment to guess. "You're Neet aren't you?"

He shrugged as if he wasn't sure, but the golden hair around his neck gave it away.

"She gave you that didn't she, Sunday?"

"She speaks of me?" he asked bashfully.

"Much." Now she felt teary with gratitude. "It was you that saved us today wasn't it?"

Again he shrugged.

"Wait 'til I get home and tell Sunday."

"You'll tell her?" he twitched his wings in excitement.

"Of course! I'll tell her all about your bravery."

He looked satisfied. "And tell her I wear it still," he said proudly and indicated the lock of hair.

"I promise."

He looked to the open hatch. "Must go now, last of snow is dying."

"Thank you, Neet."

"Neet!" he chirped, and lifted into the air and zipped away.

She listened to the drone of his wings fade, closed her eyes and lay back to sleep.

It was dark when Hathwell descended the lighthouse for the last time. As he reached the last step, he looked back along the dark spiral and marked the moment. He would never go back up there. Clovis was waiting, and offered him a hand. "Thanks," he limped along holding him for support.

"I've prepared you a bed on board The Hornet," Clovis offered.

"I'll sleep ashore tonight if it's all the same with you. I think I could sleep anywhere." He was glad to be exhausted, because the last thing he wanted tonight was dreams.

"The Beacon is clear now?"

He hobbled along watching his footing. "It is."

Clovis sensed a mystery. "Berand," he began, "earlier they burned Sef's corpse. Taal says they couldn't find his head."

"Huh! Probably rolled into the sea. As long as it doesn't roll back onto his shoulders I don't care where it's gone."

He sighed resignedly. "I suppose you're right."

Finally they came to the camp, and Clovis guessed why he wanted to remain ashore. Nearby was the mortuary enclave. Tomorrow, they would take their dead home, but tonight they rested under canvas, and Hilda was amongst them. "Ah, throw me down, I'll sleep anywhere," Hathwell groaned as he collapsed on to his blanket, looking ready to live up to that promise. Around him campfires crackled and Therions were bedding down.

"Berand, will you be alright?" Clovis was concerned.

"Right now, no. In the end, yes."

He smiled at his honesty. "Very well, wake me any hour, should you need to." He smiled wearily. "Oak Endures," he sighed and closed his eyes.

"Oak Endures." After a puzzled look Clovis went and sat by the fire, where he could keep an eye on both him and The Hornet where Kolfinnia slept. He sat long into the night looking up at the stars and thinking of Janus. Before dawn he turned to find Vega above, and slipped the relic from his robes. Janus's enigmatic face stared back at him and Clovis smiled. "Home," he promised himself.

August 11th saw rain arrive just as the fleet was ready to set sail and everyone saw something heartening. The rain turned the shattered Magnon to mud and washed them away, and the island of Thule emerged again.

Ulfar stood at the bows and navigated The Hornet out of the shallows, enjoying the rain, while Clovis, Hathwell and Kolfinnia stood on deck as they glided away from the now abandoned lighthouse.

Coven-mother Sisi was coming with them, but they would return in the spring to reclaim the lighthouse and perhaps even kindle the light. Janus had given them a quiet faith. Therions pulled at the oars and the raven sail was dropped again.

The three remaining Lions watched the imposing lighthouse vanish into the drizzle. Each made their own private wishes and farewells, and out of mutual respect none asked the others what their parting thoughts had been.

And so began a southerly sea voyage back to Hope, calling at ports where they had recruited fighters and ships, although now their pace was sedate, not frantic. Lievik, Orcadeas and Abberan came and went and as the north receded and the south beckoned, the fleet dwindled until at last it was Ulfar's twenty ships again. Clovis was heartened to see Hathwell keep up to his spell-work. He watched discreetly as the former squire sat in the bows and focused, just as Hilda had shown him.

"He's doing it for her," Kolfinnia wiped her eyes. "He adored her."

Clovis put an arm around her, but very carefully. "I understand the feeling," he empathised. She rested her head against him and thought of all she had lost, and what she might have lost.

On the evening of August 19th, they left the sea and entered the fresh waters of The Forth, and Hope was only hours away. "What have you there?" Clovis came and sat with Hathwell below the mast.

"Found it under the reflector. You know what it is?" he showed him.

Clovis took it, already knowing what it wasn't. "It's no plain stone that's for sure." It was speckled and slightly tapered at one end, and a delicate sky blue colour.

"Bird's egg?" Hathwell ventured.

Clovis pressed it to his ear. "An egg certainly, I hear a heart within." He held it up, turning it between his fingers. It fascinated him more with each passing second. "You found it on the dais?"

"Yes." A horrible thought occurred to him. "Was it Sef's?"

"Perhaps," he agreed sadly.

"Throw it over the side then."

Clovis was dismayed. "What would Hilda think!"

His mouth twisted as he thought. "You're right, that was cruel."

Clovis listened again. He wasn't sure if it was a beating heart inside or just his own pulse. "Whatever's in there we'll leave it with Bru."

"Hmm, I suppose," he agreed.

"Well, we can't take it home." Clovis attempted a smile, but Hathwell had changed these last few days. He sat looking at the deck, lost in thought. "You do want to go home don't you?"

He nodded indifferently. "Stormwood is beautiful, yes."

Clovis waited for more, but it appeared he had no more to offer. Eventually he handed back the egg. "Give it to Bru."

Hathwell took it, and they sat side-by-side under the raven and listened to the oars lapping at the river, and before long Clovis saw the profile of Hope Castle on the hill in the sunset. *We did it,* the thought finally struck him, but when he looked around at the vacant benches he wondered if it had all been worth it.

Familiarity spurred them on, and oars were pulled with mounting anticipation. They arrived back in port in the early evening, and of course Bru and many others were there to greet them, all carrying torches to light their homecoming. Clovis and his remaining Lions touched down on the riverbank again and into a rapturous crowd full of noise and activity, but which only seemed to emphasise Hilda's absence all the more.

The following day they tended the dead and Bru suggested that Hilda be buried within Hope's walls, right inside the coven where the cherry trees graced the gardens. Without thinking, Clovis and Kolfinnia, looked to Hathwell for final approval. *"I think she'd like that,"* he'd agreed, and so they set about preparing her grave and the rituals to honour her.

By noon she was back in Hethra's green earth, along with her wand and her lightning-staff. All of them lingered by the mound of fresh earth and remembered their friend. They told tales sad and happy, humble and glorious, and for a while they could pretend that Hilda was there with them under the cherry trees where the last blossom drifted down.

That evening the three took their supper with Bru in his study. "I had a dream some nights ago," he revealed as he poured more tea.

"Yes?" Kolfinnia picked at her food with her good arm.

"It was about Janus."

Now all three sat straighter and listened.

"He was voyaging across the stars, and as he went eyes opened," Bru chuckled to himself.

Clovis drained his cup and set it down. "The third eye, the voice of conscience."

"Then it's started already?" Kolfinnia asked.

"But the true effect will be years in coming, I think."

"Will we live to see it?" Hathwell asked.

Clovis regarded him warmly. "You're a witch Berand, I think you'll find you can see it already."

His brow wrinkled as he considered. "The spells I've been practising – I didn't think I could do them after what happened, but they're not as difficult as I'd feared."

Kolfinnia set down her fork and patted his knee, the good one. "That's the witch in you Bertrand."

He smiled, perhaps his first in many days. "Call me Berand."

Bru laughed softly. "A good name witch-Berand."

"You can tell Rowan how you earned it when you get back,'" she suggested.

He sighed and looked at his half-eaten meal. "That's just it Kolfinnia, I don't think I'm coming back."

She swallowed her shock. He was one of them now and she found she didn't want to let him go. "You're not?"

Bru studied him shrewdly and Clovis leaned closer.

"No," he sat back and regarded them all. "No, I think I'll stay."

To be close to her, she guessed, and saw that she'd been so wrong about this man.

"A witch and an engineer," Bru considered. "City could do with such." He clasped his staff, rested his chin on his hands and leaned closer.

"Hope-coven is just me and Hortar. You wish to make it three, Berand?"

"Yes, if you'll have me."

"You're staying," Kolfinnia realised now, and wiped her eyes.

"Yes," he smiled, bemused. He'd never made such a big decision so easily. "I'm staying here."

Clovis took his hand. "I couldn't have opened that vessel in the end Berand. You're a finer witch than I."

"I know you'll make the city proud," Kolfinnia sniffed, and took his other hand.

"It's settled then," Bru declared. "Berand stays, builds walls and teaches us magic."

"Hmm," he considered. "There isn't much magic I can teach you."

"Really?" Clovis reminded him, "what about the egg?"

"Egg?" Kolfinnia dried her cheeks. "What egg?"

He'd almost forgotten about it. "Oh yes," he reached for his coat, fumbled in the pockets and handed it over to Bru. "It's quite robust – more like a stone than an egg, I'm not sure it even is an egg."

Bru sat with the egg in his palm, and his muzzle slowly dropped open.

"Bru, what's wrong?" Kolfinnia peered at him.

He didn't answer, but licked his lips and held the egg to his ear. They all saw he was trembling.

"An egg should be in a nest, it's probably dead by now," Hathwell lamented. Bru held his breath and listened. "Not dead Berand."

"Bru, you know what it is?" Clovis shivered.

He set it down on the table, shaking too much to risk holding it further. "I dare not say." His eyes went to the banner of Astriss on the wall. "We shall see in a few days." He took the egg and set it in the basket by the fire where Rolo had languished. Now the kitten was nowhere to be seen. His health had returned and he was off doing kitten things, but his cradle hadn't lost its usefulness just yet.

Hathwell hobbled over and Clovis's head appeared over his shoulder, followed by Kolfinnia's. "What's in there Bru?" he asked.

Bru stroked the egg. "If I'm right Berand, hope," he whispered, "hope is in there."

Hathwell's decision left them saddened but pleased for him. It also left them with a new problem and Clovis and Kolfinnia discussed it the following morning. They were wandering the battlements together after visiting Hilda's grave. They left Hathwell, or Berand as they were coming to know him, there with his solitude, and came here to see the sun rise over Hope.

"So, two Lions left," Kolfinnia sighed, "soon to be one." She looked at him directly. It wasn't necessary to hide her feelings any longer, from him, herself, or even Self.

He didn't conceal his own feelings now either. "Yes, one Lion, and she'll be Stormwood's mother for many years to come."

"When will you leave then?" This still saddened her enormously, but it no longer terrified her.

He patted the relic in his satchel. "I can go when I desire."

She blushed again. "Don't use that word."

"Desire for another's wellbeing is a gift," he smiled. "But no, I won't go right away."

"Why not?" she ventured shyly.

"One last job."

"Which is?"

"To get you home of course."

She opened her mouth to protest, and it dawned on her that somewhere along the line she'd lost her disguise. "I don't even have enough to buy a train ticket to get back to Edinburgh," she laughed. "I'll have to fly instead."

"With that arm? I doubt you'd even get on your staff."

She looked down at her bandaged arm, knowing it would be like that for many weeks yet. "Once I'm well I can travel. I'll be fine," she promised.

He shook his head reproachfully. "You came with me to the bitter end, you think I'd leave you now?"

She felt tearful again, but managed a smile. "No."

"No," he emphasised, "I'll stay with you until your journey's done, back to the beginning."

"You don't have to," she reminded him, but hoping he would.

"It would be my honour."

She went and hugged him and he wrapped her in his arms, but careful not to hurt her. "Thank you Clovis," she whispered.

"No, thank *you*."

They enjoyed the rising sun, and when the streets of Hope began to come alive they went below to see how they could spend their last days here well.

Kolfinnia found herself spending a lot of time with Hathwell, like the worried parent about to send her child off into the world. She showed him the most important potions, how to say the most basic spells and told him the history of Hethra and Halla. They worked on spells together and she began to see what he meant. They *did* come easier, but whether this was the special nature of the faded-realm, or the effect of Janus, she couldn't say.

Hathwell got on with planning the city's defences. Now he'd seen Magnon for himself, he had better ideas of how to fight them if they ever came again, but Bru seemed optimistic that they wouldn't. When pressed as to how he knew this, the old fox just chuckled and said something about 'only time telling.'

Clovis had matters of his own to round off too, and on a beautiful Tuesday in late August he walked in the hills around Hope with Peri.

"I didn't realise," she admitted after he'd explained.

"I went to Thule thinking the vessel was deadly and I wouldn't survive. I just didn't want you hoping for the impossible. Can you forgive me?"

She admired his mane, his crooked smile and his ragged ear. It would be easy to fall in love with him again, but he wasn't staying. "Sometimes we hope for the impossible and we get it."

He gave her a quizzical look.

"If you'd been told two weeks ago that you'd be standing here with me now, wouldn't you have claimed it 'impossible'?"

"I take your point." And now he took her hand and they walked through the heather. The hillsides were carpeted with purple flowers and the sun was hot, but autumn was growing ever closer. They sat together on an outcrop overlooking the city. Clovis saw more dragon banners than ever before, and even the glittering course of the river looked serpentine. *Dragons*, he thought.

"What will you do, when you get home?" she asked suddenly.

It was a sobering question, and he thought hard. "The Unitari might have lost Janus, but they and their god remain."

"Will you fight them?"

He turned, and his eyes glinted coldly. "Oh yes. There's much to be set right."

"Let's speak of nicer things," she suggested. The idea of him going off to yet another battle was too painful. "What's Vega like?"

He smiled as he told her of his two sisters and how they had bossed him around as a child. He went on to speak fondly of growing up in the coven with Tiber, and how the serpent-twins that gave Vega life were known as Sun and Moon. One had scales like silver, the other gold. They talked until the sun reclined behind a bed of cloud and the shadows grew longer, and then they made ready to go back.

"Vega sounds beautiful," she thanked him.

He shook twigs from his cloak from where they had been sitting. "Despite everything, yes it still is."

"And this silver box Kolfinnia gave you, you'll open it and let the ash ride the wind?" She loved the idea.

"It'll be the first thing I do."

"I wish I had something to give you, to take there."

"Ah, but you have." He drew the pendant from under his shirt and her eyes sparkled with tears.

"You got it after all!"

He regarded it lovingly. "Aye, I got it, and it'll be making a very long trip soon."

"Vega."

They embraced, and Clovis thought that perhaps desire wasn't such a bad thing after all.

Kolfinnia's arm healed steadily, and on the last day of August both she and Skald were in the gardens, picking blackcurrants. She gathered with her good hand while Skald watched the fairies come and go, and Therions carry baskets of fruit to the storehouses. "Autumn's close now," he said with a hint of melancholy.

She looked around the gardens. "I hope Stormwood's as fruitful as this."

"Your birthing-day soon." The date had dubious significance he knew.

She stopped, remembering that day just one year ago, when she and Rowan had collected the way-bewares. "That was the last day I saw Valonia." It all came back to her now, including the sadness.

"Me too." He thought of that painful illusion in the lighthouse. *My dearest desire.* He felt angry again at how Sef had used love to trick them. "It's been an eventful year." He twitched an ear against a biting midge.

"Maybe it's over now, all that evil that began with Krast." Blackcurrants tumbled from her palm into the bowl and she went for more.

"It wasn't all evil though."

"No," she stopped, "no it wasn't."

"Without it, there wouldn't be a Clovis, or a Flowering and no Janus to give hope."

She could dwell on the darkness of the last twelve months or the light. It was hard, but she chose the light. "I look forward to some years of rest and peace," she dared to say.

Skald looked up at the sky, half expecting it to break open in defiance of her wish. "Peace," he agreed, and to his satisfaction the sky didn't fall and the world kept on turning.

In the early hours of Friday September 2nd, Bru barged into Clovis's chambers without waiting. "Clovis, come tell me my eyes haven't gone mad!"

He threw the blanket aside and dragged him out of his bed in only his nightshirt.

Clovis tumbled out of bed, already groping for his sword. "WHAT! Is it Magnon?"

"Get dressed and come see, hurry!" He scurried from the room with his lantern dangling from his fist, and Clovis stumbling after him trying to run and pull his trousers up at the same time.

When he got to the study he found Hathwell and Kolfinnia already there huddled around the fire, which was crackling away as always. "Clovis!" Kolfinnia beckoned him over. She was wrapped in a tatty gown and her hair hung uncombed around her shoulders, but her smile was sheer delight. He went and joined them by the fire, and peered down at something on the hearth. To start with all he could see was the top of Bru's head, then the old fox moved aside and Clovis caught his breath.

"Incredible isn't it!" Kolfinnia stared in wonder.

"Well?" Bru asked. "Have my eyes gone mad?"

Clovis stared down at Rolo's old box and shook his head. There was a broken shell in the bedding and two wriggling creatures. "Dragons?" he gasped.

"Twins," Bru confirmed.

"A lad and a lass," Hathwell added.

"Dragons." Clovis felt his mouth stuck around the word, but it was the only one that would come.

"Isn't it wonderful!" Kolfinnia sighed.

Clovis knelt, and Bru held the lantern higher. He looked into the box and shook his head in bewilderment. They looked like newly hatched lizards, but they had white scales, membranous wings and elongate necks fringed with tiny spines. They clambered over one another as they explored their new world. Here were the offspring of the engineered dragon that had brought Sef to Earth, and unlike their abused mother they would get the chance to live a natural life. He looked up to where Bru stood watching closely. "Your eyes aren't mad."

Bru dabbed at his tears. "Must be my mind that's gone mad then."

"If so, then all of ours too." Hathwell pulled his nightshirt tighter.

"Clovis, while I welcome this, how can it be?" Bru asked searchingly.

He heaved a sigh. "I've heard of unique dragons travelling between the stars, maybe Sef intended to use them to get home?"

"Barbarian!" he huffed. "Well, these two aren't going anywhere. Which one shall we call Astriss?"

Hathwell looked to the banner on the wall. Astriss the Lost stared down at him, approvingly, he imagined. These weren't her offspring, and they were mere tools to the Unitari who had created them, but in the end it didn't really matter, the hope they embodied was the same. "Neither," he said, "the past is lost and the future is found."

Kolfinnia listened to his words with deep feeling, and knew without doubt he was a witch equal to any of them.

With so many fairy eyes and ears news always travels fast in the faded-realm and by five o'clock that morning an excited crowd was gathering outside the castle, many of them in their nightclothes too. All of them wanted to know if the wild stories were true: finally a dragon had come to the faded-realm? The wildest tales said it was a pair of dragons, twins even, but such gossip bordered on lunacy. After generations of waiting how could they finally be doubly blessed?

Finally Bru, together with Clovis and his Lions, presented themselves at the gates to address the crowds. There was a mist on the river and the hills were taking on a rusty tint, although the heather was vivid in the morning sun. It reminded Hathwell of Hilda's Flower-Forth dress, and while Bru made the incredible announcement he pretended she was there, sharing their happiness. Sef had come to destroy, but in the end he'd brought them hope.

Their names were quickly decided as Sunné and Melté, meaning sun and moon respectively. Clovis smiled at the significance and felt flattered that Peri had taken his story to heart and suggested the names.

That night, the city celebrated and Therions flocked from neighbouring towns to join them. As the days went by, the city became the focus for thousands of pilgrims. Astriss remained lost, but Sunné and Melté were found, and with them came renewed faith. With this new awakening, Bru rightly suspected the Magnon incursion would decline and perhaps one day stop altogether. In the meantime they had new witch-Berand, and new optimism. The faded-realm need fade no more.

On September 9th, one week after dragons returned to the faded-realm, Kolfinnia awoke with the burning desire to return herself. "Home." She clambered out of bed and opened the tiny window and saw what had awoken her. The sky was dotted with migrating geese and her heart longed to follow them. "It's time to go home Skald."

He sat on the bed watching the geese, as he had almost a year ago after Wildwood's destruction. "Yes, you're right. It's time," he agreed.

She watched the geese until they were gone, and then she dressed, packed in readiness and went to find Clovis. By midday they had finalised their plans and Ulfar suggested a place where they could pass safely back to Earth without being seen, but they would need a row boat.

Bru and Taal were saddened but not surprised, and asked if they could at least accompany them when they set off. It was decided to start out the following morning at first light, and so Kolfinnia and Clovis got ready for their last night in Hope. As she curled up on her mattress that night, she listened to the geese streaming past the castle. "I'm coming, wait for me," she promised, and hundreds of geese honked in reply and she smiled, understanding them perfectly.

CHAPTER TWENTY-SIX

Last words

'You came as a stranger, but you leave us as family.'
'The Golden Trail' - traditional witch tale, 15th century

The dawn was grey and the rain was light. Bru stood at the bows of the little boat holding a lantern while Hathwell, Clovis, Ulfar and Taal rowed. Kolfinnia sat in at the stern looking like a dignitary under escort. It was September 10th, geese still passed overhead and her breath came in clouds because the first chill of autumn had arrived. She twisted about to see the castle a final time, before the bend in the river carried them out of sight. *Goodbye Hilly,* she wished silently. Hope Castle slid behind the trees and she turned back to her fellows, knowing soon that every face she saw around her would also be gone from her life. She noted them while she may; Taal's magnificent horns, Bru's shrewd eyes, Ulfar's stoic expression, and lastly Hathwell's slightly sad air. Ulfar broke the melancholy.

"Taal, you row like a baby kid with colic." Grumbling was just his shield, inside he felt as sad as the rest.

"I'm a carpenter by trade. Sooner I swap oars for saws will be a glad day for me." Taal kept snatching glances at her, they all did. That sense of departure was getting stronger she felt.

"Here," Ulfar indicated, and they rowed towards the bank where the reeds were thickest.

The boat nosed through the reeds, startling a heron, and bumped against the muddy bank. Already Ulfar was jumping out and tethering up.

Without thinking, they all kept the boat firm for Kolfinnia to step out of. She took Clovis's hand and touched down on the bank. *My first step homewards,* she thought, wondering why the moment left her more sad than happy.

They stood gathering their thoughts and checking their things, as Ulfar finished the knot and laid the oars in the boat. "This way," he pushed through the willows and was gone.

After a little way, they came to a thicket of birch and Kolfinnia saw what he meant. The trees were robust and healthy, and across the veil they would likewise be untouched. It would be a good place to arrive back. "Here," Ulfar said finally.

The party divided into two groups, split not by distance but destiny. Kolfinnia and Clovis turned to their friends and already she was tearful. Bru came and embraced her, mindful of her injury. "It's been an eventful summer," he chuckled.

"Goodbye coven-father, take care of Berand won't you." She felt his whiskers twitch as he smiled against her neck.

"He can't be as much bother as Rolo."

She stood back, smiling. Ulfar came next. "Blessings on you witch." He elected to take her hand and just when she thought he was going to give it a firm shake, he stunned her by raising it and kissing it gently.

"Ulfar!" she beamed.

"Yes, well," he coughed and backed away. "Take care."

She hid her smile. He really was the noblest werewolf she had ever met.

"Happening across Helthor that day was a great piece of luck." Taal put an arm around her and drew her close.

"Goodbye Captain." She kissed his furred cheek.

There was only one left, and while Clovis made his farewells to the others she went and embraced him.

"It was an honour having you as a daughter," Hathwell said sincerely.

"And you as a father." She took his hand. "Perhaps she never said, but I know she felt it."

The sadness in his eyes retreated a moment. "I hope so."

"She wouldn't have come here if not."

He scratched at his stubbly cheeks. "You'll have me feeling guilty."

"Not in the least. It's love that keeps us together, not guilt."

He held her hand and searched her face, and finally allowed himself a smile. "Goodbye Kolfinnia, tell Rowan to water that plum tree for me."

"Goodbye Berand," she kissed him. "Take care of those dragons."

Clovis hovered by her shoulder. He had last words of his own for Berand too. "Listen for Janus, listen to *conscience*. His song will spread through creation. This is the start of a golden age."

"I will Clovis, we all will." Hathwell offered his hand.

Clovis first shook it and then wrapped his arms around him and spoke quietly just for him. "If anyone had told me I'd one day embrace one of the men who'd marched against Kittiwake-coven, I wouldn't have believed it. You've come a long way Berand."

He leaned back and looked into his face. "The truth is Clovis, I came no distance at all. I just stopped pretending I was a squire."

Clovis grinned and slapped his shoulder, making him rock on his feet, and then drew something from his person. "Here, you must open it to send us home."

As soon as Hathwell took the pact-of-grace, a buzzing sound caused him to look around. Posit the oak-fairy, who'd waited so long in gloomy Helthor, was perched on a tree. "At last!" he groaned. "Followed you back and forth and up and down, waiting!"

"Just a few moments more, then it's all yours again," Hathwell promised.

Hesitantly, Clovis and Kolfinnia moved away. He put an arm around her and they stood ready.

Hathwell met their gazes and readied the pact. "Goodbye."

"Blessings on you," Kolfinnia wished him.

"Farewell," Clovis dipped his head.

Hathwell sprung the catch on the locket and watched as they simply faded before his eyes, leaving nothing but flattened grass. "The faded-realm," he whispered, perhaps meaning his new home, or the one he'd left behind.

Kolfinnia saw them all simply fade from view. She took a sharp breath as her sadness peaked, and in reply Clovis drew her closer. The air felt to grow heavier, more sullied, and even from so far away she sensed the noise of iron and industry swirling around them. This was Britain once more.

She drifted from Clovis's side and went and stood where Hathwell had been just seconds ago, and waved an arm through the air, wondering if he could feel her at all. "So far away," she said dreamily.

"Yet so close." Clovis took her hand and led her away, as their tears mingled with the rain.

The two Lions began their last journey, only now at least there was no battle to face at the end. For the most part they walked along country tracks, or even flew a little when Kolfinnia could manage it, usually at night. Hrafn-dimmu was their guide again. Kolfinnia could sense when they had strayed from their southerly course because its vibration changed. She even felt its constant humming through her wand-sheath, as if it was singing contentedly to itself. *It wants to go home,* she understood, and with each passing mile she shared the same longing.

The days passed, and each morning they arose after sleeping rough in a barn or stable, she pretended they were the only ones in the world and they would be together forever. When thoughts of his leaving crept into her head, she pushed them out and took joy in his company, knowing there would be a lifetime ahead to miss him, and determined to enjoy what she had now. Her desire became to simply be happy, no matter what, and just like Clovis, she found this a desire well worth fighting for.

Their path took them along the route of the Pennine Hills, the backbone of England, and she thought of Evermore, the backbone of eternity, waiting for all of them in the end.

They reached the industrial cities of Leeds and Bradford by September 21st, but gave them a wide berth and kept to the high moors. It was the equinox and also Kolfinnia's nineteenth birthday. They spent the night near a small mill-town surrounded by steep wooded hills, and spoke of the past. It was almost a year to the day that she had fled the ruins of Wildwood and met Clovis on a lonely beach in the far southwest.

Day after day Stormwood drew closer and it became harder to ignore the looming sense of loss. By September 29th she began to recognise the place names and knew they were only a day or two away. Each moment with him became more precious, and Clovis felt it too. The end was coming.

At last, after almost three weeks of wandering, lost in one another's company and wanting their journey to go on forever, they came to the outskirts of Hereford once more. The day was old and night was falling, Clovis lit a fire and they camped under their blankets in woods near Tyberton. Clovis liked the name and told her of his old friend, for whom the village could have been named. Friday September 30th was their last night together.

"Do you think he'll be alright?" Kolfinnia gazed into the flames.

"Berand? Yes, I think he'll be fine." He polished his sword as he spoke. Kolfinnia saw her face reflected in the blade that had sliced Sef's head from his body, and shivered. He saw her consternation and sheathed the weapon. "I envy him in fact," he continued.

"In what way?"

"Those full grown dragons will be an impressive sight one day."

"There aren't any dragons on Vega?"

"Only the dreaming ones that give us life, and they're safely hidden."

She hugged herself as she considered. "It's not just that though, I wonder if he'll ever be the same."

"He was devoted to her wasn't he."

"Very much."

"Then I think he'll find reason to be happy, for her sake."

"Happy," she echoed.

By the fire, Skald stretched and yawned. "I'll be happy when that arm of yours is better, I need a good long flight."

"I second that." Tempest sat incredibly close to the flames, like a cat seduced by the heat.

"There'll be plenty of flying ahead. But our fighting days are over," she turned to him, "right Clovis?"

He adjusted her cloak tenderly, keeping her warm. "I wish I could say for sure, but now Janus is free I'm hopeful."

She took his hand and leaned against him. He pulled his cloak around them both and they pretended this was the first of many nights together, not their last. As she sat there with him she wondered about her last words tomorrow. She wanted them to be perfect, wanted them to last forever. She was lost in thought searching for an answer, unaware that by her side Clovis pondered the very same thing.

The following day on October 1st they began their last journey — a ten-mile hike across the border into Wales. The Black Mountains stood silent and steadfast in the distance, and for the first time Kolfinnia felt the excitement of homecoming keener than loss.

They crossed the Black Darren again, and she remembered how they had rested there on their way to Hereford. She could even see Hilda and Hathwell sitting on the rocks, amid bags stuffed with their elegant disguises. Their pace fell from a hike to a stroll, to an amble, as neither wanted the journey to end, and each passing minute Kolfinnia felt her chest tighten. She stole glances at him, and when she wasn't looking he did the same. She felt time running away and touched her scarred cheek, thinking of him weaving right now. *Dear Champion.* Perhaps he'd kept her safe after all. She thought of Sunday and Rowan, Ben and Flora, and Farona. Excitement battled sadness and before she knew it she was standing on the hills looking over a dark forest, and in the heart of it lay Stormwood-coven. *Where did all the days go?* she wondered. The last three weeks had passed like a wonderful dream, a dream in which she wandered alone through creation with only her beloved Lion of Evermore for company.

"Come on, we're close now." He took her hand and they walked silently towards the way-bewares peeping out of the grass. "You're almost home." He wouldn't leave her until she was across the way-beware circle, and he knew she was safe. But it would be too painful to wander back into Stormwood with her. His time there was ended, he knew.

She halted a few paces short, gazing at the way-bewares.

"Kolfinnia?" he asked.

"Funny isn't it," she said without looking up, "once I cross this line I'm home." Not just home she knew. Once she crossed the way-bewares he would leave her forever.

He clutched her hand tighter. "Last step then?"

She squeezed back hard. "Last step."

Together they crossed that innocuous line and she was back in Stormwood. Her heart jumped for joy and then slumped with sorrow. Immediately she turned to him and he put his arms around her. "I'll never forget you," she whispered against his neck.

"You gave the universe a miracle Kolfinnia, but you gave me even more." He held her close, and she reached up and stroked his face, letting her fingers glide through his thick mane. She drew closer, and at last they shared the kiss they'd always longed for, before reluctantly parting. She knew their last words were upon them, and she wanted them to be perfect.

"I love you Clovis," she said.

"I love *you* Kolfinnia," he replied.

Her hands fell from his and she backed away.

He reached into his satchel and took out the Janus relic and as he did Tempest appeared and sat on his shoulder a last time. The pinch of talons on her own shoulder told her Skald was there also. She gave Clovis her bravest, most beautiful smile, because he deserved it, and he repaid her likewise. Those teeth glinted again and his eyes gleamed. The Janus relic fulfilled the god's final promise, and Clovis simply vanished.

Now she was one Lion, and she stood looking at the empty space where he'd been, expecting to cry any moment, but feeling to be carved of wood. "Kolfinnia?" Skald asked softly.

She let out a long sigh. "Come on Skald. . . let's go home."

They set off together and she walked in a dreamy kind of bliss at being home, but a shadow drifted beside her. Later, the loss would hit her she knew, but right now everything seemed unreal. After a short while she heard voices and felt Skald's excitement. "A welcome party!" he smiled.

She saw two figures approaching through the pines. One wore black and the other was a child, and she knew them at once. Sunday and Rowan picked up their pace until at last they were running and Kolfinnia felt her own legs working faster until she too broke into a run. "Kolfinnia!" Sunday ran holding Rowan's hand.

"Kol!" Rowan joined her.

Kolfinnia barged through the bracken towards them. "Sunday! Row!" Her sadness took second place to joy. She was home and these were her sisters.

They crashed into a huddle and Skald flapped away to avoid being crushed. "Kolfinnia, when Rowan said you were close I daren't hope!" Sunday smiled through her tears.

Kolfinnia finished hugging her older sister and turned to her youngest one. "Row!" She hugged her tight. "You knew I was coming?"

"I've known for days!" she laughed.

"And she only told me this morning!" Sunday pretended to complain.

Kolfinnia kissed her, and gave her a lingering hug. "I told you I'd say 'hello' again one day soon."

Rowan stiffened. "But the others aren't coming are they?" she whispered.

Kolfinnia looked to Sunday, whose smile now faded. She knew too. "No, the others aren't coming."

Sunday crouched beside them and joined their huddle. Rowan had told her this morning that only one Lion was coming home, and soon enough they would have to tell Kolfinnia that they'd lost a couple of Lions of their own: Albert and Sally.

Skald watched the three sisters become one again. It was like watching droplets run together to make something bigger, and he wondered if between them there were any challenges on this Earth they couldn't overcome. He scolded himself for tempting fate, and looked to the sky. "Peace?" he asked. The sky made no promises, but neither did it fall and that was fine for him.

****

The journey had been a 'sod', as Hathwell would have said. The December seas weren't kind and as soon as the boat ran ashore Hathwell was glad to be out of it. It was now mid-December and Thule had changed little in the last few months, except perhaps the water was colder and the hills were white.

In light of the dragons' arrival, it was unanimously decided that Thule lighthouse should be reclaimed and the Beacon relit. Its light wasn't intended for Astriss to come home, but rather to send a message to all of the faded-realm: hope was restored. Indeed, now Hope-coven comprised five witches: the usual three had been bolstered by Sisi, who had decided to stay, and Peri, who wanted to learn the ways of witchcraft, perhaps in light of Clovis, and Hathwell understood perfectly.

When the expedition to Thule was planned, Hathwell found himself volunteering to go. Bru, Taal and Ulfar thought his skills perfect for restoring the lighthouse, but they worried too what demons the place might hold for him.

"Be careful Berand!" Taal called, watching him clamber up the jetty.

"You worry too much." By now his Pegalia was very good.

Ulfar tethered the boat. There was a new jetty here now, busy with boats, and huts along the shore. Villagers from Lievik had moved up the coast to make ready for Thule's reclamation. He could hear smithy hammers and smell freshly baked bread. "Keep an eye on him," Ulfar grunted. "I don't like him wandering off by himself. Too many demons here for him."

Taal climbed out of the boat. "I'll look after him," he promised.

Hathwell was compelled to return to the Beacon to inspect the machinery. Upon entering he broke into a cold sweat and wondered at the vagaries of fate. He'd sworn never to come here again, and now look at him. He had his reasons though. He got on and told himself there was work to be done, and of course he kept her in mind as he began repairing the light.

He took leave of them during a rare sunny day, and hiked across the wintry moor to Thule's western coast, saying he simply wanted to be alone. Here the cliffs were beautiful and on the highest moors the snow was inches deep. One or two gulls drifted overhead, watching him plod his lonely way across the island.

When he got there, it took him a little while to find what he was looking for, and when he did he extracted the trowel from his coat and began digging. At Stormwood he'd planted a plum stone, but here he'd planted something else entirely. The ground was hard and cold, but still just manageable because he'd dug it over already back in August. After a while there was a mound of black earth and white snow and he reached into the hole and took out his secret. He drew out a peculiar-looking bag made of some black fabric with a metallic sheen. He'd taken three things from Thule lighthouse that terrible day, one was Hilda's body, the other was the dragon egg, and the last was this. Yes, there were demons on Thule.

He opened the bag and parted the material. Sef's severed head gazed back up at him. When he'd first hidden him here, those eyes blazed with hatred, now Hathwell saw they were mindless and despairing. He was both pleased and ashamed. He set the bag down in the snow and sat beside it.

"Much has changed Sef," he began. "Did you know your egg held twins?" He chatted as if to an old friend. "A girl and a boy, they grow strong and all of the faded-realm rejoices. In the end all you did was save the people you came to harm." He looked out over the sea. "I suppose I should thank you," he said distantly.

Sef's eyes rolled, brimming with anguish.

"I've thought a lot about what to do," he admitted. "Hilly taught me a great deal. I know the witch in me should forgive you, tip you out and let you die. That's all the forgiveness anyone could ever offer you." He rested his elbows on his knees and hung his head, looking at the snow and listening to the waves far below. "But Hilly's gone," he trailed off.

For a while, he sat thinking of all those who'd suffered by Sef's hand, aware of his tormented gaze. Perhaps if he'd known the rest of Sef's crimes he would have made a different decision; there was the murder of Sally Crook and Albert Parry, the rape of Naomi, the abandonment of Jenilla, and many more he was ignorant of. So perhaps it was best that he didn't know. The man in him wanted Sef to suffer forever, but Hilda had loved the witch in him and it was that aspect he turned to now, for her sake.

He reached into the sack and withdrew Sef's head and set it down in the snow. Sef's eyes rolled towards him and Hathwell met his gaze. Therion and witch regarded one another, knowing in a strange way each had set the other free. Sef tasted an act of selflessness, and in his last moments he knew it was the better way. Those emerald eyes slid closed, never to open again and Hathwell let out a long sigh, and then turned back to the lighthouse and his friends and his task. Someone had to get that light going again.

****

So far the winter had been kind and by the time Sunday's special day came around they had suffered only a few days of frost and snow. It was dawn, and Kolfinnia sat with Rowan in Flora's little dwelling next to a glowing fire, putting the finishing touches on her outfit. This was a lot easier now her arm was healed. All three of them were dressed in their finest, and for good reason, because today was Stormwood's first wedding.

The event was a blessing of course, but it left her feeling a little lonely. Flora had Farona, Sunday had Ben, and even Rowan had a 'special' friend in Marcus.

It was December 21st and Kolfinnia had been home almost three months, and while there was lots of heartbreaking news to share and catch up with, there were also wonderful things like weddings to plan. Sunday was nervously preparing in her quarters, and Kolfinnia wouldn't have wagered who was the most apprehensive. Sunday was getting married, but she was conducting the ceremony.

"Your hair's so thick," Flora observed as she threaded roses into Kolfinnia's garland.

"I'm growing a winter coat," she joked, thinking of Therions.

"Keep still. I want the roses to be straight."

Kolfinnia watched Rowan pinning the last oak leaves in place. They had been painted gold, and the train on her dress was festooned with them. "Will you be able to carry that whole forest behind you, Row?" she teased.

"I want to look nice for Sunday," she said absently, pinning the last leaf on.

Kolfinnia and Flora exchanged amused looks. 'For Marcus,' they both mouthed silently. The girl had grown very fond of him and if things carried on like they were, then it was likely she would live up to her promise. She boasted about how they were going to get married one day. Marcus pretended to hate the fuss, but it was just that, pretence.

"There," Flora stood back. Now her friend wore a garland of special roses, the kind Flora dubbed 'Clovis roses'. They were fiery amber, just like his eyes. "I'm pleased to say not even Sunday could have done a better job."

Kolfinnia stood slowly and smoothed her dress. All three of them wore white gowns adorned with golden oak leaves, and garlands of roses. She stepped lightly to the centre of the room under the lantern light and examined herself in the mirror. The dress wasn't quite as showy as anything Sunday had ever worn, but it wasn't far off. Kolfinnia had never seen herself look so glamorous. *Desire,* she thought, wishing her lost friends were here to share this day.

"We'd better get going," Flora advised, making hasty adjustments to her own dress. "Row, you finished those leaves yet?"

"Last one now," she sang without looking up. "There, done!"

"Well," Kolfinnia regarded them all in the mirror. Rowan was eight now and her hair reached down past her shoulders. She was a little taller and a little wiser and she was leaving her childhood behind. Flora had the air of a young woman in love and her once resented eye-patch had become a proud part of her identity. This morning on the winter solstice, the pair of them looked fit to be married themselves. Yes, she thought, they would all do Sunday proud. "Time to go," Kolfinnia sighed happily. They checked their wands a last time and took their lightning-staffs, now wrapped with flowers, and set off.

Rowan took the lead, carrying an ornate lantern. They crossed the Glade, which was crisp with frost, and to where all of Stormwood waited for Ben and Sunday. On the way, Kolfinnia bowed her head as she passed three graves and a cairn. Sally, Albert, Mally and Hilda would not be forgotten. It had taken weeks and a lot of effort, but now when she visited the graves she didn't think of Sef's evil, but of her cherished friends. She looked to the morning sky, which was clear and cold, and found Vega instantly. *Bless you,* she wished him as always.

The crowds moved aside as their coven-mother, now looking as radiant as Sunday herself, entered their midst, and admiring gasps and compliments greeted her. The trees were lined with candles, lanterns and thunder-sprites, and even a few fairies had deemed to appear and watched from the branches. In view of the cold weather a few frost-fairies sat with them, and Kolfinnia thought of Neet.

She stepped lightly onto a wooden platform with a carved dragon at either end; one of oak, and one of holly, and the crowds clapped and whistled. The lantern light sparkled across the golden leaves on her dress and the roses in her hair looked to be afire. Finally someone began singing the binding-oath, and the crowds turned to see Sunday making her way across the Glade with attendants of her own. More voices joined the song and now Ben appeared walking from the west. The two joined hands at the founding-banner and approached the platform as equals, trailing attendants, friends and family. Ben looked like a man given the whole world as a gift, and of course as always Sunday looked magnificent and it was fitting that she'd chosen black for her wedding gown. She caught Kolfinnia's eyes and winked, and they shared a knowing smile.

Here we go, Kolfinnia thought, and looked up again. Vega twinkled approvingly and she even imagined threads being woven right then, binding all their fates together. She thought of the Flowering and of Janus, and like Skald she dared to hope. "Peace," she whispered, and her wish was lost in the crowds as Sunday and Ben arrived and everyone began to cheer.

It was early on Christmas morning when Farona came to find her, scrambling up Crow-tops' ladder in hurry. His head popped up through the hatch, "Kolfinnia, there's something you should see!"

She looked out from under her blankets. "It's freezing outside, and it's taken me ages to get warm. Are you really going to make me get up?"

"It's worth it, come see." His head dropped out of sight.

She crawled out of bed, still grumbling, pulled on not one, but two cloaks and a scarf, left Rowan to sleep and went after him.

She followed him across the Glade towards the fort. The morning was still dark and the grass wasn't just crisp with frost now, it was crunchy. The wedding feast had gone on for two days and nobody had seen the happy couple since, and nobody dare go disturb them either. "I was in the fort stacking potatoes, when a section of roof caved in," Farona explained.

"Were you hurt?" she asked, suddenly concerned.

"No, just a few stones fell, but I found something." At the fort entrance he'd left a lantern. Now he picked it up and vanished inside.

She ducked and followed him within.

The fall was just twenty yards in. She smelled fresh earth, and of course potatoes, and Farona stopped and hooked the lantern on a roof beam. "Here," he said, and moved aside for her.

She pulled her dress up and knelt by the mound of stones, not sure what he meant.

"There," he pointed, watching her face closely.

She saw what he meant now. There was a craved slab lying face up. She swept the soil away, leaned closer and froze. There was a creature carved on it, and although it was stylised and softened by time it was undoubtedly a lion. It had a snarling mouth and flowing mane.

"There's a word at the bottom," Farona added.

She swept more dust aside already knowing what the word would be and tears began to fall. "Bless you," she whispered. She remembered the story of how Merlin had carved the name of the Lion on a stone and hidden it in the fort, and how he'd promised to return one day.

"Kolfinnia?" he asked, concerned.

"I'm fine," she replied between the tears, and she was.

He had promised to return, perhaps in a different incarnation, but he *did* come back. She dared hope then that one day she would see him again, perhaps not this lifetime, but others to come. She lovingly traced her fingers over the word on the stone. And the word read:

CLOVIS

The living heart of witchdom

In a place forever and nowhere, filled with doorways and untold futures, and where time was simply a matter of perspective, a spirit walked in wonderment at her new-found surroundings. She still resembled the woman she'd been in life, a woman of late middle age possessing a striking fall of dark hair. She had once been Swanhilda Bridget Saxon. Although that name and time were gone she was still a witch, and now her mortal trappings were shed she remembered what she *always* remembered when she walked between lives: that the others were waiting and they had a door to choose.

She trod the steps of Evermore without touching them, still bound by the conventions of her former life, but it was an illusion that comforted and pleased her. What she saw next comforted and pleased her infinitely more however.

Valonia, Esta and Lana all rose up from where they had been waiting on the steps. Hilda joined them and the four embraced, another vestige of their old existence perhaps but one well worth clinging to. All that remained was for the fifth and last of their number. She was young, and hopefully it would be many years before she joined them, but they always travelled as five.

The four settled down to wait, wondering who and where they would be next time, but understanding that whoever they were they would always be devoted to the twins, and they would always be witches.

ABOUT THE AUTHOR

STEVE HUTTON

Steve attained first a BA then later an MA in illustration. As a freelance illustrator he has worked for the National Trust and created character concepts for film and TV, most notably 'The Golden Compass'.

After years of illustrating for established writers, Steve decided it was time to tell his own stories. Taking his love of rugged northern lands, their legends and folklore, and combining them with other diverse interests, the resulting narrative is *The Dark Raven Chronicles*.

Steve owes as much to modern classics, like 'Watership Down', and Mary Stewart's 'Hollow Hills' trilogy, for their inspiration as he does to the 'Icelandic Sagas' and 'Beowulf'.

The *Dark Raven Chronicles* is a fantasy series blending historical facts with wild fiction to create a unique world, enhanced and enriched by Steve's own illustrations.

RAVEN'S WAND ALMANAC

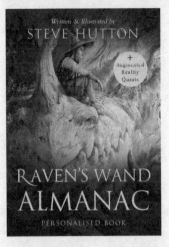

Text and illustrations © Steve Hutton

The *Raven's Wand Almanac* is full of images selected by you - just for you, making it a unique personalised picture book.

The *Raven's Wand Almanac* will take you through the beliefs, traditions and legends of the world of *Raven's Wand*. Steep yourself in the life and values of the witches and discover the Sign of your Birth & the Season you relate to.

Walk through your year in the Wildwood and learn about the characters you are most drawn to by creating your very own picture book of Steve Hutton's incredible artwork.

Visit

www.DarkRavenChronicles.com

Facebook: Dark Raven Chronicles